UNICORN WESTERN

Sean Platt
Johnny B. Truant

Unicorn Western — The Complete Saga (Volumes 1-9)

by Sean Platt &
Johnny B. Truant

For Austin, Ethan, Haley, and Sydney, who we wanted to write for before they got old enough to begin criticizing (or ridiculing) us.

And of course for Dave, who made the fatal mistake of saying we couldn't write a western without knowing the color of smoke that came from a gunslinger's pistols.

A Note About This Collection

This full saga collection contains all nine books in the *Unicorn Western* series — in other words, the entire dagged Saga.

You are about to read a story about a gunslinger who rides a unicorn. If you think that's a stupid idea, then we're on the same page. We've decided that this is the most awesome stupid idea that either of us has ever had.

The story behind *Unicorn Western* began when our friend David Wright said we couldn't write a decent western without doing a ton of research. We replied that if we put a unicorn in the story, we could get away with anything.

Kisses to you, Dave.

Author's Note

Note from Johnny: I was going to have a say in this Author's Note, but as listeners to our podcasts will understand, once Sean started talking, he never stopped. I decided to bow out gracefully and turn it over to him.

One of the first reviews *Unicorn Western* ever earned referred to it as, "The best book to ever come from a stupid idea." While I'm not sure how accurate that is — there have been plenty of stupid ideas that have made truly excellent books — I do believe there is truth in that thought. I'm sure Johnny would agree (not that he's really getting the chance, since I'm totally ball-hogging this Author's Note).

No matter what happens with *Unicorn Western*, we can never change its roots: The entire series, which will finish out at over 600,000 words, started as a joke.

Unicorn Western was born when Johnny and I were ribbing our friend David Wright during a podcast late last year. This stupid joke has since turned into one of the biggest writing surprises of my life so far, and has given me many hours of "work" where my eyes are wet with laughter.

What more could a creator ask for?

I'm not sure if it's because I have no formal training as a writer, because I'm like a monkey that swings endlessly from one tree to another, or because I came up as a ghostwriter who earned a living by writing everything from sales letters to wedding vows, but I can't tolerate the thought of sticking to a single genre for the rest of my life. This is a source of frequent debate on both of our podcasts. For the most part Dave isn't a fan of genre hopping, though I do think he's slowly coming around, and I wouldn't be at all surprised if we wrote something equally ridiculous in the very near future. During one of our playfully heated discussions when I suggested that I would love to someday write a western, Dave made one of his usual noises that sounds as if he's developed sudden, painful gas. His reason: research. Writing a western, according to Dave, would be a horrible experience (like life) because of the copious research required to write a quality western. I disagreed loudly through my laughter. Though I've not read many westerns, I've seen plenty. You need a prairie, a family in danger, and a bad guy in a black hat. I'm not looking to write a Larry McMurtry western; *Lonesome Dove* is one of my favorite books, but that's not at all the sort of western I'd be interested in writing. I want to write something simple that sticks to the skeleton so clearly articulated thousands of times already.

Dave, not knowing he would rue his next words (and deadly serious) said, "Are you familiar with the smoke that comes out of a gun back then?" This only cranked the flames of hilarity. Johnny and I are still laughing six months later — no kidding, I'm laughing right now as I type this. We agreed that the color of gunsmoke didn't matter. Even if the color of gunsmoke had somehow mysteriously changed color in the last 150 years, a writer can make his gunsmoke pink so long as he builds proper context around it.

More hilarity ensued until Dave finally raised his giant grizzly bear paws in surrender and growled, "FINE! You all go write your little western. Have fun. There's gonna be @^#*$!^ unicorns in it."

So *Unicorn Western* was (sort of) born.

This idea was hysterical, though not taken seriously. Johnny had already started another series, Fat Vampire, based on a separate but equally hilarious conversation during a different broadcast, so the idea of writing a serious book based on a ridiculous idea wasn't foreign, but I had a full plate with no room to add something stupid. Johnny would be the cowriter if such absurdity were given breath, but he and I had plans for a more serious project. I thought the exchange humorous enough to mention it to my family on the way to school the following morning, and then I put it out of my mind.

The next time *Unicorn Western* came out to graze, I was in L.A., speaking on stage about indie publishing. It was my first time on stage and I was a bit rambly. Midway through my talk I found myself discussing genre hopping, and then telling a story about the time I was talking about writing a western with my cohosts and how we thought it would be funny to write a western starring a unicorn. Standing on stage, laughing through the story, I suddenly found myself wanting to write a western with a unicorn. This wasn't a big deal: I find myself suddenly wanting to write random things many times each day.

Shortly after starting the podcast, Johnny and I agreed that we would write at least one project together. Dave and I had four serialized series at the time and one series of shorts — all dark horror — so Johnny and I thought it would be cool to write a serialized project with a totally different, albeit still serious tone. We were scheduled to start writing the new project in September, but a week before we were ready to go, Amazon's horror and sci-fi publishing arm, 47North, invited me and Dave to write a series for their new Amazon Serials division. We signed for two series rather than one and turned our next two months into a tsunami of writing.

I had to postpone my project with Johnny for those two months. By the time I finally circled back I was spent, still wanting to write something together, but not wanting to think about anything even remotely complicated. Our previous project seemed too complex. I said, "Whatever we do should be stupid simple."

It was probably the word stupid that had us crying out "*Unicorn Western*!" together.

So *Unicorn Western* was (totally) born.

Unicorn Western's narrative grew really big, super fast. So while each book can be read independently of the others, it wouldn't make as much sense, in much the same way that you could read *The Prisoner of Azkaban*" or *The Deathly Hallows* in isolation and enjoy those books tremendously, but they would be nowhere near as wonderful as if you read them as the third and seventh books in a wonderful series. We knew we wanted to have nine books total, and that we wanted to base each one on an existing western. This would give us a common frame of reference to build a story around, allow us to play with old western cliches, tropes and conventions, and help to ensure that each title could be read as a standalone piece.

The first book needed to serve as a sort of origin story; we thought the Gary Cooper classic *High Noon* perfectly served that need. Both huge fans of Stephen King's *Dark Tower* series, we wrote the first book as a mashup of *High Noon*, King's Roland, old Spaghetti Westerns, our own quirky humor, endless in-jokes for podcasts listeners, and solid old-fashioned storytelling. By the end of the first one, we were already in love. We agreed: The book was better than it had any right to be, and we couldn't wait to see what would happen next.

With the first one finished, we felt an immediate responsibility and intense desire to take our story of the Sands and Realm and Clint and Edward somewhere special. That need to make our story more daring bloomed with each successive book. By the fourth book we were so in love with our world that we knew it could never be held in only nine entries. So the prequel, *Unicorn Genesis*, and the series finale, *Unicorn Apocalypse*, were born. Knowing those two followup series were coming gave us even more freedom to write a completely off-the-wall story.

We are so thoroughly pleased with the finished book. One of the many reasons Johnny and I were so excited to start writing *Unicorn Western*, back before we knew anything about Clint and Edward or their epic quest, was because we wanted something to share with our children. Most of our time is spent writing for grownups, and I'm sometimes sad that my kids (both at prime book devouring ages) can't share my work. Reading *Unicorn Western* out loud has been an absolute joy. It's also fun to see how the story works outside my own head. The series has plenty of jokes written specifically for fans of our podcast, but the books should serve the reader just as well without the context of those jokes. I'm glad to see that the story works, even without the foundation to understand many of the gags.

Johnny and I started writing *Unicorn Western* for ourselves and for our children, but there is no doubt that the story now belongs to you. We hope you loved reading it as much as we loved writing it.

We can't wait for you to join us for the rest of the journey.

Thank you for reading,
Sean Platt (and Johnny B. Truant)
May 23, 2013

Table of Contents

UNICORN
WESTERN

CHAPTER ONE:
THE HITCHING

Clint touched his guns.

There were two of them — old, silver, and laced with scratches. Each pistol held seven bullets, as did every gun carried by The Realm's marshals. Back before Clint packed fourteen bullets, he was allowed to carry a pistol on just one of his hips, and to only fire shots from a six-bullet tumbler, like every other commoner outside The Realm. But those days, for Clint at least, were long gone.

Most of the Sands' bandits and outlaws carried two guns or more, even though doing so was as illegal as sipping from a silver flask on Sunday. But getting your hands on a seven-shooter was impossible, unless you were a marshal. Even the darkest of dealers wouldn't pass them in the shadows behind a saloon, thanks to the taboo.

In a few hours, Clint would surrender his guns for good, along with his right to marshal in any town, be it inside or outside of The Realm. He'd hand them over along with his badge and go back to being plain old Clint Gulliver, with no *Marshal* in front. He'd be left with a lone six-shooter, strapped to his right hip since he was a righty, and knew that a straight draw was always better than the crooked aim from a cross-draw done wrong.

Surrendering his guns bothered Clint something fierce, but that wasn't the worst of it. He could lose his hat, stubble, and anything else that made him a man, but along with his pistols, the gunslinger would be losing his unicorn. That was an itchy trigger finger's worth of intolerable.

And, he thought, it was the last thing he should be thinking about right now.

Clint sat in the farback of the saloon, staring into the mirror as he did about twice a year. He looked good, so far as Clint Gulliver could look good. He looked pleased, so far as his crooked, perpetually scowling face could look pleased. Yet he was torn, and that bothered him. The marshal was a straightforward, cut-and-dried kind of a guy. He was rarely conflicted. But now he was torn between two great loves, and the fact that he felt so divided felt like trouble.

What was more — and this part was as hard to believe as the breaking away of The Realm and the leaking of the magic — he was *happy*.

He wore his newfound happiness like another man's hat, every second assuming he'd have to give it back. It was a mistake, him wearing what passed for a smile. It was only a matter of time before Providence realized the truth, and took back what it should never have given the grizzled gunslinger to begin with.

Clint had seen most of the sides of the Sands, along with most everything sitting up and down the middle of the Sprawl. He had mostly been solo — and neither happy nor unhappy — prior to Mai and long before Solace. It had been that way since he first rode into the Sands with his back to The Realm.

But of course, *solo* didn't include Edward, the unicorn he wasn't supposed to have.

The gunslinger sighed, then pushed the stew in his gut down into his boots. Today was a good day. So what if being happy wasn't quite familiar? Once upon a time, turkey didn't go in pie. Things changed. Edward would be happy in his retirement, maybe even write that defamatory book about The Realm that he'd been talking on forever.

Clint listened.

Out in the main room, the pianoman was banging out "She's Got a Way" three or four times faster than the song was usually played, pouring music out from the upright in the front where the gathered townspeople sat, the music drifting all the way into the farback and into Clint's ears. The pianoman was playing the traditional hitching set, of course, working through "She's Got A Way," to "Just The Way You Are" — Clint's cue to leave, so that he could cross the saloon's main floor and approach his happily ever after.

Then, after the swapping of the vows, the pianoman would finish the set by playing "Piano Man" as tradition insisted, before concluding the ceremony and transitioning from hitching mode to party mode by smashing a pumpkin into the keys.

Clint adjusted his tie a final time, sighed, stood from his bench in front of the mirror, then walked through the batwing doors of the farback and entered the saloon's main front room.

The citizens of Solace turned to greet the gunslinger.

Most towns scattered throughout the Sprawl were relatively large. Solace was small. With the tables pushed back to allow for the hitching party to stage their ceremony, the saloon seemed downright giant.

Clint spied Mai across the room, past the waitingmen and the preacherman, standing beside her row of waitingwomen. She looked beautiful, dressed head to toe in pink. She smiled as he entered, her hand twittering at her side like a nervous bird, wanting to wave — out of character for a wedding, but plenty normal for Mai.

The gunslinger smiled — in character for a wedding, but out of character for Clint. Then his hands went to his sides, finding them slim and too fleshy.

I should have my guns, he thought.

The pianoman kept banging his upright, finishing "Just the Way You Are" with a mellow voice as smooth as any Joelsinger in The Realm. For a second, the pianoman's voice brought Clint to missing The Realm. Then he remembered his leaving, and the longing turned into a bolt of loathing. He shoved it down into his boots with the rest of his stew, reminding himself that he was at a wedding — *his* wedding, against all odds — and that a hitching was a time for joy, not anger.

The room fell into a hush as the pianoman finished, and the preacherman started with his opening words, welcoming them all and reminding them that there was nothing greater than friends gathering together to witness two souls stitching their lives together like scraps in a quilt.

The preacherman went on about the lovely day and the fair weather that would be remembered and remarked upon forever, or at least until the coming Harvest. He thanked Providence and the movements of the Sands for allowing them this great weather, then thanked Providence, on everyone's behalf, for leaving them what remained of the magic, so far from The Realm.

The preacherman finished his opening address in the traditional way, with three claps and a wink. The assembly answered his call by clapping thrice. Clint should've done the same, but couldn't bring his palms together any more than he could make himself sing along to the Joelsongs like everyone else. Margaret Partridge, who always had her nose in everyone's business, was watching Clint rather than the preacherman and gave him the reek-eye when he failed to clap. Clint ignored her.

The preacherman raised his hand. Clint walked forward at his signal and stood beside Mai. Her hand found his, squeezing it in a strange reversal of roles. Clint was usually the strong one, but today he was a fish flopping on the desert floor.

"Dearly beloved," said the preacherman, "we are gathered here today to witness the joining of this man and this woman under Providence, in the town of Solace, if the movements of the Sands so will it."

"So will it," the crowd murmured in repeat.

"The Sands have spoken, and the union of Clint Gulliver and Mai Maneau pleases them. Does it please the assembled?"

The guests, seated to the left of Clint and Mai, answered in one voice: "So it pleases us."

Mai looked over, smiling at her man. Clint couldn't bring himself to smile at the crowd, so instead he smiled at Mai. The smile, like the happiness that was worn like another man's hat, felt strange. She returned his smile, her pink headpiece framing her smooth, pale face and shining brown hair.

Mai didn't look like a Sands woman at all. She was pretty enough to grace the cover of one of The Realm's glossy books. Like the swarm of men in the saloon, women of the Sands looked beaten by gritty wind and hard life. Their skin was rough, almost like cowhide, with hair that was dull and mostly dead. Mai looked nothing like that, and Clint was clear enough to admit it was her radiance that drew him to her, like he was metal and she was a magnet.

Clint would never have shared that first slice of pie, or his tall bottle of apple brew, if Mai hadn't stood out like she did. It wasn't long before Providence let Clint know he was right. Mai *wasn't* supposed to be out in the Sands. She was supposed to be in The Realm. Her half-magick blood meant that she had a home behind the walls. That's where the gunslinger would take her again if The Realm could ever be found. He swore on his guns — be they a pair of sevens or a commoner's six.

Margaret Partridge belched from her seat. Not uncommon, but the sound still stole Clint's attention. Nosy Margaret's eyes weren't where they were supposed to be. She was staring out the saloon window, interested in something that wasn't a hitching.

"Clint and Mai, it is my pleasure to preside over your union. You wish to be joined forever under Providence?"

"We do," they said as one.

The preacherman turned to Clint. "Clint, I've known you for nearly a year. When you came to this town, it was so dirty, a decent woman couldn't walk the street without worry of falling to the grip of roving gangs. Solace was no place to raise a child. Drunkenness and lawlessness ruled, until you changed that. You are a good man,

Marshal, brave and upright. Has life prepared you for the challenge of hitching?"

The preacherman held Clint's eyes while he waited for the answer. The gunslinger buried a desire to leave him killt, which was what he usually had to do when a man dared to stare without flinching.

"Arc you prepared to tolerate Mai's friends, even when they annoy you, and feign interest in theater and dance to please her?"

The crowd should have chuckled, but something outside was stealing their interest away from the ceremony. Clint turned, spying the entire back row, which was all bodies twisted in their seats.

Mai elbowed Clint, returning his eyes to the front.

"And Mai," said the preacherman, "can you accept Clint's failure to notice changes in your hairstyle, from subtle to grand? Will you constantly pretend that the emissions from his rear don't sour your stomach and curl the hairs in your nose?"

Clint looked from the preacherman to Mai. The preacherman said, "These are the things you must consider when hitching."

Still, the saloon was missing its laughter. Behind them, Earl Lancaster, Bella Swinton, and Nicholas Willings all stood, then went outside in a line. Clint was wishing for his guns as Mai elbowed him again.

The preacherman strained his neck, trying to see where the three had disappeared — and where the remaining assembly seemed to be looking — until remembering his place and returning his attention to the couple.

"By entering into this union, you pool your strengths and shore your weaknesses. Clint, you bring grit, bravery, and a stubborn disposition. Mai, you bring compassion, stability, and a general sense of loving. If I'm right in my suspicions —" He scratched his head. "— you might even bring an increasingly rare share of magic, which even the... the..."

Bill Maynard, George Telford, and Hattie McDonnough slipped through the saloon doors and out into the street.

"... the... the..."

Robert Beltham. Nellie Peterson and her two daughters. Queer MacElroy, the town oddity. Only Teddy, the orphan in half the town's employ, still had his eyes aimed front and center.

Clint looked at Mai's uncommonly beautiful face and felt a twitching sort of nervous, like everything was suddenly slipping away.

"The vows," said Clint. "The vows are next."

Mai turned, watching the chairs and tables empty to nothing.

"There's something wrong," Mai said.

Clint curled his lip. "Ignore it."

"I want to go out and see."

"Ignore it," he repeated. Then, to the preacherman: "Come on. The vows."

The preacherman looked conflicted. Mai was distracted and wouldn't keep her eyes forward. It was pointless anyway, seeing as they were the only three people still in the saloon. Duty was the only thing keeping the preacherman from bolting outside himself.

"Do it," Clint growled. "Just finish quickly."

"This is ridiculous," said Mai. "I'm not getting married in a rush so we can run outside. We're here to be with these people."

"I don't want any interruption in my hitching," said Clint.

"We're already interrupted." It should've sounded harsh, but it sounded tender instead. Mai set the back of her hand to the rough of Clint's face.

"What do you think we...?" Clint started to say to the preacherman, but the preacherman had already gone. They couldn't get married now if they wanted to, unless the gunslinger planned to get ordained and play both the roles of both betrothed and betrother.

"Dagnit," said Clint.

Mai pulled him toward the doorway.

Outside, they found the assembly gathered around the Water Reader, his fingers dipped into one of three rain barrels that were submerged halfway into the sand alongside the main street. His eyes were rolled into the farback of his head as he chanted in readerspeak. The assembly stood in an eager semicircle, ears perked for the stray word to leave the Water Reader's mouth in plainspeak, so that they could predict his prophecy before he fell from his trance.

The crowd's faces were pinched in worry, or maybe terror. The assembly turned to Clint, as if begging him to do something — like shoot the Reader right now between his rolled-up eyes, before he could spit a prophecy to ruin them all.

"*Mnmnmnm stone mnmnm falling town mnmnmn the winds sands mnmnmn...*"

"You people are terrible wedding guests," said Clint.

Mai hushed him.

"This is how you thank your marshal?"

"*Mnmnmnm hassle return shifting sands mnmnmnm to the ends the edge mnmnmnm...*"

Hattie McDonnough looked up, her eyes wide. "No," she said. "*No...*"

"Shut it Hattie," Robert Beltham snapped. "Let the man read the

Sands."

"*Mnmnmnm coming coming with the dozens mnmnMNMNM DARK SHIFTING SANDS MNMNMN.*"

Without the slightest pause, the Water Reader's eyes snapped into place. He drew his fingers from the rain barrel and said, looking directly at Clint, "The Sands have told me that a bleak cloud is returning to Solace. They showed me dark riders. And at the front of the riders, I saw the face of Hassle Stone."

Queer MacElroy laughed. He was the only one.

CHAPTER TWO: DELAYED

The preacherman refused to continue the ceremony. He said he'd give the couple a rain check.

Mai said, "I didn't know preachermen gave rain checks."

The preacherman didn't look at her, or put apology into his eyes. He simply said, "Looks like you learned something new."

"We're to be married *today*," Mai insisted. "Tomorrow's magic is different. The moon was fullest this morning, and that made for the second moon this month, making it blue. I cannot be married except on a blue moon. Otherwise is trouble, and who knows how long we'll have to wait?"

Clint took Mai by the arm and pulled her away. The preacherman wasn't listening, and wasn't going to. He was tossing clothes, bibles, and religious trinkets into an open suitcase until it was so fat that the preacherman couldn't buckle the straps. He sat on top, forcing it closed, chuckling as if Hassle Stone wasn't galloping toward Solace when his Water of Holies vial shattered inside. The preacherman made a joke about how his wardrobe would be forever blessed no matter how fashion might change, then lifted the suitcase lid and started mumbling as he gathered pieces of broken glass.

Clint growled at the preacherman, then dragged Mai upstairs, to his boarding room in the back.

"We'll need to ride to Sojourn now so we can find a preacherman to marry us there, and we're smart to hurry since the moon'll be different by morrow," she said, standing in the doorway.

"I can't leave town," he said.

"But we're to be married."

Clint grabbed Mai gently by both upper arms and pulled her eyes to his. "I told you, Mai, I can't go. We'll still be married, but not until Hassle Stone is right-handled."

"The blue moon. Our hitching must be on the blue moon. Your friend the preacherman is…"

"The preacherman's no friend," said Clint.

"He's running from something, not even willing to take ten minutes to finish our hitching. Vows were all that remained. 'Do you? Do you? I declare you married.' Two minutes, not ten." Then she went bright with an idea. "Maybe your guns could persuade him."

Clint smiled from the side of his mouth. "I can't use my guns to force a man to marry us," he said.

"Then we must get to Sojourn. Today, Clint!"

"It'll have to be the next blue moon, Mai. I can't leave Solace. Not now with Hassle Stone leaving horizon behind him."

"Who is this Hassle Stone, anyway?" she said. "And why is everyone so afraid of him?"

Clint looked at Mai, her beautiful dark hair framing her frazzled face. She'd come to Solace after he had, and never knew a town polluted by the madness that followed Stone like an angry cloud.

"He's a bad man."

"The Sprawl is full of bad men."

"Yar'm, and a lot of them are amigo to Stone."

"Let Todd handle it. He was going to handle things while we were away anyway."

"Todd can't handle Hassle Stone."

"Why the Sands not?" Mai was nearly yelling, and practically in tears. Clint never understood how women could cry when angry. He would comfort their sadness, if that's what it was. But Clint had earned plenty a palm to his face after failing to notice a woman was angry rather than sad. Now that he knew the difference, the gunslinger might be able to survive a marriage…if he could get a preacherman to put him in the middle of one.

"Because Hassle Stone doesn't ride alone," Clint said. "He has a way of drawing others to gallop behind him, and subduing those who might fight against him. You didn't see what it was like when I first came to Solace. It was as if he were magic." Clint rubbed his hand over his uncharacteristically soft and freshly shaven jaw.

"But you have magic." Mai reached out for his hand. "*I* have magic."

"I don't have magic," said Clint.

"You *know* magic."

"It doesn't matter, Mai. You heard the Water Reader. Hassle's on his way, coming to laugh at the law. I am the law. You see what that means, don't you?"

"If Hassle Stone is bad, then of course the Reader said he's bringing lawlessness. You know how Readers are."

"Yar'm," said Clint. "I *do* know how Readers are. Several are in my family line, including Kullem the Brew. Everything goes double meaning to them. You don't know Stone, Mai. He's not back for *Solace*. He's back for *me*. *That* is what 'lawlessness' means. It's not chaos he's seeing in the water. He's reading a grudge against the local law man."

Mai shook her head, sighed, threw her hands in the air, then flopped onto the turkey feather mattress, starched undergarments rustling. Clint sat in the chair across from the bed. She lifted her head and watched him.

"If we left," he said, "if we traveled to Sojourn. If we made our home there and never came back? Hassle Stone would take this town over. Then he'd leave men to control it, like occupying armies in a game of Risk. He'd give chase, follow us until he found me. If I weren't ready when he found us, he'd lay me in my grave."

A single tear painted Mai's right cheek. Clint guessed her anger had turned to mostly vapor, and the tear a mere drop of frustration. Women cried for everything; getting learned on the various species of weeping should be part of a hitching.

"What happened with him?" she asked.

"With Stone?"

"Yar."

Clint drew a deep breath, stood, walked to the window, and looked out onto the main street in front of the saloon and boarding house, his large gunslinger's hands hanging limp at his sides.

"Stone's men used to control Solace. From the way-back, since the town was just one saloon and a pair of tall closets. Before Stone, the town had neither law nor lawlessness. Stone showed, and stepped into Solace like a key sliding into a lock. It's like the bad men were already here, just waiting for the right bandit to lead them. At least, that's what the Water Reader said, and what Todd told me later."

Clint's jaw set as his eyes went to steel.

"His roving gangs roamed the street, taking all they wanted from the stores, without a thankoo or pleasem. They chased women, and caught them often. Merchants were extorted, and left barely enough rupees to stay alive. The saloon was the only thing booming, and not with wedding business. Well, the saloon and the coffiner. Each night after the saloon went shuttered, Stone's men would spill into the streets, falling in a heap until their bodies were finished twitching from the poison."

"Sounds like the Sprawl," said Mai. "I've seen plenty of the same."

"This was worse," Clint said from behind serious eyes. "Todd said once a barber tried to help one of Stone's men up from the dirt after a long night. Got a bullet in his beak for the trouble. Smashed through his nose and sailed through the back of his head. The barber managed a final word before he fell in a pile of meat and skin."

"What was the word?" Mai asked, as if it mattered.

"Lice."

Mai was quiet, waiting for Clint to continue. Then he said, "The entire town was their private pantry, their stock of supplies earned only from the sweat of others. They invaded homes just because they could, making sure everyone knew that everything in Solace belonged to Stone, regardless of the ink on any deed. No one dared fight back, or he'd have them arrested and put on trial in the street."

"Trial?"

"More like a game of trivia. Stone held trial on the rare occasions when someone dared cross him, or sometimes to celebrate another day ending in Y. Stone'd stop men in the street, usually outside the saloon, putting his pistol to their skulls and pulling the hammer back with a quiet click you could nearly hear through the town. A crowd would gather, of course, since that's what crowds do even when they hate what they see. Stone would ask the man, down on his knees, how many posts were in front of the post office, or something else equally irrelevant. The man would either get the answer right and live, or get it wrong and die. Either way, the citizens of Solace learned it was futile to wiggle beneath Stone's heel."

Clint turned from the window.

Mai said, "Why didn't the people rise up? Weren't there more of them than there were of the bandits?"

"Who *ever* rises up?" said Clint.

"So you came to town and..."

"Edward and I came to town a while after our exile. When we found Solace, I near wanted to die. Good thing for the town, I wasn't willing to suffer a man like Stone sucking air under the same sun as me. We meant to pass through, on our way to deeper Sands, looking for a bed and pie. But the first thing that set my nerves to raw was how the place was quiet as a turkey graveyard. Then, we were welcomed into town when Stone himself stepped into the street and fired three slugs into Edward's chest."

Clint nearly smiled at the memory. Edward had looked down at his wounds, his horn glowing as the three slugs rose through his skin and fell to the dirt. The unicorn's blood-matted hair had swirled blue and red and green and yellow as Edward stared up into Stone's eyes. Both Clint and Edward realized Stone held the same fool belief as most folks — that a unicorn was only a horse with a horn.

Edward could have killed Stone with his own slugs, but Clint's unicorn thought it was funnier to watch Stone run, which he did the second he saw the slugs hit the dirt.

Edward had let him go, then said to Clint: *What a jerk. Now I need an apple brew.*

Mai didn't gasp when Clint told her Stone had shot Edward. She laughed, knowing his unicorn.

"It didn't take us long to drive the bandits out of the town," Clint said. "Edward wouldn't even help. He walked straight from the center of the street where Stone had shot him and into the saloon, then pushed all of the tables and chairs out of the way and told the barman he wanted a tall apple brew and a fat slice of turkey pie. The barman was so shocked that he served Edward his brew in a mug. Edward asked for a clutch of straws and drank it that way, then stayed there the rest of that day and all of the next one. I tried getting him to help me with Stone, but he wouldn't leave his sour mood behind. His coat was filthy, with rainbow-colored blood caked on his chest. He never washed — just stood by the bar and drank mug after mug of apple brew and ate them plum out of turkey pie. I told him we had a town to clear. He said I should try my best to avoid a mortal wound, and that he'd heal me like always if I got shot otherwise. I told him we could get done faster if he'd help, and he asked me what I was talking on since he *was* already done."

Clint told Mai the rest of the story — how he'd hunted Stone's men and taken them down, one by one. He told her about the three times he'd been shot, once square in the gut, and how each time he'd crawled back to Edward, who would only heal him after another round of ridicule. He told her about the time Stone nicked him in a lung, and how he almost hadn't made it back to Edward's new home in the saloon — and how when he had, catching up to Edward while he occupied the entire bar area of the saloon, the unicorn had laughed louder than ever, suggesting the gunslinger wear a stove plate over his heart if he insisted on continuing to fight.

Now, Clint pointed outside and finished his story, telling Mai how his final showdown with Stone had happened right there in the street below, in front of the saloon boardinghouse. He'd turned into Stone's bullet as the bandit had fired, deliberately taking the fourth shot in the shoulder and falling. Then he told her how, when Stone kicked his seven-shooter away, he'd fired from his other side.

After a faded red billow of gunslinger's smoke from the marshal's gun, Stone had fallen. Clint stood, yelling for Edward. The unicorn healed him from the saloon without bothering to emerge. Clint, standing over a moaning Stone, had fired once more, slamming Stone with a bullet in his opposite arm. He'd told Stone to go, to get out of town before he bled out, and that if he ever found the strength in his arms to hold a weapon again, Clint would find and end him by sundown.

Mai let him finish, then stood and dragged a suitcase out from under the bed.

"What are you doing?" Clint asked.

"Packing. Leaving."

"That's my suitcase," he said.

"Of course. It's you that's going. I only have a few things at the Otel. We'll go there next, and be gone before Stone shows his face back in Solace."

Clint shook his head.

"If he's at all magic — or simply not a fool — he'll be ready for you this time. He'll know your unicorn can't help you if he kills you outright. If this man is really coming back, you'd be an idiot to be here when he does."

"Mai. I can't leave. He'll end this town. All of it. He won't just take what he wants this time. He'll kill what he can't take, and he'll let the bodies rot."

"You said his grudge was with you."

"His grudge is with the world."

"This isn't your fight," she said. "Not anymore. You were to surrender your guns and unicorn in the morrow, no longer riding the Sands as a marshal. We were to leave."

"Yar'm," he said. "But we didn't."

Mai huffed, cursing the Water Reader and saying that if he could have just waited a few hours longer to disturb the town, they'd be married and Clint would have already handed his marshal's star and guns to Todd, trading them for a citizen's six-shooter and a horse. When word of Stone's return came, the couple would already be well on their way toward Sojourn, off to start a new and delightfully dull rest of their lives.

"I spent most of my life in the deep Sands," she said, "and in the deep Sands, the one thing you learn is that running keeps you breathing. Flight isn't cowardice so much as a second chance. I survived without parents in the middle of the Sprawl because I knew when to run, and therefore live to fight another day. How will you help anyone if you die?"

"How will I help anyone if I leave?"

"Rally others. Report to Sojourn authorities. You could even come back. But if you stay now, you don't stand a chance. How is that the right choice, in *any* sense?"

"Running's a coward's move."

"Your pride! By the Sands!"

"You know me, Mai. I can't leave the town nekid in a coming rain."

"They have Todd!"

"Todd's an idiot," said Clint. "And Edward will never listen to him. Edward will watch him get shot while trying not to laugh. You think *I* have pride? Unicorns make me look penitent, and *Edward* makes most unicorns look like groveling fools. I can hand someone my guns, but Edward can't be handed to any man. He has the choice to stay for the next marshal or to run back. He'll run back. He's not with me as a matter of duty, you understand. He's with me because what we have is friendship, held together by mutual loathing."

Mai's face curled in surrender. She was holding one of his shirts, and set it on the bed, neither back in place nor in the suitcase. She walked to the door, then turned back, once again blinking tears from her eyes. This time, Clint had no idea why they were there.

"We're to be married," she said.

"Someday soon, we will be," he promised.

"Come with me to Sojourn. Please, Clint. Like you promised. We've already hired the carriage. It'll be ready shortly. We can still go, just climb inside and not look back. You and me, Clint. Pretend the preacherman made it through the last two minutes of the vows. Pretend the Reader said nothing."

"But he did." Clint shook his head. "He said too much, and now that I've heard it, I can't leave Solace."

She sighed, and opened the door.

"I'm going to the Otel," she said. "When the carriage is ready, I'll be taking it to Sojourn. You have that long to do the right thing, Clint. That long to change your mind."

"I'm all that stands between Stone and these people."

She swiped a tear from her eye. "I can't watch you die." She shook her head. "I won't."

"Then don't," he said. "Watch me live."

CHAPTER THREE: THE POSSE

Clint pulled open the door to Edward's house five minutes later.

In truth, Edward's house was a barn, and Edward's room a stall, but Clint had never heard of a unicorn who used either of those base words. Horses lived in *stalls* inside of *barns*, and horses were disgusting. Horses crapped in the same rooms where they slept, whereas unicorns did their toilet business in the yard. Horses drank discolored water from plastic buckets. Unicorns lapped clean water from a foot-operated pump over an immaculate metal trough. Horses ate hay. Unicorns also ate hay, but only when there was nothing better in the offing. They loved brew and all sorts of pie, from dinner to dessert.

"Edward," said Clint, catching his breath. "We've got a problem. The Water Reader says…"

A thirty-pound bag of oats flew across the stable, striking Clint in the face and sending him to the barn's packed clay floor.

Clint stood, brushed himself off, and peeked around the corner, where he nearly ran into Edward's enormous white rump. Edward looked back at Clint over his shoulder, his spiraled horn pointing at Clint in accusation.

"It's me," said Clint.

"I know," said the unicorn. His dry, gravelly voice was eerily similar to Clint's. People often confused them, much to Edward's delight whenever he quietly sauntered up behind women, making crass come-ons in the name of the marshal, always falling into hysterics as they turned to look at and/or slap him.

"I'm your partner. You hit your partner with a sack of oats?"

Edward lowered his lips into the trough and began sucking up water. A soft glow spread in a small cloud from his head, and sent the same sack of oats flying at Clint. It struck him again, this time launching him into Edward's rear.

"Apparently," Edward said.

"I demand that you stop!"

"Good one," said Edward, his eyes still on the water. The only sounds in the stable were Clint's heavy snarl and the vague sucking sound of equine drinking. Clint slapped Edward's hindquarters lightly. "Edward. Back out so I can stop talking to your butt. Come on."

"No." *Slurp*.

"Edward."

"Clint."

"I need to talk to you. This is important."

"Tell it to your new horse."

So that was it.

"I keep telling you, you can come with us. I just can't ride you once I'm no longer a marshal."

"Didn't stop you before we came here. Before you got a new official badge, from the townspeople of Solace," said Edward's butt. "Besides, you apparently don't understand the meaning of an unridden unicorn who keeps the company of humans. If you're not a companion, you're a hanger-on."

Clint said nothing, waiting for the unicorn to finish pouting.

"When I was growing up, there was a foal with a deformed horn. His name was William, but that didn't matter since all the unicorns called him 'Stumpy'. He'd hang around with groups that didn't want him, but that didn't have the heart to reject him."

"I don't have time to talk about this right now," said Clint.

"Of course you don't," Edward said. The sack of oats hit Clint a third time, knocking the gunslinger forward hard enough to drive his face fully between Edward's cheeks just as the unicorn loudly saluted from his rear.

Clint fanned his hand in front of his face and began squeezing around Edward's bulk. He moved up toward his head, maneuvered in front, placed his hands on Edward's face, and pushed.

"Really? Really," Edward laughed. "I weigh seven times what you do and I'm magic. You're going to try pushing me out by force? Would you like me to wear a halter to make it easier?" The unicorn twisted his voice into that of a damsel-in-distress. "Yar, master, tell me what to do!"

"I'm not going to leave you alone," said Clint, still pushing.

"You're underestimating my ability to ignore you," said Edward.

"I'll urinate in your water trough," said Clint.

"I'll rinse it out."

"Really? You think you'll ever be able to get it clean enough?"

Edward was mildly obsessive-compulsive. He fussed with coasters until they were centered exactly under mugs and glasses. Even though he was a magical creature, he constantly used his hooves to knock on wood whenever he realized he might be close to counting chickens before they hatched. No way he'd ever feel comfortable enough to use a trough or spigot knowing it was peed on.

Edward sighed. It was an odd noise, hearing a unicorn sigh.

"Fine. Out in the yard. You go first or I'll crush you."

"Just be careful and you won't crush me," said Clint, sucking in his gut so Edward could back out of the stable.

"I wasn't talking about an accident that might happen," said Edward. "I was making a threat."

Clint, happy to have at least gotten Edward into a back and forth, squeezed out the way he'd come. Then he led the unicorn out into a small pasture, even though he knew it was actually a *garden* because *pastures* were for horses.

Once together in the hot midday sun, Edward faced Clint and waited for the gunslinger to speak. His always-pristine coat was so bright that he was hard to look at, and Clint had to squint until his eyes adjusted. The animosity still in the unicorn's eyes made his pearlescent, spiraled horn look extremely sharp.

Clint figured Edward wanted him to speak first — a power move, since he hadn't wanted discussion.

"Hassle Stone is returning to town," said Clint.

"Fabulous."

"He'll want to kill me. And you."

Edward laughed.

"He'll want to kill everyone in town, or make them his toys. You remember what it was like when we arrived."

"My days as a do-gooder are over."

"I'm still the marshal. I intend to do what I can. You're still the marshal's..." He had to be careful how he said this. "... *deadly sidekick.*"

"Sidekick?" said Edward.

"Ultimate weapon. Head honcho. Name your title."

Edward said, "I don't want to fight Hassle Stone. I want to go to the saloon and drink. You can come with me. We'll ring out the end of our partnership in style."

"What better way to end our partnership than by committing one final heroic act?" said Clint. "Save the town. That's how two law...

law-*beings*? should go out in style. Beings. Hmm. I'm sorry; I don't know any terms that cover both men and unicorns."

"Hassle Stone bores me," said Edward. "He was a simple bandit, and barely a challenge. You'll get on my back, I'll extend my protection, they'll shoot at us, we'll be impervious, you'll shoot back, and then he'll die or run. Once upon a time, the end, any questions, etc."

"No reason not to help me, then."

Edward scraped his hooves in the dirt, looking far more horselike than Clint dared to point out.

"Fine," said the unicorn.

"There's more to it, though."

"Of course."

"Stone won't come alone, and he'll know what he's facing this time. He'll bring men. Lots of men. *Dozens*. He can't come straight at us, so he'll go after others and hold knives to their throats or pistols to their heads. You can't protect all of them."

"You say that as though I would care to," Edward said. His horn started glowing a soft yellowish-pink, and a metal object flew toward him from the barn. It was a can of apple brew, fashioned from city metal. Edward used his magic horn to set the can in front of him, then held it deftly between his teeth, raised his head, and bit it open, drinking the apple brew as it spilled.

"You need to stop drinking if we're going to do this," said Clint.

"I weigh fourteen hundred pounds and am magic," said Edward. "Get off my back, Mom."

Clint ignored him. "We'll need men to match Stone's. Two dozen at least."

"Sure."

"Let's ride out and get them."

Edward said, "Peachy" as his horn glowed again. Clint found himself flying through the air and landing roughly on Edward's back, facing the wrong way, seconds before Edward trotted off.

Clint turned and righted himself, adjusting to find the fit between his bones and Edward's. It had taken him a long time to learn to ride bareback without reins, but the one thing even a gunslinger would never dare — and that a unicorn would never permit — would be to garb a unicorn in human paraphernalia.

As far as unicorns were concerned, saddles and reins and bits and bridles and spurs were implements of slavery, and there was an ongoing tension between unicorns and humans regarding humans' use of those instruments on horses. Horses were unicorns' dumb cousins — but remained cousins regardless of their mental ineptitude. With unicorns, the issue was straightforward: ride bareback, or don't ride at all.

Within minutes, Edward had trotted them over to Earl Lancaster's place. Earl had a small tack shop on the main street and lived in the four-room apartment above the store. Earl would help. He was big and strong and fast. Always a quick draw. He even had an illegal six-shooter — a second gun — that Clint knew of but strategically ignored. Today his feigned ignorance would pay off. He'd allow Earl to wear it openly if he'd battle with Stone.

Earl answered the door with his hair in tufts, apparently just waking to answer from a midday nap. He yawned, then saw Edward standing in the street behind Clint. He snapped awake, suddenly serious.

"What is this, Marshal?"

"'Marshal?' You were at my wedding, Earl. You've ridden with me."

"Okay. What is this, Clint?"

"You heard the Reader."

"I did. Good wedding, by the way. Did preacherman finish you up, or are you still a single man?"

"Hassle Stone is coming," said Clint, ignoring the question. "He'll be bringing men with him. Possibly many men. I need guns."

"You need guns?" Earl looked suddenly distracted. "But you have your unicorn."

"It won't be enough." The gunslinger shook his head. "Stone's coming in worse than last time. I've heard what you haven't, about things he's done after being run out of Solace. He'll burn fields if he can't get what he wants. He'll kill women if he can't have them."

"Don't take this the wrong way, Marshal… Clint… but I believe Stone's quarrel's with you, not the good folks of Solace."

"His quarrel is with the world, Earl Lancaster."

"I don't aim to invite trouble I can't hope to pardon," Earl said, scratching his head and looking past Clint, out into the street. "I just run a tack shop."

"Then you'll want to keep running it. I need your guns. You can use both of them if you'd like."

Earl flinched, probably not knowing if it was blackmail coating the marshal's tongue. He said, "I want to let him pass, Clint. He may come at you, but I've heard about his operations out on the Edge. Or rumors, anyway. He's done with Solace. And if he's not, I don't know how we'd be able to stop him."

"You don't know what you can do?" Clint felt his face flushing red. "You can fight!"

"I don't know, Clint." Earl shook his head enough to make the marshal want to punch him. Then something flew over Clint's shoulder. He ducked at the last second as a sack of oats smacked Earl in the chest, throwing him hard against the doorframe. Earl's eyes were on Edward, filled with something between anger and fear.

"Like I said, Marshal, I don't want any trouble. If you can stop Stone, you will. If you can't, us fighting will only make him angry. He'll take what he wants, then move on. Years under his heel taught us how to deal with a Hassle Stone."

"*How to deal?* And the answer is to lie down?"

The sack of oats, which had landed between Earl and Clint, twitched. Clint raised a palm to Edward without looking.

"Earl. You're a strong man and a good gun. I need strong men and good guns to handle whatever Stone's planning on bringing to Solace. Simple as that. If I can get the men, I can drive him back. If I can't, then even if Edward and I eventually root them out, it'll only be after he kills scores of you all and burns your town to the ground. Stone won't go peacefully, not this time. Before Edward and I came to town, the magic had nearly drained from this place, leaving it no better than the rest of the Sprawl. Stone had probably never seen a unicorn in person, or the flash from a marshal's guns. Now he has. He's been out in the Edge, maybe toying with darkness. This time he'll know. And if he can't fight magic, he'll burn the world down around it."

Earl shook his head, taking a long step back. "I just run a tack shop, Marshal."

"Earl."

Earl Lancaster closed his door. Behind him, Edward said, "I'll bet I can get that sack of oats through his window."

"Don't."

"So what's next, genius?" said the unicorn.

Clint remounted and rode to Bill Maynard's ranch on the outskirts of Solace. Bill raised turkeys and pumpkins. He had a few cattle, some chickens, and a small field of bedraggled crops, but as was true across the Sands, turkeys were still the stupidest and most prolific livestock there ever was, and pumpkins the only crop that continued to thrive in the Sands. There were aquifers deep under Solace, so water wasn't a problem. The pumpkins gobbled it up and grew huge. The problem was the poison soil, or so said the soil and science men. It was all a bit over the gunslinger's head.

Bill Maynard's answer was the same as Earl Lancaster's. Bill explained that the reason he raised turkeys so successfully was because he was just as stupid as they were. But Maynard insisted that he wasn't much of a gun.

Clint reminded Bill how he'd once been on the side of law and order, loathe to live under another man's boot, or do his bidding. Bill said Stone's quarrel was with Clint, not with him, and that one sure way to get yourself caught under another man's boot — the one way in which he could actually become stupider than the turkeys he raised — would be to cause trouble for himself with Hassle Stone where there currently was none.

Clint argued. Edward magicked things so they flew at him. But ultimately Bill shook his head and went inside, wishing the marshal good luck, pleasem and thankoo.

"Stephen MacElroy," said Clint as he climbed onto Edward's back. "He's a sure thing. He'll help us."

"Queer MacElroy?"

"His queerness is why he's a sure thing," Clint argued. "Earl and Bill think it's crazy to face Stone? Then I should be aiming for crazy."

Yet, even Queer MacElroy, who sometimes wore his pants backward and kept a banana in his holster, refused. It seemed that even the village idiot figured going up against Stone was a bad bet.

"Let's leave town," Edward suggested. "I'll even let you bring that woman of yours. We'll go rogue again. You keep your star and your guns, and we'll get her a nice dumb horse. These people don't want to help save themselves? Fine. Then there's no reason for us to save them."

"I can't abandon the people of Solace."

"Why the Sands not?"

"Pretend you come across a population of horses. Plain old horses, too dumb to do magic or help themselves. And a man wants to come through and cut them up for his own amusement. The horses are too dim to save themselves. Do you run off? Or do you help them because it's the right thing to do?"

"Are you saying that these townspeople are your poor dumb wards?"

"I'm saying I can't turn away. I know Stone is coming, and even if he is coming for *me*, he'll stop here first. He'll strip this town to its bones and take what he wants. He'll leave men behind like in Risk, and then he'll come after us. Either way, Solace loses, and eventually burns."

Before Edward could reply, the Water Reader came running up the street toward them, yelling and waving his hands frantically in the air. The Water Reader was an old coot; hair white and wild, and beard tangled enough to house a family of birds. His voice was high-pitched, like an old crone's from a Grimm Tale.

"It isn't just Stone who's coming," the Water Reader cried. "I couldn't see it at first, but now that they're closer, I have."

"He has men," said Clint, nodding.

"He has men behind him, yar," the Reader said. "But he also has someone in front. Someone even the great Hassle Stone must obey."

"Who?" Clint asked.

"I don't know." The Reader shook his head. "I can only see his silhouette… and his mount. Reason I ran here to the yonder was to tell you that whoever this dark man is, he's riding a unicorn of a different color."

CHAPTER FOUR: DECISIONS

Clint took Edward, who was nursing an even blend of fear and disgust after hearing of the dark rider and his mount, and walked to the Otel, where Mai was upstairs drinking a mug of Fanta from the bar.

"Fanta?" he said. "What's the occasion?"

"My fiancé has abandoned me and will be dying soon," she said. "I decided there was no point in waiting for my wedding toast. I'm going to drink it all, and damn the ridiculous price."

"Take it easy, Mai. You've no tolerance for improving drinks. You'll be on the floor."

"Don't tell me what to do, dead man," she said.

He took her arm and turned her around. She'd already had too much Fanta; he could see it in her eyes. Had she come straight here to start drowning sorrows that needn't be drowned?

"Grab hold of yourself, Mai. You're to hitch a gunslinger, yet you're acting like a trollop. Where's your grit? Where's the magic that's in your blood?"

"Enjoying itself," she said, raising her mug.

"Are you going to talk to me, or are you too far gone?"

She slapped him with her free hand.

"Better than drunk, anyway," he said.

Mai crossed to the Otel room's dresser and set the mug on its polished top, then dragged a suitcase from under the bed, unbuckled the straps, and began to fill it just as she had back in Clint's room above the boardinghouse.

"The coach will be ready in an hour. When's your date with

death?"

"Around the same time. But there's a new wrinkle."

"Is there a kitten in need of rescue?" She slurred the last half of her sentence. "Does a little old lady need help crossing the street?"

Clint came close to smacking her back, but stopped because a man should never hit a woman — only men who had it coming. But he wanted Mai back to her old self: the woman who could take what a man could. This pouty, selfish Mai was different, and not altogether good. Maybe it was the Fanta.

"You used to stand on law's right side," he said.

"I used to be on the side of *right*," she corrected. "There's a difference. You came to this town as an outlaw wearing the star of a lawman. You should've been stripped of your guns and mount back in The Realm, but you walked the Sands with both until you found a job in a small town in the Sprawl that gave you legal right. You of all people should know what I mean. Minding books isn't the same as minding sense."

"And you think leaving these people defenseless is minding sense?"

"You cannot help people who don't care to help themselves. If they want to dirty their knees to Stone, let 'em. Meanwhile my compassion and grit will be riding with me to Sojourn, searching for others who care as well for what's right, instead of settling for what's left."

"There's more at work here, Mai."

She turned, her interest piqued by something in his voice. She held a blouse above the open suitcase, pausing as she watched him, then set it in the suitcase and waited for Clint to continue.

"Stone brings with him a dark rider. Riding a unicorn of a different color."

She gasped, a hand suddenly over her mouth.

"Solace starves for magic, as does all of the Sands — all of the world since the Leaking first started. Stone and his party are close. I suspect —"

"— *I* suspect that a unicorn of a different color making you want to stay *even more* means you've already lost whatever sense you had. They aren't sensing dark magic as a sating of their thirst for magic of any kind. They have Edward in town already, with his white magic, and have for years."

"You don't understand this, regardless of your blood, Mai. Don't pretend like you do."

"I understand that when something pure willingly submits itself so fully to a master, it spits in the unblinking eye of creation! I understand that unicorn magic so totally under a human's control is dangerous indeed. And I understand that you and Edward would stand no chance against such power."

"Mai…"

"There's nothing you can do, Clint," she said. "Come with me. Maybe he'll be drawn away, and Solace will survive. Maybe not. But you cannot stand and fight, and I cannot stand to see you try."

"What I *cannot do* is run. You know I can't."

She sighed. "Yar, I suppose I do know just how pig-hearted you are. I just didn't want to believe it, since it makes you so stupid, stupid, stupid."

Clint's ire was starting to swell, but he forced himself to let it go. It was actually best if Mai left, but only after she understood that he had no choice but to stay. He would face whatever happened in Solace, live or die by his choice, and join her later if he was still breathing.

"Tell me," she said. "Have you made your rounds? Have you gone to the men of this town? Did you try to round up your posse, even before you knew about the dark rider?"

"Yar'm, I did."

"And was anyone willing to fight by your side?"

Clint was silent.

Mai flared with anger. "These people don't deserve you! This town is poisoned, like all of the rest of the Sprawl. It's the magic gone missing. Solace tolerates you, and is happy to let you protect them with Edward, but it's just that, Clint: *tolerance*. They don't change. They're sour like the air and the soil. What you see as redeemable here is all you brought with you, because of Edward. It's a facade. The town wears a false smile to hide its despicable, ruined, cowardly face."

"So I should abandon them?"

"Would you abandon rats?"

Clint stared, saying nothing.

"One hour, Clint. My coach leaves in an hour." Mai approached the marshal and set her hand on his arm. "Come with me. Please. You always said you wanted to return to The Realm, and I've not seen her walls since I was abandoned on the dusty side as a child. We may never find it — Providence says that no man or woman can — but Sojourn is at least a spoke closer on the spiral. This place is used. Discard it. Remember me, and you, and where we're supposed to be going. Don't throw it away."

"Once we left Solace as hitched, I was to no longer be a gunslinger," he said.

A half-smile crossed her full lips. "I think we both know that one way or another, with or without your marshal's star, you were leaving town on a unicorn's back, with fourteen shots across your hips."

Mai put one hand on the gunslinger's chest, then the other. Her hands were delicate and small, immaculate against the dust and grit clinging to Clint like a second skin. "Let's go. Take your guns and your unicorn. Take your woman. Let's leave. Now. It's not abandonment when folks are content to sit and stare into a setting sun. Your absence will make no difference."

His heaving chest rose and fell under her tiny hands. After a long moment, he finally said, "I can't."

Her small hands gave him a little shove. Without a word, she returned to her suitcase.

"Then go, gunslinger. Go to your death."

"I'll find you when this is over," he said. "Wherever you are."

She wouldn't meet his eyes as he stood near the Otel room door, listening to the ticking clock. He turned, and left the room to greet his doom.

CHAPTER FIVE:
THE KID

Clint returned to Edward's stall that wasn't a stall, in the barn that wasn't a barn. He was stuffing gear into his ancient cowskin rucksack when the orphan kid, Teddy, approached him from behind and jabbed a finger in his back.

Clint spun so inhumanly fast, Teddy didn't have time to retrieve his finger before Clint had a barrel from each gun digging into Teddy's forehead, both cocked. Clint saw it was only Teddy who had gotten the drop on him, then holstered both irons, lowering the hammers.

"That was a bad idea," said Clint.

"What color smoke comes out of them guns?" Teddy asked, nodding toward the gunslinger's hip. "I heard it ain't white."

"Gunslinger rounds use a special powder, highly illegal unless you're a marshal. It's a semi-magic firepowder, which makes a dull red smoke."

"You mean pink."

Clint said nothing, shoving more supplies in his pack. He'd have to shoulder the entire load when he and Edward went to the Flat Top, of course, since Edward wasn't a mule and didn't wear saddlebags, despite being many times stronger than Clint.

Edward's attitude reminded him of his own grandfather's. Clint's grandfather had lived in The Realm with the rest of them, back when what was now the Sands was still relatively magic. Grappy worked to bring home the money, so Grammy did everything else. Grappy reasoned he did enough, and shouldn't have to wash dishes... or carry cargo.

"Is it true that unicorns bleed rainbows?" Teddy asked.

"They have redundant vessels bearing many different magical elixirs," said Clint. "So yar, when wounded, before they magick themselves healed, their blood flows in multi-hues."

Teddy was poking around Edward's room, but meaning no harm. The boy was thirteen and curious, and in his mind, merely investigating cool cowboy stuff. But Clint knew that Edward, as he watched Teddy prod, saw it as an invasion of his privacy.

"What colors?" said Teddy.

"Red. Blue. Green. Purple. Yellow. Orange. More, I think."

"That's a rainbow," said Teddy.

"I guess."

Teddy poked at a stack of Joelalbums Edward had collected during his travels. "Being a gunslinger sounds really fruity," he said.

Clint said, "I assure you, the bad guys don't see it that way."

"So what else do unicorns do?" said Teddy. "Do they poop gold?"

"Yar," said Edward, breaking his silence. "Stick your hands under there and I'll show you."

"Holy Joe, you talk?" Teddy cried, rushing inside the stall toward Edward. Clint grabbed his arm and held him back, certain a stomping was imminent if Teddy violated Edward's space further.

"Of course I talk, you idiot," said Edward, turning back.

Teddy started singing an old campfire song about a talking horse named Mister Ed, glee on his face. Clint slapped his hand hard over the boy's mouth to keep him quiet. Being compared to a horse was bad enough for Edward, but a horse named Ed made the song downright infuriating.

"How come I never heard you talk before?"

"Because you're a dumb kid. Everyone else knows I talk."

"But you never go around talkin'. Like, being a member of the town. Is that because Mister Ed will never speak unless he has somethin' to say?"

Edward reared. If the stall door had been open, Teddy would have been facing two hooves in the face. Clint leaned down and whispered, "Do yourself a favor kid, and forget that song."

Teddy, unperturbed, shrugged, then resumed poking through Edward's things. After a moment, he said, "Bad guys are comin', right?"

"Yar, you could say that."

"You gonna kill 'em?"

"Yar."

"I'll help. I carry my own knife and water. I got a spyglass, for spying. And I got my gun." Teddy patted his side, where a heavy iron hung in a filthy leather holster. Clint somehow doubted that Teddy, who was small for his age, would be able to lift the thing and hold it steady — let alone summon the finger strength to pull the trigger. The only way he'd be able to use it, maybe, would be if he carried it around cocked and single-action, in which case it'd be a constant threat to blow his foot off.

"You're too young, Theodore," said Clint.

"Where ya goin?"

"The Flat Top."

"Why?"

"I want to look out across the Sands."

"You think you'll just *see* 'em coming?"

Clint inclined his head toward Edward. "I meant a different kind of seeing. Using magic."

"Say," said Teddy, "a unicorn's like a portable source of magic, right? Could you summon that magic yourself, like in a wand?"

"It doesn't work that way."

"Oh," said Teddy. "I'll bet if you could, it'd have to be a pink wand that made little pixie sparkles when you waved it around."

Clint said nothing, and certainly didn't volunteer the truth of Edward's horn, which glowed a yellowish pink when its magic was used. Or that, yes, it did sort of sparkle.

"So you going to the Flat Top right now? And that's why you're packing?"

"Yar."

"Okay. I'll come with you."

"No," said Clint. "We're going alone."

"You need help. I know it. I heard you went around to get people to stand with you against Stone. How many you get? How big is our posse?"

Clint grumbled.

"The whole town will come out, I'm sure. He's just one man, and a man can't stand against a whole town. So what can I carry?"

Clint grumbled again. Teddy grabbed two waterskins, slung them over his shoulders, then stood waiting for further orders. His innocent face wasn't endearing to Clint. It was annoying, and maybe even stupid. He'd need a lot of men to stand up to Stone and this other rider, but until he started finding some big men with fast hands, he'd prefer to ride solo. Teddy wouldn't be able to help, and it wasn't true that anything (or anyone) was better than nothing. Two was worse than one if the other was Teddy. The boy would only slow the gunslinger down, and get in the way of his bullets.

"You seem to think you're going." Clint shook his head. "But you're too young, Theodore. You'll get yourself killt."

Teddy's composure broke. "Aw, come on Marshal! Let me help. Everyone treats me like a man when it comes to earning a living, but suddenly when I want to help with something important, people tell me I'm only a kid. If I can get along in a Sands town without an ammy or appy, doing jobs and taking care of myself, then I should be allowed to help defend my home."

Clint felt bad for the kid. It was true, what he said, but there was more to it. Keeping Teddy away from the approaching quarrel had nothing to do with keeping the boy protected, or shielding him from any unpleasantness. The kid was a liability. He could help, sure, but he'd likely be helping the wrong side. Teddy was small and thin even for his young age, and had a tendency to trip over things even when they weren't in his way. Seemed as likely he'd shoot Clint or get in the way of one of the gunslinger's shots as it did that he would land a bulls-eye himself.

"I've even got my own horse," Teddy continued. "So you can ride your horse and I'll ride mine."

A sack of oats flew at Teddy's head. Teddy saw it and ducked, though he didn't seem to find it strange. It was as if people threw things at him so often that he'd grown completely used to it.

"Your horse can't keep up with us," Clint said.

Teddy made a face the gunslinger didn't quite get, but then the boy turned and sprinted for the door, yelling about how his horse was like greased lightning, and how he'd show him. Clint realized he'd made a mistake. Reject kids, and you have to reject them from feather to pie. You can't mention just one flaw in their plan. If you do, they'll assume that it's the only one, and that all they have to do is aim for a fix. But Clint wasn't used to kids, or adults. He was used to Edward, the Sands, and his own fast hands.

Clint figured he and Edward could slip away while Teddy was running off, presumably to gather his horse. He slung his rucksack over his shoulder along with the two remaining waterskins, then fought with Edward for two minutes before leaving the barn, trotting down Main past the Otel — seeing no sign of Mai — and out into the open Sands toward Flat Top.

Clint rode in silence, thinking of Mai.

When the gunslinger first arrived in Solace as an exiled marshal, astride a unicorn with two seven-shot guns hanging from his sides, everyone had stared, knowing *what* he was even if they didn't know *who* he was. Clint had gone into the saloon, practically *begging* the barkeep to challenge him or his right to drink an apple brew before using the tall closet. Clint's hand had hovered at his side, almost twitching. Fast as he was, Clint with his right hand above his holster was like a normal man holding his gun ready, cocked and well aimed.

If the barkeep was fool enough to make the wrong comment, or ask Clint a question he didn't eye proper, the man would've found himself dead on the floor in seconds. But the barkeep served Clint his apple brew and turkey pie without a word. Same for the man at the boardinghouse. Only later did Clint see that the reason everyone was so complicit was because Solace was used to doing what a man with a gun told them to do.

Even after Clint had run Stone from Solace, his distrust of its citizens lingered — along with their distrust of him. He'd ridden alone, with only a unicorn as a companion, for too long.

By the time he'd met Mai, though, he was respected in Solace. He'd won himself an official tin star, which made him their marshal. But a tin star wasn't a stand-in for friends. Clint lived with a constant expectation that the townspeople would cross him. He felt their stares, and knew they were whispering stories whenever his back was turned.

Mai changed everything. Maybe it was the purity of her magic and the way it counterbalanced Edward's jaded, cynical conjuring. Perhaps it was her beauty, or how she saw something noble in the disgraced, exiled gunslinger, even when he refused to see the same in himself.

Now she was sitting at the Otel, waiting for a carriage out of town — and, quite likely, out of his life forever. How quickly everything changed. Sure, Clint could tell himself they'd meet again in Sojourn. But how likely was that? How likely was it that Stone and the mysterious dark rider would arrive and that Clint would handle them quickly without getting killt, or that he'd be able to make it to Sojourn before Mai began a new life, moved on, or found someone else?

A narrow window was closing in front of his eyes. Maybe Mai was right.

Was Solace really worth giving up his one chance at being truly happy? He'd come to town loathing those he felt duty-bound to save. He'd always let his gunslinger's nature take precedence over his human side. Was that how he wanted to spend the rest of forever, always setting the needs of others before his own? Was he really willing to subjugate a future of contentment for a bunch of yallers who wouldn't even raise a hand to save their skins?

Clint patted Edward's neck.

Edward didn't like that Clint was bonding with Mai, but he knew, deep down, that Clint would never give up Edward (or even his guns) like the law said he must. He'd leave as he came, as a marshal who wasn't really a marshal. A gunslinger who was only supposed to sling a single gun at a time. No one would stop him when he left. They didn't have the courage to try.

But jealousy over Mai would be a petty irritation to Edward compared to the news that a unicorn of a different color was approaching. To Edward, even more than to Clint, the idea of a unicorn polluting his magic enough to mar his color away from the purity of white bordered on obscenity. The thought that a unicorn would surrender his will to any master was incomprehensible. And not just incomprehensible, either. It was bizarre, troubling, and downright profane.

Edward didn't like the idea of Mai, but he would see taking Mai to Sojourn as the lesser of two evils. All Clint had to do was make the suggestion. But he held it inside, riding in silence.

Ten minutes later, within sight of the Flat Top, Clint heard a set of clumsy hooves behind him. The gunslinger turned to see Teddy riding up on a pony that was somehow both less appealing and more awkward-looking than a mule. Its mane was frizzy, like a woman with full hair and no comb. Its teeth were visible even when its mouth was closed, and as it galloped (or maybe hobbled) closer, Clint noticed its lazy eye aimed in the wrong direction. It was panting and wheezing as if smoking a barrel of tobacco.

Of course. He'd told Teddy where he was going, so it was simple enough for the boy to follow them once he got back to the barn and found them missing.

Teddy grinned, waving at Clint when he saw him looking back. His face was half greeting and half I-told-you-so over the speed of Teddy's stallion.

"How much further is it to…" Teddy started to say, but Edward turned and shushed them. The unicorn's horn began glowing as he squeezed his eyes tight. He blinked, and after a moment said, "Okay, we can talk, but we must lower our voices. There's a party of five men over that rise, toward the base of Old Man Hill, sitting 'round a stew pool. They won't hear us yet, but they'll be able once we summit the hill."

"How do you know that?" Teddy asked.

"I'm a unicorn," Edward said dismissively. He'd been speaking to Clint about the party of men, and he resented Teddy being in earshot.

"*My* horse can't do that," said Teddy, almost sadly.

Clint flinched, but Edward ignored the insult. He was too busy taking in Teddy's mount from head to hooves to tail.

To the horse, Edward said, "You are one *ugly* mother…"

Clint interrupted him. "Come on. Let's summit the hill. You can insult each other at the top."

CHAPTER SIX:
BANDITS

Clint dismounted at the top of the hill, dropping the group's overall height to make them less visible. Teddy dismounted too, but his horse was so short that the boy's head ended up only slightly lower than when he was riding.

Edward turned to Teddy, apparently fine speaking with the boy as long as the words he spoke were insults.

"What is this creature's name? Jeb? Cletus? Eeyore?"

"Pinto," Teddy said.

"Fantastic. Reminds me of my old pal, Stumpy. He kept running into doors whenever he tried to enter a room. Liked to drink kerosene. Not good, the time he peed on a fire."

"Teddy," said Clint. "Do you still have that spyglass?"

Teddy patted a pouch at his side.

"Give it to me."

"Sure. Once we get up to the top."

"No. Just give it to me."

"We're a team, Marshal. I'll give it to you up top. You gotta let me come if you want my glass."

Clint opened his mouth, ready to tell Teddy that he could break his neck six times before the kid could raise a wrist to stop him. Instead, he closed it with a sigh and and started silently up the hill, leaving Edward and Pinto behind where Teddy had him tied to a scraggly tree. Edward was looking at the small horse as if it were an oddity at one of the Sprawl's traveling freak shows, his face a blooming rose of disgust.

Thirty feet further up, they found a spot where they could spy the hill's far bottom, maybe a quarter mile off. There were, as Edward had said, five men sitting around a stew pool, refilling waterskins.

Clint slapped Teddy's jacket with the back of his hand. Then he did it three more times, until the boy reached into the pouch, removed the spyglass, and handed it to Clint.

The gunslinger extended the glass and peered through the tiny lens at its small end. The men looked a month's worth of dirty, and were dressed head to toe in dark gear. They had five horses, all tied to hooks driven deep into several large rocks surrounding the away-facing edge of the stew pool. The horses were all carrying over-stuffed saddlebags and seemed too heavily burdened with gear.

"They're not traveling light," Clint said to Teddy. "Not a day trip. Wherever they're going, they're planning to stay."

"Solace?" said Teddy.

"Yar. Likely. I can see their path, and it stretches behind them. They'll climb this hill once they've finished resting. Unless they spin off into the Sands, which they won't, they'll hit Solace in her nose. These men are either coming to stay, or merely passing through. A stack of chips on the former."

"Is Stone with them?"

Clint adjusted the glass and scanned the short row of men.

"Nar. But they could be an advance party. The Water Reader said he saw Stone riding with a... another man. None of these men are he."

Clint didn't tell Teddy the reason he knew that the dark rider wasn't among the men: there was no dark unicorn amongst the horses. Few people knew about unicorns of a different color, and even fewer understood what they did or what they really were. A dark unicorn could get them killt like nothing else, and Clint didn't want to worry the kid. He didn't exactly care if Teddy was scared, but he figured if the kid *were* frightened, he'd be more of a liability than he already was.

"Maybe they're just travelers," Teddy suggested. "Good guys."

"I don't think so." Clint shook his head. "How often do people cross the Sands, willing to get lost in the Sprawl? How often do new people arrive in Solace? Nar, I'd say the chance of random travelers arriving on the same day as Stone are about as likely as magic true on the dusty side of the wall."

"Okay," said Teddy. "Let's kill them, then."

"Have you ever killt anything?"

"Rats. And I once had to shoot a mad cat. Winged it right across its left ear."

"A rabid cat?" said Clint. You heard about rabid dogs sometimes, but not usually cats.

"A *mad* one," said Teddy, in a voice suggesting that Clint should probably pay closer attention.

"And now you want to ride into a group of five armed men and kill every one?"

"*You* could do it," said Teddy.

"Yar, but you said *we*. Why do I have to get dragged into a *we* situation filled with stupidity when I'm not the one needing a bib to soak up my drool?"

"You just said…"

"I said they're probably *part* of Stone's party. Stone and this other rider aren't with them. Can you think of how we might find Stone and the other? It doesn't involve killing them all outright."

"Follow 'em? Spy on 'em?" Teddy suggested.

"Good for you," Clint growled. "Finding a way to use that worthless shoulder pumpkin."

Teddy turned his head, looking from one shoulder to the other.

Clint tapped the boy on his back, waited for Teddy to turn, then gestured with his head toward where Edward and the pathetic Pinto were standing. The pony was nibbling grass, eyes split in two directions. Clint could tell from the poor creature's defeated body that Edward was insulting it, and probably hadn't stopped or even slowed since they'd started up the hill.

They returned to their mounts, and Clint told Edward what he'd seen. The unicorn nodded since he'd seen most of it with his magic already.

"Now I suppose you want to go down there," said Edward.

"Yar. We need peer into their conversation."

"We?" said Teddy.

"Stone and the other rider aren't with them," Clint told Edward, ignoring Teddy. "We need to find where they'll meet, and what they're doing."

"We, like… *all* of us?" Teddy said again, swallowing. He looked like he was trying to solve one of The Realm's *problems without a solution*.

"Fine," Edward agreed. "The sooner you can kill whatever needs killing, the sooner I can return to my turkey pie, and the sleep that follows."

"*We*… including a unicorn?"

Edward said, "I'm the most important one here, seed for brains."

"But…"

"Are you wondering how a 1400-pound, bright white creature will sneak close enough to eavesdrop on a stew hole?"

Teddy nodded.

"You'll see. Watch from where we were before."

Teddy said, "Wait. No, I'm coming with you."

"No you're not," said Edward.

"I'm the only man you were able to get," said Teddy, standing tall and puffing his chest. "Like it or not, I'm number two in this two-man posse."

"I tried to ride alone," Clint reminded him, leaving out the part about Teddy being only a boy.

"And I found you anyway! Now *that's* a dedicated posse!"

Clint looked at Edward, raising his eyebrows.

"I can fit him. Plus, if he comes with us, he might get shot." Edward said the last part as if it were a bonus.

"Fine," said Clint. He accompanied Edward to the hill's edge, near enough so the men at the stew hole would soon be able to see them if they looked up. Teddy followed, holding Pinto by the reins.

"You're kidding, right?" Edward sighed, as if Teddy's stupidity was an extra thousand pounds on his back. "That thing stays here."

"But he's my mount. What if we have to ride?"

"Then you'll be lucky to not have a handicap between your legs," said Edward.

Teddy wrinkled his nose, then went back to the tree and lashed Pinto to it again. As Teddy started toward Edward and Clint, Pinto began a low, desperate whinnying.

"Shut it up," Edward ordered.

"He hates being left," Teddy explained. "Even at the barn, he's never alone. Pinto has a goat, named Cheesy."

"You can stay with him," Edward suggested. "Like Cheesy."

"I'm not staying."

Clint and Edward kept walking. Teddy seemed torn, but scampered to catch up as Pinto kept whining behind him.

"It's going to *give us away*!" Edward hissed.

Pinto made a bona-fide "hee-haw," like a donkey, and started pawing the dirt.

"*He*," said Teddy. "*He* is going to give us away."

"*He* is about to get magicked into an embolism," said Edward, his horn already glowing a dull pinkish yellow.

Teddy jumped between Edward and Pinto, as if he anticipated Edward would fire a projectile. "Don't you *dare*!" he cried, watching as the pink-yellow glow slowly faded from the unicorn's horn. Clint waved a hand at Teddy, who looked like he was on the verge of saying something new about gunslingers and unicorns being sort of fruity.

Teddy was too close to Pinto's mouth. The horse started chewing on his master's pants.

Clint approached Teddy and put a hand on his shoulder. "Look. We need stealth. I know you want to come with us, but your mount is too unpredictable."

"He'll be fine if he stays with us," Teddy insisted.

Pinto ripped off one of his pockets and chewed loudly.

"Stay here with him," Clint said. "That's an order, as your marshal. If you're my deputy, then it's your duty to stay here with your mount while we surveil. Yar?"

Teddy looked back into the gunslinger's eyes with a surprisingly mature intelligence. "Marshal, what happens if while you're down there, they pick up and decide to ride on to Solace?"

Clint's head picked up and his mouth fell open. He felt suddenly old. His oversight was rudimentary enough to hurt. The riders would crest the hill, only to find a kid and his broken pony. That might be fine — Teddy could argue he was only out riding and got lost — but even if it *was* okay, and even if the riders *didn't* kill him outright, Teddy's presence so near their meeting hole would be enough for them to stop and give a good look around. They wouldn't have to squint to see two more sets of tracks, one equine and another human.

Clint looked back at Edward to see if he'd heard what the kid had said. Edward gave a small nod, indicating that if he wasn't allowed to give Pinto a fatal embolism, he should be able to cover them as they sneaked down to the stew hole.

"Come on," Clint said, gesturing. "We'll show you how a marshal, his deputy, and two mounts can get the drop on five men."

CHAPTER SEVEN:
THE STEW HOLE

Two minutes later, Clint, Teddy, Edward, and Pinto crested the hill from the side, aiming their ride toward the men in the stew hole. Edward's horn was at the highest point in their two-rider formation, and glowing. What looked like a shower of sparks blossomed from the horn's tip, cascading over their procession like an umbrella. The surrounding magic was clear, but made everything appear pinkish yellow, making the Sands shimmer as if seen through a haze of heat, and lightly twinkle as though sprinkled with pixie dust.

"This is the manliest stakeout I've ever been on," Teddy said, staring at the fairy sparkles.

Edward snarled. "I can let you out of the umbrella if you'd like."

"I mean, it's cool, but it's just so…"

"Keep your voice down," Clint whispered. "They won't be able to see us, but they can hear us, and we're still making tracks. That's why we walked to the side and obscured our prints up top." Pinto, under Teddy, was perfectly mute now that it seemed the boy wouldn't leave him.

"How are we going to hear them?"

"By listening."

"With magic?"

"I'm occupied," said Edward, nudging his nose around at the sparkly umbra. "Use your ears."

As they rode closer, communication between the two-man posse drifted to gestures. Pinto was surprisingly quiet, making it easy for the party to get reasonably close.

The five men at the stew hole were dressed in dusty trail shirts, each with a bandana slung around his neck to help filter the endless dust and winds forever whipping through the Sands. They were all unshaven, with skin the color of cowhide. All wore two guns, which was illegal for men who weren't marshals, and which more or less validated Clint's suspicions that the men were part of Stone's posse. He was glad to see the irons were all six-shooters, comforted that the taboo of trading or using magic guns was still respected in the Sprawl.

The men sat on a winding row of rocks set around the shallow pool, dipping long stew rods into the steaming water. The gathering had the feel of friends nursing Fantas in a friendly saloon. They weren't just pausing for a spell at the stew hole. The bandits seemed to be murdering minutes. They were waiting — taking a load off until some time when they were scheduled to depart.

But what — or whose — schedule were they keeping?

One of the men stood, then pulled a wide package from one of the saddlebags on his horse. Inside the package were five smaller parcels, each roughly the size of a brick. He passed them to the other four. One of the men refused, so he took the fifth for himself and sat down to unwrap it.

"Everyone likes turkey pie," said the first man. "What's wrong with you, Roger?"

"Turkey and pumpkin mash?" The man called Roger made a face. "That was a town dish in my grappy's day. Now you take it, toss it into a saddlebag for days with a chunk of ice, and take the chance it won't infect you with a poison stomach once you get to gnawing. Nar, a real trail man eats jerky."

Roger reached into his own horse's saddlebags and pulled out a wrapped package, longer than it was wide, and peeled back the paper to reveal long, flat sicks of cured meat. Probably ostrich.

"Real man. Is that what you are?" said another of the men, fatter than the others, with a stovepipe hat, missing its top half.

"Yar. Says your mother."

A man across the group wearing thick round glasses spoke up. "The Leaking might be the best thing for manliness," he said. "People complain about it, but ponder the notion. The Realm's soft folks got softer, while the hard in the Sands've been getting harder. Even townies've been getting tough, and those who didn't get tough up and died. In *my* grappy's day, only the most desperate men rode into the Sands, be they filling their saddles with pie *or* jerky. Now it's how we all are. I say cheers and yar!"

The man with the glasses raised an imaginary mug, but nobody returned the salute. The circle's body language, worn on the group like an old coat, told Clint that the man often spoke of things no one cared about, and was so ignored.

"What time is it?" said the man with the jerky.

"You've got the watch," said a man who hadn't spoken yet. His face was long, like that of a horse.

"I have *a* watch, but it's bound in my saddle. That's why I'm asking you all."

"You have *the* watch," said the man with the glasses.

"I have the only watch?" The man looked suddenly upset. "What if it breaks? The cogs could get sullied with sand. Happens all the time. We could end up telling time by the sun."

"Then maybe we'll be late," said the man who had carried the turkey pie. He took a large bite, and spoke around the food in his mouth. "Stone isn't a train, so he ain't pulling into no station at any o'clock. He'll be there when we meet him, and we'll meet him when we find him."

The others around the circle stopped chewing their pie and jerky, apparently as aghast as the first man to learn there was but one watch in the company, and that they were trusting their timeliness to such an unsteady source.

"You haven't ridden with him before, Bradford. When Stone says 3pm at the High Rock, he means 3pm at the High Rock. Arrive five minutes after three and get a slug in the gut for your trouble. Never mind the loss to the party. I done seen him do it, too. Yar. You keep an eye on that watch, Roger. If it slips, we ride as fast as we can; we make the High Rock and we wait. I don't care if we're hours early, so long as we're not a minute late. What time is it now?"

Roger unwrapped the watch from a swaddle of cheesecloth like he was inside Castle Spires handling The Realm's most delicate plates. He stared at the watch's face before replying, probably making sure the watch hadn't stopped.

"Just after noon," he finally said.

Several of the other men glanced up at the sun and nodded, deciding that seemed about right.

Bradford studied the heads bobbing around the stew hole, chuckling through his mouthful of turkey pie. A swallow's worth of mush fell from his mouth as he said, "You're all that a'feared of Stone? He's just a man. In a party of six, he's but one."

Nobody said anything. They just traded empty glances from one to the other.

"You've not ridden with Stone," Roger repeated, his eyes not on Bradford, but rather the group's only watch as he swaddled it back in the cloth. Then, as an afterthought, he pulled another rag from his saddlebag and wrapped the bundle again.

"And you haven't yet seen Kold," said the last man.

Clint tensed from head to toe. The hairs on his neck started to dance.

"Or seen Kold and Stone together," the man continued. "It's like a haunting, I shiv you not."

"That's another thing," said Bradford. "I was hired on a six-way split. Now there's this other man handing out orders, and if I can add — which I can, up to ten — that's *seven* shares."

"Kold doesn't want no share," said the man who'd spoken earlier. "He has his own aims in Solace."

"Exactly. His own aims. Aims which will conflict with ours, thankoo and pleasem. Say his aims are the General Store. Well, that means the store's contents are less in the way of spoils for us."

"That's not what I meant. Kold wants something else. Nobody knows what, but it's something specific and nothing in our interest. Says Stone, anyway."

Bradford snickered. "Why so mysterious?"

The men around the stew hole must not have known, because they shook their heads. Bradford was the only one who seemed to find anything worth laughing about.

Beside Clint, under the umbrella of sparkly pink energy, Teddy was drawing his index finger across his throat, silently asking if they should go ahead and kill the bandits.

Clint shook his head.

Teddy repeated the gesture, pointing to Clint's guns, then his own.

Clint shook his head again.

Pinto collapsed on his side and closed his eyes, waiting for sleep, or maybe death. Teddy rolled into the dirt rather gracefully when it happened, as if it were a common occurrence.

Teddy stood up. He was acting as if Clint hadn't understood. He mimed himself holding an invisible gun, then racked off imaginary shots at each of the bandits. His invisible gun was extremely powerful. The recoil after each shot drove his hands high enough to give him an imaginary concussion. As he finished each shot, his cheeks puffed out. Even though he had to be quiet, he couldn't resist making as much of the "boom" as he could.

Clint took Teddy by the arm, guiding it until the boy had slipped his imaginary gun back into the real holster on top of his real sidearm, then he pointed at his own head and tapped it.

Below them on the ground, Pinto farted.

"What was that?" said the bandit with the glasses.

Teddy made a face at Clint, both an apology and an insistence that it wasn't his fault. Edward rolled his eyes, the umbrella still flowing out from his glowing horn.

"Phantom fart," said Roger, his voice full of tumbleweeds and mystery, as though speaking of a legendary beast.

"Don't tell me you're worried about ghoulem. They're just an old wives' tale!"

"Your problem, Bradford," said the man who'd mentioned Kold earlier, "is that you're not worried about anything."

"You bet," Bradford said. "One day you women might learn to appreciate the levity that comes from such a free mind as mine." He laughed.

"A good gunman needs to be at least a little a'feared all the time. Else what reason does he have to aim true?"

"Poetic. That's beautiful, Owen. Like a handful of sunflowers. Can you sing me a song?"

"You'd better get a little a'feared. You talk that way when we meet with Kold, and you'll find trouble."

Bradford said, "He's just a man."

Teddy tugged on Clint's sleeve, making the throat-slitting gesture more urgently.

"Look at this pie," said one of the men whose name hadn't been given, holding up the package Bradford had handed him earlier. "It's moldy."

"So eat the mold," said Roger. "It's good for you."

"No it's not," the man disagreed.

Once discussion drifted to pie and mold rather than bosses, Clint looked down at Teddy, then pointed behind them, indicating that they should regroup. Edward kicked Pinto and the horse rose slowly back to his hooves. They walked, still under Edward's umbrella, back to their earlier dismount point on the far side of Flat Rock.

CHAPTER EIGHT: DHARMA KOLD

Safely out of sight, Edward let the umbrella collapse and vented the unicorn version of a sigh. His eyes grew heavy and twitching, as his color subtly shifted from a radiant, almost glowing brilliant white to a more common bright white, almost snowy.

Clint ran a hand down the unicorn's back, starting between his ears, then repeated the gesture twice more, gently. As he finished, Edward looked at Teddy, then Pinto.

"I should kick your mount to death," said Edward. "That fart was careless."

Clint turned to Teddy. "It's hard for him to cast an umbrella that large for so long," he explained. "It takes a lot of concentration. Your horse laying down and then…being distracting makes it harder."

"He's a horse," said Teddy, as if that explained everything.

"Then get on your horse," said Clint.

"What are we going to do?"

"We're going to High Rock."

Teddy looked back toward the crest of the hill, his eyes full of confusion.

"Get on your mount," Clint repeated.

Teddy did. Clint climbed onto Edward's back and they started off as they'd come. After they'd put some distance, a scatter of sparse trees, and a few hills between the posse and High Rock (and after Edward verified that the bandits were still back at the stew hole) Clint allowed the group to talk.

"You wanted to kill those five men out of hand? Fine. Let's assume you could work that pistol. And let's assume we could get all five before they got us — which we could, and by 'we,' I mean 'me.' And I also means 'while trying to avoid getting shot by you.' Let's also assume it's okay to break Sands Treaty and spill blood at a stew hole, which it most certainly isn't and never will be. What do you think Stone and the rest of the big, bad men would have done when their soldiers didn't show?"

Teddy shrugged.

"Stone is bad. He's emptied towns without blinking; he subdued Solace for years before we arrived and drove him out. But Stone is only a man. You change this story so it's Stone and five men coming to town, and we could handle it easily. But there are things we don't know, and things we do. For one, how could we be sure those five represented all of Stone's posse?"

"I just assumed..." Teddy began.

"That's the problem with people in general," said Edward. "You assume everything. You assume that all creatures are beneath you, and yours for subduing. Do you know why the marshal rides me? Because I *allow* it. Because I *choose* to be here. He has not tamed me."

"Really? Because I always heard that —"

"You *assume*, you *figure*, and then you pass your tales from one idiot to another," said Edward, with more rancor than usual. We are not your pets. Not usually, anyway."

Teddy's face scrunched at that last part, but Clint continued before he could ask what the unicorn meant.

"Stone could have groups of men coming from all over," he said. "They could *all* be meeting at High Rock. It's a convenient place, accessible from every direction, and sitting just outside of Solace. The way trails across the Sands cut into one another, High Rock's like the hub of a wheel. If Stone has a dozen groups of five and one don't show, might they not decide someone was onto them, and adjust their plans?"

Teddy nodded. "I suppose?"

"It's what I'd do. We predicted Stone would have dozens of men, after all. But I don't think that's what's happening. Now, if I ventured a guess, I'd say it's just that half-dozen minus one, plus Stone and Kold. You heard them talk about splitting their spoils into six. They're treating it like a bank job rather than something as tangled up as the taking of a town. There might be more men coming, hired guns not entitled to a share, but the odds are against it. I'd say it's us versus seven."

"So you can handle them," said Teddy.

"It's long odds."

"Well, that'd be straight-up truth if you didn't have a unicorn," said Teddy. "But you do, so..." He started making shooting motions with both of his hands, nearly falling from his mount as he did.

"Problem is, we're not looking at seven normal men," said Clint. "You couldn't know this, Theodore, but the man they were stewing on — Kold — has gotta be Dharma Kold, who I unfortunately know too much about. His presence is troubling like a drought. You've heard of The Realm?"

"Of course. Where everyone wants to go. The city that broke loose in the fracture, and now is nowhere."

"The things you believe about The Realm are mostly true," said Clint. "It's the one place left where there's still abundant magic, without the need for unicorns to produce it and carry it. They have riches they don't appreciate, and it turns them a sort of sour they can't help, or get blame for. I was a marshal in The Realm, a long time missing, as was Dharma Kold. We were banished, and found ourselves on the dusty side of the wall. Once we were driven out a half mile into the Sands and could no longer see the wall, The Realm disappeared, gone to us forever. Even if we'd retraced our steps, we wouldn't have been able to find it. Looking drove us mad. The Realm works on you, kid, making you forget there's life outside it. So Kold and I, who once counted each other as friends, were united in anger and hatred. We plotted to return to The Realm. But we went about it different than most."

Clint squinted at the still-vacant trail spread out behind them. They were halfway to High Rock with plenty of time. He wanted to be early enough to stake out and hide, which meant getting there before Kold, Stone, or any of the others arrived.

"Kold and I walked together for many endless miles," he told Teddy. "You lose track of time and reality near The Realm and along the fault lines. It's part of The Realm's magic. I've no honest clue if Kold and I rode together for a month, a year, or ten years. We simply kept on, dipping into stew holes whenever we happened upon them, snaring game for food, and occasionally finding a town where we could pay for a shave, maybe a room, and a couple times some company. Time passed like blurs inside a dream, like one of those scenes in the flicker talkies where the view smears to show confusion. For the longest time it was hazy but tolerable, and we got along, both holding onto our marshal's guns and our companions —"

"He means their unicorns," said Edward.

Teddy nodded. Pinto placed one hoof in front of the other, taking faster steps than Edward in order to keep up.

"We were both angry when we left The Realm, and that made us dangerous. Behind the wall, it was our *job* to be dangerous — the proper sort, anyway. When we were banished, they let us keep everything that made us marshals. If they'd tried to take our guns, our unicorns, or even our stars, we'd have killt them dead. They knew they'd never see us again anyway, so they simply let us go, knowing we'd be lost a half-mile past the wall and out of their hair forever. So after leaving, we made plans. Dreamed dreams. But Kold's dreams and plans grew disturbing. His unicorn didn't balance out his human aggression like Edward does for me — one very important part of a healthy human-unicorn pairing. Kold's unicorn, Cerberus, only fed his hunger for discord. You've heard the expression 'a horse of a different color'?"

Teddy nodded.

"The expression means, 'something entirely different,' and is based on a literal change in the color of a unicorn, which makes that unicorn something very different indeed. Enough time on the trail, and I started accepting my whereabouts. Kold took to wrassling with his. Kold's unicorn fed his anger, or maybe *on* his anger. Everything changed. At first, the changes were subtle. Unicorns are supposed to be bright white, like Edward. They're fiercely independent. You don't ever *command* a unicorn, and never dare insult them. Kold's unicorn, though, became a dull white, then a dusty gray, and started to follow his say-so. That's when I knew it was time to leave. It was Edward's idea, nosing me awake in the middle of the night, casting a cone of protection around us as we trotted off into the depths of the Sprawl. That was the last I saw of Dharma Kold, though I've heard plenty stories since."

"As have I," said Edward. Clint noticed with surprise there was no scorn in his voice. He was speaking to the kid, on his crappy horse, as if he were an equal. "We have a kind of radar. There are unpaired, nomadic unicorns all over, and we're all connected. I can 'talk' to any who are close, and those I reach can 'talk' to any within their range. In this way, we can cover great distances inside our minds and magic. Sometimes we even reach out and 'talk' to horses, though it's very different. We must be up close, and horses are dumb animals, so we can only pull rough color from their thoughts — things they've seen as they've seen it, without interpretation. Based on all I've seen, across stories told by both horse and unicorn, there is a recurring tale of a dark rider, tearing through the Sands on a unicorn of pure, obsidian black."

"And that's bad?"

"Most unicorns are strong. As the marshal said, we're independent. We partner with humans of merit, but always willingly and never as servants."

Clint shrugged the rucksack that he, the human, was carrying, darkening the ink around Edward's point.

"But some of us are weak, just as some humans are. Weak unicorns wish to lose themselves to the bliss of surrender, just as some humans relish the loss of control — allowing another to take charge, hold the reins, and make all the decisions. It's tempting to do, but also a damnation. A unicorn of a different color has surrendered control of its magic to its rider."

Teddy's mouth fell open. "He's more powerful than you," he whispered to Clint. "That's why you're being so careful."

"That's an understatement, since I've no power. I'm a man. Kold's unicorn has made him more than a man. It's made him magic."

"How can you beat a magic man?"

"Carefully," said Clint. "The thing to remember is that the amount of magic between Cerberus and Kold is unchanged from the days when Cerberus had it all. It is simply under human control now, and housed at least partly inside a human. It's also influenced by a human's more base emotions and needs. Cerberus is black, like the magic itself, but Edward still holds as much magic as their pairing does now and more than Cerberus does alone. And I'm a better man than Kold, when he *is* only a man. I could always outgun him."

"So you can beat him?" Teddy looked hopeful.

"I seriously doubt it," Clint said. "It's complicated, but the short version is, purity almost always loses to pollution when the two are served in equal shares. Acceptance versus will. You can't ram purity and acceptance into something like you can with hatred. Make sense?"

"Nar."

"Okay, I'll put it this way. If you wish to keep breathing, here's what you should do: ride ahead, gather your things from Solace, and head to Sojourn immediately. If you find my woman, Mai, tell her that if I don't meet her in Sojourn, I'll meet her in NextWorld."

Teddy shook his head. "I'm standing with you."

Edward turned to the kid. "You're such an idiot. What are you going to do? I know you're a boy and believe in the fantastic, but the gunslinger just said *he* can't stand against Kold — and he's a marshal, trained in The Realm, partnered with a unicorn. Who are you?"

"I'm your ward!"

"No, you are *not*," Clint said.

Teddy stared ahead, his face tight and determined. Edward could magick him across the sands, but the kid would only ride back. Could Clint really blame him? The boy was an orphan, making his own way in a dead-end town. Adventure, in whatever form he could find it, was all he had to live for.

The kid finally broke his pouting silence. "You can't beat Kold?"

Clint said, "I very seriously doubt it."

"Then why are we headed to High Rock?"

"To find them as they meet, and disrupt what we can before we die."

"I have a better idea," said Teddy. "Let's ride back into Solace. Get the town to evacuate. Then run off ourselves."

"Your plan is to run?" said Clint. "You've a lot to learn if you wish to carry that gun like a man."

"Run and live versus stay and die. Even an orphan knows which is better."

"Then do it yourself, like I already suggested."

"All for one," said the kid. It was probably his way of saying he'd be doing whatever the marshal did, and nothing less.

"The town won't evacuate." Clint shook his head. "People never flee peril, even when the alternative's doom. Sure, they could make Sojourn, but only as paupers. They'd need to abandon their houses, possessions, and places of business. They'd march or ride into the Sands with only what they could carry on their backs. Most folks aren't that strong. Most need the warm and fuzzy of the known."

"They'd leave if you told them what you just told me," Teddy said. "And you'd have… what? An hour before the soonest they could arrive, if we ride straight?"

Clint pulled a watch from his pocket, opened it, and checked it against the sun. "Yar," he said. "An hour. But they'd never leave. Even if they did, it'd never be all of 'em."

"Is that why you're staying — to protect those who refuse to leave?"

"Yar."

"If a few stay, screw 'em," said Teddy.

"What percentage, young Theodore, is worth surrender? Where should a gunslinger draw the line at how many people die before a good man will intervene?"

"You said you can't do anything to help them."

"Nar." Clint shook his head. "I said I can't *win*. That's different."

Teddy turned to Edward and addressed the unicorn directly. "You seem selfish. Are you sure you're on board with this?"

Edward offered a small, equine chuckle in exchange for Teddy's moxie. "I'm proud, and I'm nearly immortal. I'll do what I can to assist the marshal, but how and where he choses to die is his decision."

Teddy sighed, shaking his head.

"Same goes for you," Edward added. "The one choice forever in a man's control is the way he faces his death — the one thing that is *truly* his. I would never presume to tell you how to die, either."

A few beats passed in silence.

"Although if you were to ask for suggestions —" Edward couldn't help it. "— I'd suggest getting out of town, seeing as you won't make it through the first shot."

CHAPTER NINE:
HIGH NOON

Another fifteen minutes of silent riding and they hit the outskirts of High Rock.

No one spoke. The only sounds in the Sands, outside of the wind's angry whisper, were the steady ticking of hooves — one set large and slow, and another smaller and faster — slapping the packed dirt of the trail.

By the time they were within a mile of High Rock, Clint had devised a way to get Teddy out of the way. He said that if the boy insisted on being Clint's ward and sacrificing himself on the marshal's mission, that was his business. He repeated: *You are choosing certain death and are a fool for doing so.* Then, once Teddy's defensive wall was higher than the walls of a tall closet, Clint sighed, pushed a barrel of breath from his lungs, and gave the kid his mission.

"Ride into town," he said. "You may be shot by bandits on your way, since I suspect Stone may have summoned groups from the east who will have to ride through Solace before meeting up with the others at High Rock. Be vigilant." He paused. "You sure you want to do this?"

Teddy nodded.

"Fine, fine. Your choice, even if it's turkey stupid. If you manage to survive, head to the Otel and find Mai. If she's not left town, which I suspect she hasn't despite her earlier claims, help her pack and force her onto a carriage. Use your gun if you need to, then ride with her to Sojourn. You'll be pursued, if you ever make it that far, and will surely be killt on your way. Try to get as many of the bad guys as you can before you die." Clint turned to Teddy and put a hand on his arm.

"I ask again: Are you absolutely sure you want to do this?"

The kid's face was set. "I'm sure."

"You're choosing certain death. For nothing."

"My choice, Marshal."

"Yar. So it is."

The kid tipped him a salute, then slapped his pathetic horse on the rear and rode off toward town as fast as he could.

Barely out of earshot, Edward said, "Kids are stupid."

"It's better to speak of nobility over stupidity."

"Better?" Edward said. "Maybe for you. But stupidity is so dominant in that one, I had to turn to keep from laughing. The kid will be sneaking through town with his gun drawn, hiding behind barrels on his way to the Otel. He'll try forcing your woman into a carriage if she's still around, but if I have a feeling for Mai at all, and I see no reason to think I don't, she'll likely wallop the boy and smack the gun from his palm the second she sees it. If they get on the carriage, he'll make the entire trip with gun drawn and pulse racing, eyes bugging out from his face on the lookout for bandits."

"But he'll survive."

Edward laughed. "Shall I try and convince you that your noblest mission would be to skip the Rock, run into Solace, and hop onto that carriage with the two of them?"

"Just look ahead to the Rock. See anything yet?"

"No. The Rock is clear. And I can't feel any other unicorns, either. Strange in itself."

Clint had a spark of hope, but it was squashed by Edward immediately.

"That doesn't mean Kold isn't riding Cerberus," he said. "I was losing the ability to sense Cerberus even back when he was ashy grey. I think it's because we're on the wrong frequency. Or maybe because the magic is under the command of..." Edward stopped, as if unwilling to say more.

They crossed the final stretch to High Rock, hitting the end of the trail at two o'clock — a full hour before the bandits were due to rendezvous with Kold and Stone.

High Rock was aptly named. In the middle of the Sands trails — ten minutes on horseback outside of Solace — sat a small, isolated hill. Town rumor swore High Rock was some sort of burial mound. At the top of the hill was a massive boulder, buried halfway in the sand. The rest of the rock stuck out of the sand like a finger pointing at the sky.

High Rock made no sense, and shouldn't have existed. The Sands were mostly sand, but High Rock sat at the top of a tall hill that looked like little more than a giant dune, though clearly it wasn't. The endless winds that often obscured the trails never beat down the hill. It was as if the entire hill was the rock itself, with a thin skin of filth and soil sticking to its ugly windward face.

High Rock was a curiosity, especially since stones were so small in the Sands. The Rock seemed to have been dropped there by Providence, just like the church said it was.

Kold and Stone probably chose High Rock as their meeting spot since it would be impossible to surveil without being seen. From the top of High Rock, a person could see miles of sand, broken only a by few objects that might provide some possible cover. Anyone meeting at the top would know they were being watched… unless, of course, the watcher rode with a unicorn.

Clint and Edward waited, concealed from the trail in a shallow depression behind a small cluster of cacti. A quarter hour passed, then another. Then another.

With only fifteen minutes before the scheduled meeting time, Edward cast another umbrella, and they vanished from outside view. The riders wouldn't want to be late. Based on their frightened conversation at the stew hole, Clint figured the group would arrive soon to avoid their leaders' anger.

Another five minutes were gone from the clock. It was nearly time, but still no riders crested the horizon. Clint rubbed his still-smooth chin, his brow furrowed.

"Something's been bothering me," he rasped, breaking their shared silence for the first time since hitting the top of High Rock.

The unicorn turned. His horn was glowing lightly. Sparks flew out from it and into a giant dome.

"Yar?"

"Stone knows we're in Solace, which means that Kold does too. But if I put myself in either pair of spurs, this don't make sense. They'd both know our Water Reader would see 'em coming, and that I'd ride out to meet them before they hit town, and that I'd do so only after sussing out their intentions. It'd be natural to choose High Rock as a spot to palaver since you could see anyone coming for miles, but if I were jingling their spurs rather than mine, I'd be thinking that the town marshal and his unicorn could still hide anywhere beneath a magic umbrella"

"What are you saying?"

"It's too dumb, what they're doing." Clint shook his head. "It's so dumb, it's almost blind. They're coming to Solace in plain view to anyone magic, or with access to a Reader, and riding as light as a feather. Seven men, and only one of them strong enough to make a difference. When we rode out, we predicted dozens. That many, even without a dark rider on a unicorn of a different color, could overwhelm us. Seven's a cactus without any needles."

"They're counting on Kold."

"I don't buy it," said Clint. "Kold is a marshal, which means we're kin in thought. Any man who chambers fourteen shots and rides a unicorn wouldn't do this. It's too dumb."

"Maybe the theft of his unicorn's magic has made him stupid."

But Clint heard doubt in the unicorn's words. The one thing magic didn't do was make its user stupid. Edward said it plenty of times: magic made a creature smarter, further-seeing, insightful, able to see seven steps ahead…

As the obvious clicked into place, Clint's hand fell instinctively to his gun. He turned to Edward. The unicorn, reaching the same conclusion, was staring back.

"He wanted me out of town," Clint said.

The gunslinger had done exactly what he was supposed to. He'd heard of an approaching threat, then rode out of town with barely a thought to greet it. If Kold and Stone had come from the other direction while Clint and Edward were waiting….

Edward's umbrella disappeared and the unicorn tossed his head impatiently at Clint. The gunslinger swung his body onto Edward's back as the unicorn's powerful haunches churned beneath him. Edward gathered immediate speed as Clint twisted his hands through Edward's mane and fell into his most familiar rhythm, moving with his mount, loose enough to hold his balance through the gallop.

"How long?" said Clint.

"Normally ten or fifteen minutes," Edward yelled over the wind and the thundering of hooves. "But this is a special occasion."

Edward's horn started to spark as if it were grinding against steel, glowing beyond its normal pinkish-yellow hue and into a dull, throbbing red. Sparks erupted in a cone around his horn, as if the unicorn were pushing his way through something solid.

The thundering of hooves grew distant as the world went dim around them, like someone had lowered the oil in the lamp of the world. For the thinnest sliver of a second, the world was a featureless, silent black before returning to its rightful color. The cone of sparks disappeared, and thirty seconds of riding out from High Rock, Clint found himself at the farback of Solace's high street as Edward panted and shook beneath him.

"Are you okay?" said the gunslinger.

"Yar," Edward said, nodding. "But…" His right front leg faltered, almost causing him to lose his balance.

"Can you fight?"

"I'll be able to soon. It was a shallow fold. I'll recover fast."

Clint hopped down from Edward's back, not wanting to burden the unicorn while he was already so weak — or risk being crushed if Edward's balance gave out and he fell.

Edward's head was moving side to side, taking in the town. "I don't see anything," he said. "Maybe you were wrong."

"I wasn't."

As if on cue, a shot rang out from behind the bank. Clint watched a tiny bloom of white smoke — a commoner's plume — and felt the slice of lead burn into his side. Whoever it was fired a second time, but this time a beautiful yellow flower of energy formed inches from Clint's middle. Then the bullet struck something invisible and fell to the dirt.

"I never realized it before," said Clint, clutching his hand to his side as blood gushed between his fingers, "but Teddy was right. Your magic *is* fruity."

"I see," said Edward, already starting to sound like his old self. "Would you prefer I let you die in a manly way, rather than use my fruity unicorn powers to pull that slug from your body?"

Clint winced. Two more shots struck their protective shield, and another pair of flowers (both a dusty lavender) bloomed. Two more bullets dropped into the dirt of the high street.

"Go ahead and pull it out," he said. "But if you could do it with the sounds of a mighty steam engine, I'd prefer it."

Edward's horn glowed brighter, and Clint's side became more liquid than flesh. His wound, including the clothes over it, shimmered and dipped as if a rock had been dropped into a tub of water. Then the ripples rose back to the surface, bringing the bullet on top of them. There was a small high-pitched noise, like that of a squeak toy, as his flesh congealed back into place. A blood-covered bullet fell to the dirt.

"Thankoo," Clint said.

"We should get off the street," said Edward, looking around. "Though I'll admit, this is fun."

"Nar," Clint said. "Stay here."

Another four shots struck the shield. Four slugs fell to the dirt.

Clint could see the shooters. There were four of them. After he was struck by the first bullet, the idiots had come out of hiding. The gunslinger recognized all of them from the stew hole. As he'd predicted, they had ridden around him, avoiding the High Rock entirely. But the fact that these were the same men told Clint that there probably weren't any more members joining the party, which was good. Five hoods, one leader, and one dark magician would be plenty to take over the town if the marshal stayed away. But here he was, back a half-hour early.

Sorry to put sand in your plan, boys.

Clint wasn't schooled in much more than marshaling, but could track shots better than the best sharks counted aces and kings. Two of the men had fired only a pair of shots, one had fired three, and one had fired only a single. All had extras, of course, but they'd need time to refill their revolvers once they were empty.

Clint, clutching his side and feigning injury, pointed at the man with three shots left. The gunmen kept their distance, but the farthest was only twenty yards off. They figured they had him.

"You!" Clint yelled to the man with three shots. "Are you not a man? You haven't even hit me!"

The man fired.

"Ow!" Clint screamed.

The man fired again, and the other three fired once. Now, if he was smart, the man on empty would retreat and reload. But he was as dumb as the bandit he was, and wouldn't know his status until he dry-fired the next time he pulled the trigger. So the gunslinger lay in the dirt, grabbing himself and screaming in pain, while the outlaw began to count his sixth of the town's take.

"Act more anguished," Edward suggested.

Clint clutched his stomach tighter, while screaming louder.

Outside the shield, the empty man tried to fire. His weapon went *click*, and his face turned red. He started shuffling backward.

"The clock is ticking," Edward said.

Clint hopped to his feet and lurched forward.

"Now," he said.

Edward dropped the shield.

Clint's hands were on his guns, already unholstered and aimed. He fired a shot from each of his seven-shooters, so perfectly in sync they thundered through Solace with a single report. A cloud of dull red smoke belched from each muzzle.

His outstretched arms swiveled, and he fired again. Another twin puffs of smoke billowed from the barrels.

Four men lay dead. Stone and the remaining man would now only have to spilt the town's spoils in half.

Clint holstered his guns and sighed, shoulders slowly rising and falling.

"Three left," he said.

They cut away from the high street, knowing the sound of the battle would draw the others, if it hadn't already. Edward asked Clint if he wanted him to raise the shield, but Clint shook his head. Kold's bullets would sail through it anyhow, and he'd be surprised if Stone were willing to violate taboo and try to fire one of Kolt's seven shooters. If he did, and if he was lucky, he might be able to get off a good shot before the firearm blew his hand into teethpaste.

Besides, Clint needed his unicorn sharp. Shields weren't hard, but they did require tremendous energy to make and focus to hold. It had been a while since Edward had eaten.

They slipped behind the bank. Clint unholstered his guns, refilling his four empty chambers.

"You figured out their master plan?" Edward asked. "Any idea what Kold is after? Money?"

"Nar, not money. The bandits at the stew pool said Kold didn't want a share, and I reckon that isn't wrong. The dark marshal's after something else."

"He went to all this trouble to get you out of the way. If he knew you'd return shortly after…"

"… then whatever he wants is something he can grab and easily flee with," Clint finished. "*Before* I return. Otherwise there's no point. He might as well have ridden into town and faced us."

"Maybe he wanted an early jump."

"Stone, maybe," Clint said. "Stone's eyes are likely on the town. He and his men will rob the bank and businesses, then turn this place into their own private sweatshop. But I'd wager Kold wants something specific, and doesn't plan to confront me."

"Why not?"

Clint raised his eyebrow at Edward.

No one knew better than Edward that magic battles were messy. They were always risky and never certain. It wouldn't matter what power Kold commanded. If he wanted to take a specific thing from the town, it was smarter to use subterfuge than to engage in a magical duel.

"Okay, fine," Edward said. "So what does he want? And where is Stone and the other man?"

"You tell me."

"I've been trying, but I can't see them. It's Cerberus. He must be with them."

Clint nodded. It made sense. Unicorns were supposed to be full of magic. When they allowed a human to siphon it off, they became like black holes. The effect made it impossible for other magic users to see them, or to see others nearby.

Edward's head twitched. "I can see the fifth bandit now. He doesn't seem to be with Stone and Kold."

"Where is he?"

"In the saloon."

Clint took his back from the barrel and peeked around its side. The saloon was across the high street, past the four fallen bandits.

"Why didn't he come out with the others?"

"There are people inside the saloon with him. Townspeople. Best guess is he watched what you did to his buddies and is now holed up in there with hostages, planning to bargain his way out of town without getting shot."

"Where?"

"North wall. Beside the piano."

"That's the wall over there, right?" Clint gestured to where he thought the unicorn meant.

"Correct."

Clint held one of his guns toward the building with both hands, aiming to the left of the windows. His hands became rock steady, the barrel of the heavy revolver not jittering even a nanometer.

"Here?"

"Six feet left."

"No way. That's into the outer wall."

"Which one of us has a magic horn?"

Clint inched his gun to the left, his arm moving as smoothly as a heavy iron door on a frictionless hinge. He was now sighting very near the building's corner.

"There?"

"Okay, five-feet-nine. Back up three inches."

"Told you," said Clint, his arms swinging slightly back. Griff used eight-inch posts in the walls, not doubled two-bys. He looked over at Edward, gloating.

Edward rolled his eyes, a strange mannerism for an equine. Then he said, "Two inches up."

"There?"

"Yar."

"Good?"

"Wait. He turned. Go right another two inches."

"There?"

"Yar."

"Sure? Locked in?"

"Yar."

Clint squeezed the trigger. The gun's report was thunder, but Clint's arms didn't even shake. It was as if the bullet had been fired from a rifle on a tripod rather than a handgun with a kick that could kill. A cloud of dull red gunsmoke plumed through the air.

Clint holstered his gun and crossed the street to the saloon, poking his head through the double doors and shouting to the barman.

"Is he dead?"

The barman stared.

"Is he dead?" Clint repeated.

"Something came through the wall," said the barman, his mouth hanging open. "His chest exploded."

"So he's dead."

The barman nodded, but because nobody in the saloon was moving and they were all staring at the gunslinger, Clint decided he should check for himself. He found the fifth bandit in the corner, crumpled over the piano bench.

That made five.

On his way out of the saloon, Clint tipped his hat at the barman. The barman still stared.

Clint understood the barkeep's confusion. Clint had never had occasion to shoot through a wall in Solace, so no one in town had ever seen that particular advantage of a marshal's guns — how the magic powder kept a slug spinning true until it met an obstacle it couldn't penetrate, no matter what it had to pass through along the way.

Edward was waiting outside. Clint reached the door before realizing the obvious. He returned to the bar, asked the barman for a slice of turkey pie and an apple brew, then took the food outside and delivered it to the unicorn. After Edward ate the food and drank the brew (Clint had gotten him a clutch of four straws), he looked much better.

"Thanks," Edward said.

"See the others yet?"

"No. Still nothing. They may have fled, after what you did to their posse. I can't see them at all." Then he stopped, his ears twitching. His horn pulsed a dull yellow, idling like an engine. Clint was reminded of The Realm's thinking machines, and how they pulsed when searching for information.

"What?"

"I see nothing."

Clint shrugged. "Maybe Kold found what he wanted and skipped out. We'll have to go building to building, or..."

"No," Edward interrupted. "I meant, I see *nothing*. It's like a hole where there should be something. A large and suspicious absence where people should be."

A hole?

Clint realized what Edward was saying. Solace was a bustling town for as small as it was, and most of the buildings were occupied at any hour. Even buildings with businesses usually held people inside, since most had apartments stacked onto their second floor.

When Edward said he saw "a suspicious absence," he was referring to the black hole created by Cerberus, the unicorn of a different color. He couldn't see Cerberus or anyone near him. That void where there should be people was *why* Edward could see Cerberus.

"Where?" said Clint.

"The Otel."

CHAPTER TEN: TROUBLE AT THE OTEL

Dharma Kold and Hassle Stone are at the Otel.

The thought sent a chill up the gunslinger's spine.

Mai was surely gone by now. She had to be. She said she'd be leaving hours ago, lathered in a fury over Clint's stubbornness. She was giving up, since he'd given up on their hitching. Faced with an ultimatum, he'd chosen duty, like any marshal worth his bullets was prone to do.

Mai should be safely out of town, and on her way to a new life in Sojourn, and Teddy might even be with her.

Unless she was bluffing.

Clint could see her in his mind's eye as he ran toward the Otel, on foot with Edward a few steps behind, lost in a memory from what felt like a long time ago: her smooth, clear skin, somehow saved from the ravages of the Sands' harsh weather. Her brown hair — not tied in a pink headpiece for hitching, but piled up under a common rag instead. She'd wanted to paint. To *paint*. A woman who was half-magick, abandoned in the Sands as a child, seeking and never finding The Realm as he himself had done for years.

Mai's hands were naked of scars; her legs were without a single splotch or bruise. Clint had never even seen his woman purple, and wasn't sure she could. And yet here she was, this fragile-seeming-but-not-at-all-fragile creature with a rag on her head, on her hands and knees with a bucket of paint. She held a brush in her hand like a workwoman from the Sprawl's outlying settlements.

Clint remembered how much the filthy job of changing the room's color had excited her, and how little he'd wanted to help.

"Help me with this," she'd said, handing him a brush.

"Marshals don't paint," he said, or probably growled.

"*Marshals don't paint.*" She wore a stern, over-the-top expression while mocking him. "Get over here, gunslinger. This one does."

Still, he refused, since painting a room was a task for anyone other than a proper Realm lady with her unique radiance, or for the town's marshal. Besides, the paint stunk enough to get his head to swimming. Mai kept pushing. Clint continued to refuse.

Eventually she grew angry, and told Clint that if he wouldn't help her, she'd hire Paul Wellings for the job. He'd charge more than they could afford, just to paint it brown. They never resolved the quarrel, and Clint left knowing he'd return to a brown room and a bill he couldn't pay. Instead, he found the room painted a subtle yellow by the hand of a lady working alone 'til sundown. Mai was strong-willed and liked to win her way. She wasn't above making threats to get it. Yet, in the end she was sensible, and seldom was rash out of anger.

Go, gunslinger, she'd said. *Go to your death.*

But she'd never left. She wouldn't leave, because it was the wrong decision.

Mai knew who Clint was and always had. She wanted Clint to abandon Solace and the populace that didn't deserve his protection, but she knew he never would. So when he'd left, she'd waited for the coach, stewing and hoping he'd change his mind against all odds, praying he'd meet her and they'd leave together.

But when he hadn't come back to her, she'd sent the coach away and unpacked, watching the streets and waiting for evil to arrive and for her man to face it. Perhaps her half-magick side even whispered that the men were coming too late for her to warn Clint — that they'd tricked the mighty marshal into leaving the town undefended.

Then, if Clint knew Mai, she'd probably grabbed a gun.

The marshal didn't need Edward's magic — had it managed to penetrate the nothingness surrounding the Otel — to know that all of what he'd imagined had happened. Of *course* she'd stayed. Clint wished he'd realized it sooner, before it might be too late.

When the Otel's facade came into view, Clint ducked behind a rain barrel in front of the store, his right pistol drawn. Edward moved into position behind Clint, but since Edward was nearly a dozen feet long, the lowest point on his back was five feet from the ground, and he was bright white, there was little point in hiding.

"They know you're here," Edward said. "Kold can shoot through your cover. A unicorn's magic nullifies shields and umbrellas." Edward kicked Clint in the back with one of his forelegs. "So stand up and face them in plain sight. There's no advantage in hiding like a coward."

Clint stood. Then, as if he'd been waiting for a cue, Hassle Stone's dusty shadow emerged from the blacksmith's shop to the right of the Otel, his full figure right behind. Stone walked into the middle of the street, two dozen yards from Clint.

"Marshal," he said.

Clint's hands hung at his sides, both barrels holstered. Stone's gun was already drawn, dead centered on Clint's chest. Stone had already cocked the hammer, meaning a feather's touch would fire the gun and leave Clint dying.

"Lay down your gun and I won't hurt you," said Clint, as if he were the one with the aimed gun.

"You're too late," Stone snarled. "Kold found what he came for while you were out playing patty-cake in the desert. Once you're gone, I'm taking the rest for my own."

"Taking?"

"Yar, taking. Or getting given. This town quails at the memory of me and my men."

"Your five men took five shots and fewer seconds than that to dispatch," said Clint, nodding toward the pile of bodies in the street behind him. Stone hadn't noticed. Clint tried not to smile at the outlaw's jittering gun when he did.

"Put down your weapon, Stone. I've had enough killing for today. My guns need rest."

The marshal's guns were in their holster. Stone's six-shooter was still centered on Clint's chest.

Clint started walking forward, toward Stone.

"Back up, marshal."

Clint paused. His face registered offense, as if he'd been socially rebuked.

"You're riding with the Devil," he said. "If you weren't, you'd realize how futile this is. You're under the influence of dark magic. Five men, Stone? You face me with *five men?* Have you forgotten our last encounter, and your yeller embarrassment at the end? Did you really think you could shoot me before I shot you twice?"

The barrel of Stone's gun began to shake visibly, almost violently, as if the iron were suddenly too heavy. "Your unicorn can't help you," he said. "Kold's horn carrier is preventing it."

"I don't need a unicorn to draw on you," said Clint.

"Don't you?" Stone growled. "This time I've got magic on my side."

"This showdown," said Clint. "It's not a showdown. It's amusement. I know Kold better than you ever could. He's watching

— through magic if not with his eyes — waiting to see how this will end. But he doesn't care which direction it takes. You were his distraction. And I'm sad to say it worked, that I got distracted."

"Step back."

"I know how this ends, Stone. As long as it's me versus you, I win. Put down your gun. I'd rather the afternoon not end with you killt. Not when you have information I want."

"You've some nerve, gunslinger," said Stone.

Clint watched, waiting for a crack in Stone's concentration.

Stone's eyes flicked behind Clint, probably to his pile of fallen men. It was enough. Clint drew both guns and fired twin clouds of dull red gunsmoke. The bullet from the right gun split the cylinder of Stone's pistol, causing it to spin from his hand and spilling two of its bullets into the dirt. Clint's second slug caught Stone in the right shoulder. The impact spun him like a top, giving Clint enough time to lower his head and launch himself in a sprint toward Stone. He landed his shoulder in the small of the outlaw's back and drove him into the blacksmith's hitching post.

Clint had already reholstered his guns and drawn his handcuffs. In a single fluid motion, he seized Stone's wrists and shackled them, criss-crossed, around the hitching post. The criss-cross position pulled him so close to the post that his chin pressed against it.

A clap came from above, from the upper window of the Otel. Then another, and another. Clint looked up and saw the face of his old friend, and newest foe.

Dharma Kold had changed in some way. Maybe many ways. "I'm slow-clapping in sarcastic appreciation of your victory over the bandit," he said.

Clint took several steps backward for a better view of Kold. Edward walked up and stood beside him.

"He's changed," Clint whispered.

"He's gone dark," Edward said. "Wait until you see Cerberus, wherever he is. It will be far worse on the donor's end."

"I can hear you," Kold called from the window.

"He's also gotten much uglier," Clint whispered.

Kold leaned against the window sill, making himself comfortable.

"This is the place where I'm supposed to tell you my plans and backstory, yar?" Kold sneered. He took a bite of something — a giant piece of turkey pie. Kold had liked turkey pie from the start; he'd even ordered it back in The Realm where choices were plenty. "And now, I'm supposed to come down, and we'll fight. I'll show you my new tricks — the ones my mount taught me. Your boy there counters. We fire rounds." Kold faked a yawn.

Clint said, "I don't have much choice."

"Oh, of course you do. I'm sure *this* isn't a surprise."

Kold reached to the side of the window and pulled something into view, showing Clint a fistful of dark brown hair, which was attached to Mai.

"She's lovely, Marshal," Kold said.

"Go," Clint barked. "Take what you came for and go. If I challenge you, it could kill us both. Let her go and you'll have my pardon. I'll let you leave town, and I won't pursue you with whatever spoils you choose to take."

Kold was stroking Mai's hair. She stood still, giving no resistance.

Kold laughed. "Listen to you! It *has* been forever. Our relative positions have changed more than you apparently realize. I'm not here to bargain with you, Gulliver. I'm here to tell you what I'm going to do, and what you'll have to watch."

"Take what you came for and let her go," Clint repeated, his voice losing both volume and strength. He watched Mai as she stood in the window with her vacant eyes, staring helplessly up at Kold.

Then a terrible truth dawned on the gunslinger: *There's nothing I can do.*

"Well, see, that's the problem." Kold barked another horrid laugh. "Your lady here *is* what I came for."

At that moment, a shadow spilled from the Otel's lobby and poured into the street like black tar. Cerberus was more like a hole in the fabric of reality than a unicorn. His eyes were now a bright, iridescent yellow.

That yellow stare was the last thing Clint saw before the dark unicorn charged.

CHAPTER ELEVEN: EPIC UNICORN FIGHT

The minute Edward saw Cerberus, his eyes started to flash, and what could only be described as a snarl swallowed his expression. It was beyond profane for a unicorn to surrender its magic to a human. It was an act of deep violation, like giving away a soul. What remained was more shadow than a living being, empty of all it once was.

Edward didn't just see Cerberus as a foe. He saw him as an insult to everything that he himself stood for.

Edward reared, standing on his hind legs. Clint felt the unicorn's rage, boiling beneath his skin as if it were his own. Edward wanted to destroy the dark unicorn for the perversion he represented. He wanted to punish Cerberus for the dark mark he'd put across their kind.

Edward was stronger, too, because he hadn't surrendered any of his own magic.

A blast of bright white light erupted from Edward's horn and struck Cerberus square in the chest. The impact launched him backward, into the Otel lobby.

Something flew from Cerberus as he hurtled backward. Clint stared open-mouthed as dark tentacles slithered around the white beam. Then the energies collided, crashing with an explosion that cut through the Otel's lobby like a knife.

The blast battered the Otel's walls and supports, turning it from a sound structure into a mashed stack of broken mud bricks. The top floor slid to one side and then collapsed, crumbling onto the lobby floor below.

Kold's face registered a satisfying look of genuine surprise, but then as the walls collapsed, both he and Mai were surrounded by a giant filthy bubble. The Otel's roof fell onto them, past them, into the lobby level. The walls blew out. When the dust disappeared into the late afternoon air, the entire structure was nothing more than a ramshackle pile of boards.

The dirty bubble rose from the debris, hovering above the street. It floated to the side opposite where Stone was still shackled, with the shadows of Kold and Mai barely visible inside. Then it settled onto the dirt, and the bubble popped.

Kold grabbed Mai by the arm, pulling her roughly around the corner.

Clint started to follow, but the Otel's rubble blew upward in a fountain as a pillar of black fire emerged, with Cerberus at its base. The dark unicorn marched forward, its yellow eyes wild. Edward was already galloping toward him. The white unicorn drove his entire weight, sidelong, into Cerberus's obsidian side, knocking the dark unicorn's body into the rubble.

Another flash of bright light surrounded them, and a hole appeared around the two entangled unicorns.

An explosion of snowy white blew the Otel's remains spinning toward Clint. The gunslinger fell to the dirt as a fragment of what he thought might have once been a sink whistled over his head. The flash was blinding. Once in the dirt, he looked at his hands to see if he could still see them. What he saw was something like a photo negative, or an X-ray.

It's white magic, not just light, he thought. *Your sight will return.*

For now, though, everything was backward.

Black was white.

White was black.

The unicorns had emerged and were dueling before the marshal, wrestling in a melee of legs and hocks and hooves and horns. Small spells strobed around them, meant for close quarters. Clint chewed through his panic, realizing how completely and totally Kold's black unicorn was dominating his white one. Then he realized that the black unicorn, in his backwards-sight, was Edward. And then it made sense. Cerberus would have some dark tricks, but most of his magic was no longer with him because it had been surrendered to...

Clint looked around at what appeared to be a pitch black street.

Where was Kold?

Clint couldn't get his bearings, and wouldn't be able to shoot straight even if he trusted himself to aim his guns against Kold's magic. Still, he had to try. Kold couldn't get far.

He stumbled toward where Kold had disappeared with the

spellbound Mai, but he'd not seen Edward stampeding toward him. He looked to his side and saw that Cerberus stood nearby. With his vision slowly returning, his world was sepia and grayscale.

The unicorns had taken wounds, but both instantly healed. They were painted in multicolored blood. Clint, who saw the many colors in different shades of gray, had a moment to note that even dark unicorns bled in vibrant colors.

Edward charged again, but this time Cerberus didn't counter in time. Cerberus was off balance and reeling when Edward lowered his horn and drove it into the dark unicorn's side.

Clint flinched back as the huge dark form of Cerberus flew in front of him, across his field of quickly improving vision, and then blew out the barber shop's side wall.

The wall dripped debris as Cerberus stood and shook himself free of dust. A giant blue flash lit his side where Edward's horn had struck him, and then he was whole again.

Edward's horn was now a wet map of colors. He had stopped where he'd struck Cerberus, his nostrils flaring as his chest expanded and fell. Cerberus stared back.

"Okay, enough," came a voice.

Now that the barber shop was missing a wall, Clint could see Kold and Mai taking refuge in the small alley behind the Otel. The shock was gone from the dark marshal's face, leaving behind a strange brew of amusement and boredom.

"You horses can stop beating your chests," Kold said. Edward's head jerked at the insult. "No matter who wins, I'm holding the ace." He waved his hand dramatically in front of Mai, as if presenting a prize.

Kold slapped his leg twice. In the barber shop's rubble, in front of Frank, the barber (who was cowering behind a chair in the corner) Cerberus shook his massive black head and walked over so Kold could mount him and magick the compliant Mai onto the unicorn's back. Mai wrapped her arms tightly around Kold's chest.

Thirty feet away, his hooves wearing a carpet of sawdust and cinders, Edward snorted at Cerberus's servility.

Kold turned to Clint and gave a satirical salute, then slapped Cerberus's neck. The dark unicorn reared and leapt forward, but never landed. Instead, his black coat became a smudge that wound in a gently curving trail, like smeared ink, toward the horizon. And then they were gone.

Edward shook himself off and trotted toward Clint, his horn glowing, as the gunslinger's vision returned to normal.

"Sorry about that," said Edward.

Clint had his eyes bolted to the horizon. The dark stain had vanished. "Can we follow?"

"No. I can fold for reasonable distances, and even then it's hard. But what Cerberus just did wasn't a fold. That, my friend, was a *prance*. Something most humans will never see."

Clint felt like he'd been beaten into a pile of submission.

"You can't do that?" he asked. But it wasn't a desperate question. It was an apathetic question that he felt he should ask. Despite Clint's anguish and love for Mai, he barely had enough energy left to care.

"I *could*, in the same way you *could* trade an arm for a slice of turkey pie."

"I don't understand."

"Any of us *can* do it, but only dark unicorns ever do. Think of the worst things humans sometimes do, but that the sane among you never would. It's like that."

Clint nodded and sighed, his spirit wearing a thousand pounds of defeat.

He walked to the other side of what used to be the Otel, to where Stone was handcuffed to the blacksmith's hitching post. Stone looked up into his eyes.

"Where did they go?" Clint said.

"To drink cactus juice with your grappy, gunslinger." Stone spat on the marshal's boot. The glob of saliva made a clean circle in the dust covering the weathered cowhide.

Clint raised his foot and kicked Stone hard in the ribs. The blow emptied the breath from the bandit's lungs, leaving him gasping for air.

"Where did they go?" Clint repeated.

Stone coughed, and kept coughing until the gunslinger thought he might spit his lung in the dirt.

Edward walked over and stood beside Clint, looming over Stone. Clint's boot made another visit before Edward said, "Let me try" and raised a hoof to hover over Stone's chest.

"Fine," coughed Stone. "I'll tell you. It won't matter, anyhow. Won't help you none to find them."

"Where?" Edward said, lowering the hoof so it brushed against Stone's filthy shirt.

Stone coughed again. "He's taking her to The Realm."

Clint's chin rose. He turned and looked into the distance, to where the black smear had vanished. Just because Stone headed for the hills didn't mean that was where Clint should go to meet them. There was a reason no one could find The Realm, since the Leaking had started. Lines were no longer straight, and forward was too often backward.

"That's not possible," said Clint.

"It is what it is," said Stone.

With the melee finished, the citizens of Solace surfaced from hiding and drifted out into the street. They looked to the Otel ruins, then over to the dead men lining the street. Clint saw George Telford, Nicholas Willings, and Hattie McDonnough. He saw Earl Lancaster, who just ran a tack shop. He saw Bill Maynard, who didn't want to stir up trouble with Hassle Stone where there was none otherwise.

Edward's nose poked at Clint's shoulder, urging him into motion.

Clint set his hand across Edward's back, then stopped before kicking up onto his mount. He turned his gaze to the town and its people, all of whom were staring at the gunslinger who had saved them. Again.

He took the keys for Stone's handcuffs from his belt, used the same hand to unpin the marshal's star on his chest, and dropped both into the dirt.

Without another glance or comment, Clint climbed onto Edward's back.

The gunslinger touched his guns. They felt right at his sides.

Edward's horn glowed. Space folded.

Then the gunslinger — and his unicorn — left Solace forever.

UNICORN WESTERN 2

CHAPTER ONE:
THE PURSUIT

The gunslinger and the unicorn crossed the Sands, with nothing in front and nothing behind.

After two long years of wandering the great wide open, exposed to the biting wind and angry dust that swirled through the Sprawl as though it owned it, the marshal's skin was like leather, as if he'd been tied, beaten, tanned, and then beaten again. His hands were large and scarred, with long digits that curled like a skeleton's. As big as his hands were, they were still the fastest part of him — and with Clint Gulliver, as with any other marshal of The Realm, his slowest part was faster than the fastest part of most any other man.

The gunslinger stared out at the world through the piercing blue eyes of a predator, under drawn, V-shaped brows that arched above a cruel nose. His eyes were shaded from the sun by a battered brown hat that looked a hundred years old — faded, torn, and pierced in several places as if by bullets. A scowl creased his face like a cut.

The unicorn, on the other hand, was as clean as the man was dusty. His coat was a bright white, brilliant enough to be blinding. Where the man looked weathered, the unicorn looked untouched. Where the man looked unkempt, the unicorn looked immaculate. Where the man appeared poisoned with anger, the unicorn looked purer than snow in The Realm.

The unlikely pair plodded through the Sprawl as they had each day for nearly as long as either were willing to remember. Days were never different from one another. They would walk until their legs were willing to carry them no further, and then they would make camp and fall quickly asleep. Sometimes the man would ride atop the unicorn, eyes forward and mouth set, bareback and without reins or any other tack. To keep the man in place, a filthy hand would bury itself in the unicorn's opulent mane. When the gunslinger pulled his hand away, the mane would fall neatly into place, unsullied by tangles, dirt, grit, or grease. Other times, the man would walk beside the unicorn, since even a gunslinger's legs required the occasional stretching.

Sometimes they spoke, but mostly they didn't. In the two years spent trudging from one empty spread to the next and never nearing their destination (finding The Realm was like finding a splinter in the Sands) anything that needed saying had been said at least twice.

When there was talking to be done, Edward usually started it.

"Something's wrong," the unicorn said, pausing in a cactus-pocked spot of desert behind a small rise, just as the sun was starting to set. The sun was dumping a bucket of bright tangerine all over the dusty desert — a sure sign, once upon a time, that they were walking west. But the days when a compass could be trusted were gone. Thanks to the shifting of the ground that occurred out this far, moving straight ahead could lead a man backward, and the sun might rise in any of the world's four corners.

Clint's hand twittered at his side, instinctively moving toward the stock of the seven-shooter on his right hip.

Edward said, "Not that sort of wrong."

"Wrong is if we don't make camp soon," the gunslinger said, letting his hand hang limp at his side. "I'm tired and hungry. I need a bed and a slice of turkey pie."

"Keep needing, then," said Edward. "We have jerky wraps and delicious water. The engraved canteen that's in your pack, however, is filled with apple brew, and for that, I'll thank Providence."

"Unicorns don't believe in Providence."

"Of course we do," the unicorn said. "Providence provides brew. It's the rest of your stupidity we don't believe in. Time. Space. How you think that hat looks good on you."

Clint swung his left leg over Edward's back and slid to the sand. A plume of dust spit up from the ground and re-coated the clean areas that the friction of Edward's sides had made on the insteps of his boots. That was another thing about the accursed Edge – the sand here wasn't quite sand at all.

The gunslinger tugged on his hat. "What's the trouble you mention?"

"A pain. I feel it in my chest."

Clint spit. "Too much brew."

"No. It's something else, something obscene. I can feel it as we walk — or rather as *I* walk, with a lazy load on my back. It's as if there's a wall in front of us. With every step it feels like I'm driving myself further against some sort of perversion, like I'm slowly walking into a long and rusty spike."

Clint shook his head.

"I know what you think," said Edward. "But before you mock me, think on what I've not yet said: we may finally be closing in."

Clint's icy eyes opened wider as the sun-wrinkled flesh surrounding the whites pulled back. "Mai?"

"Cerberus."

"Dharma Kold's unicorn of a different color," Clint rasped, nodding. He kept his eyes open so he wouldn't see the obsidian black mount riding across his mind. If Cerberus was near, so was Kold. And where the dark rider went, so did Mai… always assuming, of course, that the gunslinger's almost-bride was still alive.

"She's alive," said Edward, reading Clint's mind.

"You can sense her?"

"No. But Kold lost a posse and risked your wrath by storming through Solace two years ago trying to abduct her. He wouldn't do that without reason, and he wouldn't do it just to kill her or let her die. By Providence, Mai lives."

Clint's face formed a scowl. "Why did they take her, Edward? And where — for real, pleasem and thankoo — are they going with her?"

It was the oldest of their many unanswered questions. Supposedly Kold was heading for The Realm, but that was a ridiculous notion since no one knew where The Realm was — and even if a person did know where it was, he'd never find it. Clint understood Kold's quixotic pursuit, because he once nursed the same diseased longing himself. He fought it still, like a rash forever returning in his mind.

"Dagnit, I don't know!" Edward said. "I'm not *going* to know, either, and if you ask again, I'll run you through with my horn."

"Sweet relief," the gunslinger said.

"And then when I arrive at the next town wearing your corpse like a hat, I will eat all the turkey pie myself."

"Stand down, then, if pie is at stake," said Clint. "I won't ask again." It was the marshal's version of a joke, but he delivered it with all the humor of an obituary.

After a moment of standing (and sinking slightly) in the sand, Clint said, "If you sense Kold, then we should ride."

"No. They are in the same direction as the perversion I feel in my chest." The unicorn bowed his head, pointing his horn at the horizon. The horn glowed a dull yellow, tinged with pink. "There," he said.

Clint squinted into the distance and saw a crooked spark of red and yellow just below the horizon, barely visible now that the sun was almost set. In the deepest Sands, over by the Edge, sunrises were as abrupt as the sunsets. Whether that was due to the Leaking, the off motion of the planets, or the way time dilated and contracted out where the sand was slippery, none could say.

"We should continue on," said Clint. "If they've stopped, we should close the gap."

But it was a shell game — something Clint seemed to forget each time he saw Cerberus' dark smear smudging the horizon or the faded glint of Kold's fire. Every few days, they'd reach sighting distance of the outlaws, and each time, Clint insisted they push forward. But they were tailing a mirage, and as they marched closer, Kold would always vanish — and when they arrived at the spot of Kold's camp, the dust would always have swallowed their tracks, turning their presence there to a mere rumor.

"No," Edward said. "I don't know what I'm feeling in the Sands, but I don't like it."

Clint shook his head and snarled. "I'll go on. You stay here and do your nails. All four of them."

Clint took a dozen steps toward the distant fire before Edward called out to him.

"We'll never reach them, you know," he yelled. "I'd think two years of getting the rug yanked from under your feet would have taught you that. You're like that bald child in the ancient funnybooks, forever kicking at an oblong that's always pulled away."

Clint turned, struggling with something before turning toward Edward. "What would you have me do?"

"Anything else," Edward said.

"So why do you walk beside me, if you think this is a fool's errand?"

"Walk beside you? I carry your lazy bones on my back, gunslinger," Edward said. "But to answer your question, I do it because you always lead me to pie and apple brew."

Clint stared at Edward's white head and pearlescent horn for an especially long beat, trying to think of a suitable reply, until his shoulders finally sagged and he walked back.

"We'll make camp, then," he said, sitting and gesturing at the sand. "Magick us a fire. I'm cold. Not all of us are filled with magic and warm fuzzies."

Edward made a mocking, horselike sound.

"You really *are* tired. You know we can't make a fire. He'll see it."

"Behind the rise?"

"He'll see the smoke," said Edward. "There's a moon."

Clint sighed. He was a hard man, but he felt a thousand years old. He could take defeat, and he thought that when the time came, he could accept his own killing. What he couldn't accept was the constant torment of pursuing something that couldn't be caught.

"Tomorrow, we'll approach," said Clint. "Tomorrow, we'll see her."

Edward said nothing. Then, just when Clint thought he wouldn't reply, the unicorn said, "I need to understand the perversion I feel before I can go to where they are. I don't know what it is yet, but I can't walk into it. You need to understand and accept that. We may have to loop around, meet them further on. They may be crossing a place of dark magic. Such places are common out here. The Ghryst worship at them."

Time passed. How much, neither could say. Timepieces didn't work so close to the Edge because of the Leaking and Slippage. They only knew that the sun was down and the air was icy. Kold's fire still sparked, taunting them with kisses blown from the horizon.

Clint pulled his warm coat lower around his shoulders, and then both of them, once Edward laid down, squeezed beneath the giant turkey-feather blanket they'd bought from a crooked trader and his roaming donkey mercantile several months before. That was back when the weather had started changing for the worse, for the third season in a row.

"I think I may know what's ahead," said Edward suddenly.

Clint was behind Edward's head, on the far side of his sharp horn. Spooning behind a unicorn was a tad strange, but it was far better than spooning on the side that was all sharp and kicky. On that side, kicks sometimes happened by accident, when Edward dreamed, and sometimes happened on purpose, because Edward was being Edward.

"You mean the feeling in your chest?" said Clint. "Let me guess. Is it cowardice?"

Edward bucked his head back, then rolled onto his side to stand. In the process he smacked Clint hard on the jaw, probably not on accident.

"Indigestion?" Clint tried again.

Edward stood to his full height, ignoring Clint. With the moon in the sky, Clint was glad Edward had moved down the slope after standing. He was so white, he looked like a beacon in the bright light of the moon.

"You know how I said it was a perversion?"

"Like bad brew. Like ballet at game of oblong. Like a fart in church."

Edward nudged Clint with his nose — the equivalent of a slap or a splash of cold water. Magic this far out was slippery, and he wasn't sure whether Clint was merely joking or losing his grip. More than one man had been confused by the slippery magic and had been driven mad.

"I see the problem," Edward said, dead serious. "I know the feeling in my chest. I know why I thought it obscene."

"Dark magic?" said Clint.

"Worse."

"We'll go around, then, like you suggested," Clint said.

"Go around the bad spot, you mean, and meet them on the other side?"

"Yar. Like eating around an apple's sore."

Edward shook his big white head. "We haven't been this close before, and the proximity has let me see something new," he said. "This is the nearest we've come after two long years."

"Yar. And that's why we need to take what they give us, and overtake them while they sleep… once they're clear of the sore."

"No," said Edward. "It's why we *can't* overtake them. Why we *can't* get clear of the sore."

Clint said, "I don't follow."

Edward nodded toward the rise, toward Kold's fire and beyond. His horn sparked, as if underlining his speech. "They *are* the sore," he said.

"I don't follow," Clint repeated, although he was starting to believe that he actually did.

"It's Cerberus," Edward said. "He's dipped his horn deep inside of Mai's soul."

CHAPTER TWO: CHEST PAINS

Clint waited for Edward to explain, but the unicorn said no more. He waited, staring at the horizon, his head barely high enough to see above the swell they'd sheltered behind.

"Go on," said Clint.

"No." Edward shook his head, still staring into the distance.

Clint shoved the unicorn with both hands, not wanting to play the game of Sullen Edward or draw the story out any longer than needed. The unicorn was a good friend (as far as Sands friends went), but Edward carried an infuriating pride. He had to be drawn out, like a courting, before he'd give up what he had to say.

"Explain," said Clint.

"No."

It had been an endless trip through the Sands, and Clint had held himself together reasonably well, but time and futility had worn him to crust. His nerves were thinner than Sands magic, and now Edward was telling him they were close to what they'd been searching for but could inch no closer because something hideous was being done to the woman he'd nearly hitched.

Clint reared back and punched the unicorn hard in the cheek. Edward's head snapped sideways, seemingly unsurprised. Clint's hand smarted, but he wouldn't satisfy Edward with a wince. After years together and countless punches, the gunslinger refused to learn one of his most consistent lessons: unicorns had no soft spots on their bodies.

"No," Edward repeated.

Clint punched him again, this time in the nose. Edward blanched.

Then, grinding his giant teeth, he turned to look at the gunslinger. Clint thought for a second that Edward might magick him, or try to gore him with his horn. Instead he said, "Fine. Have your tantrum. I'll tell you."

Clint felt his sore hand unclench. It would require ointment in the morrow, but for now, although his hand hurt, it was a fair trade for his settling temper.

Edward shifted his weight, cocking a rear hoof onto its tip for rest.

"You know how I've told you I can't read minds, even though I can sense where people are and get a feel for their mood, even from a distance?"

"Yar," said Clint, sitting on a rock that was jutting from the Sand like a giant gnarled tooth.

"Well, it's not entirely true. I *can* read minds. Every unicorn can."

"So why have you lied, when knowledge from the heads of our enemies might have helped us? Think on Solace, Edward. Why wouldn't you read the minds of the bandits at the Stew Hole, and save us from being out of at High Rock with our pants at our ankles as if we were sitting in a tall closet as Kold and Stone stormed into town, laughing?"

"For the same reason you don't break into a person's house and rummage through their underwear while they're away," said Edward. "For the same reason you don't waylay every woman you fancy, or kill a child when he kicks you in the shin, no matter how much it hurts."

"I don't understand."

"Of course you don't," the unicorn said. "You're human. You've never dug your horn — sorry, your fingers — in another's mind and stumbled on something they've meant to keep hidden. You've never plundered the depths of a soul, which falls about a thousand lengths lower than that."

"You're saying it's taboo."

Edward nodded. "Beyond taboo. Like desecrating a shrine is taboo, or worse. It's like you're inside another, soiling their very identity. Everything they are, you pollute with your hoofprints. The thought of such an egregious trespass is so abhorrent to a balanced unicorn like myself that it causes physical pain. That's what I've been feeling. I won't probe another's soul without permission just to get information. You can't understand that. Humans have a very limited understanding of magic. You only see the practical sides of coins — what you need, versus how quickly you can get it, and sands to the cost."

Clint opened his mouth to protest, but Edward spoke over the gunslinger.

"Oh, don't even start," he snorted. "I'm not criticizing you. It's not your fault you're human and can't see how we're all connected. But whether you see it or not, that's how it is. All souls touch, in one way or another. There's a force stitching existence. Pulling at the strings of that force is how we do what we do. Those magic strings harmonize with life's energy, and that of all conscious souls. Doing magic of any sort is the same as killing, which we all have the power to do, and creating, over which we all have limited dominion."

Clint stared at the unicorn, knowing he couldn't say anything. That was the way it always was, once Edward got to speechifying.

"Every moment I ride with you, I brush against strings that, were I to pull them, would allow me to see you better than you've ever seen yourself. I could answer questions you'd once known but had long forgotten with no more effort than it takes to kick a rock. When you infuriate me as you do, I could know easily whether you're lying. But I don't, and I never will. Like every unicorn, I shrink from those strings because they're poison to the touch. We flinch from things that ought not be done far more than we act on those things that need doing. Every unicorn lives around others in constant fear of pulling one of those strings, either by accident or during a weak moment, overwhelmed by curiosity. I've heard of unicorns doing the unthinkable, but can count that number on one hand."

"You don't have hands."

Edward kicked the dirt, glancing with visible scorn toward the spark of Kold's fire. "I've hand enough to count to one."

The night was already darkening. Though Clint hadn't seen the moon descend, there it was, nearly down.

Slippage.

"Cerberus," said Clint.

"Cerberus," Edward agreed. "I didn't want to believe it. I'd felt the stabbing in my chest long before I said it aloud, keeping silent as long as I dared. Even after I told you, knowing full well what it was, I refused to admit it. Like I was looking at the red sun, trying hard to convince myself it was only a white moon. But I couldn't. Sun is sun, simple as pie. Cerberus is doing is something I've never known any to do, though I shouldn't be surprised – not when his dark hooves have ridden beneath Kold's black long enough to grow forever dark. He dares to prance, as he did when leaving Solace, as though he were no longer a unicorn. Who knows? He might actually be that dog that guards the underworld, disguised in an outward skin I'm ashamed to share."

Clint sat, his back against a rock as his mind marinated in new information. A wolf howled in the distance. As he often did when pensive, Clint unholstered one of his seven-chamber guns, and idly spun the cylinder.

"Why is he doing... whatever it is that he's doing?" he finally said.

"Information," said Edward. "What Cerberus is doing is sticking his horn — by which I mean his magic — into her soul. It isn't torture, exactly, although it's that too. It's more like ransacking. He's looking for something in her soul's house, and not caring what he breaks while searching."

"What is he looking for?" Clint asked, knowing there was more.

"Not *looking*," said Edward. "He's found what he seeks. But he can't pull the information from Mai like a book from a shelf, to read later at his leisure. Neither the soul nor the mind are so simple. He must read the information live, like listening to a record he can't touch or control."

Clint closed his eyes, not letting Edward see. This was the woman he loved, and Edward's words might as well have been literal: Mai impaled through the heart on Cerberus's black horn, her limp body hanging bloody from either side of the dark unicorn's head like damp clothes on a crooked hook. Clint supposed he should feel more anguish or anger, but Edward was articulating a despair that was too desolate for Clint to process. He wanted to surrender.

For the first time in forever, all Clint wanted to do was to lie down and die.

"You're feeling it too," said Edward. "For me, it is a literal pain in my chest. For you, it is a bottomless sorrow — a certainty that nothing will ever improve. Stick in the gummy sphere of this perversion for too long, and you'll start to feel desperate and angry. You'll hate your fellow man and distrust everyone, no matter the innocence of their intentions or bearing. It will grow increasingly worse until it becomes unbearable, either crushing us or forcing us to walk away."

Clint raised his head, which had fallen between his shoulders. "I thought you couldn't read minds?"

"I can read *you*," said Edward. "Same as you can read me."

Clint sighed, oppression draping his body like a thousand-pound blanket. He did feel exactly what Edward described — though it was hard to put a long, curled finger on, intermingled as it was with vertigo from the Sands and the simple fatigue that followed a neverending journey.

Clint had never been a cordial fellow, and two years on the Sands had done nothing to improve his demeanor. He'd long ago learned to live with a sadness that had no start or finish, hating most people, and distrusting them from their first breath. It was as if Clint had studied at the feet of the seer-cynic David, renowned across The Realm and the Sands for his far-seeing hatred of mankind.

"Do you know what Cerberus wants? What it is he's 'reading' from Mai, as you say?"

"It's not what Cerberus wants. It's what Kold wants."

"Okay then," said Clint. "What *Kold* wants."

"Yar, I know what it is," Edward said. "I don't want to know, but I can't help it. Once something is ripped from a soul's center, it pours like blood from a wound, splashing onto anyone nearby with the capacity to receive. Unfortunately, I have the perfect antenna." The unicorn wiggled his sparkling horn. "It's another reason I don't wish to go closer. I can't control it, or shut it out. It's like someone's being gutted, and the guts keep splashing into your lap. I can do nothing to stop them from doing so."

Clint shook his head, wishing Edward would answer the question rather than going on and on forever as always. The gunslinger didn't feel like asking any more questions, or dragging information out of the unicorn like a sunken wreck from the bottom of a swamp.

He was too tired, and everything felt far too heavy.

"Then tell me," said Clint. "Tell me and be on with it, you stupid horse."

The unicorn didn't react to being called a horse (and, as a bonus, a stupid one). That said plenty. It was as if Edward were too tired to protest. He probably was. They were both tired — tired through to the core of their bones. The energy of the place was wretched, and just thinking felt like trying to run through sap.

"Mai knows the way to The Realm," said Edward.

Clint stood. The fog was gone, along with his blanket of fatigue and oppression.

"What?"

"You heard me. She doesn't know that she knows, but it's in her blood, and the wind swears it's true."

"Where is it?"

Edward looked at the gunslinger without expression.

"The Realm, dagnit! The Realm! Where is it?"

The unicorn shook his neck, making his long, white mane shiver like a halo around him. "What I'm sensing is only an echo of the dark unicorn's crime. It's as if I'm looking at the cover of a book. I can read the title of that book, and I can maybe get a feel for what the book might be about. But I've no true knowledge of its interior."

"Then open the book!" Clint hissed.

The unicorn stared into the gunslinger's eyes for a long while — long enough for Edward's lack of humanity to reassert itself to Clint. He'd been talking to Edward and more or less *only* Edward through the rise and fade of two long winters. Doing so made it easy to think of him as human. But now, staring into blue eyes with oval, pill-like pupils, something settled in the gunslinger's gut. Though Edward and Clint shared much in common, they weren't at all the same.

"Have you heard anything I've said?" Edward asked.

"The *perversion*. The *taboo*." Clint grumbled as though Edward were being unreasonable.

Edward nudged Clint with his nose. "Why are we out here, Clint? What are we chasing?"

The gunslinger said nothing.

"Because I've spent two years helping you track the woman Kold took from you, and it sounded to me like you just suggested I harm her further in the interest of..."

"I didn't mean that," Clint snapped. But for a moment, that's exactly what he had meant. Though they'd been searching for Mai two years, he'd been searching for The Realm since his exile.

"They have Mai. They're going to The Realm. Our intention doesn't even matter, because either way, we pursue."

"But let's say that tomorrow, I find a way to get closer to them instead of continuing to follow from afar. If that happens, should we storm their camp? Should we rescue Mai and thus foil Kold's journey to The Realm? Should we save her, and therefore allow her knowledge about The Realm's whereabouts to remain locked within her, where it belongs?"

Clint huffed, trying to convey his indignation at Edward having the gall to ask such a question. Of *course* they'd go in and rescue Mai if given the chance!

"*Can* you go closer?" he said, not trusting himself to answer the question.

"No."

"Then don't ask stupid questions."

They were quiet. Heavy implications hung between them. Edward kept watching the gunslinger as he sat on the rock, staring at the shine long lost from his boots.

Finally, in a smaller, humbler voice, Clint answered Edward's question.

"Mai," he said. "We're out here to get Mai, Realm be riddled. If there's a chance — tomorrow or any day after — to ride in and save her, we take it."

Edward kept looking at Clint, seeming to mine any truth from his words. "Good," he finally said.

"So what do we do now?" Clint asked.

"We follow."

"For how long?"

"I don't know."

"Until what happens?"

"I don't know."

"Will you ever be able to get closer?"

"I don't know, gunslinger."

Clint kicked a small litter of rocks with his boot's toe and sent them in a skitter across the sand, down the rise, leaving snakelike trails behind them. If it wasn't Kold that had her, Clint could storm their camp and take her alone, with one gun drawn and the other in its holster, even if she were held by a dozen men. But it *was* Kold, and Kold had once been a Realm marshal, no different from Clint. A Realm marshal whose unicorn had surrendered control of its magic mostly to him — a perversion as horrible as whatever that dark unicorn was doing to Mai right now. And in that case, without Edward's help, he was facing a stalemate at best.

What Clint didn't say out loud was that as long as the stalemate persisted, following Kold would lead them toward The Realm — a not-insignificant silver lining.

"What he's doing to her," said Clint. "Will it kill her?"

"No," said Edward. "But it may permanently ruin her mind. You might have to surrender the Mai you knew. She might not be the same person, and even if she is, she might be changed such that a hitching's impossible. I don't know. There aren't enough examples in the past to draw from. This simply does not happen. Ever."

Clint thought for a moment, then rose to standing with a decision on his face.

"Okay," he said. "You cannot approach, and I cannot fight him without you. That leaves us with only one option, and that's follow, as close as we dare. We'll keep him in our sights. If for an instant his guard goes down — if Cerberus stops what he's doing — we'll ride in, and we'll fight. And if we die, we die."

"So you're saying that if you must reach The Realm in order to save her, you're willing to make that sacrifice," Edward said dryly.

"You get over your little boo-boo, and I'm ready to ride in and face them now," Clint countered.

Again, Edward stared into the gunslinger's eyes. Having a staring contest with a unicorn was nothing like holding one with a human. Since equines couldn't see straight ahead, Clint always found himself staring at Edward in profile, and often accused him of blinking the eye he couldn't see.

"Fair enough," said Edward. "I'll let you know if and when I find the will to move in on them."

They collapsed to the shifting sand without any words, and fell asleep beneath an absent moon.

CHAPTER THREE:
SANDS COOT

A month passed, and with it went sixteen nights and two moons.

It grew warm, then cold again, as if seasons were as hungry to change as the weeks.

In the mornings of the hottest days, there was frost. And on those hottest days, Edward often said it was hot enough to fry an egg on a rock. So, on one particularly trying day, Clint removed one of the turkey eggs he'd bought in a small one-pump town they'd passed about three moons past and cracked it open on a slab of rock where they sat for their midday meal. Edward laughed while Clint, who was indeed trying to be funny, never cracked a smile. The egg cooked in a few minutes, and they ate it, with the weathered gunslinger finally smiling.

That night, it was cold enough to freeze the water in the corner of Clint's eyes as he slept.

The slippage in the weather, along with slippage in the days and nights and moons, continued to play tricks on their minds. Clint lost track of time, and Edward, still more or less in constant pain from their proximity to Cerberus and Mai, grew increasingly irritable. They fought often, with Edward bemoaning the length of time Mai's rescue was requiring, especially now that he was hurting so badly. Clint said it had only been a week since Edward had first noticed the pain, and to man up. Edward told him unicorns were anatomically incapable of "manning up," and then questioned that it had only been a week, because it felt much longer.

Edward had to stop and tune into the movement of the planet to know the true time — the time the world would experience if magic were still stable, rather than leaking and slipping — to see the truth: that they'd been walking for thirty-three days since the night Edward first felt the pain in his chest.

"I can't abide this for long," said Clint, peering into a small hand mirror while shaving his face one cold morning.

"You've been ugly for forty trips around the yellow star," Edward said. "You'll manage to abide it a while longer, I suppose."

"This problem with time, I mean. The way the days and seasons change as if it were nothing."

"It's the Edge," said Edward. "We're getting close to where The Realm broke loose. You can't see it except in the days and temperatures, but I can feel it everywhere. It's as if the ground were shifting beneath our feet. You'll either adjust or go mad. Either way it'll eventually stop bothering you."

"Either one, huh?"

"Yar."

"I honestly don't know which to root for," Clint said, turning back to the mirror.

Edward often spoke of The Realm, the Leakage, the Great Cataclysm, and the slippage of worlds, and even sprinkled all sorts of conversation — polite and otherwise — with flecks of unicorn history. It seemed almost neurotic, as if Edward were the one who feared losing his mind, and was using incessant speech to hold insanity at bay. He seemed compelled to explain every small feeling to Clint, and said he felt as if he were walking on sponge, then gelatin, then as if he were climbing a cliff despite the fact that his hooves never left the flat plain. Sometimes he spoke of Cerberus's defiling of Mai — an omnipresent feeling inside him — but said he could draw nothing else about their path from the defiling, outside the fact that they were headed toward The Realm.

"I've never felt The Realm so strongly," Edward whispered with awe. "We truly are close."

"How close?" Clint asked, trying to suppress his sudden jolt of enthusiasm.

"Mere miles," Edward answered. "Or many, many centuries at a gallop."

Clint stopped, grabbed Edward's head and stared down his nose with a serious expression.

"Edward," he said, drilling his eyes into the unicorn's. "Are you okay? Be honest with me, now."

Edward was under constant intolerable stress, unable to trust even his footing. Clint feared for his safety and sanity both, especially when he said nonsensical things like he'd just said. Clint also feared for his own safety and sanity, since without a unicorn, Clint would never find his way out, face Kold, or save Mai.

"Who said that?" Edward said. "Whoever it is, I'll bet half my horn and all its ridges he's as ugly as the Devil in drag."

Clint turned Edward's head so that he was looking at only one eye.

"Oh, it's you, ugly," said Edward.

"How's your brain, other than filled with the slop that falls from your rear?"

"Addled. Confused. But I'll make it. This area is thin, but we're nearly through it. It can't be easy on Cerberus either. They're moving fast, clearly trying to cross it. Once we're past, much of this mental fog will fade. We may even return to one moon per month."

"They're almost *through* it? But you said The Realm was near."

"It is. It was. It's… hard to explain. Space doesn't always make sense along fault lines, or near The Realm. Something can be close and also far, depending on the path you take to reach it."

"Which path are we taking?"

Edward said, "The one we can."

"So it's close?"

"Yes. But more accurately, I don't know."

Clint released Edward's head, deciding for the moment that Edward's odd answers were strange because the truth was strange, not because Edward's mind had come unhinged.

Clint suddenly felt bad as he looked over at the unicorn. Edward was pursuing Mai because *Clint* wanted her, not because Edward wanted her. Edward's pain was caused by a favor granted to a friend. And sure, Edward felt that he had a score to settle with Cerberus — if for no other reason than being the obscenity he was — but under different circumstances, Edward would have let him go, and would have let the obscenity pass.

But he hadn't let it pass. He'd gone on this journey because Clint had wanted it, and now his torture seemed unbearable.

Clint himself felt fine, other than adjusting to the strange days, nights, and changes in weather. Edward assured him that he wouldn't remain stable if they stayed long. He'd adjust on a surface level, but underneath, the extreme leakage and shifting was working on his mind and soul, same as it worked on everything else.

Clint meant to ask what would happen to a person who stayed for too long in an unstable area, but he soon found out.

A few days later, the night became so frigid and the wind became so fierce that they couldn't crackle a fire. But Kold had a blaze; Clint could see it whenever he ventured far enough forward to look. Kold had found the one ridge on the entire plain that would shelter his flame. Clint and Edward had no such ridge. But just when it seemed like they might freeze to death, a square section of the sand lifted straight upward, revealing a man beneath it with wild white hair, wound in a corkscrew pointing toward the sky. Even the harsh winds of the Edge couldn't manage to flatten the tufts.

"Horsey!" said the man, pointing at Edward.

The unicorn was too cold to protest.

The odd man was standing inside a hatchway of some sort under the sand. The square section of rising sand appeared to actually be a steel trap door topped with some sort of carpeting which, when dusted with sand, entirely vanished.

"Greetings," said Clint. The "T" sound in the word came out twice through his chattering teeth.

"Howdy!" said the man. "I'm Rank. Don't smell that way, though." He said the second part like he had said it countless times before.

Clint wondered if his mind had finally cracked, or if he really was seeing a head sticking out from the sand in the freezing night, making conversation as if there were turkey pie and brew between them. He turned to Edward, who read his question and nodded in the affirmative.

Clint asked the man, "Do you live under the sand?"

The man said, "Yar. So where you comin' from?" He ran a hand through one of his tufts. There was a glow bleeding up from beneath him. Clint would've thought it a lantern, but it seemed too bright, so he decided it was probably a spark generator instead.

Clint ignored him. "I don't suppose you have more room under there?"

"And a larger entrance?" Edward added.

Rank made an odd jerking motion as a smacking rose above the wind's holler. Clint could only see his head, but was fairly certain Rank had slapped himself across the knee.

"Lawds! And where are my manners?" he said.

The trap door closed. Within seconds, blowing sand had swallowed the carpet on top.

Five minutes passed.

Finally Edward said, "I liked that guy."

Clint stood and drew both guns. "I wonder if I can shoot true enough to find that trap door."

He didn't have a chance to find out before a great shudder ran through the ground, and a large rectangular section of the sand was rising from the desert floor as if tired of being part of the plain, and planning to escape into space slowly so that nobody would notice. It raised a half inch, then a full inch. It was moving so slowly that Clint had to keep telling himself he wasn't imagining it.

After the desert rectangle raised two or three inches, Clint saw that the sand on top of it was mostly carpet, just like the top of Rank's hatch. Below the carpet, Clint saw a narrow band of yellow, maybe a flicker of lamplight, and heard a steady, rapid clanking, like chain dragged across the edge of a steel strongbox.

An inch later, Clint finally grew tired of waiting for the dramatic reveal. He walked over to the slowly growing line of lamplight, stooped low, and peered inside the giant box rising from the sand.

It was a giant liftbox, like the ones which lifted folk to the tops of tall structures in The Realm, except that this liftbox was gigantic — at least three unicorns wide and one deep.

Inside the liftbox was Rank, turing a crank with fury, so quickly it looked like he was in the midst of a fit. The clanking sound brayed from the crank, as a small catch struck a row of small grooves in the wheel beneath it. The spike of hair on Rank's head bounced with his swaying head.

Clint waited. The liftbox opening was three inches high. He waited longer, then longer. At four inches. Edward strolled over and peered into the narrow opening between the box's top and sand.

"Slow down," he said. "I don't have the stomach to ride a lift this fast."

Rank slowed down.

"I was kidding," the unicorn said.

Rank stopped cranking entirely so that he could slap his knee again, bellowing laughter and adding to the wind's whistle.

It took another twenty minutes of steady cranking for the liftbox to rise high enough for Clint and Edward to climb inside. Clint tried to drop in early, figuring Rank could use a break, but the old man yelled at him in panic, screaming at him to stay outside because the box was already incredibly heavy, and he didn't want to hoist Clint's bulk as well.

When it was fully risen, Edward and Clint stepped inside the box, and Rank started cranking in the opposite direction. Only this time, gravity made the going easier.

Clint said, "Build this lift yourself?"

"Yar. It weighs as much as the sun. I haven't used it since that one night. You remember that?"

"No," said Clint.

"Me too," said Rank. "Took me weeks to figure out the gear ratio needed to allow me to crank it myself. The answer was: Infinity! The wheel on the other side is the size of the moon. The wheel behind this crank is the size of a fly's fart."

Clint said he had no knowledge as to the various sizes of farts. Rank stopped cranking, slapped his knee, and bellowed laughter again. Then he resumed cranking, and as the liftbox descended, Clint asked Rank if he'd seen a dark man on a black unicorn come through this area recently.

"Yar," he said. "I seen him, but I kept my lids tight. Didn't like his look, and I could feel his malice through the sand, so I stayed hidden. I have a spyglass, what sees around corners, so I watched him pass. I thought the unicorn would sense me, because the riderless unicorns who come through this place sometimes can, but he didn't flinch." He looked at Edward. "Did *you* sense me?" he asked.

"In retrospect, yar, I did," said Edward. "But it was more like a smell in the air. A clot of garbage in an otherwise pure stream."

Clint flinched, but Rank didn't seem to notice the insult. "Nar, they didn't know I was here, and for that I was glad," he continued. "Just kept marching. There was something wrong with 'em. They looked stunned and weak, like you, like most who come by, because of the way things are here. But there was more to it. It was like they were… not quite there."

"Like they were in a trance?"

"Like they weren't quite there," Rank repeated louder, as if volume was the problem.

Clint looked at Edward, but the unicorn shrugged, not knowing what that might mean any more than the humans.

"They riding with a woman?" Clint asked, his heart hurting for Mai.

"Yar. Pretty lady. She looked the worst. Plodded on like the dead, she did. It was as though she was wearing a tether, but she weren't wearing no tether. She walked like her legs were in chains — didn't ride high, like her beau — and whenever she fell behind, she jerked forward like she was snapping against a rope. Looked painful, but didn't register no pain. Like she was bitten by a poison needle."

Clint turned to Edward again, and this time, he nodded. Clint didn't need an explanation of the magic involved — which the unicorn would have ordinarily been all too happy to bore him with if Rank weren't around — to get the gist: Mai was with them as a captive, and freeing her wouldn't be nearly as simple as cutting cords and shooting cuffs.

CHAPTER FOUR: KNEE-SLAPPING DOONERS

Once the liftbox settled at the bottom (Clint estimated its round-trip trip took around an hour) Rank stepped out, waved the gunslinger and the unicorn out of the box, and showed them around his home: a natural cave beneath the sand, probably a large air pocket from when the ground had cooled.

The ceiling was low, and Edward kept scraping his horn on the rock above, releasing a torrent of verbal abuse on Rank each time. Clint sat on a natural seat in the rock, accepted a mug steaming from some sort of hot liquid, and raised the mug toward Edward.

"You'll have to excuse my friend's lack of gratitude," he said to Rank. "We've been out here for too long a spell, and it plays with my friend's mind. He's barely hanging on."

"The Sands will make you crazy!" said Rank. "I've heard tales of people going two kinds of cashew!"

Clint took in the white spike on Rank's head and his patched overalls with a strap hanging loose. The shirt underneath was on backward — not a small oversight, seeing as it buttoned up the front.

"But the Sands also get into your blood," Rank went on. "People tell me to move, but I like it here. I ain't got no home nowhere else, though I could buy one sure as the hot in a dog. But I don't wanna, since I'm an Edge man. I like to be Realm-adjacent, same way some folks in Realm towers want to be adjacent to nature. I think the Castle puts out signals, and I want to hear 'em."

"The Realm is near?"

"Very."

"Do you know the way?"

"Not exactly, but I know I wouldn't travel it."

"Why not?"

"Because the path is so long."

Clint wanted to dismiss the insanity of Rank's contradiction, but he remembered that Edward had said the same thing not too long before. The Realm was near. The Realm was far. Somehow it was both.

"What do you mean by signals?" said Clint.

"He's talking about magic," said Edward, suddenly beside him.

"Magic?"

Edward nodded. "Where reality is shallow, magic is near to the surface. I can feel it."

"Does it... heal you? Help you?" He asked because suddenly the unicorn looked refreshed, as if he'd just swallowed his first bite of turkey pie after near starvation. His eyes were clear, too. The fog Clint saw earlier — the thick mist that made Edward's grasp on reality tenuous at best — was gone.

"That's not a good thing, the magic being near the surface," said Edward.

"It doesn't refresh you?"

"It does, but I'm not talking about 'good' or 'bad' being in the way it affects me or you. It's bad because it's leaking. You've got to understand that we're talking about core magic here, not surface magic. Surface magic was what used to be plentiful. It was what humans and unicorns alike tapped into and used. But core magic shouldn't be at the surface because it doesn't replenish. It can't, because it's so strong and from so deep. But out here, where the world is fractured, it flows through the cracks and escapes like air from a poorly insulated house. All the magic steaming from this hollow ultimately means less magic everywhere else."

"I do seem to feel something," said Clint.

"You would," said Rank. "I do. It's like a geyser of magic blowing up your skirt from below."

Clint decided the expression must be metaphorical, so he didn't bother to correct Rank on their status as three skirtless creatures.

But yes... Clint could feel the magic in the air. It felt powerful. He imagined that how he felt in Rank's hollow, out of the cold and with the magic touching him, must be how Edward must feel every day.

The gunslinger fell into a rare smile, suddenly certain of a new ability he could sense growing within him. He reached behind Rank, grabbed a rock from the cave ledge, then smothered it in his large left hand.

"Watch this," he said.

Clint made some magic movements over his newly enchanted hand while whispering a string of magic-sounding words, then opened his palm to reveal the metamorphosed object.

"Nice rock," Rank said, looking at the unchanged hunk in Clint's hand. He snatched it from the gunslinger's palm and shoved it deep into his dirty overalls pocket, eyes darting around, daring the empty space to challenge him and his new posession.

Edward snorted, blowing tiny flecks of mucus onto the gunslinger's sleeve.

"It's *core* magic, I told you," he said. "You can't use it, no matter how it makes you feel. You're a man, not a unicorn — pleasem and thankoo to Providence for that."

Rank continued showing them around, occasionally patting his stolen rock through the pocket of his overalls as if to assure himself that it was still there. Then, after a brief tour and some vittles, Clint asked where he and Edward could lay their heads.

Rank showed them an open room and gave them a pile of blankets that smelled like cheese. Within five minutes, they seesawed into sleep as Rank laughed and cackled like a witch from a distant chamber of the underground cave.

Clint woke with a full bladder as he did every night at precisely 3am, or the equivalent time in a world that had shifted.

The room was mostly dark, but Rank had left them a lantern, and the lantern was still burning weakly in a corner. Clint wondered if it was dangerous, leaving a lantern burning with everyone sleeping in an underground chamber. But when he reached the glow, he looked up to see black smoke licking up from the curled wick and drifting toward a small hole in the rock. It seemed to be a natural vent, and the surface wind was drawing air up and through it. Rank had already showed them his air intakes — a series of tubes meandering into the cave from the leeward side of a surface hill. The place had everything.

Rank's tall closet wasn't tall and it wasn't a closet. It was a covered bucket in a small chamber off the front room. Clint used it and then returned to his chamber to find Rank sitting on a rock ledge, staring at Edward's sleeping body. He'd brought his own lantern — a larger one, hot enough to provide some radiant warmth — and had set it on a small table in front of himself. The lantern's light threw Rank's shadow against the wall, casting it as something black and horrible.

Clint said, "It's never a good idea to let a unicorn catch you watching him unawares."

"I had a vision," said Rank. He sounded saner than he had when they'd gone to sleep, as if no joking matter were chewing at his mind.

Clint sat across from him, near the unicorn's lightly rising and falling body.

"I have them in my sleep sometimes. They let me see behind the walls of The Realm. Your friend would say it's because of the geyser of magic beneath us."

Edward stirred in the lamplight, as if he knew Rank was talking about him.

"It's crumbling," said Rank.

"What is?"

"The world. The Realm used to be the center, back when the world was whole, and now it's durn near the only place that has any magic left. Folks like you spend your lives searching for it, your minds sick with the need to find it..."

"We're after my bride to be, not The Realm," Clint corrected.

"... pursuing it over everything else, letting it destroy your lives, corrupt your souls, but it's not the place you left behind, Marshal Gulliver."

Clint's head snapped to attention and his blue eyes went steely, fierce as bullets. He'd not told Rank the surname he'd buried in Solace, and would've felt like he was spitting curses if he had.

Rank turned and met the gunslinger's eyes.

"I saw your return to The Realm tonight in my sleep," the old man said, tugging on his tuft. "Saw you arrive at the wall and watched as you breached it. Then I stared into the end."

"The end of what?"

"The crumbling, and everything else."

"Speak in sense, old man," Clint said, reaching forward to turn up the lamp. He wondered if Rank was somehow hypnotized or sleepwalking; Clint had seen stranger things.

"You were sent off for a reason, Marshal. As was Dharma Kold. You were cut like cancer from The Castle."

Clint hadn't given the old man Kold's name any more than he'd given him his own.

"But you can't always get at the cancer," Rank went on. "Sometimes traces are left, like all that you left in The Realm."

"I don't remember The Realm. Not beyond the way you'd remember an old dream."

"I have that dream," said Rank.

Clint considered telling Rank to talk sense again, but that didn't seem possible, so he let it go. Rank was a human living on a crack at the Edge, Realm-adjacent. The leakage here had driven Edward nearly insane, and the unicorn was bred to take it. Rank's mind must have splintered long ago.

"Go to bed, old man," Clint told him.

Without a word, Rank stood, grabbed the lantern, and walked out of the chamber.

Clint laid his head back down, fell asleep, and dreamed of a precious, fragile object that shattered to pieces over and over again. In the dream, Clint tried to keep the object whole, but his large gunslinger's hands could never grasp it in time.

Clint woke so groggy and bleary-eyed the next morning that he stumbled straight into Edward, who was standing in the middle of the dark room.

The unicorn was usually hard to miss, but he'd draped several of Rank's blankets over his back and head — making him look like a gigantic equine monk. Clint, not seeing him in his gray, monk-like garb, smacked face-first into Edward's rear and nearly fell to the hovel floor. Edward, just as groggy and bleary-eyed, spun with alarm, horn glowing. He seemed to remember where he was and said, "Oh, it's just you" to the gunslinger. He then returned his rear to Clint's face and backed up into the marshal, knocking him down.

Rank was back to the zany character he'd been when they'd first met. The shift into crazy guy from last night's seer/doomsayer was so dramatic that Clint almost asked him about it, but then decided not to. He didn't particularly want Rank to start reciting prophecies again, nor did he want Edward to hear them. The unicorn's mind was still too fragile. Besides, if Rank repeated what he'd said in the night's middle, Edward might decide that it was true, since his memories of The Realm weren't any clearer than Clint's.

"Thankoo and pleasem for your hospitality," said Clint. "We'll leave you with our memory, soon as we've filled the bare in our bellies."

"Ain't nothin'," said Rank. "I like the company. You want beans? I'm making beans."

Rank was cooking his beans over a tiny fire under another of the natural rock vents. The beans were still in a can, still sealed and with the label still on it. The label was burning, but Clint could tell that the picture on it was of corn.

"We've imposed on your generosity enough," said Clint. "I've plenty of rupees. What I'd like is to buy some of your stores, if you can replace and spare them."

"Take 'em!" said Rank with a hiccup, his white spike of hair bouncing with excitement. "I have more stores than I need, and the dooners are always leaving more when they raid parties coming through."

"Dooners?" said a voice gravelly with sleep.

Clint turned as Edward edged into the room wearing his gray monk's garb. He'd already used their gear and some of Rank's fresh water to brew his morning coffee in their chamber. Edward's cup was a giant metal bowl, floating before him in a wide rosy pink bubble. Edward looked surly, half-asleep, and in desperate need of caffeine.

Rank lowered the tongs holding the beans that were actually corn for long enough to slap his knee. He was wearing an ancient pair of red full-body long-johns, with only one of the buttons working hard enough to bury his rear. The flap of thin fabric bounced as he spoke.

"That's right!" he said. "I meant to tell you about them. The dooners are natives of the Sands. Lawless. Lethal. If they see you, they'll want to see you killt. You should try and avoid that."

Edward scoffed. Then his horn glowed for a moment and the bowl of coffee floated toward him until it was hovering just under his mouth. He drank, then magicked it back away.

"Don't laugh, horsey!" Rank cackled. "Not one party comes through here that the dooners don't at least watch. If it suits them, they fall onto those parties and take what they want and some of what they don't, never caring who lays behind killt. They kill their prey with sharpened metal weapons. Some say they're nar human at all. Travel in packs, small usually, but always with a larger band behind them, just over a hill should they be needed. They communicate by magic. Magic! Can you believe that? Not a lot of magic, of course; ain't like we're outside The Realm. But each dooner tribe is led by a shaman warrior who can sift what's left from the sand."

"Wow, beings who can use magic," said Edward. "That's impressive." He magicked a massive boulder away from the wall and managed to take an incredibly awkward seat on it, looking like a circus elephant perching on a tiny platform.

"Thankoo, Rank," said Clint. "We'll keep our eyes on the horizon, and high and low all around it."

Edward wouldn't be put off so easily. He'd had a rough few days, a horrible night, and clearly now an inexcusable morning. He didn't want to hear about mysterious humans or human-things that set the whole region afeared, who were more worth mentioning than wild unicorn herds that could level whatever hovels the dooners had in seconds if they had a mind to.

And besides, he really hated being called "horsey."

"Wait, wait," he said. "They're fearsome warriors, hunting with projectile weapons. Maybe swords and axes. That makes them a match for unicorns? Or even just *one* unicorn?"

Rank nodded. "Sure thing. They fight without souls or mercy. They'll surround you twice before you know what hit you once."

"How does a person get surrounded twice?"

"It's an expression."

"And are you aware I can extend a bubble of protection?"

"Is it a pink bubble?" said Rank.

"Are you aware I could cause a man to use his 'fearsome weapon' on himself?"

"Woah, boy," said Rank. "Easy."

This was the wrong thing to say. Edward didn't like being told to "woah" like a common mount. He advanced, his horn glowing. But Clint put a hand on his chest and gave him a meaningful stare. The stare said, *This man is crazy, and he's our host. Let it go.*

Edward stared daggers at Rank for a moment, then rolled his big equine eyes and took another long sip from his coffee bowl.

"You just watch out," said Rank, unconcerned with Edward's malevolence.

"Yar," said Clint. "We will."

"I'm not impressed," Edward said an hour later, staring at a distant and uninteresting ridge.

They'd left Rank's company to resume pursuit of Kold, Cerberus, and the captive Mai. Twenty of the past sixty minutes had been spent in Rank's hand-cranked liftbox with Rank cranking away at the metal wheel and refusing help. Edward kept offering magic assistance, but Rank wouldn't accept it, saying he was their host and would do his duties as such. But with Edward on board in addition to the tremendous weight of the lift itself, even the ridiculous gear ratio didn't keep the cranking from being as slow as molasses. Eventually Edward traded asking for action and magicked the lift to the top of the sand. But afterward, Rank failed to take up the slack in the chain, so when Edward and Clint stepped out and the unicorn released his hold on the liftbox, it fell precipitously, jerking to a heavy stop twenty feet below with a horrible clanging and a sound like a side of beef being thrown through a wall — probably Rank hitting the floor of the box when it stopped.

"Rank!" Clint yelled, finding the edge of the trap cover and lifting it enough to peer inside the shaft.

"I'm fine!" Rank's shaky coot voice rippled to the top. He whistled loud, cackled, "What a ride!" and then slapped his knee loud enough for them to hear it at the top.

Now, watching Edward watch the ridge, Clint said, "What aren't you impressed by?"

"These dooners."

"You can see them?"

Edward nodded. "I can sense them. They're watching us from the ridge, just as our crazy old friend said they would."

"Are they aiming to attack?" said Clint.

"I don't know, but if they know anything, they'll know they shouldn't. We're a man and a unicorn. Not only is it doubtful we'd have much of value, but their weapons are nothing next to this big pearly horn."

"I've never asked you," said Clint. "But let's just say I cut off your horn. Could you still magick?"

"Of course. My horn is Dumbo's feather."

"What's a Dumbo?"

"It's an ancient unicorn legend. But no matter, the magic is in *me*, not my horn. Or more accurately, the magic comes *through* me, rather than through my horn."

They walked for a few minutes in silence. Edward was more lucid than he'd been for weeks. He'd predicted that their way would be easier once they were past Rank's cave, and so far that had borne true.

"Rank said some of the dooner tribes are peaceful," said Clint.

"Yar."

"But if this one isn't one of those, you can protect us?"

"*Can*, yes. Whether or not I *will* is dependent on you allowing me our last slice of turkey pie."

"Sands to that; that pie is mine," said Clint. "I don't need your protection. I have my guns." He touched the seven-shooter on his right hip.

"You do. And from what I can tell, there are only seven men on that ridge. I might sit this one out and let you do the clearing for a change. Providence knows this journey has seen me shouldering most of the load."

"Yar," Clint agreed. "You've done much."

They'd found Kold again quickly, following the pain in Edward's chest. As they neared the ridge, he was barely visible on the horizon as a dark shadow, but Clint didn't fear being discovered should Kold look back. With the light brown sand, brown cliffs, and blue sky as a background, Kold wouldn't be able to see Edward's white coat or Clint in his light clothing from the same distance, and Cerberus was too occupied defiling Mai's soul to see them with magic.

"How is your pain?" Clint asked.

"Bad. But I'm learning to adjust. It's better without the mental fog. At least all I feel now is this spike in my chest."

"And you can bear it."

"Yar. And no matter how bad it is for me, I need to remember it's a hundred times worse for..."

Clint went rigid.

Edward changed the subject. "Those fools on the ridge are still watching us," he said.

Clint hopped off of Edward's back, then sauntered several paces ahead. The unicorn stopped walking, waiting to see what the gunslinger was up to, what he had up under his hat. Clint turned, walked back to Edward, and stood beside his great white head, staring into the unicorn's right eye.

"How bad is it, friend? Tell me true."

"For me, or for Mai?"

"Both."

"For Mai, it's unbearable. She's being subjected to Cerberus' evil will, and most of what I can feel are echoes of despair. How the dark steed can stand to do it — or how Kold can bear its proximity — I honestly don't know, no matter how icy their hearts, souls, and minds might be."

Clint's tight jaw twitched, his azure eyes turning a harder shade of blue. "And for you?"

"Terrible, near impossible to take. But it could go fathoms deeper before I'd drop."

"Could you bear it if we moved up on them? Can we end this, one way or another?"

"Nar to the first question," Edward said. Then he paused, breathed deeply, and spoke again: "But yar to the second."

Clint's hand subconsciously fell to one of his guns. Kold wore an identical pair. The chances of Edward and Clint exacting a win over Kold and Cerberus was remote, but so was the chance that Kold and Cerberus would triumph. Most likely the marshals and unicorns would face a stalemate, but there was at least one life that Clint could end if he had to — if doing so would cease her hurting.

"We need to ride," said Clint, slapping Edward's side.

"If she dies," said Edward, "you'll never find The Realm."

"Yar."

"And if Cerberus stops what he's doing to her and she lives, you'll never find The Realm."

"Yar."

Edward nodded, then shook his giant head. He drew a deep breath and said, "Let's ride."

Clint wove a hand through Edward's mane, readying himself to climb onto the unicorn's bare back. But before he could leap, a tremendous flare of pain erupted in his left shoulder. He looked down to see the tip of an arrow protruding through his shirt, and found himself having a whole, fully coherent thought: *I'll need this shirt laundered and sewn the next time we see a town, else I'll be riding through the Sands in long johns.*

There were hooting noises behind him. The gunslinger tried to turn, but before he could, another arrow struck him in the side and he fell to the dirt.

Dooners.

Clint looked up to see Edward battling at least a dozen men in long tan cloaks who were wielding swords and axes, some of them with hoods raised like clerics. Edward had taken several arrows and was magicking them away as fast as they ripped into his body. He was too preoccupied with triage to notice or help Clint, so the gunslinger simply lay there watching, feeling the soak slowly spread across his shirt as his head grew woozy.

A man with a raised hood appeared above Clint holding a sword. He raised the blade, but at the top of his swing, a bright yellow bolt of something blew him from Clint's view and sent him spinning hard into the sand. Clint, his head in a cloud, found the spectacle interesting — if not entirely hysterical.

After another few minutes of yellow bolts, deafening yells, sparking swords, flying arrows, and colorful magic, Clint started to close his eyes, eager for sleep.

He almost smiled at his final thought before the blackout came to claim him: *They surrounded you twice before you knew what hit you.*

Clint wanted to slap his knee at the notion, but his mind's screen went dark, and all he could do was follow his consciousness down into a deep, dark spiraling pit, filled with endless black and too much nothing.

CHAPTER FIVE: HOVEL, HEAT, AND COLD

Clint opened his eyes to a face like jerky.

The jerky stared down, female and tanned like cowhide draped on a hot rock, wrinkled before its time and dried like an old shoe. There were crease lines at the corners of the eyes and mouth, below her eyes and across her forehead. Yet, the eyes looked not much older than a child's. Clint longed to ask the blinking soul above him how old she was, but too many other questions crowded to the front.

Who are you?

Where's my unicorn?

Why are you out in the open Sands?

Then Clint realized he wasn't out in the open Sands, but that didn't happen until he had blinked enough to clear his head. There was something above him and the jerky person, gray and smooth and definitely not sky. And there was something else below him, soft but solid. Definitely not sand.

The girl (he decided she was a girl, possibly in her late teens, despite the wrinkles) patiently waited for him to get his bearings, as if she'd known he'd need these broken minutes to figure out what cloud he'd fallen down from. Clint rolled his head, slowly drifting his gaze from the girl, to the walls, to the ceiling, to the contents of what seemed to be a mostly empty room all around him.

The world spun through his brain's orbit, slowly, one impossible image of reality overlaying the top of something else, the two offsetting each other like a double-exposure. After a Sands' forever, one image finally settled into place, killing the other and making everything else come back.

The gunslinger's hand flew inhumanly fast toward his hip. Then it came back up, his finger twitching at the trigger before Clint's hand and then his brain — in that order — realized he wasn't holding a gun. Nor was he wearing his shirt, denims, holsters, boot, or hat. He was dressed in chambray that looked like... *pajamas?*

"I dislike cliches, but I have to use one," Clint rasped at the girl. "Where in the crooked gash of the Sprawl am I?"

"You're with me," she said, as though it wasn't the most unhelpful sentence in all of the Sands. Then, after two seconds, the girl seemed to realize her answer was a dud and added, "I'm Cari."

Clint stared at the smooth gray ceiling. It looked like rock. The far wall was covered by a drape of some sort. Or maybe the wall *was* just a drape. He thought he heard the outdoors just beyond, and remembered where he and Edward were walking when ambushed — the deep Sands, Edge-adjacent.

"Is this a mesa hovel?" he asked.

Cari clapped excitedly. "Yes! We're Leisei. I didn't think you'd know that, being who you are."

"Who I am?"

"You're a Realm marshal, aren't you? You were carrying two guns, and they had... *seven chambers.*" She whispered it, as if Clint might not know. "And your friend? The unicorn?"

Clint sat up, but Cari gently pushed him back to the mattress he seemed to be laying on.

"He's fine," she said, reading his reaction. "In fact, he's..."

There was a crash from outside, then a large splashing. Someone yelled that someone else didn't need to be so testy, and that he'd get him his dagged turkey pie and brew.

"... he's kind of a jerk," Cari finished.

"Was that your appy?" Clint said, meaning whoever had made the splash, possibly after being magically pushed into something by a hungry unicorn.

"Grappy," she corrected. "It's okay. Grammy pushes him into that trough all the time."

Clint nodded and laid his head back on a pillow that was approximately as soft as a carcass. But it was still better than holding it up to talk, which made him feel lightheaded.

"How did we get here?" he asked.

"Your unicorn walked up to our house with you magicked in front of him. Caused quite a stir with my grappies. Most Leisei have never seen a unicorn in person, even down in the village, in the valley, above the larger aquifer. Grammy fainted when she saw a floating man in a purple cloud coming toward her. Grappy thought it was the end, that the world had finally fractured at the fault lines, like most Leisei have said would happen forever. In fact, he thought the sparks coming off of you were trying to attack him."

"Sparks?"

"I ran outside just as he was setting you down. There were things moving between you and the unicorn's horn. Sparks."

"Phantom sprites," said Clint, nodding. "That means Edward was trying to heal me, but that for some reason he couldn't, so he aimed for sustaining until he could find a shaman. Probably means the arrows that struck me were tipped in dark elixir."

"They looked like fairies," said Cari.

"Phantom sprites," Clint repeated.

"It was all very…" Cari began.

"Then I thank you for your help," Clint said, interrupting her. "Your help, and your shaman's."

"I healed you myself," Cari said with an edge of false modesty. "It was indeed a dark elixir. We're all shaman out here, at least sort of. Only way to survive. Just enough to ward off ghoulem, and heal wounds when needed. But it's too hard to sift much more than a sprinkle of magic from the sand these days."

Clint had heard of the Leisei, but not in years he could count without thinking deep. He'd learned of them when he'd lived in and served The Realm. The Leisei were sand people, living in hovels built in gullies beneath large, flat rocks, like open-ended caves tucked under the sand. They farmed what they could, living so far at the edge of the Sprawl that you could spit into the Edge. They grew pumpkins and raised turkeys like the growers in nearly all Sprawl whistle stops, but also sifted sands and dealt in light white magic. As with all quasi-magic people, the Leisei were an odd mix of hard practicality and superstition. They learned farming and healing, but also spent an intolerable number of minutes learning to defend themselves against nonexistent wives tales, like ghoulem.

"Appy and Grappy went out to where the dooners had attacked you as soon as I gave you the potions to let you sleep and heal," Cari said, now picking clumps of sand from Clint's scratchy sheets. "They said there was nothing left but body parts. So we also have to thank *you*, since that dooner tribe has been pillaging us for months. After what your unicorn done to them, I doubt they'll trouble us again."

"I need to speak to him," said Clint.

Cari nodded, shrugged, then patted Clint's shoulder and rose to her feet. She was wearing a long, flowing lightweight cloak, but it moved with no swish. He remembered that about the Leisei too — so quiet that they were like holes in the sand, and that if they weren't so vested in the religion of NextWorld and the pacifism that galloped alongside it, they'd make fantastic assassins.

Seconds after Cari left, the drape at the far side of the small room was raked sharply aside and Edward lit the room with his bright white body. Behind him, a soaking wet old man ran over and dragged the drape closed to keep the sand out of the hovel.

"Oh, Providence!" Edward cried, looking at Clint. "The injuries to your face are ghastly! You're a monster!"

"I've sustained no facial injuries," said Clint.

"Oh, then I guess you're just ugly." Edward sprawled on the hovel floor so that his horn wouldn't scrape the ceiling.

"I heard you shuttled me back on a litter," said Clint, referring to the purple cloud, the sprites, and the magic.

"I couldn't heal you. They used helioroot powder on their weapons. We got lucky these people were here to heal you. And gunslinger, I'm sorry. The men on the ridge? They *let* me see them. They *wanted* me to see them. I should have known. These people have told me about the dooners while you've been recovering. They travel with a powerful shaman, and the shaman can make his presence 'bright' inside the magic, which makes him stand out in front of their prey… making it easier for another party to approach undetected from the rear."

"I assume that once I was down, you finished the battle?"

"They hit me many times and cut me a few, but then I gave them something special in return. It radiated out from my body like a grater of cheese. A few survived and promptly ran. Their shaman chief waited for them on the ridge, like a coward."

"Did you follow?"

"You needed my attention. And friend, you needed all I had to give."

"How long have we been here?" said Clint, dreading the answer.

Edward sighed, blowing air through his giant white lips.

"How long, Edward?"

"Two weeks," the unicorn said. "I can no longer feel the pain in my chest, nor feel the breath of Kold or Mai through my own reach, nor any of the unicorns in the area, of which there seem to be none."

"So…"

"That's correct," Edward said, anticipating the gunslinger's question. "They are gone. Their trail is as cold as the dark rider's soul."

CHAPTER SIX: THE DOOR TO NEXTWORLD

Clint couldn't convince anyone — not Cari; not Cari's grammy or grappy or ammy or appy; not even Edward — that leaving the hovel to pick up Kold's trail was in the same desert as a good idea.

He tried forcing the issue by climbing onto Edward's back and urging him out toward the open sand, but each time he tried, Edward rolled over and nearly crushed him or magicked things to fly at his head. Then, when Clint announced he didn't need any dagged horse to carry him and started marching off on his own, Edward pointed out that he didn't have his guns and wondered out loud if the gunslinger hoped to kill Kold dead by telling him knock-knock jokes. Then Edward pushed him to the ground and set a rock on his chest.

"I didn't carry you ten miles through the sun to watch you go out and get yourself killt now," he said, leaving Clint to squirm.

Edward, being a unicorn and therefore impervious to most witch elixirs including helioroot, had already been entirely healed when he'd arrived at the hovel. He wouldn't be able to completely cure Clint, who had no such constitution, until the poison fled his system. All they could do was wait and give Clint over to rest and to Cari's attention. Cari was excellent with medicines. She'd learned at the side of her grappy, who learned at the side of *his* grappy — Angus Groo, one of the most famous Leisei shaman in history.

Clint still protested, but eventually Edward squashed his enthusiasm by repeating that the trail was already cold and that if there had been another shift in the sands (which seemed a near certainty), they could no longer count on even the direction of Kold's ride to carry them toward him. If there had been a shift, *any* direction could be the correct direction. Which to take would be as random as a drop of the numbercubes. So, with Kold out of sight, there was no reason not to wait and gather strength for the pursuit — wherever and whenever they might resume it.

Cari seemed amused by Clint's curmudgeonry as he convalesced in the following weeks. His barbs and insults were constant, but Cari took each of them with an ever-widening smile. The gunslinger said that her hands were clumsy and she grinned. He told her that she was poisoning him and making him worse, and she laughed. He insulted her hovel, and she swore that she would one day live in a castle in NextWorld.

That, Clint didn't mock. Though not a religious man himself (he believed in Providence, but cottoned to no church), the gunslinger knew something about belief — and knew that a man worth his salt should never soil another's belief with his words.

And so, as the helioroot drained from his system and his strength slowly returned, as the sun crawled across the sky and turned the Edge dragonfire hot, Clint could only lay in bed while his hands slowed from lack of practice. The tedium of long, wasted days was torture, so to distract himself, Clint dragged conversation out of the family. He asked about their lives. He asked about where they came from. He asked them about their belief in NextWorld.

This last mostly happened because they kept asking *him* about The Realm.

"Our people believe the fracturing of the world and the detachment of The Realm have opened gates everywhere to NextWorld," Cari's grappy told him over a dinner of pumpkin mash and undersized turkey legs. He turned to Clint as the family always did when The Realm was mentioned and said, "What is it like beyond the wall, Clint? Do the people there wear shimmering robes and live in perpetual bliss?"

Grappy's name was Makai — a name Clint couldn't keep straight from grammy's name, Malai. He was a thin, bony man who looked frail even though he was ox strong. He was an accomplished Sands shaman, and he could sift so much magic from the leaking sand that the family had enough left after meeting basic needs to power a large spark-fueled food cooker and other appliances.

"Nar," said Clint, gnawing on turkey. "I don't remember much about my time in The Realm, but I can tell you it's only a city, same as your village above the aquifer, but larger. There are good people and bad people there, but there is also so much magic that they've grown spoilt. Few wear white robes since they spend their wealth on luxuries, including coats of many colors. Gems. Spangles. Glossy books and ample distractions. They play a lot of Risk and listen to a lot of Joelsongs. They're soft. You all, here, are better than them. A Realm man wouldn't survive a day out here."

"You did," said Makai.

"Yar," said Clint. "But even when I was in The Realm, I was a Sands man, and Edward was a Sands unicorn. We were always strangers to The Realm, which probably explains our exile. A unicorn chooses his rider, and Edward found me on a long sojourn into the desert. This was back before the first fracture, when restless souls such as mine often left The Realm to wander. It was on one of those trips when Edward found me. It was his choice that made me a marshal and gave me my guns, not a decree of the Realm. The tin star they gave me made my already-confirmed appointment official — nar more than that."

Clint realized he'd just told the family nearly everything he still knew about The Realm. There had to be a wealth of memories in his mind between his birth, meeting Edward, and his exile, but outside of a few oases in his mind, those old memories were shrouded. It was as if the great fracture had opened a matching fissure in his mind — and when that had happened, Clint's memories of The Realm had fallen into the core, into deep magic that swallowed them whole.

Makai and Malai's son was a strapping, weather-worn man named Gregori. Gregori was in charge of the family's turkeys and pumpkins, and spent most of his days while Clint was around using Makai's spark drill to tap into the aquifer below the hovel so he could give the pumpkins the water they needed. Gregori said it was a neverending battle, since the sand started spitting water a second after its sipping first started. The pumpkins took what they could, then the water sifted back down.

Gregori, like the others, seemed obsessed with asking Clint about The Realm and telling him his own theories.

"Our people believe there are wanderers who help the rest of us find our way to NextWorld," he said one day during dinner. "Even before the fracture, we believe that NextWorld moved around, and it's easy to get lost on the way to a place that moves. But a human's purpose is to find his own way. We spend our lives looking, searching for signs and guideposts, and for those wanderers in life who can guide us. When we do finally discover the way, through whatever means we can, our souls wander forward."

None of what Gregori said made a splinter of sense to Clint. He thought Gregori might be wondering if Clint was their family's spirit guide, but Clint hadn't a foggy as to how a soul could search for *anything* if its body was stuck in a Sprawl hovel. But, not being a religious man, he didn't ask questions that might be seen as disrespectful. Instead, he listened and nodded politely.

Clint stayed with Cari, Makai, Malai, Gregori, and Gregori's wife Persei for two weeks before he finally found the strength to start going on short walks. The sun was a fire in the sky, and by the end of his short walks, Clint found himself drenched in sweat. He'd been wandering the Sands under an unforgiving sun for two and a half years now — and, of course, for years beyond that prior to his time in Solace — without any trouble. But now, he could barely make it a quarter-mile.

It was the poison still in his system that caused his fatigue, said Cari, and that was a sure sign that he was not yet ready to travel.

A week after he first started walking, Clint's constitution improved and he was able to double the length of his walks, but Clint, looking back on so much wasted time, bemoaned how much the illness was setting him back. Cari explained that his old self was still there, and that the helioroot had simply slapped a mask atop it. Once the helioroot had left his system, he'd be the same as if he'd simply sat around for the same number of days. It was meant to make Clint feel better, but he'd never sat for a month before. He feared the atrophy of his muscles, his grit, and most of all his hands and fingers.

So, to exercise his dexterity, the gunslinger started doing coin tricks and using his fingers to twirl long pencils. He found hard clumps of sand to crush between his fingers. He tossed pebbles high into the air, spinning himself in a circle before snatching them with his thumb and different fingers before they struck ground.

Eventually, to further his practice and still his boredom, Gregori gave him back his guns.

"Bullets," said Clint to Gregori, inspecting the guns and finding the chambers empty.

"If I give you the bullets, you'll leave," Gregori replied. "And then, you'll die."

Clint swore sixteen curses, shaking his fist at Gregori and yelling that he was being held where he didn't belong or wish to remain. When Cari saw this, she smiled and laughed in a way that suggested that Clint would be Clint.

Still, he was glad to have his irons back. He oiled and polished them, stripping them to clear the grit and grains from deep within their works. He used a small brush Cari leant him to clear and oil each of the fourteen chambers.

Once his guns were fully restored, the gunslinger practiced his draws, pulling the triggers while trying to imagine the thick billows of dull red smoke as he fired. Soon he felt as fast and as sure as ever, leaving his aim as the only mystery. But since a gunslinger knew his hands and his guns, verifying the precision of his aim was only a formality.

Clint was practicing his draws indoors when Persei walked in, saw him, and screamed.

Clint, who saw no reason for Persei to scream, assumed a looming threat and spun toward the entrance with both guns drawn, forgetting in full that the chambers were empty. He found Persei staring, green eyes wide and aghast; mouth dragging on the dusty hot floor. She wasn't looking at Clint or his empty weapons. She was staring past him as if at something so horrible that it haunted her eyes.

She ran at Clint and began pounding her fists on his chest.

"What? What, woman?" Clint said, slipping his irons back into their holsters while fending off her blows with open palms.

"You dare! After we've taken you in and fed you and brought you to health! After we've shared table, bed, and turkey pie!"

Makai, who'd heard the commotion, ran in and stepped between the gunslinger and his daughter-in-law, holding his hands up for peace.

"He was drawing on..." Her eyes darted behind Clint.

And then he knew.

At the back of the hovel was a small, ornate arch made of dried desertwood, painted in rainbows and covered in costume jewels. Below the arch was a small door made of stone. The door's knob was cut glass, like a diamond. The entire structure stood around two feet tall, and after each meal, Makai took some small morsel of food from his plate and set it before the door, after which the others did the same.

When Edward first saw this display (he typically stuck his head through the curtain for meals, and Persei would lay a plate on the ground for him) he joked to Clint that the family must be leaving cookies for Santa, then brayed with insensitive laughter. Fortunately, only Clint was present. He shushed Edward, frantically waving and whispering that he must never make such a joke in the family's presence. Clint hadn't known much about Leisei religion when his nursing first started, but he'd quickly learned enough to know that every family had their own shrine, and that it wasn't something a man — or a unicorn — had any business mocking.

"Why not?" Edward asked. "They're putting food in front of a tiny door for no reason, and they're doing it in a part of the world where food cannot always be counted on. Don't tell me that's not ridiculous, and a waste. Who is coming through that door to eat the food? A leprechaun?"

Clint couldn't help himself. He smacked the unicorn across the nose. "Remember what you said about Cerberus defiling Mai? The profane thing he's doing to her very soul?"

Edward's eyes became serious. "Yar."

"If you want to do the same to these people," said Clint, "make that same joke in their presence."

Edward never made any jokes about NextWorld or the shrine again, either to the family or to Clint.

On the night Persei attacked him, the gunslinger stared at the shrine (which the family sometimes called a "portal") and then began to apologize to Persei. He'd been practicing drawing his guns in front of the family's single reflecting glass — but to her, it must have looked like he was pretending to fire at the portal.

"You were going to shoot at it!" she screamed, half angry, half desperately afraid.

"I beg your every pardon," said Clint. "I was practicing my draw in the glass. I meant no foul, or to draw on your portal."

Persei was still sniffling. Makai, who saw the gunslinger's mistake, was trying to comfort her while casting a crooked look at Clint.

Clint unbuckled his gun belt, fell to his knees, and placed the belt in Persei's hands.

"The chambers are empty. I meant no offense. Here: take my weapons, pleasem and thankoo."

Persei seemed somewhat appeased as she looked down at the weapons, but Clint was underwhelmed. He should have known better than to risk offense to the portal, but he could tell that she didn't recognize the symbolism of what he'd just done. A gunslinger surrendering his guns was as meaningful to him as the portal was to them, and it tore something inside of him to do it.

Makai, old enough to know the ways of The Realm, seemed to see the meaning in Clint's gesture. He took the gun belt from Persei, led her outside, then returned to Clint and handed him the belt.

"Put them back on, Marshal," he said. "You see your mistake and atone."

"I meant no offense."

"Yar, but pleasem be careful," said Makai. "I understand our beliefs aren't for every child of Providence, but I also know that life near the Edge is hard, and that faith goes a long way toward keeping a person sane. It keeps us hitched to our spirits instead of crying at what we might see when we look true."

Clint nodded, repeating his apology. He meant no offense, but he understood why Persei was bothered by the aim of his draw. The one thing you could do to a Leisei that was worse than killing was to destroy his portal. Without it, Leisei belief said that a soul was forever stuck in the sand and unable to move on to NextWorld. Such a pour soul would be stuck at the Edge forever, undead and wandering.

Persei was visibly shaken throughout the evening's remainder and into the following day. Clint felt discomfort on his head, but at the same time he felt strength and speed return to his hands. The entire event began to feel like an omen, so at the next day's dinner, Clint made an announcement.

"Thankoo and pleasem for your generosity of spirit," he said, tipping his imaginary hat since Cari, Persei, and Malai all insisted he not wear one in the hovel. "My companion and I are much refreshed and improved in health. Our spirits are thicker than on our arrival, and we agree between us that we've imposed on your household enough."

The women started to protest, but Makai was already nodding. He and Clint had shared many a palaver on the topic. It was true that Clint wasn't quite finished with his healing, but it was better for a man to risk dying on his feet than to die slowly on his back. Clint had been convalescing for nearly a month, and although he had tried to keep his mind sharp and his muscles strong however he could, the truth was that the gunslinger couldn't help but feel that he was growing softer and slower with each passing day. The longer Clint stayed in the hovel, the weller he'd be — but he'd pay for that wellness with a loss of his hardness. Skills were like butter. Once they'd softened, they never again resumed their same shape.

"Yar," said Edward, his front half sticking through the curtain at the room's far end. "We thank you. We know that more healing could be done, but we starve a little with each passing day that we stay. You are good people who live in peace. But what you must know is that a gunslinger and a unicorn need hardship like a sharp knife needs a whetting stone."

There were a few more chirps of protest from everyone but Makai, but all were half-hearted. Everyone knew that the day of their guests' departure was coming, and Clint suspected they saw a silver lining. Edward ate turkey pies as fast as Malai could bake them, and he was none too courteous about only taking a piece or three and leaving the rest of the pie for another. With their guests gone, the family would finally be able to chew their food and swallow their brew without looking behind them.

"Do you have a plan?" said Makai.

"Yar. Walk out into the sand and start looking."

"The landmarks might have shifted. You understand how common that is out here? It's not like it was near your town of Solace."

Clint felt a strange desire to clarify that Solace was not *his town* so much as a place he once kicked off his boots, but he let it go. He nodded.

"Yar. We've seen it."

"We've *felt* it," said Edward. "I've had a fault line shift beneath my feet. And when it was over, when we were past, the place we'd been the day before was no longer behind us, nor in front. It could have been anywhere. We could have *been* anywhere."

Quiet draped the table as everyone ate, after Edward's strange words killed the conversation. Truth was, neither Edward nor Clint knew which direction to head. The unicorn gave them fifty-fifty odds that heading out the way they'd come — past the site of the dooner ambush — would end up setting them in the right direction. Kold could have wandered across any number of fault lines in the past month, and any of those fault lines could have shifted in the meantime. It was as though they were heading into a giant combination lock with an infinite number of dials, hoping against hope that none of the dials had been touched.

"Get surrounded in a shifting zone, and you could end up wandering forever," said Gregori. "You won't know where you are."

"Not knowing where you are matters little when you have nowhere to go," Clint countered. All he cared about was finding Kold and Mai. Beyond that, every place was the same. His actual whereabouts didn't matter worth a fart in the wind.

The next morning, Clint rose before the family awakened and sneaked outside the hovel to where Edward was waiting. They'd already packed the meager supplies they'd brought with them, tucking them in beside the generous store offered by the family to help them get through. They were carrying so much water and dried food that even Edward, who as a proud unicorn normally refused to carry supplies, agreed to wear a humiliating set of bursting saddlebags.

They had said their thankoos throughout the previous evening so that the morrow's head-out wouldn't be drawn out and tearful, but as Clint prepared to mount Edward's back, he realized he'd forgotten something very important.

Gregori remembered too.

"I owe you something," Gregori said, approaching from behind the turkey pen and extending a fist toward Clint. Clint put his palm out, and Gregori dropped fourteen bright silver bullets into his hand. They had an oily, multicolored sheen, but felt perfectly dry.

"Thankoo," said Clint.

"They might be ruined," said Gregori. "I've had them under a sheet, beneath a pile of turkey manure for a month."

Clint had never heard anyone call turkey leavings "manure" before, but it didn't matter.

"You could have stored them in a vat of acid for a century," said Clint. "These are marshal's bullets."

"Well, that's good," said Gregori, "because here are the rest of them." He handed Clint a soggy box containing the rest of his bullets. "I thought the sheet would keep the box dry, but I was wrong. Sorry for the reek."

Clint tipped the bullets into a leather pouch, handed the box back to Gregori, and hopped onto Edward's back. Then he tipped his hat — his actual hat this time — to Gregori.

"What will you do if you don't find them?" Gregori asked, squinting into the early morning sun.

"Keep looking," said Clint.

"And if you look forever and still don't find them?"

"If that happens, I will keep looking."

"But what if you never, never find them?"

"I will," said Clint.

"How do you know?"

"Because forever is a very long time, and a man's guard gets too tired to hold up forever. Some day Kold will feel confident enough to stop, and that's when I'll walk up behind him with my pistol drawn. There was a sage once — I forget his proper name, but he was a duke of some sort — who said that a bad man never reckons on a critter that will just keep on coming. I am that critter. I will stop only when my heart does."

"You are both more patient than I," said Gregori.

"Speak for one of us," Edward said to Gregori. "I *will* give up one day and leave the fool marshal to die alone. But for now I'll ride with him, because this man is the most amusing, most hilarious person I could imagine being with."

"I am that," said Clint, in gravel and monotone.

"Go with Providence, gunslinger," said Gregori.

"Yar, and you as well," Clint replied.

"We'll see you in NextWorld."

"Yar," said Clint. "I'll be the rider following the man on the dark unicorn."

CHAPTER SEVEN:
LOST AND FINDINGS

They made a day's ride out toward the ridge and the site of the dooner attack. Edward, who didn't have a fantastic sense of direction, said everything seemed familiar but that he couldn't be sure. Clint had been unconscious during this leg of the trip and had to trust his mount.

Eventually they arrived at a rock outcropping and a ridge. At their feet, they also saw what appeared to be a skeletal severed arm sticking up from the dirt.

Edward said, "Either this is the place, or someone else has misplaced an arm."

"Dooner?" Clint nodded at the arm.

"Yar. If we sifted through the sand, we could find the other pieces. It's like a puzzle nobody would ever want to solve."

"So Kold was heading off that way," Clint said, pointing. He stopped, scratching his head, certain of a direction that didn't seem right.

The unicorn said, "I think so."

They started walking, under the ridge and past a rock shaped like a giant finger that seemed familiar enough as far as rocks shaped like giant fingers tended to go, then off past several rock formations Clint thought he would have remembered, but didn't. A month had passed, so there was no way to tell anything by looking at the ground, or by Edward's sniffing out any sort of dark magic residue. Edward said he still couldn't sense any other unicorns, though there used to be a few shrinking herds out this way. The shifting had probably sent them to greener pastures, or at least ones not made of sand.

Eventually they passed a jagged rock that was shaped like a donut on end.

"This, I remember," said Clint.

"From the dooner attack?"

"Nar. From just after we left Rank. It should be far, far behind us."

"Well, here it is again," said Edward.

"But we passed it already. Back that direction." He pointed.

Edward shrugged. It didn't seem like a unicorn should be able to shrug, but Edward managed it just fine.

"I hate to voice a cliche," said Clint, "but I think we're going in circles."

"So it's shifted," said Edward. "What do we do?"

"We go on."

"But if we do that, we're going backward."

It was too confusing. They could be going backward, or not. There might be any number of shifts ahead, and the combination could lead them forward, backward, far off, or near. They could brush within a hair's breadth of The Realm or skirt the very limits of the Sprawl. They could go forward, riding for two days before finding themselves staring up into the Otel window back in Solace, or Sojourn.

Or they could go backward and find the same.

It was even possible that a two-day journey to Solace lay both in front *and* behind, or that there were currently no trails to Solace left in the Sands.

Being blind turned them turkey stupid.

Clint said, "All we can do is go on."

So they did, following the setting sun for a week, in a straight line, until Edward, whose head was higher, saw a landmark to orient him. Clint saw it soon after — a ridge near a rock that looked like a giant finger.

"Go on," said Clint, refusing to allow either of them to state the obvious. But before the end of the day, still following the path of the setting sun, they saw clear to a large flat rock, sitting crooked atop a shallow gully, far in the distance. There seemed to be a turkey coop and a small barn beside it.

Clint sighed, and Edward matched the sigh with his own equine version.

They might as well stop for the evening, then leave again after they'd gotten a hot meal in their bellies, a soft bed under their backs, and a palaver to occupy their tangled minds. Riding on blindly wouldn't change the fact that after more than a week, they'd ended right where they'd started.

Clint, who was still somewhat weak in both body and atrophied determination, felt defeated despite himself.

He and Edward had been riding now for close to three years, including vast stretches of time during which they'd pursued nothing but rumor — whispers of a dark rider on a unicorn of a different color — seeking the path of misery and chaos that Kold left like a reek behind him. But even during the bleakest of those times, they'd known that Kold rode with purpose, and that he rode more or less in a straight line. They knew that if they kept to that line, they'd at least be riding in roughly the right direction. But now, this far out, the world beneath their feet had become a lie. It was like they were playing that game where you were blindfolded and spun three times before trying to hit a dried pumpkin with a stick in order to spill the candy from inside of it.

Now, their pursuit was no longer a matter of persistence and grit. They'd gone in a circle by going straight, and that had stripped Clint's hope to the bone. There were too many directions in the world, and all of them were probably wrong.

Instinct suddenly slapped the gunslinger on the back of his head. His thinking ground to a halt.

As they drew closer, they realized that the hovel's roof was askew, nearly caving in. The turkey pen was busted open like a dried pumpkin, and there weren't any turkeys inside. The barn looked like it had been licked by a fire; its structure had mostly collapsed, with the remainder black and painted in ash. The drapery across the hovel's front was partially ripped, and there was a piece of smashed furniture visible through the fresh hole.

"What is this?" said Edward.

Clint had already hopped off and was walking slowly toward the hovel, his stone face set. Something boiled inside him — fear or anger, he wasn't sure.

The pen wasn't completely empty. One turkey, dead and skewered by an arrow, remained inside. The arrow through the turkey matched the one that had struck Clint in the shoulder five weeks earlier. Edward saw the arrow and immediately cast an umbrella of protection over them both. If the dooners were around and struck Clint with another poisoned arrow, he would surely die.

As Edward extended his protection, Clint, heedless, walked straight out from under the umbrella, toward the barn, and was once again left vulnerable. Edward trotted closer and re-placed the umbrella over him.

The barn was still smoldering, sufficient that Clint wondered why he and Edward hadn't noticed smoke on the horizon earlier. He reached for the door handle and found the iron still warm to the touch. His fingers fell from the heat, and the entire door, still in its frame, collapsed inward and displayed the remains of the barn's broken and burned interior. Sunlight poured into the structure from every direction — through what remained of the walls and missing roof — and garishly splashed onto the hard-packed dirt floor. All of Gregori's machines and tools were gone or destroyed. His turkey feed had vanished.

Clint circled the barn. All of the pumpkins had been smashed, rather than taken.

Clint's face was still a stone of emotion. He knew not what he felt, if anything.

"Let's go," said Edward, still trying to keep up with Clint in order to keep him under the umbrella.

"No."

"There's nothing here. Maybe they were run off."

Clint stared at the unicorn. Neither of them thought that the family had been "run off." It was an insult to pretend that they did.

"Can't you sense anything?" said Clint.

"A shaman was here," said Edward.

"That's not an answer!" Clint screamed, tendons in his neck standing up like sentinels.

The gunslinger composed himself, grew stoic again as if his outburst were a lie, and resumed strolling the property without waiting for the unicorn's response.

"Can you or can you not see what happened, using magic?"

"Not yet. But it's coming." Edward's face wrinkled with effort, and his horn shifted from yellow to red to blue, then back to yellow as it repeated the sequence.

Clint strolled toward the hovel's entrance. On the way, he kicked aside a splintered piece of wood that had a second splintered piece of wood clinging to it on a bent nail. He recognized it as a piece of Cari's jewelry box. She'd told him that her grammy had given it to her, and that her grammy's grammy had owned it before that. Clint looked around where he stood. He couldn't see the rest of the box, or any of the jewelry once inside it. The baubles were worthless outside of sentimentality — common desert rocks, polished pretty. The sorts of things a poor teenage girl with nothing else would know no better than to like.

Clint raked aside the curtain at the hovel's front. The rod holding it bent in half and fell away, revealing something like a cave that gaped like an open mouth.

"Sweet Providence," Edward whispered.

The unicorn never vented surprise, nor really any emotion other than the closest thing he had, which was sarcasm and insulting wit. He also never whispered. But what he saw in the hovel shocked him as much as it had the gunslinger.

Clint stepped over debris, looking down at the vaguely human shapes at his feet. His stone face said nothing.

"Cari isn't here," he finally said.

"Clint," said Edward. "Let's go."

The gunslinger spun. He'd drawn both guns and was pointing them at Edward. Both barrels shook. "I said, Cari isn't here! Where is she, you dagged horse? Why would we leave? Why would we go anywhere without answering that question first?"

"Holster your weapons and get a hold of yourself," said Edward.

A bookcase had half-spilled to the floor. Clint kicked its wooden remainder to shards, then fired a bullet from each gun into its splintered belly, shoulders slowly rising and falling as he holstered his weapons.

"She's been taken."

"You don't know that," Edward said carefully. The unicorn was usually in charge of their palaver, but Clint had drawn the upper hand and was threatening to rip it off if Edward said anything else he didn't like.

"Of course I do. She's not here. She's young. This is what roving gangs have always done."

"Not to set you off again," said Edward, "but we should leave. There's nothing we can do here."

Clint ignored him. He kicked aside a small mountain of splintered wood. A can of apple brew. And then, when he reached the back wall of the hovel, he saw it.

Part of a small, ornate arch made of desertwood, painted in rainbows and covered in costume jewels. A rectangular chunk of stone, split in half. A cracked ball of cut glass.

The family's shrine to NextWorld had been destroyed. There was a large dent in the shape of the business end of a war hammer gaping from the wall behind where the shrine used to be. What remained of the shrine was mostly buried. Clint had to dig in the rubble to extract all its pieces.

"They destroyed this first," Clint said quietly, turning half of the shrine's glass doorknob over and over in his hands, as if worried he might break it further.

"Clint..."

"THEY DESTROYED THIS FIRST!" Clint yelled. Heat rushed

to his cheeks, making them hot. He could feel the poison still in his system like a stew, weakening his body as his blood rolled to a boil. "THEY SMASHED IT IN FRONT OF THEM! THEY MADE THEM WATCH!"

"You don't know…" Edward began, backing out from the hovel.

"This was a message. A message to us. It was payback for what you did when they attacked us out on that ridge. Cari said a tribe was adjacent. She thought you'd scared them off, but you didn't scare them off at all. They've been watching us, all this time. Waiting. When we left, they came back. She told me their shaman can sense the shifting, and predict how the world'll turn next. It's how they navigate the Edge without getting lost. They knew the way the sand was spinning, and knew we'd circle back. This is for *us*. All for us!"

Clint felt like his heart was trying to pound through his ribcage. Adrenaline coursed in an unstable current through his system. He wanted to punch through a wall, through the very roof of the hovel. The only thing reining his rage and keeping him from laying waste to his fists was the knowledge that those hands could inflict far more damage with pistols if he could keep them unharmed.

Edward was watching the gunslinger. He didn't seem to know what to think. His ears twitched and his eyes blinked. Clint thought that he'd never seen him look so much like a horse.

Clint clutched the remaining half of the shrine's doorknob in his fist, careful to neither break it further nor cut his deadly hands. He walked out of the hovel and past Edward without looking back. He stopped only once he was past the property, where he looked out into the desolate loneliness of the empty Sands.

"Bury it," he said. "Bury it in the sand before I turn around. Burn what remains. They're gone. Make it all gone, Edward. Make it a memory."

Clint closed his eyes, gripping the glass tightly in his twitching hand.

There was a flash of shamrock-colored light that Clint could see through his closed eyelids, even with his back turned. The color reminded him of The Realm, and further fueled his fury. He slowly opened his eyes, rubbing moisture from the bottom lids and coating them with hard, caustic grit.

He left the sand in his eye, painful though it was.

The gunslinger turned. The hovel was gone, and in its place a shallow dune like any other. There was no scent of magical smoke from magical fire. All that remained was a single stone marking nothing at all. It was shaped like a rectangle, and whole. Something under the rectangle had lifted one of its long edges, like a door ajar.

Shadow lay beneath, looking like an entrance to some other place.

"Now what?" Edward said. He'd just taken several commands from his rider and was asking for another. Edward had never, never, *never* taken commands from any man.

"Today we ride," said Clint. "Tomorrow, we kill."

He laced a hand through Edward's mane and swung onto the unicorn's back.

His heart rate had returned to normal.

The gunslinger felt poisoned no more.

CHAPTER EIGHT: THE SEARCHERS

The gunslinger and the unicorn rode through the Sands, with nothing in front and nothing behind.

The man's face was hard and unforgiving. His hands were large, and the right hovered perpetually — almost superstitiously — above a seven-shot firearm at his hip. He had a red bandana tied loosely around his neck, like a bandit.

The bandana once belonged to someone else, and still carried the flowery scent of her hair. Occasionally, the man would smell it, then sniff the air, like a blooddog on a trail. A piece of cowhide string was visible beneath the bandana, slapping the chapped skin at the man's open collar. From the leather, under his shirt, against his heart, hung a broken half-sphere of glass, its edges rounded by magic.

It had been two weeks since the events Clint would no longer speak of. They'd been traveling in a straight line, and the land between them stayed true and unchanging. Edward said he thought a magic influence was holding the fault lines in place for a purpose. Clint asked if he thought the magic could be a shaman's. Edward said that yar, it could be. It could be a dozen things. A shaman. A herd of unicorns. Ghoulem. A sand dragon. The Realm itself.

"It's them," said Clint. "They're holding it steady so they can cross. It means we're close."

After two weeks, Edward had regained his caustic attitude to balance Clint's subsiding fury. "Why are you suddenly an authority on magic?" he said.

"Fine," said Clint. "Then you tell me. What I just said... does it make sense?"

"Maybe." Edward shrugged — a human affect he'd learned from Clint. The unicorn's rising shoulder blades nearly unseated his rider. "But I have to ask again: What are we doing? Have you forgotten why you're out here? You've steered us from towns, and sent us into open plains following the faintest of tracks. You've not spoken to a soul other than me since... well, *since*. We've ridden away from fracture rather than towards, when we know full well that the world fractures more the closer one gets to The Realm."

"To the Devil with the Realm," Clint growled.

"Kold is heading toward The Realm. With your bride-to-be, who lives each day in mortal agony."

"Yet, she does indeed *live*," said Clint.

"Exactly. The others are gone. What have you to gain by pursuing this tribe?"

Clint removed his hat, shook it out, and set it back on his head. "The dooners have Cari," he said.

"And Kold has Mai! What is Cari to you?"

"An innocent. A girl robbed of all she's ever had, and everything she's ever believed in. A girl who did no wrong, yet now believes she's doomed to remain forever stuck in the Sands and never enter her NextWorld. She believes her kin were denied entry to their nirvana as well. Shall I go on?"

Edward huffed. They'd had this discussion repeatedly since leaving what remained of the hovel. Edward thought it made more sense to pursue Kold, but Clint's will was as unyielding as his barrels. The unicorn no longer had the strength to fight the gunslinger. Arguing with Clint was like trying to bend iron with unmagic hands.

The dooners had left a clear trail, but they didn't know it. They didn't have a unicorn among them, and apparently didn't understand them. That proved their savagery, said Edward. There had to be unpaired unicorns around even if Edward couldn't always sense them, and unpaired unicorns paired with people of merit. The fact that Clint and Edward hadn't seen or heard of any unicorns with dooner parties (Edward had asked) suggested that they hadn't found any souls of merit among them.

The dooners didn't know true white magic, which meant they didn't know about the trail that Cari was leaving in the sand. But Edward could see it — a pure, radiant blue to his eyes; magic crumbs of unbearable sorrow. Edward saw the trail immediately... after they'd set out, leaving behind the rest of what they'd found at the burned-out hovel. The trail started behind the destruction and ran out in the opposite direction. Edward hadn't said anything at first because he'd thought that if he did, Clint would want to follow. But the gunslinger was unshakable even before he'd known the trail was there.

When Edward, seeing that Clint was going to pursue with or without magic help, finally told him about the blue in the sand and admitted he'd seen it from the start, Clint came at him with his fists. Edward easily held him at bay, picking him up with magic and carrying him while he hovered six feet in the sky, yelling and thrashing. That had gone on for two days, but eventually Clint tired himself out, Edward had released him, and they'd settled into their usual routine of amiable loathing.

Clint said, "Are we at least getting closer?"

"I don't know. I can't tell," said Edward. They'd been moving quickly, but never saw the dooners on the horizon. Based on the hovel's condition, Clint figured the dooners had a one-day head start at most. But despite riding with fury, they hadn't seemed to close the distance.

"How can they move faster than us? We're only two, and you're magic."

"I don't know. But based on the few actual tracks we've seen, there can't be more than five in their party, and they know the area."

"Can't you fold to catch up?" Clint knew Edward could fold space over reasonable distances and close miles quickly. It took much from the unicorn, but he could do it, and they had plenty of food and brew to refuel him after.

"I keep telling you, no. Not in an area this unstable. Do you want me to fold us into the middle of a rock cliff? Or into a limitless void? If that happened, we'd float forever and there'd be nothing for me to do but talk to you for eternity." He shivered theatrically. "Oh, the horror."

Despite already moving at a rapid pace, Clint nonetheless insisted they move faster. They agreed that if all signs pointed to a small party of dooners holding Cari, that party was most likely heading toward a meetup with the rest of their pack. No matter what Edward had done to the dooners at the ridge, there was no way the entire pack was decimated to five.

Sand followed sand. Mesas followed mesas. Where they went looked exactly like where they had been, but Edward was nonetheless strangely upbeat. The blue line in the sand stayed fresh. They had passed the fault line area… either that, or the odd, anonymous dooner magic was still keeping the world intact as they crossed. They'd seen no signs that they were riding in circles since leaving the destroyed hovel, which tremendously bolstered their mood. It was satisfying, for the time, to simply set miles behind them.

Finally, Edward paused. His horn sparked. Then he started moving again, faster.

The gunslinger squinted. "What is it?"

"I'd prefer to be dramatic," Edward said, then closed his giant lips and said nothing more for an hour, until they crested a hill and the unicorn nodded to the valley below.

"There," he said.

And sure enough, at the very limit of the horizon, they could see a tiny row of moving shapes.

"You sensed them," said Clint.

"Yar. As with Mai, I can feel Cari's torment. It'll take us hours to reach them, but we will reach them. The question is, how far are they from their destination?"

"You mean: How far are they from rejoining the rest of their pack?"

"Yar."

"And: How large is their pack?"

Clint didn't wait for a reply. He pushed his heels into Edward's side and leaned forward as if anticipating the unicorn's launch. It was as if he hadn't been riding him for decades and thought Edward was a horse he could spur into action. But Edward was excited himself, so he let the question hang in the air and complied with Clint's quiet order, taking the hill at a gallop. When they reached the bottom, they slowed to a canter, then to a trot, and then to walking, still with hours to go.

By the time the sun moved lower in the sky (Clint found he was enjoying the increased reliability of days; the sun seemed to stay overhead, and temperatures were more or less predictable), Clint decided that they were close enough for the party of dooners to soon be able to see them approaching. So Edward cast a camouflage umbrella over them, allowing the pair to further narrow the gap. And after another hour, with dusk approaching, they were close enough that their footfalls might give them away. They could eliminate the sound by moving slower, but that would widen the gap.

"We'll attack at the next rise," said Clint, suddenly decisive. "No more hiding."

They got as close as they dared, then picked up the pace the minute the dooners (who they could now see had a captive figure tied to one of the horses, draped in a canvas hood) disappeared over the hill's top. Edward thundered to the top, knowing the hill itself would muffle the noise.

They set themselves to crest the hill and rain death on the dooners from above, but when they reached the top of the hill, they stopped under their umbrella and stared at what stretched before them.

The party holding Cari was riding into a gigantic settlement of dooner huts.

The gunslinger and his unicorn were too late.

CHAPTER NINE:
KILLING

They sat at the top of the hill beneath their iridescent, yellow-pinkish umbrella — which was sparkling and strangely beautiful in the sun — for over an hour. Edward complained the entire time about the concentration required to sustain their invisibility and urged Clint to back off and let the hill be his sightline protection. But Clint wouldn't budge.

The gunslinger watched the pack of dooners, taking in their swishing robes and weapons, counting numbers and drawing diagrams of their settlement in the sand. Finally he stood, sighed, and walked down the opposite side of the hill, where he sat to rest on a rock. Edward let the umbrella fall, magicked a slice of turkey pie and an apple brew from one of the bags, and began to eat it.

"There was a day," said Edward, "when I ate other things besides pie and brew. In the wild, we ate Magellan root. And in The Realm, we both ate breaded meat sticks with caviar."

"There are at least a hundred down there," said Clint, ignoring the unicorn. "But I see nar their shaman. There was a chief on the ridge that first day. According to Cari's family, the shaman chief sources their scant magic, and oversees the brew of their dark elixirs. They'll ride without his protection, but they don't like to. Makes them superstitious and edgy."

"So you're saying we should have overtaken them earlier by donning sheets and pretending to be desert ghoulem?"

"The shaman could be in one of the huts, but Cari also said a shaman's duty is to patrol the settlement and keep an eye on its borders to keep the pack blessed, especially when there's flux in and out of those borders. Yet a scavenge party rejoined just them, and I never saw the shaman."

"If you're not going to listen to my thoughts or laugh at my jokes," Edward said, "I'm going to stop."

"Please do."

Edward sat, then sloughed onto his side and rolled himself with sand, whinnying his contentment until he was wearing a fine sweater of grit. He stood and shook every grain of sand from his coat until he was back to a radiant white.

"Fine," he said. "I am silenced. Now what?"

"Am I right about the shaman?"

"Yar. I noticed it right away. I didn't mention it because you're stupid, and not yet entirely healed. I assumed if I told you their shaman was gone, you'd want to charge in and fight."

"Indeed I do," the gunslinger said. "I am that stupid."

"You'll die."

"It's a decent day to die," said Clint.

Edward magicked one of the remaining cans of apple brew from the sack and sent it flying into Clint's groin.

"Say more macho things like that and I'll keep throwing cans."

"Come on, you grunt," Clint growled. *"You wanna live forever?"*

Clint caught the next can before it struck him, opened it, and drank the full brew in one long swallow.

"One day I'll find The Realm," said Edward. "And it would be a shame to find it without you on my back just because you got a wild hair over a nice young girl you couldn't save."

"I can save her," said Clint.

"And if you can't?"

"Then I'll prevent the torture she'll fall to if we do nothing."

"What torture?" said Edward.

"Do I have to paint you a picture?"

Edward kicked the sand. Clint crumpled the can and tossed it into the air. Edward magicked the can apart into its base elements, which then drifted down to the sand.

Clint said, "We have to go in while the shaman is gone."

"Yar," the unicorn agreed. "If we must attack, I suppose that now is the time." He sighed. After weeks of pursuit, Clint wouldn't let go. He'd either die on the Sands, or ride away with what used to be Cari and die another day. There was no third option.

Clint checked the rounds in his guns, then pushed fourteen additional bullets into two seven-shot speed loaders. He clipped the loaders to his belt, the bullets' cones pointing out from his sides. Then he nodded, ready. The gunslinger hoped his skills were still sharp enough for something beyond shooting desert rocks.

They ascended the rise, side by side beneath a new pink-yellow magic shield. But when they reached the the top, Clint turned to Edward and said, "Drop the umbrella."

"That's stupid. At least wait until we're close."

"Drop it. Fogs my vision."

"They'll be able to see us."

"That's the idea."

Edward dropped the umbrella and Clint's vision cleared. He began walking, unhurried, down the hill.

As he got closer, he saw a tall dooner crossing from one hut to another with Cari, so he raised one of his guns and made him disappear. Thunder tore through the desert and rattled the gunslinger's hand. The dooners leapt in collective fright, most probably never having heard the report of a gunslinger's weapon before. For a moment, they all gaped.

Clint continued to march steadily down the hill. Two men emerged from huts and began running toward Cari, but their heads snapped to the side as they saw the other dooners looking toward the hill beside the camp. Their eyes fell on Clint as he swiveled around with both guns.

Two shots sent a pair of men falling into the sand. The sand seemed to swallow them, which was curious in itself. The dooners began to rally — standing, running, taking up stations. Some already carried bows. Others already carried spears, and others had rifles. Most carried nothing. These ran, one eye always on the two figures marching toward them, to fetch weapons.

"Weapon-bearers first," Edward said from behind Clint.

Clint clicked off shots in a steady, unhurried rhythm as he walked: *right-left-right-left-right*. He fired about two shots per second, regular as a metronome. He needn't have worried earlier about his unpracticed accuracy. Men fell before his guns as reliably as if the bullets were zooming along rails.

"The sand," said Clint, watching as the fallen dooners slipped beneath it.

"I see it. I don't know. Keep firing."

A spear flew toward them. It exploded in a shower of sparks two feet from Clint's chest. Arrows struck nothing and fell to dirt. Each time, Edward's horn flashed. It grew harder for Edward to track all of the projectiles as dooners began to draw rifles, but the dooners fired common shells, and Clint was too far off and too thin to easily strike from a distance. Edward, who was much larger and much brighter, made an easier target. He was struck repeatedly (Clint counted one shot in his side, one in his neck, and two in his hocks), but he simply winced and then healed himself, painting the sand behind him with a trail of multicolored unicorn blood.

Clint fired right-left and then, without slowing, simultaneously flipped his wrists downward at his sides, his guns held sideways. The cylinders fell open. Clint tipped the guns up, spilling empty shells into the dirt, then pulled the guns toward his belt, pushing the open cylinders against the rounds protruding from the speed loaders clipped to his belt. Bullets slid smoothly into their chambers. Clint twisted each, disengaging the shells from the loaders, then flipped his wrists to true, snapping the cylinders back into place.

More dooners fired pistols and rifles. Edward watched the men — and, when he could, some of the slugs they fired — and told Clint when and how to move. Their energies were tangled in the mount-rider bond, so Edward didn't have to speak out loud. It felt to Clint as if he simply wanted to move, and so he did. It wasn't perfect. He was winged twice, though Edward magicked both wounds before they finally reached the huts.

"Duck behind this first row," Edward said.

"No." Clint shook his head, continuing forward, guns still drawn and pointing. "Give me spots."

Edward sighed and seemed to concentrate. Two tiny red dots appeared on huts — one in front of Clint, and another to the left. Both were moving. Clint's fingers twitched as his eyes found the dots, then sent twin reports into the noisy sky. Two gunslinger's shells spun through wood and mortar, smashing through the huts as if they were nothing until they found their targets.

The second Clint fired, two more dots appeared in different places, on different huts.

More gunshots.

More red dots.

"You're only giving me warriors with weapons, correct?" said Clint.

"There are no women and children in this camp, if that's what you're asking," said Edward. "It's as if they reproduce from the sand itself."

Seven sets of dots came and went. Clint reloaded, still walking.

The gunslinger stopped, his back to a stone wall. He looked at Edward. "What's happening with the sand? It's firm enough to walk on, yet swallows the fallen"

"I've been thinking about that while keeping you alive," said Edward. Even during the heat of a battle, Edward's tone conveyed his burdened annoyance.

"And?"

"And I think you should double-time. Cari is ahead, just past this row of shacks. I can feel her sorrow. Grab her, and we'll go. I'll explain later."

Clint swung around the wall as three dooners appeared in the open. There were gunshots. The trio fell to the sand and were swallowed.

A moment later, Clint and Edward found themselves in the middle of an open area in the middle of the camp where the sand was especially active. The desert's floor was vibrating, beginning to churn like a gigantic whirlpool.

"If you're going to get her, you'd better run," Edward said, nodding toward the churning sand. "But go around, not through the middle."

But before Clint could move, the sand started to violently shake up and down, rotating and then rising in a small mound. The mound grew into a tower, then took on the shape of a massive head atop a long and twisted neck. A larger mound swelled below this and became a body, which then grew legs. Loose sand fell from crevices in the sand head and the sand neck, cascading the whole thing into sharper definition.

Scales. Eyes. A row of spikes along the top. Many, many teeth, and a tongue like a serpent.

And atop the back of the sand-thing was the dooner pack's shaman chief, his spear held high and his eyes bleeding murder.

"Get on my back," Edward commanded. "*NOW.*"

When Clint didn't immediately comply, Edward magicked the gunslinger onto his back. Then he lowered his head, pushing his horn into the air as if against something solid. His horn began to glow red and spark lightly. The world faded to sepia, then quickly to nothing. A moment later, Edward stepped into a quiet area away from the battlefield, surrounded by dunes and rocks and without a dooner in sight.

Clint hopped to the sand, throwing daggers into Edward's eyes.

Edward rasped, barely able to push words from his throat. "This changes everything," he said.

CHAPTER TEN:
DARKNESS AND STY

Clint was in a rage, stomping back and forth in the sand, ranting until Edward trotted a few steps forward and rammed him to the ground. Clint looked up at the unicorn, shocked.

"You don't get to throw a temper tantrum," Edward said. "Not now."

Clint stood, brushing himself off.

"That was a sand dragon. You've no idea how fortunate we are to have left when we did, or that the dragon allowed us to do so. I can only guess it didn't stop us because it was empty of energy after taking shape."

"You can't fight it?"

"I can't even fathom it. I've heard of sand dragons, of course, but only as legends. The notion that the tribe's shaman has bent one to his will is terrifying. It's an unspeakable amount of black magic they must control."

Clint sat on a rock at the depression's edge, unholstered his right pistol, and started to reload it bullet by bullet. "I don't understand," he said.

Edward began pacing. "I only know rumors and fifth-hand reports, but we believe sand dragons come from the core, where white and black are at constant war. There's always been leakage, of course. Even before the first fracture, both kinds of magic rose to the surface and seeped through. But after the fractures, both magics fell away, leaking in gushes. Sand dragons are among the forms these gushes take."

"I still don't understand. Is this about the balance?"

"In a way." Edward turned his head to look at Clint, sidelong. "Take unicorns. We're reasonably pure, but when we partner with humans, we're saddled — no pun intended — with your darker natures. That's fine in most cases, except when a unicorn gives up, which is what happens with unicorns of a different color. It was Kold's darkness — the hatred that grew in him during your exile and wandering — that polluted Cerberus. Cerberus surrendered his magic to Kold, and something had to fill the void. The violation *made* him turn. Unicorns must be turned dark. Not so with sand dragons."

"They're born as darkness?"

"Worse: they *are* darkness. But darkness has no substance in itself, so it needs to take a shape. A sand dragon is the most common form, and one of the largest."

"They *are* darkness?"

Edward walked over and drew a curved line in the dirt with his hoof. From where Clint sat, the line was like a letter C tipped onto its back, like an empty bucket. Edward drew a line in the bucket, indicating a layer of something on the bottom, then added a line of waves at the top, as if the bucket were filled with water on top of whatever was at the bottom.

"The world is like this bucket of water," he said. "The water itself is all of the layers of ground beneath your feet, between you and the core." Then Edward tapped the line at the bucket's bottom. "This, down here, is the dark magic from the core. When it tries to rise to the surface, it has no substance, like a gas. And so when darkness bubbles to the top and into our world, the bubble pops because there is nothing there to hold a shape. Make sense?"

Clint nodded, slower than he would've liked.

"But now, imagine that the bucket is filled with dirty oil instead of water. This time when the darkness bubbles up, it forms a bubble covered in black oil rather than a fragile bubble made of water. The oil gives it substance, see? It's that way with shifting sand. The darkness rises through fissures, but in order to have substance and be able to act, it needs to take on a skin of sand like our imagined oil-covered bubble. Outside, it looks like sand. But inside, it's nothing but darkness."

"Can you pop it?" said Clint.

"It's not an exact analogy," Edward muttered, resuming his pacing.

Clint reloaded one gun and then the other. Then he pulled the reloaders from his sides and tucked them into a pouch on his belt.

"I should have seen it," Edward said. "The way the sand was sinking? Sand dragons need surface magic to fuel them, and to hold their shape. Luckily for them, there's no real downside. There's plenty of magic in the sand if you're able to sift it, which they are. But sifting robs the sand of cohesion and it dissolves into something finer — more like dust. When that happens, you get dust bowls, which are almost like quicksand. We got lucky and didn't step into any of them, but the ground must have been covered with the things. When everything started to sink, I should've seen it coming. We could have dashed to where Cari was, grabbed her, and gone. I'd still have had to risk a folding to get away, but we'd at least have accomplished our mission."

Edward shook his head, looking distraught.

"I need time," he said.

"For what?"

"To rest. To recover. But mostly to think."

"To think about what?"

"Its weaknesses. If it has any."

Clint couldn't believe what he was hearing. "*You* — Edward the stalwart, the curmudgeon, the selfish — want to go back?"

"Not in the least. But I have no choice. I'm a steward of white magic, and the few unicorns I sense within reach are cowards. This dragon has been here for a while, and from what I hear on the aether, the others have slowly learned to fear it. They've convinced themselves that in a time of leaking, nothing can be done to prevent such things and that their best plan is to stay away. Maybe I'd feel the same if we wandered into this slowly, but I saw the thing rise in front of my eyes. Now I must deal with it, or live the rest of my life knowing I didn't so much as try."

"But you said you can't fight it," said Clint.

"I can't."

"Then what will you do?"

"For now," said Edward, "I'll sleep."

The next morning they awoke in the belly of Edward's protective bubble, which was faded red and perfectly spherical, extending into the sand beneath them. It wouldn't offer any protection against the dragon, but would block the unicorn's magic from outside parties, which meant that it would at least prevent the dragon from seeing him. It was only a precaution, since the thing couldn't possibly know where they'd gone. When Edward had folded back at the dooner settlement, he could have taken them anywhere in such unstable sand — something Edward said he'd known all too well when he'd done it.

The risk was acceptable because certain death was the only other option.

Edward rolled up to his feet, walked to the bubble's edge, and nudged its surface with the point of his horn. His horn sparked on contact, popping the bubble and covering Clint in pink goo.

"I thought it was a magic bubble," said Clint, wiping blush colored goo from his face.

"It was."

"Looks like an actual bubble to me," he said.

"Magic sometimes comes in foam," said Edward. "You should see the unicorn night clubs in The Realm. The unicorns wade waist-deep in the stuff."

Clint made faces, flicking foam from his face to the sand, wondering if he was desecrating magic by doing so.

Edward didn't seem to be done thinking when they rode out, presumably back toward the dooner camp. Clint said nothing and let him think, sitting atop his back and feeling out of his league. This was a unicorn matter, and he, as a man, was trapped in the middle. So were the dooners. He could only hope there was a way to keep the shaman in the middle, and squash him where he sat.

"Edward," Clint said two hours later as they crested a familiar hill. Two hills further, they should come to the top and see the dooner settlement below.

"Yar."

"You think we humans are beneath you, don't you?"

"Not fit to polish our hooves," said Edward.

"And *you're* beneath sand dragons."

"Not at all. But also yes. They have more blunt power, but we're equal representatives from our side of the balance."

Clint didn't understand, but let it go.

"So we're below sand dragons, obviously. Humans, I mean."

"Oh yes."

"So why was the shaman riding one?"

"I've been mulling that," Edward said.

"And?"

"I don't know."

Edward's hooves hit the sand with their usual hypnotic rhythm. Clint felt as though he were being lulled to sleep most times when riding for long stretches, but today he felt especially tired. Maybe it was from a close brush with dark magic, but he didn't want to ask Edward, since the unicorn clearly needed time to think.

"I can think of two possibilities," Edward finally said. "Either the shaman has something the dragon needs, or the shaman summoned the magic himself and can therefore command it. I'm hoping for the former."

"Why?"

"Because if a human can summon that much dark magic, it's a very bad thing. Maybe the worst. Fortunately, I doubt that's the case."

"So what is?"

"I'm guessing there's a bargain between them."

"What does a sand dragon need that a shaman could give him?"

"Might as well ask me one of The Realm's questions without an answer."

Edward still hadn't come up with a plan when they reached the final hill. Clint assumed he was planning to either ride to his death and be done with it, or scope the camp and see if it jogged any ideas. The dooner population had to be down a quarter or more after their raid, and the dragon might have vanished, making a second attack feasible. But when they reached the hill to see what they could see, they found the camp missing. Were it not for his honed gunslinger's sense of observation, Clint would have been certain they'd arrived at the wrong spot. The sand was completely and totally barren. Everything had vanished.

"It's gone," he said.

"Really?" said Edward. "That's a sharp observation."

"Can you sense the dragon?"

"No. Now that we're aware of one another, we'll mute each other entirely, the way a science acid neutralizes a science base. It doesn't matter," The unicorn shook his head. "I can see the trail in the sand, though. From Cari's sorrow. It goes that way." Edward nodded toward the horizon.

"The dragon doesn't realize they're leaving a trail?" said Clint.

"Sand dragons don't understand sorrow," Edward said, descending the hill.

He didn't pause at the old camp, and warned Clint to stay away because of the quicksand-like sand bowls that were everywhere at the site. Edward would see any bowls in their path now that he knew what he was looking for, but only once they were nearly close enough to fall inside.

As the sun started its fall, they saw a shimmer in the sand ahead. An oasis. The idea of false water made Clint's throat itchy, so he pulled one of the waterskins from his pack and took a long swig to scratch it.

When they arrived, they saw that it wasn't an oasis after all. The shimmer was still there and hadn't vanished at their approach. Up close, it looked like a pool of dark gray mercury.

"Magic sty," Edward explained, touching the shimmer with his hoof, watching as a series of multicolored ripples spread through the pool. As the ripples passed, the shimmer behind each grew slightly whiter. Edward repeated his touch until the pool looked like highly polished silver beneath his hoof.

"Better," he said.

"What did you just do?" Clint asked.

"I cleaned it. This is what it's supposed to look like. Some locations have these depressions, which are gathering pools of magic. Unbelievably valuable to find, but of limited practical value to anyone wishing to exploit them. It's not as though you can bottle and carry magic. You use it here to replenish yourself, then move on. If you're shot in the brain and half dead, a touch of this pool will heal you as good as new. But you can't take it with you."

"Must they always be cleaned?" said Clint, already suspecting what was coming.

"No. This one was polluted." He met Clint's eye.

"By a sand dragon."

"Yar. The dragon drank from it. It will need constant infusions of magic to survive in its current form because everything leaks, including sand bodies. Deprive a sand dragon of magic for long enough, and it'll almost evaporate. Even if they don't leave or die, they lose their cohesion. Then they usually regroup, dive back to the core when they find a fissure, and resurface with a new skin. This one doesn't want to dive, probably because it's involved with the shaman. But it needed refreshment."

Edward touched the quicksilver surface of the sty again. A rainbow of colors again rippled through it, but this time the color was unchanged. It was as clean as it was going to get.

"You don't need it?"

"I generate it," said Edward.

"Do I need it?"

"You have me."

Edward's head swiveled. As Clint watched, the unicorn seemed to grow increasingly agitated.

"Climb down," he said.

Clint did.

Edward circled the pool, nudging rocks and sand around its edge with his nose, smelling the air as his horn started glowing. Finally Clint walked to where he stood and asked him what he was doing.

"Feeling," said Edward.

Clint grunted. "Less obtuse, please."

"I feel something. Like a pain in my heart."

Clint was about to ask what that meant when his own head

snapped up to meet Edward's left eye.

"Kold," he said. "And Mai."

Edward nodded.

"Where are they?"

Edward tossed his head toward a winding path leading between two dunes. "That way."

Clint automatically took two steps toward the dunes before his hand rose to the half-sphere of polished glass hanging from his neck on a strip of leather. Even though they hadn't seen any sign of Kold's trail for months and he wanted very badly to follow, he had a score to settle with the dooners.

The gunslinger had four people to avenge, and an innocent girl to rescue.

The unicorn had a sand dragon to kill.

Clint's shoulders fell. He sighed, then returned to Edward. "Where's the blue line that will lead us to Cari and the dooners?" he asked.

Again, Edward gestured toward the winding path between the dunes.

CHAPTER ELEVEN: EPIC DRAGON FIGHT

Clint wasn't sure how to feel.

The dooners and their sand dragon were heading toward the same smear of sunset as Kold's party, after visiting the same magic sty. That was good news since it meant Clint didn't have to decide to follow one and leave the other. But on the other hand, it was bad. Were they actually together? Edward couldn't tell. If they were, it would be chewed tobaccy bad on several levels.

If they were together, were they together for a reason? And if so, what could that evil plot possibly be? Clint shivered. The dark magic of a unicorn of a different color, a turned Realm marshal, and a sand dragon all in the same place? They'd be impossible to defeat.

Edward seemed to be thinking the same thing, though he said nothing. Gunslinger and unicorn rode mostly in silence, now approaching three full years of wandering the Sands, and both bone tired — the sort of tired that rubs at the corners of a man's soul enough to turn him around.

"How's your chest?" said Clint, asking Edward what lay ahead in the only way he knew how.

"Not too bad," said Edward. "And yet, I think we're closing in on the dooners."

"You can tell by the blue in the sand?"

"Nar," said Edward, kicking at the ground. "Their tracks, idiot."

Clint looked down, feeling a kind of marrow-deep fatigue. He wasn't spry anymore, and he was feeling his age. He hadn't noticed the plain, obvious path of tracks cutting through the sand, but he looked down now. Every once in a while, in the middle of the tracks, there'd be a depression or a swell, indicating that the dragon was rising or diving, surely with the shaman on his back.

"I've been thinking," said Edward.

"That's not a good idea. Was it about rainbows and leprechauns in pink foam bubbles?"

"About the sand dragon," Edward said. "About what it could want."

Clint chewed his inner cheek, then spat on the ground.

"I partnered with you because you have fast hands and a righteous soul," Edward continued. "Many unicorns never pair with a human. I had to believe in your ability and determination to do things that needed doing before I could surrender my solo life. I wanted a partner to spread my kind of magic; otherwise I'd never be here. The sand dragon is here too, and it's paired with the shaman in what feels like much the same way. So what does it want?"

"A partner in spreading its own kind of magic, maybe."

"Maybe. And that troubles me. The darkness has no substance in and of itself. It must form itself into something such as a sand dragon before it can actually do anything. Even then, that 'anything' is almost like playing around. Oh, sure, it can cause much mayhem and killing. But to what end? Its range is limited because it'll disintegrate near cities and away from magic sties. There's only one thing that darkness truly wants, if it wants anything at all."

"What's that?"

"More darkness."

The answer bothered Clint, as much as how Edward said it. "Okay. So how would it go about getting more?"

"By making the fractures larger; by encouraging shifting and leakage. The darkness can only leak from already-existing fissures. It cannot make changes in and of itself. Change and action require hands. Human hands, specifically."

This was the first Clint had heard about the fracturing being anything other than a natural phenomenon, or about it being something that could be accelerated or made worse through deliberate effort. But unicorns were guardians of a kind, and as such, they kept their secrets.

"I'm worried that the shaman might be unduly influenced," Edward said. "That the dragon might be using him to... to get something that only human hands could get."

"What?"

"It's not for humans to know," said Edward. "Even you, gunslinger."

Clint tried to pry more information from Edward, more because he was curious than because it mattered to what they were about to do — or *attempt* to do. But Edward's large equine lips were locked tight. He seemed to have crossed a line in his mind, and on the other side were matters that were for unicorns alone. And that was in character for unicorns, even if it wasn't totally in character for Edward. Humans weren't allowed into unicorn gatherings, and were never included in — or allowed to know about — unicorn rituals. Their culture was deeply secretive. There were no human records, anywhere, ever, of unicorns sharing what they knew.

A few hours later, they arrived at a narrow pass. Edward stopped and sighed deeply.

"Okay," he said, gesturing with his hoof. "This is good. See that clump of sand?"

"Yes."

"The blue line crosses it. Now watch." Edward lowered his head until it was a foot from the clump. He exhaled slowly through his nostrils. The clump crumbled.

"Now the line is obscured. Sorrow sits on top of the sand, like a line of paint. The fact that the line remained intact across a clump that fragile means that the dooner party rode through very recently, and that Cari was at its caboose. If she were near the front or if more than an hour or two had passed since, there's no way that clump wouldn't have fallen apart."

"So we're close."

"Yar. But that's not even the good part. The good part is that my chest doesn't hurt."

That *was* good news. Still, Clint felt conflicted. If Edward's chest was hurting less, it meant that Kold and Mai were pulling further ahead. If they got too far away, the trail would grow frozen again. The gunslinger wanted revenge against the dooners and to help Cari if he could, but he'd wanted to help Mai for years and had wanted to reach The Realm ever since his exile.

"So they're not together."

"No."

"And they visited the same magic sty, then went in the same direction due to coincidence?"

Edward didn't reply. Clint could read him, though, and knew the unicorn didn't think it was a coincidence at all. What's more, he seemed to suspect the reason for both trekking across the same swath of sand, and that reason bothered him like he'd seen a dung beetle in his brew.

"One problem at a time," Edward said.

They rode harder.

Within two hours, after the sun had eaten three-fourths of the sky, a large, moving lump in the sand grew visible in the distance.

"There it is," said Edward.

As they rode closer, the lump expanded. Edward cast his umbrella of invisibility. Though it wouldn't protect them from the sand dragon's eyes, Edward felt it was unlikely that the dragon would bother to look back. The umbrella would, however, keep them invisible to the dooners and protect them from their weapons.

"Their party is smaller," Clint said as they drew near.

"Yar. I'd suspect the dragon has been eating them."

They were walking side by side. Clint stopped just for a second, processing a feeling of shock.

"This is now a traveling cult," Edward explained, seeing the gunslinger's face. "They're brainwashed by the dark magic of the dragon. They still have their will, but it's been mostly relegated to the shaman's will, and the shaman is controlled by the dragon. Of course, the shaman probably thinks it's the other way around. It doesn't matter. Either way is the same."

"Why would it need to eat the dooners? I thought it could pull magic from the sand."

"It can. But it's also traveling. Dragons aren't supposed to do that. It's probably using all of its energy to maintain its shape, so it needs more fuel than the sand can provide. The shaman probably doesn't even know what he's dealing with. He probably thinks the dragon is a real thing, when in fact it's just a giant puppet made of sand. But that's good for us; it can't dive or reconstitute without revealing its true identity. It must remain a dragon to keep the shaman on its side. And that, I've decided, is how we must fight."

"What do you mean?"

"In a battle, you can fight to win, or you can fight not to lose."

"I don't understand," said Clint.

"You seldom do," Edward replied.

Clint waited for more, but the unicorn offered nothing, so he squinted at the party ahead. The party seemed to be stopping. Clint gestured at a massive rock at the side of the trail, and they moved behind it.

"I count an even two dozen," the gunslinger said.

"Yar," Edward agreed. "With so little fuel remaining, the dragon won't last much longer. But unfortunately, if I'm right, it will last long enough to do what it needs to do."

Clint turned, propped himself up on an elbow, and stared at the unicorn. "Why don't you just tell me what it's after?"

"It's not for your ears."

"You suck," said Clint.

"Yar," Edward replied.

"I can take two dozen men," Clint said, returning his attention to dooner party and the large, lumbering, half-buried shape of the sand dragon. "So I'll get the pack. You get the shaman and the dragon."

"Yar."

"How are you going to destroy it?"

"I'm not. Don't you listen?"

Clint stared at Edward deciding that the unicorn was being deliberately obtuse. This was a good sign. Edward was a jerk by nature, so him being pleasant was worth a worry. Once, Edward had purchased a cake as a gift for the gunslinger in a town they were passing through. Clint had had panic attacks for days after receiving Edward's gift, wondering what disaster must be waiting. That turned out to be the day, not far from Solace, when Kold's trail first went completely cold.

Clint shrugged, deciding he would be getting no more from Edward.

They moved from large rock to large rock along the path, both on foot, steadily closing the gap between themselves and the dooners. The party had paused in a shallow valley. When Clint and Edward finally got close enough, they climbed up onto one of the valley's edges and peered down.

Clint proceeded to load his guns and reloaders, clipping the reloaders in place on his belt.

"It just ate one," Edward whispered, still watching the party as Clint's eyes stayed on his bullets.

Clint didn't bother to ask what had eaten what. "I barely need to bother with this second set of reloaders," said Clint. "Let's just keep following them. Maybe that dragon will eat everyone."

They'd discussed that, but had ultimately decided that one of two things could easily happen if they waited too long, and neither was good. Possibility number one was that Kold might veer away from the more or less straight path the dooners had been following, and their possibilities of finding Mai after they were done here (assuming they survived, of course) could go cold again. Possibility number two was that the dragon could eat Cari. That seemed unlikely, as Edward assumed they'd taken her in the first place because the dragon would eventually require a girl to sacrifice for some impressive bit of magic, but it was true that Cari would be eaten before the shaman, and the party was running out of third options.

"Load all of your bullets," said Edward, who knew Clint's cockiness.

They crept down the slope, toward the backs of the dragon and the chief. They approached in front of some of the dooner warriors, but the men couldn't see them through Edward's umbrella.

Clint leaned toward Edward's ear and whispered, "Do you know what you're doing?"

"I know what I'm *going* to do. That's not quite the same, but yar, I suppose." And then, Edward explained to Clint what was going to happen.

"Okay," said Clint, unholstering his guns.

"You understand I won't be able to protect you?"

"Yar."

"If you get hit, you're dead."

"I understand."

"For that matter, since I'll be so gassed, if *I* get hit, *I'm* dead."

"Maybe after you're dead, you'll move on to a beautiful world filled with elves and fairies."

Edward ignored him.

"Ready?" said the unicorn, a moment later.

"Yar. No. Wait." Clint surveyed the dooners, five in a line and four behind, gnawing on some sort of food. Another dozen or so were scattered throughout the valley. He re-holstered his left iron and held only his right, steady before him. His left hand hovered above his holster, ready to do the magic trick of making bad guys disappear.

"Okay," said Clint.

Edward nodded. "Not until it pops."

Clint nodded back.

Edward turned to face the gunslinger, then slowly backed away. The umbrella of protection elongated into an ellipse, like a long capsule with Clint at one end and Edward at the other. Edward moved ten feet back. Fifteen. The umbrella shimmered, as if held taut and barely able to take the strain. Edward's horn began to glow and spark as if struck with flint.

Twenty feet.

Edward's face was pained. Clint felt nothing behind him, but when he looked over his shoulder, he could see the umbrella stretching and shaking like a rubber band, wrapped around something invisible at his back. The same thing was happening behind Edward's rump. He watched the unicorn's head as if he were looking down a long, narrow tunnel that was just large enough for the two of them. It was as if they were both safe inside an enormous sleeve of elastic fabric, but the fabric was about to rip.

Twenty-two feet. Twenty-five. Edward was a quarter-way around the gathering, staying close. He couldn't go much farther anyway.

Once he started rounding the circle to where the dragon lay scratching at the sand, their elongated umbrella would cross the dooner circle, allowing their enemies inside.

Edward began to yell.

"Hey, dragon!" he shouted.

The dooners in front of Clint turned, and saw nothing.

"Hey ugly!" Edward yelled. "I've got a joke for you!"

The great, lazy head of the resting sand dragon rose from the sand and, after a moment's search, settled with precision facing Edward as if the dragon could see through the bubble, which was exactly what Edward had said it would be able to do.

The sand dragon stared at the unicorn with curiosity, its long pinched face seeming to say that it would get around to squashing him eventually, but didn't consider the matter particularly pressing.

"Hey!" Edward shouted. "Why did the sand dragon cross the road?"

The dragon's mouth opened in a stretch. From the side, Clint could see red and purple fire begin to glow inside of it.

"Because it sucked!" Edward answered.

The dooners were all looking toward the unicorn's approximate location, where Edward was still straining to maintain the elasticized umbrella. They chatted in dooner speak, spitting furiously across the sand as they shrugged and shook their heads. None of them could see Edward, but they could hear him… which was of course the point.

With a great heave and shudder, the umbrella finally ruptured. For a split second, Clint fancied he could see pinkish yellow bits floating in the air like a popping balloon.

In the space of two seconds, Clint had fired all seven shots from his pistol, fanning the hammer with his left palm. As soon as his left had made its last pass, it reached into his holster and drew the other pistol, which he used to dispatch the other two dooners on his side. A few heads turned, but the remaining dooners didn't know where to look. A unicorn had just appeared from nowhere at one end of the valley, and shots were ringing from the other side.

Clint moved like wind, ducking behind the large stone he'd picked out when Edward had explained his plan. The remaining dooners were grabbing weapons — arrows and spears that were surely tipped with helioroot, and rifles, which needn't be tipped with anything. Clint couldn't afford so much as a scratch from the bladed weapons, and he was unprotected. As promised, Edward's focus and energy was already set on the dragon.

The sand beast slowly rose to its feet, creating a vast sheet of falling sand that was like a massive tan waterfall. It roared as it rattled its head. The ground shook beneath its every step as it pounded toward Edward. The unicorn ran.

The dragon's neck compressed as its head pulled back. It pushed its face forward and a giant plume of purple and red liquid fire belched from its mouth. The dragonfire struck the sand a foot behind Edward as he retreated, then followed him for the duration of the dragon's exhale. Everything the fire touched melted into black, smooth glass. The dragon stepped forward, now coming after Edward. An enormous cracking shot through the air as the dragon's talons hit the black sand and shattered it. Clint watched as a sheet of nine-inch-thick glass sheared up from beneath its enormous clawed feet.

Edward was faster than the dragon, but the dragon was far more powerful. The unicorn dove behind a rock as arrows and bullets rained against it.

Clint leaned out from behind the rock. His gunslinger's eyes showed him a pair of hood-draped shapes near where he'd originally sighted them, both holding rifles. One of the dooners fired, but Clint saw from the barrel's position that the shot would miss. Clint fired his own gun twice, both shots coming from his left pistol because he'd only leaned partway out from behind the rock. Both found their mark. The dooner bullet, as he'd predicted, went wide.

With the two men cleared, Clint again emerged from behind the rock. Then, as if in slow-motion, he suddenly saw a silver metal cross seeming to float in the air ten feet from his face, with fat tufts of feathers blooming from behind. It was an arrow that he was seeing head-on, and it was a fraction of a second from striking his eye. Clint ducked back just in time, and the arrow speared the sand beside him.

The dragon made thunder, roaring as he blasted magic at Edward, the sound like a steam engine derailing. Even the dooners winced, shaking hard enough to bring conscious fire back into some of their eyes.

Still, they raised their rifles and nocked their arrows.

The next time Clint peeked out, only three dooners were visible, none with weapons raised. Clint used his guns to make them disappear, but hadn't bothered to duck. A shot ricocheted off the rock behind him, too close. Clint fell to the sand, searching for the shooter and finding nothing.

How many could be left? Clint did the math. He'd felled nine in the first volley, then two, then three. That made fourteen. He'd counted twenty-three when the fighting had started, so nine remained.

A party of three saw him lying in the dirt and stormed him. Clint couldn't get at his left iron since he was laying on that arm, so he took aim with his right. Too low. He hit one of his attackers in the leg and another in the arm, but all three kept coming at him, slowly, steadily. They watched his right pistol, ducking and dodging behind sparse trees and scattered rocks until that gun was empty. Then they advanced faster, but the gunslinger fired three times with his left, which he'd pushed through the loose sand and was holding out at his side, its barrel barely visible. He could smell the burning sand in the barrel and reminded himself that while the bullets wouldn't be stopped by sand, that sand could easily jam the cylinder, hammer, or trigger.

The three men fell, leaving six.

Clint stood, now in the open, and saw the sand dragon direct another volley of magic at Edward. Its entire mouth opened with each shot, nearly unhinging like a snake swallowing prey. A cylinder of fire billowed out, as big around as a car on a train. Just as the dragon began belching fire, Edward's horn sparked red and he vanished, appearing behind the dragon.

Edward taunted from behind. "Come on, you stupid lizard! I'm right here! Is that all you have?"

The shaman was still atop the dragon's head, riding it like a mount. He seemed furious, his mouth drawn tight in a snarl.

Edward ran directly at two dooners with rifles as they opened fire. Both bullets struck the unicorn with bright sparks, bouncing against a small, freshly raised shield — fortunate for Edward, since he wouldn't be able to summon a large shield or heal himself without giving the dragon a golden opening.

In his peripheral vision, Clint saw a dooner running toward him, his spear held high. Without turning, Clint fired his right gun, having holstered his sandy left for the duration. The man fell.

Edward yelled something else to the sand dragon that Clint couldn't hear, then charged at the duo of dooners who'd fired on him. The shaman yelled back, and the dragon, as if obeying orders, shot another column of purple-red fire at Edward. The unicorn fell to the sand as the dragon reared. The dragon tried to pull up at the last second, but was too late. The column struck the dooners instead of its target, melting the men into more black glass at their feet.

Edward's next fold opened near where Clint was standing, and they found themselves side by side. The gunslinger looked over. Edward seemed surprised, but then his horn glowed and Clint felt himself flying through the air before landing hard enough on the unicorn's back to knock the wind from his body. Without a pause, Edward galloped up, toward the lip of the valley.

"Are you retreating?" Clint yelled.

"Just getting better footing," Edward answered, unhurried. Clint looked down at the dragon still standing in the center of the shallow depression, its massive brown form nearly surrounded by smooth, cauterized black sand.

"He's turned that entire valley's sand to glass," said Edward.

"Yar," said Clint. "Great plan you had, by the way. How's it working out for you?"

"It's on track," said Edward. "How many dooners are left?"

"Three, not counting the chief."

"Not for long," said Edward, nodding. "Look."

Clint looked. The three remaining men had run toward the dragon's feet, yelling something frantically up at the shaman. The dragon reached down, grabbed all three men in its talons, and tossed them into its mouth.

The musical chewing was the soundtrack to a nightmare.

"You owe that dragon a thank-you note for doing your job," said Edward, gesturing toward the absent three that Clint would no longer need to dispatch.

It was now the gunslinger and the unicorn versus the sand dragon and shaman. The dragon was still swallowing. The chief was yelling, beating the dragon's brown sand back beneath him.

"Where is Cari?" said Edward.

"She's in the middle of where they were sitting. Heavily drugged, in a sack. Luckily she's been able to dream, giving us a trail to follow."

They waited. The dragon was still where it had been below them, occasionally looking up but not yet moving.

"What's it doing?"

Edward gave a small equine smile. "It's leaking."

Without warning, Edward charged forward, directly at the dragon. There were vast patches of glass in his way, so he leapt high in the air, skirting them with the precision of a dancer, and stopped halfway down the slope, a few feet from the dragon.

"You can't kill one lousy unicorn?" Edward shouted at the dragon.

The dragon made a noise that sounded roughly like, "Meh."

"Come on, you mighty beast!" His horn glowed and a yellow blast blew from its tip, striking the sand dragon's side. A large section of sand was blown away, revealing nothing but empty space. The dragon's side wasn't black, and it wasn't transparent. It was simply nothing, like a hole in reality.

Edward fired again, but this time the dragon parried, easily blocking it with a spell of its own. After it countered Edward, however, its giant dragon shoulders collapsed in a sigh. The hole in its side remained a void.

"Come on, is that all you have?" Edward taunted.

The dragon opened its mouth and fire came out of it, but this time, the fire only went a few feet.

Edward stepped back. The fire struck the sand below him, turning it obsidian black. Then, with one eye still on the sand dragon, Edward touched the black patch with his hoof. The glass was only a half-inch thick, and it snapped easily.

Edward fired another blast from his horn. It struck the dragon's head, knocking another section of sand from the creature, as if Edward had hit it with a pressure washer. The new hole was just below where the shaman was sitting. The shaman looked down, aghast, and shouted something at the dragon.

The dragon twitched its head upward, as if snapping at the chief. The shaman was jostled, but kept his grip.

Edward fired again. And again.

The dragon belched fire at Edward and Clint one more time, but it was a pathetic attempt to save face. The fire fell as if heavy, striking ground near the dragon's feet.

All at once, the sand that comprised the dragon's body became weightless and hovered in the air. Then it started to fall as if something had been yanked out from under it — as if the dragon were a bubble, and that bubble had popped.

The shaman found himself seventy feet in the air, sitting on loose sand. He fell through the lower sky, twisting, before he landed in a clump. The remaining sand rained down around him, creating an outline of the dragon in mini-dunes. A massive black cloud rose from the falling shape; shifting, churning, and pooling like liquid, stretching tentacles into the air like an ink-black squid.

Then, impotent, the cloud dissipated like a drop of food coloring in a glass of water, and was gone.

"We won," said Clint, his mouth hanging open.

"No," said Edward. "But we didn't lose."

CHAPTER TWELVE: BROKEN GUNS, BROKEN SHACKLES

The shaman chief slowly returned to consciousness, his eyes confused. Clint cocked a pistol to help him become less confused.

The dooner shaman chief looked up, his eyes turning into saucers, and then scooted back in the sand, away from Clint and Edward, until his rear wedged against the leg of a fallen dooner. He started babbling in a long string of noises that didn't sound like more than gas and gurgles escaping from his throat.

"Edward," said Clint. "Translate."

The unicorn approached the gunslinger and the shaman. His horn glowed briefly, and suddenly the shaman was speaking in Clint's tongue.

"… didn't know what I was doing! It came to me and I…"

Clint interrupted him.

"The girl you took. Is she alive?"

But Edward was already answering the question. Clint saw movement in the corner of his eye, then turned to watch as the girl was magically lifted out of the sack the dooners had been carrying her in.

"Yar," Edward said, "she's alive."

"Her family isn't," said Clint, his attention returning to the dooner below him. There was a loud blast from the gunslinger's pistol and a tiny fountain of sand erupted beside the shaman's ear.

"Blood for blood!" yelled the shaman, holding his hands up. "You killt ours! We claimed vendetta!"

"We killt yours only after you attacked us," said Clint. His pistol went off again, this time striking a small semicircle of sand in the hollow between the shaman's chin and his shoulder.

Clint looked at the gun. "Why does it keep doing that?" he said. Then he pointed the gun at the shaman's groin and added, "Hopefully it doesn't do it again."

The shaman tried to roll away, but once his body found motion he groaned sharply, grabbing his left arm.

"You hurt?" said Clint.

"Yar."

"Good."

Clint used his other hand to reach into a pouch on his holster. His hand returned with a toothpick. He nudged it between his teeth and started to chew, staring placidly down at the shaman, his gun aimed and unmoving.

After a few moments of silence, Edward spoke to the shaman.

"This creature you thought you commanded. What did it want of you?"

"It didn't want anything," said the chief. "I summoned it as a weapon."

"A weapon that slowly devoured your people?"

"A weapon that was all I needed, with or without packmates."

Edward made an impatient grunt. "Listen closely," he said. "You didn't summon it. It summoned *you*. It took the form of a dragon, but it wasn't a dragon. Do you understand?"

The shaman said nothing, his expression stuck somewhere between disbelief and anger.

"It lied to you. It took the form of something you thought you understood, but it wasn't that thing. It was darkness wrapped in sand, but it stayed topside too long in one shape, and it traveled too far. Once it was exhausted and out of magic, it abandoned its shape. It's still out there, though you'll never see it again."

"Why not?"

"Because you'll be dead," Clint answered.

"I want to know where you were going," said Edward. "Tell me that, and maybe we'll let you go."

"To make war with the East Edge dooners," said the shaman.

"And why are you following a dark rider on a unicorn of a different color?"

The shaman looked confused. "I... I don't..."

Edward turned to Clint. "He's worthless," he said.

Clint aimed his pistol higher.

"Wait!" said the shaman. "It wanted to steer us through Precipice.

It didn't talk, but I could hear it in my head. We don't like towns; we prefer staying in the Sands. My will tried to steer it around Precipice, which is a more direct route to the East Edge and into our rivals' pack, but the dragon resisted. Precipice! Maybe that's what you seek. But I know nothing of this rider of whom you speak."

"He's ahead of you," said Clint. "A half day at most."

Edward was circling the clearing, gathering supplies from the fallen dooners and adding them to the saddlebags he'd reluctantly started wearing to handle their load. Clint turned to the unicorn for confirmation of Kold's lead on the dooner tribe. Edward nodded.

"I know nothing of this rider," repeated the shaman.

"Do you know how to rouse the girl?" said Clint, nodding toward where Edward had uncovered Cari's sleeping form.

"She's being given a smelling potion that causes sleep," said the shaman. "As long as it stops being given, she'll wake on her own within a day."

"And when she awakes, what will you tell her about the murder of her family?"

"Sands Law!" shouted the shaman, obstinant. "Blood for blood! We were justified!"

"Your interpretation of the law concerning the murder of innocents is shaky, considering that the conflict was between your pack and mine, not theirs," said Clint. "I should know. I'm a marshal."

Clint drew several deep breaths, his gun centered on the shaman. Edward was still picking up supplies and had already magicked together a travois for Cari, to drag her until she awoke. Finally he walked over to Clint and said, "I have all of the food and water. There is nothing else of value here. We can go."

The shaman looked up at the gunslinger. His arm was at a funny angle, and now that Clint looked down, so was his leg. Maybe both legs. He'd fallen quite a distance from the dragon's back.

"What are you going to do with me?" the shaman asked.

"Arrest you, of course," Clint told him. "Can you walk?"

"No," said the shaman.

Clint reached deep into his bag and pulled out an ancient pair of shackles he'd had since years before Solace. They weren't rusted and seemed to work fine. He locked one of the manacles around the shaman's wrist, then the other around the dead dooner's ankle beside him.

"Oops," Clint said, looking at his own wrist as if expecting a second shackle. "I guess these are broken, too."

Clint stood and climbed onto Edward's back. Then the gunslinger, the unicorn, and girl on the travois rode up the next rise, following the pounding ache in Edward's chest.

CHAPTER THIRTEEN: PALAVER

The gunslinger, the unicorn, and the girl rode through the Sands, with nothing in front and nothing behind.

The next evening, when the sun started to set, they made camp. Cari already felt her strength returning, so she helped by breaking down the travois on which Edward had carried her until the dooner potion finally wore off. After waking, she'd ridden behind Clint, wrapping her hands around his slim, dusty waist. At first, her grip was weak and tentative, but after a few hours, it grew stronger and tighter.

When she felt a little better, she'd started to cry. Clint said nothing. Sometimes, tears needed husking, and until she asked for the gunslinger's comfort, he'd let her shed them in private, onto the shirt covering the backs of his shoulders.

Eventually she stopped and they rode on, none among their trio eager to break what felt like a period of quiet meditation. The day offered no distractions. There was sand and there was more sand — and there was the unicorn's pain, growing harder to bear with every passing mile.

Eventually, as the sun dipped below the horizon and the sky gathered an angry smear of red inside it, Edward told them that Kold had stopped. They walked slightly farther, until they could see the glow of the dark rider's fire, then backed up a quarter mile, out of sight, so that they could build their own.

"I have something for you," Clint said to the girl.

Cari looked up at him, the firelight running across her face like something liquid.

Clint reached behind his neck, untied the leather string beneath his shirt, and pulled out the polished half-knob that once adorned the door of Cari's NextWorld shrine. He held it out to her, and Cari's hand flew to her mouth as her eyes rimmed with tears. One spilled onto her cheek as she reached for the simple necklace with both hands.

"I watched them destroy it," she said. "Now my people will wander forever."

"Yar'm, they destroyed it" said Clint. "But there's something you don't know."

Cari looked up at the gunslinger.

"Do you remember how your grappy kept asking me about The Realm and what was behind the wall, because I'm a Realm marshal?"

"Yar."

"And do you remember what your father said to me over dinner that one night, about how there are wanderers in the Sands, here to shepherd the worthy to NextWorld?"

"Yar."

"Remember the parts of the legends about how those wanderers from the magical cities are guardians? How not only would they act as guides, but as protecters… and, if necessary, as avengers? And how the judgment of the wanderers trumped the need for a shrine, since they could guide departed spirits to NextWorld?"

"Yar," she said, nodding faster as a fresh tear fell onto her cheek.

"You will see your people there one day," he said.

He rose from the fire's perimeter, then laid beneath his blanket for sleep without waiting for Cari's reaction. A marshal, no matter what crossed his mind, was never supposed to show weakness.

When Clint awoke at 3am with a full bladder and walked with gummy eyes to the edge of their campsite to do his business, he ran into something large and white.

Edward said, "Right on time."

"Give me a minute," said Clint, rubbing at his eyes.

Clint returned to Edward a minute later, sat on a rock, and waited to see what the unicorn wanted.

"We need to talk," the unicorn said. "And what we need to discuss is not for her ears."

"We can trust her," said Clint.

"This isn't for your ears either," Edward said. "But I have no choice. You're all I have."

"Thanks." Clint yawned, not at all awake.

Edward paced, tossing his head. "I've been trying to figure out why the sand dragon would go to so much trouble to partner with humans, and all I can figure is that it needed human hands to get into a place that it couldn't reach, and to do things that a dragon's hands, such as they are, can't do. A place of doors and locks and shackles. A place where something might be locked away that the dragon would want, but that it wouldn't be able to reach on its own."

Clint nodded.

"I had ideas from the time we first encountered the dragon, but I dismissed them as fancy. But then, back at the magic sty, we saw that Kold and Cerberus were on the same path as the dooners. Then both parties left, headed in the same direction, neither aware of the other. Quite a coincidence, wouldn't you say? They're not together, so the only explanation is that they're seeking the same thing. They are both headed to the same place, to get something that a sand dragon and a unicorn of a different color would need to achieve what they wanted."

"Precipice?"

"The *Holy City* of Precipice, as it's known amongst unicorns," Edward said, nodding.

Clint shook his head. Precipice was the proverbial one-horse town. There was absolutely nothing interesting or special about it. It was smaller than Solace and Sojourn, and with less civilization. There was a bank and businesses and people, and from what he heard, there was little law and constant fighting. It wasn't near gold or anything else of value. Why would unicorns consider it holy?

"What would they want in that dump?" said Clint.

Edward sighed as if weighing a difficult decision. Then, apparently reaching a reluctant conclusion, he answered.

"Dragons want to open faults and release darkness. Kold and Cerberus want to reach The Realm, but even once they reach it, they'll have to breach the walls. Either task calls for an unthinkable source of black magic."

"I don't follow," said Clint.

"Regardless of the discomfort I feel in my chest, we must charge on until we overtake Kold," said Edward. "We have to reach him before he reaches Precipice — before he can find what I'm afraid he's after."

"What's he after?" said Clint.

"I think Kold has discovered the resting place of the Orb of Malevolence," said Edward.

Clint's breath caught in his throat.

Somewhere in the darkest part of the Sands night, a coyote howled to mock them.

UNICORN WESTERN 3

CHAPTER ONE: THRESHOLD

Clint only fired on the Asian man wearing banker's clothes and dark eye shades after he strutted forward, yelling in some garbled language, and failed to heed the gunslinger's orders to retreat. The shot sounded like a cannon as a billow of faded red marshal's gunsmoke belched from his seven-shot revolver. A bullet screamed into the yelling Asian man and he vanished with a puff.

"What is Gangnam style?" said Clint, perplexed.

The unicorn turned a disdainful blue eye toward the gunslinger. "What are you talking about?" he said.

"That easterner was yelling about style," said Clint, gesturing to where the man used to be.

Edward looked, then turned back to Clint. His horn looked sharp and malevolent. The unicorn himself seemed deeply disinterested.

"There is no easterner." He looked the gunslinger over, head to toe, taking in his dusty, road-weary desert-walker's wardrobe. "No style, either."

"Don't tell me you've not seen him," said Clint. "He's been on the horizon for miles. Hiding behind cacti, and the wrecks of those flying machines."

Something changed in Edward's large equine eye. Clint would have called it a "softening" if he didn't know Edward, and knew him to be mostly incapable of such. The unicorn stared out at the open expanse of sand, then at Clint, then again at the sand.

"Do you see wrecks of flying machines *now*?" he asked.

"Of course," Clint said, pointing. "Are you blind?"

Edward looked, then turned to Clint. "Give me the map," he said.

Clint rummaged through his pack, eager to make use of the map despite his annoyance at the unicorn's obtuseness. After spending the previous year wandering the unstable lands near the Edge, the gunslinger was always happy to touch the map, to consult the map, or to even catch sight of the map when rummaging in his pack for pie or brew. The Edge had shifted constantly, changing and moving every time they turned around. That shifting had abated somewhat by the time they'd dropped the girl Cari off with her remaining kin in a Leisei settlement, and it had disappeared entirely several weeks after that. Where they were now — desolate and dusty as it was — was blessedly *mappable*. The simple luxury of traveling in an area that remained the shape it was supposed to be was deeply, soul-pleasingly satisfying.

Clint spread the map on a flat expanse of stone at a rock outcropping that offered shade from the angled afternoon sun. They'd purchased the map in Beauregard, a town they had passed through a week before. The thing was closer to leather than parchment, and unrolled with a whisper instead of a crinkle.

"I was afraid of that," said Edward. "Where do you reckon we are?"

"Here," said Clint, pointing toward a red dot on the map. The dot said, YOU ARE HERE.

"Not even close," said Edward. "We are actually *here*." A new dot appeared on the map. Edward was projecting it from his horn and using it the way a man would use his finger to point.

"But *this* dot says we're *here*," said Clint, pointing at the YOU ARE HERE dot. "It moves, because this is a magical map."

"There isn't another dot," said Edward. "Just like there are no wrecked flying machines or style man in the sand."

"Yes there is," said Clint, insistent. "It's right here, near this chicken."

Edward looked down at Clint, seeming to weigh whether or not Clint was joking. Clint was not. He put his finger on the drawing of a chicken on the map, then tapped it, increasingly agitated.

Clint felt something like a hand under his chin and could make out a dull yellow glow at the limit of his vision. The invisible hand gently turned his head up to look at Edward.

"No dot," said Edward, looking into his eyes and then releasing the magical hand. "No chicken. No wrecks. No man. Look at me carefully, gunslinger. Do you believe I speak true?"

Clint knew that unicorns couldn't control minds any more than they could truly read them (unless they were willing to cross into perversion, of course), but their gaze was persuasive enough to earn the nickname, "The Look of Truth." Clint felt his head start to clear. Because unicorns were such pure sources of white magic, staring into their eyes was like seeing the world as it was supposed to be. It was like hypnosis, except that subjects could not be manipulated.

"You speak true," Clint repeated dutifully.

"Now look at the map."

His head slightly dazed, Clint returned his eyes to the battered tan map. There was no giant red dot or drawings, save the ones that were supposed to be there. His eyes found the smaller dot projected by Edward, showing their location as just outside Beauregard. He also saw the ink dot near the map's top left corner, which was marked PRECIPICE.

"Okay," said Clint. "I see the truth."

"Do you see the region we're entering?"

Clint looked at the nothing between Edward's dot and Precipice.

"No," he replied. The area was entirely blank. Suspiciously so, seeing as the rest of the map was flooded with irrelevant landmarks.

"Seems like there should be something in there, right?"

"Must be empty desert," said Clint.

"I don't think so. Hang on."

Edward's eyes fell shut as his horn started glowing a soft purple. It was rare for the unicorn to close his eyes outside sleep, and Clint could count on one long-fingered hand the number of times he'd seen Edward close his eyes to make any sort of magic. Shuttered lids meant he was doing something especially delicate or thoughtful.

Clint looked out into the sand where he'd seen the man in banker's clothes and could almost sense the magic reaching out from Edward into the sand, as if he were using a long hand to search for something beneath it. A large section of sand maybe three hundred feet away began to vibrate and shimmer. Then, as Clint watched, something massive emerged from beneath the desert's surface. The massive thing was a dull, smooth white, easily as large as Edward.

"Do I see that?" said Clint, already doubting his vision.

"Yar. I'm raising it from the sand."

"What is it?"

"It's a dinosaur bone."

"Bollocks. Dinosaurs are legends, like leprechauns."

"No," said Edward. "They were real, and they looked just like in your storybooks. I'm afraid we are entering the Dinosaur Missouri." The unicorn reached out and tapped the map with his front hoof. "And unfortunately, we're going to have to cross it to get to Precipice. The ways around are months of detour. We'd have to go around this lake if we went east, and around the river canyon running from that lake if we went west. It's why the dinosaurs bottlenecked here. They were held back from the holy city, and many died."

"I don't understand," said Clint.

Edward said, "Well, get used to that."

He used his magic to re-roll and stow the map, then resumed walking. Clint scampered to catch up, feeling as usual that he was the lackey in their relationship.

Suddenly the gunslinger's eyes went wide and he drew both pistols, but before he had a chance to aim them, they were lifted from his hands. The guns hovered in the air for a second, then sailed back down into his holsters. Immediately following this perversion, Clint felt himself be picked up and flown through the air. He dropped to rest on Edward's bare back.

"What are you doing?" he spat, aghast.

"Letting you ride," said the unicorn. "You poor, stupid man."

"And why did you stay my guns?" His tone was angry, indignant.

"What were you going to shoot at?"

Clint opened his mouth but nothing came out. He didn't remember. What was essential a second before had withered to something he couldn't put his finger on.

"You don't remember, do you?" said Edward from beneath him. "There will be a lot of that until we ford the river and cross out of the Missouri. You're going to need to develop some mental muscle. Everything you think now requires a filter. You must think before you act until we're through this area, and you must also think before you think."

It was a simple imperative, but Clint's brain and training both wanted to refuse. A gunslinger relied on his eyes and hands to share a lightning-fast exchange. Such signals bypassed his brain and went straight to his spine. It had always been the way he was most effective. Asking his thinking mind to weigh in on every fired bullet would make him slow, and an easy target.

"What is this place?" Clint asked, eyeing the massive bone that Edward had unearthed. As they drew closer, he could see that it curved up high until it ended in a point. It looked like the rib of something titanic.

"This is a graveyard," said Edward.

Clint shook his head dismissively. "I've laid many graves."

"Not like this. Dinosaurs were magic creatures. Forebears to unicorns. They held a primitive, ancient magic. When magic dies, it leaves an echo. This area's bottlenecks are a massive dying ground for dinosaurs. More died here than anywhere else, by many-fold. This place is unthinkably ancient, and polluted with that old magic."

"Polluted?"

Edward shook his head slightly. "Matter of perspective. Let's just say we're out of tune with it. Or it with us. You especially. It will act on you like any other time you've encountered out-of-tune magic, only much more strongly."

Clint said, "I've not encountered out-of-tune magic."

"Of course you have. You'd call it a haunting."

"This desert is haunted?"

"The Dinosaur Missouri is, yes. And I'll be frank with you, gunslinger. You may not be able to take it. Any human would be in danger here. This magic is older than older than old. It came before what you thought of as white and black magic, or surface and core magic. Here, the darkness inside our friend the sand dragon would be an infant, as would the darkness it was trying to assist in bleeding through the fissures."

"Will it affect *you*?" said Clint.

"Yes," said Edward. "But I am better than you."

They plodded on. Edward's truth trance hadn't yet shaken from Clint, so he felt sure the bones he was seeing on the horizon were real. There were a few to the east and west, but most were up north, where they were headed. In that direction lay Precipice — the town in which Clint and Edward hoped to intercept the dark rider and his unicorn of a different color before they reached the Orb of Malevolence, which Edward felt certain Dharma Kold was pursuing.

"We're only on the apron of the Dinosaur Missouri," said Edward. "It will take us days to enter its heart. We must be vigilant with our thoughts. And we'll be fasting."

"Why do we need to fast?"

"Because the Missouri's ancient magic is like wet tar, trapping the thoughts of those who go through it, then showing those thoughts back to everyone who follows like carnival horrors. The Missouri is a crossroads penetrating many worlds, like an axle through many wheels. Some of the thoughts we'll see, having come from other worlds, will be foreign and terrifying to us. But what's worse, the magic will pluck thoughts from *our* heads and leave them behind for *others* to see... but only after showing them to us. And because of how any being — but especially humans — are wired, you can expect your mind's most dominant thoughts to share space with your fears. You will see what terrifies you. And you will see dinosaurs."

Clint was a hard man, and it scared him to think that the stones in his mind might betray him. He had to make it through with his sanity.

"And the fasting?"

"What would you rather think on — demons, or your own

hunger?"

Clint saw his point.

"How long will we be inside the Missouri?" he asked.

"Not long. A few days in its center at most. But it will feel much longer than that."

"But you say that Kold crossed it?"

Edward managed a horselike shrug. "He went through, or he saw what I saw and decided to go around. Either way, we should proceed. If Kold went through, he could be in Precipice by now. If he went around, he'll be months getting there and we can arrive before him."

Clint saw a trio of small, green men fifty feet off, at the base of a cactus. Leprechauns. He forced his twitching hands away from his guns, then closed his eyes, breathed deeply, and exhaled. When he opened them again, the leprechauns vanished.

"Do you want my guns?" said Clint, reluctant to make the offer, but thinking of what might be most safe.

"Either way. You won't fire on me, and you can't hurt me anyway because of my white magic. All you could fire on that would do any harm would be yourself. But if you lose that much of your mind, putting a bullet in your brain would be mercy delivered. So you may keep your arms, or you may surrender them. Whichever makes you feel better."

Knowing he was making a foolish, childlike decision, Clint said, "I'll keep them."

After a few more minutes' walk and a few more bones passed, Edward said, "There's something else you should be aware of."

"What?"

"In the interest of full disclosure, I mean."

"What?" Clint growled.

"There's a good chance that you may emerge from the Dinosaur Missouri insane."

"If I lose my mind, then I lose it," said Clint, keeping his eyes on the big picture.

"That's the spirit," said the unicorn. "And on the upside, at least there's not much there to lose."

CHAPTER TWO: INSIDE THE DINOSAUR MISSOURI

The day ended and a new one began. Then that day ended and a third began, and a fourth and a fifth followed.

On the morning of the fifth day, gunslinger and unicorn passed through a massive ribcage like parasites through a monster's intestines. Edward declared that based on what he could feel in the magic, they were entering the Dinosaur Missouri's ancient heart.

"Look at me," said the unicorn, emerging at the far end of the ribcage, near where the skeleton of the huge thing's tail had sheared off from a shattered pelvis. "I'm poop."

Clint couldn't bring himself to answer Edward's juvenile humor. He was too hungry. The trail had turned Clint hard, but never had he ridden with food in his pack yet denied himself access to it for so long. They'd subsisted on sips of water from their canteens and waterskins, but Edward wouldn't even allow a single swallow of brew.

"Nutrition will at least nourish the body and clear the head," Clint said, dying to at least replenish some of what his body was expending.

"Exactly," said Edward. "So, no brew."

On their first day of fasting, the gunslinger's stomach had rumbled, and he had willed the feeling from his body as he had many, many times before. By the end of the second day, while they palavered over a fire with turkey pie from Beauregard's Restaurant going bad in his pack, his stomach churned into an angry knot, and still he willed the feeling away. But by the third night, a deep weakness started to set in, and so for a reason he couldn't explain, he sneaked a few pinches of extra salt with his dinnertime water just to feel something drop into his stomach. The salt didn't help. Instead, it almost made him want to vomit, but he held it down. Water was precious, and would stay so until the Missouri was cleared.

"Walk faster," Clint grunted at Edward after they'd passed the huge, skeletal tail and Edward had made his fecal joke. They were both walking, and Clint had taken the lead simply so that he could yell at Edward.

"I can walk plenty faster," said Edward. "I've been sandbagging out of consideration for your slow corpse." He increased his gait to a trot and put ten yards between himself and Clint.

"Finally, some progress," said Clint, breaking into a jog.

The day was hot. Clint felt himself starting to sweat as he ran. He looked around, saw giant bones of deceased monsters, and wondered if the bones were actually there. He also wondered how the dancing Asian man in the banker's clothes and eye shades had caught up, and again what Gangnam style was.

There were giant signs everywhere around him — the kind of things they called billboards back in The Realm — but the signs displayed things that Clint didn't understand. One sign showed a woman smoking a tiny white tobacco pipe and read, "You've come a long way, baby." But the woman didn't appear to have come from anywhere, and Clint imagined himself being on the sign because he *had* come a long way, and then suddenly the woman from the sign was walking beside him, except that she had the low, deep voice of a saloon blues singer, and she said, "You've come a long way, gunslinger" before punching him in the face and sending him sprawling to the dirt.

Edward didn't look back until he was a good distance ahead. Then he stopped and turned and laughed. Clint looked around. The woman was gone. Nobody had punched him. He'd tripped on a rock.

Edward said, "Humans are so slow and clumsy."

"Hurry up, horsey," whistled Clint, regaining his feet and, suddenly furious with the unicorn, breaking into a sprint.

Edward ran. Clint ran. Then they hit a stiff downward slope and both fell, rolling to the bottom. Clint stood and found himself totally brown, covered in clay and dirt from head to toe. Edward, by contrast, looked pristine and spotless, like the sun.

"Such a pretty boy," said Clint, staring with disdain at the unicorn.

"Look at yourself," said Edward. "You're perfectly filthy."

"You think you're better than me?"

"I don't even think that's a real question."

Clint shoved both hands hard into Edward's side. Not even one of Edward's twelve hundred pounds budged. Clint's strong arms felt like twigs about to snap.

"You're pathetic," said Edward, huffing, trying to catch his breath after the sprint and the tumble down the hill.

"No, *you* are," said Clint, also huffing.

Then something clicked inside his mind, cutting through the Missouri's fog, sinking its fingers into the soft meat of the gunslinger's brain.

"It's hunger," he said. "We shouldn't be fighting. We're just hungry." He hoisted the pack from his shoulder and started unwrapping a slice of turkey pie.

"Don't eat that."

"Sands to you," said Clint.

"You're weak. *Mentally* weak. Don't be such a wimp. Be a unicorn."

Clint gave him an insolent look. "So you forfeit your half then." He raised the unwrapped pie in front of him and licked his lips, his eyes on Edward.

"Don't."

"You aren't my mother."

"If you're fed, you'll be able to think of demons."

Clint stuck his tongue out at Edward — something he'd never, ever done, and which he marveled at even as he felt himself doing it — then opened his mouth to invite the pie inside. But before he could, something heavy knocked the pie from his hand, grazing his face on the way. There was a very hard, very blunt pain that Clint barely registered. He watched the turkey pie fall into the dirt, into a desiccated pile of manure.

"You think I won't eat manure pie?" said Clint.

But Edward was staring at it too, and not just to keep Clint from grabbing it. Clint could see his lips and mouth working, trying to fight the urge to extend his neck and swallow it.

"Don't you dare take it," said Clint, watching Edward's white lips smack.

Then Clint dove toward the pie, which had broken apart on impact and become enmeshed with manure and sand. Edward was faster. He extended his neck, but then seemed to regain some control and spun, sitting down hard onto the pie. There was a squelching sound as it mashed underneath him.

"You think I won't eat unicorn-sat-on manure pie?" said Clint.

A diffuse glow came from below Edward's enormous rump.

"What are you doing?" Clint blurted.

"Baking it," said Edward. He stood and what used to be the pie fell from his rear in charred black flakes.

"I have more in the packs."

Edward looked Clint fully in the eye, but something inside the gunslinger was already starting to shift. He'd had a moment of delirious weakness, but he knew the unicorn was right. Spiritualists had used hunger and fasting as methods for self-control since humans were barely humans. If he couldn't resist hunger, he'd never be able to resist whatever mental slide show the Dinosaur Missouri had in store.

"Fine," said Clint, sighing and re-shouldering the pack.

Edward kept his eyes on Clint, as if he were trying to decide whether to trust the gunslinger. Finally he said, "You are so totally ugly."

"I'll bet you're ugly on the inside," said Clint, "without all your pretty magic."

"I'm beautiful everywhere," said Edward.

"Rainbows and fairies and gumballs, right? Would you like me to tie ribbons in your hair? How about if we paint each other's nails? How can you walk out here without an entourage applying lipstick and braiding your mane with bubblegum pink ribbons?"

"What color smoke do your pistols make, gunslinger?"

They stared at each other for sixty full seconds, neither speaking, Clint looking into Edward's profile so the unicorn could see him. Finally, Edward blinked lazily.

"I win," said Clint, thinking of the staring contest he felt they were having.

Edward resumed walking. Clint didn't follow. After Edward put twenty yards between them, Clint just stared after him. Then he felt an invisible snare grab him by the ankle drag him foot-first through the dirt on his back. He scrambled to his feet and walked, and the snare vanished. Soon, they were walking side by side again, neither speaking.

A few hours farther on, dinosaur bones exploded in number until they were everywhere. The many beasts from Clint's childhood, all mystical and made-up in his mind, were suddenly in reality around him — the skull of the T-wrex, the long and curving backbone of a bronosores. He even saw the giant head crest and horns of the mythical land rhino, which human legend said was the great ancestor of the unicorn. The bones, Edward kept assuring him, were real. Very little else seemed to be. Clint, in his delirium, kept seeing living dinosaurs, multicolored like in the fireside tales he'd heard as a child back in The Realm. He saw people everywhere, and he shot at several before realizing that he should ask Edward about their reality first. Edward, whose head seemed to be clearer, always told him the phantoms weren't there.

Worse than the visions was the noise.

Clint felt as if he were inside of a giant hive mind, hearing every thought that had ever been thought by every person who had ever crossed the Missouri. There were times when they'd have to double back on their path, and when they did, Clint would hear his own thoughts in an echo, or he'd see something he'd been imagining when they'd crossed the stretch earlier.

The gunslinger heard music that had previously been heard by millions of other ears. So much of it (probably because it had come from other worlds) was unfamiliar. Other songs were very familiar indeed. He heard Joelsongs that could have come from his own hitching ceremony when he'd nearly wed Mai back in Solace. He heard "Just the Way You Are" and even the non-hitching titles "My Life" and "Moving Out." He also heard dark music he'd only heard rumors of, full of wailings and sounds that could only come from thinking machines — unholy noises deserving of Providence's damnation. He heard melodies he couldn't imagine existing, with no clues to their creation. Much was profane or spiked with innuendo. He heard a woman singing about a Disco Stick, then heard the same woman singing about a Poker Face. Worst of all was a girlish song that seemed to be called "Baby."

His head swam with noise and sight and taste and smell. He saw people that Edward explained were probably the friends, relatives, and enemies of people who'd passed through the Missouri. Some of these phantoms attacked. When they did, they struck the travelers and evaporated into mist. Others simply strode by without heeding them. Many of the figures were mangled and injured, and Edward said that those represented the death fears of other travelers. They even saw monsters that had never existed and had been born solely out of someone's terror: ghoulem, yandas, and even a crowd of dead-eyed walking corpses that could have been Clint's own mental idea of xombies.

"They can't hurt you," Edward told Clint during a particularly nervous moment that caused the gunslinger to draw both guns and wave them around wildly. "They are mere memories."

But for the most part, the depths of Clint's mind seemed to understand that he was seeing things that weren't actually there. Ghosts approached and vanished without heed. Phantom banshees howled at them before becoming giant spiked lizards, and Clint shrugged them off easily. Mostly, the visions held no horrors for Clint (or for Edward, as far as Clint could see) because terror is highly individualized, and the fears of others didn't resonate with the gunslinger. They mostly seemed childish to him. Many involved death — and these left Clint, who'd dealt his share of death and didn't particularly fear his own, puzzled.

Through the worst of it, Clint rode on Edward's back.

Clint wanted to stretch his legs, but Edward felt that riding was more prudent. The Missouri's illusions kept threatening to separate them. Clint would see a path and follow it, but he'd quickly fall into a false trail made from someone's memory. He'd see an expanse and cross it, but just in time the unicorn would pick him up and he'd find himself hovering above a chasm he hadn't seen. He even saw Edward in his mind, and the mental unicorn projected back to him by the Dinosaur Missouri blurred with the real one. One time, he watched Edward dissolve into blood and sinew and decay. Another time, he saw him sprout wings and fly. One time Edward's mouth became an alligator's mouth a second before trying to bite the gunslinger in half. Each time, as Clint screamed and ran, the real Edward grabbed him with his magic and righted him.

"Is it even possible for a man to cross this area without a unicorn?" Clint asked once he was safely atop Edward's back, plodding forward.

"If he's very, very lucky," said Edward. In Clint's eyes, he saw a false vision as Edward spoke: the unicorn looking directly at him, his head twisted backward on his neck, his eyes and mouth full of fire. Then Clint blinked and they were again a rider and a plain old white mount with a non-twisted neck, plodding steadily forward in the blazing sun.

As they walked, Clint heard everything thought by everyone whose head had ever passed near his. Being up high, on the back of a unicorn, kept him above the worst of the noise, but the assault on his senses was still deafening. He couldn't shut out all of the images, words, music and thoughts that bombarded him.

"What is a star track?" asked Edward at one point.

"I don't know," said Clint.

"It's a human memory I'm seeing and hearing. Someone who came through this place thought that the Missouri was like a timeless ribbon of energy that existed in a star track."

"I don't know what that means," Edward repeated.

"The memory involves a huge flickering screen, and a man upon that screen named Kirk. This Kirk wore a kind of man's wig. There was another man named Malcolm who once had a mechanical orange, filled with clockworks."

"I hear the memory," said Edward, "but you humans are such idiots. It could mean anything. Or, more likely, it could mean nothing."

" 'Where no man has gone before,' " said Clint, quoting something he heard in his mind.

"The man whose memory you're hearing fell and broke his leg over there," said Edward, gesturing. "Then he died of thirst."

Clint looked toward the unicorn's gesture, and his heart leapt. He tried to scramble from Edward's back, but Edward's horn glowed and Clint felt himself pushed down hard.

" 'Twinkies! Twinkies!' " Edward yelled, repeating the voice that Clint himself could hear in his head. "That's what our star track man thought as he ran over there. Do you see them?"

Clint did, and his mouth watered at the sight. To the left side of the trail was a pile that looked like stones on a burial mound, but instead of stones, the mound was made of oblong yellow sponges. Being human, Clint connected enough to the memory of the star track man to know that the oblongs were a snack food.

"They're not real, Clint," said Edward. "However, the hole filled with sharp rocks that you can't see below it is very real indeed."

"Hole?"

"The hole with our star track man's skeleton at the bottom. Perhaps you'd like to go down there and ask him about Twinkies and that man named Malcolm?"

Clint fought his hunger, kept his eyes away from the mound, and waited until the impulse to gorge himself faded.

After a few moments (or was it days? Clint was losing track of time), Edward stopped and sniffed the air. Then Clint watched as a man wearing a bright purple suit and rhinestone-studded eye shades walked into Edward and evaporated into mist. When he did, Clint had a foreign thought he didn't understand: *Crocodile rock.*

Edward's ears twitched, swiveling as if on hinges.

"Good news," said Edward.

"You know which direction to go?" said Clint, staring forward at three distinct paths he suspected might not actually be there. Down one path was a lake filled with aquatic dinosaurs. Down another was what looked like an enormous carnival tent. The other vanished into literal nothingness. Beyond it, Clint saw the dark of outer space.

"Yar," said Edward. "But that's not the good news."

"Then what is?"

"I've found Kold," said Edward. "And Mai."

CHAPTER THREE: THE BUBBLE OF GLEE

Clint stared at the back of Edward's neck. They couldn't look one another in the eye unless Clint dismounted, but the gunslinger knew the unicorn could feel Clint staring him down. Overhead, a terrydaxl bird dinosaur screeched, swooping low enough for Clint to feel the ghost's breath on his neck.

"What do you mean, 'I found Mai'?"

Just in front of Edward's huge white head, Clint saw Mai appear as if blown together by swirling sand. She was wearing her hitching dress. She smiled like the last time Clint had seen her happy, back during their botched hitching ceremony in Solace three long years ago. She gave him a tiny wave, then her eyeballs fell backward into her head and her face became a dried, gray skull. The phantom Mai blew apart into thousands of pieces.

Clint cringed. Edward said, "I can hear her thoughts. Not in the perverse way that Cerberus hears them, by dipping his horn into her soul, but on the wind, from when she left them behind."

Clint tried to still his mind and pull Mai's thoughts from the millions assaulting him, but it was no use. He heard a thousand songs and random thoughts. He watched monsters surround him and Edward from all sides. Edward could filter out the Missouri's racket and hone in on individual thoughts, but Clint was only a man. Instead of mastering the air inside the Dinosaur Missouri, the Missouri mastered Clint. Every monster and every dinosaur and every walking apparition became Clint's almost-bride Mai, who this instant was Dharma Kold's tortured captive. He watched her scream and die from every side, in every possible way. Other thoughts vanished, alongside their noise. Everything was Mai, and her curdled screams of torture and torment. It was as if the place's old magic saw Clint trying to earn an upper hand and said, *Okay, you want Mai? I'll give you all the Mai you can handle.*

Clint closed his eyes and pressed the thumb and forefinger of his right hand against his eyelids.

"Master yourself," said Edward, trying to turn his head to look back. "I can hear your fear in a holler. Shut it out. The memories I sense are at least a day old. She's probably clear by now."

Or dead.

Or she's been ravaged by the dark unicorn's torture.

Or they fell into a pit, like the star track man.

Clint opened his eyes and ugly thoughts took form: Mai being killed in a million new ways before his eyes, all in stark color. Vivid like a moving picture.

"I can hear all of the thoughts you're making now, too," said Edward. "Focus on your hunger."

Clint did, again closing his eyes. It was hard at first to *not* think of a thing, so he instead tried to feel the details of his hunger. He felt his stomach churning, and the acid wanting to eat him from inside. He felt his own weakness.

He opened his eyes and every instance of Mai had become a slice of turkey pie.

"I guess I'm better," said Clint. In front of him, a slice of turkey pie became a skull and exploded. A slice of turkey pie fell into a pit and broke its leg. A slice of turkey pie was subjected to the manipulations of a dark unicorn until it went insane, spilling pumpkin mash from its innards into a pool in the sand.

"I guess I'd better not dwell," said Edward. "Let's just say we're on the right track. I can sense all of them. They came through not long ago. It's easy to get lost in here, even for a unicorn, but now I know where to go. If we get lost, at least we'll be lost with them."

Several slices of turkey pie snarled as they turned into Dharma Kold. The Kolds advanced, growing large and indestructible, the way Kold had seemed in Clint's imagination years before. Clint had wondered how he could possibly best Kold, and the Dinosaur Missouri knew it. It magnified Clint's doubt, twisting the reality in front of his face. The Kolds grew huge, firing poisonous spells and deadly bullets, looming large as carriage wheels.

Clint closed his eyes. When he opened them, the Kolds were still there.

He cringed. He curled into a ball perched atop Edward's back. His hands fell to his revolvers, though he knew they were useless. He drew one and cradled it like a child.

"You okay back there?" said Edward.

"We're all going to die in here," said Clint.

Edward sighed. "Okay," he said. "I don't want to do this, but I don't have much of a choice."

There was movement, and Clint suddenly found himself so distracted by the sight of a large pink balloon growing from the tip of Edward's horn that his mind unclenched and the giant Dharma Kolds (and the proliferating dying Mais) vanished. The ballon grew larger and larger, now standing straight up. It was as if Edward's head were a tank of lightgas and he was filling the balloon through his horn, which was the nozzle.

The balloon grew bigger, becoming gigantic, until it was as tall as Edward was wide. Then it was as tall as Edward.

Clint felt his head clear. "What is that?"

"Don't move," said Edward.

The balloon jumped from the end of Edward's horn like a leaping cat. It struck Clint in the face with a force that seemed like it should have unhorsed him, but he managed to stay in place, barely, atop Edward's back.

Clint opened his eyes and found that everything around him seemed rosier. He felt better. And strangely, his skin felt taut, like he was wearing a skintight but very stretchy suit.

Then the initial burst of near-euphoria retreated and Clint's sharp gunslinger's instincts reasserted themselves.

"What the Sands is this?" he said, staring down at his right hand — which, the way it looked now, could never fire a pistol. There were giant pink webs between each of his fingers. The same substance ran down the length of his body, creating webs wherever his body should have had angles. All of his skin and all of his clothing blushed with pink.

"It's a bubble," said Edward.

"A bubble *of...*" said Clint, annoyed despite a strange and pressing joy that was threatening to suffocate him.

"Glee," said Edward, sighing. "It's a bubble of *glee*."

"I don't want to be in a bubble of glee."

"It's that or go insane," said Edward.

Clint tried to hold back the euphoria being forced upon him by the bubble, but its magic was strong. He felt as if he were swashbuckling a puppeteer who was bound and determined to cheer him up with an exceptionally dull-witted puppet show — and he was losing.

Clint heard himself giggle, hating the sound.

"What is it doing to me?" he said.

"It's called a 'bubble of glee,'" said Edward. "Figure it out."

Clint looked around. Where the landscape had been stark and desolate, it now looked open and inviting. The sand looked like powdered chocolate. The cacti looked like giant striped lollipops. He saw no fewer than five rainbows, even though the air held not a drop of moisture. Movement in the corner of his eye made him turn to the once unforgiving sun, and he saw that it was now wearing eye shades, that it had a mouth and two hands, and that it was smiling at the gunslinger and waving.

Before Clint could stop himself, he waved back at the happy sun.

"This is intolerable," he said.

Edward exhaled loudly. Then he said, "Xombies. Mai dying. A million sand dragons with teeth of steel."

Everything Edward said entered Clint's mind as a coherent thought, but then the thoughts twisted into something else. Clint realized that he didn't care about xombies. He was distantly aware that xombies were terrifying, but that didn't seem important right now.

Through his pink haze, he watched as a parade of corpses walked toward him holding bouquets of daisies. He watched as Mai was shot, but her wound bled sprinkles like the sort meant to garnish a cupcake. She ate them and was healed. The gunslinger watched as sand dragons blew him kisses, which he felt compelled to reach up and catch.

"Fine," said Clint. "Glee it is."

Despite the annoying cheeriness he felt, Clint found that the bubble wasn't all bad. He could at least think inside of it, for one. His thoughts were of puppies and colorful mushrooms. The Missouri's soundtrack became the pleasant tinkle of a nickelodeon. Only one piece of music managed to penetrate his pink prison — a bassline that snared his mind. He found himself alternately singing to Edward that Edward couldn't touch this, then chanting about an unknown object called a superfreak.

Time passed. Rainbows dissolved and surrendered to new rainbows. Fuzzy creatures scampered. Giant billboards now bore phrases like YOU ARE LOVED and FRIENDSHIP IS SPECIAL. On several separate occasions, Clint found himself telling Edward to "chill out" when he stepped around a thing in their path that Edward deemed treacherous, but that to Clint appeared cute.

Eventually they mounted a gradual rise (Clint saw it carpeted with neon green grass and studded with a bed of bright white flowers that were smiling up at him), and when they reached the top, Edward shook his head. A tiny red spark shot from his horn and struck Clint's body. And when it did, the world snapped back to ugly and brown and desolate. But the music and the noise were gone, and no ghosts rose to confront them.

"We're clear of the Missouri," said Clint.

He said it like a fact, his stony demeanor reasserting itself with the bludgeon-like blow of a hammer. He was embarrassed by what he might have said under the influence of glee, like a regretful man who has consumed too much brew.

"Yar," said Edward. "See that river?"

Clint looked. The river was wide, but didn't seem deep. The path from the hilltop where they were standing sloped down toward it, into a kind of valley that rose around it on all sides.

"Yar."

"In the old times, that river filled this valley. The dinosaurs couldn't ford it, so after being funneled into this space, they died. But the river is now quite shallow, and it's where we are headed."

"And we can eat once we're on the other side?" said Clint, still unsure of his bearings. He hadn't felt like himself for a week, and was just a few chews away from starving.

"Yar. But there's something else."

"Nar. There's nothing else mattering as long as there's food."

Edward started walking, still with Clint on his back. After a moment, he said, "You remember the Darkness?"

"No."

"The Darkness from inside the sand dragon. When the dragon lost its form, you watched the Darkness disperse."

Clint hadn't understood what had followed their battle against the sand dragon a month prior. He knew only that he'd watched a huge black cloud emerge from the disintegrating dragon's body. Edward had explained that dark magic sometimes escaped from the core, filtered up through the sand, and took on forms like sand dragons. But Clint hadn't understood that, either.

"If Darkness is what I saw, then yar," said Clint, slowly finding his familiar (and gleeless) rhythm of bouncing atop Edward's back.

"Do you remember how I said that the Darkness wasn't gone? That it would escape and find a new host or a new form? That it had become a dragon in order to lay its hands — its *talons* — on something in the physical world, and that it would surely return in a new form and resume its quest, and that we would face it again?"

"Sort of," said Clint, though he still didn't really follow.

"I sensed it in there," said Edward, jerking his head toward the Dinosaur Missouri. "While you were gleed. I could feel its passage."

"The Darkness must travel on foot, as we do?" said Clint. The idea seemed ludicrous. It was like saying that clouds could get sore feet.

"Yar. Do you remember nothing?"

"Very little," said Clint, content to let Edward believe he had forgotten rather than admitting he'd never understood in the first place.

"Anyway," said the unicorn, "I sensed it in the Missouri, as I sensed the others. But then I lost it."

Clint cocked his head and adjusted his hat. "So what does that mean?"

"I don't know," said Edward.

They were already halfway through the river. It was barely deep enough to cover the unicorn's hooves. Clint waited for Edward to say more, but he said nothing.

"Why are you telling me?" Clint finally asked.

"Because you are unfortunately the only one here for me to talk to," said Edward.

They plodded through the rest of the stream, then climbed the rise on the opposite side. From the crest of the new hill, Clint could see that they'd reached a small town. Nearby was a well, with a bucket wound to the top of the crank. He could see the handle of a dipping spoon poking over the bucket's top edge.

"Precipice," Edward announced.

"And Mai," said Clint.

"Maybe," Edward replied. "The Orb's magic would mask the pain I've been feeling from what Cerberus is doing to her, so I cannot be sure. But yar, I'd bet my pie that she's here, and so are Kold and Cerberus."

Clint cracked his knuckles.

"And the Darkness," Edward added.

Clint stopped, his arms out and fingers intertwined.

"I can no longer sense it," the unicorn continued, his lips drawing into a scowl. "But it's here, all right."

CHAPTER FOUR:
A FISTFUL OF DOLLARS

They walked up to the well, their throats dusty and their waterskins near empty. Clint unpacked a shallow dish that Edward used for drinking and set it on the ground near the stones of the well. He removed the dipping spoon and lowered the bucket to the well's bottom, filled it, and wheeled it back up. Then he took a long, slow drink from the spoon before spilling the bucket's contents into Edward's dish. And finally, while Edward drank, Clint drank more, then began to refill their water supply.

Clint had the dipper to his lips when he noticed movement in the otherwise still town below. A child of maybe ten years spilled through the door of a ramshackle mud brick structure, stumbled, and fell to the dirt. A huge figure wearing criss-crossed bandoliers and a wide-brimmed hat came out after the boy, yelling at him in a local dialect Clint didn't recognize. The boy, penitent, tried to protest, but the big figure kept coming. He delivered a kick to the kid's side and yelled more. The big man wore guns on his hips — six-shooters, tarnished nearly brown. He was fat and slow, but had the unmistakable bearing of co-opted authority.

The kid held up his hands and said something. The man yelled a string of hollers clearly meant as a threat, or a warning. The kid came to his feet and scampered away, toward a building from which a thin man had emerged. The man held his hands out to the kid, who ran into them.

Then, looking up, the thin man did not walk out to confront the bandit. Instead, he said something in the strange language that sounded almost like an apology. The fat bandit yelled something back and waved an expressive, warning hand. Then the thin man, with the child clasped against his abdomen and legs, vanished inside the building.

Clint still held the water dipper to his mouth. His lips were cracked, and his stomach was rumbling. They still had their supplies, but they'd agreed it would be more appetizing to break their fast at the town's saloon rather than with dried-out jerky and wraps.

The man with the bandoliers took several steps toward the building where he'd emerged, then noticed Clint and Edward at the top of the rise two hundred feet away. Clint finished his drink, returned the dipper, and met the bandit's gaze. Then, because there's always town business in which a stranger nar should interfere, Clint let his eyes drop from the bandit's and turned to retrieve Edward's empty drinking bowl. By the time he'd looked back up and re-mounted, the big man was gone.

Edward, with Clint on his back, began to plod unhurriedly down the shallow slope toward Precipice.

"The magic here is incredibly strong," said Edward. "Can you feel it?"

Clint scanned the buildings as a bell rang nearby. His eyes found the bell, atop a three-story tower that barely rose above the dull and monochrome one and two-story buildings surrounding the main street. It was an old-fashioned bell, pivoting in the middle with a rope tied to its top. Somewhere below, someone was ringing the bell by hand. To herald what, Clint couldn't imagine.

"It's a hole," said Clint. "All I feel is poison. Look at this place."

Edward did, but his glance was perfunctory. Apparently the unicorn was awed by something the gunslinger couldn't sense.

Clint felt himself overwhelmed by the town's desolation. A few of the buildings were boarded, and the rest might as well have been. Clint's sharp eyes could see people watching him through windows as he passed, trying to hide behind draperies. Closed doors with peep-through slots had their peeping slots open, displaying glaring sets of fear-stricken eyes. The street was silent, with no foot or carriage traffic to mar it. No children playing. No sounds of working. Nothing at all.

"It *is* poisoned," Edward agreed. "But it's also magic. To me, the strength of magic here is like a cloying odor that masks everything else. Cerberus could be violating Mai's soul right around that corner and I wouldn't be able to feel the pain that we've been following for years. In a way, it's a blessing... but in another, it's disorienting. I don't like to be surprised. And there's still the matter of the Darkness. Its presence here frightens me most of all."

"How do you know it's here?"

Edward's lips curled. Clint could barely see it from his position on the unicorn's back, but saw it he did.

"I *know*," he said. "Just as Mai and everyone else left parts of themselves behind in the Dinosaur Missouri, so did the Darkness. I saw its stuck memories and thoughts, and recognized its soul from when we fought it as the sand dragon. It wasn't the dragon anymore... but in a way, it also was. I sensed something like what humans call déjà vu, where you seem to recognize someone you've never met. That's what it's like for me, and even though I can't sense it, I can still sense it. It's traveling. It's *here*. Somehow, it is right here with us — in some form or another, since Darkness can't act without a form."

They were halfway down the length of the main street, moving slowly. Dust billowed up from Edward's hooves with every step, but the dust failed to stick to his pristine white coat and hooves. To their right, a child sat on a building's stoop. The door to the building burst open and an adult rushed out, pulled the child back inside, and slammed the door behind them. Clint watched the display, then turned his eyes placidly forward, between Edward's ears and on the street ahead.

"Why would that frighten you more than Kold, who carries two marshal's seven-shooters and the stolen power of a unicorn?"

"Because Kold is a man. The Darkness is not. It will have gone to great lengths, after losing the dooner shaman as its servant, to take a new form in order to do its searching. But both of our adversaries were headed here, and both are likely here now. The Orb of Malevolence is still in town; I can feel it on me like heat. Both Kold and the Darkness need the Orb, and the Orb is frightening in either of their hands. But if you ask, then yes — between the two, I'll take Kold, because what the Darkness wants to do with the Orb is far more terrifying."

"What does it want to do?"

Edward turned his head, trying to give Clint a scornful eye. "You never pay attention," he said.

Before Clint could reply, a filthy man in chinos and stringy long black hair ran up beside them. Clint didn't bother to draw his guns. The man seemed harmless, and if he turned out not to be, Clint could surely draw quickly enough to dispatch him.

"You are new in town!" the man yelled up at Clint in Clint's language, ignoring Edward as if he were a common horse. "A man could get rich here; you will see!"

"Is that so?" said the gunslinger, still looking straight ahead.

"Yes," said the man, trotting beside Edward's flank. "Rich, or dead. One or the other."

"Nar in between?"

"Not for a man who brings his own guns," said the man. "You will see."

Edward, tired of being ignored, paused and looked over at the man.

"And who are you?"

"I am the bell ringer," said the man, turning his gaze to Edward.

"Quite the career choice," the unicorn said. "How many years of schooling did that require? And does your specialized knowledge provide you with the job security you deserve?"

"I am the bell ringer," the man repeated.

Edward turned his head toward Clint, who was dismounting. "We need food," he told the gunslinger.

"Where's the saloon?" Clint asked the dirty man.

"It's around the corner there. But watch out, because Dean's men sit outside. They won't like you none. They are with the boss. They run this town, and will run you out."

"The boss, huh?"

"Yar. They won't like you and won't want you in town unless you join them."

"Or kill them," said Edward.

"You will either end up rich or end up dead!" the bell ringer blurted.

"I think we get it," said Edward. He resumed walking, now with Clint beside him.

The bell ringer followed them for maybe ten steps, then vanished.

"Do you think he's the official greeter too?" Edward asked. "He's so charming."

"So the town has a boss," said Clint, looking at everything around the dusty road with new eyes. "That explains the mood; it's like Solace was when we arrived. How would Kold fit into this, do you think?"

"Maybe Kold is the boss, under an assumed name. *Dean.* Has a folksy ring to it."

Clint shook his head. "It's not Kold who runs the town. This town has been subdued for a while now. The question is, what happened between Kold and this Dean *after* Kold showed up?"

Before Edward could answer, they rounded the corner and found a carriage parked outside the saloon with three men perched atop it, drinking. A fourth leaned against the hitch, which had long ago been untethered from the horse that had once pulled the rickety box. The men all wore clothing that looked as if it had once been brightly colored, but was now muted beneath a brown sweater of sand and dust. Each man wore a gun — just one six-shooter, of course — on his right hip.

Edward said, "Maybe we could ask these fine gentlemen?"

One of the men looked into his cup, then to the man beside him. He said, "Did that horse just talk?"

Edward started to reply, but Clint extended a hand and placed it on Edward's chest to stop him. His look said, *Let me handle this.*

Clint walked around and stood in front of Edward in his most non-threatening posture: hands clasped with fingers intertwined, hovering in front of his buckle. Other than surrendering his guns or raising his hands over his head, entangling his fingers was the most encumbered and hence slowest a gunslinger could appear.

"I'd like to see the boss," Clint announced.

"And who the sands are you?" said the man leaning against the hitch.

"I'm a stranger."

"Don't you have a name?"

"Sure. I'll tell my name to the boss."

The man, whose body language told Clint that he was the leader of the men on the carriage, set down his cup and took a step forward. His hand rested on the butt of his gun. Clint's hands stayed clasped in front of him, encumbered and unthreatening.

"That's a big gun you carry," said the man.

"You like it? Because this one is the same." Still with his hands clasped, Clint shrugged his left shoulder. His waterskin had been covering his left gun, but the shrug shifted the waterskin enough to expose it.

All of the men gave a satisfying reaction, but the man who almost fell from his perch on the wagon's top earned the bluest ribbon. That one almost choked on his drink, then grabbed the carriage's seat to regain his balance, suddenly looking like he was made of rubber.

"They're big because they have seven chambers," said Clint, his stoic expression giving no indication of just how much he was enjoying this dramatic reveal.

The leader's face shifted into a sort of snarl. His hand was already brushing the butt of his gun, but now his index finger began tracing circles on the stock.

"You have some nerve violating taboo, mister," he said.

Clint lowered his head about an inch and peered into the man's eyes. He was watching all three of the men, of course (each was fondling a gun), but the leader was the most important out of all of them. As the head of this particular beast went, so would its body.

Behind Clint, Edward began drinking from a trough. He wouldn't interfere unless Clint needed him, understanding that this was a matter of men.

"The trick to firing such big guns is to have big hands." Clint unclasped his hands, then held up his right in admiration. He did the same with his left. "But as to taboo, have you ever heard the rumors about how only a marshal can fire marshals' guns? Well, yar it's true."

"You ain't no marshal."

"What if I was? What if I was a rogue who left The Realm in search of... of better employment?"

"But you ain't," the man repeated.

"If I *were,* though," said Clint, the tiniest of smiles flirting with the corner of his mouth, "I'd be able to prove it. I'd be able to draw on you even if, say, my hands were up — like this! — and yours were on the butts of your guns. I'd be able to take you all down before your fingers found the triggers. And what's more — and this is just for example, you understand — I'd be able to brag to you about it first, and explain what I was about to do."

The man who'd called Edward a talking horse suddenly blurted, "You won't find no work with the boss if you kill us!"

The man beside him shot him a look, but the first man was undaunted. He hissed, *"Look at those hands!"*

"We'll go for a trick shot, then," said Clint. "Do you think you could fire a gun without a grip?"

The front man squinted. "What?"

Clint's hands dropped to his guns and drew. He raised them and fired each twice within a second, pulling both triggers at once. What sounded like two single shots rang out through the empty streets. He'd re-holstered both pistols before the first man's hands dropped to his side and found his gun handle missing. He'd have to hold a skinny metal protrusion with a few splinters clinging to it if he wanted to attempt to return fire.

Slowly, carefully, the lead bandit said, "You want to see the boss?"

"Later," said Edward, shoving his way past Clint and into the saloon without slowing. "I've been without food for a week, and right now, I want pie and brew. And because there can only be one brain to this outfit, what I want is what the marshal wants too."

The four men stared at Edward as if they'd never before seen a unicorn.

"That *is* what I want," said Clint as if the thought had just occurred to him.

He turned to follow Edward. After a few steps, though, he turned back and bored his cool blue eyes into the lead bandit's brown ones.

"You tell the boss that there's a new gun in town. *Two* new guns, in fact. Tell him that those guns would appreciate a chance to meet with him about a job." Then he shrugged, eying the remaining three men, all of whom were looking helplessly between Clint and the shattered handles of their revolvers.

"A man told me on the way in that this town was the sort of place where a man either gets rich or dead," said Clint. "And I aim to grab me a fistful of dollars."

CHAPTER FIVE:
TWO BOSSES

The barkeeper was a stocky man with a strangely jolly temperament, given the poison and dust that otherwise covered the town like a blanket. He wore a gigantic mustache and went by the name of Yardley.

Unlike the bandits outside, Yardley was totally unfazed by the sight of Edward squeezing his bulk between the saloon's batwing doors. Clint, however, fazed him. He saw the marshal, noted his two guns, and then greeted him like royalty, running from behind the bar to pull out a barstool for Clint to sit on. He nodded to Edward and smiled, offering to drag a mattress down from upstairs. Edward declined, so Yardley pushed several barstools out of the way to give Edward room to stand beside Clint at the bar.

Yardley had surely heard the shots outside, but he didn't seem to care. *Clint* was the one who entered the saloon, so clearly *Clint* had won whatever confrontation had occurred out front. And from that — from Yardley's gleeful greeting of a stranger who'd bested the town's bandits, Clint drew an expected conclusion: whoever this Dean fellow was, the townspeople didn't particularly like the feel of his thumb.

Yardley brought them brew and two full turkey pies. He poured Edward's brew into a bowl and made a small bow before apologizing that his barroom needed attending. He then busied himself behind them, wiping tables and chairs with a dry rag.

"Neat line you fed those fellows outside," Edward said to Clint. "So now we're going to work for the town boss?"

"Mayhap," said Clint. He'd already shoved half of the pie down his throat and was feeling both sick and, paradoxically, much, much better. "I really just want to meet him to get the sprawl of the land. I figure the 'rogue lawman in search of profit' story might be a good angle that will get us in without getting us killed. After all, the man who *runs* a town *knows* the town. He'll know where Kold is and what he's been up to. We'll be able to see if he's teaming up with Kold, or if Kold has recruited his men to help find the Orb. And we'll be able to see if Kold or Cerberus is possessing them... or doing whatever else a turned marshal can do."

"The men outside reacted to you as if they'd never even *seen* a marshal. Or a unicorn," said Edward.

Clint shrugged.

"You know who else usually knows the things that a stranger might want to know?"

Clint looked at Edward, his eyebrows up. In answer, Edward cocked his big white head toward the barkeeper.

Of course.

"Mister Yardley," said Clint, turning on his stool.

"Yar, sir!"

"Who is 'Dean'?"

Yardley stopped his cleaning. His eyes darted around the saloon, which was otherwise empty. Then he ran to the batwing doors and looked out and, once he'd satisfied himself that the bandits had left, returned to where Clint and Edward were sitting. He sidled behind the bar and poured himself a shot of something from a brown bottle. He downed it before speaking.

"Dean Dylan," Yardley whispered. "He's boss in this town. Well... one of the bosses."

"*One* of the bosses?"

"The other is the preacherman, Parson Jarmusch. And yar, a preacherman makes for a strange boss, but he's a boss, all right. You see, Dean Dylan is a very religious man. Dean was raised by the church as an orphan, then went bad in the convenient way that a religious man goes bad — which is to say that he stayed holy by attending services, but also began killing men and robbing caravans and organizing roving gangs, never seeing the opposites of his two lives' bucking horns. He thinks he's waving a ticket into NextWorld because he kneels and prays, rather a one-way pass to LowerWorld for all the souls he's dispatched. He's the most dangerous sort of man — one who does bad things with a clean conscience, thinking he's doing Providence's work."

"But how can the preacherman be a boss over a man like that?" said Clint.

Yardley gave an exasperated shrug as if Clint were being

exceptionally dim-witted. "Because the only way to hoist a bad man of faith — other than killing him, of course — is upon his faith itself. The parson is in his sixties and has known Dylan all his life, since he was dropped on the church's doorstep as a babe. Dylan runs the town, but Parson Jarmusch still has the power to tell him whether or not he's in Providence's good graces. And usually, because the parson is normally a good man with a level head, he tells Dylan that he *ain't* in good graces, and is headed straight for LowerWorld."

Clint nodded.

"Dylan controls the town, but Parson Jarmusch controls Dylan," Yardley continued. "Or at least, he keeps him on a leash. Ain't nobody *controls* Dylan. But because of that leash, they hate each other. The parson hates Dylan because Dylan is an evil man who kills and robs. Dylan hates the parson because the parson holds the power of NextWorld over his head. He can't bring himself to *not* believe the parson, and he can't bring himself to end the parson. That's how Dylan is. He's funny. The holy is in his bones like a cancer, and though he wants to cut it out, he can't. So he hates the parson, but he still listens to most every word the parson says. He would never draw on the man because it'd curse his soul."

Yardley sighed, looking around his empty bar.

"But as bad as that was, it's gotten worse. Used to be, Parson and Dylan squared off a fair share of sundowns but mostly held their calm. But over the past few weeks, something's gone sour. Soured even more than you'd think a two-boss town — a town where the common man ain't no boss even of himself, and can count on dying young and poor and defeated — would be *able* to sour."

"What happened a few weeks ago?" Edward asked, nodding for Yardley to refill his bowl with brew and his plate with pie.

"A man came through. I seen him. He was a marshal, like you. Rode a unicorn, too," he said, nodding at Clint and then Edward.

Clint almost jumped, "A few *weeks*?"

"Yar," said the barkeeper.

"I was afraid of that," said Edward, answering the question in Clint's eyes. "I felt another slip as we crossed the river. The cracks that used to be near the Edge? They're spreading to wherever the world is thin. Like it or not, it seems like Kold got a nice head start on us after all."

"Kold," said Yardley, nodding. "He's your man? Well yar, he looked *cold*, at that. He was somehow wrong. The air around here went bad the second he showed his face. And his unicorn weren't white, neither. It was black. And on the black horse, the man had a woman. She was all skin and bones and white as a sheet. Haunted and beaten. She sat freely behind the marshal, but her look was like she was tied. And your man, he went straight to Dean Dylan, like I heard you saying you were aiming to do. And after that, Dylan and his men both changed. For one, should anyone dare to ask them about the dark rider, they acted like they didn't know nothing at all, like they'd never even seen him. But they stopped their robbing and killing and hoarding, what were good at first, but then they started tearing the town to pieces. Storming into homes. Kicking people out into the street. Burning buildings. Rummaging through the bank and the store like they was looking for something."

Edward gave Clint a meaningful look. They'd seen this before. Dylan and his men were enchanted, as could be done to men of weak character. It wasn't as bad as what Cerberus was doing to Mai, but it came from twisted unicorn magic all the same.

"But that ain't all. Parson Jarmusch, he watched it and started speaking of the dark rider in his sermons, which of course Dylan attended. It was uncomfortable, since no one else would talk about the other, and nobody other than the parson would dare imply Dean Dylan was doing what another man told him to do. But Dylan was so erratic after the rider came to town that his hatred of the parson started to win out over his holiness. He confronted the parson. Beat him something fierce. And then the parson, who's supposed to be holy himself, didn't back down like you'd think an old man would. Instead, he started railing harder against Dylan and the rider, getting worse and worse. It's like something snapped inside of Parson Jarmusch. His sermons have gotten frightening. All about old-world vengeance. And because the parson has sway in the town, he started to do as Dylan did: he asked *his* people to rise up, and he formed his *own* little group, and though I don't blame him with Dylan being so newly violent toward him, it shocks me. The parson went from being a preacherman who could control the bad man to being something closer to an outlaw himself. I stopped going to his church and have been praying at home all week. It's becoming like a... a whatsit...?"

"A cult," said Edward. Clint looked over. He'd never heard the word, but he caught its meaning just fine.

"If that's what you call it," said Yardley, shrugging. "Whatever group it is that Parson Jarmusch has formed for himself, it behaves like a gang, and when Dylan's men started tearing up the town, Parson said he knew what they were looking for, though he wouldn't tell nobody what, and vowed to find it first... so that he could protect it from Dylan and the dark rider."

Clint exhaled as he pondered Yardley's story. He stabbed a piece of turkey pie with his fork.

"Two bosses," he said.
"And us in the middle," Edward replied.

CHAPTER SIX: RUMORS

Based on his encounter with the bandits outside the saloon and their subsequent reactions, Clint supposed he had an open appointment with Dean Dylan whenever he chose to take it. But because the dark rider had been his nemesis since before he was dark, Clint decided it might make more sense to find the parson first and attempt to enlist his group's help against Kold... hoping all the while that the adage "the enemy of my enemy is my friend" was true.

"The parson is not going to turn out to be your friend," Edward said as they left the saloon and walked down the high street toward the church. Strangely, the church wasn't under the bell. The town's bell was simply a bell, and they had a dedicated man to ring it. It made no sense to Clint, but he'd seen stranger things aplenty.

"How do you know?" said the gunslinger.

"He's a crazy holy man. You know many crazy holy men you'd want to sit with for brew?"

"Maybe the barman's perception isn't how things actually are," said Clint. "Or maybe Dylan's actions *drove* the parson to craziness. Maybe whatever he's doing is justified. I once heard a story about a pacifist who vowed revenge because doing so was righteous. This might be like that. It's a mistake to dismiss Parson Jarmusch as useless without at least talking to him."

The unicorn sighed, knowing better than to argue.

A few minutes later, they arrived at a barricaded church. Edward gave Clint a look, silently asking if he thought a barricaded church seemed normal and friendly. Clint ignored him and knocked, and after a few minutes (and a few repeated knocks), a short man with a bald head and wearing a white robe opened the door. There had been much noise and clanking prior to the door opening, which seemed to suggest that he'd just unlocked many bolts and moved some furniture away from the door.

"Are you Parson Jarmusch?" asked Clint.

"Providence, no," said the man. His tone sounded affronted, almost offended. "I'm Parson Willick." He extended a tiny, pudgy hand. Clint shook it. His giant gunslinger's hand swallowed the parson's like a goliath spider encompassing prey.

"Where is Jarmusch?"

Willick sighed — a gesture that took over his whole body. "I have no idea, marshal. Have you come to arrest him?"

"Arrest him?" said Clint. He shook his head. "Nar, I'm not the law proper here. Don't you have a sheriff or a marshal of your own?"

"Yar," said Willick. "He's out in Ever Rest Cemetery, under a nice gray headstone with a star at the top. His deputies didn't get such nice sendoffs. They are in the woods somewhere, but we're not sure where exactly. Nobody — not even the deputies' widows — had the guts to ask Mr. Dylan where he disposed of them." Willick shook his head, which seemed as heavy as a saddle. It was a gesture of resignation, as if he'd completely lost faith — in law, order, Providence, basic decency, and apparently his fellow parson.

Clint could tell how loose Willick's lips already were, and knew how to make them looser. The man had a story to tell, probably because nobody else would listen. But before Clint could say anything, Willick jumped as if stuck with a pin. He extended his arm into the church, apparently realizing how rude he was being to his guests.

Clint started to follow Willick's arm, but the small parson held up a hand to gently stop him.

"If you don't mind, Marshal, I'd like to extend my invitation to enter to your friend first," he said.

The small man looked directly into Edward's eye, side-on as if he were used to conversing with equines. And then, after a quiet moment, Edward blinked his big blue eyes and did something Clint had only seen him do once before: the unicorn bowed his head.

Edward followed Willick's arm into the church. Clint followed. Then Willick climbed over a pew that was resting on its back near the door and secured four separate locks, barricading them inside.

"Used to be, we'd never dream of locking this sanctuary, but times have changed," said Willick with a shake of his head. "You saw how I thought you were here to arrest Jarmusch? Well, watch me betray my fellow clergy even further: the parson *deserves* locking up,

Marshal. You'll see that I've locked the door against him."

Clint frowned. The door to the church was locked against *its parson?* Clint had assumed that the precautions were in place against Dylan, or against Kold.

"When did you do this?" Clint asked.

"Two weeks ago. The change in him was so dramatic and so rapid that at first I failed to believe he might be a threat — even after some of the things he'd said, and some of the measures he seemed willing to take against the newly heinous actions of Dean Dylan and his men. He used to be a calm man, but he's different now. He stood right here, at the altar, and told the assembly that you couldn't be afraid to get your hands a little dirty when it came to fighting evil. So he told the assembly to arm themselves, and beseeched them to march out with him to the rancho at the edge of town to take on Dylan's men. He did this *here*. In a place of *worship*." The parson shook his head.

"So you locked the doors?" said Edward.

"He was gathering followers like a madman gathers lost souls. When I told him to leave — that it was my church too, and that it was Providence's church above all — he grew furious. He broke things. He threw whatever he could find. He grabbed one of the tall candlesticks and came at me. Some big, sturdy men in the assembly pulled him outside, and since then, yes, I've been locking the doors." He shrugged, extending a hand toward the multiple locks.

"Question for you, then, parson," said Clint. "Who would you rather have after you and in your town — Dean Dylan and his men, or the new and unimproved Parson Jarmusch?"

"Impossible to say. Providence help me, I fear and hate them both. The rancho that I mentioned? This town used to be prosperous, and we used to have our own small breed of magic royalty here. They once lived on a huge and beautiful stretch of land at the edge of our borders called the Rancho Encantato. Guess what happened to them when Dylan got old enough to carry a gun and get people to follow him? He saw what he wanted and took it. This town used to bloom, Marshal. I believe even your people —" He looked at Edward. "— even consider this place to be of some magical significance?"

Edward nodded.

"Well," Willick continued, "you see how Precipice is today. How it's been for years under Dylan's rule. Law can't bloom here any more than a wet palm can bloom in dry soil. And since that stranger came to town… well, it's grown so much worse."

"The barkeeper told us about a dark rider on a unicorn of a different color," said Clint.

Willick nodded, shifting his gaze between the two of them. "Yar.

A black unicorn. I'm versed enough to know more or less what that must mean. The dark rider went to the darkest part of town, straight to the Dylan gang's abode. I think he spellbound them. They don't remember the rider, if you can believe that. They only know they have to kill more and destroy more and... and apparently *search* for something. Do you want to know what I think? I think this all has to do with black magic."

"It does," said Edward. "But Jarmusch? You think that what's happened to him is due to black magic?"

Willick looked around the empty church as if deciding whether or not he should admit to something, then seemed to figure that the not-quite-legal marshal and the white unicorn were the best he was going to get when it came to confidants.

"There are rumors," said Willick. "Very, very, *very* old rumors. Rumors so old nobody believes they have nar any truth. The rumors speak of this town as a holy place. They say there's something here that can never be taken, though it *can* indeed be taken and used to do terrible things by the proper dark soul. They say our magic royalty were guardians of that thing, and that when they were murdered, the secret they guarded went with them. Dylan, who doesn't put much stock in legends, searched the rancho when he first took it over, then settled into being a common thief and killer. But when the rider arrived, we heard noises from the rancho that sounded like Dylan's gang were tearing it in half. Then the dark rider left, and last I heard he was searching an old copper mine outside of town, leaving Dylan's men to do his work in Precipice. That's around the time Parson Jarmusch grew truly obsessed with stopping Dylan. I think at first it was a noble, holy errand in his mind like a halo on his head — to stop Dylan from finding whatever the dark rider had tasked him with finding. But then the air's black magic infected Jarmusch. I think he quit trying to stop Dylan out of righteousness, and instead started trying to stop Dylan in order to take the black magic for himself."

A beat of silence held Clint and Edward's consideration.

"Where is Jarmusch now?" the gunslinger finally said.

"I hear he started a new church with his followers — followers who are more like an army than a holy assembly, armed and willing to do whatever their leader asks. They're said to meet in the old town hall. There hasn't been any need for the town hall for years around here anyhow, seeing as there's no law."

"And yet," said Edward, looking with respect at the small parson, "*you* have stayed."

Willick shrugged. "There are people even in the darkest places who need someone to help them keep hoping."

"And do those people still attend your services, since the rider arrived and Jarmusch tipped?"

Willick gestured into the sanctuary. "It's Sunday, and my pews are empty," he said. "Just as there are always people who need hope, so is there a limit to hope's allowance."

Edward, who seemed to command Willick's respect, took a step forward. "What if I told you that you could yet make a difference?" he said.

"What do you have in mind?" Willick asked.

Edward told him.

CHAPTER SEVEN: DOWN TO BUSINESS

After parting company with Parson Willick, Clint and Edward walked side-by-side down the center of Providence's main street. Willick had told them that the street headed directly toward the bank, then curved to the left and sloped gently downward for a winding half mile until it finally dead-ended at the Rancho Encantato, where Dean Dylan and his men made headquarters.

The rancho itself was enormous, sprawling for untold acres, but Clint and Edward could see from a long distance that most of those acres had gone to scrub and desert. Back in the days when the rancho harbored magic owners, those magicians might have been able to provide water for crops or magically cause their land to blossom, but between the magic owners' departure and the negligent Dylan gang's arrival, everything seemed to have fallen into disrepair. There were three sheds and a barn that Clint and Edward could see, and the roofs had caved in on all three. One additional structure seemed to have been burned. There were skeletons of what might once have been livestock in the fenced yards, now free to roam if they wished because the fences had been felled by wind, wanton behavior, or other forms of destruction.

The main house, where the gang made its beds, was in far better shape. It was three stories tall, making it taller than any building in Precipice's town center. Clint and Edward had a long time to study the house as they approached because it was huge enough to be visible well before they arrived at its door. Clint counted twenty-six windows across the front on one level alone, many of them large picture windows. The rancho wore the look of an old estate that had been curiously unbrushed by time.

The appearance of harmony started to vanish as they drifted closer. The house itself was old and classic, but its front yard was studded with dead machines made of a new-looking alloy that gleamed like diamonds in the sun. The largest alloy object had a huge handle that gleamed so fiercely that it seemed to be generating its own light. The gunslinger and unicorn were forced to squint, shielding their eyes to see past it. The estate was covered in white split-rail fences, and had a manual well with a bucket wound to the top just like the town's well — except that the base of this one was made from a shiny silver substance that looked like crinkled minerals. The front door of the house was a quaint ranch red, but the accent color was repeated in strange arches and angles that protruded whimsically from the structure. Clint's eyes, which were sharp, even picked out flashing lights on a contraption mounted to the rancho's side wall. It almost looked like something from The Realm — a sort of spark pack that might once have powered a thinking machine.

Clint's eyes picked out something else while they were cresting the final hill, too, but Edward was first to mention it.

"They're watching us," he said.

"I see them," Clint said, nodding. He'd been watching the drapes shift for several minutes. He also thought he might have seen the glint of reflected light up ahead, from the lens of a spyglass.

"Should we approach in some way other than walking straight at the front door?"

"Of course not," said Clint, still marching. "I earned my invitation."

Edward gave an annoyed grunt. "The suspense is killing me."

Edward was being sarcastic, but Clint was indeed beginning to find their march tiresome. The approach to the ranch was so long that the house had been in front of them for over fifteen minutes and didn't seem to be drawing closer. He could feel the eyes of Dylan's gang on them, and it annoyed the gunslinger that the men inside probably thought they were being subtle and sly. He wanted to let them know he wasn't fooled if nothing else, and to get the meeting underway as quickly as possible.

"I'll bet I can rush it along," said Clint. "Watch this."

He drew his right gun, sighted, and fired a single shot.

The ranch was easily five hundred yards distant. The best Sands rifleman couldn't have hit the house (let alone hit it accurately), but Clint was a marshal, and even the best riflemen didn't use a marshal's gunpowder or have Realm rifling in their barrels.

There was what appeared to be a tiny puff at the front door and, a few seconds delayed, the sound of splintering wood. Immediately, the door was thrown open and a man began sprinting toward them, yelling, waving his hands above his flopping hair. It took several minutes for the man to arrive, but when he did, Clint saw that it was one of the bandits from in front of the saloon. He was holding a huge metal mug with a bullet hole through both sides.

"Wait! Wait!" the man shouted. "Don't shoot!"

Clint was still holding his pistol, more because he liked the feel of it in his hand than because he had any intent to use it again. He looked at the shouting man, amused, then re-holstered the sidearm.

"We're expecting y'all!" the man shouted. "No harm. Friends! You want a job and we have one, pleasem and thankoo. Come yonder." He tried to smile, but the smile was too large and looked about as carved on his face as one on a statue. "We could use a man like you, yes sir. Let's ride up to the house together, what d'ya say? I'm beat. Think your horse could handle two riders?"

This was the wrong thing to say. Edward lowered his head and, without hesitation, directed a fierce purple flash at the bandit. The bolt struck him in the chest and he flew sideways, perpendicular to the ranch road, as if flung from a catapult. He struck a six-inch tree, sheering it clear in half. Then there was a second flash from Edward's horn — this one yellow — and the man groaned and rolled over.

"Don't worry," Edward mumbled. "If I didn't plan to fix his back, I wouldn't have broken it."

Clint said nothing as they marched past the moaning bandit, never breaking their gaze from the house.

"He had a point, though. May I ride?"

Edward sighed. "Fine."

Edward broke into a trot and arrived at the house a minute or two later. The bandit had left the door (with its bullet hole) open, and Clint noticed a strange seal around the door's edge that glowed with an odd light. *Techem*, he thought. *This is Realm magic — the sort that isn't actually magic at all.*

"I can't fit through that door," said Edward, staring at the rancho's entrance.

Clint dismounted, and, in deference to Edward's inability to enter the house, sat down on a white-painted metal chair beside what used to be a garden. He turned the chair so that it faced the house and then leaned back contentedly with his legs crossed, looking up at the windows as if the house were a stage show. He pulled two apples from his pack — rather extravagant gifts from Parson Willick — and handed one to Edward. He began to munch the other, taking huge bites and letting the sweet juice spill down his chin.

They waited.

A few minutes later, when it became apparent that the new arrivals wouldn't be entering the house, a large man with broad shoulders stepped through the open door and stood in front of them. He pulled a chair from the garden for himself, then turned it around so that he was facing the gunslinger and the unicorn.

"You're quite a gun," said the man after a few long seconds.

Clint took a bite of his apple.

"It's nice that you have skills and all, and believe me, I want us to be friends," the man continued. "But at the same time, I don't want you forgetting who's boss of this town. And that's *me*, Dean Dylan."

"Seems to be some debate on who runs this town," said Clint.

"Right now," Dylan continued, "there are no fewer than ten guns trained on you. You might be able to find and disable most of 'em, but I guarantee that if you do anything funny, one of those bullets will take you down."

"If he does anything *funny*," said Edward, "rest assured you'll find yourself laughing uncontrollably."

Dylan ignored him. "Are we clear?"

"Because he's so hilarious," Edward clarified. "I mean, just look at him."

Dylan looked at Clint's long, ugly face. He was sitting back with his legs crossed, chewing his apple. He took a bite and said, "A man walks into a bar. Next time, he ducks."

Edward raised his eyebrows at Dylan. "See?"

"I said, *'Are we clear.'*"

"And if he tries anything *dangerous*," Edward continued, still ignoring the question, "you'll be dead."

Clint made a gun out of his right index finger and thumb, pulled the imaginary trigger at his host, and said, "Boo!"

A chorus of loud mechanical clicks came from around them like clockwork cicadas. That would be at least ten guns being cocked, Clint thought, and the man was right — he couldn't see them all. He could make out four or five men without turning his head, but no more.

Clint gave a wry smile, then leaned forward, uncrossing his legs, and put the heels of his palms on his knees. Juice from the apple still clasped in his hand dripped into the dirt.

"Yar, we're clear about that," said Clint. "But another thing to be clear about is that my friend and I are here because we *want* to be here. Your men seem to think my friend is a horse. And they don't seem to have ever met a marshal. I've given them ten percent of what I have, and Edward here, save that one unfortunate fellow further up the hill, has given them none of what he has. So let's dispense with you pretending to be the big man, and if you'd like, you may pretend that if you tried to kill me right now, you might succeed. And then, with all of that aside, let's talk business."

"Business?"

"Dollars," said Clint.

"How many dollars?"

"As many as you can afford. See, I left a lot behind when I turned my back to the wall. There's a lot I'm accustomed to, and I ride with a bounty on my head. I have valuable skills, and I deserve to be paid well by the right employer."

"Maybe I don't need you."

"I think you do," said Clint. "You have a problem with your friend the parson. I assume you've heard what he's up to?"

Pause.

"Yar," said Dylan finally. "He's gone around the bend a bit."

"You've known the parson for years. Apparently, you've had your troubles with him."

"Everyone knows that."

"Thinking of the man you know, can you believe that he's lost his mind so entirely? And can you imagine *why* he might lose his grip on reality and on control? He attacked the church; did you know that? It's true. I've spoken to Parson Willick, who these days locks his doors to Jarmusch. Willick says Jarmusch is building an army of armed men who will do whatever he says."

"I have that situation in hand," said Dylan.

"You're missing the point," said Clint. "What matters isn't his army. What matters is what might cause a good, kind-hearted, pacifist of a parson to build an army in the first place."

Dylan looked at Clint. "I don't know what you're talking about," he said, both eyes singing a different song.

"You're looking for something," said Edward. "You're searching the town for a dark magical object that is desired by the dark rider."

Dylan said nothing, but his unshifted expression implied agreement. At least Dylan himself knew who was actually in charge in Precipice.

"But despite all that looking, you haven't found what you seek," Edward continued.

Again, Dylan said nothing.

"So I ask again," said Clint. "Can you think of anything that might turn a quiet parson so bad, so fast?"

Dylan chewed at his lip. "You're saying that *he* found the dark object we've been looking for?"

"What we're saying," said Edward, "is that *if* he's found it, you don't have a needle's chance in sand of fighting him and taking it back before the dark rider returns. So here we are — a gunslinger with fast hands and a unicorn bursting with white magic — for hire."

Dylan stared from Clint to Edward. Edward to Clint.

"So," said Clint, spreading his arms and leaning back in his garden chair. "Let's talk business."

CHAPTER EIGHT:
BLACK CHURCH

Edward said, "He's sitting on it."

They were in the cleared hollow of an abandoned house on the far opposite side of the town from the Rancho Encantato, a half mile outside of what passed for the city limits. The house had a barn, but Edward, who refused to bunk like a common horse, had blown out a crumbling wall of the ramshackle structure and magicked several bales' worth of straw inside to lay on. Then he'd made himself comfortable on the floor, looking extremely horselike (though Clint would never say it) as he rolled back and forth, his heavy hooves swaying in the air and crashing back down onto the wooden planks. Clint lay on what had once been a padded bench along the opposite wall.

Both gunslinger and unicorn looked tired. They'd set out from the Rancho with a wad of Dylan's cash and with the intention of going directly to find Parson Jarmusch, but they'd detoured here instead out of exhaustion and by unspoken mutual consent. Edward said it seemed that they were always walking, carrying palavers with their six feet still moving. From Solace to the Edge to the Dinosaur Missouri to Precipice, it felt like all they'd done for the three years on Kold's tepid trail was to *walk*. They'd had their stay-over with the Leisei family, but Clint said that didn't really count, seeing as he was sick at the time, and everything had ended in death.

They'd stopped at the house because they wanted a place of their own to rest their weary bones... just for a while.

Clint longed for the stability he'd felt in Solace prior to Hassle Stone and Kold's arrival. He also longed for the emotional security he'd nearly felt with Mai, and which he hoped he'd one day feel in full once he and Mai had been properly hitched. On the day of their intended hitching back in Solace, it had struck Clint how strange it felt to feel happy. Now, soul-tired, he missed that strange happy feeling. He'd been so blinded by vengeance and rage over the past three years that he'd grown calluses on his heart. Still, deep down Clint longed for Mai, for the hitching, and for the life he wondered if he'd ever have.

"What do you mean, 'He's sitting on it'?" Clint asked.

The unicorn's giant white form dominated the floor of the small, broken-down house. He replied without lifting his head. "I mean that Dean Dylan sits on what he seeks," he said. "The Orb of Malevolence is at the Rancho. Couldn't you feel it?"

"Nar."

"I know you're not magic, but... *wow*," Edward said. "I could barely speak for the power I felt there."

"So why did Cerberus lead Kold to the mine outside of town that Willick mentioned, if its presence at the Rancho is so obvious?" Clint said.

"I don't know. Perhaps he's clouded by the perversion he is perpetrating on Mai. Or perhaps because this is the Orb of *Malevolence*, its power is less obvious to Cerberus, who radiates a stupendous amount of malevolence of his own. That would make feeling the Orb like trying to hear a coin hit the ground in a room filled with the blasting of Joelsongs. But regardless, it's obvious that none of Dylan's gang knows it's there. They're randomly tearing through Precipice as if they have nothing to lead them."

Clint nodded. "So we bust our way in. We search. We find the Orb. And then we take it, before they realize it's under their noses."

Edward rolled halfway up, now in the equine version of a sit. Then, because he was never comfortable in a half-laying position, he rolled up to his feet. He looked down at Clint, who was still on the couch.

"That may not be a good idea. Malevolence breeds malevolence. I know you could feel the men's menace when we were there."

"Yar," said Clint. "That, I felt."

"There are dozens of his gang there. They have a whole house to hide in, and they're being influenced by a dark force they don't understand. That's making them jumpier, angrier, and deadlier than they'd be otherwise. We could take them in an open area, but attacking them in that house would be like attacking bees in a hive. We also don't know exactly where the Orb rests, which means that we will need time to search for it." He shook his head. "No, we need to get them out of there."

Clint stood, checked his guns, and shrugged. "We were on our way to see the parson, so let's do that," he said. And then, with no preamble and without consulting Edward, he rose, stepped through the open end of the house, and hooked back onto the road leading into Precipice. Edward trotted behind until he caught up.

Ten minutes later, they found themselves standing in front of the town hall, which they wouldn't have recognized as such if Parson Willick hadn't told them exactly where it was.

The town hall had pillars and official-looking architecture, but beyond that, it seemed nothing like a house of government. The building gave off an intimidating odor of decay, and it looked as if it had been burned in a fire that hadn't managed to destroy a plank of the actual structure. Its facade was black, covered in what appeared to be soot. And, Clint thought, that soot had come from a peculiar sort of non-fire, because the structures to each side — a bank and the courthouse, which Clint used to confirm it was indeed the building Willick had described — were dusty but otherwise untouched by whatever had struck the town hall.

"This looks promising, for a church," said Edward. "I'd totally worship here."

Clint rubbed his forefinger along a column at the building's front. His finger came away black, and the lighter hue of the building's wood grew visible in a streak where the gunslinger had wiped it clean. Clint sniffed it.

"This is what's creating the odor we smell," he said. "It smells burnt, but a fire would have destroyed the building."

Edward made a disgusted face. "I think the fire killed a million eggs."

"Sulfur," said Clint.

"Brimstone," said a third voice.

Clint looked up, his hand flying toward his right gun, and saw a tall, gaunt stranger standing in the town hall's doorway. Clint hadn't seen or heard him approach, yet he was only fifteen feet off. Clint's eyes went to Edward and the unicorn gave a silent reply: *I didn't know he was there either.* Clint didn't like to be sneaked up on and hadn't been often, seeing as doing so was nearly impossible.

"Brimstone," the man repeated. "The dark rider's curse did it, to brand us with a black mark."

He was dressed in a long white robe much like Parson Willick's, though he was unlike Willick in every other way. Willick was short and bald. This man was tall, with a full head of wavy gray hair. Willick was fat, and the man in the doorway rail thin. Willick was young with a rosy, water-fat complexion. This man was older and dried out, like he'd been left in the sun.

"Parson Jarmusch?" said Clint.

"Yar," the man said, then made no further measure of greeting. He simply stood in the doorway, gazing more directly into Clint's eyes than a gunslinger would normally tolerate from a man who wished to keep breathing. His gaze was an assessing one. It seemed as if he didn't like Clint and resented his presence, but hadn't yet reckoned how to wipe him away.

"We'd like a palaver," said Clint.

"Fine," said Jarmusch, unmoving. Clint could see past him through the open door. The entire entranceway was covered with soot, as was the front of the hall, yet there wasn't so much as a smudge on Jarmusch's pristine white robe. Clint wondered how he could possibly move around inside a building so covered in grime without soiling a garment so white.

"May we come in?" said Clint.

"Nar. This is a holy place."

"You mean '*Holy c…*'" Edward started to say.

Clint cut him off. "But this is the town hall. It's a public building, is it not?"

"It is not," said Jarmusch. "We've not had law in Precipice for decades. The town hall and courthouse have invited the elements for years. When I was cast from the church along with my flock, we were forced to find a new place for our work and our worship. We settled here, where only the faithful may enter."

"I'm plenty faithful, Parson," said Clint.

"New days require new degrees of faithfulness," said Jarmusch. He said nothing more, still staring directly at Clint with wide-open eyes before shifting his gaze to Edward.

"You have fantastic stage presence," said Edward. "Have you ever considered a career in puppetry?"

Clint let it go, relieved that the unicorn hadn't gone for the more obvious joke of offering the parson a tithe, then pooping in the street as his offering.

"No offense, Parson," said Clint, "but we've heard around town that you've been conducting black mass over here. People fear you."

"Might they should," said Jarmusch. "In the old books, Providence was vengeful and full of wrath. My old church — Willick's now — was soft. We tried things that way for years, and in answer, we watched as Dean Dylan took what he wanted from this town. Tell me, Marshal," he said, looking at Clint's twin guns, "what would you do in my shoes? Would you continue to preach pacifism, promising lies, saying Providence would protect the flock if they remained weak? Or would you take up arms and do what had to be done?"

It was a good question. Clint found himself unable to disagree with the parson's direction.

"A dark rider came into town a few weeks back," Jarmusch continued. "I know you know that. I could feel you behind him before you were separated by a time slip, as sure as I could feel the dark rider himself. He is evil incarnate, and his mount is a wellspring of the darkest magic. This was once a holy place, this town, and there's something in it that they want. That something has long been lost, but the rider enchanted Dylan and his men, and they now all seek it without knowing why. They *will* find it, and when they do, it will be the end of days for all of us. So I ask you: am I so troublesome and frightening in my desire to prevent the end, even if I'm willing to do it by any means necessary?"

Clint chewed his cheek, looking at Edward. "So do it," he finally said.

"Do what?"

"Storm the Rancho Encantato. Do what's necessary. Take out Dean and his men. You say you want to fight evil, but according to what we've heard and seen, all you've done is bunker into a black building and keep on with your preaching."

"And you're incredibly creepy," Edward added.

Jarmusch, not softening, shook his head. "They're too many, and they have the dark rider behind them. Even you couldn't defeat the dark marshal and his unicorn of a different color."

It was true. The best Clint and Edward could hope against Cerberus and Kold would be a stalemate, and that was their best-case scenario. But then Clint remembered something: for the time being, Cerberus and Kold were gone from the picture. He saw an opening.

"The dark rider is out of town, searching an old mine," he told Jarmusch.

"There are still too many men."

"Not for us," said Edward.

Jarmusch seemed to consider. He looked from the gunslinger to the unicorn, thoughtful.

"You would help our righteous cause? You would help to vanquish evil with your white magic, and protect the object the dark rider seeks?"

"Of course," said Clint, his head slightly tilted. "For a price."

CHAPTER NINE: MOVING PIECES

After leaving Parson Jarmusch, Clint insisted on detouring by Willick's church. When they arrived, Clint knocked on the large doors, but no one came to answer. Shrugging, he pulled the yellow envelope Jarmusch had given him from an inside pocket and transferred its contents to the much larger envelope of cash that Dylan had given him. He took enough money from the ponderous stack to buy himself and Edward vittles for a few weeks, tucked the spare cash deep into his bag, and shoved the bulging envelope through a slot beneath the church door for Willick to find later.

This done — and with stunningly little commentary from Edward on the futility of charity — they retraced their path back to the Rancho Encantato.

They found Dylan on the front porch, his massive form crammed into a tiny rocking chair. He had a drink by his side as if he had been spending his day in an idyllic paradise sipping lemonsweet. Dylan had removed his gun to squeeze into the chair and was spinning it idly on his finger when Clint arrived on Edward's back.

"What color smoke comes from those guns?" said Clint when he saw them.

"White," said Dylan, setting his gun on the chair's arm. "Is that a serious question?"

"I've not done research on the matter, and was curious," said Clint. "I seldom see gunsmoke other than my own." He hopped to the dirt, but didn't approach.

"Have you done your job?" said Dylan.

"Not yet. We must wait for the parson to return from an errand.

We'll be waiting when he does."

Dylan stood. He'd been wedged quite tightly into the small chair, so the chair rose with him, only falling back into place on the deck once Dylan was mostly standing. The chair was heavy, and a leg broke when it struck the deck's planking.

"His *errand*?" Dylan said.

To see what it felt like, Clint unholstered one of his own guns and twirled it on his finger. Despite his dexterity with a pistol, the motion felt clunky and uncomfortable. His guns also didn't have safeties, and he feared pressure on the trigger might cause the gun to fire. He put it back.

"We arrived at his little black church to find it empty," said Clint. "The Parson and his army of fanatics were gone. But don't worry. They'll be back. Edward sniffed out their magic trail. He could tell where they went, and when they were likely to return."

This was pure fabrication. Edward couldn't trail people's intentions like a magic bloodhound, but Dylan and his men didn't know that. Clint could make up whatever he wanted. When they'd rehearsed earlier, Edward kept petitioning to insert a "boogie boogie" into the conversation to demonstrate how mystical and magical he was, but Clint struck it down, insisting that it was over the top.

Dylan's face appeared disturbed. "Where did they go?"

"It's nar a problem," said Clint, attempting to twirl his second gun with his other hand with no better luck. "They'll be back tomorrow. Edward could read their... intention?" He looked at Edward, who nodded subtly. "... on the sand. And it's a quick thing that Jarmusch is doing. Boom-boom-boom — almost literally, seeing as their intention involves violence. Nar that we care. The more of 'em die out there, the fewer we have to kill back here. Maybe the Parson himself will lay killt by sundown. Chop off the head and you kill the body, and all that."

"Sands," Dylan muttered. He turned and pressed keys on a small alloy pad near the ranch entrance. The door opened, and Dylan yelled for someone inside to come out. He turned to Clint and repeated his question: "Where did they go?"

"An old mine outside of town. He found a foe out there, or something. Edward reads... wrath? ... in the sand."

"Boogie boogie," said Edward.

Clint shot the unicorn a look, then turned back to Dylan. "He doesn't know the what or the why of the errand, but he does know that there was an awful hurry behind it, and an equal hurry to return."

"And when they do, we will be waiting," said Edward, to put a finer point on the matter.

Dylan spun himself into a tizzy on the rancho's long porch, checking and holstering his weapon several times as if by compulsion. One of his men emerged from the house (a man Clint hadn't seen before), and Dylan shouted for the new man to rally the others. He shouted that they had five minutes to ready themselves, and that any man who failed to get ready in that time would be shot.

"What's going on?" said Clint.

"Copper mine out by the old magic-sifter, right?"

Clint shrugged.

Dylan looked furious and panicked. He stabbed a finger into the distance, past the ranch. "That way, dagnit! Is that where he's going?"

Edward's horn glowed. He followed Dylan's finger, then feigned a magical sort of trance and took his time to reply. Dylan's eyes remained fixed on the unicorn.

Finally, his voice heavy with drama, Edward said, "Yar. A copper mine. And I see a magic-sifter that was abandoned before."

"SANDS!" Dylan roared.

"What?" said Clint.

"Look, all you need to know is that there's going to be a scuffle. I paid you well, Marshal. Are you a man of your word?"

"Of course," said Clint.

"Then ride. Follow your unicorn's... *sense*. Ride fast. If you see the parson or his men, start killing them. No need to be picky over who you shoot."

"But they'll be back tomorrow," said Clint. Even spreading his naiveté thick, Dylan was too panicked about a potential Kold/ Jarmusch dust-up over the Orb to see through Clint's lie. Men poured from the rancho and streamed toward the barn, pulling horses from stalls already saddled and swinging onto their backs. Dylan ran around rallying them with big circles of his right arm.

He turned to Clint. *"Just ride!"* he screamed.

Clint's eyes followed Dylan's finger. Then Edward complied, and began running as fast as he could.

Once they were out of sight, the unicorn stopped, caught his breath, and said, "Hold onto your hat, Mary."

His horn started sparking and popping as if pressed against a spinning grindstone. The world went black, and when the darkness cleared, they were once again in front of the town hall. Edward collapsed. Clint managed to avoid being crushed by his falling bulk, having hopped deftly to the side.

Jarmusch was on the porch and saw it all happen — the unicorn and gunslinger arriving from nowhere with Edward in a heap. They hadn't staged the collapse; Edward was simply fried, as always occurred after a folding. But watching the big white unicorn fall had a nice effect on the parson, whose creepy and disinterested expression fell from his face as Clint ran toward him.

"They've found it!" Clint gasped, making long, clumsy strides toward the steps of the town hall, staring up at Jarmusch with what he hoped was a desperate expression. The gunslinger didn't have much experience in the dramatic arts, so it was possible he might simply appear constipated.

"Found what?" said the parson.

"What they've been searching for!" Clint yelled up at the man in white. Then, because his story required validation, he ad-libbed something the parson hadn't mentioned the last time they'd spoken. "I heard them say something about an orb. 'He's found the orb,' Dylan shouted to a group of men as they rode off. We arrived right as the house was going empty. The men were leaping onto horses and storming off —" The gunslinger looked around for his bearings, then pointed. "— in *that* direction."

Jarmusch jumped. It satisfied Clint to see him react after so much posturing.

"The mine!" Jarmusch blurted. "That's the direction of the old mine where the dark rider has been searching!" Jarmusch ran into the town hall, then back out. Just as had happened at the rancho, activity swarmed behind him. People began to rise and run inside of what Clint had suspected might be an entirely empty hall. But it wasn't empty at all. Based on the stirring crowds he could see, Clint figured there might be fifty or more armed people inside.

As Jarmusch's followers poured into the street — all of them with sallow, drugged expressions painting their faces — Clint saw that there were both men and women among them. One woman, probably in her seventies, had a giant gray hairdo. She was stooped and held a shotgun, a downright terrifying expression across her wrinkled features.

"How long ago did they leave?" said Jarmusch.

"Seconds," gasped Edward from the dirt, still recovering. "I can travel instantly between spots a certain distance apart, but I pay a price to do so. We just left them."

The parson looked off in the direction of the mine, then in the direction of the rancho. His eyes dilated with calculation. The mine was more or less straight out from where they were standing, but Dylan's men would need to take an angled approach to reach the same spot from the rancho. If both posses left at the same time and rode at the same speed, the group leaving from the town hall would get there first.

Edward lay motionless in the dirt. Clint stood at the foot of the steps, affecting an air of concern. The parson ran inside and grabbed a gun belt, which he strapped over top of his clergy robe in what had to be the most ridiculous display of gunfightership Clint had ever seen. Still, the pistol in his holster gleamed as if it had been polished to a sheen, had been well-oiled, and had been fired regularly.

The parson's dull-eyed followers began to flow around them, finding mounts to ride off into battle. They even looked like churchgoers — some of the women in flowered hats — but all of them carried or wore guns. It was a hard and determined-looking group, unforgiving despite their finery.

A man in dusty slacks and a pressed shirt brought a brown horse to Jarmusch. The parson mounted and, from the saddle, called to Clint.

"You will follow?" he said.

"As soon as my unicorn has recovered," Clint replied.

"I need pie," Edward gasped. Clint looked over. The gunslinger had dropped his pack as he'd leapt from the unicorn's back, and there had been a slice of turkey pie near the top of the bag. Clint could no longer see the pie. He suspected Edward had eaten it, was already mostly recovered, and was now doing a poor impression of a swooning dramatic actor.

Jarmusch looked for a moment as if he wasn't sure whether Clint and Edward were speaking true. But then he spurred his mount and the horse and rider ran off, Jarmusch holding the reins with surprising competence for a church man in his sixties.

CHAPTER TEN: ZAP!

They found Parson Willick at the church, exactly where he was supposed to be. This time, Clint didn't have to knock. They were barely at the steps when the doors swung wide and the short, bald preacher greeted them with what Clint suspected was the first genuine smile the man had worn for years.

"I saw you coming," he said.

"And you heard the hooves of Jarmusch's others as they rode out to the mine?" said Clint.

"Yar. And I stand ready now to do what I can."

Clint had left a note for Willick inside the envelope of cash that briefly explained what he aimed to do with the day. It wasn't much of a departure from the plan they had laid after first meeting him; details and times had simply been added. And so when they arrived, the pastor was already prepared. In one hand he held an oversized shotgun that was almost as long as Willick was tall. In the other was a sledgehammer.

"What we're after has managed to remain hidden for time eternal," Willick explained, hefting the sledgehammer. "I can assure you, we'll need to smash something to get at it."

"True," said Edward, "but I have five implements that are much more powerful." He stomped his hooves. His horn glowed.

Willick shrugged and set the sledgehammer inside the door of the church beside a long brass candle snuffer. The two implements looked odd together, and Clint wondered if that was where the hammer had always been stored. He got a sudden mental image of the stocky priest lighting candles during a church service, then pulverizing a watermelon like an ancient Realm funnyman whose name he couldn't recall.

"And that?" said Clint, gesturing toward the shotgun.

"For leftover bandits," said Willick. "I've lived in Precipice long enough without raising a finger. Maybe there's a bit of Jarmusch in me after all."

"Wouldn't you prefer something smaller?" the gunslinger asked, referring to the gun.

"Precipice is *plenty* small," said Willick, referring to the town.

Clint shrugged. If the parson wanted to lug an eylifant gun on their errand, it was none of his affair to say otherwise.

Once Willick had closed and locked the church doors, the two men prepared to climb onto Edward's back. The parson, however, was too small to climb up by himself, so Edward magicked him up. Then, to spare Willick his dignity, he magicked Clint on as well, as if this were the normal way things were done. Then the unicorn ran.

It took ten minutes to reach the Rancho Encantato. It bothered Clint to spend the minutes (they didn't have long before the parties at the mine saw the ruse and returned, probably with Kold and Cerberus), but Edward was far too spent to attempt another fold. When they arrived, a single bandit dressed in cliche black ran out and fired at them. Clint returned fire and the man fell quickly. After that, the ranch was theirs.

They searched the house first, but it quickly became obvious they were wasting time. The Dylan gang had lived in the house for years, and every room and facility had been used in full. The house also had a human feel to it, and Edward assured them that those who had hidden the Orb would have given it more dignity. That was the word he used: *dignity*. Clint, who had been a human all his days, repressed an urge to reply to the unicorn's oft-implied suggestion that "human" and "dignity" were downright opposite.

Edward, who couldn't enter the house unless he blew out its walls (something he'd suggested but that Clint had vetoed) stood outside yelling commands. As he did, Clint found himself recalling what Edward had said about the sand dragon during a middle-of-the-night palaver just prior to entering the Dinosaur Missouri:

It needs human hands to get into a place that it can't reach, and to do things that a dragon's hands can't do. A place of doors and locks and shackles. A place where something might be locked away that the dragon would want, but that it wouldn't be able to reach on its own.

And suddenly, as they searched the house, Clint realized that *they* — the two human men — were *Edward's* hands.

Dragons and unicorns.

Darkness and light.
Dharma Kold and Clint.
Cerberus the ebony and Edward the ivory.

The dragon had required the dooner shaman… but so had Edward required Clint — both in the short term and for the duration of their partnership through life.

It was all very Yin and Yang. There were always two sides to everything.

"Come out!" Edward shouted through a window. Then in a lower voice when he saw Clint approach: "It's not in there, which I more or less knew from the start."

"What about the basement?" Clint asked.

"It's not in there, I said."

"Then why did we waste time searching the house at all?"

"It's taking me a while to tune in," said Edward. "This is ancient magic. Now that we're here, I can feel it and think I might be able to home in on it, but when we first arrived, I was flying blind."

Clint and Willick emerged from the house moments later. Edward tossed his head toward the rancho's rear. "Come on," he said. "I think it's this way."

Edward began walking with his nose to the ground as if sniffing, but it seemed like he was actually leading with his horn. As he marched forward, its tip, pointed directly forward, pulsed like a heartbeat in deep maroon. The color of blood.

"You're going to lead us directly to it, aren't you?" said Willick.

"Yar. So it seems."

"So how has the Orb remained hidden so long?"

Edward stopped and briefly considered Willick. It was the first time the parson had said the word "Orb," thus revealing he knew more of the lore than Edward had thought. Clint watched the short, bald priest and the unicorn as they looked at each other. With each of them in bright white, they looked like malformed twins.

Finally, Edward seemed to reach a decision about Willick. "Because it wanted to stay hidden," he said.

"And now it wants to be found?"

Clint winced. The wincing was instinctual. When *Clint* asked Edward questions, he was answered with scorn, denial, and sarcasm. But Edward seemed to have decided on a short-term species of respect for the parson, so he answered him straight.

"I guess it's more correct to say that we unicorns didn't want to find it," said Edward. Then, when he saw the perplexed look on Willick's face, he went on: "No offense, but you can't understand unicorns because you are a human. Humans could never keep a secret that any human was capable of knowing, but we can. Any white unicorn, unclouded by dark magic, could have come to this place and found the Orb. But only now, for the greater good, has one decided to look."

"I can't believe that," said Willick.

"You don't have to believe it," said Edward. "But it's true."

He led them through a pasture, past the barn that had housed Dylan's horses, over a fence (Clint climbed it, but Edward simply obliterated it when it was his turn), and into an untamed area that had probably once been rolling acreage for livestock. The notion that the magic royalty of this place had kept actual livestock beyond a gaggle of turkeys was absurd, but the evidence was in the barn.

"How can 'pure' unicorns be so in-tune with such a dark object, while black unicorns like the one ridden by the dark rider be unable to sense it?" said Willick. "I mean, you speak like it's a unicorn artifact, which would make it pure, but the thing is called 'The Orb of *Malevolence.*' "

"Nothing is quite that simple," said Edward.

Clint smirked. It was as obtuse an answer as the unicorn would have given to him. The parson, however, was undaunted.

"What do you mean?"

"What is in your hands, Parson?"

Willick looked down. "A rifle."

"Could you use it to obtain meat for your family to eat?"

"If I had a family, yar."

"Could you use it to kill a good man who has done you no harm?"

"A bad man could do that, yar."

"There you go," said Edward.

Minutes passed. They parted tall grass, passed an outer fence, and began walking along a short but steep hillside. As they walked further, the hill's grassy side crumbled to rock and they found themselves with a sheared-off section of land to their right, as if Providence had cleaved the hill down the center to expose its granite center. Eventually, Edward stopped where a sheer expanse of rock was embedded in the hill. It seemed a massive boulder had fallen to the ground from the sky, and that the hill on either side had grown out away from it.

The rock was perfectly flat, like a wall in a throughway between two of The Realm's massive buildings of stone and metal. A huge mural covered every inch of its surface. To the left side of the mural was the head of a tiger, its mouth open, its sharp white teeth frozen in a snarl. To the right was a wizard wearing blue robes. A pointed hat was atop the wizard's head, and both of his hands faced forward, palms up. One hand held a crystal ball. The other fired a lightning bolt. Between the wizard and the tiger's head was a lithe woman in a two-piece garment that exposed her stomach and long legs. This woman wore black boots with very long, spiked heels and was holding something in her hand that looked kind of like a pistol except that it appeared more plastic than metal and had lights painted all over its curvy surface. The word *ZAP!* was written near the barrel of the weapon in a pointy yellow starburst.

"I was wrong," said Edward, looking at the mural with disgust. "Apparently unicorns *couldn't* be trusted to keep away from the Orb. So the ancient ones created this painting to drive them away."

"I like it," said Clint, admiring the woman's firearm.

"You would," said Edward.

Willick was about to weigh in with his opinion when there was a huge sound in the distance that shook the ground under their feet and caused a scree of pebbles to fall from the top of the fresco painted on the rock. It was a deep, hollow booming of massive proportions — the sound of a small world ending.

"Look," said Willick. He was pointing toward the horizon, the sleeve of his long white robe dangling below his arm like a flag. Clint didn't need to follow Willick's finger to know where the sound had come from. He'd seen the flash of orange out of the corner of his eye and now saw black, acrid smoke rising from the same spot in the distant hills.

"Dynamite," the parson explained. "They don't use it often these days, but there's plenty still out there, and it makes a noise you don't forget. Judging by the color of the smoke, I'd say that boom ignited — or was ignited by — a few barrels of oil."

"Is that the direction of the mine where the dark rider was searching for the Orb?" asked Clint, who'd lost his bearings.

Willick nodded.

"Then I'd say our ruse was discovered," said Clint.

"What do we do now?" asked Willick.

Edward turned to face the mural on the rock. "We hurry."

CHAPTER TEN: THE UNDERGROUND CATHEDRAL

They were in a long, wide tunnel covered in blue and white tile. Except for a few weak spark lights in curious metal cages overhead, the tunnel's length was devoid of illumination as they descended the slow downward slope. It was like burrowing into the center of the world. Everything echoed — including the light, which bounced off the brilliant tiles like a firefly's glow. They moved quickly. After the explosion, Clint theorized that one of the warring parties at the mine must have blown its entrance, and the clock running against them would now be ticking.

He could even see those distant events unfold in his head:

Kold is inside the mine with Cerberus. Jarmusch's group arrives first and storms down the mine's dark throat to find Dylan's men, who they believe are already inside. Dylan arrives and ignites the dynamite. The rock collapses. Kold and Cerberus, who can fold space, escape. Shots and magic are exchanged. Those who aren't trapped or killed realize they've been set against each other and that the Orb has not been found. They realize that the stranger with the fast hands hasn't shown. And the jig, such as it was, is up.

It was only a matter of time before survivors returned, furious like a nest of rattled wasps. If Kold still lived — which he almost certainly did — the situation would become bad quickly. Kold would assume that Clint had lured the others away because he or Edward had found what they all sought. Kold and Cerberus could close the distance from the mine in seconds, and if they did, the gunslinger, the unicorn, and the parson would find themselves outgunned and trapped, like flies in a bottle.

The painted fresco of the tiger, woman, and wizard had concealed an underground chamber. Edward had said that he could feel it, and that he could feel the Orb inside.

"Blow it," Clint had said in a nervous voice, nodding at the mural.

"I'd blow it even if there was nothing behind it," Edward had replied, lowering his head and giving the wall a small tap with his horn. The rock face exploded inward, rumbling down the tunnel in an avalanche of rocks no larger than a man's fist.

That was ten minutes ago. They'd been moving downward since, with no end in sight. The only difference between the way they'd come and the way they were going was the slope under their feet.

The tunnel was floored with smooth, gray rock that had a gritty surface that made their footing sure and easy. It looked artificial. Edward's hooves clicked when they struck it, and the sound bounced off of the walls and surrounded them like cicadas in chatter. The walls curved up from the floor until they met overhead, turning the entire tunnel into a near perfect semicircle.

Willick kept walking to the tunnel's edge and touching the tiles, marveling at how they gleamed so brightly considering their age and the fact that they'd almost certainly never been polished. He wondered aloud whether the tiles actually repelled dirt through an ancient magic. The wondering was probably meant for Edward's ears, but Edward seemed lost in thought.

They followed the tunnel down, down, down. It made Clint nervous to watch daylight disappear from overhead. He wanted one of them to stand watch at the entrance in case their enemies returned, found the Rancho purged, and followed their trail back through the fields. Edward told him that leaving someone behind was a stupid idea. They didn't know what they faced, and each of the three in their party were needed. Edward understood the magic that had created the place and guarded the Orb. Clint was needed to protect their backs, wherever their backs might wander once underground. And Willick (setting aside the fact that he'd make a terrible guard, which Edward was at least kind enough not to mention) was there because he knew Precipice and its history, knew of the people who'd once lived at the rancho, and knew the characters comprising both warring posses Clint and Edward had sent to the mine.

Once fully underground, the downward-sloping tunnel evened out and they continued walking horizontally, now seemingly headed back toward the rancho. The frequency of the spark lights — and, thankfully, their brightness — increased, allowing the trio to see their surroundings better. There were framed placards on the wall, and the placards were so lifelike that at first Clint feared they were real people, or enchanted windows. One showed five scantily-clad women with garish clothing and worse hair frozen in the act of jumping. Across the top was the legend THEY DON'T JUST SING. Below this, in a black oval: SPICEWORLD. Along the bottom, taking up nearly half the placard, were the words THE MOVIE. Another placard was black and displayed only a strange text character Willick identified as a letter in a distant tongue called *pie*. Below this were the words FAITH IN CHAOS. Clint objected that the strange letter wasn't pie at all, but the mention of pie made him hungry, and he had to resist the urge to dig into his pack.

Every once in a while, their path branched off into other paths and chambers. Clint attempted to peek into these, but they were all entirely dark. The sounds of rushing air and, sometimes, a distant and great engine-like roar, came from the darkness. The sounds were disturbing, and soon all three of the travelers stopped inspecting side chambers and simply kept walking along the straight path through the center, which the makers had clearly meant to be the main one.

"Do you still feel the Orb?" Clint asked Edward. Three rats scampered over his toes, seemingly unafraid of the gunslinger's tromping feet.

"Yar. Its presence here is suffocating."

"Are you okay?" asked Willick.

"It's suffocating like the air in your face when you run very, very fast," said Edward. "Suffocating in a way that isn't unpleasant — as if you can't breathe, but for some reason, you don't mind."

Clint, who'd ridden atop many a galloping horse and exactly one unicorn, knew the feeling.

Barely a minute later, just as the gunslinger was about to remind Edward that it wouldn't take the mine stragglers long to find them and that they needed to set awe aside in favor of hurry, the long tunnel and its odd, whooshing side chambers opened into a massive room with a high ceiling. The ceiling was so high, in fact, that Clint could barely see its top. He looked up for a while, trying to see the roof of the cathedral-like chamber, but eventually he looked down because it was raining in the room, and the grit from his face was running into his eyes.

"How far did we go down?" asked Willick, also looking up.

"At least that far," said Edward, jerking his head toward the ceiling. "I'd guess we're back under the house. That's why I felt it so strongly when we first came here. It was right under us."

"So we *should* have checked the basement," said Clint.

"I don't think so," said Edward. "This is a magic place. I'd wager if you dug straight down under the house, you'd find nothing but dirt."

"But you said we were under the house right now."

"Yar," said Edward. "We are."

Clint waited for further explanation, but as usual, the unicorn offered none.

Edward strolled away from the two humans and across a small but sturdy bridge that crossed a small, natural river running through the cavern in which the massive cathedral-like structure was housed. The bridge was wide, just like the tunnel. It was as if the place had been made for unicorns.

In the center of the room was a massive stone dais. Atop the dais was a cage with an elaborate latch on its front. It seemed as if it closed and opened with no key required. In the center of the cage was a simple stone cup. The cup appeared to be empty.

Edward and Willick, side by side, walked to a small altar near the dais. There was a large, ancient book open atop the altar. Edward was gazing down at it and Willick, who was too short to easily see the top of the altar, was attempting to gaze up. Finally he found a rock, stood on it, and looked at the book's pages.

"I can't read this," he said. "Though I dearly wish I could."

Edward, over his shoulder, said, "It's written in the Old Language."

"Can you read it?"

"No. But I understand now where we are and what all of this must mean."

"Do you know where the Orb is?"

"Yar," said Edward, walking over to stand beside the cage. He dipped his head toward it. "It's this cup."

Clint looked at the cup. It was singularly unremarkable, chipped around the rim and looking like it had been dragged up from the bottom of a muddy ditch.

"Go ahead," said Edward. "Take it out of the cage."

"Get it your dagged self," said Clint.

Edward was right beside the cage. The unicorn was the one who knew what was going on and, as usual, was playing coy rather than simply telling them what he knew. Edward held all of the cards. The fact that he wanted Clint to retrieve something that was right beside his nose was infuriating.

"I *can't* get it," said Edward.

Across the chamber, footfalls echoed into the cathedral space. All three of the travelers turned to find the source of the noise.

It was Parson Jarmusch, his body broken into an inhuman shape of twisted terror.

CHAPTER ELEVEN:
THE ORB

Jarmusch was still in his parson's robes, but only barely. The white garments were shredded to tatters and blackened with soot. His neck seemed to turn in a sharp hook to one side, his ear flat against his left shoulder. His right arm was in front of him instead of at his side. His right leg had at least two more joints than it should have, and the foot on that leg was facing backward. From where Clint stood, Jarmusch's left arm appeared to be totally gone. His torso was twisted and bent, like a corkscrew that had failed to penetrate rock. His skin, visible below his scorched robes, appeared raw and blistered.

"I'm beginning to suspect that someone may have lied to me," said the Jarmusch-thing.

Clint drew his guns, but Jarmusch laughed.

"Don't bother," he said. His voice was somehow different and strange, as if it had doubled but that the two halves of his voice hadn't synchronized correctly. The effect was strangely alien, almost mechanical. "You can't kill me, and none of those you *could* have killed came with me."

"Where are your people?" asked Willick.

"Dead," said the thing that had once been Parson Jarmusch, flapping a broken hand with a disinterested air. "Or trapped, soon to be dead."

"Trapped where?"

"In the mine. You played a good game, gunslinger. You got almost all of us… with a little help from your friend."

Clint hadn't lowered his guns. Each was trained on one of the monster's eyes. "My friend?"

"The dark rider. Our party and Dylan's party went in. The rider and his mount alone came out. Then the rider blew a great load of dynamite and burning petrol at the entrance to the shaft, as if he'd been expecting us and had set it up from the start. The mine collapsed. Petrol spilled. Everything burned. You can guess the rest."

Clint stared at the creature across the cathedral chamber. "And you?"

"I crawled through the cracks," he croaked. His body convulsed. Something cracked. A small black belch of what looked like smoke drifted from a rip in his robe before striking the skin under his chin and vanishing again.

Jarmusch advanced. Clint fired. The shot struck him in the chest, but he continued to advance.

"Like I said," the Jarmusch-thing growled, "don't bother."

Clint eyed the cup in the cage — the thing Edward seemed to think was the Orb of Malevolence. Jarmusch was eyeing it too, shambling straight toward it.

"There's more," he said, and this time, black smoke poured from his open mouth before circling his head and re-absorbing into his scalp. "The Orb wasn't in the mine. But it also was. Now the dark rider has it. I saw him on the horizon after I came through the rockfall at the entrance."

Two more shambling steps. Clint stepped in front of the cage, as if to hide it.

Clint whispered to Edward. "What's he talking about?"

"It's the water," the unicorn whispered back.

"It's the water!" Jarmusch echoed, apparently having heard just fine. "The entire dagged aquifer that's been under the town the entire time!" He laughed with a corpse-like rattle.

Clint looked over his shoulder at the cup, confused. Wasn't the *cup* the Orb?

"There are degrees to everything," Edward continued, seeing Clint's glance. "The spring in this chamber is enchanted, and its 'Orb nature' is stronger the closer you are to the source. I should have known, by reading into how the legends are written. Malevolence can't be contained, so they put it in a form where everyone could sip it but none could wholly possess it. It can be disseminated in such a way because it's not the whole of the picture. That's what I meant about how the legends are written: 'The first Orb spreads chaos. The second regulates and focuses it.'"

"The second?"

"The second!" the thing stumbling toward them cackled, its voice rising to a maniacal laugh.

"It's okay," said Edward. "I think he already knows."

Willick was looking from Edward to Jarmusch to Clint, then back in a circuit. His mouth hung open with the weary look of a man who couldn't believe what was before his eyes.

"Your man had a large waterskin slung around his shoulder when he rode off," said Jarmusch. "I guess this underground river must run out and under the mine." He looked down and stepped across the bridge. "He found that the mine draws direct from this river, but miles out. I guess he put two and two together around the time we showed, or maybe figured it out and was waiting to kill us. That's okay. I don't want what's in the mine. *I want what's in here.*" He tried raising his head to sniff the air, but his neck was clearly broken and useless. Instead his head flopped on his shoulder. "It's so strong. So *dark*," he said, his features twisting in pleasure. "*I* want to drink from the Cup of Ages."

Clint looked to Edward, who shook his head, promising a later explanation. Then Edward, finally tired of Jarmusch's monologue, stepped up beside Clint, putting himself between the parson's walking corpse and the cup. His horn began to glow and he said, "I don't think so."

"Oh, step aside," said Jarmusch, annoyed. Billows of black smoke spilled from his mouth. "You didn't beat me out in the Sands, and all you could do here would be to pulverize this body further. Haven't you ever heard that energy can't be created or destroyed? It only changes form."

Jarmusch was now only thirty feet away and not slowing. Edward lowered his head, and a blast of blue light erupted from his horn. The blast struck Jarmusch in the chest and burned the front of his robe away. Behind it, Clint saw a black hole opening into nothingness. He couldn't see the chamber through Jarmusch. He only saw blackness, as if Jarmusch were *made* of blackness. It was all so familiar.

"It's the Darkness," said Clint. "From the sand dragon."

"I figured that out when he walked in as a corpse that had forced itself through a wall of rock and then began belching black smoke," Edward said with scorn.

Willick was still staring. He took several steps backward and stumbled against the back wall of the cathedral, falling to a hard sit. The butt of his rifle struck the hard floor, jarring the weapon from his grip. The rifle clattered to the floor, forgotten.

Edward struck the thing again with another blast of blue light. Half of its head vanished, leaving a large part of him as only silhouette.

"Thish ish *poinlessh*," hissed Jarmusch, now speaking from half a mouth.

"It's not pointless at all," said Edward. "Kold could at least walk off with less-than-pure water. But after I blow off your cover and leave you without human hands, what are you going to do?"

Jarmusch stopped and tried to incline his half-head thoughtfully. He failed, and the head lolled.

"True," he said. There was a chaotic stirring, and the half-head of Parson Jarmusch seemed to vanish into the neck of his robes. Parts of him began to twist and shift and drop to the ground. At first Clint thought the body was simply crumbling to pieces. But it was actually collapsing into a pile of rats.

The rats filled Jarmusch's clothes like a sack stuffed with living stones. The robes writhed, gray and brown forms spilling from the sleeves, underneath, and up from the neck. There were hundreds — greater in total size than Jarmusch. Clint found himself remembering the gargantuan sand dragon, and wondered just how large the darkness could make itself.

The rats began to climb Clint's legs, biting at him in a thousand places at once. It was impossible to defend against them all. They bit his fingers. He tried to swat them off and keep his big hands clenched, but the bites were too many. His guns fell to the floor and made a sound that broke Clint's heart. He tried reaching for them, but rats swallowed them with their bodies. Then, in a rush, there were rats up his pants, down his shirt, and in his hair.

Darkness from Jarmusch split into too many pieces to fight. Edward wore a sweater of rats. He magicked many away, but the swarms were nearly as thick as the air, and already inside of whatever shield the unicorn might raise. His legs were three times wider than normal, covered in fluid moving bodies. He stepped high, stomping the ground to jostle them. Some fell, but whenever a few scattered, more climbed up.

Clint clawed at his body. The pain was disorienting. The rats were on his head, climbing toward his face, his mouth, his eyes.

But then everything stopped.

There was a brilliant blue flash and a thousand rats squealed at once. Clint saw piles of the creatures fall dazed to his feet and to Edward's hooves. Not one rat remained on them. A few were trapped in Clint's clothes, but they were stunned as if hit with sleeper gas. Clint shook them out, looking down. He kicked rats aside until he could recover his guns. They felt good in his hands, and he promised himself that no matter what came at him in the future, he'd never drop them again.

He looked at Edward, silently asking how the unicorn had

managed a spell to repel the rats, but Edward shook his head. It hadn't been his magic at all.

Below them, the dazed rats stirred. They looked up, seeming to regard the man and the unicorn before diving in vast waves into the river spilling from the Orb spring.

"Step on them!" Edward shouted. "Shoot them if you can!"

Clint began to stomp as Edward, with his heavy front hooves, did the same. The gunslinger drew his pistols and started to fire. His hands were lightning, but there were way, way too many rats. Between the two of them — three, once Willick summoned his strength and raced over — they put an end to dozens, and each time they smashed or shot one, black smoke puffed from the small bodies like from a boot tip kicked into a spore fungus.

The river filled with rats as their guns and stomping feet went silent, and shortly thereafter the creatures emerged from the underground river on the other side, soaking wet.

Then they turned — a thousand tiny heads rotating at once — and regarded the unicorn, the gunslinger, and the parson. They seemed to smirk, and then the entire gray and brown mass ran back through the tiled passage toward the exit, leaving a slick of wetness on the ground behind them.

Clint quickly reloaded and holstered his guns. It was finished. Whatever this had been, it was over. Dead rats lay in a carpet. The river seemed momentarily polluted, but quickly cleared. Willick retrieved his rifle.

Edward sighed. "When those rats squeeze themselves off, it's going to make the last cup of water I'd ever want to drink," he said.

Clint mopped his brow. "I don't understand what happened here."

"What happened is that the bad guys both managed to seize the Orb. But it's okay." The unicorn nodded toward the ornate cup still on the dais, as if they hadn't just been rudely interrupted. "Get the cup."

Clint turned. The latch on the front of the cage was like nothing he'd ever seen, and it took him several minutes to figure his way into opening it. Doing so, once he reasoned it, required six fingers and two distinct hands. He had to slide two fingers of each hand through brass loops on either side of the door to raise pins that kept the latch closed, then use another two fingers to pry against one another and free the catch.

Once the door was open, Clint reached inside and grabbed the simple stone cup.

"Use the cup to fill a waterskin, then mark that waterskin carefully," said Edward.

Clint did as Edward told him.

"Now, shatter the cup."

Clint waited a moment to be sure Edward wasn't going to change his mind about destroying a timeless unicorn artifact, then shrugged and threw the cup hard against the floor, where it broke into shards.

The gunslinger turned to the unicorn. "Now what?"

"Now we ride," said Edward.

CHAPTER TWELVE:
THE SECOND ORB

They left the subterranean cathedral and rode out of the rancho the same way they'd entered, then rode to Willick's church to drop him off before resuming their journey. Willick sprinted up the steps when they reached their destination, unlocked the doors and threw them wide, then removed the furniture barricading the entrance. Then, once Edward assured him the Darkness had better things to do than possess another of Precipice's townfolk, Willick vowed to do what he could to help the town move on and restore its hope. He said it had been a long time since Precipice had last managed to hope, but that with both warring bosses out of the picture and with a fat stack of their cash, anything was possible. Clint was skeptical of such shameless optimism and Edward made a biting remark about how Willick could fart rainbows, but secretly both were pleased, and rode on as satisfied as a gunslinger and a unicorn could be.

As they rode from town, they passed the stone well where they had paused to drink on their way in. Edward nodded toward it.

"I understood once I saw the book in the underground cathedral — which I couldn't read, but which I recognized the symbolism of — and once I saw the spring," he said. "The spring itself is the purest source of 'Orb of Malevolence' in Precipice. The mine, fed by the same underground river, is third purest. Kold must have figured that out, and decided that 'third purest' was good enough for his purposes, and it is. Between the two, this well — which taps directly into the aquifer without filters or intervening stone and is closer to the source than the mine — is second purest."

"We drank from it on the way into town," said Clint. "It was here all along."

"Yar, and drinking from it may have saved our lives. Energy from the old artifacts isn't passive, just as magic isn't passive. It has its own intelligence, and it responds to the will and character of those who use it. The Darkness can take its share of the Orb to use for nefarious purposes. It *did* take its share on the backs of those rats, and it *will* attempt to use it for nefarious purposes... but at the same time, Darkness can't stand against that same energy if the energy is within noble souls — which in this case was a Realm marshal and a unicorn."

Clint looked at Edward. Then he said, "The bright flash that stunned the rats and made them stop attacking us. That was Orb magic in our blood repelling the Darkness?"

"Yar, it was."

"You're saying that The Orb of *Malevolence* was on *our* side?"

"There are two sides to everything," said Edward. But beyond that simple sentence, he said nothing more.

They came to the top of the hill and looked briefly out at the river separating Precipice from the madness of the Dinosaur Missouri. They wouldn't be heading in that direction, but would instead be skirting the Missouri to one side, hoping to loop back and make up some time on Kold — and, if it was traveling mortally, on the Darkness.

"What about the cup and cage?" said Clint.

"It's complicated."

Clint leaned forward and punched Edward below the ear. "It's time you started trusting me, and time you stopped shilling this puzzle a piece at a time."

Edward, unperturbed, kept walking. "Don't punch me again, and try to understand that you may not be able to understand what I'm about to tell you."

"You've made your thoughts about the stupidity of humans abundantly clear," said Clint.

"It's not about stupidity," said Edward. "What I mean is that some unicorn matters are beyond the actual human *capacity* to understand. You are limited. It's not a bad thing, but it's how you are. To take a simple example, humans can't understand infinity. What is beyond the stars? And then what is beyond that? You are literally unable to comprehend the idea of forever. You've nar the power to grasp it."

"I get it. Go on."

"The answer to your question begins with the fact that *intention* matters to magic," said Edward. "Earlier, Willick asked how we, as pure creatures, could be associated with an Orb named for its power to cause chaos. But we don't see things as black and white. The Orb was once part of a powerful force of creation, but like all powerful things, the Orb can be twisted and perverted in the wrong hands. You're wondering why there was an elaborate, hidden cathedral beneath the Rancho Encantato to house the Orb when any man could have simply sipped from the well? It's because anyone can take possession of the Orb, but only the sort of soul that the Orb would want to possess it would be willing to go to the trouble to find the cathedral. Those who built the shrine beneath the Rancho wanted a team of two to carry the Orb — a magical creature who'd be able to breach the wall at its entrance, and a mortal man with fingers able to open the cage. Drinking from the cup is only symbolic, but in the case of magic, symbolism matters enough to make the difference. Do you understand?"

Clint didn't totally understand, but figured he would in time, as he processed.

"Yar," he said. "But the Darkness could have opened the cage, had we not been there."

"But we *were* there," said Edward.

"We might not have been. And if we hadn't been, it would have gotten the cup."

"It didn't, because we were there."

"But we might not have been," Clint repeated.

Edward shook his head. "I'm trying not to mock you, but it's difficult to refrain."

They rode in meditative quiet for many minutes, with no sound save for Edward's hooves in the sand. Finally Clint said, "But the Darkness *did* get the water. And right from the source, even without the cup."

"Yar. It got the Orb in the way Kold got the Orb — which is the same way your idiot companion Yates got his schooling back in The Realm."

Clint didn't remember much from his time in The Realm. Most of his early years were a void in his mind, as if erased by a chalk wiper. But he remembered Yates.

The highest schools in The Realm conferred special papers which decreed that a man was schooled once he'd completed a certain number of years. Yates hadn't completed his years, but his wealthy family had used their money to purchase a paper for him. Yates would be able to do anything with his paper that a properly schooled man could do with his, but it was nar the same.

"You're saying they cheated," said Clint. "That their Orbs won't 'work,' whatever that means."

"Yar. And nar. They'll 'work' just fine."

"So what does it matter? How is the water in our sack any different from theirs?"

Again Edward shook his head, as if bearing the blunt weight of a ride with such stupidity.

"I'll just sit back here and be an idiot," said Clint, hearing the pout in his voice.

"You do it so well," said Edward.

"And I'll let your brilliance take us to wherever. To get the second Orb, which will probably be some magic dirt we can use to plant magic beans."

Edward stopped.

"I haven't told you about the second Orb," he said. It wasn't a question.

"What about the second Orb?" said Clint, still pouting.

"Kold already has it."

Clint looked down at Edward's neck, saying nothing.

"I felt it when we left the cathedral and took new sips of the pure Orb. The energy of one Orb shows you the way to the next, and what I saw when I drank was Kold. The second Orb is already in his possession."

"When did he get it?"

"He's had it all along. He apparently took them out of order."

"What is it?" Clint asked. His voice had changed from pout to plea. The sky's colors were suddenly wrong, starting to swirl.

"It's called the Orb of Benevolence. It controls the action of the first — or, if its user wants, refrains from controlling it."

"But what *is* it?" said Clint, afraid he already knew.

Edward dropped his head, his nose close to the sand, almost apologetic.

"It's Mai," he said.

UNICORN WESTERN 4

CHAPTER ONE:
THE REALM MACHINE

"Look at this," Clint said, stretching a leg from his mount's pristine white side to kick a leaning, faded sign beside the trail as they passed. *You are approaching Nazareth Shiloh, home of the Sands' best chili brewfest.* "Now that's a blast from the past. When's the last time you heard of anyone brewing chili?"

Edward grunted. There were many things across the world that had turned to legend and gone missing forever. Chili was the most appetizing among them. The sign did indeed advertise a long, long, *long* forgotten and delicious event, but Edward's grunt seemed to suggest that Clint was pointing out the sign specifically to irk the unicorn. Which, of course, he was.

"That sign means we're entering the Lakes," said Edward, "and there are other things that the Lakes are home to that you should be more concerned about than chili."

"Mmm, chili," Clint said, rubbing his stomach theatrically.

Edward said nothing. It felt as if the two of them had been riding together forever. It was almost true — in Clint's mind, anyway. He was no longer sure how long it'd been since his exile from The Realm, but he knew the few memories from before his exile were tumbleweeds in the sands, probably at least in part from all of the leaking and slippage. As far as the gunslinger's memory was concerned, he and the unicorn *had* been riding together forever. Just one very long trail, pocked with brief stops for a chance at love and the certainty of sorrow.

The days recycled, never ending. Even after his years in the Sands, Clint never grew used to it — at least not entirely. Day followed day. One mesa chased the next. Nothing changed, save the occasional one-horse town. When they passed through a dusty burg for a belly full of turkey pie and brew, they never stopped longer than needed to refill their supplies and for Edward to insult the local horses. Then Clint would pat his replenished belly and they would head on out, one day again following another, with one mesa chasing the next.

"You're magical," Clint said to the back of Edward's horned head below him, suddenly feeling the weight of his endless journey sitting on his heart as they arrived at Buddha's Thumb — a giant freestanding boulder out at the edge of the Gobe Forest. The Thumb was near 6,000 squared lengths, and rose almost eight Otel floors straight to the sky. "So because you're magical, maybe you can tell me: does this ever end? Or do we wander forever?"

"We wander through the Lakes O Plenty as planned, then on to the Meadows. That's all I know," said the unicorn.

"And after the Meadows, we catch the bad guy."

"*Catch. Catch,*" Edward mocked. "That's your fantasy, not mine. If you ask me, we're never going to *catch* Kold and Cerberus. Or save Mai. We're just going to walk until we crumble to dust."

Clint tittered, suddenly feeling giddy in the face of such unending tedium. "Tell me the name of the Meadows again," he said.

"The Meadows," said Edward, shaking his big white head, as pristine as if he'd just come through a Realm conveyance washing station. Edward could walk through a sandstorm and come away clean enough to sleep on silk bedding — assuming he could lose the brown-coated rider on his back.

"*What* Meadows?"

Edward sighed. "*Elf* Meadows."

Clint cackled a dry, humorless laugh.

They'd been heading steadily for a region originally frolicked by the unicorns and which, according to legend, had been Realm-adjacent back before the first fracture. The entire region, having been settled by unicorns, had names that Clint found imminently mockable: *Rainbow Fields. Puff Valley. The Plains of Delight.* Making fun of unicorn nomenclature was all Clint had to counter Edward's constant insults.

And now they'd entered the Lakes O Plenty, which Clint was already mocking-o-plenty since there were no lakes. But despite the mockery, the feeling that their quest had run forever and would never end, and Clint's suspicion that Kold's captive — Clint's once-bride-to-be, Mai — could no longer be the woman he'd once known, Clint couldn't suppress a spark of hope. Rumor surrounding Elf Meadows suggested that the land there never shifted. *Ever*. If that was true, it would mean that despite the fractures and the leaking, Elf Meadows would still be Realm adjacent, even today.

Nobody can find The Realm, said a voice in his head.

Somebody can, because people still live there, Clint answered himself.

He let it go. It was an argument for another day. If The Realm couldn't be found, that was both good news and bad. It would mean that Clint would never find himself back behind the wall, but it would also mean that Kold wouldn't, either. It would mean that Kold might not find the third Orb, thus possessing the entirety of the Triangulum — an object that Edward still refused to fully explain. If The Realm couldn't be found, it would mean that both the gunslinger and the unicorn might die on the sand… but at least the world, such as it was, would march on.

Edward stopped, so suddenly that Clint found himself pitched forward and had to grab Edward's neck to keep from spilling to the dirt. If Edward had been looking up, Clint would have been impaled on the unicorn's horn, which Edward would likely have found hilarious.

Because Clint was feeling irritated, he used the backs of his heels to kick Edward's sides, clicking his tongue at him like he would a horse.

"Witty," said Edward, not looking back at his rider. His eyes were fixed in the distance, as if he'd just heard or scented something.

"What is it?" said Clint.

"Magic. A lot of it. It suddenly filled the air like a strong cologne."

Clint wanted to enter into snide banter with Edward, but they'd seen too much of magic's dark side over the past years to take it for granted that Edward sensing magic was a good thing. He might be sensing the Orb of Malevolence (a vial filled with water that they carried in their saddlebags) reacting to the presence of another, even more malevolent Orb. He might be reacting to the presence of Cerberus, Dharma Kold's black unicorn. He might even be sensing the Darkness, which they'd last seen fleeing the old cathedral under Precipice in the form of hundreds of soaking wet rats.

"Is it the Orb?" said Clint.

"No. It's so familiar I almost didn't recognize it. *White* magic. The kind that once permeated the world's surface, back before the leaking. It feels sweet." Edward's nose moved up as if scenting the breeze, as a man would to draw a particularly fine fragrance to his nostrils. "Oh, it's been *so long*," he said with something like a sigh of pleasure. "This was what it once smelled like everywhere. Back when I was young."

Clint, who only smelled dung, said nothing to sour Edward's nostalgia.

"It's ahead," said the unicorn.

Edward sounded like he'd been transported back through many years, perhaps to a time before he'd grown so cynical and jaded. He sounded — and Clint had to triple-check his mind's assessment before allowing the conscious thought — *happy*.

The unicorn's feet began to move. Clint, on his back, found himself wanting to drop back. He'd never seen Edward like this.

Within a minute, they reached the edge of a tall cliff where Clint found himself looking down into a deep valley. There appeared to be a party far below, but Clint couldn't make out a single detail. He could see a scatter of people, but couldn't tell who they might be or what they were doing. There was something large in the center of the milling figures, big and winking in the sun's bright light, as if made of gems or mirrors.

Looking down, Edward's demeanor flipped like a switch.

"I should have known," he said. His moment of euphoria had popped like a bubble.

Clint carried a spyglass, so he fished it from his pack while Edward kept staring, a scowl starting to form on his mouth. Then Clint put the glass to his eye and saw what Edward saw below.

There was a long, winding crack along the valley floor that looked as if it were made of light. At first, it had blended in with the sand and sun, but with the glass to his eye, Clint could see there was something glowing beneath the crack — a sort of blue-white fog that was emerging in a light haze, like the smoke from sublimating scientist's ice. After a moment of observation, Clint could see the smoke wasn't simply wafting from the crack. The glass was strong and Clint's hands were steady. His eyes were sharp, and he could see the ghostlike vapor curling up into the air in what looked like tentacles, beckoning to the blue sky above. It looked almost alive.

There was a large alloy machine straddling the largest part of the crack. The machine had great treads like a Realm groundmover, and one tread was positioned on either side of the chasm. The machine's belly was a man's height from the ground. What looked like a giant mandible hung below it. The mandible looked like the mouthpiece of a beetle.

There were five men circling the machine, seemingly making adjustments and setting controls. Three were dressed in what appeared to be alloy themselves, but of a mesh, see-through sort.

These men wore alloy helmets as well. The two others looked like workmen, dressed in clothing that could have been from any Sands town, albeit much cleaner and not yet worn to threads.

"That's a Realm machine," said Clint, still peering through the glass.

Edward, who didn't need a glass to see every detail Clint could see and more, made a noise from below that sounded like a scoff. "Yar."

"It's not running on steam or spark. There's no smoke pipe."

"It's running on magic," said Edward. "The magic sitting below it."

Clint took the glass from his eye and looked down at the unicorn. Then, when Edward didn't acknowledge his surprise, he hopped down and stood beside him.

"You're saying that's a magic vein."

"Yar," said Edward. "An open one."

"You don't seem very happy about it."

"That's because it's not naturally open. *They* opened it."

That snagged Clint's interest. Magic ran beneath the surface of the sand, and like a river system, tiny runnels and tributaries always funneled back to bigger streams of magic. The largest magic streams were like mighty waterways, but none was accessible to a man with a shovel. It took magic to open magic, and based on everything Clint had heard from Edward and other sources, it was never supposed to be opened, especially in a time of great leaking. The fracturing of the land did plenty of opening on its own. One day, to hear Edward talk, what remained of the magic would all evaporate. Making more openings on purpose seemed tantamount to a crime.

"Why did they open it?" asked Clint.

Edward nodded toward the machine. "That's a seam-stitcher. This land must still shift out here. The Realm is the only place where magic's still abundant, but this is their dirty little secret as to why. When the lands shift, it opens fractures and leads to more leaking. But The Realm doesn't want its flow interrupted, so it uses these machines to seal the fractures."

"But that's good, right?"

"Nature finds its own way when it isn't interfered with," said Edward. "Even a great fire has a purpose."

"How about you just tell me what you mean for once instead of speaking in riddles?" said Clint.

Shooting erupted before Edward could reply.

Neither gunslinger nor unicorn, engaged in conversation as they were, had seen the attack party approaching. Clint raised the glass back to his eye as a group of men circled the seam-stitcher and its crew. All but one of the attackers had lassos, and each of the lassos was spinning like a storm overhead. Only the remaining man — an odd-looking fellow with bushy, fiery orange hair standing out from his head like an oversized helmet — had weapons. This last man brandished a pair of what from Clint's vantage point looked like very long and bulky pistols.

The lasso-bearers demeanor was strange. They wielded the ropes as if they were guns, and the Realm men around the machine backed up, their hands in the air, as if the ropers might shoot them with lassos. But that didn't make sense. The seam crew had to have weapons among them. If their opponents carried only ropes, why didn't they retaliate?

The standoff (Clint counted a dozen men with ropes plus the man with the large orange hair facing the stitcher's crew) held for perhaps thirty seconds before another man ran out from the machine with his hands up, waving frantically and apparently yelling, though Clint couldn't hear more than faint mutters from this high up. The new man seemed to have been inside the machine. He was wearing a suit that gleamed even more than the mesh suits on three of the others — more even than the seam-stitcher itself.

"That man is covered in metal," said Edward.

"It's not a man," said Clint, scattered memories of his time in The Realm resurfacing in his clouded mind. "It's a thinking machine."

The thinking machine was mostly golden in color, with accents of brown and other muted tones across its body. It had the shape of a man, but Clint had seen similar machines before and knew that up close, it would be all alloy and bolts, painted to appear as if it wore human clothes. Clint had never seen a seam-stitching operation before, but he recognized a commissioner when he saw one. Commissioner machines were in charge of every operation outside of the walls because they could be programmed to be authoritative, responsible, and loyal — while also being entirely expendable. The three men in mesh (which Clint assumed were Paladin Infantry soldiers) were there to protect the operation, but Infantry were the lowest level of knights and held no authority. They were grunts in need of a boss — even if the boss was made of cogs and clockwork and operated on steam.

The commissioner machine ran to just past where the two men in common clothing and paladins were holding their ground. All three of the paladins had dropped their hands to their sides like gunslingers, but none had drawn. They were watching the men's lassos around them, and again Clint found himself wondering why. Their weapons were *ropes,* for Providence's sake. Clint could fell a town full of men even with one hand bound. But part of Clint's reaction was probably due to old prejudice because back in The Realm, there'd been a constant power struggle between knights and marshals. Knights thought that marshals were mercenaries fit only for dirty jobs involving killing. Marshals, in turn, felt that the knights were soft.

A long blue beam of light appeared at the hip of one of the paladins. He'd drawn his scimitar. The closest rope man reacted, but he wasn't fast enough. The paladin covered the distance between them in three long strides and spun with his light weapon, which lashed like a whip as it neared the man with the rope. The beam seemed to glide right through the rope-bearer, sending him straight to the dirt. Clint couldn't help but admire the man's grit. He'd reacted like a marshal.

Immediately, a rope man across the circle flicked his arm toward the knight. The rope in his hand seemed to defy physics, becoming more projectile than lasso, and simultaneously wrapped itself around the paladin's neck, arms, legs, and torso. The knight's weapon seemed to cleave in half and turn off, falling to the sand as a useless cylinder of alloy. The rope was taut across the standoff circle, and the commissioner, who had stopped waving his hands in surrender when the paladin had charged with his scimitar drawn, backed away as if the rope were poisonous.

The other two paladins broke their paralysis and drew their own scimitars — slender cylinders at their sides which burst into long weapons of bright blue light. But instead of charging, these two ducked behind the stitching machine, dragging the two workmen with them.

Ropes flashed, shooting like bullets behind the fleeing men.

The man who had already lassoed one of the knights gave a tug and the rope returned to him, leaving the knight in a pile. From the cliff, Clint couldn't tell what had happened to the paladin, but he wasn't moving.

The man with the orange hair had his great pistols pointed and, as they watched, fired a shot at the commissioner. Clint almost laughed. Realm alloy was impervious to such as bullets. But then the almost-laugh caught in his throat as the gunslinger saw a spray appear behind the thinking machine. Whatever the man with the red hair was firing, it was strong enough to pierce the skin of a commissioner.

The machine fell. The man with the orange hair re-aimed his weapons. From the dirt, the machine raised its arms then sat up, looking around as if mildly inconvenienced. But commissioners, in every instance Clint had ever heard of, were beyond docile. It was not a threat. If the entire human complement of the stitcher crew were killed, the commissioner would likely offer to clean the gang's boots before they rode into town.

"If they're smart, the knights will stop trying to slash those men and will use projectiles instead," said Clint, still peeking through the spyglass.

They did. Still hiding behind the stitching machine, the two remaining knights began to fire what looked like balls of light from the ends of their scimitars. The first projectile shot straight at one of the roper's chests, but the man sprung into the air and flipped backward, allowing the light ball to pass directly below him. Then, when the ball circled around and homed back at him, he cartwheeled to the side, jabbing out with his rope. The rope grabbed a rock and flung it toward the ball of light. The light struck the rock and the rock exploded. The man sprung away on one hand, his rope still moving.

The knights continued to fire projectiles, but the rope gang continued to weave and dodge. It was like watching a circus. While the paladins and workmen cowered, the eleven remaining rope men sprung around them like acrobats, effortlessly evading the light balls and using their ropes to grab objects to deflect them.

The rope men circled the machine. Their ropes found the workmen and dragged them out and began using them to deflect the paladin projectiles. The paladins couldn't recall the projectiles once they'd been launched, and the balls of light struck the workmen. The workmen fell.

The two remaining paladins, finding themselves alone and outgunned by men without guns (the orange-haired man had re-holstered his weapons and was now leaning against a rock, watching the battle while smiling from behind a toothpick), ceased fire. From the dirt, the commissioner stood then scooted off, eventually hiding behind a large rock outcropping far from the stitcher.

The rope men surrounded the paladins. The paladins climbed into the stitching machine.

"I guess they're going to drive away," said Edward.

But then the rope men all started to strike out with their ropes at once. The ropes slapped the the stitcher's side, twitched, then seemed to fall to the dirt. One rope looped itself around a handle used to climb to the machine's top. The man pulled and the entire side panel came away.

They were somehow using ropes to disassemble a Realm machine.

Within minutes, the stitcher's side panels lay on the sand. The treads were pulled away. One of the men used a long throw to pull off the canopy of transparent alloy at the thing's top, exposing the two cowering paladins. Then the paladins, to their credit, stopped cowering and leaped out into the dirt and, all restraint gone, began firing ball after ball of light at the rope men. But the eleven rope men parried effortlessly, picking up and using pieces of the disassembled stitcher to deflect the projectiles.

It looked to Clint like the rope men were playing with the paladins. They seemed amused, not actually trying to end the fight.

One of the knights broke out and charged at the closest of his opponents, his scimitar wielded like a sword. He almost made it, but before he reached his target — who didn't attempt to defend himself — three ropes circled the man and three bandits pulled, and the man fell to the dirt.

The last paladin, defeated, suddenly stood, tossed his scimitar aside, and held his hands high.

Three ropes circled the man.

Three bandits pulled.

The man found himself bound to what remained of the stitching machine, unable to move.

Then the bound man watched — as Clint and Edward watched from high above — as the orange-haired man walked to the open magic vein and lowered something into it.

CHAPTER TWO:
SLY OF THE FAMILY STONE

After the bandits had gone, Clint and Edward made their way down to the valley floor, to the mostly-disassembled Realm machine and the two remaining members of the stitching party. During the long descent, Clint and Edward took turns chiding one another for not intervening in the

(Assault? Robbery?)

events they'd just witnessed. Clint said that Edward should have folded them down to the valley floor so they could take out a few of the rope-bearers. Edward retorted that he'd be too weak after folding to help, but that Clint should have fired a few of his marshal's bullets from up on the cliff. Clint claimed they were too far for shooting, even for marshal's bullets.

But really, both knew the other hadn't intervened for one simple reason: there was too much wrong in the Sands for any one man or any one unicorn to solve all of it. The facts of "right" and "wrong" were seldom obvious. A man — even a marshal — had to choose his battles carefully.

But perhaps most important in their decision not to intervene was the fact that the attacked party had been Realm folk. The Realm had exiled Clint. Edward distrusted The Realm's decadence, and had often implied that The Realm's manipulations sullied and exploited magic. Edward seemed to think that what the stitching crew had been doing to the magic vein bordered on a sort of sacrilege. So why should they stop anyone who stopped The Realm's work?

So they waited. And after the bandits had gone, Clint and Edward went down to see what was what.

The valley was nothing but metal pieces and decay. There was a thin ribbon of pure blue energy pulsing through its center. As they drew closer, Clint inspected the rift. It looked like liquid fire. Now that Clint was near it, he fancied he could see it reaching up from the ground with snakelike tentacles. He had a strange thought that was close to fear: Might it try to grab him if he got too close? Might it suck him down into the ground?

The commissioner machine had begun to creep out from behind the rock, but it slinked back the second it saw Edward approaching with Clint on his back. The surviving paladin, who'd unbound himself, was picking around the scene with a sullen air. The gunslinger was reminded of a man who compulsively checks his pistol after missing a shot as if to imply the revolver was at fault. When the paladin saw them arrive, he didn't bother to dive for his scimitar. He'd apparently been too distracted (Clint thought "incompetent") to pick it up after the bandits had left, and now he seemed to decide it was too far away and that if the stranger was going to kill him, then kill him he would. That was how knights thought. At heart, they were all cowards and quitters. So Clint thought, anyway.

"I didn't know commoners rode unicorns," the man muttered without looking up. He was wearing an odd sort of a skull-cap helmet and a full suit of chain mail — both a shirt and long pants that belled at the bottom. The wide-bottom pants on paladins were just getting started when Clint was exiled. He was sad to see that they'd endured.

Clint drew his revolver, sighted down the barrel, then re-stowed it in his holster. He'd held it just long enough to show the man his sidearm, and let him see the seven chambers in its cylinder.

"Fine, don't answer me," said the man.

"I'm not a commoner," said Clint. The knight was stupider than he thought.

"Yar, yar... everyone is special in their own way."

Clint was preparing to respond when a rapid clanking of metal came from one side. He looked over to see the commissioner machine running forward on stiff-jointed legs. Its makers had seen fit to paint blue jeans and chaps on the thing so it wouldn't appear naked, but hadn't seen fit to give it decent knee joints that would allow it to run in a natural way. Realm thinking at its best.

When the commissioner reached the circle where the ropers had first made their lassos, the machine fell onto one knee. Because of its stiff joints, this was awkward at best, but once it was settled, its position made it look like it was about to offer Clint a ring and propose a hitching. Its chest was painted to look like an open-throated trail shirt with a terrible approximation of a cowhide vest over the top. A Realm logo was painted on one side of its chest, on top of the vest. Its face was gold, like its hands and arms and neck, and its features were roughly humanoid. As a final absurdity, it had been fitted with an enormous alloy handlebar mustache, painted brown. A pocketwatch was painted on a chain, in its vest "pocket."

From its knees, the machine said in an artificially low, drawling voice, "A thousand thankoos for your presence, Marshal!" Then the glass spheres that passed for its eyes rotated toward Edward and it added, "And for yours as well, magical sire!"

The paladin looked over, vaguely interested. "You know these guys?"

Clint dismounted and looked Edward in the eye. Edward muttered, "I was wrong up on the cliff. It's him you should shoot."

The paladin finally did make a lunge for his scimitar, but Clint's right gun was out so fast he barely had time to flinch. The knight had committed on the lunge, though, and when he stopped his feet, momentum carried him forward too far, and he fell.

"I'm not here to kill you," said Clint. "So kindly don't make me."

"This gentleman is a marshal, Mister Havarow!" the machine called from its knees. "A marshal true, all the way out here in the Sands! We are saved!"

The paladin stood. As a gesture of goodwill, Clint re-holstered his firearm for the second time. He wasn't used to drawing and not firing, so he muttered a silent apology to his pistol as he stowed it.

"*Former* marshal," said Clint. "Now exiled to walk the Sands forever."

There was a mechanical sort of whirring from the commissioner and a belch of steam wafted up from somewhere behind his head. The thing's facial expressions were rudimentary, but Clint could sense discomfort no matter its source.

"Nonetheless, we thank you," the thing drawled in its low, thick backwoods voice.

"Call me 'sire' again," said Edward.

"Si..."

Clint interrupted him. "Get up. You don't bow to us. What are you?"

"Timekeeper and commissioner for Stitching Rig 104, sir," said the machine with what sounded like pride. Then he looked at the stitcher, which was in shards above the deep blue vein of fire that crossed the valley's floor. "Now defunct." Then he stumbled to his alloy feet and shambled a few feet forward, extending an arm toward Clint in a series of spastic jerking motions. "My official designation is

Commissioner 104-13, but informally I am called Buckaroo."

"Buckaroo?" said Edward.

Buckaroo's face couldn't convey emotion, but his manner and his voice could, and did. He made a small steam-gear noise and a puff of white vapor rose from the back of his neck. Clint felt suddenly sure the noise was Buckaroo's version of a laugh.

"An appropriate nickname, sir," said Buckaroo." I am a Sands machine and I ride a —" He gestured toward the rig, as if he kept forgetting that it had been stealthily disassembled. "Well, I rode what used to be a mechanical horse."

"Looks like a horse to me, all right," said Edward, using his magic to poke at the pile of rubble from a distance. His horn sparked lightly. The paladin was watching, but nothing seemed to have clicked. It was as if he'd never before been in the presence of a marshal, or had never seen a unicorn.

"What are you doing out here?" said Clint, even though Edward had already told him. "With this... whatever it is?" Edward gave him a look, but Clint gave it right back, urging him to play along. Either Buckaroo would believe that a Realm marshal and a unicorn wouldn't know what a magic vein looked like or he wouldn't. The paladin's thoughts (or lack thereof) didn't concern either of them.

"Stitching, sir," said Buckaroo, fidgeting and moving toward the wrecked pile of alloy, then deftly stepping over the chain-mail-clad figure of one of the fallen paladins. "And now? Oh, dear. We'll never make the shimmer. This vein is exposed, and without a rig to stitch it." He shook his head with a clank. "They'll have to send out another."

Buckaroo reached into what Clint had thought was a painted-on pocket in his side to retrieve what he'd thought was a painted-on pocketwatch. But the pocket turned out to be a real cavity in the machine's side, and the pocketwatch appeared to be real. The chain on the watch was attached to Buckaroo's chest, so it was probably a readout device rather than a watch true, but Buckaroo checked it like a train conductor. "Oh dear. Oh dear. And that was him who attacked us, you know. That was Mister Stone."

"Stone?" said Clint. "Not Hassle Stone, surely..." He was thinking of the bandit he'd left to the people of Solace — the man he'd driven out of the dusty town before meeting Mai, then faced again just before Kold had ridden off with his almost-bride. Was it possible that this was Stone again, and that he'd made a fatal mistake in letting him go? Should he have left him killt?

"Of the family Stone," Buckaroo clarified. "Hassle is this man's brother. This is Sylvester, though he goes by Sly. You've not heard?"

Buckaroo made fussy, nervous gestures while the remaining paladin, who still hadn't formally introduced himself or reclaimed his weapon, looked at him with scorn. "Oh, no, dear, of course you wouldn't. How long have you been exiled? Oh, I'm sorry, that is insensitive of me to ask. But you wouldn't know, would you? Of Sly and his roving rope gang?"

"I've not heard," said Clint.

"He's been raiding our operations. We have to open the veins before we can stitch them, see?" said Buckaroo, gesturing and talking more rapidly, his stiff legs pacing the site. "It's like setting a bone — sometimes they have to break it open further before setting it. And seven times over the past five years, this gang has sabotaged operations like this. He's stealing magic."

Edward gave the machine a condescending look. "You can't travel with magic."

"Oh, but you can, sire," said Buckaroo, now shambling toward Edward. "With Realm technology, you can. Stone has a set of casks. He dips them in, see, and he uses the magic he takes in his guns and possibly in other..."

"Realm technology," Edward muttered, turning away.

But Buckaroo was either too obtuse to read moods or simply didn't know Edward, because he continued to explain, still coming closer. "Yar! It's an amazing age. Except that you have to refill those casks from source, and out here, source is rare. The only way to access source out in the Sands is to draw directly from the veins, but you need a rig to do so. It puts us in a difficult position, sire. We must stitch these fractures, or else in less than a thousand years, they may spread to The Realm. You are familiar with the phenomenon of cancer, in humans?"

"I am very familiar with human cancer," said Edward, but Clint was sure he was speaking figuratively. He was looking out along the blue rift with its spilling magic. His face wasn't visible. Buckaroo shambled up beside him.

"We have to fix the rifts to contain the spread, see, sire, but every time we do, we do exactly what Stone's gang wants — we open a rift to expose the source magic. We were just about to begin the stitching when his gang fell on us. And now, look!" He gestured at the wrecked pile of Realm alloy. "Worse than it was. Now it's not only opened; it's exposed. But we cannot simply ignore the fractures, sire!"

"That's why we're here," said a voice beside Clint. He looked over. The paladin had stopped pouting. Clint had been keeping an eye on him, and he'd seen the man strip the weapons from the two dead knights while retrieving his own.

"Good thing you *were* here," said Edward. "Look how much you helped."

"Yar," said Buckaroo before the paladin could respond to Edward's sarcasm. "Used to be, stitching crews were just a commissioner and two cleaners." He gestured at the two plainclothes men in the dirt. "We added guards to all operations. But…" He trailed off. "Soon we'll need to start sending marshals, I suppose."

He looked up at Clint as if Clint were the answer to his mechanical prayers. A puff of steam plumed out from the back of his neck. The giant brown-painted handlebar mustache on his gold face rose and fell — probably some machinist's attempt to add an outward expression of humanity to a machine's hotly debated soul.

Buckaroo had re-stowed his pocketwatch, but now he pulled it back out and consulted it. The behavior of looking at the watch had to be something the engineer had programmed into him, because Buckaroo was a machine. If a machine couldn't recall what he'd read only a minute before, nothing could.

"This is intolerable," said Buckaroo. "The shimmer! We'll never make it. We can't seal this vein. We can't take the stitcher with us."

"What's a shimmer?" said Clint. But Buckaroo didn't hear him, and Edward, who'd returned from looking wistfully down the blue magic vein, nudged Clint with his rump, silently telling him that they'd discuss it later.

The paladin, finally finding himself after scavenging the site and pouting, moved until he was directly in front of Edward and Clint. He pulled something from his pocket. It was a badge — much smaller and less ornate than the one Clint once carried, but a badge nonetheless. He had the air of a man reaching an important decision.

"I need your mount," the man announced, speaking to Clint.

"Pardon?" said Edward.

"And I claim one of your sidearms, too," he added.

"Pardon?" Clint repeated.

"My scimitar is contaminated with sand. All of them seem to be," he said, patting a pouch around his waist that apparently held his fellows' weapons. "So I'm going to need a weapon." He extended a hand.

Clint ignored both hand and request. The layers of ineptitude and inappropriate behavior were downright baffling. The man wasn't authorized to carry a seven-shooter; it violated the taboo; his hands weren't large or strong enough to fire one; his shoulder wasn't sturdy enough to handle its kick. The magic in Clint's guns would, in all probability, blow off his unauthorized hand purely for spite. Asking a gunslinger for his guns was like asking a woman for her undergarments. And Edward? Edward would gallop through a sea of razors before he'd ride below a man who's soul he didn't know and trust.

"Friend," said Clint, putting his huge hand on the paladin's shoulder. "I'm going to do you a favor and ignore everything you've just said."

"I need to ride in. I need to pursue Stone."

"Because you did so well against him just now?"

"We were surprised."

"Yar," said Edward. "You were."

"There is a standing order," said the paladin. "Stone is wanted. *Badly* wanted. I need to find him. And I need to bring him in."

"That would be a neat trick," said Clint.

The paladin pushed Clint's hand from his shoulder. "I just lost two of my fellow knights!" he blurted. Clint found himself glad to see a genuine reaction from the man. "We've lost four rigs to this bandit and the fractures are spreading. You can't keep pulling at a tear in fabric or it will all fall apart." He jabbed a finger at the horizon, and the direction Sly Stone had ridden with his gang. "They're headed toward Nazareth Shiloh. I aim to follow. Are you so stubborn as to keep me from my duty? Stand aside!"

Edward had walked to the side of the ambush site, between the paladin and Nazareth Shiloh. The man's finger was still pointing; it looked like he were accusing Edward of a crime.

"Stand aside yourself," said Edward.

The man's face grew red as he started to march toward Edward. The change was so complete, Clint couldn't believe it. Maybe this dumb, incompetent knight had some life left in him yet.

"You will try to keep me from doing my duty? You once served The Realm! You are bound by Realm law — not to mention natural law, if I understand your kind — to..."

"No," said Edward, his voice calm. "I mean, *stand aside*." And he nodded toward the ground, toward the blue-fire rift in the ground, and to the remains of the Realm stitcher.

Clint saw Edward's meaning. He stepped back a few paces, away from the open magic vein, then grabbed the paladin's forearm and pulled him back as well. The man, unused to being commanded by the stern voice of a unicorn, complied. Buckaroo was already away, looking at his watch and fretting about things that made no sense to the gunslinger.

Edward lowered his head. His horn started to glow — turning purple and red before settling on a sunny, delighted orange — and then blasted a massive bolt of energy from its tip. The bolt swallowed the machine sitting atop the fracture. For a moment, Clint thought it would explode. Instead, it blew into a billion microscopic pieces, like sand-sized confetti. It looked like the whole thing was made of dust, and someone had just breathed on it hard enough to make it fall apart.

Then a stronger bolt — one that made a clap like thunder — shot from Edward's horn and struck the magic vein. The blue hands Clint had seen in the fissure all reached up at once and seemed to grab it from both sides, then pulled the rift together like slamming a door. All four of them shook as the ground jerked and rattled beneath them. The fissure vanished in a fine spray of shaken rock.

When the rattle was finished, Buckaroo walked to where the fissure and his rig used to be. There was nothing there now but a small, hair-thin line in the clay that would disappear forever once the sands blew across it for an hour.

"You're welcome," Edward said.

CHAPTER THREE: CLOWN WITH SHOTGUNS

Clint couldn't quite figure where Edward's loyalties lay with respect to The Realm and the magic — which, according to Edward, were often more or less at odds — so he asked. He asked why Edward had sealed the leaking vein of magic; he asked why The Realm didn't use unicorns for stitching jobs all the time (though he suspected it had to do with unicorn pride and their general level of jerkiness); he asked why they were escorting Paladin Havarow and Buckaroo into Nazareth Shiloh and whether or not they were *just* escorting, or whether Edward actually had plans to help the man and the machine apprehend Sly Stone.

Clint asked Edward all of this, and Edward's response was puzzling.

"HOLY GUNS, THERE'S CHILI HERE!" Edward blurted.

There were two levels on which Clint was confused. He didn't know how to react because it was strange to see such unbridled excitement from Edward. He also didn't know how to react because the notion of a town having chili was as stupid as that of a flying unicorn.

Clint looked levelly at Edward, but he could pry no further because Havarow, who was walking a few paces ahead with Buckaroo, turned his head at Edward's *gee-whiz, pa!* exclamation and quickly had his nose in the gunslinger and unicorn's business.

"Did you say chili?"

"He's kidding," said Clint. Then to Edward: "You're so silly, Edward."

Havarow, after a moment's indecision, returned his attention to the trail. Nazareth Shiloh was only a few miles off, so they all agreed to walk. Edward was tired from stitching the vein, so Clint walked too. Havarow seemed to think he was in charge, and Clint let him believe it. If they encountered bandits along the way, Clint's bullets would make things clear. For now it was irrelevant.

Edward's lips were flapping and loose. His eyes wore a wild look, almost divided and staring in two directions at once.

"Don't mess with the paladin and the machine," Clint told him. "Let's just deliver them into town. Then we can go — back through the rest of the Lakes O Plenty and to your Elf place." After a second he added, "By the way, there are no lakes here."

"That cactus is *mean*," said Edward.

Clint looked at him. "What?"

Then, suddenly, the fog vanished from the unicorn's big blue eyes. His vacant expression cleared. He looked at Clint for a long moment as if angry, like the gunslinger had done something to offend him.

"We should be on the trail toward Kold and Mai," Edward said finally, the *gee-whiz* gone from his voice, his manner once again surly. "He has two of the three Orbs in the Triangulum. Why are we with these fools?"

"Exactly," said Clint.

His hoofs beating a slow tattoo on the hard-packed clay of the ground, Edward continued to stare at the gunslinger.

"What?"

"I asked you a question," said the unicorn.

Clint looked at Edward for a moment, then shook his head and ignored him. Edward was being obtuse. He was *always* obtuse. He still hadn't explained what in the Sands this "Triangulum" thing was, and knowing Edward, he never would — at least not entirely. And now, for some dumb reason, he was playing games.

Annoyed, Clint walked faster. He left the unicorn behind and strolled up next to Havarow, deciding to try his luck at pulling Realm news from the paladin. He may never find The Realm again, but at least he could gather some of the latest gossip.

"Do you think it's true?" the paladin asked without preamble as Clint came up beside him.

"I know nar of your man Stone or what might be true or false about him," the gunslinger said.

Havarow cleared his throat, scratched his dusty skin with a dirty fingernail, and spit into the sand.

"I meant what your unicorn says about chili," he said. "They can see far, can they not?"

Beside him, perhaps listening in, Buckaroo made beeping noises. The vent on the back of his neck belched white steam.

"Edward is an idiot," Clint said. Then he decided that wasn't fair. "Okay, he's not an idiot. But he *is* a jerk."

"But could it be true, though? Could there really be chili?"

Clint thought. He'd heard the rumors. He'd heard the reports from travelers, and he'd always regarded them in the same way he'd regarded reports about the Fountain of Youth. He'd heard from seers, from those who dealt in magic.

"Of course not."

Havarow spit into the sand again.

"Do you think your man will be there, though?" said Clint, changing the topic away from absurdity.

"Why? Are you feeling like a lawman again?"

Clint shook his head. "Just curious."

They were passing a large cluster of signs. One said, *You are entering the land of Abraham and chili.* Havarow looked lightningstruck when he saw it, but Clint made a casual remark about how superstitious the outlands were about their gods and about chili, and Havarow fell silent. Later, neither remarked on a crooked, ancient sign ten feet further on that read, *Providence saves; blessed is the chili.*

Havarow spat. The glob struck Clint's boot, and Clint resisted an urge to leave the paladin killt in the sand lying beside his saliva. It would be easy, and he doubted the thinking machine would judge him for it, giddy as it had been to see them back at the seam.

"He'll be there," said Havarow. "He's cocky. He's walked right in front of us before, just to flaunt his supposed power and authority. And that hair? Those shotguns? It's all showy, since he figures…"

"Shotguns?"

Havarow rolled his eyes. "He carries two magic-enhanced sawed off shotguns in his holsters instead of pistols. Kind of hard to miss. Some marshal you are."

"I'm sorry, Paladin," Clint said. "I was too busy watching your men get slaughtered to make out the insignia on his barrels from a quarter-mile above you."

Havarow's eyebrows drew together, but he said nothing.

"Butterflies!" Edward yelled from behind them.

"What is wrong with your mount?" said Havarow, looking back.

"He's messing with you," said Clint.

Buildings were becoming visible as they crested a rise. They passed two more signs. The signs were identical, flanked by crosses, one on each side of the road. They both said, *Believe in chili.*

"I think it's true," said Havarow.

"Oh, it's true," said Clint. "He messes with *me* all the time."

"I meant the chili," said the paladin. "We've worked these lands before, though I've never been to Nazareth Shiloh proper." His eyes darkened with superstition. "The shaman here whisper of chili."

"I ain't heard nar a person who believed the rumors of chili were true," said Clint.

But the rumors *were* true, or else the town of Nazareth Shiloh was suffering a grand delusion. When they entered the town itself — passing a well not unlike the one outside Precipice, then a blacksmith, then a cobbler's shop — they began to see signs for chili everywhere.

Clint was reminded of a time he'd accompanied a friend to a revival. The friend had been acting strange (not unlike Edward was now, in fact) and had told Clint all about how his new friends could sift magic like a shaman and were planning the return of the magic. Though Clint knew it to be untrue, he went to the revival anyway. And at that revival, he'd found crazy men and women dancing and singing and circling a washtub, burning candles and branding themselves with cattle irons. Crazy people, brainwashed into a dream.

The chili aura of Nazareth Shiloh town felt like that revival.

On a storefront: *Our chili has seven spices.*

On the storefront across the street: *Forget how many spices a chili has — ours has simmered for hours!*

On a post outside the town hall: *Serving chili here! Believe in chili!*

And at the town marshal's office, at the head of every hitching post: *In chili we trust* and *To protect and serve chili.*

"I hesitate to ask for help from a chili-based lawman," said Clint.

But Havarow didn't hear him. He was licking his lips, picking up his pace as they neared the marshals' station. Then he started to run.

But there was something wrong. Clint could feel it.

"Paladin!" he shouted. "Stop! It's a trap!"

The gunslinger sprinted after him, diving to catch Havarow in a tackle. But the paladin was too fast, his chili lust too strong. He was a half-step ahead, and Clint only caught his ankle.

Clint fell to the ground. Urgently, he turned to summon Edward's help, but it was in vain; his vision was met by a semicircle of keratin descending toward his face. He rolled to the side and the keratin — a unicorn hoof — slammed into the ground beside his ear. Another set followed, all somehow miraculously missing their stomp.

He rolled in the dirt, his heart thumping.

Edward's enormous white rear and swishing white tail passed him, running behind Havarow. The paladin jumped onto the porch outside the station and through its door. Edward stayed close, but he was too big; instead of passing *through* the doorframe, he slammed hard into it. The doorframe shuddered and shook. Wood splinters flew.

Along with being too wide for the doorway, Edward was also too tall. His horn caught on the top, knocking his head backward. Then something gave — presumably the threshold — and Edward's large shoulders jammed to a stop. Then he stopped, jammed in the doorway with his head jerking around as if confused about what had just happened.

"Edward!" Clint shouted, scrambling to his feet.

"I seem to be stuck," said Edward's rear.

"It's a trap! Create us a bubble!"

A small pink bubble formed at the tip of Edward's horn, then fell to the wood planking underfoot and popped.

"A bubble of *protection!*" Clint snarled, equally panicked and annoyed.

Edward didn't give any indication that he'd so much as heard him, but Clint was already realizing that it didn't matter. Nothing had happened. Despite Havarow and Buckaroo's mad dash into an obvious trap, there had been no gunfire.

He approached the unicorn, who was still wedged into the doorframe, and tried to peek around him. But then Edward's head snapped around and he stared daggers at Clint, wordlessly accusing the gunslinger of causing his predicament.

Edward's body shimmered with light. There was a sharp pop, like the noise of a woman's tiny pistol, and an inch of space appeared all the way around Edward where the doorframe had been pinching him. The wood that had filled the space sifted to the deck in a billow of sawdust. Then Edward backed up, minding his horn, and continued to stare sidelong at Clint.

Clint met Edward's look of loathing, then looked past him into the police station. Buckaroo and the paladin were both inside, speaking to a man behind a desk. Clint could see several paintings on the wall of bowls heaped with chili. None of the people in the room gave any indication that they'd noticed a unicorn getting stuck in the doorway.

"Everyone okay in there?" Clint shouted.

"Why wouldn't we be?" said Havarow.

Edward was still staring wordlessly at Clint. He backed off of the wood deck and into the street. He started to pace. Clint, leaving the lawmen behind, followed him, more confused about Edward than ever.

"Why did you bring us on this fool errand?" asked the unicorn.

"This was *your* idea," said Clint.

"I've no recollection of that."

Clint grabbed Edward's long face and stared into his right eye. "What's wrong with you, Edward? Something is wrong in your head, isn't it? Tell me true."

The big blue eye blinked, its expression turning to exasperation. Edward sighed. "It's the magic. I was worried about this. Have I been saying strange things?"

"To put it mildly."

"Even unicorns are not meant to be so near a pure source of magic, or at least not one that is so completely exposed. I'm afraid it has left me addled."

"Will it go away, now that we're further from the magic and the vein is sealed?"

"It's like catching a sneeze," said Edward. "I'm afraid it will have to run its course."

Clint sighed. "Fine. Then let's get this 'fool errand' over with and be on our way. Look around for the bandits we seek."

Edward turned his head, looking around.

"Using your magic, I mean."

But Edward just looked at Clint uncomprehendingly, a fog across his eyes.

"You're back into 'addled,' aren't you?" said Clint. "You don't know how to use your magic, do you?"

Edward looked at the gunslinger for a moment longer, his expression vacant.

So Clint started pacing. He walked to one side of the street. He turned, then walked back to the other. Edward remained rooted, his head low like a common horse. So Clint walked further, peeking in windows, and when he returned, he saw that Edward had magicked a piece of turkey pie from the pack. It was floating in front of his face.

The unicorn eyed Clint and took a bite.

"You remembered how to use your magic, then," said Clint.

"Yar. I also remembered how ugly you were," Edward replied, chewing.

"Come on. Let's try the saloon."

So they walked down to the saloon, which had a sign posted outside advertising free chili with brew. It was the sort of place where any outlaw worth his salt would hang out if he came through town, and once Havarow and Buckaroo rallied their posse, it would probably be the first place they'd look for Sly Stone and his gang. It's where Clint would look first, anyway.

Slowly, minding his footsteps, Clint peered inside. There was a huge sphere of orange at the bar. It looked like a magical floating orb until he realized that it was the back of Stone's head.

Clint's hand fell to his gun.

"You can't kill him," said a voice.

Clint turned to find Edward behind him, the piece of pie still floating in front of his face.

"You heard what Havarow said earlier," he continued. "They need to know about this man's operation. He needs to go to The Realm and stand trial, and he can't do that if he's dead."

"And he *will* stand trial," said Clint, tapping his head with a long, bony finger. "I'm not as dumb as you think I am. I don't know if you were in your stupidity when the machine mentioned a way they had to return to The Realm, but they have one, and I intend to see it."

"And *use* it?" said Edward.

"Maybe they could use the help of a marshal in escorting their man, is all I'm saying."

Clint nodded at the unicorn, then rotated his gun belt so that his left pistol was behind his back. He pulled a bandana from his pocket and casually draped it over his right pistol. Obscuring his sidearms was humiliating, but a common man could only carry one pistol, and the bandana would conceal the visible gun's size and seven-shot cylinder. With luck, Stone would believe it to be ordinary.

The gunslinger entered the bar, leaving his unstable companion outside.

Clint and Stone were the only two men in the bar and the clack of Clint's boots on the floorboards was loud. After a long moment, Stone turned slowly around to look at Clint — but when he looked, he *looked*, up and down. And Clint, keeping his scrutiny low-key, did the same of Stone.

Stone's giant orange hairdo looked fake, but Clint could tell that it wasn't. He had pale, freckled skin that looked entirely too fragile for the Sands sun and air. (Clint theorized that perhaps his large hair acted as a brimmed hat, shielding his face.) He wore two guns on his hips (illegal enough), but Clint could see right away that they were actually shotguns with the barrels and stocks mostly removed (*very* illegal), slung into oversized holsters like giant pistols. To make the illegality complete, Havarow had said that those two big guns were powered by magic — and sure enough, Clint could see a small device, like a reload capsule, buried in the grips of each. The magic capsules glowed in a steady, pulsing rhythm.

"Hi there, fella," said Stone.

Clint looked at the man's guns. They were in their holsters with the handles facing forward. It meant that Stone drew across his chest rather than straight from the hip. A cross-draw would be clunky with guns so large, so it had to be something he did for show, not unlike his giant hairdo.

"I saw you from a cliff in the desert," said Clint. "You and some men with ropes."

Stone smiled as if he were a celebrity meeting a fan. "Yar."

"How can those men do what they do, with mere ropes?" said Clint. He was pitching his voice in an imitation of awe, as if he himself were aiming to learn to rope.

"Practice," said Stone.

He took a sip of something from his mug. Whatever was inside was too chunky to be brew. His lips parted from the cracked porcelain flushed in a deep red. He wiped his mouth on a dusty sleeve and then looked again at Clint, taking him in. He paused at his single gun, draped with a bandana. He smirked, and his eyes rose to Clint's face.

"And what, may I ask, is your interest in roping?"

"Just curious. As I'm curious about those sidearms you carry." Clint tried cracking a tiny smile — a quiet promise to Stone that this was all just casual banter, that he was a shy man who'd found someone he admired.

Stone tapped the shotgun on his right hip. He smiled and was about to answer when he suddenly stopped, his eyes narrowing as a small noise broke the quiet.

Clint had heard it too, but he pretended he hadn't.

Stone reached toward the bar. He pushed the mug away. They were standing in the middle of the saloon, a few feet from the bar's polished edge, with Clint's back to the door. Something in Stone's expression had changed. Clint's hand wanted to go to his (single) gun but he held it, some deep intuition telling him that no matter what, he must not engage until and unless he had to.

This man will be taken to The Realm, he told himself. *Kold is going to The Realm. We want to go to The Realm. The third Orb is somewhere between here and The Realm, and so is Mai. Stay your hands. Whatever chance there is to reach The Realm, that chance rides with Stone.*

His hand twitched, wanting to make murder. But he held it. He waited.

"These are *magic* guns," said Stone. A small smile twitched at the corner of his mouth. "Here," he added. "I'll show you."

Stone's hands moved fast.

Clint, repressing every urge in his honed gunslinger's body, stilled his own hands and dove for the floor.

CHAPTER FOUR: BY THE SEVEN SPICES OF CHILI

As Clint suspected, Stone's draw was, by marshal's standards, slow and clumsy. His sawed-off shotguns were at least three times as long as Clint's seven-shooters and easily five times as heavy. Clint saw every rattle and shake that the giant guns made as they emerged from their holsters. Alloy clattered on rivets. The barrels flicked the leather, not coming out clean. Stone had to fumble and adjust his grips during the draw, and as the guns crossed — that big, showy double cross-draw — they nearly collided. The guns were so long that Stone couldn't rotate their barrels toward his targets until they were clear of each other, which was something a straight draw would eliminate.

Despite all of that, Stone's draws were by most measures clean and fast. Within a flicker of a second he'd aimed and pulled both triggers, shouldered two incredibly large kicks, and blown matching holes in the saloon walls — one on either side of the swinging batwing door.

Of course, Clint had seen this coming.

He'd seen Stone's eyes flick toward the door as he'd heard the tiny sound from outside. He'd known Stone anticipated an ambush, and he'd known that Stone was right. He'd known that although Clint was a wildcard in the bandit's eyes, the targets outside were *for-sure*. Clint was counting on a hunch that Stone wasn't intending to fire on him, and that he'd leave the stranger alone as long as he didn't seem like a threat. But if he was wrong, he'd be dead. Edward was right outside, but he was flickering in and out of awareness. He might not be able to help if Clint got himself wounded or dead.

Stone's shotguns flashed. They belched forth two swirls of purplish smoke in the saloon's dry air (Clint was relieved to see the smoke wasn't the pink of a marshal's weapon, so at least there hadn't been a total breach of taboo) as his targets — two lawmen crouching outside — evaporated into a churning green mist. Then Stone moved again, turning a third lawman into mist as he tried to enter. Then, immediately after the third shotgun blast, a volley of shells crashed into the saloon. Stone fell to the floor as lead slugs blew splinters from the wooden bar. Then he came to his knees, knocking two stools down in front of himself as a makeshift bunker. The stools were meager cover, but they stopped at least one shell, which annihilated a cross-brace and narrowly missed his leg.

Clint, who found himself nearly in the line of fire, crawled away from the door and made his way to the side, now more or less behind Stone. Stone was crouched low, almost in a ball. All Clint could see were guns and a giant sphere of orange hair. Purple haze filled his eyes as Stone continued to fire.

The front wall of the saloon exploded with tiny holes as splinters tumbled to the floor. Distantly, Clint wondered just what the lawmen were thinking. They couldn't see what they were shooting at and their shells wouldn't spin true like a gunslinger's rounds, so they could hit anything. The bartender, who'd been in the back, was safe. But was that just luck, or had they known the saloon would be empty?

Or did Havarow not care if the bartender — or Clint, for that matter — were struck?

Low on the ground, Stone had the advantage. A fourth and fifth Nazareth Shiloh lawman stormed into the saloon, immediately ducking behind large alloy signs advertising chili. But they'd either forgotten that Stone's shotguns were magic or Havarow hadn't told them, because the outlaw stood tall and blew twin holes in the signs. Green mist puffed from around the edges.

Clint could hear Havarow outside, yelling at the others to go in and do his job for him. The marshal felt his irritation with the paladin — with paladins in general, based on his experiences — grow. Havarow was commanding other men to go into *his* conflict, to apprehend *his* responsibility, and to be killt so that *he* could live. It was just like them. Bullies and cowards, all.

Stone raised his guns to fire again, but they clicked empty in unison. He rushed to reload, frantically ducking back behind the barstools and fishing shells from his pockets.

He got one into the chamber.

Two.

Three.

He hadn't closed the chamber and was unprepared when the batwings burst open and Paladin Havarow, finally showing his face, entered with what had to be the only three lawmen left in town. All four ducked for cover. Stone, finally loaded, racked one of his guns and raised it, leaving the other on the floor. Havarow drew, but Havarow was slow. Stone was faster... but there were too many lawmen, too many targets, too many guns turning toward him.

He held his fire. Havarow, a half-second behind, held his. A moment later all five of the battling men found themselves with their firearms pointed at each other in a standoff.

Everything stopped. One heartbeat passed. Everyone saw who had the drop on whom. Stone had a bead on a man who had a bead right back on him. But very close by, Stone had two others — including Havarow — dead in his sights. It was possible that the man who Stone was centered on could kill Stone before Stone killt him. But it was more possible that Stone would win the exchange between the two — and if that happened, the three lawmen and the paladin would never fire their guns in time.

"You can kill me," said Stone. "But rest assured, at least two of you will go with me."

One lawman looked at Havarow. Havarow looked back. Stone shifted his gun, seeing who was in charge, and focused his barrel on Havarow's chest. Now only one man on the side of law was in danger, but it was the one who was giving the orders.

Havarow slowly lowered his gun and set it on the floor. Then he waved for the others to do the same. A moment later, one man with one gun held four others at bay, their eight hands held high in the air.

That was when Clint cocked the gun he'd set against the back of Stone's skull.

The room exhaled.

Across the saloon, the lawmen reclaimed their guns. Havarow crossed to Stone and placed him in shackles, but Stone, instead of looking at Havarow, turned to look at Clint. He smiled, giving the gunslinger a small, congratulatory nod.

Stone was in shackles and being led toward the batwings by Nazareth lawmen when two ropes entered the saloon, seemed to turn at right angles through the door, and grabbed the lawmen by the necks.

The lawmen fell as the ropes tightened, dragging them toward the door. Their hands went to their necks, digging fingers under the ropes, gasping for air. Then all of a sudden there was a flash of yellow light from outside. The ropes went slack. And at the same time, two men screamed.

Clint ran for the door, passing Havarow (who'd manage to pin Stone) and the two lawmen (who were unroped and breathing again). Outside, he found a group of four men grasping at their chests as if they'd been punched. Someone had disarmed them, just in the nick of time.

Edward.

Clint looked around and saw the unicorn across the street, eating grass from a small patch near a trough. Edward *never* ate grass. Eating grass was something horses did.

Clint sighed, unsure whether to be thankful for the rescue or frustrated by the reversion. Edward had stopped four of the bandits, sure. But it seemed that his switch had already flipped back.

Four bandits. But that wasn't enough, was it?

Clint looked around for the rest of the gang (by his count, there had to be at least seven more), but the streets of Nazareth Shiloh were nothing but dust. The rest of the gang was gone or was hiding.

The men on the ground had dropped their ropes. As Clint watched, they got up and began reaching for them again. They had their hands on the ropes and were already starting to form new lassos when Clint removed the bandana at his waist and rotated his other pistol into view.

"By the seven spices of chili," whispered one of the men. "He's a *marshal.*"

The man immediately dropped his rope and raised his hands, backing away. Another watched him and did the same. Then both men, seeing that Clint wasn't moving, turned and ran.

One of the two remaining bandits — a scrawny man with the alabaster skin of an albino — continued to work his lasso. He wielded the rope like a weapon that was already drawn and aimed. It looked as if he thought he could rope Clint before the gunslinger could shoot him. Or as if he thought he could catch bullets.

The remaining bandit looked at the albino. "Teedawge," he said. "Don't."

"Yeah, Teedawge," said Clint. "Don't."

But Teedawge did. He whipped his arm forward, and the rope shot at Clint far, far faster than the gunslinger would have imagined possible. It circled his right gun and began to tug it from its holster. Just in time, Clint got his big hand around the pistol as well, fighting to pull it back. His face twisted into indignant rage. Whether a man used a rope or his hand, it was death to touch a marshal's guns.

While his right hand fought the rope for a grip on one gun, Clint dealt death with the other. Teedawge hit the dirt. The rope went slack.

The other bandit looked briefly at Clint and then ran.

Clint freed his right pistol from the slack rope, shaking a little at how easily the man had almost disarmed him. He looked at the rope, expecting it to be magical. But no, it was just a rope. Nothing fancy.

From the doorway, Sly Stone — still in both shackles and Havarow's custody — chuckled. Then Havarow twisted the shackles, turning Stone's chuckle to a sharp groan of pain.

Then Buckaroo walked up to Clint, steam belching from behind his neck.

"Thankoo for assisting us with apprehending our man, sir," he said, giving a small bow to the gunslinger. He turned and gave a deeper bow to Edward, who was still chewing grass and not paying the slightest bit of attention. "And thankoo, sire," he added.

Edward was silent, save for the munching sounds coming through his large teeth. Clint nodded. Havarow grunted.

"What will you do with him?" Clint asked the machine.

Buckaroo tittered nervously, checking his pocket watch. "Take him to a shimmer, sir, in Aurora Solstice. Tomorrow. He will be returned to The Realm, where he will stand trial." He looked to Havarow as if for confirmation, and got it from the paladin in the form of a small nod. The gesture said that Havarow was annoyed to be asked.

"A shimmer?"

"None of your concern," said Havarow before Buckaroo could respond.

Clint let it go. Edward would explain it later.

"Pardon sir," said Buckaroo, addressing Havarow, "but it may indeed be his concern, or perhaps it *should* be. Meeting a 3:10 shimmer tomorrow will be difficult as it is, given the hour. And there is also the matter of Mr. Stone's gang, which is still at large. You are one man — be you noble and deadly of course, sir — but I am of little value in ambush. We could use the help, should trouble resurface."

Havarow glanced at the body of the bandit Teedawge, then looked at Clint with something like heavy, sighing irritation.

"Where do your travels take you, Marshal?" he said.

Clint smirked. Havarow had called him "Marshal." And Havarow, who was a minor knight of The Realm himself, would never call an exiled marshal "Marshal" lightly. Knights of all levels were proud and superior, and paladins and marshals had never much gotten along. He wouldn't be giving Clint a title he didn't feel Clint deserved if he didn't need something — whether he was willing to admit it or not.

"We are pursuing a rider," Clint replied. "We have reason to believe he may be headed toward —" He paused, then continued. "—

toward Aurora Solstice."

That was a bit of a lie, because they no longer held a definite trail on Kold and had last assumed he'd be heading through the Lakes O Plenty and on to Elf Meadows. But the bigger truth was that Kold was headed to The Realm, and where routes to The Realm were concerned, the fastest path — seemingly Havarow's — was best. Havarow would never let Clint and Edward near whatever this "shimmer" was, of course, but Clint could deal with that particular problem when it arrived. One challenge at a time.

"Your passage back to The Realm. It's tomorrow afternoon?" said Clint.

Buckaroo removed his pocket watch, on its chain, from the cavity that served as his vest pocket. He consulted it for the millionth time and replied, "Yar, sir. By my calculations, which I currently believe to be accurate, the window opens at ten minutes after three."

"Opens at?" said Clint.

Havarow shot him a look. "You'd be an escort. Nothing more."

"And what is my incentive to be an escort?" said Clint.

Havarow chewed his lip. He was a minor knight and had virtually no authority to offer Clint anything.

"Magic, perhaps."

Clint nodded toward Edward. "I have magic."

"Money, then."

"I have no need for money."

Havarow rolled his eyes. "Absolution. Forgiveness. They wouldn't revoke your exile, I'm sure, but maybe they could... *forgive* you. *Maybe*."

Clint's eyes narrowed. His lips formed a stiff-lipped frown. Listening to his own voice, he was shocked and almost frightened by the ice he heard in it as he said, "I don't want your forgiveness."

"Then how about entertainment?" said a fourth voice.

Clint turned around. Havarow had taken Sly Stone's guns and shackled him to a post while they were gearing up to leave, and now Stone was, against all sensibility, laughing behind him.

He smiled, then shook his giant orange afro and said, "Hey, everybody loves a clown."

CHAPTER FIVE:
AN UNEASY PALAVER

As they set out for Aurora Solstice and their rendezvous with whatever a shimmer was, Edward went in and out of lucidity. Clint did his best to hide Edward's condition from the others, but he wouldn't be able to for long.

During his more present moments, Edward told Clint that his thoughts were becoming increasingly foggy. He was having a hard time holding his concentration. He sometimes forgot the trick of using magic — but more troublingly, he also sometimes flat-out forgot the trick of *being Edward*. He spoke of elves and turkey pie and of things that didn't exist. He spoke of his colthood, which sounded like it might have been millennia back... and that's assuming that the unicorn was speaking true in the first place. Edward himself soon couldn't tell which thoughts were real and which weren't, and took to quizzing the gunslinger to find out.

"Cerebrus defiling Mai?" said Edward.

"Real," said Clint.

"Chili in the last town?"

"Rumor," said Clint. "Superstition."

"An easterner wearing eyeshades and singing about style?"

"That was my hallucination, back in the Dinosaur Missouri. How can you know *my* hallucination?"

"I don't know. But somehow it infected me, because he's right beside you."

Clint looked over, saw nothing, and continued to ride.

Clint feared that his opportunities to speak with the real Edward were growing fewer with each passing hour, so he, in turn, tried to gather whatever information from the unicorn that he could while there was still time. He asked about the Orbs, about Kold, and about the object that Edward had alluded to called the Triangulum Enchantem. But Edward was already too far gone. He could barely remember the Triangulum. He could barely remember the Orb of Malevolence. He could barely remember fighting Jarmusch, or the Orb they still carried in a vial, heavily protected inside of Clint's pack.

"If Kold finds the third Orb before we find Kold," said Clint, "will he be too powerful to stop?"

"I don't know. I don't remember. I think so," said Edward, his eyes distant and helpless.

"So we should pursue Kold, and we should abandon these fools."

"Kold is going to The Realm, and they are going to The Realm. So where we are is not insensible." He blinked. "I mean, I think it's not."

"Yar, but this group is going through a shimmer, whatever that is," said Clint. "Kold is taking the long route, and he might be finding the Orb right now. By the time we meet him in or near The Realm — if we meet him — he may be unstoppable." Clint paused, then added, "And while we're at it, what *is* a shimmer?"

"I don't know." Edward shook his head, making his mane dance. "I mean, I did know once, but I no longer do. It's so hard to concentrate. The magic in me is too rich. It's like a disease, eating me alive from within." He took a deep breath and seemed to concentrate. Then he said, "I believe that a shimmer is like a door."

"Why have you never told me about shimmers before? We could have been searching for them, taking shortcuts."

"They're a product of decay," said Edward. "They are not supposed to be here."

"So is it that you don't know where they are, or are you being elitist and refusing to use doorways that are somehow perverse, even though they might speed our journey?"

A moment passed. Clint waited for Edward to answer, but then he looked down and saw that the unicorn's big blue eyes were vacant, gazing at the dusty trail ahead.

Edward's vacantness became the norm as the day grew long. When they'd left Nazareth Shiloh, Clint had been riding Edward the unicorn. But after a few hours, Clint was riding something or someone else. Edward forgot Clint. He forgot The Realm. He forgot that he was magic, and that he was a mighty unicorn. He became an unresponsive, blindly obeying mount. Like a horse.

So, to quiet his panic about Edward, Clint spent the rest of the afternoon trying to draw information from Havarow and Buckaroo — the only two beings from The Realm he'd met since his exile.

Havarow was useless. He was tight as a drum, and refused to talk to Clint beyond the necessities. He seemed to feel that an exiled marshal — one who thought he was above The Realm's forgiveness, could such forgiveness be given — shouldn't be offered more information than he already had. He seemed to think that Clint Gulliver had been exiled for a reason and should be handed nothing that might help him to return.

Buckaroo, however, wouldn't stop talking. So after a few miles, with Havarow in the lead on a horse he'd purchased in Nazareth Shiloh and with Stone tied securely to a horse beside him, Clint slowly fell behind and lured Buckaroo to the rear of their convoy with him.

Then, he and the thinking machine started to chat.

Buckaroo was of limited help because he'd never actually been to The Realm, but he was miles better than the silent paladin. He was a mere service machine, tasked with leading stitching crews to repair damage before it could spread to The Realm. The offhand way Buckaroo spoke of the rest of the world — nobody cared if the fissures spread *away* from The Realm, for instance — irked Clint, but Buckaroo spoke so matter-of-factly and innocently that it was clear he was programmed (quite literally) to think only of The Realm. His prejudice wasn't his fault. Buckaroo had no malice toward the rest of the world, but he definitely loved The Realm above all else. The fact that he himself had never been allowed behind the wall didn't seem to faze him.

As they rode — always watching for Stone's roving rope gang and never seeing it, though constantly assured by Stone that it was following — Buckaroo also told Clint about his other function.

"I am a timekeeper, sir," he told Clint, patting the alloy pouch on his side and thus affecting a pat of his pocket watch.

Specifically, what Buckaroo "tracked" were tears in the fabric of the worlds. As a timekeeper, his job was to calculate the timing, location, and duration of tears. Buckaroo, being a low-level machine, didn't understand exactly how or why the world *had* tears, but Clint had heard enough rumor (and pried enough from Edward over the years) to fill the gaps in Buckaroo's knowledge.

During the first fracture, the Realm sheared loose from the rest of the world in a way that no man could see, but that unicorns could. The physical roads leading to The Realm didn't crumble, but the roads nonetheless grew confused. The Realm, so it was said, became impossible to find. The ways in — which had once been concrete and distinct — became vague. A path to The Realm could be long or short depending on a traveler's perception, the day and time, or shifts in the magic. A man could brush the wall of The Realm and not know that it was there — and, in a way, might not actually *be* near it at all.

It was all very confusing, but the way Clint imagined it was this: it was as if The Realm had fallen out of phase with the rest of the world. Edward talked about frequencies of magic and of "tuning in," and told the gunslinger that The Realm was no longer at the same frequency as the rest of the world. Edward also used some of the same terms Buckaroo used: *fabric* and *tearing*. Edward often spoke of loose threads, and about how you should never tug on a loose thread lest the whole of the fabric unravel. And so, Clint's mind had formed a picture of the worlds as a large bolt of fabric with many folds in it. Sometimes — and Buckaroo seemed to agree with this metaphor — tears in various places on the fabric lined up. When that happened, something from one point on the fabric could instantly travel through the tear to an entirely different place.

To The Realm, for instance.

Buckaroo, as a timekeeper and tracker of aligning tears, was equipped with instrumentation that he himself didn't understand. All he knew was that the pocket watch device he carried gave him data, and that his intuitive processors were capable of making rather precise estimations about the location, timing, and duration of tears — called "shimmers" — based on that data.

"What's to stop a bandit from taking you apart and stealing that machinery for his own use?" Clint asked, making sure they were well back from Stone when he did.

Buckaroo tapped his golden head and replied in his polite, down-home, syrupy voice. "Intuitive processors," he repeated. "Magic can't just be read, sir. It must be thought out, like a logic puzzle."

When full dark fell, they made camp. Edward fell into and mostly out of lucidity, spending the majority of his time sullen and disconnected. Clint was concerned. He wondered if the real Edward would ever return… if the poisoning he'd received from the magic was like a passing illness that simply had to run its course like a fever, or a lingering one that would result in lasting damage.

With Edward addled, there were only four coherent souls around the fire that evening. Buckaroo was so subservient and by-the-rules that his presence was closer to that of a spark cooker, and so, despite their differences, Clint, Sly Stone, and Paladin Havarow made palaver as if, for a desperate moment, they had become friends.

Stone was disarmingly pleasant for a man in shackles who was on his way to trial and then to death. He made jokes. He asked politely for food. He ate neatly. He said pleasem and thankoo. When Clint dropped a fork, Stone picked it up, cleaned it, and returned it with a smile. This happened several times, because the forks Havarow supplied were tiny, and Clint had gigantic gunslinger's hands.

Stone also told them about his gang — not because he wanted to make threats, but just for the practice of spinning yarns. His tales treated the gang's deadliness as matter-of-fact. He explained that he'd allied with the rope gang's leader, Gunther Jethro, because they had the same aims. They were not innately tied, and would remain allied only until such time as their aims diverged. But Stone added that *until* that time, the gang remained fiercely loyal to him. They were *absolutely* on their trail, probably watching from the weeds, waiting for the right time to pounce. He quite calmly told the paladin that he'd never make it to the shimmer. The gang, including Jethro, saw Sly Stone as a co-leader, and they'd see his taking — from them, proud ropers that they were — as a direct affront to their honor. And they did not stand for affronts to their honor.

"Gunther Jethro," said Havarow, spitting into the dirt. "I'd say that's as stupid a name as Sly Stone."

"My full name is Sylvester," said Stone, nonplussed.

Havarow chuckled. "That's even worse."

"What's your first name, if I might ask?"

Havarow cleared his throat and raised his chin. "Nigel."

"That's a fine name for someone with his head up his own butt," said Stone, nodding.

Havarow stood, his suit of chain mail jangling. He pulled his scimitar from his belt and lit it. A sword of light extended from the alloy cylinder, casting shadows that danced across the campsite, counterpointing the shadows made by the flickering light of the fire.

"I wonder if I'd be praised or reprimanded if you died on the way to your trial," said Havarow.

"I wonder if, with that hat on, you look like a bedpan from above," Stone countered.

"I think they'd be disappointed that they couldn't try you, but that they wouldn't chastise me too harshly," said Havarow.

"Do birds ever pee on your head?" Stone asked placidly.

Havarow, who had been ready to boil from the moment Clint had met him, lunged for Stone. Clint managed to get his hands between the men, holding them apart. Havarow's teeth pulled back in a snarl.

"Oh, of *course* birds don't pee on your head," said Stone, leaning back as Clint fought with the paladin. "How silly of me. Birds urinate in a paste. So do birds ever *paste* on your head?" He made a curious face. Then he squeezed a sausage from his dinner between his fingers, shooting a lumpy stringer of grease onto the paladin's chest.

Havarow, barely restrained, renewed his lunge toward the bandit. This time, Clint couldn't get between them. Havarow began throwing punches at his prisoner. Stone tried to hold up his shackled hands in defense, but it was no use; blow after blow landed until Clint pulled Havarow away, still kicking and thrashing. But the paladin still needed a target, so he turned his rage on Clint. He tried to swing at the gunslinger, but Clint easily deflected his blows.

Stone, beaten and bleeding, laughed from the dirt. Havarow hurled insults. Across the fire, heedless, Edward slept on his side.

Eventually Havarow calmed down, and after casting a few final glances at Clint, he tied Sly Stone to a tree. Stone's hands were shackled; his cheek and eyes were already starting to puff. Then Havarow spread his bedding in a clear area, rubbing his bruised fist. Clint, still quietly fearing for his unicorn companion, laid down beside Edward.

Eventually, the reluctant companions — now turned combatants — fell into uneasy sleep.

CHAPTER SIX: NO TEARS FOR THE PALADIN

Clint awoke to a sensation he almost never felt: a hand lightly slapping him awake. It was so odd that at first, he had no reaction. Even though it had happened in his sleep — someone had gotten the drop on him.

"Wake up."

The campsite was dark, three shades from pure black. Clint had no idea of the time. Buckaroo was normally studded with lights, but he'd extinguished them when he'd put himself into sleep mode. The fire had burned down to embers and was now glowing with a vacant, haunted orange that peeked between the remains of the logs in an abstract lattice.

The hand continued to slap him. The voice he'd heard was a whisper, so whatever was happening, Clint's foggy mind reckoned that quiet and discretion were warranted. And the owner of that hand hadn't killt him yet.

Clint had a pack of matches in his pocket. He pulled one out, lit it with his thumbnail, and held it up to see the patient face of Sly Stone haloed by bright orange hair. The hand that had been slapping him was now visible in the matchlight. Stone's other hand was at his side.

(!!!)

Clint shuffled backward fast, his back colliding with a sleeping unicorn. Edward didn't stir. The gunslinger's hand flew to his holster and within a fraction of a second, his gun was out and pointing at Stone. He'd even managed to do it quietly.

"How are you free?" Clint hissed. The last time he'd seen Stone, before sleep came to drag him down, the bandit had been tied to a tree with shackled hands. Somehow, in the midnight hours, Stone had freed himself from his shackles and, quite separately, broken his tether to the tree.

Stone held a finger in front of his lips.

"How?" Clint hissed. He was panicked. It was wrong of a marshal to be panicked, but he'd also just been surprised while sleeping. It was a miracle Stone hadn't reached his guns. But that hadn't been a real possibility, had it? His hands and hips would feel a man fooling with his sidearms... wouldn't they?

Stone jabbed the finger more insistently in front of his lips. Clint's own fingers, holding the match, were getting warm; the match had almost burned to its end. His other hand moved his pistol into the light, in case Stone had missed it.

Stone's eyes rolled. "The fork, okay?" he whispered. "Your fork from dinner."

Clint felt his head clearing. He moved his gun forward. "Where is it now? The fork?"

"In the paladin's neck."

The flame from the match touched Clint's thumb and he jerked his hand. The match went out and fell to the dirt. Clint felt it strike his leg.

With the matchlight gone, the night suddenly seemed unfathomably black. Clint's eyes had adjusted to the flame, so now he couldn't see a thing. *Where was Stone? Would he try and take Clint's gun now that the darkness was full?*

With his heart beating a drumroll, Clint fumbled until he found another match. Every second felt like minutes, hours, days. He could imagine the outlaw's hands finding him. He could imagine Stone's hands grabbing at his gun.

The match popped alight and Clint saw Stone exactly where he'd been, in exactly the same position. Clint's gun was still aimed at Stone's forehead.

"The fork is in his throat?" Clint whispered.

"Yar. He's killt."

Clint nudged Edward, immediately behind him, with his elbow. The unicorn grunted but didn't stir.

"Here, for Providence's sake," said Stone. He ripped a piece of fabric from Clint's sheet and tied it around a stick. He held the fabric-wrapped stick out to Clint, who surmised that he was supposed to light it. He did, then waved the match to a thin line of smoke and the scent that went with it. Stone stuck the end of the tiny torch in the sand, and the campsite was cast into a weak orange light and severe, ominous shadows. It was just enough light to make out the form of the paladin, slumped in a corner with the gleam of a fork below his chin just as Stone had promised.

"We have company," Stone whispered, his comical face with its comical hair suddenly dead serious.

"Your gang?"

"I wouldn't wake you if it were my gang," said Stone. He looked around and then went on, his voice even lower. *"Dooners."*

Clint sat up. Now he nudged Edward harder, and the unicorn started to stir. Clint planted a hand on Edward's neck, their trail sign to move carefully. A moment later Edward was standing and awake, but by the light of the tiny torch, Clint couldn't tell if Edward's usual self was present in those giant equine eyes. He didn't think so. It was too much to hope for a window of lucidity when it was most needed.

"I woke you because you have the only weapons. Believe me, I'd like to run. But I'd never make it."

Clint wrinkled his brow at Stone. "I'm supposed to *save you?* After you ended the paladin?"

"You won't cry for the paladin," said Stone.

It was true. During the entire trip, Clint had spent many a minute wondering which side he was rightly on. Was he on the side of The Realm, which had cast him aside? Or was he on the side of the outlaws, of which he was technically one?

"Besides," said Stone. "You're supposed to save me because it's saving yourself. Here's the situation, Marshal, in case you haven't reckoned it true: we work together, or we die."

Clint looked at Edward, then at the sleeping form of Buckaroo, then finally back at Stone. Stone's hair was picking up the flickering light and seeming to distribute it, like a beacon. Clint's eyes had almost adjusted. Around him, he could see the campsite, rocks, bushes, and the sheer wall of a cliff that they'd sheltered behind. Even with fully adjusted eyes and a torch, he could see nothing beyond their own little nest. The dooners, if Stone was telling the truth, could be anywhere.

"I need my guns," Stone whispered.

Clint looked at him unbelievingly.

"We work together or we die," he repeated.

"It's a trick."

"My guns are in your unicorn's saddlebags. I know better than to try and steal from a unicorn. This is the only way. Get them and give them to me, and maybe we'll survive."

Clint's senses were back, the night's fog having lifted from his mind. He squinted into the weeds, still seeing nothing. Hearing nothing. The night was preternaturally quiet, like they were in a hole in the middle of nothingness.

His mind began to figure, his wheels turning.

Even with the paladin killt and Clint asleep, Stone couldn't leave unarmed because he'd have too far to travel alone in hostile territory. He couldn't take Havarow's scimitar because the scimitar would be keyed to work only in Havarow's hand. He couldn't steal guns from a gunslinger. Edward had Stone's shotguns, and Edward, even addled, was too big of a risk to rob.

Which meant that this was a ploy. There were no dooners.

Clint, proud of seeing through Stone's ruse, smiled a crooked smile and said, "I'm not as stupid as Havarow."

But at that moment, an arrow streaked between them and struck Edward in the hock. He whinnied like a surprised horse and rolled up, kicking sand all around in a frenzied cloud. Another arrow split the night, landing at his feet, and Edward then rose onto his hind legs, his front legs pawing the air, making the men duck and hold up their hands. The unicorn's eyes shot wide. Clint could read his expression: something in him wanted to run, but there was still enough unicorn in him to stand his ground as if obeying instinct. Multicolored blood — all of it orange by the light of the fire — streamed from his wound. Then there was a spark and the arrow fell to the dirt. The wound stitched closed. With it gone, Edward calmed somewhat, his eyes wild but his feet reluctantly rooted. Somehow he'd healed himself. But it didn't seem that he knew it, or that he'd done it consciously.

"Give me my guns!" Stone hissed, holding out a hand. "Do you really think I can outdraw you?"

It was a good point. Havarow was dead. Buckaroo was asleep and would remain that way until six in the morning or until someone hit a button on his chest. Stone couldn't harm Edward and would never outgun Clint, even with his giant guns. With or without his weapons, there was little Stone could do to harm them. The risk of arming the bandit was minimal, but the upside was substantial.

Clint ran around Edward, who didn't react, and pulled the two large shotguns from his saddlebags. Then, as an afterthought, he returned one of them. He tossed the single sawed-off through the air sidelong and Stone caught it with one hand, immediately racking it to chamber a round. Then held out his other hand, waiting.

"And the other!" he shouted.

"*One*," said Clint.

Stone gave Clint an annoyed glance, but then a brief high-pitched whistling wiped the snarl from his face and sent both him and the gunslinger down to the dirt. Another dooner arrow raked through the night sky, careening within inches of Clint and striking the sand behind him.

Stone made a circling-around gesture with his finger, then pointed for a notch between two massive rocks to his rear, indicating the way out of the valley in which they'd sheltered. The camp was in the middle of a clutch of scrubby, ugly trees. The brush provided nice shade, but it also blocked what little moonlight there was. Clint looked up, between the trees, and saw that the moon had fallen behind a wall of thick clouds. The dooners had probably waited for the clouds, wanting it to be full dark before their attack. Clint couldn't see in the dark and neither could Stone, but he was betting that the dooner shaman chief, who could sift magic from the sand, could. The good news was that if that were true, only one among their party — the shaman — would be able to see well enough to shoot. The rest would have to run in and fight close with war hammers. Which meant that if they could make it to the notch in the rock and there was a break in the clouds, they'd be able to see the warriors coming.

Or, if they had Edward.

As quietly as he could, Clint snuffed the torch with his boot, drooping a curtain of ebony. Then he punched Edward in the side. The unicorn didn't react.

"Edward!" Clint hissed.

Edward turned his big white head and moved his lips over his teeth, looking very horselike.

Clint punched him again, this time higher. Stone had sneaked into the brush with his guns, seemingly expecting Clint to cover the other direction and follow him around, so they could meet at the notch in the rocks. Apparently he was planning to retrieve his horse later. Clint, on the other hand, wanted to take his own mount with him. And to wake him the sands up.

"*Edward!* Get your wits! I need your magic!"

Edward said, too loud, "Horses aren't magic. You must know that."

Clint ignored his words and pushed his body hard with both hands. "Make a bubble! Make light! Make anything!"

Edward's lips moved and a bubble of saliva formed, then popped.

"Best I can do," he said.

There was a burst of green light across the valley and the sound of a shotgun reporting through the night's silence. Edward jumped, his big blue eyes registering fear in the scant light of the hooded moon. He was too dim, too confused. Clint would have to lead him, but Edward didn't wear a halter, so there was nothing to grab. He tried reaching for the unicorn's mane, but Edward was too spooked, and jerked his head hard. So Clint got behind him and pushed, knowing he'd need to move fast if it looked like Edward was going to kick.

A shadow crossed in front of the embers of the campfire.

Clint froze. Something — something he couldn't quite explain, yet intimately trusted — told him that the shadow wasn't Stone. His hands flew to his belt. Irons rose. Hammers fell. The shadow dropped at the same time as a sliver of moon peeked from behind the clouds.

Dooner.

Two more blasts of green light exploded across the valley. Two swirls of purple indicated that Stone had scored hits and that two bodies had just vanished. Green and purple appeared again in quick sequence, one like an echo of the other.

Clint pushed Edward. Then Edward *did* kick, and the gunslinger found himself on the ground with a hoofprint on his chest. But when he looked up, he saw something in Edward's posture that heartened him. The unicorn hadn't been spooked into kicking. He'd done it to be a jerk.

"Never push a unicorn," said Edward.

"Are you back?" Clint hissed up at him.

Edward looked around as if he weren't sure. He said, "Seems that way. For now."

"Can you cast an umbrella?"

"I don't think so. It's hard to explain."

"Can you do *anything?*"

"Yar," said Edward. "I can do this."

Suddenly it was like someone had turned on all of the lights on the world. A brilliant ball of white appeared above them — and in its glow, Clint could see everything. He saw Sly Stone in the scrub on his belly. He saw three advancing dooners as they paused mid-step, shocked and frozen. He saw the dooner shaman chief, recognizable by his garb.

Clint's guns came up. He fired two gunshots, and two of the men — both foot soldiers — fell. The remaining warrior and the shaman dove for cover. Clint told Edward to run to the notch, that he would follow. After a moment, he did, but halfway to the notch, the illumination overhead vanished and Edward's purposeful trot, visible ahead, became a panicked canter. Apparently the unicorn's window of lucidity had vanished, and he was once again just a spooked equine.

There were two quick blasts of green light and two more roars from the shotgun, and immediately after, Clint heard a set of running feet. He thought he had a bead on their location and made himself ready, but then the feet stopped and he lost them.

There was a barely audible breath at his rear.

Clint spun to see the inhuman face of a dooner warrior with his hatchet held high. An arm circled his torso, pinning Clint's own arm to his side. But then there was another blast of green light and the arm loosened, and the dooner slid down his body like a man down a pole. The dooner's shape became indistinct and fizzled away into purple smoke.

The moon emerged, and in its slim white light, Clint saw Sly's face and ridiculous hair. He nodded once, curtly.

There were running footsteps in the other direction, back toward the trail they'd taken into the alcove.

Edward had vanished — seemingly through the notch and into the open. Clint followed, his guns out. But there were no more arrows, no more men. There was no way to know how large the dooner party had been, but beneath the ball bright light, he'd seen only four. Stone had dispatched at least four others, maybe more. There couldn't have been too many of them.

Clint ran through the notch. Beyond it, the sky opened. The gunslinger found he could see more of his surroundings as his eyes again adjusted to the dark. He located Edward, who had stopped and was chewing at sparse sawgrass. Then he turned back to the notch with his guns drawn, waiting to see what might emerge.

Seconds ticked by.

Where was Stone? Clint thought he'd been right behind him. But then he realized that the campsite hadn't been a dead end; if it had been, they wouldn't have chosen it. There were other ways out.

More time passed. There was no sound. And there was no Sly Stone.

Clint wondered how long he should wait before returning to the campsite. There were still horses in there. Buckaroo was still by the fire, asleep, oblivious. They also had supplies, assuming the dooners hadn't survived and grabbed them. Food. Water. Things they needed.

Maybe Stone had been killt.

Maybe he'd dispatched all of the dooners and, now duly armed, had run back out the way they'd come in, looking for his gang.

Clint's lip creased. Either scenario was more likely than Stone walking out to join him. He cursed himself for being so stupid. Of *course* Stone would flee. Why would he want to return to Clint — to the authority — to be re-shackled and taken again as prisoner?

Clint wondered if he cared at all about the errand Havarow had set them on and decided that yes, he sort of did. Buckaroo knew how to find the shimmer — the way back to The Realm — but Buckaroo, who now no longer rode with a paladin knight, was unlikely to take *anyone* to the shimmer unless he felt he was on official business, with a prisoner to escort. Clint didn't care what crimes Stone had supposedly perpetrated, but he cared plenty about seeing The Realm. And Stone, unfortunately for Stone, was his ticket in.

But Stone was gone, and the night was again silent.

Clint crept back toward the notch in the rock, his guns at the ready. He peered inside and saw nothing. The overhead trees blocked most of the moon in the alcove. It was like peering into a cave, with embers from the campfire at its center.

There was a dead pine branch at Clint's feet. It was desiccated and brown. Clint holstered his right gun, pulled a match from his pocket, popped it alight with his thumbnail, and touched it to the branch. The branch lit immediately, becoming a beacon in the dark night. Clint picked it up with his match hand, his other still aiming his gun into the blackness. He waved the branch around, illuminating the campsite. He could see Havarow's body with Buckaroo asleep beside it. He could see fallen dooners. He could see the horses — who, strangely, had barely reacted to all of the gunshots. They were battle horses from a battling border town, and apparently didn't spook easily.

He didn't see Stone.

Clint moved further in, waving his branch and holding his gun. Then, seeing himself from outside, he decided he was being stupid. Yar, he could see. But he could also *be seen*. He hadn't noticed the dooner shaman — the archer — fall. He might still be out here. He might be nocking his arrow right now, aiming at Clint, preparing to fire...

He dropped the branch, then started to stomp out the flames. It was big and didn't go quickly. He considered running, abandoning the branch, but before he could, there was a deafening shotgun report behind him, and the area in front of him, already awash in orange firelight, became tinged with green.

Clint spun. Disturbingly close, he saw the body of the dooner shaman puff into mist as his bow clattered to the ground in front of him. Then he saw the giant orange afro of Sly Stone and the smoking muzzle of a magic sawed-off shotgun.

"Thankoo for drawing him out," said Stone. "You took a big risk of him laying you straight dead."

Clint, who hadn't been trying to draw anyone out, nodded his you're-welcome.

CHAPTER SEVEN:
THE ROVING ROPE GANG

Clint, who never felt bad, felt bad the next morning about re-binding Stone's wrists after Stone had saved Clint's life... twice. Stone did nothing to make him feel better.

After the campsite had been cleared, they'd roused Buckaroo, who'd voiced many wild west cliches in a thick backwoods accent after realizing that they'd been ambushed. Then they'd gathered the horses and supplies, consulted Buckaroo's timepiece (which did, in fact, have a Realm-time chronograph built into it), and determined that the sun would rise before the moon would set. So they'd mounted up and rode, but before they had, Clint had pointed his gun with one hand and requested the outlaw's gun with the other. Stone had surrendered his weapon with a shake of his head, seemingly unable to believe the gunslinger would demand it. And then, out of habit as a lawman, Clint had bound Stone's wrists.

But by sunrise, the bandit's complaining and protesting had weakened Clint's will, and so by the day's early light, Clint removed the man's shackles.

It was a small risk. Stone had no weapons. He'd saved Clint and Edward's lives twice now — three times if you counted the fact that Stone had woken them before the attack had even started — and he hadn't run off when given the chance. Clint was sure that he hadn't run because until the rope gang showed, Stone was far safer in dooner land with the marshal than without, but a non-escape was a non-escape nonetheless.

Once freed and able to hold his own reins, Stone again grew talkative. It was an odd sort of talkative. He spoke to Clint like an old trail friend, but he simultaneously implied that Gunther Jethro and the rope gang were stalking them and that when they finally struck, Clint would probably die.

Confident that he could easily handle Stone should he decide to flee, Clint allowed Stone and Buckaroo to ride a few steps ahead and tried again to glean information from Edward. But it was in vain; the unicorn's lucid moments had dimmed to nearly nonexistent. Throughout most miles, Edward plodded along beneath the gunslinger without saying a word. Occasionally the true Edward shone through, and when that happened, he confirmed that the rope gang, as Stone suggested, was indeed close. And Stone knew it, too; he kept looking around with a smile, as if meeting eyes with his posse and telling them to wait for a weak moment.

The two men, the two mounts, and the machine marched on, and the gunslinger waited.

Stone prattled on about the gang, as if it were impossible to surrender too much information. There were a dozen men, he said — a fact that caused Clint to start planning his gunshots. The gunslinger told Stone there were eleven, since he'd dispatched Teedawge back in Nazareth Shiloh. But without conceding Clint's one-man-down clarification, Stone went on to say that Clint hadn't killt Gunther Jethro, who was the gang's beating heart.

Gunther Jethro, Stone continued, wasn't the name the gang's leader had been given at birth. His true name was either Gunther or Jethro, but nobody knew which. He'd grown up as one of a set of identical twins, and the two boys — Gunther and Jethro — had taught themselves rope tricks from the age of six out of necessity. They'd been orphaned and had, after the orphaning, returned to their family homestead to tend to their family's herd of cattle. In order for two six-year-olds to subdue cattle, they'd needed ropes. But time was short to learn those ropes, and so they learned fast, always fighting a ticking clock marked by the few supplies they had on hand. If they wanted to eat, the boys realized, they'd need to learn to rope a cow. And so they'd practiced, and practiced, and practiced. They learned, they caught, they ate, and still they practiced, eager to improve. Soon their skills grew beyond the needs of their bellies. They learned to rope men, who they could then rob. And with that realization, the gang began. Their ropes became their arms and their singular weapons. They trained others. Together, the gang learned to tie people up without getting near them. They learned to nab weapons from a distance. They learned how to pull their foes into pieces. But the skill was a double-edged sword, and on one unfortunate day, one twin accidentally killed the other during a stunt. Nobody — including the survivor — knew which twin had lived, and so Gunther Jethro had taken both names just to be safe.

The rope gang, Stone promised, were some of the most dangerous men he'd ever met. The ropes of the gang were to be feared as much as any weapon wielded by any man.

"They're just ropes," said Clint, chewing a toothpick, his shoulders bouncing slightly as he rode atop Edward's back. "I have guns."

"I do too, normally," said Stone. "But I wouldn't cross the gang. Sure, they're 'just ropes.' But rope gang ropes are lassos of a different nature."

"Are they magic?"

"In a way."

"In a way?"

"Either the men are very, very good, or they're very, very good *and* have ropes infused with magic. I nar know which, and don't think they do either. We hijack magic together, and they use the Realm devices to take their share. I know they need it, and I know they use it. Whether it's in the ropes or not, I couldn't tell you. But this, I *can* say: back at the campsite, had the gang been there, they could've snatched the dooner arrows right out of the air."

"I don't believe that," said Clint, staring forward and not giving Stone the satisfaction of meeting his eyes.

"Believe it," said Stone. "Because I've seen 'em catch bullets."

Clint sorely missed Edward's biting wit. Edward would never have allowed Stone to say the ridiculous things he was saying. But Edward had gone stupid. He'd become a walking, talking contradiction.

"What kind of a rider are you?" he chided Clint when they stopped at a stew pool to dip some water for their waterskins and to moisten their lips. "All you carry is turkey pie and jerky. Why don't you carry anything for your horse? Don't you have any oats for me?"

Clint just looked at him, trying to decide if Edward was actually back to himself and just messing with him. The unicorn's eyes never wavered.

"You're not a horse," Clint replied.

"Of course I am. Hooves." He stomped a forehoof on the ground. "Big lips and teeth." He flapped them. "Big tail, and a sturdy back you ride upon."

Clint made a grand gesture. "You're a *unicorn*."

Edward laughed.

So Clint pulled his shaving mirror from his pack and showed Edward the horn on his head and the way he didn't wear any tack like horses did. But Edward wasn't buying it, thinking it all an elaborate joke. But then finally, Clint thought of an unassailable argument.

"Horses don't talk," he said.

"Of course not."

"But... *you're talking*."

Something lit Edward's eyes. It looked like a realization.

"Then I must be a man. Give me a hat like yours," he said.

Clint put his face in his hands. It was no use.

For the next mile, Edward tried to talk either about horse matters or his perception of human matters, but eventually he forgot entirely what he was, then forgot that he could talk. Only every once in a while (usually when Clint said something directly to him) did the unicorn bother to say anything. He looked shocked every time, as if surprised by his own words. Then he'd ask for oats, and poop on the trail.

Still, the rope gang stayed hidden. Clint could almost feel them watching. From time to time, as they rounded corners in the trail, he drew one of his guns and waited, ready for ambush. Stone watched him and laughed, swearing that one good rope could easily snatch that gun from his hands before the gunslinger was even aware that something had gone missing. So Clint pulled his second gun and rode without hands and Stone laughed harder. Clint knew he was giving the outlaw an upper hand by giving him something to laugh at, but he let it go. And as they drew closer to Aurora Solstice, they stopped and Clint wrapped him back in the shackles. Stone looked hurt, again reminding him that he'd saved the gunslinger's life. At least twice.

Buckaroo consulted his timepiece and said that while a shift did indeed appear to be occurring, he still predicted the shimmer on time, at 3:10pm local time, right there in Aurora. He said the shift was muddling his read of an exact location and that he'd have to wait until closer to departure to be sure. They still had plenty of time.

Around noon, as they rode into the town, Clint decided to pay for a room at the Otel using Havarow's money so that they could rest and refuel in peace while waiting. The Otel even had a barn. Normally, Edward would blow up buildings at the thought of being placed in a common barn beside horses, but the unicorn seemed to have virtually no lucid moments left, and the likelihood of him snapping out of it and becoming suddenly offended seemed remote. Clint was beginning to fear for Edward, wondering and seriously doubting he could complete his journey without a clear-headed unicorn. He certainly couldn't face Kold and Cerberus. He couldn't rescue Mai. He couldn't find the third Orb, or prevent Kold from doing so. He couldn't return to The Realm. Which, now that he thought about it, made this whole errand sort of pointless. Clint had been nursing vague plans to force his way through the shimmer behind Stone, but was it worth it without Edward? What would he do once he was through, other than face the authorities and be exiled for the second time?

He didn't have long to think on it because as soon as Clint, Stone, and Buckaroo got comfortable in their second-floor Otel room, the shouting started outside.

Clint looked out the window and saw that the street had filled with men twirling ropes. It was the gang, with a clear ringleader at the center. They appeared to be putting on a sort of show for the townspeople, circling their lassos into familiar shapes. One rope somehow made a square in the air. Another made a heart. Another made the outline of a pistol.

The townspeople gathered to watch.

"Who among you has a coin!" shouted a man in a striped vest at the center of the group.

Over Clint's shoulder, Sly Stone said, "That's Gunther Jethro. You'll like this coin trick."

Clint shouldered Stone roughly away, cuffing him to the floor.

Outside, a woman in a blue dress and a large flowered hat held up a coin.

"Toss it into the air! High!" shouted Gunther Jethro.

The woman did. Then there was a flash of Jethro's rope, which shot out and then returned to his hand like a bird. He held up the coin for all to see, then tossed it back to the woman.

"You, boy!" Gunther then said. "Those two strips of alloy there. Pick them up."

The boy stooped to the town's dusty street and picked up two thin strips of alloy.

"Toss 'em both in the air. One here and one there. At the same time."

The boy did as Jethro asked. This time, two other men shot out a pair of ropes. One rope seemed to strike each of the strips, and then the ropes ran into each other. Jethro reached up and snatched something from the air. He held it up and the crowd *ooh*ed and *aah*ed. The two strips of alloy were formed into two interlocking circles, like two links in a chain.

"More! More!" the boy yelled.

"You want to see more?" said Jethro, addressing the crowd.

The crowd applauded, cheering their agreement.

"And do you want to see just how much harm we can do to all of you with these ropes?"

The crowd began to mumble, unsure what Jethro could mean and taken off-guard by the lightning-quick change in his tone.

Gunther Jethro began to circle his rope overhead. It again formed the outline of a gun, then changed to a dagger before settling into the shape of a noose.

"There's a man in that Otel named Sly Stone," Jethro said, pointing and pitching his voice for all to hear. "He's being kept by a lawman who has no right to waylay him. We can't approach because the lawman's hands are too fast, and because being the murdering thief he is, won't hesitate to leave us killt. But *you* can approach. And because there is something we need here today, you must know one thing, and it's this: *we* can approach *you*."

The skin on the back of Clint's neck tightened behind a hundred rising hairs. From the corner of his eye, he could see Stone watching from the window beside him, a knowing smile widening his face.

"In two hours," Gunther Jethro yelled to the crowd, "we will begin taking some of you at random. When we do, we will see what our ropes can do to those people. But there is a way out! You see, anyone who so much as attempts to subdue the lawman holding our brother will make his or her whole family immune to our ropes. And anyone who manages to *free* our man will receive ten thousand rupees, or ten thousand dollars. So you understand — I am a fair man! If you help me, I will help you."

Murmurs rumbled down the street. Many of the people wore pistols on their hips. Hands naturally fell to their guns.

"Help us free our brother and you will live," said Jethro. "But *fail* to help us… and you will die."

The heads of the townspeople turned to the Otel windows, up toward Stone in one window and Clint in the other.

It was 1:02pm.

CHAPTER EIGHT: TICK TOCK

An hour passed. Clint split his time between the window and a large chair across the room, where he sat while staring at his prisoner.

The ultimatum in the street had changed the town's demeanor. When they rode in, everyone had waved to the man on the unicorn, knowing who he was and what he represented. Out at the Edge, few people had seen a Realm marshal. The same was mostly true in deep Sands towns like Solace, Sojourn, and Precipice. But Aurora Solstice was a fair step closer to the old center, and while most people still hadn't seen a marshal, they knew true what he was, and considered him a force as white as his unicorn.

But all of that had suddenly changed. The twin promises of retribution against the town and a reward for anyone with aggression enough to try stopping Clint had turned every person on the dusty streets into a sworn enemy. So far, no one had tried storming the Otel, but it was only 2:00. As time grew short, the people outside would become desperate.

The gang had remained outside, shouting through the windows, performing more and more ominous rope tricks. One roper demonstrated how his lasso could squeeze a wagon wheel into splintered kindling. Two others had pulled a thick alloy faucet in half as easily as stretching taffy. The gang had roped several townfolk — pulling them from inside buildings and through an open second-story window — and had brought them into the circle they'd made in front of the Otel, then laughed and let them go. The people of Aurora Solstice knew the men with the ropes meant business, and were currently more afraid of the twelve of them than of a vaguely-remembered tall and dusty man with a gun.

Clint had poked out the window at around the hour mark. The ropers had turned to watch him, curious, as he'd leveled his weapon at a very white, almost-albino looking man and used a bullet to knock him down. Both the man and his whirling rope fell to the dirt. One man shouted, "He killed Teedawge!" and several of the others seemed mildly annoyed, but mostly they did nothing other than to lasso themselves some thick alloy shields. Otherwise, there was no reaction. They'd watched him take aim. They'd watched him fire. They'd watched one of their own fall. But it had been very transactional, as if they'd been willing to sacrifice a man to see what Clint's guns looked like and what he would do with them.

It made Clint's already jaded blood run cold.

With an hour to go before the gang's deadline, Stone sat in an overstuffed chair in the Otel room's corner, his back straight and both feet flat, shackled hands curled in his lap. He looked nothing if not in command.

"Why are you doing this, Marshal?" he said. "Why are you carrying out that idiot paladin's mission? You're no longer with The Realm. If anything, you're against it. You're like me. We're both riding on the other side of the wall, with the same if not similar aims."

Clint sat in a chair on the opposite side of the room, away from the windows. He could hear shouts from the gang amid surprised exclamations from the town outside. He kept the room door in his sights, should someone try to barge inside. He didn't answer Stone. He sat with his face set, mentally willing the chronometer in Buckaroo's pocket to move faster.

"You have nothing to gain," Stone continued. "You'll take me to the shimmer, and you'll push me through. Realm authorities on the other side, in Yuma province, will take over. They'll put me on trial, and declare me guilty before the second blink. It will be easy. I *am* guilty. I've stolen untold amounts of magic to sell on the black market. And for my guns." He nodded toward his matching shotguns, sitting beside Clint's chair. The gunslinger had removed them from Edward's saddlebags before leaving him in the barn.

Stone continued. "Why does The Realm deserve sole dominion over the magic? There's hardly any left in the whole of the Sands, thanks to the leaking. All that's left, save what can be sifted, is in the veins. The Realm splits the veins, repairs what is in their — and only *their* — best interests, and keeps fractures from spreading toward their precious city while simultaneously diverting magic toward them — and only them. Where are *our* magic veins out here in the Sands, Marshal? Don't we deserve to have use of them? Don't those people out there deserve it?" He gestured toward the window.

"Are you referring to the people currently being terrorized by your rope gang?" said Clint.

"They're Gunther's gang."

"Are they yours or are they Gunther's? Make up your mind, Stone."

Stone sighed. "Fine. I've ridden with them. And they are no good, but they are good *for me*. Without them, I'm one man. One man can't split veins, and one man can't take over a stitcher by himself."

Then, with an oddly sincere gesture of attrition and apology, Stone tipped his hat to Buckaroo, who'd run such a stitcher, and taken many losses.

"Are you claiming to be Hood of Legend?" asked Clint. "Stealing the magic so you can give it to those who need it?"

Stone laughed. "If you trade 'give' for 'sell,' then yes. A man must pay for pie and brew somehow."

Again, Clint wondered why he was still holding tight to this mission — now to the point of putting a town of innocents in peril. What did it matter if he could get Stone to the shimmer? Why did he care if Stone was brought to trial? *Did* he care? But then he decided that the truth was that yar, he *did* care — but only because he had once been a man of the law, and such instincts ran deep.

"You're a criminal," said Clint. "Just like your brother, Hassle."

"We're nar alike, beyond sharing parents. And if you ever imply I'm like him again, I will cut you in two and spit on each half."

That surprised a chuckle from Clint.

"You aren't looking to right wrongs," he said. "You're stealing magic to suit you."

Stone cocked his head and replied, "I can do both."

Clint wasn't sure what to say to that, so he said nothing.

The clock crawled forward. Buckaroo consulted his timepiece as if by compulsion. He declared that he'd calculated with a relatively certain precision that the shimmer would be not quite a quarter of a mile away. He gave Clint the location and told him that blessedly, the shifting seemed to have stopped. So Clint traveled the route to the shimmer in his mind. They'd come by it when they'd ridden into town; he knew exactly where it was and how difficult it would be to get there. Then he peeked out and watched the ropers, all of whom ducked behind their shields the moment his deadly eye showed through the window.

More time passed. The gang continued to shout the time out to the nervous townspeople at regular intervals.

You now have a half hour to seize the marshal before we sacrifice one of your own.

You now have twenty minutes.

You now have fifteen minutes.

The gang's deadline would be up a few minutes after three. The shimmer that would briefly connect Aurora Solstice to The Realm's Yuma province would appear at precisely 3:10 and would, according to Buckaroo, last for 131 seconds. If they left at three sharp, they could diffuse the gang's time bomb and then maybe... *maybe* make it to the shimmer. Buckaroo could take dozens of gunshots without harm, but things would be harder for Clint. Clint would be making the trip with a man in shackles who he'd practically have to drag, and without a unicorn to heal him if he got roped or shot.

Or perhaps more accurately: *When* he got roped or shot.

"You're still trying to work out how to transport your prisoner, aren't you?" said Stone, sitting placidly in the large chair. "Let me go, Marshal. Let me return to my gang."

"The gang that you say is full of bad guys, despite your being Hood of Legend?"

"The gang that helps me get what I need, because nobody else will give it."

Clint rubbed his chin, thinking. There were only a few minutes left before the deadline. If he surrendered Stone, all of this might go away. The gang might release the town. He might still have to face the gang itself, but he could handle a bunch of men with ropes. And without Stone, the shimmer — and hence the need to hurry and probably make dumb mistakes — didn't matter. He couldn't go through to The Realm without Edward anyway.

But something about it still wasn't right, and after a moment he realized why.

"We will go to the shimmer as planned," he told Stone, "because if I don't hand you to The Realm, you will continue to split seams. You will continue to unravel the fabric of the world."

"So?" Stone sat forward in his chair. "So what if I do?"

"Rips will widen. The world will crumble. There are only a handful of veins left, and Havarow told me you'd sabotaged stitching operations on most of 'em. It may take a thousand years, but the unraveling will grow inevitable."

"And what if it does?" said Stone. "What if the fabric rips apart?"

"Armageddon."

"Then what?"

Clint just stared.

"Your unicorn mutters in his sleep. Are you really after the Triangulum?"

"We seek to keep it from the wrong hands. Yar."

"Ah," said Stone. "And what will the *right* hands do with it? Hasn't your friend told you of the balance? About why unicorns partner with humans? About why there is *always* light and dark, purity and pollution?"

Clint shook his head. "What are you speaking of, Stone? Plain English preferred, pleasem and thankoo."

"I don't have time to explain. Let me go, Marshal. Have faith for once. Trust what your gut says over the rules set down by a dead paladin you didn't even know. If Edward the Brave were awake, he would tell you to let me go. Or *has* he told you that, along the way?"

"Edward the Brave?"

Stone groaned. "Let me go. Release me, Marshal."

Clint was torn. It made perfect sense to let him go. But to the gang on the street — the ropers terrorizing the town? Nothing good could come of that.

He turned to Buckaroo.

"How long until the window opens?"

"Twelve minutes, sir."

"So it's two minutes until three o'clock high."

Buckaroo gave a mechanical nod, the room's spark light glinting from his golden skin and brown-painted mustache. "Yes, sir."

"Okay," said Clint, standing and walking toward Stone, then removing his shackles. "I'll let you go, but not to the gang. You're going to the shimmer."

Sly, still seated, spread his hands and shook his head. "So how is that letting me go?"

Clint returned to his chair, reached down, and tossed Sly one shotgun, then the other.

"Because you're entering The Realm armed. With me."

CHAPTER NINE: 3:10 TO YUMA

The Otel's lobby had a sheltered breezeway leading to the barn. They stormed through it in a dead sprint, Sly Stone at the lead with one of his shotguns drawn and Clint behind. As far out on a limb as Clint had gone, he wasn't willing to go so far as to allow a man with a gun to run behind him. Buckaroo kept shockingly close behind, proving his stiff joints could unloosen and be plenty agile if needed.

Nobody was in the hallways, the lobby, or the barn. The citizens had distanced themselves from the criminal and the marshal. The gang hadn't entered because they knew the marshal had a unicorn. If they'd known the truth about Edward's confused state, they probably would have stormed the place already.

The rope gang, Stone explained after Clint realized they might be rushing and ducking for nothing, was still very much a problem. They considered Stone to be its second leader, and instrumental to their getting of magic. Without Stone, they'd want for magic to use in their ropes, and to sell. Whether Stone went with Clint willingly or as his prisoner was immaterial. If Stone was leaving the Sands for The Realm, they'd want to stop the gunslinger. They wouldn't want to kill Stone, but they wouldn't stand aside, either.

"Keep pretending I'm a prisoner," Stone told Clint as they took the Otel stairs four at a time. "That way, they'll only shoot at you."

"That sounds like a win-win," said Clint.

The two men and the machine burst into the barn and all three of them climbed onto Edward's back. The unicorn was napping. He startled when Clint opened the stall and backed him out, but he roused when Clint slapped his rump like a common mount. All three climbed aboard. Clint rode in the middle, sandwiched between Stone in front with Buckaroo in back. The thinking machine could be shot with no foul; he'd easily repaired even a blast from Stone's magic shotgun back at the vein. And they were protected from the rear because the gang wouldn't shoot at Stone.

Edward had no idea who or what he was. Clint shouted that he was a mighty, noble, all-powerful unicorn. The unicorn laughed and said that unicorns weren't real. So Clint shouted, angrily now, that Edward was a horse, a horse who talked, and that his rider was telling him to RIDE, and then Clint kicked Edward hard with the backs of his heels, wishing for spurs. The white, horned horse threatened to rear and topple his riders, but then he broke forward and began to move.

The door to the barn was closed. It opened into the square, where the bandits were. So Clint yelled again at Edward as he crossed the barn, kicking him again, telling him that his rider needed his mighty horse strength and to trust him. Edward, muttering that it was a horrible idea, moved faster toward the closed door. Clint grabbed Stone around the middle — to steady Stone rather than himself — and Stone drew both shotguns, both across his chest from the opposite holsters, and blew the barn door's heavy wooden cross brace to splinters in a flash of green fire. Edward barreled into the fire, trusting his rider through a loyalty that was buried deep inside him. Edward didn't know what he was, but the doors did; they exploded outward and fell from their heavy hinges into the dirt. And then suddenly the gang was in front of them, twelve men

(twelve?)

looking back at the barn in shock, their lassos never ceasing overhead as if on autopilot, their mouths dropping open. Stone had already holstered his guns. Clint held one of his pistols to Stone's head for show and used the other to fell three bandits in quick succession: a short and fat man with a mustache, a man wearing an orange bandana, and a man who was almost pale enough to be an albino. Then, before the other nine could react, they'd turned and were headed back down the street. Shots were fired — not from the bandits, but from citizens. Several hit Buckaroo, who acted surprised, as if the impacts tickled. Clint turned as best he could, now sighting with both his guns, and fired them twice. Four more bandits fell.

Five men ran to their horses and, with barely a pause, were up and pursuing them at a full gallop.

Clint craned his neck toward Buckaroo, who was holding onto him with a death grip as if he weren't made of alloy and nearly indestructible. Buckaroo hadn't wanted to go on this suicide mission and had protested the plan, but they needed Buckaroo to track the shimmer and, frankly, he made a fine suit of armor, so Clint had berated him into coming. It wasn't hard; Buckaroo was used to following orders. And now, with the thundering of hooves underfoot, bouncing hard enough to make the men's teeth rattle, Clint shouted to the machine, *"How long?"*

"Five minutes, sir!" Buckaroo shouted back.

A rope shot out from nowhere and caught Clint by the wrist. The world flipped topsy turvy and he felt something solid hit him hard in the side of his face and ribs. He thought he heard a bone crack. He was on the ground, with the gang bearing down on him. His hand was still snared from the side, from a man who'd managed to get around him. He'd held the gun in that hand, but couldn't move his arm or aim it. He looked over and saw the bandit at the other end of the rope, pulling it taut while laughing.

The group of four remaining horsemen approached and two stopped, one quickly roping and stretching Clint's other arm akimbo. The other two men thundered on, still pursuing Edward. Clint turned and looked back, still fighting the rope on his wrist. He could see Edward retreating in a cloud, the blue back of Stone's shirt atop the unicorn. But that was wrong, because Buckaroo's back was brown. And then Clint realized that of course Buckaroo would have been unhorsed because he was behind Clint, and so he looked over and saw the machine lying at the side of the road, severely dented and muttering daintily.

The new man on the horse approached Clint and looked down. Both of Clint's arms were out, both large hands holding guns he was unable to aim. The ropes squeezed, and Clint found himself thinking of the alloy faucet they'd torn apart as if it were taffy.

The man in front of Clint had his own rope circling overhead. Clint looked up as the circle turned into the outline of a sword.

"I heard there's gold inside gunslingers," he said, moving the rope faster. "What do you say we open him up and find out?"

The man hitched forward with his rope hand, but then there was an incredible booming sound from behind Clint and the bandit flew backward, soaring through one massive stone wall of a building and then another. The building, cleaved, tottered and tipped forward, its roof slamming down onto the packed clay of the street.

The noise had startled both the other rope men and their horses. For a split second, the ropes slackened. It was enough. Clint straightened his wrists and fired both guns to his sides, dropping the remaining men to the dirt. Only when finished, and after he'd pulled the ropes from his wrists, did Clint turn to see Buckaroo standing behind him. His chest had dilated open, and protruding from it was what looked like the smoking muzzle of a cannon. As Clint watched, the cannon retracted and Buckaroo's chest irised closed.

"I see you carry a weapon," said Clint.

"We work dangerous sands, sir," said Buckaroo.

"What else can you do that you've nar told us?"

Buckaroo grabbed Clint hard by the back of his belt. "This, sir," he said.

There was a great rumbling sound as twin belches of white fire came from beneath the machine's alloy boots. Clint felt himself yanked up and off his feet, then was suddenly flying through the air with the buildings of Aurora Solstice floating beneath him. The balance, with Buckaroo holding his belt, wasn't perfect, and Clint's body kept wanting to pitch forward. He thought he might slide out of his pants and fall to a hard death below, so he gripped his belt from the front, swung up, and grabbed Buckaroo's arm.

Thankfully the flight finished quickly and Buckaroo set them down in the middle of a cluster of three buildings, right where the shimmer was supposed to appear. The space was almost a courtyard. Blessedly, for the time being, they were alone. There were maybe two minutes left to wait.

"You could have flown us here from the beginning?" said Clint.

"I cannot carry a unicorn, sir," Buckaroo replied, delicately running his alloy hands across his alloy clothes as if to free them of dirt.

"And you could have helped us during that dooner raid?"

"I have a verbal wake command, sir," he said. "Perhaps you should know it if we are going to work together. It is, 'Awake, Buckaroo.' "

Clint's attention quickly circled back to the present danger. There were still two bandits out there, and Stone was who-knows-where with Edward. If the shimmer was due in just over a minute and would only last for another two after that, their very narrow window was closing fast, and Stone was yet to return with Edward.

But of course, Clint suddenly realized, Stone *wouldn't* return.

The moment's absurdity would quickly reveal itself to Stone. Without Clint and Buckaroo, the situation had changed such that Stone was now fleeing from his own men. Once that dawned on him, he'd stop and join them, and they'd ride off. Clint would watch the shimmer open and close but would be unable to enter it. Maybe at some point in the future Edward would realize that he wasn't a horse and would remember Clint, and at that point he'd ditch Stone and they'd find each other again... but for now, another man was riding the gunslinger's unicorn partner and could do as he pleased. A commoner riding a unicorn was taboo beyond reckoning, and it made Clint feel both sick and deeply saddened.

But as Clint mulled, there was suddenly a great cacophony and what Clint had at first taken for a draped wall revealed itself to be a sheet of bedding on a line. A giant spike pierced the bedding. The courtyard grew crowded as Edward thundered into the circle with Sly Stone atop his back.

Sly hopped down from the unicorn with an apologetic nod to Clint for riding his mount.

"Are they killt?" said Clint.

"Nar. But I lost 'em. It won't take long for them to find us. Are we in time?"

Clint turned to the commissioner. "How long, Buckaroo?" he asked.

"One minute and six seconds, sir."

Clint's chest was rising and falling. He hadn't realized until now just how exhausted he was, and how hard his heart was beating.

"We made it," he said. He looked at the open space in the courtyard as if anticipating a visitor.

Buckaroo was still staring at his timepiece. "Yar, sir," he said. "But..."

"What?"

"There's been a shift, sir. It's..."

"A *shift?*"

"Yar, sir. I thought it had stopped, but I was wrong. The magic has its own mind, and the calculations aren't always precise. But it hasn't moved far. It's..." He paused a moment, seeming to calculate, and Clint could feel the seconds ticking off with agonizing slowness. Finally Buckaroo jabbed a golden finger back through the torn sheet. "*There*, sir. Almost line of sight. Three thousand and fifteen feet."

Clint did the computation in his head. Over half a mile straight out. There were maybe forty seconds left until the window opened, then 131 seconds until it closed again. Just under three minutes total. They'd never make it.

He shoved at Buckaroo and Stone, hopping up onto Edward and then pulling the others after him. Once they were all three on Edward's back again, Clint leaned and yelled into Edward's pure white ear at the top of his voice: *"RIDE, DAGNIT! IF THERE IS ANY OF EDWARD LEFT IN THIS STUPID HORSE, YOU'LL RIDE UNTIL YOU DIE!"*

Something clicked. Horse or unicorn, Edward turned and ran. He ran hard. The wind battering Clint's chest — in front this time — threatened to unhorse him. The others held to him hard as he lowered his torso to wrap his arms fully around the unicorn's neck. The movement of Edward's haunches and head battered Clint in a neverending series of concussive blows, but he held on. This was The Realm they were after. *The Realm.*

Buckaroo, in the middle, shouted out times. He was a machine; he didn't seem to need the chronometer.

"The window has opened, sir!"

Clint yelled at Edward to move faster. Amazingly, Edward found a way to comply. They passed houses. Businesses. People. Citizens jumped back as if from lightning. The world was a blur.

"Ninety seconds to closure, sir!"

Faster. *Faster.*

"Sixty seconds, sir!"

He could see it. By providence, he could see it. At first it appeared to just be a window of white light in the middle of nothing. But then as his eyes and brain adjusted to the jarring ride and the approaching light, he could see details: a haloed entrance from one world to another. Aurora Solstice's dusty, forgotten street gave way to verdant, lush and rolling knolls. He could see small flowers waving in a gentle breeze. *Yuma Province.* Maybe even behind the wall.

"Thirty seconds, sir!"

The doorway in front of them grew and grew as they rode. The shimmer was as large as a barn door, easily big enough for all of them. The could simply ride right through. It was barely across a square now. *They were going to make it.*

Suddenly there were twin flashes of brown, so perfectly synchronized that Clint at first thought The Realm's beauty had reached out into Aurora Solstice to greet them. But it wasn't beauty. It wasn't Realm magic. It was ropes — two of them, each screaming from one side. The ropes met in front of Clint, in front of Edward, and seemed to shake hands. They made a knot and pulled taut.

Edward was going too fast to stop. His chest struck the ropes with tremendous force. Clint had time to see walls on either side of the square crumble and collapse in unison; the ropers must have tied the ends off because they knew they couldn't hold them against Edward. Even the bindings on the walls gave way, but it was enough. Edward's feet tangled under his body. Clint, Stone, and Buckaroo found themselves airborne.

Buckaroo collided with the corner of a dry fountain and bent nearly in half. Clint and Stone had the training or presence to tuck, and the gunslinger felt himself beaten by the ground for the second time in ten minutes, his core and neck protected but his skin grated raw. Edward took the brunt. He had been so committed to the run that there was no controlling his collapse. He became a deadly ball of hooves and momentum. He struck a wall. With a sound as big as the world, Clint looked up in time to see his horn snap at its midpoint, now cleaved in half.

Clint rolled up to a sitting position as two dusty men emerged. His big hands immediately went to his belt, reaching for his guns but realizing too late that they'd been pulled off as he'd fallen. He could see them now, halfway across the square.

The men walked forward, ropes still entangled. Clint realized that each man did, however, carry a sidearm. Six shots. Less than half of what a marshal had, but plenty to do the job.

Silently, without ceremony, the window into The Realm closed. It slid down from the top, Aurora Solstice's backdrop replacing Yuma's grass fields inch by inch.

Then it was gone, as if it had never been there.

The men stood above Clint. He hurt. His leg might have broken, or his back. He looked toward his guns — too far to retrieve. He looked at the white lump that had to be Edward, stirring vaguely and covered in multicolored unicorn blood. He could see half of Edward's horn laying in the street. It looked dusty and dirty, as if being shorn from its source had turned it into a mere spiral of ivory. Buckaroo hadn't stirred. He was halfway into the fountain, his carriage bent almost in two.

The men above Clint didn't draw their guns. They had all the time in the world.

Sly Stone stood. He was scratched and battered and his hair had flattened, but he seemed otherwise whole. One of the men turned to Stone. Stone's guns had come off as well and had landed at the bandit's feet. He stooped to retrieve them, still in their holsters.

"You okay, boss?" said the man.

"Yar," said Stone, rubbing his neck. "I think so."

"Sorry for the tussle. It was the only way to stop the unicorn. We couldn't get him earlier. When the other two fell off, he was too fast and lost us."

"I'll be fine, Gunther."

The man handed the guns to Stone. Stone buckled them back in place, then stretched.

"We kept you from the window," he said. "I'm sorry. But the situation changed. We didn't reckon on no lawman's unicorn. We reckoned on a sheriff. It was too risky."

"They didn't send a sheriff," said Stone. "I figured they wouldn't. It would have been the paladin, and that machine over there." He nodded toward Buckaroo.

Clint, still on the ground, still hurting, still casting his eyes from the dazed Edward to the beaten Buckaroo to Stone and the bandits, folded his brow.

Gunther Jethro looked at where the shimmer had been. "You gonna wait in town, or…?"

"We'll take out another stitcher. Maybe this time, they'll send someone more competent."

Clint sat up on his elbows. His leg burned fire, but at least he could still move. "You wanted to get caught," he said.

Stone nodded, almost apologetic. "Yar."

"Because they'd take you to The Realm, for your trial."

"That's the size of it, Marshal."

Gunther Jethro surveyed the scene, waiting for Stone to say more, to lead them, to give them a course of action. Clint found himself wondering if Jethro was a co-leader at all, or if Stone had headed the gang, fully, from the beginning.

"We've got to clean up these loose ends, boss," said Jethro, nodding to Clint, Edward, and Buckaroo.

"Yar," said Stone. He looked at the gunslinger, an apology on his face.

"So you *are* a criminal," said Clint.

Stone nodded. "Yar, I am."

Still looking down, Stone drew both of his shotguns. He pointed both at Clint, but then he swung them around, one to each side. One found the chest of each of the rope bandits. There was a belch of green fire, and both men evaporated in twin swirls of purple smoke.

He looked down at Clint.

"Can you walk?" he said.

It took a moment for Clint to say, "Yar, I can."

"Then go to your partner. Wake him. And we'll ride."

CHAPTER TEN:
BLUSH COLORED TATTERS

Clint's leg didn't seem to be broken, but some of the bones in his left hand as well as a few ribs most certainly were. One felled hand bothered Clint more than two broken legs. Some of his tendons seemed to have snapped, and he found that he couldn't move his thumb or grip a pistol.

Sly Stone was much better off. They didn't visit anyone who could tell them for sure, but it appeared Stone was only bruised and cut after their tumble. Buckaroo, given the time and the space, easily unfolded himself and returned more or less to full function, except that he had a wrinkle in his front that would probably remain for the rest of his service lifetime. Once he'd buffed out what he could and had run several rounds of redundant checks on his processors, Buckaroo looked at the wrinkle and said that it was okay, since every Sands man should have a scar to show the world what he was made of.

Edward had taken the brunt of the injuries. He'd hit the clothesline at full gallop, and after stopping and spilling his riders, he'd rolled over and over and collided with a wall. He'd fractured his horn, so he'd insisted that Clint stow it in a saddlebag for sentimental reasons even though he was still addled and didn't know what it was — except that it had once been a part of him. He'd risen from the rubble, covered in the reds and blues and yellows and purples of his own blood, thick with stiffness and in pain. He seemed to have somehow magicked his own flesh wounds without realizing how or why, but he didn't understand the trick well enough to fix the rest of himself, or to fix Clint. None of his legs were broken, though, and he could walk. So he did.

The men and the machine didn't try to ride the broken unicorn. They left Aurora Solstice on foot, directly through the town's center, through a crowd of townspeople milling along Main. The townspeople's eyes were hard to read. They no longer looked menacing, probably because Gunther Jethro and the rope gang were no longer a threat and could offer no reward. Still, they averted their eyes and watched as the party of four limped past. They didn't menace them. Clint's single drawn seven-shot pistol and Sly Stone's magic shotguns convinced them that doing so would be a very bad idea.

Strangely — possibly because a thinking machine's emotions were different from a man's — Buckaroo seemed to hold absolutely no resentment toward Stone for what he'd done to his crew or the stitcher. Buckaroo, in fact, seemed to be coming into his own. As they marched out, he kept talking about the fact that as a damaged machine, he'd never be allowed to work on a Realm operation again. He was an appliance, nothing more. If he reported to his chief, the chief would scrap him and send in a new commissioner for stitching operations in the sector. And, said Buckaroo, he normally wouldn't have been bothered by being scrapped. It was a machine's duty to do its job until it was no longer needed, and then to shut down when its term of service ended. But for some reason, he no longer felt quite that compliant. He was no longer identical to the other commissioners. Now he was marked. He was no longer just a metal man. Now he was the metal man with the scar — the scar he'd gotten when his sir and his sire had led him into battle, where he played his part proper.

Under Buckaroo's direction, they left Aurora Solstice and walked out into the Sands. Their course was hard to reckon and Buckaroo knew little of absolute locations that would make sense to Clint (The Realm didn't care about town names; they gave all locations outside The Realm as coordinates), but Clint looked at the sun and traced their path backward through his mind: Aurora Solstice, to Nazareth Shiloh and its rumors of chili, to the outskirts where they'd first encountered Stone and his former gang attacking the stitcher. He determined that wherever it was that Buckaroo wanted to take them — to the next shimmer for sure, but he couldn't explain where or when because too much was in flux — it was all the same to him.

In the end, they found themselves headed in the same direction that he and Edward been heading before the incident at the stitcher. They would travel through the Lakes O Plenty. They would cross into Elf Meadows. Then it would be just like they'd never left their path, slowly closing in on Dharma Kold. Kold would have gotten a much larger head start by now, but at least it all kind of made sense and wouldn't be subject to shifting. Kold would cross into stable lands. They would follow. Perhaps Kold would find the third Orb before they reached him and perhaps he wouldn't. The consequences of Kold reaching it first were unthinkable, but Clint was all thought out. Whatever would happen would happen. He was hurt. Edward was hurt. He simply couldn't expel the energy needed to think on it. And for the time being — despite the fact that the fate of the world might well hang on what happened next — he simply didn't care.

After about a week of wandering and hurting and not knowing where they were going ("I simply don't know yet, sir, but it's in this direction," Buckaroo replied politely every time he was asked), Edward finally began to have growing moments of lucidity. Neither Stone nor Buckaroo could offer advice, but this seemed like a good thing to Clint. The windows of "true Edward" grew larger and longer. During one, Edward wondered why he was in pain, and then immediately healed himself — starting by restoring his horn. He cleaned himself, magically whisking away his multicolored blood. And when he was as pure and white and whole as he'd ever been, he did what he normally would have done immediately, healing Clint's hand and ribs.

Being healed was, for Clint, like finally coming up for air after a long time holding his breath underwater. His left hand was finally able to move, and so he drew, reholstered, drew, reholstered. He fired his gun, because nobody other than their party was around to see or hear. He thanked Edward, but the unicorn just whinnied and nibbled at the leaves of a small, pathetic tree because he'd already reverted. It was a start. Clint was willing to wait.

Within another few days, Edward became more and more himself. He noticed, for the first time, that Sly Stone was apparently a permanent member of their party and berated Clint, demanding the entire story. Clint told him. Edward made some remark about how one human was the same as the next to him, and scoffed, saying that both Clint and Sly were incredibly ugly. Clint smiled. He couldn't help it.

They passed through town after town. They ate turkey pie. They drank apple brew. They trusted no one, and always made camp far out, blocked from naked eye and spyglass alike. The lands remained dusty and dry but the skies grew more stable and less ominous. The shifting stopped. Yet still they walked, and still Buckaroo could not tell them where the next shimmer was. "I simply don't know yet, sir, but it's in this direction," he'd say.

Because he was a machine, he'd answer in the exact same way, using the exact same words, every time. It became a joke between Clint and Stone. Clint would ask where Stone had stored the spyglass because he needed it. And Stone would reply, in a down-home, syrupy accent, "I simply don't know yet, sir, but it's in this direction." Buckaroo would only smile in the small way a thinking machine could smile, because he didn't understand that the joke was on him.

Clint began to suspect that Buckaroo didn't know where the next shimmer was because there were none. But Buckaroo didn't know. There had always been a shimmer, because he'd always commissioned a stitcher rig and a crew. Now he was a rogue. The idea that new shimmers might no longer open or respond to his calculations was beyond him. Clint asked, trying to provoke him into new ways of thinking. Buckaroo didn't evade the question, but was unable to answer. It wasn't in his programming.

Fifteen days out from Aurora Solstice, they came to a small, ramshackle lean-to amidst a clutch of cacti. It had the look of a waystation constructed for travelers and used when needed, but long ago forgotten. The thing was barely large enough for two men to sleep, but it had its own little well. It was too small to use as shelter for their party, but Clint took it as a sign that they were on the right path.

There was a hag inside the lean-to when they passed it. The hag radiated a magic presence that Edward, who was nearly back to normal, could sense. Magic sought magic, Edward explained, and along the correct path, they were sure to run across many seers and fortune tellers.

The woman in the lean-to was deeply wrinkled and appeared to be a thousand years old. She wore an ancient dress that was once probably bright pink but was now nothing but blush colored tatters. She smelled like death. When she looked up at Clint, he saw that one of her eyes was either sealed shut or had gone missing. Her lips were wilted like dead leaves. A dry, rasping noise croaked from her throat as she breathed.

Edward, eager to follow the magic and always looking for Kold's trail, walked over to the crone. Clint and Stone stayed back, half out of respect and half because the old woman's decayed appearance frightened them in a way neither would admit, but that each could see in the other's eyes. Edward spoke to her for a moment, then walked back to the men and the machine.

"Fashion a travois," said the unicorn. "She's coming with us."

Stone looked at Clint. Clint looked at Stone.

"Do it," said Edward. There was something in his voice that Clint couldn't quite grasp. It was almost fear. It was almost compassion. It was almost desperation.

Stone looked at Clint, Clint looked at Stone, and both looked at the unicorn.

"Why?" said Clint.

"Because, gunslinger," said Edward, "we haven't seen the woman in that lean-to for over four years. She's sick, she's hungry, and she won't last long — and such that we can give it, she needs our help."

Clint felt his mouth come open. He didn't move, despite the unicorn's stare.

"Do it," Edward repeated. "You near hitched your gunslinger's heart to her once, almost promised your fealty through sickness and health. Here's your chance to prove it, to prove whether there's still a man left inside the marshal."

The gunslinger fell to his knees in the dust.

Blood coursed from his human heart to his deadly hands.

Mai.

UNICORN WESTERN 5

CHAPTER ONE: BONES OF AN AMBUSH

The woman on the travois was fragile, beyond frail. She was a doll made of thin porcelain — or spun from spiderwebs, given her apparent age — and the trail's every bump and jostle had the gunslinger worried that she would crumble to pieces and spill her innards like dried detritus to the wind.

When they'd discovered Mai in the roadside shack, she'd seemed old, at least at first. She looked like a hag — a witch roughened and aged by a life spent stirring potions in pewter cauldrons. But when they brought her to the travois that would drag behind Edward (the unicorn, unlike Stone and Buckaroo's horses, could cushion her passage somewhat with a sort of magical pillow), they found that she was more than old. Mai was *used*, barely a husk. Carrying her was like lifting a scarecrow made of dust. Even with his hands beneath her, Clint worried that Mai might break, and that the woman he'd traveled the Sands for four long years to find would be gone and lost forever.

After weeks of riding, the fields of pure sand around them began to surrender to plains of tumbleweed, but the change of scene did not break the monotony. The posse rode mostly in silence. Clint thought back on the Mai he'd known, and the life with her he'd pondered while inspecting himself in the farback of Solace's saloon on their hitching day. The Mai who, back then, he'd thought of as imperturbable. Women of the Sands were like the men — dried like raisins. But Mai was different and always had been. Her skin had always looked glowing and water-fat even during the driest of days. No lines on her face, nor a scar on her hands. Rough Sands living hadn't impacted Mai in the way it had impacted everyone else. She looked radiant enough to grace the cover of one of The Realm's glossy books, her smile rich and white, comforting like a crackling fire. Mai had always sought the best in everyone — even a particularly grizzled and pessimistic gunslinger — and had found it. That optimism left its mark on Mai like a dimple. She looked like what she expected in all others: *radiant.*

The woman on the travois was none of that. The frail woman was so diametrically opposite the Mai Clint once knew that at times, when he looked back on the thing that didn't have the strength to moan as its body boiled in inhuman pain, he refused to believe it was the same woman he'd been so near to hitching. But it was. He knew it. Could feel it in his bones just as Edward felt it everywhere.

The first time Clint realized what Cerberus, Dharma Kold's unicorn of a different color, was doing to Mai, the unicorn warned him they might never get her back. He hadn't meant that they'd never *literally* get her back, but that she might never again be the same as she was. She might be irreparably damaged, as she now seemed to be.

Edward was doing all he could to stabilize Mai. A shimmer of light blue energy flowed back from his horn, surrounding the unicorn's rear half, Clint's lower half, and the travois. Clint asked if the energy was healing her. Edward said it wasn't quite healing. More like propping her up.

"Nothing can repair the damage from such a deep soul-plunging as Cerberus has done to your Mai," he said. "All I can do is to keep her from getting worse, and hope she'll find a way to repair herself."

Clint sighed. The end of Edward's sentence, once upon a time, might have heartened the gunslinger and given him hope, but he had seen little to make him believe in hope since leaving Solace to chase Kold through the Sands and recover his captured almost-bride. The trail had brought him little but heartache. Every task seemed to finish in a way that left him with a new and larger wound.

Nonetheless, he asked: "*Will* she repair herself?"

The unicorn sighed. "Nar. Kold has drained her very essence. Do you understand that?"

Clint nodded, knowing Edward wouldn't see him while he rode atop the unicorn's back.

"Mayhap her soul will grow stronger now that she's free of Cerberus's work," Clint said, not believing his words true even as he heard himself say them.

Edward stopped. For a few hoofbeats, Sly Stone and Buckaroo's horses kept walking, until the riders noticed the pause and reined their mounts into a halting. The unicorn turned his great white head.

"Clint Augustus Gulliver," he said, looking at Clint sidelong, his voice shockingly compassionate. "Noble Marshal of the Realm. *Gunslinger*. You must understand a soul cannot be regrown. If you don't come to grips with that now, your pain will only be greater once it sinks in, and then two souls will be gone. Kold carried Mai because…"

"Because she carried the Orb of Benevolence," said Clint, looking at the dirt. "I know."

"Nar. Because she *was* the Orb of Benevolence. You wondered how she could know her way to The Realm without knowing she knew? This is how. The Orb knows magic. Magic knows The Realm. Magic can see through the shifting; it can focus the myriad worlds our one world has become and perceive them as them whole again. It can draw a straight line where there is no straight line. Mai didn't know her true nature except that she had magic to some degree. Now we know to what degree — she *was* magic. Magic incarnate. And if Kold has removed the Orb, he has removed all that she was. There's nothing left in this woman to grow stronger. Nothing in her to regenerate. Kold has scooped her empty like a gourd."

"But you said you felt magic," said Clint.

Edward again looked at the trail ahead, at the fields of dead grass and brown shrubs peppering the open desert.

"Magic is in her skin and bones," he said. "But Kold has taken the Orb. There is still magic in her, yar. And life. But there is no *Mai* in her anymore. Her body may yet recover, which is why we've taken her. We owe her that much, given what we've been party to putting her through. But she will not be the woman you knew. She will be ordinary, and nar will she know or love you. She will no longer stand out, and will appear to all as perfectly plain."

Clint said nothing. Edward started walking, moving past the other horses. The riders nudged their mounts to follow the unicorn, both the criminal and the thinking machine knowing better than to speak.

Clint turned his thought to Mai's body, hoping it would recover, offering up a plea to NextWorld. It was a pointless hope. It was vain, with no fruit on its tree. But that small hope, such little of it as remained, was like glue for the gunslinger's soul. Without hope for Mai, Clint would crumble to the dirt, dry up, and blow away. Through four long years, they had ridden with only a glimmer of hope that they might catch Kold and rescue the woman Clint nearly hitched. But it *had*, nonetheless, been hope. If that hope was gone — if Mai true was dead forever — then what reason would remain for riding on?

"Don't forget," said Edward, reading the gunslinger's mind, "we can still stop Kold from finding the third Orb and uniting the

Triangulum."

"Yar," said Clint. "I suppose that's something."

A few days later, with absolutely no improvement from the dried-out corpse on the travois, three mounts and three riders came to the outskirts of San Mateo Flats — the first town at the edge of Elf Meadows, where they hoped to catch scent of Kold's trail. There were no meadows and no elves (creatures Edward assured the humans were not at all cuddly), but dead vegetation now swapped space with sand more and more often. Clint, either recovering his spiritless spirt or deflecting, joked that soon they would discover a blade of grass and worship at its dewdrop.

"The whole world isn't a desert," said Edward. "Believe me, my people know."

Next to Edward, atop an unspotted black appaloosa named Socks, Buckaroo belched steam from the back of his neck. The gold-skinned thinking machine checked what looked like a pocket watch on a chain and said, "It's true, sir. I've not been to The Realm, of course, but I've seen towns near it through many a shimmer. The closer to The Realm, the greener."

Sly Stone huffed. His own mount (also an appaloosa, this one brown, named Leroy) snorted as if echoing Stone's sentiment. "Sounds very Realm, all right," he said.

Clint said nothing. Edward, strangely, was also silent. Since the unicorn had regained his wits following his magic-addled fog, he and Stone had formed a strange sort of friendship that was somehow based on both shared goals and loathing. They didn't like each other (since Edward didn't like anyone), but whenever Stone told tales of his gang's days stealing magic and subverting Realm operations in the Sands, Edward chimed in with some Realm vitriol of his own.

The path to San Mateo grew more funneled, less open. This concerned both gunslinger and unicorn, as following a narrow path exposed them to ambushes that weren't possible in open sand. But there was no way around it, so they drew their guns and held them at the ready as the trails wound between dead underbrush, across packed dirt that had been trod by many feet and carriage wheels.

The party of riders stayed wary. Clint and Edward watched their front. Sly, with his twin shotguns, watched their rear. And eventually, then they found the ambush they'd feared... but the ambush they found wasn't their own.

Off to the side of the trail, nearly in the brush, was a stagecoach with one door hanging ajar like a pouting lip. The big wagon was slightly cocked, the wheels on one side brushing the trail's shoulder. The traces at the front of the coach had been cut, and whatever horses had once pulled it were long gone.

Clint's sharp gunslinger's eyes read the dirt like a water reader read the sands: close-set, heavy hoofprints deeper at the open end told him that when the ambush had happened, at least two horses had reared. A distinctive pattern of prints heading toward town (again with a deep-stomped set at the rear) said that the horses had run — not walked or trotted — in that direction. Around the severed traces and in the path's center were undisturbed human footprints. There were only three sets. One set belonged to a man they found killt near the front of the coach. His coat marked him as its driver. One of the other sets had been made by boots that looked too narrow for the tracks' depth, indicating a man who was lean but heavy, meaning that he had to be especially tall. The final set was made by a shoe Clint hadn't seen in a long while, but which he recalled from a wisp of memory from his almost-invisible Realm days. These last tracks had been made by the shoe of a fancy man.

Clint waved the others back and dismounted. He circled the stagecoach on foot, soaking in details from the dirt. Then, once he reached the far end, he found a man under the coach who was lying somewhere between killt and alive.

"Pilgrim," said Clint, noting the man's fancy shoes. "You alive enough to warrant a saving?"

The man groaned. He tried to roll over to look at Clint. After a quarter roll, he yelped in pain and settled.

Clint turned to Edward, but the unicorn's horn was already glowing. Under the stagecoach, the man lifted an inch straight up as if on an invisible skiff, with no part unsupported. He moved smoothly out from under the coach and settled on the dirt where Clint could get at him.

The man was beaten past beaten, his clothes ripped and filthy. Both eyes were already blackening and his body was covered in scrapes, scratches, and friction burns. His scalp was split, and beneath the split, his skull appeared to be partially caved, as if he'd been struck by something heavy. Seeing it, Clint was shocked that the man was still breathing, let alone conscious.

"Can you speak?" said the gunslinger.

"Leave me," the man croaked, his breath falling from his mouth in harsh gasps. "I can see the reaper."

"Don't fear the reaper," said Edward. "He's not met a unicorn."

Edward's horn glowed again — this time a dull yellow. The magic haze gathered on his horn like a giant balloon, then floated toward the man in the dirt. The glow brushed the man. Then it seemed to empty into him, puffing his body up. The glow dispersed and the puff subsided. When the yellow was gone, the man's eyes turned a proper color, and his scalp stitched with no crevice. Only a cake of dried blood remained, crusted across his neck and tattered clothing.

"Wait," said the man.

"I don't have time to wait," said Clint.

"I..."

"Stop being dramatic. You are healed. Stand up."

The man stood, looking down at himself, shaking his limbs as if expecting parts to fall from his torso. He seemed unwilling to believe his lack of pain, and wouldn't speak until he'd verified that somehow, he was no longer neighboring death.

"What happened?" said the man.

"*I* happened," said Edward. "You're welcome."

"Thankoo," said the man, still looking at Clint. "I don't know how you helped me just now, but...*thankoo!*"

Edward turned to Stone and Buckaroo and said, "Think I should un-heal him?"

Clint took the man by both shoulders, squared him, then gave a gentle shake to clear his awe. Awe was embarrassing, and neither a gunslinger nor a unicorn would ever expect a pleasem or thankoo. Except for Edward, that was.

"Who attacked you, and why?" Clint asked.

Instead of answering, the man started looking around the disaster until his eyes found a battered black satchel with some papers spilled beside it. He snatched nervously at the papers, then stuffed them into the satchel. Then he dove toward the brush behind the stage to recover more pages, gasping with relief at every new find. It was as if they were Orbs — too vital to leave in peril.

The man was everything Clint wasn't. He was short and plump, and had small hands that were so soft they seemed naked without gloves. His face was smooth and unscarred. His clothes would be perfect if they were clean and untorn — a white shirt with a string tie; pearl buttons; a dour deep blue overcoat. His hair was combed and parted (possibly oiled), and he had a small, pencil-thin mustache drawn above his full lip. As Clint watched the man scamper, the man located his hat and donned it. It was a dented brown bowler with a small blue feather in its band.

"Pilgrim," said Clint.

"*Alan*," corrected the man. Then he seemed to realize he was being rude and ran toward Clint with his armful of gathered papers. With the satchel and vellum clasped to his chest, he thrust a hand clumsily toward Clint. Because his elbow was pinning papers to his body, he couldn't fully extend the arm. Clint shook the man's small, soft hand. The gunslinger's large hand devoured it like a bird of prey.

"Alan Whitney," the man said. "Attorney at law."

"Where is Law?" said Clint.

"Nar. I mean I'm a lawyer."

"I don't know what a 'lawyer' is, nor do I care," said Clint. "I want to know what happened here."

"Attorneys enforce the law," said Whitney, answering the question Clint hadn't asked. But once answered, Clint couldn't help but look the man over with fresh eyes. He carried no gun and had no muscle. Plenty of meat on him, but none of it tough. And nar any weapons, at the scene nor on the man. How could one such as this *enforce the law?* But he let it go.

"What happened to you?" he repeated.

Behind him, Edward grunted. Sly, smelling Realm on the man, grunted a disapproving echo. Buckaroo, ever dutiful, said nothing. He did, however, check his faux pocket watch. It was a compulsion, if machines could be said to have compulsions.

"I was robbed, sir," said Whitney. "I was riding into San Mateo when the horses stopped, reared, whinnied, whatever. I couldn't see them because I was inside, but I heard it and I felt it. The coach rocked. I heard a great rustling and a scuffle, and by the time I came out the... oh, dear, I forgot. The poor driver." The man looked over, removed his hat, set it across his heart, and then after a thoughtful moment returned it to his head. "When I came out, there was a man here dressed all in black, and nothing else to indicate the great noises I'd heard earlier, though there *was* an ominous sound — like a thousand maracas shaken at once — from off in the brush. The man himself was very tall and thin. He had a weapon like a heavy alloy ball on a stick. He robbed the coach's strongbox — not much in there, anyway — then told me to run off. But I stood up to him."

Whitney's chest inflated with what looked like pride. Or stupidity, as Clint saw it. A coward ran when he could make a difference. Idiots failed to flee when they couldn't.

"You stood up to him?"

"Yar. I told him I would see to it that he paid for what he'd done to the driver, who was in my employ and hadn't hurt anyone, and who hadn't so much as threatened the bandit from what I heard. I demanded his name. He laughed. He wore a bandana across his face to hide his features, but I knew he'd be easy to identify anyway on account of his stature, and told him so."

"Well," said Edward from behind Clint. "We'll be on our way.

You're obviously too stupid to save. Would you like your injuries back?"

Whitney ignored Edward and kept speaking to Clint — the only one in the party who, in Whitney's eyes, apparently looked like an upstanding lawman. The great white equine, the gold-skinned machine, and the clown with the giant orange ball of hair didn't come close, it seemed.

"These lands are wild," Whitney said. "I've seen things you wouldn't believe since coming here."

"I doubt it," said Sly Stone, tracing the short grips of his sawed-off shotguns with a pale finger.

"Lawlessness everywhere. Well, it won't stand. I told the man that law was coming to the wild Sands whether he liked it or not, and that men like him would answer for their crimes."

"That's when he tried to kill you, I reckon," said Clint.

"Yar. He hit me with his weapon, then cut the traces and freed the horses. He punched me and kicked me, then hit me again with his large alloy ball. Here." Whitney rubbed the spot on his head which, a moment earlier, had been concave. "I crawled under the stage. After kicking my papers around, the tall man left. When he went, that terrible rustling from the bushes went with him. Then I stayed for... I don't know how long — Minutes? Hours? Days?... until you came along."

"What was the rustling you heard?" Edward asked.

Whitney ignored the unicorn and turned to Clint, his eyes full of begging. "Will you escort me into town?"

The gunslinger took hold of Whitney's head, then forcibly turned it so that he was looking back at Edward. "If you ignore my friend again, I will leave you here," he said.

"I'm sorry," said Whitney, looking at Stone. "I..."

"He was talking about me," Edward said.

Whitney clutched his chest. "Providence! A talking horse!"

Edward's horn glowed purple.

Clint stepped between them, arms out. He looked at Whitney, then Edward, then Whiney. After a moment, something seemed to settle into Whitney's head and Edward paused his ominous magic.

"Tell you what," said Clint. "We'll palaver as we ride."

CHAPTER TWO:
ALL SEVEN SPICES

They spoke while riding into San Mateo Flats, but Whitney wasn't much help beyond what he'd already told Clint. He rode behind Buckaroo, the most accommodating in the posse, while casting suspicious glances at Sly Stone and his massive guns. He looked at Edward with something slightly different than suspicion, but no more flattering.

Eventually he realized Edward was a unicorn ("What gave me away?" the unicorn had asked him, waving his horn), but Whitney explained that his usual territory was well into Elf Meadows, much closer to The Realm, in a kind of lawful middleground where marshals and unicorns were seldom seen but things were relatively civilized. He'd heard of unicorns, of course — who hadn't? — but he'd never met one. Clint advised him quietly to watch his step and do his best to keep from insulting Edward. Doing so could make things unpleasant.

Whitney had no more to say on the strange rustling from the bushes. He just repeated what he'd said earlier, about it sounding like a thousand maracas. Clint asked him to guess what it might have been. Whitney didn't have a clue. *Men?* Clint asked, already knowing from the number of distinct footprints on the scene that the man with the large alloy ball rode alone. Whitney said he couldn't be sure. It was possible the man who had attacked him came with a gang, that the gang had approached without stepping on the path, and that they'd waited in the bushes during the attack before leaving, also without stepping on the path. But why? Why would a man have a gang if they didn't show themselves?

Stone, who'd noticed something Clint hadn't, asked about the lacerations on the coach driver's face and why his eyes seemed destroyed. Whitney shook his head, repeating that he didn't know, that he wished he could add more, and that he'd been inside the coach when the driver was killt.

Stone, to make conversation with the nervous lawyer, asked about his business in San Mateo. Whitney replied that his business was in Aurora Solstice, where Clint's crew had just come from, and that he wanted to establish a law practice. Clint wondered again how someone like Whitney could be a lawman and was near to voicing his ponder when Stone beat him to it by telling Whitney that Aurora Solstice was in the other direction.

"I know that, Mister..." He paused, waiting for Stone to give his name.

"... Bozo," Stone answered.

"... Mister Bozo. But I need to return to San Mateo to report this crime. I saw a constable's office when I rode through earlier."

"Report this crime?"

"He wants him killt," Clint told Stone.

"Nar, sir," said Whitney. "I want him convicted."

The riders understood the concept (Stone had been on his way to trial in The Realm before he and Buckaroo joined Clint's posse, after all), but it didn't make sense. The bandit Whitney sought had killt the coach driver and had intended to end Whitney. That called for killing, not accusing.

But Whitney was a strange man, so the riders let it go, falling silent. Unfortunately, Whitney seemed uncomfortable with silence. He yammered on, and on, and on. He told them about how the Sands were lawless and needed order. He told them about his hometown and his education. He told them about the law practice he wanted to start in Aurora Solstice. He raged and ranted about how bandits in the Sands must be captured, tried by a jury of peers, and jailed.

"And what if the local law won't arrest him?" said Edward.

"Then I will face him myself," said Whitney.

Edward grunted. Whitney took it for a noise of support, which it wasn't.

Because they were going through San Mateo anyway, Clint agreed to wait for Whitney to lodge his complaint with the local constable — just long enough to make sure the idiot didn't get himself laid out dead. It would be a quick stop. They would head in, stop to reload their supplies, and be on their way.

San Mateo Flats, however, merited a few hours' delay. The town was unlike anything Clint had seen other than vague, barely-there almost-memories of his days in The Realm. The buildings were larger than those in towns they'd come through, and were built of alloy as well as wood and brick. There were machines in the streets — nothing so complex as Buckaroo, but a few spark-driven engines and a smattering of food suppliers who sold out of steam-driven carts. In addition to riders and stagecoaches, there were also odd carriages in the streets that were pulled by horses now, but that seemed as if they might at one time have been self-locomotive. The roads were dirt but were packed hard, keeping the air mostly free of dust. The people on the streets wore fancy clothes. Shoes such as Whitney's were common. The men wore hats that were tall and made of felt, not rough and beaten and flat like Clint's. The women were draped in large dresses. Some carried parasols and wore gloves.

As they looked around and got a better feel for the whistle-stop, the town took on a strange tinge in Clint's mind. It looked as if San Mateo had boomed, then stopped mid-explosion. There were many buildings, but many were unfinished and without a crew to work them. Some of the streets were coated with crushed stone rather than packed dirt, but the stone surfaces ended abruptly, as if the crews resurfacing them had suddenly surrendered. The main square's skyline — if buildings two stories tall could be said to be a skyline true — was speared with alloy members. It looked as if several buildings were supposed to keep growing upward, but the subsequent stories had gone missing.

The constable's office was on the main square. The square, in contrast to the half-finished buildings outside of it, was thriving. It was filled with coaches, pedestrians, and riders, and had been built around a large central island with a bandstand and a giant stone fountain. The bandstand was clean and white and new, but the fountain held no water. Shovels and picks circled the base, with bags of cement and sand stacked around it.

They pulled up and walked toward the constable's office. On the front door was a sign that read, *Gone for chili*.

"Chili?" said Stone. He laughed at the absurdity. "Is this a joke?"

Clint, already feeling skeptical after his brush with chili-believing lawmen in Nazareth Shiloh, followed a large hand-drawn arrow on the sign that pointed to the left. There, beside the constable's office, was an eatery with its name writ above the door: THE LIBERTY VALANCE. Below that: *Best chili in Mateo!*

"This is absurd," said Clint. "The lawmen leave in the middle of the day to engage in some bizarre ritual?" He looked at Whitney. "Head out, Whitney. You don't want San Mateo justice. They'll insist on simmering your man for six hours in the mysterious seven spices, and never arresting him."

Whitney climbed around Buckaroo and hopped down to the street.

"Fine, I'll find the constable myself," he said, heading for the saloon door. "Pleasem and thankoo for the ride."

Stone looked at Clint, then raised his eyebrows. Despite his mockery of the chili notice, Stone was curious. Chili cults perpetuated false hope, but Stone, Clint, and Edward were all hungry. Bizarre rituals or no bizarre rituals, the travelers were in need of pie and brew. Stopping in at the Valance wouldn't hurt.

Clint gave Stone a nod.

"Hey Whitney," Stone called.

Whitney turned.

"Stay your feet a moment. We'll go with you."

Whitney smiled, then came back over and helped Buckaroo tie his horse to a post. He watched Stone hitch his, then managed to refrain from reminding the gunslinger to tie his own mount.

"I can't fit in there," Edward said, nodding toward the building's batwings.

"So you'll stay out front, then?"

Edward shook his head. "Nar. Mai and I will check out the town. Won't we, Mai?" His horn glowed and Mai's inert body rose from the travois, gently coming to rest on the unicorn's back inside of a protective pink bubble. He looked at Clint. "Now that *your* wretched carcass is off of my back, *the lady* can finally ride. Are you comfortable, Mai?" Using the bubble, the unicorn made her head nod. Then, in a squeaky falsetto from the side of his mouth, he said, "Yes, Edward! I'm quite comfortable, thankoo!"

Clint gave the unicorn an annoyed look, but he and his partner had lived through too much seriousness and sorrow lately. It was hard to be irritated by any levity, no matter how inappropriate.

"Oh, relax," said Edward. "She'll have fun. Bring me some chili."

Clint laughed. *Hard.* He didn't know what had broken his armor — Edward's quip or his absurd mention of chili — but in an instant the dour gunslinger had gone from annoyed to giddy. For years, he'd been near his breaking point. Maybe he'd finally tipped past it, into maniacal dementia.

"I will stay with you, sire," Buckaroo said, addressing Edward. "This town is still far from The Realm and equally far from anywhere we've stitched seams. These people will likely have more questions about me if I go in than they will for Mister Whitney."

"We'll bring *you* some chili too," said Clint, still giddy.

"I'm not hungry, sir, but thankoo," said Buckaroo.

Clint laughed harder — and then, with a scintilla of panic, suddenly found himself unable to stop. So after a moment, Stone took him by the arm and pulled him into the crowded saloon, shoving Alan Whitney ahead of them.

They found the town constable at a table with six other lawmen, all wearing stars. The constable was a greased sow's worth of fat and spoke with a long and lazy drawl. He was unshaven and jawing on a fatty steak when they arrived, dripping grease down onto the front of his shirt. The lawmen didn't look much more promising than the constable; all were either fragile or slow. Clint, whose mood sobered when he'd seen the state of law enforcement in San Mateo Flats, estimated that he could kill all seven before one touched his sidearm.

While Clint stood by like a chaperone, Whitney told the constable about his encounter outside of town. He started by mentioning a robbery, and the constable listened politely. Then he described his assailant and the table fell hushed. The party to the left, sensing the mood at the constable's table, fell into a hush. The table to the right caught the quiet, and then it spread through the room like a disease.

"I don't have jurisdiction out there," the constable said. "And if you didn't see the bandit's face, you couldn't identify him anyway."

"Of course I can identify him!" Whitney blurted. "He was as tall and thin as a railpost. Easily six and a half feet tall, skinnier than that man there. He carried a sidearm, but the weapon he hit me with was like a ball on a stick. Heavy alloy on one end, abutted to a black handle. He attacked alone, save for the strange rustling in the weeds."

"I'm sorry," said the constable. "That could be anyone."

"That's Independence Lee, that is!" blurted a man at the next table, unshaven and with a single snaggletooth sticking out of his upper gum. His hat was brown, beaten, and torn. "Constable, that's Independence! He's the only one what carries a mace!"

"That's it," said Whitney, pointing. "A mace. Caved my skull in with it. I'd be dead if not for this man's unicorn." He touched Clint's shoulder, and Clint resisted an urge to snap the man's arm from his body.

At the mention of a unicorn, the lawmen looked from one to the other. Then they looked at Clint and noticed for the first time that he wore two guns, both with large, seven-shot cylinders. The constable's eyes found Clint's, but he silently refused to acknowledge the true he'd just learned of the gunslinger's identity. The presence of a Realm marshal complicated things in a thousand different ways.

"You don't know that it's Lee, Marley," the constable said to the unshaven man. "He has no proof."

"Proof? You act like I'm accusing you. Aren't you the law in this town?"

"Yar," said the constable, "but…"

"But nothing," said Whitney. "Your office is next door. Let's head over there and I'd like to file a report, and…"

"Mister," said the snaggletoothed man, "you don't 'file a report' on Independence Lee. You stay away. And if you face him, you prepare to kill him … or die yourself."

"Probably the latter," said a man beside him. Then he looked into his mug of brew and added, "So far, anyway."

"Where's the law in this town?" Whitney railed, raising a hectoring finger. "What kind of lawmen are you? I'm an attorney, sir, and let me tell you, I…"

But at that moment, a server slid a bowl filled with a red substance in front of the constable. Stone grabbed Whitney's arm to stop his speechifying and said, "Is that chili?"

Whitney quickly recovered. "… I will not stand by lawlessness! You have a bandit who assaults people that you seem to already know about, which means you're turning a blind eye to…"

Stone mopped the fresh sweat from his suddenly beaded brow. "It is, isn't it? It's… holy guns; *it's chili!*"

"It's Fool's Chili, you fool," said Clint.

"I can smell it. *All seven spices.*" Sly Stone's voice was wet and full of yearning. He stood on his toes, craning over the table and the rich, red bowl like a vulture over prey. His eyes were wide, mouth smacking in a way that had to be subconscious.

"Stand down, Stone," said Clint. "We're here to do a job and to help Mr. Whitney to…"

"It's true! It's always been true!" Stone crouched over, reaching for the bowl. The constable pulled it back. "Providence, it's true! I can smell it! Let me have it, Constable. Let me have just a little…"

"Get your own!" the constable snapped, eyeing Stone's huge ball of orange hair.

"Constable," said Whitney, "I want to file my complaint, and…"

"GIVE ME THE CHILI, FLATFOOT!" Stone screeched, pulling both shotguns from his holsters and aiming them at the constable. Movement stirred from behind and Stone swung one of his guns around, now pointing one barrel at the terrified constable and the other at a table of men who were, now, cowering low, ducking below their table.

Clint put a hand on Stone's gun, pointed at the constable to remind Stone who he was threatening, then pushed it slowly toward the floor. But Stone shook him off and turned a wild gaze to the gunslinger. Forgetting all semblance of himself, he yelled, "THEY HAVE CHILI! THEY'VE ALWAYS HAD IT!"

"Put down your guns, we..."

"What is wrong with you people?" Whitney stuttered. "This Lee, he..."

"Here!" spat the constable, shoving the bowl forward and spilling it onto the plaid tablecloth. "Here! Take it! Take the dagged chili!"

Stone leapt for the bowl, but a fast hand snatched it from him. Clint looked down to see who'd taken the chili from Stone and realized he'd done it himself. He could smell it. It wasn't Fool's Chili. It was chili true.

"Oh, so now you believe?" said Stone. "GIVE ME THE CHILI!"

Clint flicked at Stone's gun barrel with his free hand. "Or what, you'll hit me with your pop guns?" He brought the bowl closer to his nose and deeply inhaled. "Smells good, Stone. I'd say this has *eight* spices."

Stone started to bring his gun around, but it was too big, too clunky. Clint had his pistol out, cocked, and aimed as Stone attempted to shift his grip. He poked Stone in the forehead with his iron and said, "Go ahead. Make my day."

"I WAS THE BELIEVER!" Stone yelled, his eyes bugging out.

"With hair like that? I don't think so." Clint raised the bowl to his mouth and touched his upper lip to the fragrant red liquid. A tiny drop entered his open maw and detonated pleasure in his brain.

"SANDS TO YOU!" Stone kicked his foot upward, meaning to strike the precious chili and spill it — if he couldn't have it, nobody could — but Clint was too fast. He wasn't going to actually shoot Stone, but he wasn't going to let him have the chili, either. He lowered his gun and fired a shot at Stone's boot, knowing it would fly harmlessly between his toes with only a burn. The shot was on target but threw off Stone's kick. His boot landed in the gunslinger's groin.

Clint almost collapsed, but was still holding the chili. He winced and staggered back, gripping the table behind him. Men scattered. Then, fighting seething pain, he raised his gun and whacked Stone across the head.

A server girl who had missed the commotion came out from the kitchen carrying a tray laden with at least eight bowls of steaming chili, then chose the wrong moment to say, "Chili up!"

Stone, seeing that Clint hadn't faltered, was frozen on the floor with a gun in each hand. His eyes flicked toward the server. Clint, still holding his pistol and fighting discomfort, saw Stone's eyes and followed them.

Stone's eyes said, *That's my chili.*

Clint's eyes said, *Like sands it is.*

Stone lurched to his feet. Clint lunged. The girl flinched, nearly spilling her tray. Clint caught Stone before he could rise and they fell to the floor. The first bowl flew from Clint's hand to the floor and shattered like the world was ending. A wave of rich meatiness flowed toward them, coating Clint's sleeve. Stone licked at it, moaning.

"I'll kill you for that," said Clint.

"Try it," said Stone.

They paused, staring at each other. The girl was frozen, and backing up, looking at the men. The other patrons of the Liberty Valance watched the fight, frozen. Time stopped.

"I'm going for the chili," said Stone.

The door exploded and something gigantic bowled through the saloon, upending tables, scattering diners and sending them diving, causing the girl to trip and spill her tray, which rained like meaty blood around the room.

It was like a bomb had gone off — a massive white bomb, yelling about chili while shooting bolts of purple and blue light, causing cataclysmic damage. Whitney's problem mattered nar, and neither did Independence Lee. Nothing mattered.

The saloon held its breath and waited for the tumult to end.

CHAPTER THREE: THE BANDIT AND HIS MURDER

"Once again," Clint said, "we're sorry."

William O'Hanorhan, the Liberty Valance's owner, glanced sidelong at Clint, then turned to Sly Stone, then finally to Edward. The unicorn had indeed been too big to fit through the door, but once he'd broken in (leaving Mai outside with Buckaroo) and trashed the place in a fit of chili lust, Edward figured he might as well eat his fill of hot, steamy chili. So now the unicorn was sprawled on the floor, half on his side, complaining about how uncomfortable it was to sit that way. But he couldn't stand unless he wanted to keep clanging his horn on the saloon's decorations — most of which were hanging portraits of a thin-faced man who O'Hanorhan explained the saloon was named after.

"Yar," said O'Hanorhan, unwilling to totally commit himself to accepting Clint's apology. Edward had already fixed everything they'd broken and had even magicked the chili squeaky clean from the floor, but O'Hanorhan still didn't like them. *Outsiders*, he seemed to think.

After a long glance, O'Hanorhan returned to the kitchen. Edward, not to be out-ignored, announced that he'd had his fill of both chili and local hospitality (unlike Clint, Edward hadn't apologized) and stood, broke through the doors again, fixed them again, and left to rejoin Buckaroo and Mai. He said over his retreating rump that he had to explore a hunch he'd been pursuing anyway. Now that he'd eaten, he said, Clint could "Be dumb with the dumb townies" on his own.

"You have some bridges to mend if you're aiming to stay, I'm afraid," said the fat constable after O'Hanorhan and Edward had left Clint, Stone, and Whitney alone with the table of lawmen. The constable's name turned out to be Paulson, and he wasn't seeming any more brave or competent to Clint as time passed.

"Yar," said Clint.

"It's just chili," said the constable. "What sort of fool has a bowl of chili set in front of him one day and gets some stupid idea?"

"We've nar heard rumors of chili were true," said Clint.

"Tomatoes. Peppers. Spices. Meat. There's really nothing special."

"You're not from the deep Sands," said Clint.

"I mean, my mother used to make it every…"

"We get it," said Stone, wiping his lip with a bare wrist. He was trying to sound annoyed by the patrons' overreaction to their group's irrational response to what had turned out to be a rather common bowl of hot food, but his bliss was true. He was on his fifth bowl of chili, which placed his consumption behind only Edward, who'd eaten thirty-four.

"Look," said Paulson. "We're simple folk, not used to such commotion. We're not familiar with outsiders. Your man here —" He gestured toward Whitney, who astonishingly didn't care about the chili and hadn't had any. "— what he yammers on about? That's just not something we talk on here in San Mateo. Yar, I'm sure he came afoul of Independence Lee. He's the only man what carries a mace and is tall and thin as such. Dressed all in black, weren't he? Yar. But Lee and his murder? They're our cross to bear. A nest we don't poke."

"Maybe *we* could poke it," said Clint. But as soon as the words were out of his mouth, he wondered why he'd said them. They had a man to pursue, yet it seemed that over and over, they kept getting sucked into other people's problems. Curse of being a lawman true, he supposed.

"Nar, you won't!" Paulson said, pointing an accusing finger at the gunslinger. "You're not from here. You don't know how it is. You thought chili was worth killing for? Wait'll you see Independence Lee. You don't understand San Mateo. Things is different here."

"We could *make* them different, is what I'm saying," said Clint. "Lee couldn't touch my unicorn."

"Yar," said Paulson. "But what on his murder?"

"Exactly," said Stone.

"There will be no murder," Whitney declared. "This is my complaint, and I won't have vigilantes on its account. I am a man of law. Not 'law' like you, though. I'm law and order. You're law and *dis*order."

"Strange thing to say to those who saved you," Stone said. "Maybe you'd rather we left you with your 'orderly' head wound to die."

Whitney held out a pacifying hand. "And I appreciate your help, but towns like San Mateo will never prosper so long as they're lawless. Man killing man?" Whitney shook his head. "That's no way to live. You need men like your Lee to nar start trouble — and for that, you need law."

Someone cackled behind Paulson. It was a man playing poker at the next table. He turned, then nodded to Stone and Clint. He said, "Sirs? No offense, but you don't know Lee and his murder. He ain't gonna abide no law. When he attacked you — did that go lawly-like?"

Whitney just stared.

"Did he seem like a man what'd be upset by a fella like you?" The man laughed, tickled by something in his head. "Mister, I'll bet you told him you'd see him in jail. Did you?"

"I told him I'd have him arrested for assault."

"How'd that go?"

Whitney said nothing, but he'd already told Clint, Edward, Stone, and Buckaroo how it'd gone. During the entire encounter, Lee seemed to have three goals. Arranged in order from most important to least, the goals seemed to be insulting Whitney, causing chaos and inflicting pain on Whitney, and, as a by-the-way, robbing Whitney.

"Mister," said a man at the poker table wearing a hat big enough to be a twenty-gallon, "did you meet his murder?"

"What are you talking about?" said Stone.

"His soldiers. Did they get at you?"

"His gang?"

The table looked from one man to another, then laughed. "I suppose you could call 'em that," said the man with the big hat.

"Nar," Whitney said. "I heard noises in the bushes, but saw no men."

"Nar, you wouldn't have." Paulson rubbed at his chin. "Had you seen them, you'd never see anything else ever again. Lee is crueler than cruel, see. The foulest kind of man, who loves to cause pain more than he even loves his own pleasure. Your squirming, it must have been like..." He looked around the table at all of the empty, red-stained bowls and laughed a deep, throaty laugh. "... like *chili* to him. So he'd want to pound you himself. And the way you lived until your rescuers arrived? I'd wager that weren't no accident. Probably let you live on purpose, because more life after a pounding with that mace means more pain. Means more cruelty."

Clint shook his head. This was absurd. He didn't want to put his foot where it didn't belong again, but Lee had attacked Whitney alone. Based on the other stories he'd heard so far, Lee usually attacked alone, and only called on his gang when he needed the help. *One* man. Clint could dispatch a lone troublesome outlaw in an afternoon. When he did, his gang — if he knew gangs, and especially ones that were used to just standing and watching — would disperse.

And now, after the chili and saloon debacle, he felt he owed the people of San Mateo Flats a favor. Maybe a lot of favors.

"Constable," he said, "maybe your town has been beaten to fear this man Lee, so if *you* don't want to scuffle, fine. I'll scuffle for you."

"Nar," said Whitney, "I want him tried according to…"

Clint held up a hand. "Now hold on a second there, Pilgrim. I understand you want to do law your way, but I don't have time for it. The way I help is with a bullet. That's the only way quick enough to get me back about my business. We're months behind our man already, and getting further behind with each minute."

Paulson considered, took a spoonful of chili, then shook his head.

"It's a fine offer, Marshal, and I appreciate it, but it's like my friends said: Lee's only half the problem. The rest is his murder. You saw the town? The way nothing's finished? Weren't always like that. This town was bustling once upon a time, with new buildings going up every month. This close to the Meadows, we're right on a through-route for rich folks wanting to explore and rough it in the grit. We were expanding the Otel, building out businesses, putting in a casino, creating new stores and whatnot. Repairing roads. Parks. You get me. Then Lee sent his murder to park themselves on every project, and when they're there — standing on an alloy beam with their black eyes on yours, you *know* not to build. There've been times when men have tried starting up on old projects. Plenty of times. They'll go for a while, but then the murder shows. Men get killt with their eyes gone. Travelers won't take our roads, not with the murder lining its way. The paths are treacherous and folks stay away. So you see, even if you take out Lee, we've still got the murder to contend with."

Clint shook his head. "I've seen plenty of gangs, Constable. They talk big, but they're all weak. Sever the head and the body collapses."

"Mister," said one of the lawmen at the table, "don't you listen? This ain't no *gang*. This is a *murder!*"

Clint squinted, nearing anger at the obtuseness of law in San Mateo. "What the sands are you talking about, 'murder'?"

"Wait," said Whitney, realization creeping into his eyes.

"What's that sound?" said Stone, cocking his head at something outside.

"Wait," Whitney repeated, still grasping for a thought.

"It sounds like…" Stone paused.

Clint listened. A low chattering sound began to grow louder. In the space of a few seconds, the relative quiet outside the Liberty Valance was shattered by a tremendous squawking. It sounded like a thousand maracas.

Or a thousand birds.

"A 'murder,' " said Whitney, "is a word referring to a flock of crows."

A whipcrack sound made every head in the Liberty Valance turn to look toward the batwing doors, where a very tall, very thin man dressed entirely in black smiled his way into the saloon.

At his feet was a spreading pool of black birds.

CHAPTER FOUR:
THE MAN WHO SHOT
LIBERTY VALANCE

Lee sauntered into the Liberty Valance like he owned the place, twisting his head in a series of small, assessing glances, sucking in his surroundings like a man making sure things are in order.

The man was gigantic. He had to duck as he stepped through the doorway — and still the top of the doorframe tipped his hat back on his head. He was thin enough to blow over in a heavy breeze. His fingers were longer than Clint's, and those fingers were caressing the handle of something in a holster that wasn't a gun. It had to be the heavy ball — the mace — that the others described. On his other hip, he wore a pistol. Its grip and the edges of the black cowhide holster looked worn, as if the weapon had been drawn over and over and over again.

Every man in the saloon reacted to Lee's presence. Some physically backed away. Others turned their chairs, eyes wide. Conversation stopped at every table. Men who didn't back away at least watched the bandit, fear in their eyes. Lee clearly felt in control and apparently usually was; his manner said it, as did the manner of every man and woman inside the Liberty Valance. Even a giant of a man in the corner that Clint had been eying earlier — a behemoth who was easily eight or nine feet tall and five feet wide at the shoulders, about the size of a tall closet — had set his brew to the wood and made his face wary.

Lee took a few slow, measured steps across the wood plank floor, clearly enjoying the effect he was having on the townsfolk. Birds milled at his feet, deftly avoiding the toes of his boots as he walked. There were ten birds at first, then twenty, then thirty, then forty. Once they'd covered the entryway like a black tide, they began to bird-hop up onto chairs, shelves, and tables. They squawked randomly, causing diners to jump. One flapped into the middle of a table filled with coins and cards, and all six of the poker players at the table shambled back as if the birds were bombs.

Lee pulled the mace from its modified holster and twirled it in his hand.

"Well, don't stand on ceremony," he said to one of the servers. "I came for chili."

The girl immediately pulled out the nearest chair, then returned her body to its ramrod-straight position.

"Thank you, sweetheart," said Lee with a mock bow. He walked to the chair, crows following behind him. Here and there they flitted around the room, effectively surrounding everyone in it. They were only crows — ordinary crows — but they were clearly bent to Lee's will. It reminded Clint of the rats in the cathedral beneath Precipice.

Halfway to the chair, Lee stopped and looked to his right. A table of men wearing beaten-up hats and mutton chops stumbled back, two of them tipping onto the floor. Another man with his back to the bandit was too engrossed in something to see him approach. So Lee grasped the man's chair by its back.

"I'd prefer a chair closer to the window," he said to the server, yanking on the seat and sending the man crashing to the floor. The man rolled to face his attacker, then crawled back like a frightened animal when he saw who it was. He had trapped himself under the table, and so had to scamper around another man's feet to get free. Lee watched and laughed, now swirling the large weapon within inches of the table's top.

"You don't mind if I take this table, do you?" he asked the remaining men.

"No, Independence," said one. "It's all yours!" The man stood and backed away from the table until he found himself in front of the doors. He squeezed by the crows and ran. The other men backed their chairs from the table, joining their neighbors to give Lee his space.

Instead of sitting, Lee took another long look around the room. He stretched, looking at the giant in the corner before seeming to decide that the big man wasn't going to cause trouble (birds were at his feet and on the bar beside him, and Clint couldn't help but admire him for not flinching) and moved on.

When Lee's glance reached Clint's face, he paused. What sounded like thousands of crows made an increasingly loud racket outside. When Lee wasn't speaking, the murder's squawk was the only sound in the air, and it rang aplenty.

"Well, now who are you, stranger?" he said.

Clint remained seated, his guns hidden. "Just a traveler. And you?"

Lee chuckled, ignoring the insult of ignorance. He looked at Stone, sitting beside Clint. "And you travel with a clown?"

Stone flexed to rise, but Clint held a subtle hand to his arm. There would be plenty of time to take out this one man — this *only* one man — in a moment. For now, Lee might have things to say that the gunslinger wanted to hear.

The bandit shrugged at Stone's impassive face. Then he saw Whitney and broke into great gales of laughter. "Well, if it isn't my old friend!" he bellowed. "It's been a long time. We've played games before, yar?"

Whitney didn't have Clint or Stone's restraint. He popped up from his seat, knocking his chair back. His posture and face were righteous and indignant. He shot an accusing finger toward Lee.

"Constable!" he said. "This is the man who attacked me on the path outside of town. I would like to file a complaint!"

Lee threw his head back, erupting with laughter. The birds began to titter and ruffle their wings as if laughing along with him. Then Lee stopped, and the birds stopped too. He took a few steps toward the fat constable with both of his arms forward, wrists up. One hand still held the mace.

"He's right, Constable! He'd like to file a complaint, so I guess it's your duty to do so. Take me into custody!"

The constable looked up. His face twisted through a range of emotions, most of which were kin to fear. "Really?"

Lee laughed harder. The birds laughed with him. "You're a spitfire, aren't you, dude?" he said, taking a long step toward Whitney. Whitney looked up at him, defiant. "Well, I'll make you a deal. If you can catch me, you can take me in. Same goes for you, Constable. And same for any of you. Catch the big man and make him go away. Sound good?"

"I'm not afraid of you," Whitney declared.

"Really, dude? Then you're dumber than you look. Maybe my mace could teach you a lesson." And with that, he slammed the heavy ball onto the table between the Constable, Whitney, Stone and Clint. It made a satisfying crack and splintered through the table's center.

"That's not a very impressive mace," said Stone. "It doesn't even have any spikes."

Clint elbowed him, but Lee was already looking over.

"Oh, but you're wrong," said Lee. "A ball with spikes is a morning star, not a mace."

He slammed the ball into the table again, directly in front of Stone. Stone didn't flinch, and held the bandit's gaze.

"And a ball on a chain? That's called a *flail*."

Again he slammed the table. The ball had to be unbelievably dense and heavy. This time, the impact broke an entire section from the table. The wedge of wood fell into Stone's lap.

"I have all three, but this is the one I like best. It does damage without killing, and is easily controlled. It has a way of persuading people that I'm right about things. How about you, dude? Do you think I have a point?"

Stone sniffed. "It's always nice to learn new things."

Lee smiled, jerking his head in satisfaction. He stood tall. Very tall.

"You're new to town. Not hard to see that. You with your hair and those big guns. I'll bet you couldn't draw before I caved your head in and turned it to chili. And *you*, with your dumb flat hat." He nodded to Clint.

But Whitney was behind him, still remonstrating. In an astonishing display of stupidity, he tapped Lee hard on the shoulder. Lee spun, his mace held high. But when he saw who he was facing, he just laughed again, taking a few steps toward the door and into the murder of crows, taking his time, enjoying the show.

"Your tap startled me," he said. "I figured maybe Pompi finally decided to get up and face me. But he's smarter than that. Aren't you, Pompi?" He raised his eyebrows to the giant in the corner. The huge man met Lee's eyes, said nothing, and took a sip of his brew.

Whitney was undeterred. "You can't tell these people what to do. You've no right. You killt my stagecoach driver, a man who never did anything to hurt anyone. This isn't the wild Sands! This is on the doorstep of Elf Meadows! They're building railroads through here soon, and when they do, your kind won't stand. They'll need law and order and…"

Lee started walking toward Whitney, bumping him with his chest, forcing him to back up.

"I told you, dude. You want to take me in? Then take me in. I promise I won't kill you. Just hurt you real bad. You're too entertaining to kill."

Clint was about to stand and confront Lee — who only held a mace, after all — but something else happened first. From the bar's corner, the giant stood. He was much, much larger than Lee, and as he stood — unhurried, brushing his mug of brew down the bar as if it were a flea — it became apparent just how much bigger he was. Not only did he have to duck every time he passed one of the roof beams, but he was as wide as eight Lees standing side by side.

Something flickered across Lee's features as he watched the giant approach. It wasn't quite fear or concern — more like indecision. He wasn't going to face the big man with a mace, and even if the birds could be summoned for attack, they would probably only be an inconvenience to the giant. Lee didn't back up, but his expression did. He stowed the mace by reaching across himself to place it into his left holster. Then, seeming to not know what else to do, he pulled his six-shot revolver from his right hip and leveled it at the advancing wall of man.

"Well, look who grew some hair," said Lee, chuckling in a way that didn't sound at all confident.

"You are too mean, Mister Lee," said the giant.

"Sit down, Pompi."

"You go. You take your birds and go. Leave us alone, Mister Lee."

"I said, sit down, you big idiot."

The giant bared his hands, which had thus far been behind his back. Clint, who usually couldn't be shocked, gasped. The man's hands were half as wide as his chest. Clint wondered how he could have held his mug of brew.

"I said..." Lee began.

"Go away, Mister Lee," the giant repeated. His right hand moved behind his back and re-emerged with a gigantic hammer. It was as long as Edward was tall, with a beveled block of stone on its end. It had to weigh a literal ton. Looking at the thing, Clint couldn't imagine how he'd been wearing it on his back and sitting at the bar at the same time.

"Now, Pompi, do you really want to..."

"Your birds don't scare me," Pompi said, tapping the hammer in his giant palm. It was astonishing — his hands had to be mighty powerful to tilt something so large up from one end so casually. "Those birds are full of the bad stuff from Meadowlands, but it's all just little bits."

"My quarrel isn't with you," said Lee, but now he was the one falling a step back. His gun was still out, still leveled at the giant's chest. But how much damage could it possibly do?

Lee cocked his gun. "Don't make me hurt you, Pompi."

Across the room, Stone barked laughter.

"*Go,*" said Pompi, still advancing. He held the big hammer in one hand so he could make dismissive shooing gestures with the other. The gesturing hand was, when open, as big as the poker tables in the saloon. The fingers on it were as big around as Clint's legs.

Lee — probably because he knew shooting the giant would only make things worse — fired a warning shot to the side, into the saloon. Patrons gasped and shrieked. The bullet struck one of the framed portraits of the thin-faced man directly between the eyes.

"Back off, Pompi," said Lee.

But Pompi gave no indication that he realized a shot had been fired. He shifted the hammer and slowly raised it.

Lee looked at Pompi with defiance, then holstered his gun. Pompi lowered his hammer, but continued taking small steps forward. The crows around the room began to flutter back to the pool on the floor, and soon the entire murder was shuffling out the door. Then, once the birds were gone, Lee began to back out as well. It was as if the birds knew what he was going to do before he did it.

Before leaving through the batwings, Lee turned and shouted across the saloon.

"This big galoot knows he can't end me!" he yelled. "Don't forget that! And don't forget that he won't always be here to protect you!"

Clint stood. Lee's eyes darted toward him, then widened as he took in the twin seven-shooters on the gunslinger's hips.

"But if that happens," said Clint, "they'll have me."

CHAPTER FIVE:
WHAT BREWS IN
THE MEADOWLANDS

Once Lee and his murder were gone, the big man called Pompi swung the hammer behind his back, where it seemed to vanish. Then he plodded to his seat at the bar, picked up his brew, and resumed drinking.

"Your head is too hot," said Clint, looking over at Stone. He reached into Sly's lap, picked up the wedge of sheared table, and tossed it aside.

"Mine?" Stone retorted, not particularly annoyed. "*Your* head is too cold. In case you missed it, that was the bad guy we were just talking about ending. You could have done him in before he blinked. And so could I, if you hadn't backed me down."

"Yar," said Clint, "but so could that giant." He gestured to the big man, who'd more or less vanished back into shadow and obscurity. "But he didn't. And he had something going that neither of us did. You saw Lee. He knew the giant had him and wasn't afraid. So why didn't the giant end him?"

The constable, who'd ducked under the table during the standoff, came back topside and sat in his chair.

"Like I said, you fellers don't understand the way things is here," he said. "That's Pompi Bobo, one of the giants what used to work on the railroad up in Elf Meadows, in the city of Meadowlands. What you just seen? That's happened before. Lee can't hurt Pompi. Not even a bit. His birds probably couldn't hurt him if they tried, even all at once, and they *won't* try because those birds are afeared of him.

Every once in a while, Pompi gets his britches up and puts Lee in his place, but he won't poof him off with that big hammer of his because he's afraid of what we was talking on earlier — that the murder, who aren't like a normal gang, would come back at the town once their leader was gone. Right now we have a man controlling all those birds. But with him gone, we might face a flat-out bird epidemic and never be able to go outside again."

"Absurd," said Clint. "I've seen this kind of dark magic before. Its brain is in Lee. Kill him, and it will flee."

The constable cocked his head. "You sure about that, friend?"

Clint realized that nar, he *wasn't* sure. Back in Precipice, the Darkness had become rats and had run off with its own Orb sample, but they hadn't seen it since. It could be anywhere, but he couldn't be sure where. Was the Darkness in Lee? Or could it be in the birds? Could it be in both? The birds, all together, were much larger than Lee. If he killt Lee, might there not be more than enough shaped Darkness left to avenge the mace-wielding bandit?

"I guess I'm not," said the gunslinger. He glanced at Stone. "I suppose leaving him killt might not have been wise." He stood, nodded to the constable, then gestured at Stone to follow him. They crossed the bar and stood in front of the giant man in the shadows.

"You're Pompi," said Clint.

"Pompi," said the giant, sipping brew and staring at floor.

"I'm Clint Gulliver," the gunslinger said, extending his hand.

Pompi looked up — first at Clint's face, then at his hand. The giant's hand was holding a mug that looked like a toy. The other hung at the stool's side. Loosely clasped with his knuckles brushing the floor, the hand looked like a massive boulder. Clint lowered his arm.

"I'm a marshal of The Realm," he added.

At this, Pompi Bobo bolted to his feet, careful not to move toward Clint as he did. Because there was nowhere else for his body to go, he pushed back against the bar as his legs straightened, splintering the stool to kindling. His eyes went wide.

"Marshal!" he said. "Pompi had to go! Pompi had to leave! There's something wrong there, yar there is. Please Marshal, don't..."

"*Exiled* marshal of The Realm," Clint clarified, holding up his hands. He looked to Stone, sharing a confused glance with the outlaw. The giant could squash either of them with a thumb, and Clint doubted anything other than a few perfect shots — even from his marshal's guns — could fell the big man. Yet here he was, cowering before them.

"Oh. You're not here to arrest Pompi?"

"*Could* a man arrest you?"

"Yar, if Pompi let him," said Pompi.

Clint watched the giant, waiting for more. Pompi was silent. So the gunslinger said, "Nar. I'm not here to arrest you, but I might be here to make you a deal."

"What kind of deal?" asked the giant, lowering his hands.

"Sit," Clint said, gesturing toward one of the tables. "Let's have us a palaver."

Pompi, seated on top of the sturdiest table in the room and plied with a 65-quart stock pot full of chili, settled down once he saw that he wasn't in trouble. Clint and Stone shared their own stories to make him more comfortable. Clint told him how he and his unicorn partner had been sent beyond the wall many long years ago. Stone told him how he'd sabotaged Realm vein-sewing operations and was wanted more than any other man in the Sands.

Pompi told them that he'd come from a city in Elf Meadows called Meadowlands — which, as Edward had said, was Realm adjacent, verdant and still relatively rich with magic. A new land baron had taken up residence there, commissioning the kinds of improvements that remained unfinished in San Mateo, only on a far larger scale — new buildings, vehicles, machines, spark lines and steam factories. The baron's reasons for all of the improvements were unknown, but the showpiece of the entire Meadowlands project was the massive new railroad Whitney had spoken of to Lee.

The train, Pompi explained, led from the Realm, through (or *over*, or *past*, or *around* — whatever) the wall, and then traveled outward into the Sands. It would, rumor said, connect the Sands and The Realm, but only for people who actually rode inside of the train. The whole system was magic. The engine was magic; the rails were magic; even the ties and spikes were magic. A passenger in the train would traverse the fracture separating Realm and Sands, but if a man ran down the tracks in the direction of The Realm, he'd never reach it. Pompi couldn't explain how it worked, and neither could Clint. Edward probably could — but knowing Edward, he'd never deign to.

According to rumor, the train was a bullet-shaped, magic-fueled, glimmering silver machine while it was in The Realm, but as it traversed the wall, it became a black steam-driven engine with camber-linked wheels and a tall stack shaped like a funnel. Because the rails were magic and nailed into the ground with magic spikes, the job had to be done with magic hammers. At this point, Pompi pulled his massive hammer from behind his back, again seeming to draw it from nowhere, and explained that the giants' hammers were the only way to drive the spikes — something any decent giant worker could do with a single swing. And because the hammers were magic, he said to answer Stone and Clint's widening eyes, they could collapse into small pouches that giants wore on the backs of their belts. He stowed the hammer again to show them.

The giants, he went on, had been called down from Colossus Hollow to work on the railroad. He added rather casually that this was a mandate from the land baron and considered compulsory. The baron was apparently a representative of The Realm who'd been tasked with opening trade between Sands and Realm. As a Realm man, his word was law. The giants were paid a fair wage, but there was no question of compliance. They were required to work for the good of all worlds, "to heal a festering sore across our land."

Pompi said that under normal circumstances, he had a giant's compliant temperament and would have been perfectly happy to work the railroad and earn his fair wage forever. But, he went on, he sensed something in Meadowlands that shouldn't have been there. An evil presence, mayhap. So one day, he sneaked out in the middle of the night and headed east. He had only planned to stop in San Mateo Flats briefly for chili, but once he saw the way Independence Lee controlled the town, he felt he had to stay. Lee feared the giant, and Pompi figured that fear might be enough to keep things from leaping from bad to worse. And so, in return for his protective presence, the town kept Pompi employed on the few projects that Lee's murder didn't interfere with, and kept him in chili and brew.

Stone, Clint noticed, took a liking to Pompi immediately. Not only did the giant's defection from Meadowlands make him an outlaw, but he also seemed to have an innate moral compass that somehow co-existed with his otherwise dim-witted manner.

"The train," said Stone. "Does it run over a magic vein?"

"Yar," said Pompi. "It's the only way to power it. It draws from it by in…" He paused. "Pompi forgets."

"Induction?"

"Yar. That's the word. Like the magic in the vein speaks to the magic in the train. It follows the vein from The Realm and will come out here, to San Mateo Flats, then to Aurora Solstice and Harper's Knee."

"You mean Nazareth Shiloh," said Stone. "The vein doesn't go to Harper's Knee." It goes to Nazareth Shiloh. Then past Baer Manhattan, then to Precipice, then to a few Edge towns and beyond."

Clint cocked his head. They'd been through Aurora Solstice. They'd been to Nazareth Shiloh, outside of which they'd met Sly. Did that mean Stone had been sabotaging stitching operations on the same vein upon which the new railroad would ride?

"How do you know where the vein goes?" Clint asked Stone.

"It's my business to know," said Stone. The gunslinger supposed he meant his "business" as an outlaw who stole magic, but Clint had been suspecting for a while that there was more to what Stone did than theft. Back in the Otel at Aurora Solstice, Clint told Stone that if he kept pulling threads in the fabric of the fractures, the worlds might finally and irrevocably tear into two or more. Stone had dismissed the implication, essentially saying, "So what?"

Then Clint realized something else.

Baer Manhattan. Precipice.

"The vein," said Clint. Does it go through Leisei territory?"

"I think so, yar," said Stone.

Clint's heart beat faster. "And Sojourn?"

"Yar."

"Solstice?"

"Yar. Beyond Solstice is the delta. But of course, thanks to fractures, those towns never see the magic flowing beneath them, and couldn't reach the vein no matter how deep they dug." He shook his head and said with venom, "*Realm*. It's all *The Realm*. Oh, *they* could tap it anywhere they wanted. But instead they dam it up, use it for their own needs. For their railroads. They stitch only those fractures that matter to them, letting it spill to the Core at the delta — down, not up, into the sand."

Clint's head was spinning. Based on what Stone was saying, he and Edward had been following the magic vein from the start. The *same* magic vein that, if Pompi was to be believed, would soon power a railroad connecting the Sands and The Realm — the *unreachable, unfindable* Realm. Clint didn't know what it all meant, but it couldn't be a coincidence.

He stood. Stone and Pompi looked at the gunslinger.

"Let's go, Pompi," he said. "You've got to palaver with the rest of my friends."

CHAPTER SIX: BIG NEWS

They found Edward, Buckaroo, and Mai out at the town's edge, on the opposite side of San Mateo Flats from the road they'd ridden in. The streets and buildings were empty of birds.

Edward was at his most theatrically thoughtful, gazing out across an open plain studded equally with cacti and scrubby, dry trees. Rough desert grass sprouted in clumps. He was looking west, where the sun had just descended behind a rolling set of hills, spreading crimson light across the horizon like blood.

"Very nice tableau you have going here," said Clint. "Would you like me to sing you a traditional cowboy trail song? Something from the Z collection, like 'Sharp Dressed Man?' Or maybe you'd like me to ask Ma to fry you up some grits."

"I'm thinking."

"I see that. I brought a friend. His name is Pompi."

Edward looked, seemingly unsurprised to find that they'd gained a giant. Pompi nodded back. Clint remembered what Pompi had said about the giants' relationship with magic and wondered if unicorns and giants shared any kind of kinship. It wouldn't be the first time Edward had withheld information from the gunslinger.

"We booked a room in the Otel for the night," Clint said. "Havarow's treat." He jingled a bag of coins that had once been owned by the paladin, back before Sly Stone had killt him. Out in the Sands, it was hard to say who were the good guys and who were the bad. But regardless of what Havarow was, he hadn't needed his coins, so Clint figured they might as well use them for pie, brew, lodging... and now chili.

Edward looked from Clint, to Stone's outrageous halo of orange hair, to Pompi, to Buckaroo the thinking machine, to the dry husk on the travois that had once been Clint's bride-to-be, Mai.

"Tell me the truth," said Edward. "You're deliberately trying to add one of everything to our crew just for the shock value. At the next town, you've made arrangements to have something else ridiculous join us. A giant floating baby head mayhap?"

As usual, Clint ignored Edward's sarcasm and went to Mai. He knelt on the dirt (dirt more than sand; that would take some getting used to) and bent over her. She turned her head, slowly. Then her eyes opened. Clint gasped. Those tortured eyes looked into Clint's and then closed again, her breathing the rattle of dead leaves.

Clint said, "She opened her eyes."

"She's dying," said Edward.

"But she opened her eyes."

"Her eyes were open when we found her in the shack."

"But nar since."

"Fine," said Edward, sighing. "Don't believe me. But you will do your heart good to consider her gone. Even if she somehow becomes better…"

"Yar, yar. I know." He stood, turned to the unicorn, and drew a spyglass from the saddlebags Edward loathed so much. He extended the lens and peered toward the horizon and setting sun. Behind him, Stone and Pompi sat on a rock in a low palaver. Buckaroo was either sleeping, standing, or in some sort of standby mode. It was strange, not knowing how to treat a machine that looked like a man.

"I don't see anything," said Clint.

"I'm sensing, not looking," said Edward.

"Sensing what?"

"The Darkness. We haven't seen it since Precipice, but now I sense it again. Can't you see how jumping-up-and-down excited I am to see you and tell you this big news?"

Clint looked over at Edward, who slowly swiveled his big white head and looked at the gunslinger.

"Yar," said Clint.

"I can tell it's out there. In that direction."

"Birds," said Clint. "It's in a flock of birds. And it's also in the man who beat Alan Whitney nearly to death. I met him after you left." He told the entire tale to Edward, including the detente that seemed to exist between Independence Lee, his birds, and Pompi Bobo.

"Birds?" said Edward.

"A murder of crows."

Edward thought for a moment, then shook his head. "Nar."

"Nar?"

"Nar. I sense something farther off. In the distance." He nodded his head, gesturing with his horn.

"The birds flew off. They must be nesting out that way."

"Mayhap," said Edward. "But the point is, we found the Darkness again."

"This is good news?"

"I said *big* news," the unicorn replied.

Beside Edward, Buckaroo stirred. He made a beep, then pulled the device that looked like a stopwatch from the chest cavity that had been made to mimic a vest pocket. Commissioner to the end, he checked the device constantly, as if he were still commanding a crew of stitchers.

"Sunset, sir and sire," he said. This was one of his affects. He announced the exact moment of the sun's rise and fall. It was, Clint thought, one of the most useless functions a machine could have.

"Anything on a shimmer?"

"Nar, sir. The shimmer in Aurora Solstice was the last I've seen. Mayhap The Realm has stopped feeding me information, and that's the reason we haven't found another."

"Is that how you work?" Clint felt suddenly paranoid, thinking that if The Realm had been sending information to its machine, it might be able to collect information from that same machine... perhaps about a party of outlaws and its intentions.

"It's *not* how he works," said Edward, rolling his big blue eyes. "He doesn't know how he works. He's partially powered by steam and the rest by magic. The Realm are the ultimate users. They have no idea how magic functions; they just stick it in machines and see what happens."

"True, sire," said Buckaroo. "It's more likely that there simply aren't any shimmers this close to Meadowlands. We can approach, and then hope for the wall to allow us inside."

"That's likely," Clint muttered.

"Nothing changes," said Edward. "We'll have to walk, same as always. Tonight."

"Tonight?" It was Stone, who'd been listening. He sprung up and trotted over, apparently eager to get going. "Good. I'm tired of this town. It's freaking me out. All those birds." He shivered. "Let the cowards who live here deal with their own problems." He hopped onto Leroy the horse, who Buckaroo had moved to Edward's spot of thoughtful meditation, and waited.

"Wait a minute," Whitney said, turning to Clint. "Wait a minute, Marshal. We can't leave. We can't go and leave this town to that man

Lee. You saw how he was. You saw those crows. We can't just go."

"You want to put his crows in prison?" said Stone.

"Pompi can't leave," said Pompi.

"Then Pompi can stay," said Edward. "I don't recall anyone inviting Pompi to come along, after all."

"Wait, he's got to come," said Stone. "You need to hear his story, Edward. About the train and what's happening in Meadowlands. We're going to need him. Tell him, Pompi."

"Pompi used to work over in..." the giant began.

"I don't care where Pompi worked," Edward snapped. It was the first time in a long time that Clint had heard an emotion from the unicorn other than dry, biting sarcasm — or, apparently, out-of-control chili lust. "I also don't care if the rest of you go with us. This started as a marshal and a unicorn, and as far as I'm concerned, that's all it has to be... plus our friend on the travois, of course. We don't need a lawyer. We don't need a giant. We don't need an outlaw with shotguns."

"Edward," said Stone. "You know that I..."

"You *can* come. So can the giant. But we're leaving. Whoever goes, goes. Whoever stays, stays."

"But this town needs your help!" Whitney blurted. "*I* need your help!"

"We saved your life. That's help enough. The marshal will give you enough money to buy a horse. You can ride east, staying off Lee's roads, and consider yourself twice assisted."

"But justice...!"

"Perhaps he has a point, sir and sire," said Buckaroo. "Law and order is one of the key components of Realm society that..."

Edward spun on Buckaroo. "Oh, I'm sorry. I forgot one. We also don't need a thinking machine. You uphold the ways of The Realm? You said yourself that they'd scrap you if you tried to return to the service you've loyally done for years. And for what? A dent in your chassis?"

Buckaroo beeped. Steam belched from behind his neck.

A soft, alien voice said, "He's right."

Edward spun, eager to tell another dissident that he could go or stay, but that the unicorn and the gunslinger were heading out tonight, here, as the sun set. But when he turned, he found himself looking at Clint.

"He's right," Clint repeated, now sounding more like himself. "What's happening here is part and parcel. You agreed the Darkness is in the birds and Lee, and the Darkness is after..."

"I didn't agree to that at all. I said I could sense the Darkness in the desert."

"Which is where the birds are roosting. This isn't just another random outlaw, Edward. You didn't see him. If it were, I'd have laid him flat back at the saloon. Lee is afraid of Pompi, but Pompi — who I'll remind you sensed that same dark power in Elf Meadows and is in touch with the magic as you are — wouldn't engage him. There's more to the story here. This isn't like Solace. I stayed in Solace for duty, but I've had four years to see new shades in old resentment. This isn't about a lawman's duty. This is something else."

Edward stared at him, nostrils flaring. Clint knew he was trying to decide whether or not to storm off with Stone, but the gunslinger knew he wouldn't pair with Sly even if he didn't have an orange ball of hair. Clint was his and he was Clint's, two halves of a whole.

"Fine," said Edward. "We sleep. We end this. And then we leave tomorrow."

"We leave when the job is done," said Clint.

Edward stared at him for a second longer, then turned away, annoyed.

"So," said Stone, climbing down and apparently not as perturbed as the unicorn, "back to the Otel?"

Clint nodded.

A few minutes later, the most motley crew ever assembled was up in the Otel room, magically levitating the wheezing Mai (whose eyes kept flapping open, creeping Clint out) into the soft bed. Whitney planned to bunk in the second bed. Stone would make himself a nest on the floor and Buckaroo would lean in a corner and power down to recharge. The only place Edward could bunk was in the barn, and the only way Edward would allow himself to bunk in a loathed *horse barn* would be if Clint bunked there too, thus pretending it was suitable for all species. Pompi, who was uncomfortable in confined spaces, said he'd join them. Clint didn't understand that, but when they were inside, he saw why Pompi considered bunking with the gunslinger and unicorn so acceptable: one of the stalls was filled with Pompi's belongings, indicating that he'd been staying in the Otel's barn since he'd come to town.

On the trail, it usually made sense to rise and settle with the sun, regardless of the hour. So they all laid down in their rooms and stalls, ready to sleep and wake early to learn what they could.

An unknown amount of time later, they awoke to the sounds of birds.

CHAPTER SEVEN: THE BIRDEMIC

The sun had set. The barn was black. Clint hadn't thought to bring a lantern. He'd left his matches in his bag, and his bag was up in the room because at first he'd been planning to bunk there. The gunslinger had his guns as always, but what good would they do when he couldn't see?

"Birds," said Clint, groping around the barn for Edward or Pompi, unable to find either of them.

"I hear them," came Edward's groggy voice. Clint couldn't see the unicorn, huge and white as he was.

"Make light. Give me a ball of light."

"Nar. Light will give us away. Nobody knows we're here. They'll be focused on the Otel."

"The Otel!" Clint blurted. "They'll get Mai!" He scrambled to his feet, suddenly desperate. But before he could get proper footing, a hoof struck him square in the chest. The blow was precise, as if Edward could see exactly where the gunslinger was.

"Sit down, you fool. Think. If you run out there screaming, they'll be all over you. Same if we make light. These are birds, not bandits. They won't be afraid, and there will be many of them. I can't protect you from all of them if they're the Darkness. Remember how they overwhelmed us under the Rancho in Precipice, back when they were rats? You'll have to reach the others and rally their help, but you must do so quietly. Like a big, ugly mouse."

There was a stirring to Clint's right. He heard a voice. The voice was muffled, and he remembered why he hadn't been able to grope to find the giant. Pompi was in the next stall, a wall of rough-cut boards away.

"Pompi help," said the voice.

Clint reached out, still seeing nothing. The dark was a black velvet curtain. His hands felt along boards toward the voice. He set his face to the planks, and whispered through a crack.

"Not yet, Pompi. I need to tell the others. We have three more guns up there, and one is a canon. The birds will go for the others first, and they will require help. I need to bring them down here, or at least make them ready. Lee might not know where they are, and probably thinks he'll find me or you up there with them. I don't know if the birds are capable of knowing anything."

"Mai," said Edward's voice from the blackness.

"What about her?"

"You can't carry her down without killing her. And I can't float her all the way down from here. Even if I could reach that far, I'd rack her into every wall on the way down. I can float something, and I can steer blind. But I can't do both at once."

"You'll have to go up there and get her, then," said Clint.

In the dark, Edward actually snickered. "You're funny."

"I'm not losing her again!"

"Don't worry, hero," said the deep, disembodied voice. "I can project a small bubble from here. Enough to keep the birds away from her, but not enough to stop bullets. Keep Lee away from the Otel room and we can leave her where she is. But doing so will make me somewhat useless, so you get to decide. I can protect Mai and not help the rest of you very much, or I can do my best to fight beside you, and leave her exposed."

"Protect Mai."

"Okay." Something was wrong with Edward. He'd agreed to something without judgment, mockery, or irritation.

"You agree?"

"Yar. It's the right choice."

"Why?"

"I don't know."

Clint shuffled to his feet, then stretched his arms blindly around in the blackness. His eyes had adjusted as much as they ever would, and he still couldn't see. A sliver of moon sliced the night, and as San Mateo slept without spark, it took little to snuff the scant light.

Straw rustled underfoot and made the gunslinger unstable without eyes to keep him level. Eventually he found the wooden stall door, which was open, and shambled through. Pompi started to say something behind him, but Clint shushed him and said to stay back. He had to make it to the Otel. He had to do it without letting Lee —

or his murder, if it were capable of thought — know that he was afoot. He had to get the others' guns ready, and had to prepare them to fight. Mai couldn't be extricated. If they fled, the birds would have her. And the gunslinger, after all of this time, wouldn't allow that.

Clint stumbled through the pitch black barn, one hand in front of him and the other on his right gun. The bird noises were growing — not as if the birds were becoming agitated and speaking louder, but as if there were more birds gathering. And when he reached the barn door, he saw them.

Birds were everywhere.

Ominous shadows pocked the dark courtyard past the barn. Clint could see what looked like thousands of black crows, like a pound of pepper scattered across a swath of snow. They freckled every building, stumbling over one another for footing and milling on the ground. They perched on lantern posts; they crowded the now-quiet horse-drawn vehicles. They filled every doorway and haunted every bin, storage box, and roof.

Beyond the courtyard, a single lantern was lit. That had to be where Lee was since the birds steadily increased density in that direction. The path from the barn — which was situated well behind the Otel — to the back door was clear. Lee didn't know Clint rode with a unicorn. He'd seen a man, and must either not know that Realm marshals had unicorn companions or had assumed the marshal had lost his mount along with his star. But shouldn't the *Darkness* know about Edward? He didn't know how it worked. Edward said the black magic had to periodically submerge back to the Core for refreshing. When it did, did it resurface with memory? Was it exactly the same bit of Darkness in the way that Clint was the same man he'd been yesterday? Or was it more generic — dark magic instead of "The Darkness" as its own unique being? Would it remember Precipice? In Precipice it had remembered meeting Clint earlier, as a sand dragon. So it *did* have memory.

Regardless, the way from the barn was clear. He'd be able to cross the courtyard on foot.

Clint shook his head, his vision improving slightly. It didn't matter why the birds were filling the street. In time, they'd spread to the barn. He could see them still arriving, hundreds a minute, flying like a great black manta from the west.

The west.

Clint looked to see that they were coming from where he'd predicted — from some roosting spot in the thinning desert between San Mateo and Elf Meadows. From where Edward had said he'd felt an ominous presence, from out of the dark and toward the light.

From the other direction, past the gathering flock (*murder*, he reminded himself; it's called a *murder*), the sun was just starting to rise. It seemed only a short time ago he'd been watching the same muted red blush the horizon toward Meadowlands. Now he could see it in the other direction. They were supposed to send Whitney off, headed that way, today. If, that is, he was still alive.

Sunrise seemed in a hurry, so Clint scuttled across the courtyard while he still had the cover of darkness. Five more minutes and San Mateo would be awash in a dull red — plenty enough to see a running gunslinger by. He made the back door, slipped through it, and ran up the back stairs. The travelers weren't used to locks, so the boarding room door opened on the knob.

When he opened the door, Clint found himself staring at two circles of alloy.

"I didn't ask for a wake-up," said a voice.

Clint pushed the circles apart, feeling cold iron under his hands. Sly Stone's pale face stared at him from behind them, with its sideways grin and giant orange hairdo.

"You've been up all night?"

Sly scoffed, insulted. "I was dead asleep. You think I'm so unfit to guard this group that I'd need to be awake to do it?"

"Good. You'll need your energy for Lee."

"Lee?" His ears made a report to his brain: *the bird noises outside.* "I see. How many?"

"Many." Clint looked around the room, surveying the sparse arsenal to see how far he could stretch it. Mai was motionless on the bed beside the window, Edward's yellow shimmer already visible around her. Whitney was in the closer bed, between Mai and Clint. Stone's nest on the floor was at Clint's feet. Buckaroo stood in a shadowed corner, dark like an appliance without any spark.

He kicked at Whitney. "Wake up, Pilgrim."

The lawyer grunted, trying to turn over and sleep. Clint kicked him harder, making no effort to spare his toe. Eventually Whitney popped up, his hair in corkscrews. His eyes were afraid. After a few moments of resistance, he'd snapped from sleep to full awareness in one gestalt leap. He could hear the birds. He'd drawn the lines and connected the dots. Of course he was terrified.

"Birds," he whispered.

"Yar," said Clint. "A world of them. Like a bird epidemic."

"I'll fight them."

"Don't be stupider than you usually are," Clint hissed. Then, louder: "Awake, Buckaroo."

In the corner, small lights pocked the shadows. Steam belched through an exhaust vent. Alloy clanked.

"Yar, sir," said Buckaroo. "Good morning." His metal head looked around in a way that, were he human, would seem confused. "Sir?"

"We have a bit of a bird issue," Clint said, explaining.

"I don't do well with birds, sir. The acid they spew is one of the few things that will erode Realm metal. Fatally so... such as the word means to a machine."

"Birds don't spew acid."

"Oh, but..." Buckaroo started to say, but stopped when he saw how Clint was staring at him. The older thinking machines wouldn't have known how to interpret a look like that, but the newer ones were intuitive. Buckaroo lowered the arm he'd raised in protest.

Stone was clicking something into the butts of his guns. It was a sort of glowing pod, throbbing in the dark room like a heartbeat. Finished, he looked up at Clint and nodded. The gunslinger looked at Whitney, whose hair and fussy professional's pajamas were an absurdity. He sat on the bed, waiting for a command. His feet, for a man who'd just awoken, were strangely filthy.

"You," said Clint. "Watch her." He nodded toward Mai.

"With what?"

"Your eyes."

"I meant, using what? I don't have a weapon. How will I protect her?"

"I don't recall saying to protect her," said Clint, managing to stifle his insult by wrapping it inside a laugh. The idea of Whitney *protecting* Mai was worse than ridiculous.

"What good will *watching* her do?"

"It will keep you out of the way."

"I want to fight!"

Clint shook his head. "That's noble, Pilgrim. But you don't have a weapon, and if you had one, you'd be just as likely to kill one of us."

"I want to fight!" he repeated.

"You'll be a target."

"Marshal," said Whitney in an earnest voice that he probably used in the courtroom, "if it's Lee out there, he'll be after me as much as you. And if he doesn't find me, don't you think he'll search? And if he sends his birds through the buildings to find me, don't you think your woman here will be in danger?"

Clint opened his mouth to retort but found himself with nothing to say.

"I know." Whitney ran to the closet, yanked it open, and grasped a rod that was mounted between the walls inside it. The small man began to yank and pull, apparently trying to break it away. Stone and Clint watched as he wrapped both hands around the rod and propped one foot against the back of the closet. Still, the rod wouldn't budge. Finally he climbed up inside the closet, with both feet now off the ground, prying against the rod. If it gave now, he'd collapse to the floor in a heap. But it held firm.

Whitney dropped to the floor, put his hands on his hips, then perked with inspiration. Several triangles of twisted wire were in the closet. They had been a mystery to Clint on arrival, but Whitney had used them to hang his clothes. Now, he pulled one of the heavy wire triangles from the rod, held it by the corner, and wielded it like a machete.

"This will do," he said. His ears perked toward the window, where they could now see the dark forms of birds flying by through the dawning morning. The sounds outside were changing. They could still hear the chatter of crows, but another odd sound had joined it — a sort of screeching, dying noise like diving flying machines.

"Those aren't just birds," said Stone, looking back.

"You heard me tell Edward about the Darkness?"

"Yar."

"Well, let's just say they're magic birds, in a way. They might bite and scratch, but who knows what else they might do?"

In the corner, Buckaroo clattered with fear.

Stone racked one shotgun, then the other. The auxiliary packs he'd added to the stocks glowed as the large weapons sat at the ready in his holsters. "Well," he said, "I have some magic, too."

They made their way downstairs, closing the door behind them and leaving Mai in her bubble. Clint took the lead. Sly was behind him, then Buckaroo (who, being both alloy and poorly jointed, wasn't quiet on the stairs), then Whitney at the rear. Whitney held the wire triangle (he called it a "coat hanger") as if it were the most deadly instrument known to man.

When they emerged into the square, Lee was waiting.

The tall bandit stood in the street's middle. The birds had given him a small, cleared circle about the width of his spread arms. Lee held the circle, standing in its middle as the sun rose behind the buildings. He twirled his mace on a lanyard attached to the bottom of its handle. In the early light, the mace looked blood red.

"Aah," he said. "Nothing like waking to the sound of chirping birds, am I right?"

Clint looked around. The crows were everywhere, but were no longer sitting and watching as they had back in the Valance. They circled overhead, swooping, diving. It was all for show; there was nothing to dive into. Not yet, anyway.

"I guess this is the part where you deliver a speech," Clint said.

"Nar," Lee disagreed, shaking his head. "This is the part where I either kill or drive you out of town. I'm in charge here, see. And after last night, I think you and that big galoot might've left some of the townspeople with the thought that I wasn't. That won't do. They might start failing to listen, and mayhap start their little projects again."

Birds rustled, flapping feathers and cawing, as if this were all a performance, and the birds were playing their rehearsed parts.

"Just so we're clear, Marshal," said Lee, "you *did* take me by surprise the other day. A Realm marshal! Here! That was a head-scratcher. But as you see, I've quickly recovered." He spread his arms as the birds chattered. One started circling Whitney, who stabbed at it with his coat hanger as he looked wildly around.

"You know I could kill you before you could draw that rusty sidearm," Clint said, nodding toward Lee's weapon.

"Oh, sure," said Lee. "But then, what would happen with my birds? Would they lose their cool? Destroy this town? Could you kill all of *them?*"

"*I* could," said a voice.

A squawking noise sang from the rear. Clint's head turned to see Edward emerge from the barn. He'd just stepped on a bird. Pompi, ducking to clear the barn door, appeared beside and towered above him. He slapped his hammer into his palm.

Lee blanched — long enough for Clint to wonder if Lee knew that Edward *couldn't* kill all of the birds any more than he'd killed all of the rats under Precipice — but then he recovered quickly.

"Well," he said. "I suppose you feel that with a gunslinger, the giant everyone thinks I'm afraid of, and a magic horse, that I'll just turn tail and run. That about right?"

"Mayhap," said Stone. He'd unholstered both guns in the Otel stairwell and was holding them vaguely upward, his fingers on the triggers. Beside him, Buckaroo did nothing. Clint urged him to open his chest to free his canon, but Buckaroo seemed frightened, if not downright terrified. He kept muttering about "bird acid" and how deadly it was. The foursome stood with their backs together, but they'd had to shift so Whitney and Buckaroo weren't standing beside one another, since both were so useless.

"Well," said Lee. "You're right, and I'll be running now. Have fun without me."

Lee started to move. Clint's hand flew toward his holster. He was fast, but not fast enough. All at once, all of the crows on the ground between Clint and Lee began to flap and take flight, blocking his vision.

The big black birds lumbered into the air, then began to scream toward the foursome. Every crow in the square had flown in unison, as if someone had fired a shot to send them off startled. Lee was no longer remotely visible, but still Clint fired, watching birds fall in a line below the perfect trajectory of his marshal's bullets. There was nothing behind them.

Clint fired. And fired.

"He's gone!" Edward shouted. "Save your ammunition!"

"He became birds?" said Stone.

"He became *gone!*" said Clint.

A beam of red light shot toward Clint, Stone, Buckaroo, and Whitney. The beam widened, pushing away birds like a strong arm, and a tunnel appeared between their two parties. As the foursome ran toward the giant and unicorn in front of the barn, glass began to shatter above them. Clint looked up. Birds were breaking every one of San Mateo's windows, streaming into every house. Screams trumpeted above the chatter of beaks and the strange dying machine sounds of swooping birds.

Stone ran behind Clint. Buckaroo passed them both, screaming by Edward and the giant, then into the barn. Whitney didn't make it. The tunnel closed as Edward's concentration faltered or the bird attack grew too intense. Last they saw, the lawyer was swatting at birds with the hanger, using his other hand to protect his head.

"Again!" said Clint.

Edward seemed to summon great concentration, then blasted another red shot from his horn that again blew birds to the sides, sending them crashing into each other and into walls and ground. Glass continued to break. Above them, it was as if a stream of birds had pierced the buildings, preparing to thread giant strings through them before lifting them up. A black line of crows streamed in one side and out the other as if taking shortcuts.

The tunnel turned Whitney visible. He was scratched but otherwise unharmed, still swatting at birds with his hanger.

"Run!" yelled Stone.

But Whitney either didn't hear or was being stubborn.

"Pompi get him!" bellowed the giant.

He stormed forward. His hammer rose and fell over his head, crashing into the square's packed clay with a sound like armageddon. The birds seemed to whiff away in its wake, popping like heated kernels of corn. Each vanished in a puff of white smoke with a sound like *POOF*. When Pompi struck many at once, the air thickened with the whickering sound of a large fire in the wind.

It took Pompi two giant strides to reach Whitney. He scooped him up in one hand and then — Clint didn't believe it until Pompi returned — tucked the lawyer into the waistband of his pants so he could return while fighting two-handed.

Beside Clint, Stone made a curious, almost ritualistic series of motions with his gun barrels. Both jerked up twice, then down, then both barrels to the left, to the right, to the left, to the right. He pushed two buttons on the stocks and, in a final display of showmanship, spun both shotguns on his fingers before starting to fire.

Stone's guns became the blaze that Clint's were, except that Clint could only fire each gun seven times whereas Stone's guns seemed to be able to go much farther. It wasn't hard for Clint to count shots while firing his own, and he heard Stone tally sixteen shots, eighteen, twenty. The way cleared, but the birds were a swarm, and any gaps they made refilled in an instant. Birds were swooping and diving, but most hovered in a cloud around them — up and down the street like an opaque cloud. Visibility was nearly nil.

Stone fired, fired, and fired again. Green flame belched from the barrels of both shotguns. Birds puffed into clouds — purple, in sharp contrast to Pompi's white. Buckaroo had vanished; they could hear him whining from somewhere back in the barn. Edward tried blasting the birds away, but with his attention held on Mai in the Otel, he couldn't manage much more than to repel them. His frustration came out as an equine bellow. He retreated, backing into the barn beside Buckaroo. Waves of birds dove at them. Splinters of wood flew as the birds struck the barn, digging into the wooden meat with their beaks. Clint felt a stabbing pain, and looked down to see the birds' talons were shredding his shirt and scratching his face. He swatted them away.

The gunslinger fired. First one gun, then the other. Dead birds rained from the sky as Clint's imperturbable rounds tore through bird behind bird like a skewer through meat. Beside him, Stone fired, fired, and fired again.

Clint tried reloading his guns while taking scratches and failed, dropping his bullets. He had filled his reloaders, but birds kept knocking them from his belt. He ducked, feeling for the devices and the shells, finding his hand scratched long across the top, swiping the veins. He pulled his hand back. The reloader skittered away, too far to see.

"Edward!" Clint cried out.

"I'm doing all I can," the unicorn spat, annoyed.

"Fetch me my reloader!"

"HERE," Edward grunted, sounding angry. The seven-shot reloader flew toward Clint, struck him in the knuckles, and sent his entire hand into a dull ache. It fell to the ground and Clint squatted, birds beneath him. He kneeled on one, making it scream, and found the bullets.

Beside him, Stone continued to fire. They were most of the way into the barn. The birds were bottlenecked, now only able to attack from the front. The barn didn't have windows, and the back door was closed. They could hear the sounds of birds attacking the frame, pinging onto the roof like hailstones, pecking at the walls like woodpeckers.

A few birds had flown by them, into the barn. Stone held a gun in front of him and another one backward, toward the stall where Edward, Clint, and Pompi slept, and started firing both.

Green fire. Purple smoke. Birds vanished.

Clint chambered his rounds, feeling slow. Birds were all over him. He used his guns like clubs, feeling the heavy clunk of his arm against body, claw, and beak. He cleared the way and fired again, but it wasn't close to enough. There were too many of them.

Pompi was at the front of their group, using his great hammer like a fan. The birds gave no resistance; the giant swung and the birds *poofed* with a trail of smoke behind, curling in the weapon's wake. Back and forth, back and forth. Pompi swung away, clearing the air.

Clint's hands refused to work. They dripped red, cut and scratched. His thumb was tired; his trigger finger wasn't fast enough.

But Stone was equipped; he fired without tiring, moving like the engine their party's machine couldn't bring itself to be. Guns roared. Birds vanished. Still he wasn't making a dent.

"Why do you never have to reload?" Clint shouted, clubbing another bird from his arm.

Stone's teeth were gritted, his gums showing. He fired while shouting back, "*Magic!*"

Edward was beyond frustrated. Birds struck him, drawing multicolored blood. Given his magic's distracted nature, he couldn't always repel the crows and he couldn't protect the others. He tried blasting the birds with his horn, but too much of his attention had gathered in the Otel room and the shots were too weak. Clint turned his gaze to the second-floor window where Mai was still in her sleep or trance. The glass there was shattered. The draperies waved as a stream of black birds flew into the room like a torrent. Clint could imagine them circling Mai, landing on her bubble, trying to snap at her. He looked at the unicorn, silently urging him to not worry for their party. Protecting Mai was the most important task.

"She's fine," said Edward, reading the gunslinger's face. "It's us who are in trouble."

Stone spun in place and fired three shots at a trio of crows that had been crawling inside the barn and approached them from behind with their talons bared. Purple smoke wafted by like machine exhaust.

"We need to get into the barn," Clint said, still edging backward. They were almost there; another few feet and they'd be able to close the doors. The only problem was that they were barely holding the birds at bay; if one of them stopped working (Pompi was keeping most away with giant swings from his hammer, but would crush the barn if he didn't stop before backing in), the birds would rush them.

"Yar," said Edward. "Because then things will be peachy."

"I'll keep them back!" Whitney yelled, still swashbuckling with his coat hanger.

Edward turned an eye to him and, using a kind of invisible hand, grabbed Whitney and flung him far into the barn. He rolled to the other end, into a pile of loose hay.

"Good idea, stopping to help that guy," Edward said to Clint.

Clint didn't reply. His hands were scratched and battered and dripping, but Edward couldn't heal him. Everything on him was too slow. They were overwhelmed. *He* was overwhelmed, suddenly feeling old.

"I know what to do," Edward said. "Get your guns ready. And if you laugh, I will impale you."

Clint, feeling not the least bit jocular, didn't even look over. He kept firing, and kept struggling to reload. Beside him, Stone still hadn't reloaded. His guns and Pompi's hammer were all that held the murder at bay.

A weak, poofing sort of spell puffed from Edward's horn in what could only be described as a spreading rainbow, like multicolored ripples in a pond. When the waves touched the huge, menacing crows fronting the party, they turned into tiny chirping bluebirds.

Clint stopped firing, cocking his head. Several of the tiny birds began circling his head and tweeting merrily. One dove and speared a hole in Clint's cheek with its beak.

"YOU STILL HAVE TO SHOOT THEM!" Edward bellowed, furious.

But the tiny birds were too close, so Clint batted at them with his hands. The tiny things fell to the ground, still chirping. Then the birds stirred and flew at them, sharp beaks out. Clint had to shield his face.

Pompi shifted his hammer to one hand (for the crows) and swatted with the other (for the tweety birds), doing double duty. Clint, reacting purely from self-preservation, stepped on the things that didn't poof away as Pompi felled them.

Edward hit another wave of birds with a second burst from his horn. Being attacked by small birds rather than large ones was a definite improvement, but not by much. The giant crows with their sharp beaks became tiny bluebirds with teeny beaks — small, but sharp, and still constant.

Clint stomped. Stone fired. But the smaller birds were harder to hit, and eventually Stone turned his guns around and started using them like clubs, knocking the tiny bluebirds from the air.

Pompi was still swinging his hammer. Stone tapped him with the butt of one of his guns. The giant turned, still swinging. His eyes asked Stone what he wanted, and Stone, resuming swinging himself, jerked his head inside the barn. Pompi didn't hesitate; he stowed his hammer in its tiny pouch and practically rolled into the barn, bringing thunder with him.

Pompi sheared a post, collapsed a wall between stalls. The barn's frame shook. A new wave of birds screamed forward — still crows — sending Clint and Stone to the doors, sliding them closed.

A few cleanup shots dispensed the final crows that had come inside, and then five sets of lungs and one set of mechanical bellows heaved for breath. Outside, a rain of beaks struck the barn, slowly pecking their way inside.

CHAPTER EIGHT: BEYOND INFURIATING

According to Buckaroo's chronometer, a half hour passed before the birds paused their assault on the barn. The sound outside during that time became cacophonous, sounding more like an artillery attack than a flock of birds trying to peck their way in. There were sounds like flying machines streaking down from the sky — a sort of descending, paralyzing squeal of noise. There were explosions, like incendiary powders. And on top of that, there was the neverending chatter of birds and the scratching of a million talons and the clicking of a million beaks.

The barn's roof was alloy; they could hear the birds clacking across it like rain plinking into a can. They could hear the crows dive-bombing into the barn's wooden sides. They heard them clawing the vents, trying to get in. Edward was able to extend small protections to keep them out, but with the protection he still held for Mai, he became like a boy with his fingers and toes in many holes in a leaky dike, spread too thin and too exhausted to so much as think. The unicorn couldn't even get his own water, so Stone brought it to him in a bucket.

By the time Buckaroo's chronometer showed that a full hour had passed, the birds outside had started to settle and diminish (ruffling noises replaced the sounds of bombs and shells, and even the more mundane sounds of angry pecking beaks), and after two hours were gone, every sound had ceased. The barn took on an ominous quiet, like a waiting storm. They were all imagining the birds sitting patiently outside with their beady black eyes, ready and willing to outlast the four men, the unicorn, and the machine for as long as they had to.

After a full hour of quiet — now into proper morning in San Mateo Flats, when citizens should be up and stirring — Whitney stood, brushed off his pants, and announced that they should move on with their mission. There was a bandit out there who must be brought to justice.

"You're kidding," said Stone.

"Of course I'm not kidding." Whitney picked up his coat hanger and gave its end a twist as if checking the sights on a fine revolver. "Do you plan to stay in here forever?"

Clint looked at the lawyer. His hair was wilder, having grown from sleepy corkscrews into wild points and tufts, his scalp now pocked with scratches and scabs. He was still in his pajamas. Stone, who had slept in his clothes (and didn't, as far as Clint knew, *own* pajamas), was still sitting on the dirt floor, his eyes on the closed barn door. His knees were up. He sat with his arms crossed atop them, fingers brushing the holstered stocks of his magic guns — the ones that seemed to carry unlimited ammo. The lawyer looked ridiculous and out of place in the company of his five strong and battle-scarred companions. Yet, the ridiculous lawyer was also most eager to resume fighting. Clint couldn't decide whether he admired or loathed the man.

"I plan to stay until the birds are gone," Clint said.

Whitney shrugged, then climbed a cobweb-covered ladder mounted to the barn's wall and peered through one of the vents. A pink shimmer wavered in front of the vent, projected by Edward. Whitney touched it and it sent a shock into his hand. He pulled the hand back, startled. Then, keeping a safe distance, he peered outside.

"I think they're gone," he announced.

"Well... do you know why they stopped?" said Stone.

"I don't know." Whitney shrugged. "Maybe they got tired."

Stone, still half-statue, shook his stoicism away and stood. He avoided eye contact with Clint, Edward, and Whitney, glancing only at Pompi briefly. Finally he said, "It's a trap."

"It's not a trap," said Clint. But he wasn't feeling himself. He felt weak whenever his hands were wounded, and hadn't asked Edward to heal them since he was spread so thin with his protections.

"What do you mean?" Stone asked.

"Edward," said Clint. "You may drop your protections."

"Except around Mai," said the unicorn.

"Except around Mai," Clint agreed.

Edward looked at the gunslinger, measuring his gaze. They'd been partnered for most of Clint's life. As much as it was possible for a unicorn and man to know each other's souls, Edward knew Clint's and Clint knew Edward's.

The shimmers vanished at the vents. "Done," Edward said.

Stone unfolded his arms and stood. "What's on your mind?"

"This isn't a trap. Never was," Clint said. "This was a distraction."

Whitney hopped down from the ladder and walked over, brushing cobwebs from his arms and, ridiculously enough, from his fancy shoes.

"He loosed his birds on us, then ran off," Clint said. "So where did he go? If this was about us, why would Lee leave? The birds came up like a magician's poof and when they scattered, he was gone. He didn't even stay long enough to gloat."

"Trap, diversion," said Stone. "What's the difference? A villain is a villain. Birds are birds. How does this change anything? We should have left when Edward said."

"Yar." Clint nodded, then shook his head. "And nar. Yar, we should have left. But nar, we *couldn't* have left. We thought this was an errand of mercy? That our duty was to keep this man —" He nodded to Whitney. "— from getting himself killt? Well, isn't it convenient that we found him practically under our feet? That he wasn't killt outright? Isn't it convenient he wanted to run off to confront a man in the town that we were headed toward?"

"You're saying we were *supposed* to face Lee," Stone said, fingering the butt of a shotgun. "That he *wanted* us here."

"Yar. What better way to keep us from the Meadowlands?"

"But if Lee is your 'Darkness'," Stone said, handling the word deftly, using it in the way Edward had explained it while they'd ridden together, "then that Darkness would want to move on toward The Realm too, not stay here. And yet, he's settled in as the Mace-Wielding Bully of San Mateo."

"Exactly," Edward said. He was laying down to conserve energy, but with his protections folded, the unicorn was coming back to himself. He stood, now entering the rough circle of men and immediately dominating it. "That's because he's not the Darkness."

Clint raised a hand in protest, but it had already become Edward's conversation.

"I told you earlier that he wasn't the Darkness, but nobody listens. I told you we had to ride on, to make Elf Meadows, which is where I felt menace true, but who wanted to come on this errand? Who wanted to *stay* on this errand? I'll hint you gunslinger — it wasn't the one who understands what it is that we're facing. Nar. It was the men, who thought they knew best. It's the men who *always* feel they know best."

"Now wait a minute," said Clint.

"When I was a colt," said Edward, cutting him off, "The Realm didn't exist. Humans came, and at first we were curious. A bit of dark to our light — and there was good in you, too. In a way, we fit. Unicorns have always understood the balance. We're pure white. You had dark inside. We didn't flinch from that, and found souls that became the precursors of gunslingers, and at first those pre-gunslingers wielded magic before they could wield iron. That magic worked through you as it worked through us. Then men learned to manipulate magic, and they built. Before we could stop it, or knew that we should, the balance had tipped. The Realm thought it was doing the work of the white. But they wanted more and more of the white for themselves, to do their work and make The Realm like NextWorld here, on this plane. In doing so, they grew greedy. Do you see? They wanted only good, but even doing that upset the balance. They caused the first sparks of unrest in the Core. Their overabundance of white set the dark to leaking."

"I don't understand," Clint said. He didn't want to say it, but it was out of his mouth before he could stop himself. Edward didn't rise to the obvious bait. He would usually make a quip about how of *course* Clint didn't understand; he *never* understood. But now he seemed past jokes. And in a way, that made things worse.

Instead of replying, the unicorn shook his head.

"I do," said Stone, stepping forward. "I *do* understand. This is about the vein."

Edward nodded. Understanding passed between him and the bandit like a secret.

"Your man. He's been following the magic vein. He's been following the one remaining true source of magic in the Sands straight to its wellspring. Now you think he's found it, or that he's close."

"That's what I fear," Edward said. "And while we've been here, fighting another villain of the week, he's found what he's after. The vein pointed the way. One in Solace. One in Precipice. One in Meadowlands."

"The Orbs," said Stone. "The Triangulum."

"A way in," said Edward. "A way to end it all."

Clint looked from one to the other. Off to the side, Whitney seemed confused. Buckaroo belched steam. Pompi, looking large and strong and clueless, sat on the clay and picked at fingernails the size of dinner plates. Stone and Edward understood something Clint didn't, and the gunslinger repressed a flash of irritation for being excluded.

"He needs for Meadowlands to prosper," said Stone.

"Which means that San Mateo can't," said Edward.

"What are you two talking on?" Clint asked, annoyed. His fingers, duly healed as a by-the-way when Edward had dropped the protections on the barn, felt itchy. He fingered the grips of his pistols compulsively.

"There won't be any more shimmers, will there?" Stone asked Edward, ignoring Clint.

"Nar," the unicorn said. "Only one way in. One way out. With Armageddon in between."

Clint's patience snapped. He shoved Stone hard with one hand, and Edward with the other. He stepped between them, eyes wild, staring death into both of the others. He scowled and said, "You *will* tell me what's happening here and stop playing at secrets or so help me I'll..."

A gunshot rang out in the distance.

"What's that?" Whitney cried out, as if he'd never before heard a firearm discharge.

"Our cue," said Edward.

Clint was still furious, unwilling to be interrupted. "Our *cue?*"

"Our cue. To play our part," said the unicorn. "Lee is calling to us. We're supposed to go to him, and we will."

"And what will we do when we find him?" Clint asked, thinking of the birds, and how narrowly they had escaped the first attack.

"Then we'll end him," said Edward.

"Really. So simply?"

"Oh," the unicorn said, shaking his giant head. "I doubt it will be simple. But this is the way out. Because we must follow the vein, and on the vein between San Mateo Flats and Meadowlands — between us and both Kold and the Core's dark magic — stands Independence Lee."

"He'll be ready," Clint said.

"Of course he will. It's his purpose."

"Then why should we go after him? Why not ride out of town and let him be?"

"Gunslinger." Edward looked him in the eye. "Do you trust me?"

"Nar."

"Yar, you do. You don't want to, but you do. And one day, when there's time and we've played enough of our part, I will explain all of this to you. But I know what's happening now. I know why Kold has done what he's done. I know why he drained Mai and left her. I know what will come next. And in order for it all to happen, you must do as

I say."

Clint had never been more livid. Edward always seemed to know more than he let on, but this was the first time the unicorn had so clearly dangled such an insulting carrot. He knew so much, yet refused to tell. And yet he expected Clint to obey him mindlessly like a slave? It was beyond infuriating.

"I'll nar do as you say," the gunslinger growled.

"Yar, you will," Edward said. "You must. And right now, we're following Lee's call, and we will heed it, and we will end him. We'll clear this town so that it can bloom without this dark cloud above — a cloud not made of black magic, but of simple malevolence."

"I won't go." Clint sat in the dirt, pouting like a child. Edward never treated him as a partner. He treated him like a lackey instead.

"Yar, you will," Edward said.

"Why should I?"

"Because," the unicorn said, staring the gunslinger in the eye, "if we can clear San Mateo, you may yet get your beloved back."

Clint's hard expression dissolved. He thought of Mai, alone in the Otel. Mai, a husk of who she once was.

"You said a soul can't be regrown."

"It can't," said Edward.

"You said she was empty, and that there was nothing in her to regenerate."

"Fight," said Edward, "and you may yet live to see me proven wrong."

CHAPTER NINE: STREET FIGHT

Clint held a palm up to Whitney. "Stay."

Whitney, who'd watched the exchange between gunslinger and unicorn, said, "I won't do what you say."

Clint punched Whitney very hard in the face. He was furious with Edward, furious with Stone, and furious that he had to battle a man who wouldn't fight for himself but commanded thousands and thousands of birds. The last thing he would accept was insolence or insubordination from a civilian hanger-on.

"*Stay,*" Clint repeated. This time, he didn't hold his palm out to Whitney. He held it down as the man lay with a bloody nose on the deck outside the Otel.

Whitney nodded, assenting. Then he stood and walked back into the Otel, silently agreeing to watch Mai while the others faced Lee, just as Clint ordered.

They had emerged from the barn slowly — all but Edward, who emerged without hesitation. Sly Stone, who seemed to share much of the unicorn's knowledge, came out with only a cursory glance around. Whitney cowered across the courtyard with his coat hanger out and ready, his eyes darting in tiny circles. Clint had drawn both of his guns and was watching the roofs, skies and corners. Pompi ducked through the door and pulled out his massive hammer. Buckaroo, who for some reason refused to unsheath his chest cannon, shambled behind them all, muttering nervously. Not a single bird squawked.

The streets were vacant.

Clint said, "Where is everyone?"

"In their houses, I'd wager." Stone drew one of his guns and racked it, then held the one weapon with two hands, keeping it ready.

They cut through the town's middle, headed down Main. Clint looked around at San Mateo's arrested progress with fresh eyes, Edward's words clanging in his mind. The fat constable had said that Lee and his birds kept projects from being finished. Edward had echoed the sentiment, saying that San Mateo couldn't be allowed to grow so that Meadowlands, which otherwise might compete with it for resources, would. That meant something. Clint tried to understand, but couldn't.

The Darkness. Independence Lee. Kold, who might already have his hands on the third Orb, ready to reunite the Traingulum. And, Edward had said, Armageddon in the balance.

The morning was overcast and chill. A slight breeze roamed the streets, wicking between Clint's hat and the tops of his ears. The town was entirely quiet, with only the occasional flicker of activity inside houses and businesses. No one came out to greet them. Clint couldn't blame them; the bodies of crows still littered the streets, and all of San Mateo's windows were shattered. The Otel, like all the other buildings, was littered with broken glass. Inside, apart from broken furniture, glass, and disturbed papers, the building was no different than it had been. Clint had run upstairs to check on Mai before commanding Whitney to stay with her, and had found her the same as he'd left her — unconscious but alive, now speckled with shattered glass from the broken window.

Clint didn't know where their group of five was headed. Edward didn't even seem to know, but walked at the head of their group as if he held the world's purpose at the tip of his horn. Eventually, he reached the road where they had entered the town, sniffed at the ground, and kicked at a few dead crows with his hooves. Then his ears perked up and he sort of snorted, turning toward the saloon.

"The Liberty Valance?" said Clint. Beside him, Stone was about to say the same thing, but the gunslinger tossed him a look to remind Stone that the unicorn was *his* partner, and that *he* was the marshal here, and fully in charge.

"I think so."

They rounded the corner and discovered that San Mateo's every machine and vehicle was now parked in front of the saloon. They were three carts thick, and the carts were piled high with alloy scraps, steam devices, and fragments of wood and stone. Inside, they could see Lee's hat atop his tall head as he paraded back and forth.

"He has hostages," said Stone.

"So what?" said Clint, raising his right pistol and leveling it at a stagecoach. He was firing marshal's bullets. He could punch through every obstacle, and Edward could tell him exactly where to aim. If they hadn't already decided Lee wasn't filled with the Darkness (he seemed to be merely directing it, though the birds themselves clearly were influenced), this would have been the clue. Lee wouldn't have bothered to bunker in because bullets wouldn't harm him, and he'd know obstacles wouldn't stop Clint from shooting true.

"You can't shoot," said Edward.

"Why not?"

"He's in a crowd. You'll hit him, but you'll hit someone in front of him… and probably someone behind him, too."

Clint, his gun still aimed, pulled back the hammer. "And?"

"Don't be a fool," said Edward.

Clint looked sidelong at the unicorn. "I've been a do-gooder for four long years. Longer if you count marshaling in Solace. Where has that gotten me?"

Edward's horn flashed. Clint felt his gun slapped downward. It had the feeling of a disrespectful reprimand, and Clint felt his cheeks redden with anger.

"I've about had it with you," said Clint.

"Save it."

"Aim me true. I care nar for hitting innocents."

"Yar, you do," said Edward. "Spare me your pride. I know you feel wounded and belittled. Get over it. There's more at stake here."

Clint turned his gun toward Edward.

"Nice," said the unicorn. "At least we're through posturing."

"I know I can't kill you," said Clint, "but I'll bet it would hurt."

Stone, making sure the gunslinger could see him, put a hand on Clint's arm and slowly lowered it. Then he put a hand on Clint's chest, tapped it, then tapped Edward's great white chest as the unicorn stared arrogantly down at Clint.

"Good guys," said Stone. Then he slowly pointed a finger at the saloon. "Bad guy," he added.

Clint snarled, "I remember a clown who used to be a bad guy."

"Well, that man in there isn't as charming as I am," said Stone.

Clint slipped his pistol back into its holster. "Fine. So, what? Our all-knowing unicorn host blasts all that out of the way?"

"He would," said Edward, "but our ugly and far more stupid co-host thought the woman in the Otel needed protection." His horn glowed, casting a faint beam of yellow light back the way they'd come. As they'd headed away from the Otel, they'd begun to notice crows watching both the posse and Mai's Otel window. The message in their eyes couldn't have been clearer: *We know what you're doing, and we know how to handicap your most powerful member.*

"You're useless," said Clint.

Edward refused to nip at the taunt, and instead began to use what unencumbered magic he had to see inside the saloon.

"Buckaroo," said Clint. "Blast that stuff away with your canon."

But the thinking machine didn't hear. He was twenty feet off, hiding behind a stagecoach.

"Fantastic," said Clint, putting a hand on his narrow hip.

They were hiding behind a hay wagon. As Clint huffed, a hand the size of a table reached up and casually pushed a huge stack of hay aside, providing a better view.

"Pompi help," said a voice.

Clint looked over at the giant. "Pompi. Do you think you can clear the way so I can take a shot?"

It was their best option. With Edward occupied protecting Mai, Clint and Sly were the only ones capable of fighting their way inside. Pompi's hammer wouldn't be precise enough, and even Stone's weapons would probably be too scattershot. It was Clint's pistols or nothing, and he had to be able to see to do anything.

"Pompi smash," said Pompi quietly.

"*I* smash," Edward corrected, just to be a jerk.

"*I* smash," Pompi repeated.

"On three."

Stone unholstered his guns.

"One…" said Clint.

But Pompi apparently didn't understand the idea of counting down, because the minute the gunslinger said *one*, the giant jumped up, placed his enormous hands flat against the side of the wagon, and shoved. The entire hay wagon shot toward the mess in front of the saloon, colliding with stagecoaches and machines and exploding into splinters. The hay hung in front of them like glasses atop a yanked-away tablecloth, then spilled back on Clint, Stone, and Edward. The unicorn deflected the spill with a small umbrella, but Stone was knocked flat, one of his shotguns discharging and turning three falling bales of hay to purple vapor. Loose hay sprinkled down on Clint, itching him madly.

Before the hay hit the ground, the huge giant with his disproportionately huger hands had reached the pile in front of the saloon. Clint waited for him to draw his hammer from its sheath, but instead he raised his hands like two boulders, bellowed, *"I'M GONNA WRECK IT!"* and brought both fists down on top of the pile.

The mountain flattened, slamming into the dirt like a fencepost driven by a sledge. Pompi was sweeping his big hands back and forth, legs bent, clearing the way. A stagecoach flew across the side street and crashed into a second-story window. Someone screamed. A hunk of alloy and stone slammed into the barber shop next door, shearing its posts. Wood and rocks filled the air, and as Stone and Clint ran forward (leaving Edward behind to shoot whatever paltry spells he could while occupied), they held their hands overhead, ducking low to avoid being struck. Something that might have been a bureau or a dresser slammed into the street beside Clint, opening on its joints like a blooming flower.

The front of the saloon was cleared in a second. Pompi moved forward and, with one huge swiping motion to the right, severed all of the vertical posts along the saloon's front deck, causing its roof to sag. That didn't escape Pompi's attention; he knew he was supposed to clear the way and the roof was now in it. So he reached up with one hand and, like snapping a twig, ripped the huge hanging section of roof away and tossed it aside. With it came the saloon's front window and facade, and then there was nothing between the occupants and the giant.

A sudden scatter of gunshots from inside the Liberty Valance sent Pompi retreating around the corner.

There was no time to check on the giant. Clint and Stone were at the saloon's front, ducking behind the remaining debris. Pompi had almost done too good of a job, leaving precious little shelter. Stone hunkered behind a piece of plywood barely large enough to cover half of himself and not nearly enough to stop a common bullet. Clint, seeing his options were few, stood tall and sighted directly down his barrel. But there was no shot.

"Neat trick!" sang Lee's voice from behind a huddle of three Liberty Valance servers. "But if you like tricks, check this one out!"

The crows weren't gone. They'd been hiding.

At some unspoken command from Lee, they spilled from every corner, building, and eve. They'd been crouching in wait like humans in ambush. All at once, like a black tide suffusing a pond from its edges, the crows raced toward them.

Pompi saw it coming and dove, wrapping one giant arm around the two gunmen. Clint felt himself pinched against the giant and against Sly Stone. One man looked at the other. The birds were close; they came with their beaks open and talons out. Pompi reached behind himself with his other hand, unsheathed his giant hammer, then started to spin it. The world became a blur. The giant was shockingly fast. As he spun, the birds struck the hammer and puffed into white smoke, the sound of a thousand sequential *poofs* like the purr of a steam machine. Smoke filled the air, obscuring their vision. Clint felt himself becoming dizzy, and beside him, Stone held his free hand over his mouth. When Pompi stopped, the first wave of birds dispatched as a billowing cloud around them, Stone stumbled off and vomited. Then he had his guns out, just behind the marshal, and the three of them stood back to back to back.

Lee yelled something inside the saloon and the birds started to come again, but by now Edward had nudged closer and was able to blast the second wave into smaller birds, which the men thrashed and knocked to the dirt, stomping them below their feet. Small spells shot from the unicorn's horn — a mere fraction of what he'd have been able to do if he weren't holding an umbrella over Mai a hundred yards away — and turned a few into cinders. Pompi swung his hammer. Stone fired with both guns, never reloading. Again, Clint, marshal and senior knight of The Realm, felt himself the least useful of all. His guns were accurate and fast and deadly, but there were too many birds for them to make a difference.

Talons struck the gunslinger's shoulder, tearing the fabric. They scratched his cheek. As they'd done before, they found his hands and clawed at them, turning them slow. The same was happening to Stone, and even to Pompi. The giant also seemed to be bleeding from his side — probably the result of Lee's earlier gunshots.

"Hang on," said Edward. "I want to try something."

Clint had the distinct sensation of a double beat, of Edward doing something with his horn that went *one-TWO*, and a flash of orange fire spread out from the center of their circle. It went fast, like lightning, and then was gone. When it passed, every bird the wave had struck fell to the dirt, sizzling. The air filled with the scent of a working kitchen.

The remaining birds began to circle, keeping their distance. Several hundred made a cyclone around them, like a whirlpool.

"Do that again," said Clint, aiming his weapon around, unsure where to sight his guns.

"I had to drop my protection for a beat," said Edward, seeming to look inward. "They won't let me do it again. There are now two crows sitting atop the umbrella directly over Mai's eyes, ready to peck them out if I give them a second."

"*Don't* do it, then," said Clint.

"Oh, come on," said Stone, waving his shotgun at the circling birds. "There are only a few hundred left. The problem with you two is that you've had it easy for too long. You have no appreciation for a true challenge!"

Inside the saloon, Lee laughed. Clint tried to aim him down, but he was still behind the three servers.

"Come out, you coward!" Clint shouted.

"Coward, maybe," Lee shouted back. "But stupid? Never!"

"Do it," Stone told Clint. "The girls would understand. It's for the greater good."

Clint aimed. He could do it. He could end Lee easily, if he was willing to take an innocent in the doing.

"I can't," said Clint.

"Do it and the birds will leave," said Stone.

"You can't be sure about that."

"Don't do it," said Edward. "Lee doesn't control the Darkness in the birds."

Clint was still sighting, still waiting for Lee to give him an opening. But his cover was impeccable, his cowardice total and complete. Clint waited for one of the girls to elbow him and step aside. That's all he'd need. Just one clear shot. But none of them did.

"Yar he controls them just fine," said Stone, sounding annoyed.

"Nar, he doesn't," Edward insisted.

"Edward is wrong," Stone said. "Shoot."

"I'm not wrong," the unicorn said.

The birds stopped circling and started to gather into a single large and flapping mass. From where the men stood, it looked like a dense, undulating cloud — the sort of cloud that might strike with lightning at any moment. Something orange began to drip from their collective body. Clint couldn't tell where it was coming from — whether the birds were generating it from their mouths or somewhere else. But when the stuff struck the ground, it smoked like science ice. Everything the strange liquid struck went fizzle and snap.

"Acid," said Clint, recalling Buckaroo's fears. The birds were preparing to spew the strange orange acid at them. To douse them, and make *them* fizzle and snap.

Clint fired at the mass, and so did Stone. But there were too many left, and Pompi's hammer couldn't reach them. There was nowhere to hide. Inside the saloon, Lee remained buried in cowardice, still laughing. Clint sighted on the girls in front of him. He couldn't do it. He couldn't harm an innocent to save himself.

"Do it," Stone hissed. "Not for *us*, but for the worlds! If we don't stop your man Kold, who will?"

Clint waited for an opening. Lee gave him none.

"Do it and the birds will stop," Stone repeated, his voice becoming panicked. "Don't you see? *He controls the Darkness!*"

Before Clint could decide, there was a huge booming sound. The black cloud of birds exploded in fire. Acid flew with it; it struck Clint on the arm and started to smoke, causing him to lose his pistol to the dirt. He gripped his arm above the wound, gritting his teeth. A moment later the wound glowed and the gunslinger looked up to see Edward healing him, healing them all.

"I see you took a risk," Clint said to the unicorn.

"Not me," said Edward, jerking his head backward. Clint turned. Buckaroo was behind them, shivering nervously. His chest was open, his canon out. He had several fizzling holes eaten through his golden alloy skin. The holes were slowly growing, quenching, preparing to stop and become permanent. But as Clint turned to thank the machine, Buckaroo made an about-face and ran.

"I couldn't do it," Clint said, looking at Stone.

"Good," said Edward. "Because there were specks of Darkness in those birds, but as I said, it wasn't being controlled by Lee, and if you'd killt him, they wouldn't have stopped attacking."

"What controls the Darkness then?" said Clint.

Edward shook himself off, making himself pristine and spotless.

"If I had to guess," he said, "I'd say Dharma Kold."

CHAPTER TEN:
FOLLOWING ORDERS

"Stand back!" yelled a voice from behind the three serving girls, now holding a note of fear. "I'm calling more birds right now!"

Clint leveled his firearm, aimed, and shot a glass figure hanging from the saloon ceiling. It exploded like a bomb and rained glass onto Lee's head.

"Hey!"

Clint fired again, this time making it rain ceramic as a plate shattered.

"Stop it!" he yelled. "I'll kill these women!"

One of the girls heard the panic in Lee's voice and must have read the writing on the wall. She turned around and punched Lee hard in the gut. The bandit, dressed fully in black, was suddenly visible, bent over with the top of his glass-and-porcelain-covered hat showing as the girls ran off.

Roaring, Lee unholstered his weapon and aimed it not at Clint, Pompi, and Stone, but at the retreating girls. But Clint was too fast for him. A single shot had Lee wincing and staring at his arm, at his empty hand.

Pompi stowed his hammer and marched forward, his face changing and contorting with rage. From what Clint could tell of Pompi, the giant had the righteousness of Alan Whitney, but not his false perception about his ability to do damage. Pompi could and would flatten Lee if given the chance. And here it was.

Lee held up his hands. "Okay, okay!" he shouted. He tossed the heavy mace aside as a sign of concession, as if he'd thought they expected him to use it against four gun barrels and two enormous fists. "Don't hurt me!"

Pompi stopped, looking at Clint.

"Oh, I think we'd rather hurt you," the gunslinger said. Pompi took a step before Clint stopped him with a gentle hand.

"I was just doing as I was told!" Lee blurted.

The gunslinger's pistol erupted. A bullet whizzed by Lee's ear, making him wince.

"That's the problem with the world today," Clint said, using his free hand to park a toothpick in the corner of his mouth. "Everyone does what they're told." A long thumb rose to cock the pistol he still held at his hip.

"Don't kill me. Please!"

"Why not?"

"Because I can give you information!"

"Edward!" Clint called without breaking eye contact with Lee. "Do I need any information?"

"Nar," said the unicorn, looking toward the Otel. "You're good."

Clint straightened his arm.

"Look, look! I know what was in those crows. It was some sort of old magic. But I didn't control those birds, okay? I could send them messages with my head is all. I don't even know how it worked. It was like they did my bidding without my asking. Like they were serving me... like you and your unicorn and how he serves you! You..."

Clint's gun erupted again. This time the bullet severed Lee's gunbelt, sending his holsters to the floor.

"You're making it awful hard not to leave you killt," said Clint.

"Look... a man came to me. A baron, working up in Meadowlands. He had a partner. A man without a name, or at least nar given. I got the impression he was more than a man. Like a dark wizard, controlling the birds. And the entire town, just ask them! They'll tell you about the... the ominous dark in Elf Meadows. Sometimes the sun goes down wrong if you look out that way, like it's shrouded by a black cloud that has no business in nature. Sometimes there are strange sounds, strange colors. They say the baron is building something. They say he's making a railroad into The Realm. They say that soon there'll be a way for us to trade with The Realm. Can you imagine that?"

"Yar. It's a world of possibility for a bandit with no conscience," said Clint. "Just imagine robbing that train. It'd be the last thing you'd ever have to rob."

"I didn't have a choice!" Lee blubbered, sinking to his knees. "I was already in the area, already robbing coaches with my gang. I had to eat! But this man who came to me, he killt my gang. He said, 'The birds will be your new gang if you do as I say. And they'll be *my* gang if you don't.' Then he gave me a look, and I knew what that meant. What would you do?"

In answer, Pompi smashed one of his fists into the opposite palm.

There was a rattling noise from up the street. Clint turned to see the gold-skinned Buckaroo running toward him, his chest cannon re-stowed but bearing several new wounds from corrosive bird acid. He shambled up to Edward and the two exchanged words.

While they were talking, the townspeople slowly started to stream from the buildings and into the square. One of these was the constable, now making his way over. Clint couldn't stop the bile from rising in his gut. How many times had he watched this same scene unfold? How many times had he seen timid faces resurface into a scene of chaos after he and Edward had done all the dirty work?

He shook the thought from his mind. This was the life he'd chosen. An ordinary man couldn't help his nature any more than Clint could help his.

Edward's horn was softly glowing. The gleaming stopped and the unicorn went over to Clint, Stone, and Pompi as the constable arrived. Several yards distant, Lee still cowered on his knees in the middle of the frontless Liberty Valance saloon, his hands held high. He seemed almost inconsequential.

"Mai is safe," Edward reported. "Buckaroo took out the birds over her. With a broomstick, no less. But Alan Whitney?" He shook his head.

Clint shook his own head, sighing. Why one man's death should matter to the grizzled marshal more than another, he couldn't say, but this one did. Whitney had been irritating and righteous and pompous, but he'd stood up for a sort of good Clint couldn't fathom. Whitney had wanted an end to killing. And look where it had gotten him.

"I guess Whitney's death makes you a killer one more time over," said Clint, talking to Lee.

"I never meant to kill him!" said Lee, shuffling a few steps forward in penitence. "I was even told *not* to kill him. 'Waylay the attorney. Injure him but don't kill him.' Those were my instructions. *I WAS ONLY FOLLOWING ORDERS!*"

"Pompi smash," whispered the giant, again striking one hand into his opposite palm.

"Don't let him kill me!" Lee cried, his eyes on Pompi.

"I'll do it," said Stone, re-drawing one of his shotguns.

Clint set a hand on Stone's arm, pushing it down as Stone had done before the battle, when Clint had sighted on Edward.

"Nar," he said. "This is Alan Whitney's battle."

Stone raised his eyebrows. Pompi watched Clint. Clint gave him a small look. Pompi returned it, understanding despite his seeming dimness.

Clint turned to the fat townie who'd joined their group.

"Constable," he said pointing to Independence Lee, "arrest that man."

CHAPTER ELEVEN: ROLLING FIELDS

They marched into the Sands for weeks. As they walked, the Sands became less and less sandy. The travelers' feet tromped on packed clay, loose dirt, and the occasional patch of topsoil. Around them were scrubby trees and vegetation that was harsh and dry but still alive, thriving despite the tough land. And as they walked further — as they traveled the path of the vein, laying distance between themselves and San Mateo Flats — they found more and more green, and less and less sand. They walked through fields that were harsh and hard, but that were, in the end, *fields*. Rolling hills began to sport what looked like farms. They spotted small villages in the distance — villages that would surely have fresher fare than turkey pie and apple brew.

Clint could hardly recall the idea of lands fertile and moist enough to grow a crop other than pumpkins, and support livestock less hearty and stubborn than turkeys. They even saw cattle in the fields, which Clint licked his lips over and said would cook right nicely. The cows — perhaps sensing the gunslinger's hunger — kept their distance.

Pompi the giant had decided to travel with them, feeling that he yet owed a debt in Meadowlands. He'd deserted his post there because he'd felt an ominous darkness, but he now had companions who were driven to face that darkness. He'd served San Mateo Flats, which no longer needed him, and so now, with the help of the others, he would return home.

The giant was able to walk lighter than any of them would have suspected, but he absolutely towered over the group. This was both good and bad. He could serve as their lookout from high up, but he also made their posse easy to spot. There would come a day when that would become a problem — when they neared the city in Elf Meadows, where a man was building a train to unite the Sands and Realm — but for now the way was still open, comprised mostly of miles and miles of nothing.

They stopped to rest under a tree with small, oval-shaped leaves that were a desperate shade of green. Clint tied the horses to the tree while Stone and Buckaroo made themselves comfortable beneath it. Buckaroo's fear of the birds, it turned out, had been justified; he was scarred with new acid burns that Edward had been unable to fix. But the burns were only cosmetic, and Buckaroo said that they, like his old scar from Aurora Solstice, gave him "character."

Clint passed out turkey pie and water while they rested, wondering if it would be the last time for a while that he'd be seeing turkey pie.

"Kold is in Meadowlands," said the gunslinger, readjusting his battered brown hat.

"And the Darkness," Edward added.

Clint sat below the tree beside Mai, who seemed to be slowly improving. Her eyes were open more often, and her skin was filling out, not looking quite as deflated. She'd said a few words. There was still no way to tell what was living inside her, but Clint took it all as guarded good signs.

The gunslinger said, "What's he doing? Kold, I mean."

"Looking for the Orb," Edward replied. "For a way into The Realm. He's run straight, and we've detoured and become lost. By now, he's months ahead of us. My guess is he's already found the Orb, but not his way into The Realm. You heard the people. He's settled. He's a baron, building a city."

"And the railroad? Is that his way in?"

"Mayhap. But something bothers me about that. About the railroad."

"Misters," said Stone, "ain't *nothing* about that railroad that *doesn't* bother me. Trade with The Realm? What does anyone hope to attain by that?"

"Same as usual," said Edward. "Power. Wealth."

"But at the expense of the magic."

"Also as usual," said Edward.

The unicorn looked across the hills, seeming to think. Then he laid down in the grass and rolled, scratching his back. After satisfying his itch, he stayed that way, on his side, two hooves occasionally popping up into the air.

"Edward," said Clint. "You said you understood what was happening."

"In a way. Yar."

"So what's happening?"

"I also said that when it was time, I would explain it all."

"Yar." But Clint already knew what was coming next.

"It's not yet time," the unicorn added.

Clint swore. He wanted to echo what Edward had said: *Also as usual*.

"We ride to the city in Elf Meadows," Edward said. "To Meadowlands. We find those we seek, and we see if they have found what *they* seek. We know things we did not know before. A city is growing. A new man is in charge, and that man is in league with the Darkness. The growth of the city and the building of the train are so important to both of them that together, they are sabotaging towns further down the vein in order to allow the city to grow without competition for resources. Now that we've been through, San Mateo Flats will start to grow again. They will finish their buildings and pave their streets and create their businesses. Soon they will thrive. How this will upset the baron's plans, I don't know."

"I thought you knew everything," said Clint.

"I know plenty, but free will keeps getting in the way."

Clint shook his head, annoyed, and took a sip of his brew.

They sat under the tree for longer than they should have, but it was hard to summon urgency after nearly four and a half long years of pursuit. It was perfectly true, what Edward had said about the many-month lead that Kold already had on them. Every step along the way, they'd wandered and meandered and become lost, forced to deal death, while Kold had marched forward with purpose and haste. What difference could another half hour possibly make?

Soon the time came to leave — to push on into Elf Meadows, to the doorstep of The Realm and the railroad being built upon it — so Clint stowed their gear and packed it away, overburdening the horses because with so many backs at the ready, Edward had resumed his refusal to carry saddlebags. He cleaned the site, brushed himself off, and went to work re-securing Mai's travois behind the unicorn.

Clint knelt in the dirt to look at her. Once upon a time, she'd been so strong. He knew she had magic inside her, and he'd always told her that one day, they would return to The Realm. He'd come from The Realm; she'd come from The Realm; they'd found each other like two needles in one big, sandy haystack. Their meeting was so fortuitous that it sometimes seemed too good to be true. That's what he'd felt back in Solace as he'd stood in the saloon's farback, staring into the mirror on the day of his hitching: he wasn't meant to be happy. How had he managed the trick of it? Out of all of the men in the Sands, how had this beautiful woman found him? *Why* had she chosen him? But for whatever reason, she had. The gunslinger had nearly found solace in Solace, as appropriate as it seemed. He had almost hung up his guns for her. But it hadn't been meant to be.

Before re-securing the travois, Clint cocked his head at the woman he'd almost hitched, trying to see her as she'd once been, on that day long ago.

"Mai Maneau," he whispered, too low for the others to hear. "What has a gunslinger's love done to you?"

Her eyes fluttered open, as they now often did when people spoke to her. Her skin was still like paper, but her eyes were alive inside that dry and dead hull, just as he remembered them. He tried to see past her desiccated lids and cracked lips. Tried to see the woman she'd once been.

A dry hand reached up. He took it, held it briefly, and set it gently at her side. He gazed at her for a long, silent beat.

Her lips parted. Her eyes watched him as he watched her.

She drew breath and said, "Clint?"

UNICORN WESTERN 6

CHAPTER ONE:
HUSK

"It doesn't mean anything," Edward said. "Unless, of course, it means everything."

Clint was in the dirt, on his knees, surrounded by the first true grass he'd seen since leaving The Realm. He leapt to his feet in a single fluid motion and, carefully leaping over the travois that carried his once-bride, Mai, flew at the unicorn. His fists were up and out, and he didn't care if Edward could instantly heal wounds, if there were no soft spots on a unicorn, or that he'd bloody his fists trying to fight. He was sick and tired of being in the dark, and being toyed with.

He slugged Edward hard in the eye, causing the unicorn to fall an unlikely and impossible step back. Then the gunslinger yelled, his fist throbbing and his face just inches from Edward's.

"YOU WILL STOP TOYING WITH ME AND TELL ME WHAT I NEED TO KNOW!"

"Clint..." said Sly Stone from behind him.

The gunslinger turned, planted both hands on the outlaw's chest, and flung him hard to the dirt. Stone looked up without an iota of anger in his eyes. He carried two sawed-off shotguns in his holsters, but he didn't flinch toward them. He held his back to the ground, looking up at Clint in shock.

The gunslinger was usually about as emotional as a stew hole. This was the first true crack Stone had seen in Clint's dusty armor since they'd first found Mai's husk outside of Aurora Solstice, left by Dharma Kold after he'd sucked her essence — also known, in Mai's case, as the powerful Orb of Benevolence — from her like juice from a fruit.

Above Stone, the gunslinger spun back to Edward.

"YOU ARE HIGH AND MIGHTY AND I AM LOW AND STUPID BUT THIS IS MY WOMAN AND IF YOU WITHHOLD INFORMATION, PROVIDENCE HELP ME I WILL... I WILL..." He paused, then screamed in inarticulate rage and punched the unicorn again, this time in the other eye.

Edward said nothing. He hadn't bothered to heal the first eye Clint had punched, which was already starting to puff and bleed. The unicorn could make Clint boil from the inside; he could hurl him across the valley; he could disintegrate him into his component elements or pull him into pieces. But right now, the power he was using — and it was a mighty power indeed — was the power of restraint. This confrontation was four and a half long years coming, and Clint never vented. It was time. Edward seemed accepting of the gunslinger's rage, being strong enough to take it.

Stone remained on his back, lying in the ratty brown grass with his hands at his sides. Pompi Bobo, the giant, had turned to look at the commotion but had otherwise barely moved. The Realm thinking machine, Buckaroo, had powered down for a brief rest and was still in repose, oblivious. A trickle of steam billowed from behind his neck as he leaned against the tree.

Clint's shoulders rose and fell. His hands balled into even tighter fists. He could hear his heart hammering through his chest. After a too-long moment, Edward finally addressed him.

"I mean this only as a question," he said. "But are you finished?"

Clint's mind processed the unicorn's query. A part of him was still red-hot, but his more logical side considered and decided that he could settle down from high alert. So he did. His breathing started to slow and his fists unclenched. He looked down at Mai, who'd fallen back into something like sleep after saying Clint's name — the stimulus that had gotten Clint worked up in the first place. Her ability to recognize him, to know him, or even to know herself was supposed to be impossible, seeing as Kold had siphoned out the core of her soul along with everything that made Mai *Mai*. If she recovered, Edward had said, it would be a recovery of body, not mind or spirit.

Then later, the unicorn had added that there was more to Mai's situation. He knew more — including what might happen next — but in Edward fashion, he refused to share that information with Clint.

"Yar," Clint said. "I think I'm finished. But you need to tell me what's happening with her. *Now*."

"I'm not entirely sure, but I have an idea," he said, speaking as if Clint had never punched him. "Let's just say there's a small chance Mai has some of herself left inside that shell. Are you aware of a bird called a phoenix?"

"A mythical bird, you mean," said Sly Stone, judging it safe to move.

"A *bird called a phoenix*," Edward repeated, looking sidelong at Stone to let him know this was Clint's conversation, not his. "It dies in fire, and then is reborn. Mai had magic lineage. We always knew that. *She* knew that. But magic lives in the blood, and magic calls to magic. Understand?"

"Nar."

"We're on The Realm's doorstep. We're nearly to Elf Meadows and into the Lakes O Plenty — named so back when there were still lakes instead of so many patches of land. We've traveled atop the strongest remaining vein of magic, direct to its source. She *came* from here, Clint. You knew that. You've promised her you'd return her to The Realm from the start, have you not?"

Clint nodded. Looking back, it seemed like a vain, stupid promise made between lovers. *Of course* he'd return her to The Realm, he'd told her. But of course that was impossible — just something they said to one another. The Realm couldn't be found. Questions without answers, fracture and leaking. Mai knew it all, and knew she'd never return. But still Clint promised, because that's what a man did for his woman: he attempted the impossible.

"You're saying she's being… restarted from the ground up? And that she might return to herself, like your phoenix?"

"Mayhap. But — and you must prepare for this possibility — it could also be a stir of echoes. Memory buries itself in flesh, and flesh is temporary, even for unicorns. The magic will start something inside of Mai as we get nearer to the Meadows. But whether that something will be her nature true or false memories without association, no one can say."

"No one but Mai."

The unicorn nodded.

Clint said, "I'm sorry about the punches."

Edward's horn glowed. The swelling, discoloration, and blood marking Clint's strikes vanished. A moment later, the unicorn looked as pristine as he ever had.

"What punches?" he said.

Clint reattached the travois to Edward, watching Mai for new signs of stirring, but she remained impassive. He gave her a long look before circling to mount Edward. They'd found Mai a few weeks back, and every time Clint looked at her, he couldn't keep himself from cringing at her appearance. She was so weak and dried out. But now, after hearing his name come from her lips, he looked upon her with fresh eyes, trying to see her for what she was rather than seeing how little she'd changed in the past hours or days.

She *did* look better, if Clint could bring himself to compare Mai to the shell they found in the shack rather than the one he'd known when the two of them had held hands in Solace. Her flesh was firmer than that skeleton's flesh, as if it held more water. Her lips were fuller. Her color, in skin that still appeared as brittle as old parchment, was more robust. Her wrists and ankles seemed sturdier, less sharp and bony. Edward fed her magically, placing masticated food in her belly, and her body saw benefit from the nutrition. Her clavicles protruded less. Her shoulders seemed slightly rounder, less angular.

The others packed up the site, pretending not to notice Clint as he knelt and whispered.

"Mai. Are you in there?"

But there was no sign, no stirring, no opening of eyes, no saying of his name.

He pulled away and looked at her face — so unlike the face he'd seen four years before in her pink hitching veil.

Then the gunslinger sighed, climbed onto the unicorn's back, and rode.

CHAPTER TWO:
THE GROSS OF GRINGOS

The rolling hills passed underfoot as if being fed toward the travelers on a belt. Each rise surrendered to a valley which then gave way to another rise. Farms in the distance rose and fell as if the land was breathing. The path curved and wove. Everything was round and soft — not sharp like in the deeper Sands. San Mateo Flats began to feel like a memory. The land they saw was still sparse, but it was no longer dusty or dead. They saw only a few cacti and a few tumbleweeds. There were crops everywhere, and there were clumps of trees. The farmers of the crops were likely slaves to weather — a warm summer would kill their entire harvest unless they hauled buckets of water out from a well on donkeys — but *there were farmers*. Crops could grow out here on the Meadows' apron where Edward steered them. Whether it was the water, magic, or magic in the water that allowed them to grow, Clint couldn't say.

Eventually, Edward nodded forward with his horn and said, "Look."

The unicorn could magically see farther than anyone else in the party, so Pompi (on foot), Stone, and even Buckaroo (on horses; Buckaroo was tireless but seemed to love playing cowboy) were unable to spot what Edward saw for another five minutes. But then eventually, a small dot appeared on the trail far down the path, walking with purpose toward them.

Clint said, "Does he have a gun?"

"Nar. He's a kid. Farmer's kid, judging by his clothing. Loose whites from head to toe. He has a hat in his hand rather than on his head, where it belongs. Just like a kid, being stupid in the sun."

Clint kept his sidearms holstered. Five minutes later, the kid was near enough to start running, waving his big floppy hat at the travelers. He arrived in front of them, gave Edward a long look, and then started shouting up to Clint, who sat atop his back.

"Señors!" said the kid, speaking in farm dialect, "You are riding to Baracho Gulch, sí?"

"Yar."

"We need your help. Will you help us?"

"Kid," said Edward. "We've helped at least five groups of helpless people out of five separate situations. I'm all helped out."

"You talk?" said the kid, gasping as he stared at the unicorn.

Suddenly, almost nostalgically, Clint found himself remembering the kid Teddy from a lifetime before in Solace, as Teddy had reached the same shocking epiphany about Edward. Teddy had insisted on joining Clint's "posse" back when this all began, back when Sly Stone's outlaw brother Hassle had returned to Solace with Dharma Kold and his unicorn of a different color. Clint never found out what became of Teddy. In order to save the brave but fool kid's life, he had sent him ahead of what he'd thought would be a confrontation in the Sands with the bandits, ordering him to get Mai out of town. It was a fool's errand, and Mai turned out to be the target. But through all of that, he'd heard nar of Teddy. Clint wondered if he'd survived, and whether Dharma Kold would hurt a kid.

Clint smiled at the memory, wishing Teddy well and picturing him at seventeen, the age he would be now.

"Yar, seems I talk," said the unicorn.

"Amazing," the kid whistled. But then it was as if this "amazing" revelation evaporated from the front of his mind as he immediately pushed on, rushing into his business with the unicorn and rider. "We need help. You'll be going right by our village if you stay on this road. You *are* going to Elf Meadows, sí?"

"Yar," Clint said.

The kid shrugged, then looked around at the farms lining the road. "Many people go that way now."

"What sort of people?"

"Realm people. You can tell them by their clothes. They bring big machines, both ways. It didn't used to be that way. But you are not Realm people."

"Not totally," said Clint, shifting so the kid could see his twin seven-shot revolvers.

"We cannot pay for your help," the kid said, either unimpressed by or ignorant about Clint's guns. But as he listened, Clint realized how smoothly the kid had shifted his way of speaking so they *were* now helping and simply needed to settle upon the matter of proper payment. "But we can feed you. Give you beds. Water."

"Thankoo," said Edward. "But nar. We are used to the trail. Our party is well-supplied and rides in haste."

"You are passing near us anyway," the kid insisted. "You could sleep on the hard ground under trees, or you could have peaceful dreams in our village's beds. And our frijoles? Our guacamole? You've never had better than my abuela's." Then he considered the unicorn and added, "I suppose we could put a mattress under a shelter for you." He turned to Stone and Buckaroo's horses. "For all three of you. How does that sound, amigos?"

Stone's horse whinnied and blew a snot bubble from its giant nose.

"Muy bien. Come. Come." The kid began trotting down the trail.

"So now we're helping him?" Clint asked Edward as they started to follow.

"Nar. We're going down the road. Only now we have a target out front to draw fire, should we run into bandits. That's a win."

The village was a good twenty minutes away, and the kid used that time to work on Clint and Edward, who he correctly judged as the group's leaders. He was respectful to Stone, who seemed to like the kid, and put his hat back on just so that he could tip it to the giant, whose kind he said he knew from working the Meadows. He even asked after Mai, lying on the travois. Clint gave him the truth so succinctly that it hurt to say it: "She's sick."

The kid seemed to be in his lower teens — around thirteen or fourteen, the same age as Teddy had been way back when. His name was Rigoberto Montoya, or Rigo for short. He had been born and raised in Baracho Gulch, and he said he was growing to be a good man in the warmth of its bosom. He worked on his father's farm and would take it over one day. He even had a horse, which Clint (and, the gunslinger was positive, Edward) immediately saw in his mind as resembling Teddy's flap-jawed, googly-eyed mount, Pinto.

Even though Clint and Edward insisted many times that they wouldn't be stopping in Baracho Gulch or helping the kid with his problem, Rigo told them every detail anyway.

"Our town is just south of the Rio Verde river. Everything north of the Rio belongs to Elf Meadows, which is where you amigos are headed. You will cross the Rio either way, and you will pass the outskirts of Baracho — directly by my father's western field — if you stay on this road. There is law in Elf Meadows, but Baracho is the town nearest the border so we are the first stop for bandits who don't dare disobey Realm law. This is the way it has been since before I was born. Each year a man named El Feo rides down to Baracho from the north. El Feo is a very bad man. His gang is an army: The Gross of Gringos, who all wear masks modeled to look like our crop demons. They are meant to frighten us, and do. Because El Feo and that many men with guns keep our pueblo in terror, our fathers do as they say."

"And what do they say?" said Stone.

Clint shot his companion a glance. The last thing they needed was to encourage the boy, or to give him false hope that they might help.

"They say we must surrender our crops. They collect our corn and wheat and whatever else we have. We are left with enough to survive, but only barely. Our bellies still rumble. They do this each harvest so we are forever scraping by. We have no money, or anything other than what we hold in our hearts, since even a man so ugly inside as El Feo can never take that away."

"You have to fight, kid," Stone said. Clint shot him another look.

"Si, we must! But with what? Fight guns with machetes? Even if it were only El Feo and not his Gross, we cannot. He laughs when men try. The last time he came, a man named Sancho ran from his house bearing a machete. El Feo shot him twice, once in the heart to kill him dead and another just because. We cannot fight, señor." The kid shook his head. "We have nothing."

"Buy guns, then," said Clint. After saying it, he wanted to throw himself a look. But he couldn't help it. The kid was charismatic.

"With what, amigo? We have nothing. We have crops, but in a week or two, El Feo and his army will return and then we will not even have those. My father has a watch. Some other villagers have trinkets. We could perhaps offer a few coins as payment. But for what? One gun? How can we face that many men with only one gun?"

By the time Stone argued that hiring men was cheaper than buying guns (which, he reasoned, the villagers wouldn't know how to use anyway), the conversation had begun to assume that the group would be stopping in Baracho. So to break the chain, Edward paused, waited for the kid to turn, and said, "Kid. *Rigo*. We feel for your town's quarrel. But we cannot help you."

"Oh, but señor," said Rigo, "you are headed that way anyway."

"That way, then past," said Clint. "You can hire other gunmen. We are not for hire. We need to reach Elf Meadows, on a mater of urgency."

"Why so urgent, señor?"

"There's something there. *That*'s the fight we must fight."

"Bad magic," said Pompi.

The kid looked at the giant, then Clint.

"But don't you see? The bandit, El Feo, he comes from the north. Our priest, Father Sebastian, says that one of the reasons El Feo has so many men is because they aren't really men. They are demons wearing masks. Father Sebastian says that El Feo dances with black magic. El Feo, he claims to want our crops for riches, but what man robs for riches and then robs and robs again, every year, while never growing richer? And El Feo, in the last years, he has become less and less rich-looking. Father Sebastian says it is because El Feo owes a fealty."

"Fealty?"

"A debt. And he is repaying that debt in the service of dark magic. It's why he wants our grain. There have been great green fires lighting the horizon. My village, they are scared of these fires. We wear old masks and dance against the demons. Father Sebastian sees this and grows angry, but even he believes in secret. My friend Mauricio and I snuck into his casito and found his mask. My abuela asked the Father what the fires were for, if not for summoning demons. And the Father, he says the fires are our crops burning with the fury of UnderWorld."

"Why would he take your crops only to burn them?" Clint asked. But already this was sounding familiar.

"The same reason a man would terrorize a town in order to prevent its growth," Edward said, seeming to read Clint's mind. "By using a flock of birds, for instance."

Clint shook his head.

"We have to stop," said Edward.

"We *can't* stop."

"We *have* to stop," Edward repeated, this time more emphatically. "The errands are one and the same."

"But Mai…"

This time, Rigo interrupted, already excited by what he read as a definitive win. "But señor, that is all the more reason to stop!"

Because Rigo wouldn't shut up, the party's mouths had grown loose around him. They'd told him the safe-to-tell parts of their journey; they'd told him about the bond between humans and unicorns; they'd told him Stone was wanted by certain authorities but was actually one of the good guys. And of course, they'd told him about Mai and how she'd been hurt by a unicorn of a different color. They'd explained that originally, they hadn't expected her to recover… but that the closer they inched toward the magic of Elf Meadows, the better she seemed to be.

"Mister Clint, your woman, she needs magic, sí? And so you go toward the Meadows? But the Rio Verde, it is gordo with magic. Its source is —" He lowered his voice conspiratorially. "— *inside The*

Realm."

"How is that possible?" Stone blurted.

During their travels, Sly Stone with his ridiculous orange hairdo had proven to be a rather non-ridiculous authority on leakage, shifting, magic veins, and The Realm itself. Clint had never met a man who knew more. It was strange to hear such well-deliberated theories, thoughts, and conjectures regarding the alignment of worlds from a man they'd first encountered sabotaging an operation supposedly intended to keep the worlds from crumbling.

"You can swim upstream forever in the Rio and you will never reach the wall, of course," said Rigo. "But the water, it comes from inside all the same."

Clint leaned low so he could see Edward's eye. The unicorn glanced at him and said, "It's true. Before The Realm built the wall, water from the Rio Verde flowed into the Lakes O Plenty. Then the lakes ran dry, and for a while, we wondered what would come of the Rio. Would it form a lake inside the wall? A kind of moat? Water always finds its way, and this water found itself in a sort of permanent shimmer, though different. It flows out in a way I cannot explain, but does flow out, probably because it must go somewhere. It's only water, you understand. But it is also a controlled, safe form of leakage. The current carries magic."

"Could we drink from it?" asked Clint. "Like from a sty?"

"You could, but there's no need," Edward said. "*You* have me. But I cannot give magic to Mai because there is nothing left inside her that I can touch. Right now, she's being lit by the magic in the air in the way you'd be warmed by a fire. The closer she gets to the magic's source, the more awake she may become. I'd planned all along to have her drink from the Rio. I can't touch whatever is in her, but water? Well, that can go anywhere. It becomes part of you. That's why we've come this way, as opposed to the other. I... suspect we may benefit from the diversion."

"What other way is there?"

"We could have kept south of the dry lake for longer, then skirted the edge and headed north. Instead, we went up farther west, toward the middle of the lake bed, where the Rio Verde still fills a basin before vanishing underground. It was a bit out of the way, because after drinking, we'd have to head south again — *then* west — before resuming our trek to the north."

"But señor!" said Rigo. "You can cross the river. You do not need to head south."

Edward considered the boy. "Ridiculous."

"Not by swimming or fording, of course. By boat. My uncle, he has a flatboat he uses to ferry goods from the rare Elf Meadows trader who wants what El Feo leaves us. It is a large and stable boat. I'm sure he'd be happy to take you across."

An unspoken "if" hung in the air: *He'd be happy to take you across… if you help us.*

Clint turned in his saddle and addressed the gold-skinned thinking machine. Buckaroo was now severely battle-worn. He had a huge ripple across his front from being bent nearly in half back in Aurora Solstice and a spattering of unrepairable acid burns from the Darkness-filled birds back in San Mateo Flats. But none of the scars bothered Buckaroo. He wore his flaws as badges of honor — as life experiences he'd earned through hard-fought adventures.

"Buckaroo. How long would it take us to reach Elf Meadows if we went to the river, turned south, then skirted the lake as Edward described?"

Buckaroo beeped, calculating. "Twenty-one days, sir."

"And how long if we can take a boat across?"

"It depends on the boat, sir, but based on a hand-oared riverboat at the Verde's narrowest known point — and this is based on the old maps, you understand, so I cannot verify that the land hasn't shifted…"

Edward said, "Elf Meadows has never shifted."

"Three days, sir."

Clint looked down at the unicorn. "You want to stop anyway."

"I don't want to stop. I *am stopping*."

"And if this errand costs us fewer than eighteen days, there's no loss in time."

"Nar a loss," Edward said.

"And how do you know this El Feo will show while we're in town?" said Clint, addressing Rigo as his final reluctant objection.

"Oh, do not worry, Señor," said Rigo. "He left us a bell to ring."

CHAPTER THREE: BARACHO GULCH

It took only another few minutes to reach Rigo's village on horseback, once Stone pulled the kid onto his mount and allowed him to ride behind him.

They would have passed within a half mile of Baracho Gulch if they'd headed directly to the basin where the Rio Verde vanished underground as Edward had planned. But instead, rather than passing within a half mile, they swerved down a worn dirt road bordered with bright white marigolds and rich pink lavender, then entered the dusty town.

Clint's reservations about helping the village — despite Edward's argument that El Feo was likely as in league with the Darkness (and maybe Kold) as Independence Lee had been — vanished the minute he saw the place and met the men, women, and children who lived there.

Their shacks were built of mud brick and topped with thatched straw and wood. Rigo said the village didn't get much rain but that the roofs did a good job of keeping the bricks together on the rare occasions when it did. He explained that water for the crops and drinking came not from the sky but from the river. They didn't need to run hoses; the lake's bed extended below the village in the form of an aquifer their wells tapped after a mere ten feet of digging. It was a wonder that their village hadn't spilt and washed away given that it was practically sitting on a lake, but when Clint made that observation, Rigo said, "The water is magic" as if pointing out an obvious fact to a very dense and unobservant person.

The village was meager, with a handful of houses in what passed for its "town center" and a small mercantile for trading. There was also (of course) a saloon specializing in frijoles, chili, and a drink called tequil. From the town center, farms sprawled out like patches on a blanket. From the mercantile, they could see other houses below, perched in the middle of vast, hand-tended fields. Some of the fields were already reaped, the corn stalks formed into cone-shaped bunches instead of growing in rows. Other fields were being reaped as they watched — all by hand rather than with the help of Realm technology. The traffic through town and on the farm roads was comprised solely of donkeys pulling carts or hefting riders. The village was so poor, it couldn't afford even the skinniest horses.

"It is okay, amigos," said Rigo. "Donkeys are better for farm work. Donkeys are not smart, but horses are."

Edward laughed loudly, then made a series of jokes about how stupid horses were, going so far as to butt the other two horses in the party (Socks and Leroy, ridden by Stone and Buckaroo) with his nose to goad them. The horses didn't object, which made Edward laugh harder. Then he made more jokes about wanting to meet some of these donkeys so they could all play cards together, allowing Edward to earn a fortune. Clint and Stone rolled their eyes. Buckaroo beeped. Pompi didn't notice. Rigo laughed along, although it was obvious that he didn't remotely understand why what Edward was saying might or might not be funny.

When they reached the town's center, Rigo pointed to its tallest structure — a three-story bell tower with an ancient, ugly-looking bell at its top.

"There it is, amigos. That is the bell El Feo gave us."

Rigo explained that the bell was simultaneously the village's most holy and most loathed relic. It had been in the village since before Rigo was born and was, said Rigo, magic. It had been carted from the north, from beyond Elf Meadows, from a monastery deep in giant territory.

When Pompi saw the bell, he immediately verified Rigo's story, explaining that the bell was made for summoning. He made a delicate hand-shaking motion with his table-sized hands to underscore his point. Eventually Stone laughed and said it must be like when a rich man wants something and rings a tiny bell for his servant. In a giant's hand, the massive bell in the bell-tower would indeed be easy to ring like a hand bell, despite how large it appeared on the streets of Baracho Gulch.

"Summoning, yar," said Pompi, nodding. He then explained that in the mountains, magic was so common that it had become an inexorable part of giant culture. The bells didn't just *make noise* to alert one group of giants about something needed by another. Instead, the bells conveyed signals by magic. Ringing one bell caused another bell — its twin — to ring, no matter how far apart the two bells were. Then Edward, eager to show off his superior knowledge, jumped in to say that the bells were actually *the same bell*, not two distinct bells, so of course ringing one would ring the other. Nobody understood, so Edward tried to further explain via spatial folding and complex magic concepts, but nobody cared. So the unicorn huffed off, choosing instead to insult a group of nearby donkeys.

"El Feo has the twin of this bell," said Rigo. "When our harvest is finished, we ring the bell from our side, and his rings to tell him to come."

Clint was thunderstruck. "You ring a bell *to tell a bandit it's time for you to be robbed?*"

"Yar, señor," said Rigo, shrugging. "This is how it has been for always. El Feo will come anyway, but in this way we benefit. If we ring the bell, he can come at a time of our choosing, take his supplies, then be gone. If we are honest and give him the proper amounts, we can even leave his take in the streets and never face him or his demons."

"And if you are dishonest?"

Rigo's happy face grew dark. "El Feo always knows. We have learned not to try and deceive him."

"What happens if you don't ring?" said Stone.

"We *always* ring," said Rigo, his expression small and guarded. There was so much unspoken pain in the kid's simple answer that neither Stone nor Clint felt the need to pry.

After showing them what little there was to see of the town's geography, Rigo led the posse to a small, two-room mud dwelling where he introduced them to a man named Jose, who wore a giant drooping mustache and who Rigo identified as his father. Rigo then introduced them to Maria, his gray-haired grandmother. They smiled with their emaciated faces, reminding Clint of beaten animals that were too stupid to know that life could and should be better than it was.

Not that the gunslinger found Jose, Maria, Rigo, or any of the other villagers stupid, though. It was quite the contrary. None appeared to be learned in the educational style of The Realm, but all had a deep understanding of farming and the things that blossomed with life.

Privately, Edward told Clint that these people were magical — quite literally — but that they would likely never know that they were, or allow themselves to see it. They drank from one of the purest sources outside of The Realm, and because of that, their bodies were saturated with magic. When their crops grew, they grew in part because the villagers expected them to grow and believed that they should. This idea perplexed Clint, but then Edward said something that Clint had heard him say many times before: *Intention matters to magic.* With every seed planted, the village farmers were performing tiny acts of wizardry — particularly powerful acts because they were returning the magic to its source for use by other life, rather than siphoning it off for their own selfish desires.

"Like others have done, and still do today," Stone said, waving a hand at the river.

Stone and Clint sat in small, handmade, fragile-looking wooden chairs surrounding a block of bricks draped with a tablecloth. Atop the cloth were clay mugs filled with tequil and wedges of bread. Edward stood beside the men, making a place for himself at the table and drinking tequil from a shallow dish beside the clay mugs.

"What is it with you and The Realm?" said Clint. "Edward and I were exiled. But what did they do to you?"

"What did they *do?*" said Stone as if he couldn't believe Clint would need to ask.

"To make you hate them so much. Most people in the Sands regard The Realm as an unreachable paradise, like a NextWorld that they might — but of course never will — reach without dying. Others hate it in a jealous way, because The Realm has so much and the Sands has so little. But your hate is different. You carry the loathing of a radical."

Stone kicked back on his chair. Clint was suddenly sure it would collapse beneath him. "Oh, I'm a lover, not a fighter," he said.

"What were you doing back beyond Nazareth, when we found you with the rope gang? Were you just thieving magic for your guns? Or was it something else?"

Stone settled all four legs of his chair on the ground, then looked from Clint to Edward, then back to the gunslinger.

"I'll put it this way, Marshal. My guns use magic, but they would fire just fine without them."

"So?"

"The people in this village? They work their hands until their callouses are bloody. But if there was no magic, do you think they would starve? Nar. They would dig roots from what survived. They would hunt. They would collect dew to drink if they had to. They would work harder. Magic makes them better farmers, but if it vanished from the world, they would still farm."

Clint hated indirect answers and fancy metaphors. Edward's

diatribes were thick with them, and it was obnoxious. The gunslinger was a straightforward man. Walking with Edward was like walking with a riddler, and walking with Stone was like walking with a riddling lawyer.

"And?" he said.

"If the magic vanished," Stone continued, "these honest people would survive. *You* would survive. *I* would survive. But what would become of The Realm?"

Clint shook his head.

"Isn't it interesting that in any sustained economy, it's those who have the most that are soon the only ones who truly need the currency?"

When Clint said nothing, Stone stood, tipped his hair like another man might tip his hat, then left the casito and wandered into the pueblo's center.

Over the first twenty-four hours, the gunslinger, bandit, cynical unicorn, slow giant, and even the thinking machine fell in love with the people of Baracho Gulch. The villagers worked in the fields as long as they could and returned as the daylight dimmed, dirty and smiling, to greet the newcomers as if they'd been born in the Gulch themselves. They shook hands with their rescuers, thanking them for coming, and whenever they did, Clint found their palms rougher and even more callused than his own. The simple people seemed to truly need almost nothing. They ate a few spoonfuls of beans for dinner and were joyous. They woke at dawn to work the fields and were near to giddy. The town children — timid at first, then increasingly curious about the white men, sleeping woman, machine, talking horse with the horn, and the giant — began to follow all of them around and hide behind corners when someone caught them looking.

Stone began playing into this, turning quickly when the children followed, then drawing and firing imaginary guns in their direction. This was immediately popular. Within two days, some of the village children were packing their hair with clay and teasing it out in an attempt to replicate Stone's giant hairstyle. The effect was always comical. Stone showed them gun tricks while Clint watched with crossed arms, uninterested in having children hang on him but attentive to their like of Stone.

It would be dangerous to grow attached, Clint thought. The last time Clint had become truly attached to innocents, he'd seen them buried in their mesa hovel near the Edge. That was a rough time, and had torn him in a way he swore he'd never again allow himself to be torn. So through Precipice, then Nazareth Shiloh, Aurora Solstice, and San Mateo Flats, Clint had kept his distance. It was like a game for the gunslinger. Townsfolk were numbers to count, nothing more. As long as the numbers at the end were more positive than negative, the encounter was a win. It was nothing personal.

Still, Clint and Edward spent most of their time with Stone (at least when the gunslinger wasn't wetting Mai's lips with river water, readying her in the ways that Edward instructed), and so the children followed the man and white horsey as well. Clint shooed them off. Edward pretended to be offended by being called "horsey." But over time, the hard man found himself softening. Since their stay with the Leisei, they'd felt nothing but dryness and scorn through their travels. Since *Solace*, Clint hadn't felt like he truly mattered to anyone. But they mattered to the children, and the children were innocent, and there was no helping or stopping their reluctant attachment, and so Clint soon started drawing phantom guns the same as Stone had — but only while Edward wasn't watching. And once, after whittling a trail whistle from a reed, Clint was playing it as a girl approached him, watching. He handed it to her and she took it, running off with it clutched in her small hands like a jewel.

Three days passed. Little changed. Clint started showing the villagers how to fight so they could help the posse help them, and so they wouldn't be defenseless when the visitors left. But there was little to show them without guns.

The villagers fed them what they could, including the most amazing (yet most commonplace — at least among the villagers) chili any of them had ever imagined. They polished Buckaroo like a relic, until he shone despite his flaws. They fashioned a bed for Edward made of their own mattresses, in a sheltered alcove rather than in the barn with the donkeys.

Through it all, Clint wet Mai's lips with the magical water from the Rio Verde. Clint wanted her to drink, but Edward said that as long as they had the time — and they did, since they wouldn't summon El Feo until the harvest was completed — it was wisest to wait until she recovered more on her own before shocking her system with the water. So Clint moistened her lips, and watched as her skin tightened and began to improve. He watched as her bones filled out, and he brushed her hair when no one was watching.

On the third day's dusk, Edward came to find Clint sitting beside Mai. She was asleep as usual, though she'd been waking more and more often. She hadn't repeated Clint's name or given any further indication that she was anything other than a husk of her former self and was still waxy and wrinkled, but she was better. Clint wouldn't allow himself to hope, but it was something.

The unicorn stood beside the gunslinger. Both the man and his almost-bride were on cots in a breezeway, a large drapery parted to the surprisingly warm outside air. The sun had set but there was a moon, and the sky was clearer than they'd seen since leaving Solace four and a half years before. Clint could smell the river's water on the air.

"It's time," said Edward.

CHAPTER FOUR: INTENTION MATTERS

The water was a bright green that Clint could see even by the moon's sparse light. He'd seen the Rio Verde during daylight, but the color had scarcely changed despite the loss of the sun. Clint didn't see how it was possible. Edward said it was the magic.

According to the unicorn, the river, in addition to being magical, was also insanely dangerous. Just shy of the village, the Rio Verde dove underground, rushing away as a subterranean river. The southernmost point of the north/south river was a pool slightly wider than the river's body above. All around the pool was the scabbed, impassable cavity of what had once been a massive lake. The river's current was fast — but because the pool marked the point where the river went underground, the current at the pool was also *downward*. Previously, Edward had warned Clint to hold his distance and to dip water from the river using the long dipper that the villagers left in the crook of a tree. Anyone who fell into the pool would be taken on the magical ride of a lifetime, but they'd only get to enjoy it for the minute or so they could hold their breath.

So on the moonlit night when Edward suggested Clint take Mai to the river so she could drink, the gunslinger raised a bucket he'd dipped that afternoon and said that there was no need to go anywhere. Edward shook his head and repeated what he'd said many times before: *"Intention matters to magic."*

Edward's decree that Mai would have to sip from the pool with her own lips may have been a symbolic act of contrition, but the logistics involved scared the gunslinger silly. She would need to regain consciousness and semi-lucidity long enough to sip. Clint would have to convince her to do so, despite the obvious peril. He'd have to make certain that in her addled state, she didn't simply roll into the pool and drown. She couldn't walk. She couldn't even crawl. Clint would have to drag her to the pool's edge himself, and place her in position.

When they were within fifty feet of the bright green, moonlit pool, Edward wished them both good luck.

"Wait," said Clint. "You're not coming with us?"

"I weigh twelve hundred pounds and the pool's lip is fragile. I'd just spill us into it."

"Then magick us over to it. Make us hover."

Edward shook his head. "Intention matters. If you want what's in the pool, you must humble yourself to get it."

"But the pool's lip is strong enough to hold us, surely."

"That's the spirit," Edward said.

Clint breathed deeply several times, then unhitched the travois from behind Edward. He rolled Mai from it, then painstakingly dragged her limp body to the pool's edge. As Edward suggested, the lip was incredibly fragile. The current in the pool created a slow whirlpool that had eroded the land under its edge. As they drew close, a clump of tough brown grass broke off and dropped into the water under Clint's hand, almost causing him to pitch in after it. He watched the clump of sod swirl downward into the fathomless green depth.

"Careful," shouted Edward, keeping his distance.

"Thanks!"

"Stay flat," said the unicorn.

Staying flat, of course, was pretty much all that Clint would be allowed to do. Edward's instructions had been specific. Mai must drink from the pool with her lips. *With her lips*. She couldn't reach in with her hands. Clint couldn't dip it out for her. All of this was why Edward had wanted her as strong as possible before they attempted what they were attempting, but now that Clint was at the pool's edge and gazing down into forever, Mai's slight "improvement" seemed absurdly inadequate. She couldn't even hold her head up. Clint would have to thread his fingers through her hair to hold it high, thus keeping her face from dropping into the water and drowning.

After a few minutes by the pool, Mai's eyelids began to flutter. She looked up, then at Clint. Her head itself didn't move.

"I had a dream," she said.

"Mai," said Clint. "You need to do something. I need you to take a drink."

"Okay." She blinked. "Are you the one who will give it to me?"

"I'm Clint."

"Okay."

"But you must take the drink yourself."

"Okay."

"You are too weak to move. I'm going to roll you over so that you are face-down, then push you to the edge and hold your head up. You'll need to sip the water directly from the pool. Then I'll pull you back. If you can move, don't. You will fall into the pool and die."

Mai looked up at him. "Okay."

"Do you trust me?"

"I don't know you," she said. "But I've always trusted you."

"Let's try, then."

"Ever since Solace."

Clint had one hand across her, grasping her far side at the ribs, and was preparing to roll her. They both had to stay flat, to distribute their weight. It would be awkward at best. But now the gunslinger stopped, his hands tensed to pull. "What?" he said.

Mai closed her eyes, then deeply inhaled. "It smells so nice here. Like memory."

"What do you remember?"

"Roll her over!" Edward shouted from behind.

"What do you remember?" Clint repeated, speaking more softly.

"I remember a dream."

Clint waited a moment to see if Mai would say more, but Edward yelled again, and she said nothing. So Clint flipped her. It was easy, light as she was. He positioned her above the pool. He threaded his hand through her hair and repeated the instructions. Then he lowered Mai's face to the pool, sliding up to watch her lips and ensure he wasn't submerging her nose. The pool's lip faltered and Clint tried shifting his weight, but it crumbled away and he had to tense his back muscles to stay up, to keep Mai alive.

Finally she finished and Clint wiggled back, terrified to move. He asked her if she'd gotten any drink, then looked at her lips and into her mouth. He saw her weathered throat working, then slowly pulled her further away. When they arrived at the unicorn's feet, Clint stood and looked down at Mai. She had again fallen unconscious.

"What now?" Clint asked.

"Now we wait," Edward said. "And hope."

CHAPTER FIVE:
FIST OF FURY

The next day, Mai didn't wake at all. Edward told Clint not to worry, that this was how things were with magic and that if the water from the Rio Verde had helped her, time was required to show it. Clint asked Edward if he was telling the truth, or simply telling the gunslinger what he wanted to hear. Edward didn't answer. Instead the unicorn left the room, heading out to meet Stone after suddenly remembering he had an appointment.

Regardless of Mai's lucidity or lack thereof, Clint soon decided that sitting and hoping by her bedside wouldn't speed up her recovery. The marshal had a well-hidden soft side, seldom indulged, and after the adrenaline of the poolside encounter and the subsequent night of disappointing unconsciousness, Clint chastised himself for being too soft.

Speaking tenderly to a dying woman. Hoping for the impossible. Making whistles for children! Get ahold of yourself, gunslinger!

Attachment and softness were both absurd. The marshal had a job to do, and part of the job was preparing for a bandit and teaching villagers — all of them only numbers, nothing personal — to fight. Not because he cared about the villagers, found them noble, or sympathized with their plight. Not because it mattered to him whether they lived or died. He must do it because the Darkness was now El Feo's employer, and was working him like a puppeteer as he had with Independence Lee. Kold and the Darkness were keeping settlements south of Meadowlands from thriving, and it was Clint's job to throw a wrench in those plans.

Still, in spite of Clint's newly cold stance on the detachedness of his task, his party wasn't helping. Pompi seemed to be courting Rigo's sister, Paloma. The courtship was hilarious, because Paloma was petite even amongst the villagers and Pompi could pick her up in his hand. Rigo, despite his affection for the visitors, was protective of his sister and took to stalking Pompi and Paloma on whatever they did that passed for dates. Buckaroo, who was a source of unending fascination since he was both artificial and built by The Realm, began to gather the townspeople and tell long-winded stories of life behind the wall — which, given that he'd never actually *been* behind the wall, ended up being stuffed with Realm propaganda that painted it as an enviable paradise. Stone watched these gatherings and heckled from the back, throwing anti-Realm sentiment into Buckaroo's stories wherever he was able.

Even Edward was forming attachments, despite the unicorn's grating nature. Unsurprisingly, Edward's bonds were founded in mockery. He mocked the donkeys, especially to the villagers who owned them. He wandered the countryside, ostensibly scouting, and reported finding a group of wild horses who drank from one of the Rio Verde's less-perilous (but less pure) offshoots and hence, thanks to the magic, had learned to talk. According to Edward, these horses were irretrievable idiots who ran around being clotheslined by low branches and telling each other tired humorous observations about their world. One would say, "Have you ever noticed how rabbits hop?" and another would say, "Hey... *RED CAMARO!*" and then they would both laugh, despite the fact that there was nothing Edward had ever heard of called a "Camaro."

The dumb horses' antics were a source of unending entertainment for Edward until the sixth day, when the horses began explaining to him how smart they were. They told him horses were fathers to the unicorn, but that it was okay if Edward didn't understand and that he should never be embarrassed by his horn. This made Edward go from enjoying himself to wanting to gore the talking horses. To make things worse, the horses had somehow heard the ancient song about the horse named Ed, and they sung it to him because his name was Edward, and he was almost as good as a horse.

All of this bonding irritated Clint beyond measure, but he couldn't control the others. He could only control himself. And so, when Mai failed to wake on the second day following the pool incident, he closed his eyes and promised the gunslinger inside of himself that he would harden his heart enough for all of them. The best way to face reality and squash innocence, he decided while chewing on a toothpick, would be to do his dagged job — to teach the villagers to fight and kill.

So Clint pulled Stone from heckling Buckaroo and enlisted his help in gathering a group of able-bodied men and women. Infuriatingly, Rigo was ready and smiling at every gathering. Clint said he was too young, that he should protect the younger children and stay hidden once the fighting started. Rigo argued to the point of screaming (the only display of aggression among the villagers; Clint couldn't decide if this was good or bad) that Clint was being ridiculous. El Feo cared not for age. He'd steal Rigo's food just the same as anyone else's, and leave him killt if he stood in the bandit's way. Besides, fourteen among farmers made him a man already. He added that he could fight well. *Very* well. Clint scoffed, asking how well a farmer's son could possibly fight, having been raised in a village of pacifists who had lived under a boot heel since before he'd been born. Then Clint sent Rigo off and resumed trying to teach the villagers, which was mostly pointless.

There were no guns to be had, but Stone knew how to build bows, so he did. He had a few reservoirs of gun magic (the recharge capsules that had allowed him to fire without reloading against the birds in San Mateo Flats) and sprinkled each bow with the special Realm magic resin when finished. He claimed that he hadn't always slung a gun, and that he'd once been a woodsman. This all seemed bogus to Clint, but the bows Stone made were shockingly easy to fire. They were also very accurate. Soon the villagers were hitting targets fifty yards off on the nose, over and over again.

Rigo was relentless. He insisted he was old enough to carry and fire a bow. That he was old enough to wield a machete, or at least a club. He told Clint that the villagers might lose their bows during the battle, and should therefore learn how to fight hand-to-hand. He repeated that he would be an excellent teacher, and begged Clint to let him try. But Clint cuffed him away, hardened beyond affectionate rebuke.

Then one day, Rigo arrived at a gathering of warriors-in-training ahead of Clint and began class without the gunslinger. What the farmer's son could do made Clint's eyes nearly fall from their sockets.

The kid was ridiculously fast, ridiculously agile, ridiculously intuitive in his fighting. While Clint watched, Rigo asked the farmers to charge toward him holding pillows in front of their chests to deflect his retaliatory blows, to throw things at him, to strike at him with sticks. Rigo dodged the objects, ducked or leapt over the sticks, parried around every attacker and planted his foot or fist in every pillow. When one man who seemed to be particularly enjoying the play-fighting came at Rigo, Rigo tucked and rolled twice before springing up ten feet away, came to a strange one-footed crouch (his other foot shot outward in a sweep, sending another man's feet flying from under him), and struck at a third attacker's pillow, which the man had fortunately or unfortunately held in front of his crotch.

As the demonstration progressed, Rigo's practice attackers started throwing more and more items at him, determined to find the kid's breaking point. As far as Clint could see, Rigo had none. His opponents threw heavy clumps of dirt, rocks, and even melons. Rigo dodged the dirt, struck at the rocks with fists and feet, and caught the melons. While continuing to parry, he then rolled the melons toward the spectators because something as rare as a melon should never be wasted. He improvised with what he had on hand. When one man dropped a stick, he picked it up and turned it into a fighting staff. He jumped and swung across the fight circle using overhead branches. He ran up a skinny tree trunk, rolled overhead, and landed flatfooted behind his attacker.

Clint watched Rigo fight for a long time — longer than he should have, because he was only encouraging the kid — and then finally called out to end the melee. The fighters stopped and looked over, panting for breath. In the middle stood 14-year-old Rigo, his bare chest heaving, his grin so wide that it seemed to touch his ears.

"Okay," Clint said. "I will admit that you can fight. But how did you learn?" He'd never seen a style of fighting like Rigo's. Gunslingers fired guns, and the deadliest fighters Clint had ever known did the same. The idea of inflicting so much damage only using one's body was inconceivable. Clint found himself wondering how the kid would do in a gunfight. Would he be easily felled, rendering his fancy feet and hands useless? Or would he adapt and find a way to survive... or even win?

"I doubt you will believe this," Rigo said, "but it came from a dream."

"You learned all of this from a dream?" Clint said, gape-mouthed. "You're right. I don't believe it."

"Some of us, as we sleep, see visions that we believe come either from behind the wall of The Realm, or directly from the magic. In my mind I see a man, clad in black and often shirtless, who can do these incredible things and battle multiple attackers. And as I watched those dreams night after night, my body learned to do what he did."

"That's your *mind*," said Clint, shaking his head. His own hands hadn't learned quickness because he *thought* on quickness.

"The possession of anything starts in the mind," Rigo said. "As you think, so shall you become."

"What does that mean?"

"Just that in this case, seeing it in my head was a start to what became a bodily habit." Then the boy's steely gaze faded, and he stopped being the deadly phantom from his dreams. He became Rigo again. His shoulders slumped, almost bashful, but his smile stayed fixed. A deep, deadly confidence could still be seen swelling from deep down inside him — like a man inside of a man.

"Okay," said the gunslinger. "If you can train the others to do what you can, you may fight with us when El Feo comes. And I daresay you'll make for a formidable weapon."

Rigo smiled. "Gracias, amigo!"

"So that's how many? There's you, me, Edward, Stone, Pompi, and Buckaroo… as long as there are no birds."

Rigo ticked them off on his fingers as Clint counted. When he finished, the kid was silently holding up an open right hand a thumb on the left: *Six*.

"It's not enough," said Clint.

"We will train the others before the harvest is finished, señor," said the boy. "They will fight too, once they know how."

They were standing in that tableau — the gunslinger in front of the boy, with happy and exhausted men behind them, picking up debris from the sunny street — when a man wearing twin bandoliers rounded the corner on a white horse.

Behind him rode row after row of ornately masked men.

CHAPTER SIX: EL FEO

The man not wearing a mask (but wearing a pocked face, a small mustache, and a wide hat) approached, then paused without bothering to dismount. The other men, all masked and riding horses of their own, spread around the practice area until a semicircle had formed facing Clint, Rigo, and the villagers. Then the villagers slowly backed away, leaving only the gunslinger and the boy to face the bandit.

"I guess you've got more visitors," said Clint, looking at El Feo and his Gross of Gringos.

The Gringos' masks were all painted and decorated to look like colorful skulls. The masks themselves were varied, but the men behind them looked as if they'd been cut from a common mold. They all seemed to be the same height, weight, and build. They all held their reins in exactly the same way. The small motions each made with their heads and bodies, Clint thought, were identical from man to man. And there were many, many men.

"So when you said 'Gross of Gringos'," a deep voice to Clint's left said to Rigo, "you meant it literally."

Clint turned to the voice and found himself staring at Edward's big white head and horn.

"Yar," said Rigo. "A gross. One hundred and forty four men, señor. I thought you understood."

"By 'gross,' I figured you meant they didn't bathe," said Edward. His nostrils flared. "Which they don't seem to," he added.

"So Baracho Gulch has found itself some guardians!" El Feo announced with a smile from atop his horse, looking down at Clint and Edward. "That is nice."

"We haven't finished the harvest," Rigo told the bandit.

"Oh, I know that. But I sent a few advance men, and they told me that your harvest slowed when some strangers came to visit. I decided to come see these visitors for myself. And look what I find! A Realm marshal true and his trusty sidekick! But señor," he said, lowering his chin toward Clint, "you've nar enough bullets in your guns to handle a tenth of us."

"I have more bullets," said Clint, his hand hovering above his belt. Beside him, Edward's horn pulsed red, then blue, then green.

"Oh, sí, sí. And your big horse, he can shoot fireballs at us! But let me ask you, amigo: Who will protect the villagers while you are busy fighting?"

Clint looked around the semicircle and estimated that only half of El Feo's men were present in the square. The others might be in other parts of the village with hostages, or in the dry fields with lit torches. Or mayhap in the hills, with rifles aimed.

"Fourteen bullets is less than a tenth of what would be needed to shoot one hundred and forty-five men," Edward said, repeating El Feo. He thought for a moment. "That's right. I didn't think bandits got learnin.' " He looked up at the bandit. "Hey, chief: What's the capital of Yuma Province?"

"Seattle."

Edward frowned, then turned to Clint. "He's right. Don't be fooled by his odor."

There was the creak of a door, and Sly Stone sauntered out of the mud-brick saloon, his guns drawn and aimed at the bandit's head. Other than the presence of two giant magical shotguns in his hands, Sly looked like he could be out for a stroll. He walked to Clint's side and stood there, looking around with a smile on his face. Several of the Gringos drew their firearms in answer, but El Feo didn't draw. He chuckled instead.

"Three is not enough to fight so many of us, no matter who those three are," he said.

"Four," said Rigo.

El Feo laughed hard enough to send a hand to his belly. Once calm he said, "Oh! The Montoya family has assured for itself matching graves instead of supper! Good for the village, I suppose. More supper for the rest of them."

A clanking noise came from beyond the town fountain. A few of the Gringos turned, the skulls' teeth painted on their masks seeming to grimace. Then a drawling, proper-sounding voice said, "Five, sirs," and Clint looked over to see Buckaroo stepping into the open, his chest parted and his canon out.

The smile stayed on El Feo's unshaven face, but something subtle shifted in his expression. Clint attempted to put himself in the man's shoes, to see the village's new arrivals as El Feo must be seeing them. There were many more Gringos than fighters, but there was also so much about the hired guns that would be unknown. Would bullets harm the thinking machine? What could the machine's large weapon do? What might the pulsing capsules in the orange-haired man's shotguns be? How much damage could the unicorn inflict? Clint had no idea how much a Sands bandit would know about unicorns, but the presence of one in the village had to be daunting. As Clint watched the man on the horse, he seemed to be weighing his odds. He might be estimating his ability to fight shields, folding, and a unicorn's devastating assault spells.

Still, he held his ground, and held his pride.

"I see we are surrounded!" he said with a sarcastic laugh, looking around and waving his arms. "But alas... even five, I think, is not enough."

Clint looked around too, but not for theatric value. He was calculating positions, odds, and losses. He'd been watching the body language of the men in the ornate masks, and unless they held a secret weapon he couldn't fathom, he felt he could read them perfectly. These men had come on this errand year after dusty year, and each year, the village had offered the resistance of a sponge. Even if a new decree from a dark power had made them desperate, they would still be complacent. That complacency would make them slow.

Clint estimated he could empty his guns and take out fourteen of the masked men before they fired a single reasonably aimed shot. Edward could take scores easily, and protect their group — all but Buckaroo, who was too far away but who wouldn't need protection from commoner's bullets anyway. If anyone mortal took fire, Edward would be able to heal them once there was a lull. Stone wouldn't need to reload and could fire scattered rounds that, at close range, would likely take two of the gross at once. Buckaroo's canon could do significant damage, and Rigo could handle any men who lost their firearms — not much, but it was something.

Clint was reasonably confident they could take out the bandits he saw without casualties to their own. But the problem was the bandits he *couldn't* see. *Those* men might do anything — burn, pillage, kill innocents... anything.

Seeming to read Clint's mind, Edward whispered to Clint, low enough that nobody else would hear: "Stand down. He wants the crops. Let him leave with them, thinking he's won. We can catch up with them later."

Clint whispered back, "We can beat them."

"Of course we can. But we need to know more, seeing as these men are in league with…"

"… the Darkness," Clint finished.

"Mayhap," said Edward. "But I don't sense Darkness in these men as I have in others. Before you interrupted me, I was going to say Kold."

El Feo was watching them, waiting to see what came next. He didn't seem at all worried.

"Kold?" Clint hissed.

"You're slow," whispered Sly Stone, butting in. "Your man Kold is the Meadowlands land baron."

"How can you possibly know that?" Clint said.

But before Stone could answer, a huge booming noise came from behind the bandits and Pompi Bobo tromped onto the scene with his enormous hammer in his hands. His kinky giant's hair stuck out at odd angles. He yawned, appearing mildly bothered to be awoken but otherwise ready for work.

"Pompi makes six," the giant said, his footfalls causing the mud buildings to shake and rain dust. Clint, who knew that Pompi could walk like a feather when he wanted, figured that this was for effect.

Several of the horses — including El Feo's — started to stutter backward, spooked. The bandit held the horse, his hand falling to his sidearm. He didn't draw. He watched Clint, refusing to give him the satisfaction of looking over at Pompi.

"So, Baracho has found its spine," said El Feo. "But we are one hundred and forty five, and you cannot watch us all!"

Behind him bandits rattled weapons in the air.

"Showing off is the fool's idea of glory," said Rigo, a serious look on his young face.

"Ring the bell to summon us when the harvest is finished, and have our share ready," the bandit replied. "Do that, and you may live to see another year. Don't, and we shall all see what happens."

Then, with a final menacing glance around the square to remind everyone who was boss, he circled his hand in the air and the masked men turned their mounts around, leaving the way they'd come.

CHAPTER SEVEN: UNWINNABLE

"We cannot win this fight," said Edward.

"Make up your mind," said Clint.

The gunslinger sat beside Mai's bed in her open-ended room after the sun had set, brushing her hair from her face. Her body seemed greatly improved, but she'd still not regained consciousness. Her skin had lost its papery appearance and was now mostly smooth. Her flesh had filled out, replenished with some of the fat back where it was supposed to be. Beneath that, her muscles seemed to be returning, hardening even beyond the lithe strong presence she'd had before. Her beauty was slowly resurfacing. Her shoulder blades no longer protruded. Most of this had happened in the past half-day. It was as if the Rio Verde's magic was accelerating in Mai — increasing not just her healing, but also her *rate* of healing. Whenever Clint went to her bedside, he thought of Edward's metaphor of the phoenix bird, and had frightening visions of Mai erupting in magical fire.

"I was wrong," Edward told him. He'd pulled back the heavy drapery that formed the room's fourth wall and was sipping from a bowl of tequil he'd magicked from the saloon. "There are too many men to watch and follow all of them. We can fight, yar. What we can't do is keep them from causing the village irreparable damage *while* we fight."

One of the villagers had given Clint a heavy alloy coin. The gunslinger tossed it up and down, up and down, snatching it from the air to practice his oversized marshal's hands. "This was your idea!" he snapped.

"Yar, and there were three reasons for that. The first was that we were coming here anyway to sip from the river. That, we've done. The second was to stop a bandit who was being controlled by the Darkness. But I sensed no Darkness in El Feo or his men."

"He could still be working for Kold, like Independence Lee," said Clint.

"Yar, he could. But we could also just be fools wasting time while Kold increases what is already nearly six months' worth of lead on us. And as far as saving time by crossing the Rio instead of going around? Well, I've looked at the crossing more closely since we've been here. We wouldn't actually be crossing the dangerous part, where the Verde dives underground. We'd be crossing a tributary that feeds into the river's main body. That's barely magical water. It's not rapid, just deep. I might be able to swim it."

"Might."

"Honestly," the unicorn said, "I'd prefer to take the boat Rigo mentioned."

"Which he said he'd let us use if we could help this village."

Edward took a sip of his tequil. "We could take it without his permission."

Clint glared at Edward, the coin momentarily halting in his hands. "You'd do that? You really are terrible."

"Fine. But I'm not swimming with you on my back. Can you swim?"

The gunslinger, who'd spent his life in the desert, stared at Edward.

"Mayhap I could float you. Or magick a boat, for that matter." He rolled his eyes, shocked that they hadn't figured this out earlier. "There it is. We can magick a boat and cross at our leisure. Tonight, if we want to."

But Clint, as much as he'd wanted to pass on this errand and as much as he'd refused to bond with the locals, shook his head. He looked away and resumed his tossing, flipping the coin high in the air. He caught it between two fingers, balanced it on his thumb, and rolled it across his knuckles.

"Coward."

"It's not cowardice. It's sense. You want to help this village? Then don't start a fight you can't finish, that won't make things worse for them for years to come. All it would take for this to go sour would be for a single bandit to set a torch to any of these thatched roofs once they felt that we were winning. They could destroy the crops. Capture their women and children. Kill villagers. We can protect ourselves, but what about them?"

Clint was about to retort, but the same concerns had been in his mind for hours. It wasn't simply a matter of fighting. If their troop met El Feo's in a canyon with no one around, Clint would be willing to battle until everyone on one side lay dead. His own side would probably be victorious, but even if they weren't and were killt, it wouldn't mean the end of the world. The gunslinger wasn't afraid to die, or to lose. What bothered him about this fight was that only one side would play fair. There were too many unscrupulous shortcuts in a fight like the one they were facing.

"So what are you saying?" he asked the unicorn. "Cut and run? Let El Feo keep brutalizing and pillaging the village?"

"We have a larger errand in Elf Meadows."

"Allow the forces we're after in the Meadows to have their fill in Baracho Gulch? Strengthen Kold by letting him weaken this village?"

"Gunslinger," said Edward. "You have known me for longer than any man. I am not one to run or surrender. But this is a fight we cannot win. *Six fighters are not enough.*"

Clint sighed. He tossed the coin, but it never landed. Instead, it made a sharp angle in the air and shot like a bullet toward Mai, who raised a hand to catch it. The coin struck her palm with a sound like snapping leather.

"Seven," she said.

CHAPTER EIGHT: THE AWAKENING

There was no slow and gradual improvement in Mai's recovery upon waking. It happened all at once. It was as if her body and mind had been organizing themselves as she slept, healing her entirely before returning her to consciousness, like a mad genius completing his machine backstage before dropping the curtain. Within minutes after she caught Clint's coin — or, more accurately, after she called Clint's coin to her hand from out of the air — the last of the pallor fled her skin. Her wrinkles vanished. There was no glaze in her expression, or softness in her muscles.

Her body, as she rose, was a work of art. She was beautiful and soft where she was supposed to be, but hard everywhere else. She immediately seemed to be far faster and stronger than she'd ever been since Clint had known her — faster and stronger, it seemed, than Clint himself. She literally leapt up from the bed. When Clint told her that she was weak and should settle, Mai gave him a sly look and then ran through the door at a sprint. The gunslinger wasn't fast enough to follow, but Edward pursued her into the hills, up toward a rocky cliff where his heavy, clumsy hooves finally couldn't follow, and he lost her. Mai returned ten minutes later, barely winded and still wearing nightclothes, her expression flushed with euphoria.

"Mai?" said Clint.

" 'Mai?' " she said, mimicking the gunslinger's dry voice.

"Do you know who I am?"

"Nar. Because you never open up and talk about yourself. It's infuriating."

Clint looked the smiling woman over from head to toe. She wore no shoes, yet had sprinted up hills to summit a peak, losing both a marshal and a unicorn in bare feet. Her nightclothes, intended for a convalescent, were loose and full of frills. She would need a fighter's outfit to replace them. The woman before Clint and Edward was no convalescent. Her expression was bright, her bearing strong. Her hair was smooth and dark and shiny. Like Edward, she seemed to repel dirt and sweat and grime, and looked as if she might forever appear radiant and clean.

"Are you mocking me?" Clint asked.

"Yar."

"Then you *do* know me?"

"Clint Gulliver. Proud marshal to The Realm. Gunslinger. Exiled. About to hitch a woman — that's me! — named Mai Man..." She stopped in the middle of her last name, thinking. "*Did* we hitch? We didn't, did we?"

Clint couldn't help himself. Instead of answering her, he crossed the room and wrapped his arms around her in a stunning display of unmanliness and weakness, entirely unbecoming of a gunslinger. The pistols on his belt clapped into her sides, useless and soft and beneath mention.

When Clint released her and pulled back, Mai looked at him, shocked. "You've changed," she said.

"*I've* changed?"

"I can feel it in you. In your energy. You've always been polluted by sorrow, but this — this I feel in you now — is so much worse." She sniffed the air as if overwhelmed by fresh sensations. "Oh, I can feel it wafting from you, Clint. So much scratching at your soul. So much..." Her eyes went moist, and a tear spilled over her lower lids and trickled onto her cheek. "It's almost too much to bear. How long has it been since Solace? Since our hitching day?"

"More than four and a half years," he said. Then he glanced at Edward, silently asking how any of this was possible. Mai wasn't supposed to remember. Her soul was supposed to be in a vessel packed low in Dharma Kold's saddlebags. But Edward only shook his head. His expression was just as shocked as the gunslinger's.

"Four and a half years!"

"You don't remember any of it?"

"Nar a bit!"

"You don't remember Dharma Kold?"

Her expression darkened. "I remember Kold just fine, but not the interim. Where have I been?"

"With Kold. With his dark unicorn, Cerberus." He couldn't bring himself to tell Mai what Cerberus had been doing to her over the course of that time, though. Not yet. It was too soon.

"And you...?" she said.

"We followed."

Her tears began to fall more freely, but she didn't seem weakened by them. If anything, she seemed overwhelmed. In a few moments, Mai had gone from nothing to everything, from unknowing to full of dreadful awareness. Delight, sorrow, relief, and euphoria all rushed across her radiant face. She hugged the gunslinger. She stalked the room. She gave Edward knowing looks that spoke volumes, promising plots and plans and more, once the time was right. And Clint, seasoned fighter and walker, discovered that in the shoes of those she wanted to plot and plan against, even he would be terrified to face Mai as she was now.

"Something has changed in you," he said. "Was it the magic?"

"She's always been magic," Edward reminded him.

"Not like this." said Clint, shaking his head. "This is new. Something's been added."

"Not added," said Edward. "Awoken."

"Awoken?" Mai sounded angry. Her personality had been completely repressed for nearly half a decade, and now it was all spilling out at once. In time, hopefully, it would equalize, but for now it was like a busted faucet. "*Awoken?* I've never been like this. I've never felt like this."

"Mai," said Edward, "what Kold wanted from you... it was very powerful. Something you didn't know you had, called..."

"I've never been like this!" she shouted. "What have I awoken from, Clint? What is this feeling inside of me, Edward the Brave?"

Clint flinched, hearing her speak that name and knowing she'd never heard it from him. He himself had never heard of Edward being "Edward the Brave" before Stone had said it outside of Nazareth Shiloh, and he still didn't know what it meant.

Clint put his hands on her shoulders. "You've just woken," he said. "Sit down."

"Sit down? I haven't just woken from *sleep.* I've woken to find I'm something different than I was! What do I feel inside of me? Can you tell me that? And what, pray tell, is *this?*"

Mai held out her hand and, as she'd done earlier, called Clint's coin to her palm. She caught it and glared at him. "And what is *this?*" She held out her other hand. An alloy cup left the dresser and shot into her hand. The cup wasn't empty; its contents sloshed onto the sheets of the bed in which, forever ago, Mai had slept. "I've lost four years, and I wake up to *this?* I don't want it, Clint!"

She huffed, anger wafting from her body. The cup flew back

where it had come, forcefully, shattering a clay vase. The coin shot away and blew a hole through the casito's brick. At that, all three of them stopped, Mai now looking as shocked as the others. Clint walked over and put his eye to the hole. The coin had gone all the way through.

"Well," he said. "That could come in handy."

Mai's temper seemed to diminish after that, and Clint and Edward were able to dress her in some appropriate clothes from the closet. Duly clothed, she sat back down on the bed and slowly returned to her old joking, upbeat temperament, having purged a sort of emotional plug. Once she was settled, they started to palaver. She told them she'd heard their last discussion as she'd lain in the bed, as well as much of what had been said above her while the magic water was doing its work. She understood roughly where they were, the present threat, and the decision at hand. And Mai, fresh from her sick bed, found dying as a fractional husk of a human not terribly long before, wanted to fight with them.

"Nar," said Clint, pacing the room. "You cannot fight."

"I want to fight, because it's a fight that must be fought."

Clint shook his head. "We've all but decided to leave."

"That was before I woke up," Mai said.

Clint repeated: "You're *not* going to fight."

"You don't understand," said Edward. *"We can't win."*

Mai seemed meditative. "I once knew a man before Solace," she finally said. "He was bound by an immobile body, but his will could move mountains — not literally, but by persuading others. He once told me something about unwinnable fights. He said, 'If you can't win the game, change the rules.' "

"What are you saying?" said Edward.

"I'm saying that you should stop being so noble for once. If you can't win by being fair, then stop worrying about being fair. Fight dirty. *Cheat.*"

"I won't fight dirty," said Clint, skulking around the room, his hands itchy and his fingers twitching.

" 'I won't fight dirty,' " said Mai, again mocking the gunslinger. Then, in her own voice, she said, "Then you will lose. This is a righteous fight. It's better to win a righteous fight by cheating than to lose it by fighting fair. And besides, *I* plan to cheat. So your side will be sullied by my actions anyway."

"You are not fighting!" Clint blurted.

"Why?"

"Because you're a woman!"

Mai lowered her brow. It had been nearly half a decade since

Clint had last seen that look, but he recognized it all the same. It meant that he'd said exactly the wrong thing, and that he was about to pay for it.

Her hands came up. Both of Clint's pistols left their holsters, flew through the air, and landed in her palms, the barrels leveled at the gunslinger's chest.

"Oh, come on, let me play," she said, putting a pout on her lips. "I'm the fastest draw across the Realm and Sands."

CHAPTER NINE:
THE MAGNIFICENT SEVEN

There was no more arguing with Mai. She stepped up, took her place as the seventh member of the posse, and — much to Clint's consternation — took a large if not dominant role in the planning of their attack on El Feo.

The gunslinger's doubts were many. In his mind, men were fighters and women were not. He didn't want Mai at risk so soon after finally returning to him. He didn't want to attack El Feo; Edward had convinced him moments before Mai awoke that there was no way to win. He didn't believe the villagers were ready. And perhaps most of all, he didn't want to cheat.

But Mai, in the way that only Mai could, good-naturedly made fun of the gunslinger's sense of honor and duty until the idea of cheating became almost tolerable. *How honorable was El Feo?* she asked him. *How kind and fair had he been to Baracho Gulch over the years?* The bandit had taken nearly all they grew, none of which he had any right to. He marched in with guns while the villagers had nothing but machetes. He rode with a gross of men at his back — all wearing masks intended to frighten the men, women, and children into submission. Insisting on fighting an unfair man in a fair way was beyond absurd, she said. It was like playing a game of oblong with animals, adhering to rules that the animals were incapable of understanding.

Once Clint was convinced, the rest of the posse fell in line. Edward, who had always been a jerk, took to the spirit of Mai's plan immediately. Stone, outlaw from the start, had zero qualms. Buckaroo would believe whatever he was told to believe, and Pompi was too slow to do much other than what the majority of his friends wanted. Rigo was infatuated with Mai and would have lit himself on fire had she told him to.

So they renewed training the villagers of Baracho Gulch, determined to win the coming fight by any means necessary. Stone made more bows and taught the villagers (both men and women; Mai insisted) how to use them. Edward carved clubs and slingshots using his magic and showed the people how to wield them in unfair, dirty-fighting ways — clubbing knees, groins, and backs when they were turned. They sharpened machetes. They made knives. They rigged nets and tripwires. They hid the supplies they had to keep, then buried their treasures. They sent those unable to fight into the hills, where Edward had hollowed them a sturdy cave for refuge and decked it with camouflage.

Rigo taught the villagers his fighting skills. It wasn't possible for them to learn everything in the time they had, but he taught them punches and kicks, focusing on basics and not stretching the fighters beyond their new potentials.

"I fear not the man who has practiced ten thousand kicks once," Rigo explained to his students as they repeated the same set of actions on bags of flour over and over and over again in an endless loop. "I fear the man who has practiced one kick ten thousand times."

Rigo himself focused on impossible striking routines, fighting anything that anyone could literally throw at him. He wanted to see if he could evade bullets — this time *not* literally, but by using his skills to approach a fighter by stealth. Clint refused to indulge him, declaring that he didn't fire his weapons to miss.

Rigo's students complained that they couldn't do what he did. Rigo said they didn't have to. They had to repeat the same actions over and over until they became automatic.

"Take things as they are. Punch when you must punch. Kick when you must kick," Rigo said. "Less effort makes you faster."

Mai worked on perfecting her own new skills — levitating, drawing, and propelling metals — which she was unable to explain and which Edward could only guess about. Rigo, still smarting from Clint's refusal to shoot at him for practice, asked if she thought she could catch bullets. She told him that she she seemed to only be able to use metals that were attracted to magnets, and lead bullets were not. Rigo seemed disappointed. Bullets, he said, shouldn't be so final.

Once the pueblo's harvest was finished, the villagers found themselves as prepared as they were going to get. Still Clint was reluctant.

"Don't ring the bell," he said. "We may have scared him off, now that he knows this village will fight. There are other villages. San Sebastian. Salazar Valley. Other places for El Feo to pillage instead of Baracho Gulch."

"And if you are wrong?" said Maria, Rigo's grandmother. "If we do not ring the bell and he comes anyway… mayhap after you have left us?"

"She's right," said Edward. "We can't stay here anymore, sitting back and allowing Kold to grow stronger across the river. If this is Kold's doing, we must try to end it, then move on. If they ring the bell, at least he'll show now, while we're still here."

"But they'll be expecting a trap," Clint said. "It's nar a mystery that we're here."

"Yar," said Maria. "They will expect a trap. And they will expect right."

CHAPTER TEN:
C FOR CONCEDE

They rang the bell, then rang it again.

Nobody came.

The gunslinger was checking over his shoulder six times an hour when Rigo came running down the main street with a holler. Clint ran to the boy, but Rigo pushed at him, saying he needed the other señor, the other. At first Clint didn't understand; Rigo was flustered and couldn't catch his breath. Then he found his words and shouted, "EDUARDO!" Clint understood, and ran with him to the unicorn's quarters under a large overhang outside the saloon.

Edward was lying down, taking a siesta, when the gunslinger and boy burst inside. At first the unicorn was annoyed, rolling up and making no effort to keep from kicking at them as he did. Rigo took a hoof in the chest and Clint took one to the chin, and then Edward was up and mumbling. Rigo cut him off, shouting about his sister, Paloma. At this, Pompi Bobo stormed in through the opposite overhang, as he was also too large for indoor quarters. Rigo cast him an eye, left over from his earlier animosity about the giant dating his sister, then seemed to remember his priorities and turned back to the unicorn, explaining.

"She's hurt, señor! In the hills! It was El Feo. They made me tell you! We were walking in the east field, gathering loose corn stalks into bundles, and the masked men surrounded us. I did what I could, but they had guns, and after I'd struck three or four of them down, one simply leveled his gun at Paloma and shot her in the side. Then he leveled his gun at me and asked if I understood and would behave. I am not afraid, amigos; I am ready for NextWorld if Providence wills it true that I go, but for Paloma, I was afraid. So I let myself be tied and they took us into the hills, far, far up, and on the ride I started to see — thank Providence — that her gunshot was merely a flesh wound and that she would survive if patched. Still, she was losing a lot of blood and looked pale by the time we arrived. When we reached the ravine — it is way up; I can show you where — they cut our ropes and let us go. Paloma collapsed. I went to her, and she was weak. Then the men on the horses, with the masks, they said, 'The unicorn can cure her. If you hurry.' Then they rode off. I ran as fast as I could, but the ravine is at least fifteen minutes away and she may not last long. You have to come with me!"

Rigo started to climb onto Edward's back, ready to ride the unicorn to the ravine, but Clint put a hand on his shoulder and pulled him down. He was just a kid, and didn't realize the offense of what he'd done.

Listening, Pompi thrashed, beating his massive hands on the ground. Clint held out a hand, needing to think.

Edward looked at Clint. "They want me out of the picture," he said.

"Yar."

Rigo looked from Clint to Edward with panicked eyes. He tugged on the unicorn's mane, urging him forward, muttering.

"I must go," Edward said. "It's what El Feo wants, but I have no choice. I must go anyway."

"Señor! We must hurry!"

Stone had seen Rigo running. He stepped in as Edward was speaking, looked from one to the other, then asked what was going on.

"Paloma is hurt," Edward said. "I can heal her, but I must fold to reach her in time. I can be back within seconds, but when I do, I will be useless."

Stone said, "It's a trap."

"Of course it is. The minute I leave, that's when El Feo and his men will attack. They think they can take the rest of you, but I, like all unicorns, am too powerful for them. So they are pulling me from the equation."

"Don't go," Stone said. "Send someone else."

"She may already be dead," said Edward. "It must be me. Nobody else can make it in time. Nobody else can heal her instantly on arrival."

"Then let her die. She is one person." It was what Clint was preparing to say — just numbers, nothing personal — but Stone had beaten him to it.

"You can hold the town until I return."

"She is *one person*," Stone repeated.

"And *you*," Edward snapped, "do not understand the nature of magic where it comes to sacrifice... although you, of all people, should." He gave Stone a look that seemed to imply more than was being spoken, but Clint didn't understand it and didn't bother to try.

Behind the unicorn, Pompi continued to rage, now crushing boxes of clay pots and screaming. Rigo was still tugging at Edward, not hearing anything beyond *She may already be dead*. Clint and Stone were stoic, attempting to calculate the scenario before it unfolded.

"Go, then," said Clint. "We will hold them off."

"You understand that I cannot fold back? If I do, they'll shoot me where I collapse, and I may nar be able to heal. I will need to fold to the ravine, then return on foot. That will give me time to recover. but in the meantime, you will be exposed. Are your irons ready?"

Clint nodded. "Yar."

Edward stepped onto the street. Clint, Stone, Mai, Rigo, and Buckaroo ran around the pueblo, letting the villagers know that El Feo was approaching and that they would need to be ready. Pompi, who couldn't contain his agitation over Paloma and insisted on going along with Edward to save her, beat his fists on the ground and yelled impatiently.

When the warnings were done, the boy, unicorn, and giant stood in the middle of the street in front of the saloon. Edward turned to Rigo and Pompi and told them to hang on tight, then strode forward. His head bent; his horn sparked; his posture became one of pushing through an obstacle. Then a light surrounded him and he vanished into a slit in existence itself, leaving Rigo and Pompi staring at nothing.

"We must go!" said Rigo. Pompi slammed his fists together.

"You are needed here," said Clint.

"WE MUST GO!" Rigo yelled.

Clint grabbed the boy by the collar. "By Providence, she is already healed! What would you do? Leave your village undefended so you could skip back home beside her yanking daisies on the way? Do you believe what you say, Rigo Montoya, or are you a selfish coward? Are you man or boy? El Feo is on his way!"

And then they came — around the corners from the hills, just moments after Edward left. They came from the other end of town, from the river side. The six fighters found themselves surrounded. The gunfighters drew their guns. Pompi drew his hammer, focusing his upset on the newly-arrived men — the men who had done what they did to his love.

"Pompi smash," he murmured.

"Soon," Clint whispered.

But El Feo and his gross of masked men seemed to know all about unicorns and their weaknesses, because they took their time. They knew Edward would not be able to return immediately. El Feo nudged his horse forward slowly, chuckling.

"So, back to five," he said. He looked around, seeing that there were many more than five, but ignoring Mai and the villagers. The villagers, who had seemed so confident while training, were already slinking back in the face of their oppressor and the demons.

"Or more," said Clint.

"Oh, let us not play this game," said El Feo with a wave of his hand. "You cannot match us. Certainly not *all* of us. Things were once so easy here. All you are doing is adding casualties to the inevitable. Do you really think these farmers are prepared to fight us? Do you really think you can win? Do you really doubt we will leave without the supplies we came to take?"

"Nar," said Clint. "I don't doubt it at all. I just don't like it."

El Feo cocked his head. He had surely anticipated that Clint and the others would stay, and he had surely anticipated that they'd try training the villagers. He seemed to have anticipated the ease with which the villagers' formerly fervent determination would wane once the bandit was actually in town. But he hadn't anticipated this. He hadn't anticipated the sneakiest out of all sneaky plans: giving El Feo exactly what he wanted.

The bandit smiled. "You are quite a comedian, gunslinger."

"I'm not kidding. Although my friend, who you sent on an errand, often tells people that I am indeed hilarious."

El Feo studied Clint's stoic, lined face.

"It's true," said Stone, standing beside him. "He's hilarious."

El Feo shrugged atop his horse. "Okay, comedian. Tell me what you are not kidding about."

When Clint's group had first arrived in Barucho Gulch, Rigo had explained that in order to minimize contact with El Feo, the village often set El Feo's take in the square across from the church. And so, a day earlier, the town had done exactly that. It was Mai's secret Plan C — C, for "Concede."

Clint told El Feo about the supplies waiting in the square.

"You are joking," said El Feo.

"Do I *look* like I'm joking?"

El Feo peered into Clint's eyes, sensing a trap.

"He's not," said Mai, stepping to the front of the group. "But to be fair, this *is* what he looks like when he's joking. Although his jokes, I have to say, are absolutely terrible."

"Knock knock," said Clint.

"Don't ask him who's there," she warned.

El Feo turned his gaze to Mai, soaking her in. She'd donned man's clothing to train, but the garments did nothing to make her look mannish.

"Oh, and who is this?" said the bandit, his smile widening. "Mayhap I will take more than supplies this time. What kind of a man do you prefer, señorita? A man who gives up, or a man who leaves with what he wants?" He winked. Mai said nothing.

"It's not giving up," said Clint. "It is creating a way for both of us to win. If we fight, both sides will lose. So I would like to propose a deal."

"A deal?"

"You were right," Clint told El Feo. "You are too many, and we know that you won't play fair. So we will give you what you want, but this will be the last time you come to terrorize the Gulch. We will surrender the supplies. That's how you win, and keep breathing. But you will leave Baracho alone after this. That's how *we* win."

El Feo snickered, then stretched his neck and looked into the square. The way was blocked, so he jerked his head toward one of the masked men. The man ran his horse toward the square. A moment later he returned and said, "Sí, it is true, El Feo."

There was a moment of indecision during which the bandit's squinting brown eyes met Clint's piercing blue ones, but eventually his stern expression crumbled and he laughed.

"Okay, amigo. I will take the supplies. And I will promise never to return here." Then he raised his eyebrows, spread his hands, and repeated himself, his voice dripping with sarcasm. "I *promise*."

The Gross of Gringos, followed by El Feo, made their way into the square. In the center were wagons laden with barrels filled with unmilled corn and wheat, beans, avocados, tequil, many bales of straw and hay, and other supplies.

"You *are* a funny man," said El Feo. "You are hired to protect this town, but then you hand it over. Would you like to pull my wagons as well?"

"Actually, sir," said a drawling but proper voice, "I will pull the wagons for you."

El Feo looked for the source of the voice, then found it in the form of something he'd probably taken for a piece of farming equipment. Buckaroo was sitting atop two stacked bales of hay, his golden alloy legs crossed.

"Don't let him get out of control as he pulls those wagons," said Clint. "He's clumsy."

"Time to go, then, sir," said Buckaroo.

He stood. The boosters under his boots ignited, and the bales of hay beneath him immediately caught fire. He stumbled, his boot still ignited. The floor of the wagon caught. Then the barrel of corn, which started to pop. Then the wheat, straw, and crates.

El Feo stormed forward, shouting. His men followed, rushing the wagon.

"What is it doing?" El Feo yelled. "*No deal!* No deal if your idiot machine can't even..."

The gunslinger drew two pistols and started to fire.

CHAPTER ELEVEN: THE BATTLE OF BARACHO GULCH

When El Feo and his men had seen the supplies, they'd dropped their guards because they'd thought they'd won. That had been one level of distraction. But then, when the village showed him they'd rather destroy their supplies than keep handing them over, the gap between El Feo's overconfidence and his confusion grew wide enough to shoot a pistol through — or swing a giant's hammer at.

Clint backed away, both guns drawn and centered on El Feo. But before he'd committed to fire (he enjoyed watching the bandit chief's reaction a bit too much, and lingered too long), some of the Gross stepped between him and their chief, and Clint sighted on them instead. His guns blasted dull red smoke. Men fell from horses. Clint reached out with his foot, kicked the horses' hindquarters. The horses jumped and jerked their heads around. Clint kicked them again. Now riderless, the horses reared, their forelegs flailing in the air. The motion spooked some of the other horses, who then also reared, unhorsing their riders. Guns came out of holsters too slow — way, way, *way* too slow. Clint easily evaded the bullets, diving behind a barrel. A shot cracked; wood splintered; water began to pour from the barrel in a tiny waterfall. Clint turned his head up and took a drink, wetting his face and stubbly chin.

Buckaroo had fully ignited his boosters as instructed after lighting the bales of hay, taking flight. Clint looked up and couldn't see him. The thinking machine couldn't fly far, so he'd landed (or would land) somewhere nearby, at which point he was supposed to come back with his chest open, his canon out and ready.

The villagers had buried nets in the dirt at every entrance to the square, and as the wagon began to burn and the Gringos ran forward (led by El Feo, who then quickly turned from the flaming booty and began looking for enemies like a disturbed wasp), the townspeople grabbed the nets, pulling them tight, blocking the horses' way. Most nets could be climbed over, of course... but *these* nets couldn't be climbed over because they'd been magicked by a unicorn.

At least a third of the Gross was inside the square, trapped, when the archers appeared along the tops of the buildings and began nocking their arrows. The Gringos fought well. Once they realized what was happening, they drew their irons and pointed them at the archers. Bullets fired. Archers fell.

As the seconds ticked forward, the Gringos began to lose their masks. Some of the masks had been knocked askew; some of them had broken; some of the Gringos had ripped their masks aside to allow for better peripheral vision. Behind each demonic visage was a face almost as frightening as the mask covering it: alabaster skin pocked with pink eyes. Each man was the same size, all with identical builds and identical features.

Every one of the Gross of Gringos was the same man.

On schedule, Sly Stone climbed from the roof of a casito onto a lantern post and slid down behind Clint. Clint didn't bother to acknowledge him. He knew how Sly sounded when he moved, and knew the pattern of his breath.

"These men are all Teedawge," Stone said in the casual tone of voice he might use to acknowledge a man's new shirt.

"I noticed," Clint replied, still not turning. He vividly remembered the albino member of Stone's old gang. Teedawge was the one who kept popping up no matter how many times Clint killt him.

"I never liked that guy," Stone muttered.

Clint continued to watch the battle, still hidden. The few Teedawges who had seen Clint dive behind the barrel had already been shot by archers. In front of them, the scene was all confusion. Archers fired. Gringos fired. Clint felled El Feo's gang as unfairly as he could, picking them off like a sniper and tipping the odds forward one man at a time.

"Where is Rigo?" he asked.

"In place."

"Pompi?"

"Ready. And absolutely *furious*."

Stone peered around his own water barrel, then began to shoot his guns as the bags of black powder the villagers had hidden around the square exploded, deafening the combatants. Stone's shots were lost in the tumult of noise, and still none of the Teedawges had noticed them hiding and firing. Their every pull of the trigger was a potshot, unfair and dirty. Which was, of course, exactly the idea.

Clint was eying the Gringos as their masks came off: the pale skin, the pink eyes. All of them exactly the same.

"I *thought* I killt Teedawge more than once," he said. "You rode with the man. He was in your gang —"

"Gunther Jethro's gang."

"— so you had to know. You knew, right?"

"That he was an archetype? Nar, I didn't know. There are rumors about these things, but nobody I know has ever seen one — or at least seen one and known it for what it was. I'm not surprised, though. I suspected we had a mole in the gang." He sneered, making a noise of disgust. "*Archetypes*. Realm magic at its finest. Edward will lose it. You just watch."

"Archetypes?" Clint looked puzzled. The wood above him, part of the casito, splintered as a bullet struck it. The slug was a stray. Not an aimed shot.

"Uniform living machines," Stone explained. "They all look the same for the reason many guns look the same — they're cast from the same mold. But nar, I had no idea. We got into some tough spots with Jethro's gang, and Teedawge was always the most aggressive, diving right into hails of bullets. He seemed to survive through impossible odds. There was a time or two we even thought he was dead and left him behind, but then he'd show up later, totally fine. Looking back, it seems obvious. But at the time, we just figured he was tough."

"Very tough," said Clint. "Watch this."

He reached over the water barrel and fired a single shot at a Teedawge who was aiming at an archer. The bullet struck him square in the chest, and he fell. But a moment later, the man was back to standing, sighting again, now with a hole through his middle.

"Like xombies," said Clint.

"Dispatch them like xombies, then," said Stone. "Rumor says they have a machine thinkbox where a man's brain would be."

Clint fired again. This time he struck the back of the thing's head. A shower of black smoke plumed from the hole and this time when the Teedawge fell, it kept kissing dirt.

On cue, the nets on the southern end of the square fell. The Teedawges were focusing on the archers, who were all at the north, so dropping the net simply freed the riderless horses. Baracho Gulch needed horses, and it was high time the village stole something back from their tormentors.

"Go," said Stone.

"Not yet."

"Go! They're regrouping, and soon they'll…"

There was a deafening thunder and a blinding flash of light as the gunpowder on the flaming wagon caught. Clint stayed down. Stone had stood, but now ducked. A wagon wheel struck the casito wall behind him and embedded itself halfway in, breaking into a misshapen half-oval. Splinters as big as a man's fist pocked the front of the barrels.

"Okay," said Clint. "Go."

They marched into the square, guns drawn. Many of the Teedawge machines were covered in flames, still firing relentlessly toward the townspeople. Stone shot round after round, his guns belching green fire. Teedawges in front of him evaporated into swirling purple smoke. Clint fired both guns in unison, each echoing in a single report. He fired them together; he spread his arms and fired them in each in opposite directions. Neither man slowed. When they reached the wall below the archers and the stone was littered with archetypes, Clint estimated that the Gross, as a whole, was half dispatched. The square itself was cleared. El Feo was nowhere to be seen, but that meant little. If Stone had shot him, he'd have turned to smoke.

"Did you hit El Feo?" Clint asked.

"I don't know."

"We have to be sure. These other things are only drones."

But they couldn't be sure, so they signaled for the villagers to drop the nets and ran north, to a large courtyard where the pueblo's children often played games.

As Clint and Sly approached, Rigo ran in front of them in a sprint, left to right across the courtyard, pursued by a huge group of Teedawges. Stone raised his guns and fired, but instead of turning to smoke, some of those he struck simply kept coming. His guns were magic and were responding to the Teedawge's non-human nature, refusing to render them purple smoke until they were killt true. So he aimed for the thinkbox and made a few go away, but the pack behind Rigo was still too many and too fast.

The mass of identical archetypes overtook the boy and fell on him in a pile. Rigo emerged from the bottom of the pile, shirt torn off and black pants belted above his navel. He waved his arms around his head, made faces, and screamed a war cry.

The archetypes had thus far seemed plenty capable of fear and surprise. They fell back in a wave, seeming to forget that they were clinging to weapons as Rigo screamed. They remembered their weapons around the time an enormous alloy wagon axle careened across the space, knocking a huddle of archetypes to the ground like a sweeper bar, crushing them into the wall behind Rigo. The boy escaped easily; he ran up the wall and backflipped over the axle. Then he turned and nodded curtly to Mai, who'd hurled the axle. She still had her hands out, seemingly trying to decide if she should use the axle again or turn her magnetic magic elsewhere.

The axle had smashed many of the machine-Gringos beyond recognition, but it hadn't totally destroyed their thinkboxes. It seemed to have addled them, though, and they'd become pure aggression, little logic. Beyond searching for their guns, they stormed toward Rigo with their fists out. But Rigo was too fast, too good; he dealt blows with his fists, feet, and a leg that swept like lightning from the sky. As he battled, the dirty-fighting townspeople streamed in behind the attackers, beating at them with clubs and farming implements, smashing their thinkboxes and causing them to barf stinking black smoke.

Archers scampered from roof to roof, firing at the Teedawges as the things swarmed toward Rigo. But there was no need; Rigo spun and leapt from obstacle to obstacle, one foot here and another there, up the corner of a building, scampering like a rodent, snatching up a piece of shorn debris and using it as a staff, twirling it as he struck his attackers.

The staff snapped in his hands. One piece hung from the other, the two shorter lengths still attached by an internal bit of something flexible, like chain. Rigo flawlessly adapted to the surprising new weapon, spinning one stick around and using it to bludgeon Gringos as they piled toward him. He swung it behind his back, then from hand to hand across his chest, then under his legs. The archetypes formed a ring around him and the scene became a standoff, but then suddenly the air was split by a voice yelling *"STOP ATTACKING ONE AT A TIME, YOU IDJITS!"* and Clint turned to see that El Feo had indeed sneaked out like any self-respecting cowardly leader.

Clint turned his guns to fire, but the bandit vanished around the corner before he got himself all the way around. Clint started to give chase, but Mai beat him to it. The wagon axle rose up and sheared into pieces. A hunk landed at her feet and she straddled it like a witch straddles a broom. The thing took off like a shot, Mai holding on, her hair streaming in a flutter behind her, and then she was gone around the corner and after him.

Clint pointed at Rigo, then at Stone. "Help the kid," he told Stone. Then he ran after Mai and El Feo.

How many could possibly be left?

The answer was: *a lot*. Worse, they seemed to be getting smarter, and adapting their attacks. Shots came from windows. Fires blazed across rooftops — whether from the exploding wagon or from new fires, he couldn't tell. The Gringos — some still wearing masks, some with their pale faces showing — were peering out from everywhere.

A shot struck Clint in the arm and spun him like a top. He slapped the dirt, his teeth clattering hard together. Mai was nowhere. The bandit who'd shot him ran out, smelling a killing, and aimed his weapon. He stood above the gunslinger — who, incidentally, found his guns pinned beneath him — and then established that the Teedawges had a collective memory by saying, "I owe you for that day in Nazareth."

Clint could only stare up as the albino cocked his weapon, but then something huge fell on the man and he vanished, pounded into the ground like a stake.

"Pompi smash!" boomed a huge voice behind him.

The huge object that had crushed the Teedawge rose with a feather's weight. No man squirmed below what turned out to be Pompi's magic hammer — just a whiff of smoke rising from the empty crater with a quiet *poof*.

Clint saw Mai. She was still riding the wagon axle, but had either dispatched or lost El Feo. The mass of Gringos converged, grabbing her leg and pulling her to the ground. The axle fell, then lay still.

"Pompi!" Clint yelled, pointing.

He didn't need to point because Mai, as always, could handle herself. There was a great rattling from every casito on the square as knives flew out of every kitchen drawer in the pueblo, screaming in a great river toward the Teedawges, ending many and dropping the rest.

Quickly, unkillt, most of the felled started to stand, now sporting new spikes of iron.

There was a tremendous explosion two buildings away — like the gunpowder blow in the square, but more hollow and less like fire — sending eruptions of mud into the sky.

A prim voice bellowed, *"Take that, sirs!"*

Mai ran to Clint. Teedawges followed her with knives protruding from them, now mostly weaponless and shambling like xombies.

"How can there be so many?" she shouted at Clint as he joined her in a dash for cover.

"They respawn! You have to hit the thinkbox!"

Mai stopped. Clint shambled a few more steps before turning back.

"Oh," she said.

She flicked her hands. In all of the pursuing Teedawges, the knives shimmered and shifted positions, moving toward their heads. Black smoke belched from their thinkboxes. What remained fell in untidy piles.

Another blast from Buckaroo's canon. This time, Clint thought he might have heard a *Yee-haw*.

"Did you get El Feo?" Clint asked her.

"Nar."

"Why is it that in these confrontations, the leader is always the last to die?"

"Because they're the most cowardly, and they run the fastest."

"Or maybe it's a trope," said Clint. "That's Edward's word for something that the universe sees as unbending. Something that must be."

"Like fate?"

At that moment, Gringos poured into the street behind them and something struck Mai hard in the head, knocking her to the dirt. She didn't get up, maybe *couldn't* get up. Archetypes surrounded them, pointing guns and yelling, but Clint didn't listen. He knelt. Mai wasn't dead. She was unconscious.

Clint stood, intending to draw his guns as he did, but then bodies pressed around him and he found himself boxed in, held tight, his hands pulled roughly behind his back. In front of him, one of the Teedawges who had managed to keep his skull mask stepped forward and slapped Clint with the back of his hand.

Where was Stone? Where was Buckaroo?

Clint could hear Pompi, a ways off and causing untold damage with his hammer. What about Rigo? Had Rigo escaped?

"We may be artificial," said the masked archetype, "but we still have feelings. And you've hurt a lot of our feelings today." He smacked again.

Clint spat at him.

"See, now something like that won't improve my hurt feelings," he said. He pulled off his mask. His pink eyes were full of menace. He wiped spittle from his neck, grimacing.

"You're cowards," said Clint. "Mindless. Where is your fearless leader?"

"Oh, he's not fearless," said another of the Teedawges in the circle around Clint. "He's just the one the big man speaks to."

"The big man?"

The Teedawge in front of Clint slapped him again.

"El Feo is safe. He's the only one who *needs* to be safe, so we aim to keep him that way. We won't be a *Gross* of Gringos for a while thanks to you, but…"

Another of the men picked up his sentence. "… the great thing about being us is that there are always more where we came from."

Mai lay at his feet. Her breathing was slow. Clint looked up and saw Stone, held by another six Teedawges. He didn't have his shotguns, nor did any of the men holding him. He seemed unhurt. He thrashed, but the archetypes held firm. Stone managed to get a foot into the gut of a Teedawge and had a moment where Clint thought he might wrestle himself free, but then his captors tightened their grip and again the orange-haired ex-bandit was bound.

Clint's arms were pinned. Stone was held. Mai was out cold. The gunslinger knew not where the others were. In the opening were only a handful of the Teedawge things, but it was enough to stop them.

They had done well in the battle of Barucho Gulch, but not well enough.

Stone yelled again and kept kicking out, but the Teedawges held tight. One of his captors punched him in the gut and left him gasping for breath.

Clint felt one of his pistols pulled from its holster. The feeling of an enemy touching his guns was worse than a violation. It felt like a piece of himself being ripped from his body. He looked up and stared into the pink eyes of the man who'd slapped him, now holding one of his pistols. The man turned Clint's iron over in his hands, smiling at its deadly shine. Clint could feel neither his own heart nor his own breath. They were in a duel to the death, yar. But it was unthinkable to ever, ever touch a marshal's guns. *Ever*.

"It's so heavy. Feel this, Teedawge," said the man with the gun, handing it to another.

"It *is* heavy, Teedawge," said the other, handing it back.

"It's full of lead poisoning," said Clint.

The first archetype fingered the cylinder, lifting the hammer, spinning the tumbler through its seven chambers. "Seven shots," he said. "And yet all I need is one."

"You can't handle a gun like that," said Clint.

"Oh, I think I can." Teedawge took a pair of steps back, using two hands to heft the large gun. Clint watched his hands shake, and couldn't totally suppress a smile at how he was unable to hold it steady.

"Nar," said Clint. "I mean, you can't fire a marshal's guns."

"I know about the taboo." He pulled the hammer back. Clint heard the click. Every moment the pale man's fingers were on his gun was torture for the gunslinger. "But the beautiful thing about being what we are is that there is so little we care about."

"Nar, I mean…"

The Teedawge pulled the trigger. But instead of firing one slug forward, the gun split like a shotgun, folded up, and fired the other six shots backward. There was a massive belch of dull red fire as six magic slugs rammed backward through their casings and propellant, then ripped straight through Teedawge.

The gun re-folded as the Teedawge fell and dropped it. Clint caught it before it struck the ground, then used the remaining shell to end another of the men in the scrum around him. The blast had shocked them all, as well as the men holding Stone. There was a beat of held breath and they flinched.

It was enough.

Clint still had seven shells in his second gun. There were two men left in Clint's group. He dropped them, then ended five of the six surrounding Stone before his chambers clicked empty. Stone kicked the remaining man in the chest, stumbled backward in search of a weapon, any weapon. But the Teedawge simply looked at Clint — not Stone — and fired a slug into Stone's chest.

Sly Stone fell.

Clint reached for his belt, for a loose shell.

The gunman turned.

Clint's big fingers deftly pinched a shell while tossing his gun's tumbler open. Spent casings rained to the ground in slow motion.

The gunman aimed.

Realizing he couldn't load in time, Clint dove as at least twenty Teedawges came from the east, guns up and ready.

The gunslinger grabbed for Mai, then pulled her back behind a high stack of boards. Only the one gunman knew he was there; the others had yet to see him. But the others *did* see the gunman turn and fire, missing Clint and striking dirt. The man fired again. Then again. He couldn't hit them where they were, but he would be able to in a few steps if Clint didn't reload, and he hadn't. His hands were full of Mai, keeping her free from the line of fire. Her breathing was steady but deep. He tried peering out for Stone, to see if he'd crawled to safety or if he lay killt, but the gunslinger saw nothing.

He tried again and a bullet streaked by his ear.

In the distance, Clint could hear Pompi and Buckaroo, but still nothing from Rigo. He hoped the kid was okay. He hoped *Stone* was okay. But he doubted it.

There was no standoff. Stone's shooter yelled to the new men, and they all came forward at once with no hesitation. Clint wondered how there could be so many of them left, but knew it mattered nar. He pulled the filled reloader from his pouch, snapped the shells in place, then did the same with the other gun and second reloader. He pulled the hammers back, to make the triggers lighter. The gunslinger tensed. They were too many, and they were already halfway to him. Clint had fourteen shots. Even if he hit every thinkbox, he'd never be able to reload before the remainders were on him.

Get them to line up, he told himself.

The idea was absurd. Yar, if they lined up with one man behind the other, he could hit more than one with a single shell. But where? How? There were no bottlenecks, and no way out behind him. He was in a corner, and he doubted they'd answer his call to form an orderly line for a neat and tidy extermination.

He popped up, fired once with both guns. Turned. Again. Four fell, but the others held no pause. Too many. Too fast.

Teedawges raked the boards aside, and Clint found himself and Mai with no cover at all.

Clint, in a ball, started to stand, refusing to die in a crouch.

Hammers cocked. One barrel aimed at Mai. Another found him.

Behind them all, a great noise held the Teedawges' barrels in hesitation. Eyes twitched.

Then in a great crashing of dust and clay, Edward reared and kicked behind them, flailing his forelegs in the air with a noise that was less like a whinny and more like a battle cry. His horn flared with the deep blood red of anger, and a great wall of orange fire swept through the archetypes, turning them to ash. The fire struck Clint. He could feel it thinking, assessing him, judging him worthy. Then it passed through him and Mai both before it was gone.

Edward's head flicked toward Stone, lying motionless at one end of the space.

Teedawges at the ends of the open area turned and ran toward the unicorn. But the fight was over before it started; Clint could see a deep crimson churning in Edward's eyes — the look those eyes made when his white magic had been turned dark by raw fury. Some of the Gringos fired. Their shells glanced off of Edward's shield like gnats. The unicorn marched forward, his horn cycling through hot and angry hues. The men began to turn, but Edward shot another wall of fire and sent them flying like debris into the swirl of a tornado, sending them crashing through the village's walls and over rooftops. Where the archetypes hit, they exploded like fireworks, their machine souls dispatching in thin billows of reeking inky smoke.

The great white unicorn turned, his nostrils flared and heaving, his eyes slowly cycling back to their usual blue. His head jerked around. He kicked at the dirt testily with one hoof.

Clint walked forward, leaving Mai on the ground behind him.

"I ran," said Edward. "But I wasn't fast enough."

"You still saved one gunslinger. And his magnetic bride."

They walked over to Stone. He lay in an uncomfortable-looking position, one hand up and the other down, torso twisted and one leg crossed over the other. He was gone.

"Not fast enough," Edward repeated.

CHAPTER TWELVE:
HERO

Sly Stone wasn't the battle's only casualty. The villagers lost twenty-three of their number, including Rigo's father. His grandmother survived, as did Rigo, giving them at least some good news.

The other bad news was Buckaroo.

A mass of Gringos had advanced on a group of villagers attacking with machetes and pitchforks and clubs. The Gringos were furious and gave chase, but Buckaroo flew from the sky, landing between the fleeing men and women and their attackers. The villagers behind him squeezed through a narrow slot between two buildings, so Buckaroo plugged the slot, forcing the Gringos to run all the way around if they wished pursuit. The Gringos were furious — being archetypes didn't make their emotions any less human — so they drove at Buckaroo instead of circling to chase their original quarry. Buckaroo fired his canon, clearing wave after wave of men, but they rose again and again and beat him and pinged at him with their tiny commoner's bullets until the sheer relentlessness and number of their attacks finally dented and disabled his weapon. But even after he was disarmed, Buckaroo continued using his metal body to dam the gap, allowing villagers to flee.

The Gringos fired their weapons, but still their bullets weren't strong enough to do more than ping like a song against Buckaroo's Realm metal. Eventually one of them lit and tossed a half stick of dynamite, and the explosion broke something inside the ex-commissioner. Rigo, who'd been with the villagers, circled back and found the thinking machine still functioning after the Gringos moved on. Buckaroo's final words were that he didn't mind dying, since dying proved that unlike other thinking machines, he'd actually lived.

Mai hadn't known Buckaroo or Stone well, but she cried for them both just as she cried for Rigo's father and the other twenty-two villagers. Clint didn't cry, because a marshal couldn't. Gunslingers had to harden their hearts, since there was always killing ahead.

Edward had found Paloma with no problem and had healed her. He'd then stumbled back toward the town, trusting that she could find her way on her own... but after the battle, she still hadn't returned. Pompi was beside himself. Rigo sat with the giant, stroking his hip, which was as high as the kid could reach. Pompi paced the village, causing the water in saloon glasses to ripple. He knotted his enormous hands. Rigo walked with him, to keep him company. Edward said they hadn't let enough time pass and that she could yet return. He added that he'd told her to hang back and be certain the battle was finished before she stepped into town. But Rigo pointed out that El Feo and his few remaining Gringos (mayhap six or seven) had been seen running off in that same direction.

"And the bandit escapes," said Clint. He looked at Edward. "One of your tropes."

"Yar," said the unicorn.

"Like fate?" asked Mai.

"Mayhap," said Edward.

"And Stone? Also fate?"

"I don't know from fate," said Edward. "It's a human concept. More of your mysticisms — your way of trying to make sense of things you don't understand."

"But we have to follow the men who escaped," said Clint.

Edward was silent for a moment. "Yar."

"Because if he lives, he'll regrow his army and return."

"Yar."

Clint let it go. All he cared about was killing El Feo. It didn't matter why. The bandit was doing the Darkness's bidding or Kold's, and so long as he lived, he'd keep on with that bidding. But also, his army had killt a man and a machine that Clint had come to think of as friends... although, of course, gunslingers had no friends.

So they cleaned up the village and Edward restored their burnt supplies to new. As long as they could keep El Feo from coming back, the supplies would make the village richer than it ever had been — which wouldn't be very rich at all, though it would feel that way after starving for so long.

Clint dug two graves by hand, refusing Edward's magic help. It took him the entire night, working by lantern light as the village slept, before he had them deep enough. At the next day's dawn, they buried the outlaw who'd become an honorary marshal and the machine with a heart of gold to match his skin. Edward didn't mock Clint — not about burying a machine, not about digging the graves himself, and not about his sentimentality. The unicorn would never admit it, but Clint knew that Edward felt the loss the same as the others, and grieved in his own way.

By morning, Paloma still hadn't returned.

Edward and Clint were tired and didn't need another errand of heroic mercy, but if Paloma was anywhere, she had to be with El Feo. Taking a village girl as they fled would be the ultimate revenge — until next year, when they'd return with a new gross of archetypes, take the entire harvest, and burn the village to dirt, thus rendering their party's two deaths meaningless. Finding Paloma and El Feo was but a single errand, and Clint meant to handle it.

And so, with their dead buried, Clint, Mai, and Edward packed up and prepared to ride out of Baracho. Pompi had become a permanent part of their troop and packed as well, but his real drive was to find Paloma. Rigo's was the same. Clint argued that the boy needed to stay with his village instead of heading off on some fool's errand with the wrong sorts of people, but Rigo said that if Pompi was after Paloma, then he was too. If revenge was to be dealt at El Feo's table, Rigo wanted his seat as well.

So the three humans, the giant, and the unicorn set off with two horses — the same two they'd rode in on, except that now Mai rode Leroy and Rigo rode Socks. The horses seemed to notice the difference in riders after so much time under Sly Stone and Buckaroo, but they were horses, and they did as they were told.

They headed up into the hills, following a confused and scattered trail left by El Feo's men. Edward said that this proved it, that El Feo and his remaining Teedawges were riding with the help of black magic. Nothing else could twist a trail so thorough.

One hour passed with no sign. Then another. They reached the ravine, and both Edward and Rigo confirmed the last place they'd seen the girl. Rigo argued that they should continue searching between ravine and village, but Edward asserted that they should keep moving toward Elf Meadows since that was where El Feo came from, and where their ultimate quarry was located. He said he could feel it more and more with every passing hour — an oppressive black sensation from the north. And, finally again, the presence of the unicorn of a different color, Cerberus.

They searched the site and soon found a note, pinned to a tree with a small knife. It read: WE HAVE THE GIRL. SEND THE

MARSHAL INTO THE VALLEY ALONE. NO WEAPONS.

Mai snatched the note from the tree, leaving the knife in place. She read it again, shaking her head.

"So he knew," said Clint. "He knew we'd follow."

"Yar," said Edward.

"This was a final ploy. To get me."

"*Kold* wants you," Edward corrected. "You will know that to be true when El Feo places you in Realm shackles, and when he takes your bullets from your pouch but handles them with a rag. Kold will have told him that if he touches a marshal's bullets with his commoner's hands, he'll find himself killt."

"So what do I do?"

Edward looked almost amused. "You go, of course."

"If they're in the valley, we could set an ambush. We could…"

"You go, of course," Edward repeated.

Clint was too tired to argue with anyone, especially Edward. If he marched alone into the valley, the worst that could happen would be his own death by El Feo's hands. But after everything he'd been through — nearly five years of wandering and hardship — he'd managed to do the most important thing he'd set out to do by rescuing Mai. Now, truth be told, he longed for rest. It was only Edward's insistence that there was much work ahead for the gunslinger that kept him plodding painfully along.

So he took off his gun belt and placed it in the only other place in the world where it felt right: buckled around the unicorn's neck.

"Don't worry," said Edward. "I won't eat the jerky you keep in the place where you once kept extra shackles." Then he magicked the jerky out and ate it right there, in front of Clint. Mai couldn't suppress a giggle.

Clint walked out of the rocky, tree-strewn hill region, over the crest of the next hill, and into a dry valley.

The descent to the valley's bottom was long, and in the open. He felt alone and exposed. His hips felt light; he missed the comforting presence of iron. His hands wanted to hang at his sides, but he held them up, mostly crossed. The absence where his guns should be was too much to bear.

When he reached the bottom and dipped his walk into the center of the valley, he found a cluster of several large boulders. Behind these was El Feo. He had with him seven horses and six Gringos — far from his original gross. But he also had Paloma.

"Hey, you made it!" said El Feo, standing and waving as if greeting a long-lost friend. "How are you doing, amigo?"

Clint said nothing.

"So you decided to give yourself up for the girl, eh? That's not too smart. You just taught a whole village to sacrifice itself for your cause. That's not selfless. And *this* is the time you chose to be selfless? When it's one girl versus your entire mission?"

"My unicorn told me to come."

"Ah. And you always do what your horse says? Hey, I understand. Me too." He leaned close to the nearest horse's mouth and put a hand behind his ear as if listening. Then he straightened, said, "Okay, whatever you say, Freddie," and slugged Clint across the jaw.

El Feo struck hard, but Clint bore the pain and gave him no satisfaction by flinching.

The bandit pointed his thumb toward the horse. "Freddie here, he didn't like the way you killed one hundred and thirty-eight of our friends and ruined our livelihood."

"Dumb horse," said Clint.

El Feo hit him again. "Aren't you going to fight back, lawman?" he said.

"I don't want to hurt my hands," said Clint. "I'm going to need them to kill you later."

El Feo laughed, then glanced around the circle at the Gringos, sending them a message to join in his laughter. They did.

"Big man. Well. I will take you to see a bigger man." From behind his back, El Feo pulled out a pair of Realm shackles, then used them to bind Clint's wrists.

"Dharma Kold."

El Feo's brow wrinkled. "Diamante. I don't know a Kold."

"Well, he wouldn't tell you his real name. He'd lie to everyone unimportant."

El Feo hit him again. Clint's lip was bleeding and he could already feel his skin starting to swell. Still he said nothing.

"Let the girl go," said Clint.

" 'Let the girl go,' " El Feo mocked. "Always the hero. Do you ever say anything that isn't cold and heroic, *hero*?"

"Here's one: you're ugly."

One of the Gringos laughed. El Feo shot him a look.

"I was going to release her anyway, but you're making me want to keep her, just for spite." He stared at Clint for a long moment. Then he shrugged, put another insulting smile on his lips, and said, "Eh, it's okay. I can't argue with a hero like you. She can go. I don't need her, and I'm too kind to kill a pretty girl for no reason. And besides, now I have my real prize." He gestured toward a rock, urging Clint to sit. The hand on his six-shot revolver said that if Clint didn't sit, he'd make him.

Clint sat. One of the Gringos freed Paloma, and she ran up the hill the way Clint had come, toward her brother and beau. Clint's eyes followed her. The valley was wide open with nowhere to hide. Nowhere for a kid fighter and a giant, anyway.

"So now I tell you, sí?" said El Feo.

"Tell me?"

"This is the part where I tell you my plans. So here they are: I will take you to Señor Diamante, then I will find new Gringos and I will return. Your friends won't bother to protect the village this time, because they will be off trying to free you. But they won't be able."

"Why are you robbing the village?" said Clint.

El Feo stabbed a scarred finger at one of his men. "Because this fat man needs to eat, and eats a lot!" he blurted, then laughed as if it was the most hysterical thing anyone had ever said. The man he'd pointed to was identical to the other five. All were thin.

"Because this 'Diamante' tells you to," said Clint. "That's all you know, is how to do what you're told. But now you must split what you take with him. So how does that help you? And why are you so weak as to take such a poor bargain, seeing as you've been robbing that village yourself for so many years?"

El Feo frowned. "You think you're smart, don't you, amigo? Think I'm dumb and that you know it all. But you are wrong; I don't split what I take. Diamante lets me keep everything, and I burn what I don't need. He pays me to do it. He gives me protection, and men, and guns."

"Why?"

"I don't know!" El Feo threw up his hands as if annoyed by the gunslinger's query. "But he does. And he traffics in magic. Magic that's building Meadowlands into something like you've never seen. You know how they speak of The Realm, sí? Well, Meadowlands is like that now, only better since it's in unfractured land. There are *roads* to Meadowlands, even though there are none to The Realm. And soon, a railroad. You can find it. You can get there. The Realm's days are finished, my friend. Meadowlands will quickly eclipse it."

Clint took mental notes, comparing what he was hearing now with what Edward and Stone had said about the city in Elf Meadows. What Edward described was less impressive than the picture painted by El Feo, but El Feo was a man of the land, and perhaps more easily impressed. And of course, impressions of The Realm were just that: *impressions*. Nobody knew what it actually looked like. Well, except for Clint and Kold, though Clint's memories were mostly gone.

"Sounds like a pretty fantasy," said Clint.

El Feo chuckled. "So brave. But you may chatter all you want, because I find you entertaining. These six are boring. You know? I think you did me a favor. Six are a bore, but a gross were terrible. And all those creepy eyes always watching me. So thank you for clearing my extras, hero."

Without warning, the six Gringos around the circle collapsed. Somewhere off to the right, there was the sound of something wet being caught in a mitt. El Feo looked from the Gringos to the sound, then to the gunslinger.

"You're welcome," said Clint.

"What are you doing?" El Feo stood, now jerking his head nervously around. "How are you doing this? Who is with you?" He turned to the valley and shouted. *"Where are you?"*

The bandit looked down at Clint, who hadn't moved, still sitting motionless on the rock, hands still bound behind his back. Clint looked up innocently at El Feo.

"Where are your friends?" He turned and shouted again, but there was no answer. He pressed his gun's barrel to Clint's forehead, then looked around with small jerking motions of his head, trying to see something that wasn't there.

"I will shoot him dead!" he shouted to the empty valley. "You hear me?" He cocked the hammer, pressed his finger against the trigger. "You hear me? My gun is cocked, amigos! My finger is on the trigger! One light touch and he's dead. *Do you hear me?"*

Clint, placid, rolled his eyes upward. He saw the barrel, then El Feo's stubbly, panicked face.

"Who are you talking to?"

"Don't play stupid with me!"

"What makes you think that those six men didn't simply have heart attacks?"

El Feo fogged heavy breath from his lungs as his finger jittered on the trigger. It was entirely possible that he might kill Clint by accident.

"Have they shot at us? There is no way! We are protected! There is no line of sight! What voodoo do you deal in?"

The gun left El Feo's hand. It flew behind him, into Mai's hand, as she stepped out from under Edward's umbrella. The barrel settled against the back of El Feo's head. The trigger settled under her finger.

"We deal in lead, friend," she said.

A shot sounded across the valley. A group of birds took flight, startled by the sound.

Baracho Gulch's worries flew away with them.

CHAPTER THIRTEEN: ACRES OF GREEN

Rigo was relieved to see his sister alive, but Pompi was even more so. When the giant saw her, he crushed her in a hug so severe that the girl was left moaning, and Edward had to heal three cracked ribs. Their tearful reunion, however, was short. Pompi felt duty-bound to remain with Clint, Mai, and Edward — not only to deal with the Darkness he'd felt during his days in Meadowlands and his lingering guilt over his desertion, but also to avenge those he'd ridden alongside. If he could use his hammer to fight beside Stone and Buckaroo, he said, then he owed it to their memories to use it to avenge them. So he had to go. Paloma couldn't ride with them, and none of the party — especially Clint and Edward — would allow it. The gunslinger and the unicorn were exhausted. Their refusal had less to do with protecting the girl and more to do with not wanting to be annoyed as they rode. So Paloma remained, and Pompi prepared to leave, with promises to return when his task was complete.

Rigo had planned to ride to Elf Meadows with Clint, Edward, Mai, and Pompi, but with Paloma found, he had purpose and a mission back in Barucho. And with her beloved Pompi riding in the opposite direction, Rigo was also required to pull Paloma, kicking and screaming, back toward the village. So he did, thanking the party as they left.

"I am eternally grateful to you for stopping," Rigo said. "We all are. You have saved us."

"It was our duty," said Clint, feeling grizzled. "Go out. Serve your pueblo. Make us proud."

The boy gave a sideways smile. "I will do what I can," he said.

"But I'm not in this world to live up to your expectations, and you're not in this world to live up to mine."

"Be well," said Clint, nodding at the appropriately noncommittal nature of Rigo's reply.

"Vaya con Dios," he said.

So they rode. Clint was exhausted to the pit of his soul. Edward, who was magic, seemed to be entirely his jerky, normal self, and tried bolstering Clint when he could. But short of putting him inside another bubble of glee — something the gunslinger loathed — Clint would simply have to ride out his weariness. So he ate the guacamole and traveling packs of invigorating chili supplied by the villagers, and little by little, as they crossed into Elf Meadows, he felt his vigor and purpose returning.

Mai was tireless. While being entirely back to herself, she was simultaneously very different. *Purified*, almost. The magnetic species of magic she now wielded grew stronger by the day. She could lift ferrous minerals from the earth. She could weave alloys into art. And she could kill like a marshal, as she'd shown when she'd ended the threat of El Feo forever.

"What did you do to the Gringos?" Clint had asked her back on that day as the three of them had climbed out of the valley to rejoin Rigo, Paloma, and Pompi.

"I pulled the iron from their blood," she'd said, showing him her left palm. It was coated with a slick, metallic residue.

They walked for a week after using Rigo's uncle's boat to cross the Rio's western tributary. They were now in Elf Meadows, Edward explained. They could say goodbye to shifting lands forever. And, he added with a heavy dose of sarcasm, they could say hello to prosperity and magic.

"And hello to Dharma Kold," Clint added.

"Yar, and that," Edward agreed.

But the dark specter ahead seemed distant and unreal as the land spooled out in front of them, becoming less desolate by the mile. Brush became weeds. Scrubby pines became leafy trees. And eventually, as they cleared a rise, they found themselves entering an area with rolling hills covered in short, grazed grass that was new and thick and as green as emeralds.

They tied Mai's horse to a tree and sat in its shade. A few paces off, the big unicorn lowered himself and began rolling in the dirt to scratch, moaning with what sounded like nostalgia. When he came back up, he looked almost pleased. Almost.

"It's been *so long* since I've seen grass," he said. He gained his feet and looked at Clint for a long moment, seeming to decide something. Then with a warning look, he said, "Don't you say a *dagged word*." He bent down and tore off a hunk of grass with his big teeth. He swallowed, then spat as best as he was able.

"Okay, it's official," he said. "I may be nostalgic, but I'm still not a horse."

Leroy, tied to the tree, whinnied and bent his neck down to show that *he* still was.

"Sly would have wanted to see this," said Mai. "He seemed so interested in the magic."

"Beyond interested," said Edward. "He was a savant."

Clint was chewing on a piece of jerky. He looked up at the unicorn.

"A mnemonic agent. Like a living library. He had vast stores of recorded knowledge about the history of The Realm, the Sands, the Great Cataclysm, magic — everything — coded into his genetic material. His whole line does. You've heard of a Rosetta Stone?"

"Yar."

"She was the first. She's where the expression comes from. Their line was one of the original seven. Much, much older than humans realize."

"Sounds like a noble line," said Mai. *Noble like her own,* Clint added in his head.

"Yar."

"So how did he end up as an outlaw?"

"Because there was a leak. Genes drift, but the archive sequence was protected and was never supposed to purge unless deliberately accessed by an archivist. Savants aren't supposed to know the information's there. Sly did. He began having suspicions about why the Cataclysm happened, suspecting The Realm wasn't just a paradise where magic was still plentiful, but rather that The Realm was the *reason* magic had vanished from everywhere else."

"Like the Conspiricists."

"Yar. Except that Stone wasn't *believing.* He was *remembering.*"

They sat on the hill, chewing jerky, enjoying the feeling of the soft grass beneath them after so much time spent amongst rock and sand and dust.

"He knew another thing, too," said Edward. "He didn't tell you, because you were human and wouldn't understand. You'd try to stop it."

Mai and Clint looked over.

"He knew he was going to die before reaching Elf Meadows."

"We should have protected him," said Mai, her voice regretful, chastising the unicorn. "We *would* have protected him, had we known."

Edward sucked on his chili packet. "And that's why neither of us told you."

There was nothing more to be said, so they finished their rest and food, then moved on.

Green hills rolled into more green hills. It took days to cross Elf Meadows' southern apron, but none of them minded the time spent. The land was lush and beautiful and scented fresh, unlike the death and decay they'd been smelling for so long. They could all feel the magic working inside of them. Pompi said that being in the Meadows was like going home, which for him was literally true.

Three weeks after crossing the Rio Verde, they came to the top of a hill and stopped. Clint's mouth hung open. Beside him, Mai looked like she'd been slapped. Even Edward looked taken aback, though he quickly tried to brush it off. Only Pompi appeared completely nonplussed.

In front of them, maybe three miles distant, was an enormous city with a huge glass tower at its center, surrounded by countless acres of green, green grass.

UNICORN WESTERN 7

CHAPTER ONE:
OPEN RANGE

Clint, the gunslinger, sat atop Edward, the unicorn.

Mai, the almost-bride (now restored to her old self after being scooped out and left hollow by the dark rider), sat atop an unspotted brown appaloosa named Leroy.

Pompi Bobo, the giant, sat atop a rock.

The four of them sat together on the crown of a hill high above Meadowlands, which sprawled below them unlike anything else they'd ever seen.

Pompi Bobo had seen Meadowlands before, of course, but the city had grown significantly in the two months he'd been away. When he'd been called down from the mountains along with the rest of the giants, Meadowlands had been nothing more than an unremarkable berg whose only claim to fame was that it sat at The Realm's doorstep insofar as The Realm — unreachable by any conventional means — could be said to have a doorstep. The city had grown during the time Pompi had worked on the railroad, but what he saw below them now was, he said, nothing like the place he'd left behind.

The town, he explained, had a new land baron who'd boasted that he could build a way back into The Realm. The baron said that the people of the Sands would finally be able to open trade with the unfindable and unforgettable kingdom. Pompi said that at the time the baron made it, the claim had sounded bizarre. Everyone knew The Realm couldn't be found. There were, of course, people who claimed that The Realm appeared in the sky to the north of Meadowlands on the brightest days, but nobody would admit to believing them lest they be thought a fool. But rather quickly, things changed. Even before Pompi had left for Baracho Gulch, the city's skepticism had begun to shift. More and more people admitted to seeing flashes of castles and green in the sky. The city grew. New trade items came in as if from nowhere. Riches began to fill the city, spilling from some magic or another. And in the stockyards, an enchanted train that ran on magical rails was being built bolt by bolt, giving no indication that it had any purpose other than the one the baron had claimed.

The group went as close as they dared. Thanks to information yanked from the bandit El Feo before his untimely demise, they were reasonably sure that the land baron (who went by the name "Diego Diamante") was actually Dharma Kold — the man who had captured Mai and scooped her dry, and the man Clint and Edward had been pursuing for nearly five long years. Kold was the man who wanted to breach the wall to The Realm, careless of whether or not he fractured all the worlds along the way. If Kold was Diamante — and if Diamante was as powerful as Pompi said he'd been just two months earlier — then Kold would flat-out control the town by now. A town controlled by Kold promised no equity, even if it glimmered with illusion. There would exist only the mirage of balance… and beneath it an iron fist.

Regardless, Clint couldn't help but be astonished by what Kold had done with the six months of distance he'd set between himself and his pursuers since shaking Clint and Edward in Precipice. The city was every bit as impressive as Clint's scant memories of The Realm prior to his exile. It was at once foreboding and bucolic, its older section buffered by vast green pastures and its newer section buttressed to the north by sharp mountains. The new construction — mostly tall buildings huddled close together — was all glass and silver alloy. From the city's center protruded a shockingly tall crystal structure, like a clear finger pointing at the sky.

They could also make out a gleaming track of alloy circling the city. The track weaved between the buildings, cutting through the city at angles. Pompi explained that the track was for a spark train that ran twenty feet above the ground on a single rail of alloy. The elevated train, he said, was the creation of Nikolai Peculiar, an inventor who believed the city should be strung with thin alloy wires that would carry spark to houses from a central generator. And yar, the train was impressive (they watched it circle the town from their hiding place behind several large boulders), but Pompi found it underwhelming. He scoffed, saying that engines were meant to run on steam, as did the train that would ride atop the giants' newly-laid rails. Spark trains were slow and flimsy. Steam trains, by contrast, were mighty and strong. Strong enough to require two magic rails, in fact.

Pompi's opinion was shared by Thomas Boehringer, the inventor who'd designed the conventional, steam-driven parts of the train that would one day open a path between Meadowlands and The Realm. Boerhringer, in fact, wanted the whole city to run on steam. He'd built a network of tubes running from his steam plants to all parts of the city. From where Clint's group sat, they could see what Pompi said were steam mains running beside the streets and above stone paths he called sidewalks. According to Pompi, the argument over spark versus steam was the city's central debate. Peculiar didn't like the steam mains, or the smaller lines that serviced steam-driven houses owned by Boehringer's customers. He said having giant pipes throughout the city was unsightly (in this beautiful city they all shared, pleasem and thankoo) and dangerous. He spoke publicly, cataloguing laundry lists of scalding injuries and deaths. Boehringer, on the other hand, retorted that all of the steam-tubes were insulated and double-walled and that it was spark — which might stop a man's heart — that was dangerous. Smart citizens knew that the mains were cool to the touch, and that steam was cheaper.

Clint listened to Pompi's descriptions (all recounted in third-person Pompi-speak: "Pompi did this," "Pompi heard that") and felt his interest in Meadowlands turn to scorn. It was as if an artery inside The Realm had been cut, then bled and clotted all over Meadowlands. The debate of "steam or spark" spoke volumes about a soft decadence previously known only to The Realm. How easy must life become before people would fight over the power source for machines that didn't exist in most of the world? Clint remembered Solace, and remembered watching a water reader dip his fingers into a rain barrel to read the shifting of the sands. He recalled how the town's people had hung on that man's words as if they meant life and death... which, in fact, they did. Would their town be pillaged and robbed and burned? Would they die soon? And when the people of Solace *had* worried about their machines, they hadn't worried over the speed of a steam vehicle. Instead, they'd worried over a warped wringer on a hand-cranked washer, because a warped wringer might tear a man's only suit of clothes. Or it might fail to expunge the blood that was spilled through regular living, and daily battles with the dusty sand.

Meadowlands, if it was debating steam versus spark, must harbor few such worries. They wouldn't feel the constant threat of death at their collective door. In Meadowlands, there would be no need for gunslingers. An inept breed of civil lawman would protect them instead. That was the way it always was when there was enough magic and dollars to go around, when even the most annoying trivial pain could easily be healed by the magic in a doctor's kit — at least for those who could afford it.

As dusk descended, they watched the city light like a fire. A soft yellow glow gleamed from glass fixtures along the streets and in the smooth alloy-and-glass buildings. Pompi didn't know whether the night lights were powered by spark or steam, but no one in the group cared.

When the day's light was mostly gone (and after Clint had crossed to the other side of the grassy hill to light a fire in a cleared spot on the prairie), they watched as the steam train in the outskirts lit up and started moving back and forth, chugging down a small track that cupped the city's southern edge and then headed south. The track's southernmost spur was nearby, so Clint and Edward left Mai and Pompi by the fire and walked over to watch the great engine as it passed. It was massive and black, lumbering and slow, and it moved along the tracks tentatively, as if testing itself. Clint could feel power radiating from the engine, even all the way up on the hill. Edward said that the power came from the magic inside of it. The steam was there to start the train, to steer it, and to provide extra power when needed. But the magic vein running beneath the train's tracks (beneath, but inaccessible to any ordinary shovel) was the train's true power source.

"The wealth in this city…" said Clint, letting the thought steep in the cool night air.

"Yar," said Edward. "There is great wealth among thieves."

Clint let Edward's comment go without offering a response. Edward missed Sly Stone, because Sly would always agree with his anti-Realm, borderline-anti-human rhetoric. The Realm was rich with magic but refused to share, they both agreed. To hear Stone talk, he himself was the modern-day Hood of Legend, who'd made it his mission to rob the rich of magic so it could spread down the vein to those who needed it more.

"Which came to Meadowlands first?" said Clint. "The wealth, or Kold?"

"No way to tell."

"Do you think he's found the third Orb?"

"I suspect it, now that I see what the city is becoming. Based on what Pompi said, Meadowlands' growth has been faster than non-magical means could account for. Something must be powering all this expansion, and it's not steam or spark. The air is as thick with magic as the scent of a barber's aftershave."

"Might the magic you sense be coming from the leaking?" Clint asked.

"Nar. The magic I feel is not simply leaking out. It's being generated."

"By the Triangulum Enchantem?"

"Mayhap."

"So you *do* think that Kold has found the third Orb."

"You ask a lot of questions."

Clint was in no mood to play games. He looked the white unicorn in the eye. "Tell me, Edward," he said. "Tell me what you know."

Edward sighed. "The third Orb is called the Orb of Synthesis, and it activates the other two. The Orb of Malevolence represents the dark. The Orb of Benevolence the light. The Orb of Synthesis acts as a catalyst, allowing the others to blend and work together, as they are supposed to."

"And create the Triangulum."

"Yar."

"Which is the deadliest, most dangerous magical item ever to exist."

"*Most powerful* magical item," Edward corrected. "Whether it is dangerous or not depends on who commands it. The same balance that rests in the Triangulum exists everywhere, including between the two of us. In the beginning, there were only unicorns. When humans came, the universe grew polluted with the darkness inside of you." He looked over at Clint, saw his eyebrows furrowing, and added, "Don't be insulted. It was an intended pollution. The magic at the core was always dark and light. You moderated us; we moderated you. Balance. *Synthesis.* You understand?"

"For a change, I think I do. But if Kold has the third Orb, then he has the Triangulum and commands its power, yar? And yet he hasn't breached the wall."

"He's building a railroad that will be able to travel between Realm and Sands."

Clint removed a toothpick from his shirt pocket and parked it in the corner of his mouth. "I figured the completed Triangulum would work more like a bomb that would blow a hole in the wall."

"Maybe it would," said Edward, "if the wall were actually a wall."

"So he just needs time? For the Triangulum to gain power? For the train to be completed? And *then* he'll go inside?"

"I don't know."

"But if that's the case, why would..."

Annoyed, Edward sighed and repeated himself: *"I don't know."*

Clint made his own voice annoyed in retaliation. "Well, what *do* you know?"

"I know that I am better than you. And I know that you are very ugly."

"Mai doesn't think I'm ugly."

"Yar, she does. She just tolerates ugly. She's into ugly. She's an ugly-chaser. She'd take trolls and rub them all over herself. She'd kiss a butt if it spoke to her kindly."

"That's my woman you're talking about," said Clint.

Edward chewed at his big tongue. "Mayhap."

There it was: the same old issue that they kept refusing to discuss. Clint looked toward Edward, staring at the unicorn's big white side.

"You don't know what it was that happened to her," he said. "With Kold, with the magic from the Rio Verde, with the transformation she's undergone... none of it."

"I know *exactly* what happened to her," Edward replied, not looking at Clint.

"What?"

"You wouldn't understand."

"What?"

"She fought Kold's will. She wouldn't give her nature to Cerberus. I was wrong, months ago. I said she'd be a husk forever, and that Kold had stolen who she was when he'd stolen the Orb from her soul. But I was wrong. He took the Orb and left you Mai. A harder Mai. A *better* Mai. A faster, stronger Mai. He ran her through a filter."

"Like coffee through a strainer."

Edward rolled his eyes. "I don't know why I tolerate you."

Clint resisted the urge to retort. They'd had this discussion before, and no matter how many times and in how many ways Clint tried getting Edward to explain, Clint never understood. He only knew that the unicorn saw something different in Mai. It wasn't a bad difference. Edward didn't distrust her, or feel that she was somehow corrupted. Quite the contrary. But there was something in what Edward kept saying (about how the difference in Mai was good and fine but still worth watching) that Clint didn't understand at all. But then again, the gunslinger *never* totally got what Edward said, and had grown used to it in the same way a man could grow used to a loud noise that went on for too long.

"We have to get into the city," Clint said, changing the subject. He watched the train as it passed them, heading south. It would return. They'd followed the rails and knew the spur ended just a few miles further on. The giants would quickly lay rail in both directions — into the Sands toward San Mateo Flats and into The Realm though means that even Edward couldn't conceive — but for now, the train only seemed to make trial runs in order to find its metaphorical legs.

"Yar," said Edward. "But Kold runs the city."

"Diamante," Clint corrected. "Best to start thinking of him as Diego Diamante, entrepreneur and tradesman. Calling him Kold will only raise eyebrows."

"*You* raise eyebrows anyway," said Edward. He gave Clint a small glance. "… ugly."

Clint ignored the insult. "It has to be Pompi who goes into the city."

"I'd figured that much out, genius. Kold knows you. Kold knows me. He rode with Mai behind him for well over four years, so I'd say he knows her, too."

"And Pompi is supposed to be in Meadowlands anyway. He's a giant."

"WOW are you observant."

Edward, who'd never been particularly friendly, had been especially caustic lately. Clint knew Edward well enough to recognize his testiness as nerves, but he didn't know what was bothering the unicorn. Even if he asked, Edward would nar answer him true. Edward carried his own pride, and it weighed a ton.

And then suddenly, watching the sulking unicorn, Clint found himself recalling something Edward said months earlier, in San Mateo Flats: *One day, when there is time and we've played enough of our part, I will explain all of this to you.*

One day.

Meaning: *Not yet.*

It wasn't the first time Clint had felt like his unicorn partner was deliberately withholding information, but it was the first time that Edward's withholding had seemed so willful. It was as if he were teasing Clint — dangling a carrot and taunting him with some kind of foreknowledge, refusing to share what he knew while Clint stumbled stupidly along in the dark.

Clint pushed the stew of frustration in his gut down into his boots. It would do no good to argue now.

"Something has been bothering me," he said. "Can I ask you something without being insulted?"

"It's so hard not to insult you," said Edward. "But I will try."

"Kold is working with the Darkness."

"I believe so. Yar."

"And the Darkness controls the birds. Some of them, anyway."

"Yar."

"So Kold should know we're coming, because we've seen many birds."

"Yar. He should."

"But if he knows, then why haven't we met any resistance?"

Edward sighed. "The answer to that might be complicated."

"He's evaded us for years. He's practically run from us. So if he knows we're here, and he has power, he should send minions to intercept us before we can organize and attack him. Or he should come himself. Or he should erect a shield, or put up some other kind of magical protection. He'd should do anything other than simply let us come, but he hasn't. Why?"

Edward sighed again. He was staring into the distance, watching the retreating spark lights on the back of the Realm train — the one that, if Pompi was correct, would soon cross the wall. Its magic, if that were true, would be beyond comprehension.

"Unless you're implying that Kold doesn't care if we come after him. That he has the Triangulum now, and it makes him so powerful that we're no longer worth noticing. But that can't be it, right?"

The unicorn snorted. He stepped forward and touched the magic rails, tapping them with his hoof, seeming to test their permanence.

"But you're *not* saying that, because that would mean we're too late," said Clint. "We wouldn't just keep going, heading into a losing battle, if it was too late. So we're *not* too late. Right, Edward?"

A breeze ruffled the unicorn's mane.

"Edward?"

Edward chewed his cheek, watching the distant red lights turn to white as the train circled and started rolling back toward Meadowlands.

CHAPTER TWO:
A FANCY PARALLEL

"It's called a what?" Clint said. He heard his own voice as gravelly and low. It also sounded farther away than it should be, like an echo.

Edward mumbled, "A 'fancy parallel.'"

"Everything you do is fancy," said Clint. Then he raised his hand to point. In front of him, the man with the long, lined face raised his own hand, also pointing.

"Look, he sees us," said Clint, his own voice somehow coming out of the man he saw in front of him. "Wow, this is weird."

"You'll get used to it," said Edward.

"Wait, that's not right," said Clint. "It's not 'weird.' It's *fancy.*"

Edward grunted with irritation. "Let's get started."

"Hang on," said Clint. "If we're going to be fancy, let me get my tea." He used two fingers to grasp a tiny imaginary ceramic cup, extending his pinky. He feigned drinking tea. In front of him, the man with the long face (and the surprisingly large hands with surprisingly long fingers) did the same thing.

"Do you want to get into town or not?" Edward huffed.

But Clint wasn't listening. He was too fascinated by whatever Edward was doing to him. He raised his arms, made odd gestures and faces, stood and turned around, and waved a hand in front of his eyes. In front of him, the man he was looking at did all of the same things. Then Clint closed his eyes, and watched as the man in front of him closed *his* eyes. But even after Clint felt his own eyes close, he could still see. Specifically, he could see the man with the long face sitting across from him with his eyes closed. But it was too strange. Clint shot his eyes open again, and when he did, his vision didn't change.

"You still in there, Pompi?" Edward said.

"Pompi here," the giant replied. Pompi's voice sounded incredibly loud. Clint could hear it boom inside his own head like thunder.

"And what do you see, Pompi?"

"Pompi sees Mister Clint. Being funny."

"Do you see me?" the unicorn asked.

"Yar," said Pompi

"What about you, Clint?"

"I see you," the gunslinger answered.

"Pompi," said Edward, "hold your head still. Clint, close your eyes."

Clint closed his eyes. As had happened the last time he'd closed his eyes, he continued to see just fine. He saw Edward and the long-faced man — the man he was still having a hard time believing was himself. He watched as Edward backed up until he was no longer visible. Then the unicorn said, "Can you see me?"

"Nar," Clint said.

"Pompi?"

"Nar," said the giant.

"Tell me when you can see me," Edward instructed. Then Clint began to hear the unicorn take one step forward at a time.

"Pompi sees you, Mister Edward," said Pompi.

"Clint?" said Edward.

"Nar. I can't see you."

Edward took another step. Then another. Then another.

"Anything yet?" the unicorn said.

"Nar."

Clint heard Edward take a fourth step, then a fifth. Finally he saw the tip of something bright white appear at the left side of his field of vision.

"Okay," Clint said. "Now I can see your nose."

Edward came fully into frame and looked at the gunslinger, but Clint actually saw Edward look at the long-faced man rather than back into the eyes he was now using — Pompi's eyes.

"Giants' eyes are much larger than humans', so your brain is not used to processing the extra information," Edward explained. "At a distance of twenty feet, you seem to have lost about two feet of peripheral vision all the way around, so you're only seeing the center of the full picture. Something to keep in mind." The unicorn turned to look at Pompi. "Pompi, try to look directly at what you want us to see. Clint won't see it if it's near the edges."

"Okay."

"What about you?" said Clint, looking at Edward. It was odd not only to hear his own gravelly voice (did he really sound like that?), but to hear it from so far away. Usually it was right there in his head.

"I could see myself when Pompi could. I can assimilate all of the information."

"Great." Another reminder of how unicorns were better than humans. That was all Clint wanted, especially now that Edward was withholding information he needed and acting belligerent about their mission. "And what if bandits come by while we're out here sitting on the rocks with our own eyes and ears turned off?"

"I see and hear both sets of senses — Pompi's and my own," the unicorn said.

Clint rolled his eyes, but because he was seeing through the eyes of the giant, the movement was awkward. Pompi was too far from Clint to determine if he'd successfully rolled his eyes. It was unsettling to roll his eyes and not have his vision roll with them.

"One other thing," Edward added. "Pompi can hear me in his head. But because it's entirely too tricky to establish a connection with you too — giving you his sight and vision are taxing enough, but I'd say it's necessary — you won't hear me when I speak to Pompi. You're an observer, nothing more. Understand?"

"Yar."

Edward explained that it would be like watching a flicker talkie back in The Realm, sitting in a dark room and seeing sights and sounds that had been recorded by someone else. Clint reminded Edward that he remembered almost nothing of his time in The Realm. Edward reminded Clint that he didn't remember much either but asked how he could forget flickers.

"Stop talking to me, Edward. Talk to Pompi. This is so disorienting."

"You will sit and watch. I will be talking to Pompi inside of his head, telling him where to go and what to say. Like this, Pompi." He apparently said something to Pompi, inside his mind so only the giant could hear.

"P.T. Anderson," Pompi said out loud.

"That was a joke," Edward said. "I didn't think you'd ever been to The Realm."

"They show flickers in Meadowlands. Sometimes outside at night, so the giants can see too."

"Don't try to reply to me once you're in town," Edward said. "I can't hear thoughts without trying, and I refuse to try. I don't want you speaking to me out loud. Just listen and do. Then come back when I say. Understand?"

"Pompi understands."

Pompi entered town, walking down the long and shallow rolling grass hills into the outskirts.

It took Clint a while to adjust to the viewpoint since Pompi's eyesight showed him as standing so much taller than normal. Then he realized that the viewpoint wasn't all that different from riding atop Edward's back, so he forced himself to ignore the clumsy two-step of Pompi's walking and mentally superimposed Edward's four-beat walk instead. With that adjustment, things seemed more normal. As he sat on the rock in the prairie, Clint couldn't feel the vibration coming through Pompi's legs as he walked (or what Edward telegraphed up into his crotch as they rode) but could instead feel his own human hands on his human legs, but as long as he didn't move his human body much and pretended he'd gone numb, Clint found he could fall into the role as if he were right there with Pompi.

He/Pompi entered the newer section of Meadowlands (an area Pompi had called NewTown) and walked down a street covered in a flat, perfectly smooth surface that was a bit like rock. He stepped up onto a slightly higher surface covered in the same rocklike finish (one of the paths Pompi had called a "sidewalk" earlier), now closer to the glass and alloy buildings. It was like walking along the boardwalk in a Sands town, but Clint wanted to see the entire area. He wished he could tell Pompi to look around, and wished he could urge the giant to walk on the street instead of off to the side.

There was a humming sound from behind him and something like a stagecoach passed Pompi, except that the stage had no horse to draw it — similar to the wrecks they'd seen by the sides of the streets in San Mateo Flats, but newer and slicker and actually working. It rolled by on wheels made of a black substance, and its innards made a sort of purring noise. Another of the machines followed the first. Then another came from the opposite direction, and Clint realized that Pompi, who'd spent time in Meadowlands, understood something Clint hadn't — a man walked to the side unless he wanted to be in the vehicles' way, and unlike a stage, these vehicles looked like they might run out of control and strike you if you stepped in their path. There were stagecoaches on the streets, too — slick, new-looking stages — and riders on horseback, but even these stayed to the side, in special lanes.

Pompi either knew where he was going or was being directed effectively by Edward. He reached a point where one street crossed another (there were strange posts at the corners where Pompi stood, watching before crossing; the posts would ding and swap one flag for another before the giant would cross), turned, and walked further. He turned again and again, losing Clint entirely. Buildings grew larger and smoother. Clint wondered what the air there smelled like. The vehicles (which were now more plentiful) belched thick black smoke. He wondered if the billows carried the scent of gunsmoke.

Pompi came to a larger vehicle, open all the way around like a coach with only side rails, no windows, and a large rectangular roof. A fair number of people were inside it, some sitting and some standing. A few held onto vertical poles made of a yellowish alloy.

The people wore fancy clothes. They looked like church clothes back in Solace, but cleaner and newer, not beaten and worn down by Sands wind and a thousand washes. Many of the women wore large hats bedecked with bows and ribbons. The men wore hats as well, but not trail hats like Clint's. These people's hats were clean — bright bowlers and the occasional top hat. The women had golden hoops and gems dangling from their earlobes, and wore strings of alloys and gems around their necks. The men wore similar (but smaller) accoutrements on pins adorning their vests and piercing strips of fabric hanging from the fronts of their shirts. The women's faces looked powdered. The men's faces were smooth, and amidst all of that clean skin, a few wore fussy facial hair. Clint saw big bankers' handlebar mustaches, small pencil-thins, and large waxed fancy mustaches. The men who wore beards wore them neat and immaculately trimmed. Clint wondered how they could afford a daily barbering.

Pompi stepped onto the car, stretching two giant fingers to grasp one of the vertical alloy poles. The minute he did, the passengers started to protest, waving him off. One pointed to a sign that Clint could read but that Pompi probably couldn't. It read, *No giants or laborers*.

Pompi stepped off the strange vehicle and it pulled away with a dinging noise, seeming to ride on tracks buried in the street itself, like a train. Something above it touched a set of overhead wires, which sparked.

"We aren't supposed to," Pompi said, apparently speaking to Edward. Clint heard the giant's voice both outside and inside his head. It seemed loud. But after that, he said nothing more. Edward had probably just reminded Pompi not to reply to him.

Clint watched Pompi's vision turn as he climbed a shallow hill in the street, the gunslinger still pretending he was riding Edward instead of seeing through the eyes of a giant.

Pompi wound through the streets of Meadowlands NewTown as vehicles passed. The buildings continued to grow larger. The giant looked up. Pompi either hadn't come into the city much before or things had changed a lot since he'd left, because his gaze was lingering and pondering, as if he were awed by what he was seeing. He looked ahead, then around the street. Many people walked, and the giant had to turn sideways on the sidewalk to avoid crashing into them. He saw a few other giants, but not many. The humans looked at him and at the other giants with expressions that were somewhere between suspicion, fear, and annoyance. Several times, a walker crossed the street to avoid Pompi. Clint found the behavior irritating (he wished he could control Pompi's hands and that he had guns to draw) but the gunslinger could only watch.

Eventually, amidst all of the glitz and chrome, Pompi found a side street where everything was large. Not large like the other buildings (which were tall), but large in proportion. Doorways were enormous, and the businesses' ceilings high. Pompi walked down this new street — again either following Edward's direction or his own memory — and entered what was unmistakably a saloon. Clint felt something inside himself relax. The place wasn't as unfamiliar as everything else he'd seen during the fancy parallel. It had a lot of glass and alloy and far less wood than was common, but at least it looked like a saloon. Clint suddenly wanted an apple brew and a slice of turkey pie more than anything, and considered rummaging for some in his pack by feel but decided against it. Eating and drinking while not being able to see or hear seemed too disconcerting to try.

The saloon's tables and chairs were triple the normal size. But because *everything* in the bar was three times its usual dimensions, Clint barely noticed. The mugs, however, caught his attention. They had relatively normal-looking cups on them, but the handles were gigantic by comparison. The handles were three times as large as the cups they were attached to, and the cups were already large. As Pompi watched, one of the saloon's giants clutched his mug and took a swallow. In his titanic hands, the handle no longer seemed huge. The cup it was attached to now seemed petite and delicate.

Clint saw Pompi approach the bar and raise a finger. The bartender — who was human and the only thing not three times bigger than normal (something that made him look small and elflike by comparison) said, "You have to pay first."

"Okay," said Pompi, seeming to fumble in his pocket for money. Eventually he found some and slapped it onto the bar. The bartender took it and drew Pompi a brew in one of the huge mugs. Pompi sat in front of him. Clint couldn't see the stool because Pompi never looked down, but it had to be enormous.

"It's the owner's policy," said the bartender.

Clint's vision shifted as Pompi looked up. The bartender had hair around his ears and the back of his head, but was bald on top.

"I'd allow you to start a tab. But the owner, he's... well, you understand."

Edward had probably orchestrated all of this. Clint didn't know how, but Pompi had ended up in a giant saloon with a sympathetic human bartender. A stalwart human would have been useless, and a giant bartender would also have been useless because giants were so slow. Pompi's own bovine pace was the reason they'd done the fancy parallel in the first place. Pompi would never have remembered what to ask, wouldn't have noticed the same details as a gunslinger or unicorn, and would have forgotten what he'd observed before he could return and tell Clint and Edward about it.

"Pompi is new in town," the giant said.

"You'll find that humans are rude to you everywhere here," said the bartender, shaking his head disapprovingly. "I don't like it, personally. Giants dug the foundations of these buildings. Giants lifted the girders. Giants are building the railroad. You work on the railroad?"

There was a pause. Edward was probably telling him what to say in reply.

"Pompi works on the railroad. And on the baron's new project — the project for trade."

The bartender's eyebrows rose. A man didn't become a bartender unless he was interested in gossip and hearsay, if only for the sake of catching his share and passing it on.

"The big thing? What they're talking about on the flickershows?"

"Yar."

The bartender whispered low. "What is it? The project, I mean."

"Pompi can't say."

The bartender straightened, pulled a rag from his shoulder, and started wiping the bar top. "Oh, of course you can't. Of course. And it's not like I need to know. Diamante keeps things secret for a reason, you know. For our common good. I understand that. Everyone's upset, saying 'Diamante shouldn't keep secrets from the people in his city,' but if everyone knows everything, those things get messed up. Because it has to do with The Realm, right? And without Diego Diamante, would The Realm even be talking to us out here at the lip of the Sands? How long has The Realm been just a shimmer on the brightest days, no more than a mirage? How many people have tried to reach it, only to find that a year's worth of walking didn't bring it closer? How many of those people went out in search of that mirage, fell asleep, and woke up to find the mirage now *behind* them? But now? The other day, I looked up and I could see parapets. Actual parapets! My wife and I told my kids the fables about Castle Spires, of course, but they're just fairy tales, right? Now, with The Realm growing clearer and clearer by the day, it's like the unreachable fairy tale city is a haven true, and we might someday actually get there!"

Clint felt his human heart beating hard in his human chest outside of the city, up on the grassy hill. *They can see buildings in The Realm!* The gunslinger had never heard of anything like it. Not this level of surety. Not this level of detail. Not this plainspoken, non-rumor-laced, factual recounting of seeing The Realm true as if it were just another place to which one might travel. It was unheard of.

What the bartender described about men seeking The Realm was painfully familiar. Clint and Kold had found themselves chasing the same shadows and the same vague outlines in the clouds from the second they'd surfaced on the wrong side of the wall. They would chase the city's halo for days, then find it suddenly behind them. Then they'd turn and chase it again, but it never drew closer, regardless of their ride's fury. The most difficult thing Clint had ever done had come after a few weeks of that back and forth: he, Kold, Edward, and Cerberus had turned around, putting their backs to the city in the sky. They'd walked off as The Realm loomed at their rear, seemingly just a few days' away behind a thin cloud. It had taken tremendous faith — no, it was the opposite of faith — to convince themselves they would never reach it, and that all they were doing was driving themselves mad. So they'd walked, refusing to look over their shoulders, and a few hours later they'd found themselves staring around at nothing but sand. Looking back, Clint thought it was probably the turning away that had finally broken Kold and started the chain reaction that ended in his co-opting Cerberus's magic, turning both of them dark. Deliberately turning their backs on the kingdom's promise had been like abandoning a child of their own blood. It would have been easier if there had never been a choice — if The Realm had simply vanished. But nar, giving up had required a conscious decision, and that decision had felt like a knife in the gut.

Through their many travels, Clint and Edward had never heard of a city that could faithfully and regularly see The Realm. Yar, Meadowlands was thought of as Realm-adjacent. But that had come before the fractures and the leaking. Today "Realm-adjacent" meant simply that it was still rich with magic — and even that was only a relative thing. But as Clint listened to the bartender, he found himself believing things he'd previously thought impossible. Was Kold actually doing what he'd set out to do? Had he truly found a source of power capable of building a bridge?

"Pompi is a good worker," the giant's voice said. Listening, Clint sharpened his focus. He could almost hear Edward behind those words. Edward, like Clint, had gotten a good bead on the bartender's temperament and biases from what he'd just said, and was surely now crafting a way to mine information from him.

"Sure, sure," said the bartender. "Every giant I've ever met is a good worker. That's why I don't understand the way you're all treated."

"Pompi wants to stay out of trouble."

"Of course."

"But Pompi sees things on the secret project…"

"Yeah?"

"Pompi wonders if some of it is okay by the law, and Pompi has thought about going to the marshal…"

The bartender looked appropriately concerned, but in political situations like in Meadowlands, there was always a love/hate relationship with those in charge. Clint (and of course Edward, who was feeding Pompi his lines) would understand that half of Meadowlands' citizens would hate Diamante and complain about what he was doing to change things in the city, but would trust him because they had to — because they relied on him. Those who complained couldn't sift sand or carry guns or do hard work. If not for Diamante, what would their lives be like? So it was perfectly reasonable for a giant to find something about his job questionable while doing it anyway, and it would be sensible for a bartender to express doubt about the baron's upstanding nature while still praising his work.

"Old Fat Ziggy? Nah, don't go to Ziggy." The bartender looked around conspiratorially, holding his voice low so that only the worried giant who worked on the big man's secret project would hear. "Fat Ziggy is in Diamante's pocket. How can a man do the things the baron has done in the time he's done 'em — right up to opening relations and trade with a floggin' *fantasy world* — without greasing a few wheels? Not that I blame him, understand. Great men, they don't always pay heed to law. Look at Nikolai Peculiar. I heard he has a spark generator in his loft that durn near sets the building on fire when he turns it on. But he's got the whole place to himself so he ain't nar hurting no one. Folks say half of Nikolai's research budget goes to Fat Ziggy, to the building inspectors, to the judges, whoever else he has to pay to keep them off his back. All black money, see? But I say that without Peculiar, we wouldn't have nar a spark of light here. And without Boehringer, who has the same issues, we wouldn't have steam washers and engines to power our flickershows. They say you have to break a few eggs to fry an omelette. Well, with Diamante, it's the same. If he has to do some borderline stuff and pay the marshal in order to do what he does for the city, I say yar, that's okay."

It was too much information, but that was without question why Edward had Pompi speaking to a bartender rather than someone more official. Bartenders were used to talking, and often ended up with many a foot in their large mouths.

"Oh," said Pompi.

"What's the problem, if you don't mind my asking?"

There was another pause. Clint imagined Edward instructing Pompi, telling him what to say. Finally the giant said, "Pompi doesn't know how the big man has the power to do what he's doing."

"Nobody does, do they, friend?" said the bartender. "But you're a step ahead of the rest of us. At least you know what you're working on. The rest of us get the tease on the late flickers. 'Imagine free trade with The Realm!' 'Imagine the ability to partake of The Realm's majesty!' 'Imagine the return of magic to the Sands!' They've got us 'imagining' everything, but seeing nothing. It's enough to drive a fellow mad. Does it have something to do with the train? Can you tell me that? Me and my buddies, we think it must, since they speak of trade, but then there's the thing about magic's return. But that's not possible, is it? How can it be? But then, they used to say The Realm couldn't be reached, and out in the Sands, they still say it can't even be *found*. So is the big project related to the railroad you work on?"

"Yar, Pompi drives spikes on the rails, but…"

"I know, I know, you can't say," said the bartender, waving his dishcloth like a flag of surrender. "But if you lay rail, that tells me more than I knew before you came in." He winked. "Pleasem and thankoo, as they say in the Sands."

Clint, who'd spent most of his remembered years in the Sands, made a mental note not to utter 'pleasem and thankoo' once he himself entered Meadowlands. Or 'tall closet,' probably. Or speak of water readers. Edward could magick them new clothes and make them scrubbed and clean when the time came, but Edward couldn't change Clint's way of speaking, which would give him away just as easily.

As Clint watched, the world became suddenly black. For a moment, Clint thought his connection to Pompi had broken, but then the world returned and he realized that the giant had just winked back at the bartender. Because giants weren't known to be coy, Pompi wasn't especially good at winking. He'd done it with both eyes at once.

Pompi upended his brew, and then Clint saw his vision move up and down as the giant nodded to the bartender. "Thankoo for the brew," he said.

"And thanks for the insider information." The bartender winked again. This time Pompi didn't try to wink back.

The giant stood. Clint saw his vision swing around as Pompi turned and walked toward the door. The same giants he'd noticed as he'd come in were still there, still staring moodily into their mugs with the giant handles.

Pompi left the saloon, turned right, and resumed walking down the road into NewTown Meadowlands. A man on horseback passed him, tipping his hat as he did. The man must have been from out of town, since the locals didn't seem to feel like kindness to giants was necessary. Pompi returned the nod, then rounded the corner and moved back out of the giant-scale alcove. Humans began to avoid him again. Clint pictured himself riding high, atop the unicorn's back.

Toward the center of the city, the already-tall buildings grew even taller. The air became louder. Clint caught snippets of conversations as the giant breasted the crowd. Twice he heard debates involving steam versus spark power. Once he heard a woman blabbing on to another woman about a magic cooker she'd purchased for an absurd price. Three other times he heard groups talking about matters involving The Realm, Diamante and his train, trade, or all of the above. The crowd was excited. Meadowlands was booming; the rich were getting richer; the horizons held nothing but promise.

Once Pompi made it through the crowd's thickest ribbon in the largest alloy-and-glass part of the city (which still boasted many horses and carriages; their contrast against the slick, speedy vehicles was downright bizarre), the citizens walking the stone walkways became fewer again and the buildings shrank again in size. Glitz slowly gave way to older structures, and Clint realized that Pompi was now headed back out of town, nearing Meadowlands' original section, which he'd referred to as OldTown.

As he rounded a corner, two giants, six albinos (Clint recognized them as more of the Teedawge archetypes they'd faced in Baracho Gulch), and a small, fat, bald man stepped in Pompi's way.

"Hold on there, feller," the small man said, flashing a star. "I'd like you to come with me."

"Why?" said Pompi.

"Ain't nothin'," he said, extending his arm to indicate a shallow alcove between two buildings. "Just step in here for now, and we'll go down to the station later if the situation warrants."

Pompi paused, then said, "What did Pompi do?" Clint found himself amused to note that although Edward had surely fed him the line, Pompi hadn't been able to recite it without substituting his name for "I."

The plump man didn't answer. Instead, the giants and Teedawge archetypes came to Pompi's side and nudged him into the alcove, where the sky was mostly hidden and it was darker. Pompi looked down and watched as the small man sat back to lean against the wall. The archetypes milled, chuckling, staring down at their hands. The giants drew large tarps from a concealed pocket and started to shake them. Clint realized with surprise that the tarps were actually gloves, and that they were pulling them onto their massive hands.

"Your name is Pompi Bobo," said the fat man. It wasn't a question.

"Yar."

The man touched his chest, fingers tented. "Harvey Ziglar," he said. "Call me Ziggy. Marshal of Meadowlands. Since way back when Meadowlands was but a hollow haunted by you whoppers rather being than served by you, in fact." He gestured at Pompi and his two largest escorts.

Pompi said, "Elf Meadows doesn't belong to humans."

Clint winced. Edward had probably muttered that line subconsciously, with no intention for Pompi to repeat it.

Ziggy cocked his head. "That so?"

"Pompi didn't do anything wrong," he said, back to the script.

"Well, see, I disagree. We got a ring from a giant friend of ours, says he heard you saying some funny things about my friend Diego in the saloon. Maybe saying too much. The bartender said too much too, but never mind him; one of my deputies is paying him a visit. He also said your name was Pompi, so I looked it up. Turns out we had a deserter a while back with that name."

"Pompi didn't do anything wrong," he repeated.

"Maybe Pompi came with a group. With other dissenters."

"Nar."

"Maybe Pompi isn't telling me everything he knows."

"Nar."

Clint's vision jerked toward the alcove floor as something massive struck Pompi's midsection. The thing pulled back and Clint realized that it had been one of the other giants' fists. His vision jerked to the side, sent there by a giant's knee.

Fist. Knee. Foot. Fist.

A massive hand flew toward Clint's vision, struck Pompi hard in the face, and sent his world to black.

CHAPTER THREE: DULY DISGUISED

Thanks to Pompi's tutorial about Meadowlands' layout, they knew where Fat Ziggy and his crew would take their oversized prisoner. And thankfully — because among the three of them, only Mai was remotely comfortable in larger towns — that prison was outside the tall buildings of alloy and glass.

From the hills outside Meadowlands, they could make out the town's odd geography. It had started much like every other town in the Sands — small, dusty, and poor — and that vintage town still existed in the area Pompi had called "OldTown." The newer, shinier city had blossomed from its northwest side, up where the magic was strongest, nearer to the mountains. The law and oldest businesses clunked on in OldTown while the fancier ones grew out in NewTown. It was like a country and city mouse had set up residence as neighbors, each with a different impression of what living quarters ought to look like.

After Pompi's fancy parallel connection went black, Clint felt himself tumbling down a deep corridor of nothingness until he struck the bottom — a rock seat where he found his hearing and vision return to join his tactile sensations, which had never left. His eyes fluttered open, then flinched back to shut as he fought disorientation. His own eyes seemed tiny, his vision incomplete. Everything too low to the ground.

Slowly he came back to his senses, opening his eyes and ears to see a beautiful, brown-haired woman kneeling in front of him, reaching forward to take his hands.

"Clint."

"It's okay. I'm coming around now."

"You looked like you were going to faint."

"Gunslingers don't faint."

She mimicked his voice: " 'Gunslingers don't faint.' Yar, they almost do. What happened? What did you see?"

Edward walked into the circle of their dead fire, tossing his head, snorting. "They got him."

"They got him?"

Clint squeezed Mai's hands before standing — standing slowly, because he was still fighting disorientation after his time as a giant. Her hands were the same, despite the changes she'd undergone. But the things those hands could now do were amazing. Brilliant. Unthinkable.

"They got Pompi," Clint explained. "The local marshal and his cronies — two giants and a bunch of those xombie things we fought in Baracho. They beat him up, then…. what?" He looked at Edward. All he knew was that suddenly, Pompi had been unable see.

"They knocked him out," said Edward. "One of them probably hit him with something on the back of the head."

Mai shook her head. "Why?"

Clint rummaged in one of the packs, found a waterskin, took a swallow, then returned it. "They knew who he was. And they heard him talking about Diamante."

"Ruthless land barons don't like subversives," said Edward. "Now I feel responsible."

Clint didn't reply. Edward usually acted like a jerk, but in the end, he was strangely loyal. Of course he felt responsible for getting Pompi in trouble, and of course they'd need to ride into OldTown — where the marshal's station sat — to rescue him.

"I'll go," said Mai.

"Nar." Clint shook his head. "Kold barely left you living."

"I've changed since then." Mai extended her hand and a can of beans zoomed into her palm.

"Mayhap too much," Edward said. "That's the problem. I suspect Kold does indeed control the Triangulum. My guess is that he found the third Orb months ago, and has been using it to power the city. But that poses a problem for us. The Triangulum will call to you and you will call to it."

"So I can help you find it," said Mai.

"In time. But you can and will also expose us while we're trying to rescue Pompi. Try to understand, Mai. To the Triangulum, you shine like a beacon."

Mai put her hands on her hips. Clint knew that look well. It meant that she understood, but that understanding didn't fence her irritation.

"I see. And nobody else here is enchanted?" Mai stared at the magical unicorn.

"I was getting to that." Edward looked at Clint for a long, serious moment. "I must do something to hide myself. And just so you're warned, this will disturb you."

Edward's coat started to shimmer. Then from its bright white, dirt-repellant color, it faded to a dusty gray. Light smoky spots began to blot his rump. He left a white splotch — now an ordinary, non-glowing white — down his nose, creating a blaze amidst the gray.

"That doesn't disturb me," said Clint.

"I'm not done."

The unicorn's horn began to glow, then shrink. But nar, that wasn't right. It wasn't *shrinking*. It was *retracting*. The entire horn was descending into Edward's head as if being pulled down from the inside. Clint watched it happen, his mouth open. Edward's horn was longer than his head was thick. Where was it going? Into his neck?

When the horn was gone, its old spot shimmered and became gray hair. Edward, the magical unicorn, was now a horse.

"I don't know what to say." It was as if Clint were looking at someone else. He felt stupid even speaking to Edward, since the equine before him clearly wasn't a unicorn. Who spoke to a horse, except for that talking horse of the old songs — coincidentally also named Edward?

The horse said, "Don't say anything."

"I didn't know you could do that."

Edward grunted. "It wouldn't be the first time unicorns have had to hide their true appearance."

"You look like a horse."

"I can still magick you into every rock on the way down," said Edward. "I'd have to peek my horn like a turtle from its shell, but I'll risk the exposure to hurt you if you say that again."

Mai couldn't stop herself from slowly circling the no-longer-a-unicorn and stroking his sides. Luckily Edward appreciated the touch of a human woman, or else he'd see what she was doing for what it was — assessment of a common mount.

"This will hide your magic?"

"My horn is like an antenna. Without it, I don't broadcast."

Clint slapped Edward's gray neck. "You're going to need a saddle."

"I know."

"And a bridle. And reins. Ooh! And a bit!"

"If you try to put a bit in my mouth, I will bite off your fingers and swallow them without chewing."

"What kind of cowboy rides without a bit? And spurs?"

"The kind that rides with commoner's guns."

The remark felt to Clint like what Clint's "horse" comment must have felt like to Edward. His mouth hung open. He felt his belt seem to lift, looked up to see a small glowing spot on the top of Edward's head with a tiny tip of horn peeking out, then looked down and saw his gun belt unbuckling itself. It fell without ceremony into the dirt.

"Leave them with Mai," Edward said. "And Mai, don't try to shoot them."

Clint's jaw was still open. "I need my guns!"

"We're entering Meadowlands. No magical Orb woman, no unicorn, no marshal's guns with their magical powders. You can't sense the strength of the Triangulum's enchantment. Even if you could hide the fact that you had two guns and that they had seven-shot tumblers, the mere presence of your bullets' powders might give us away. And if we get into trouble and you fire a shot, that *definitely* will. So now you're a commoner. Pretend it's the academy days. You can still fire a six-shot iron, can't you?"

Mai reached into her saddlebag and extended a new gunbelt to Clint. It was El Feo's.

"Come on," said Edward, annoyed. "Take it and put it on. At least you don't have to be a horse."

Clint buckled the bandit's gunbelt around his waist, withdrew the shooter, and found it to be light ("like a toy") but accurate. He climbed onto Edward's saddled back and they began their approach into town. Both of Sly Stone's shotguns were tucked into Edward's saddle, but the magic in them had been keyed to his hand. Clint had tried them on the trail, finding the guns plenty handy but now entirely conventional. They would act as handy backup weapons.

Clint wore a new shirt with curly stitched accents at the top of the chest. The shirt was a light shade of blue, almost periwinkle, and made Clint want to vomit. Edward had magically shined his boots, bringing out a glimmer that Clint had nar seen in them before, and Mai had given him a stiff hat she'd picked up at a trader's stand. Under the hat, Mai had combed and oiled Clint's hair, and had wiped the trail grime from his face. With his makeover complete, Mai assessed him and declared him quite dapper. Clint gandered as best he could in a small hand mirror and declared himself ridiculous. Edward said that he didn't want to hear a dagged thing about anyone looking ridiculous. Then he began making dumb-horse jokes in order to deflect.

Mai stowed Clint's seven-shot guns, promising to protect them with her life. Given what they'd seen of Mai lately (she didn't seem to have paused her transformation and was still somehow improving), that was a promise with teeth.

The fancy man and his gray horse, duly disguised and both mumbling, made their way across the green, grassy plain and down a set of rolling hills. They crossed a valley, skirted the alloy, steam, and spark metropolis of NewTown, and entered the more familiar-looking OldTown. The first building they encountered was a livery stable. Clint dismounted and hitched Edward to a post. The unicorn who was now a horse threatened to disembowel the gunslinger, but Clint said that no respectable fancy cowboy would ever leave his horse untethered, given that horses were so stupid. Then, snickering, he walked into the barn and called up into the hay, looking for the proprietor.

After a few shouts, a balding man with wild hair sticking out above his ears and a crazy graying beard matted to his chest shambled down a ladder and approached him, broadcasting his welcome.

"Yar!" said the man.

"Evenin'," said Clint, touching his hat and trying to sound appropriately yokelish. "I'm looking for a man of mine. Came into town to inquire about some supplies but hasn't returned. Big man. Giant, in fact."

The man scratched his head, then his rear. "Lots of giants around here."

"This one came from outside, not from the mountains. We fear he might have gotten himself into some trouble because he wasn't officially employed and wouldn't know the ways of the town. He's hot-tempered." That was a lie, of course, but Clint already knew where Pompi was. He was merely fishing for whispers.

"Well, he'd be the one in with Fat Ziggy, then. They brought a giant in just a bit ago, in fact. Needed a wagon to do it, so everyone came out to watch while they dragged the giant inside. Was a bit of a spectacle since giants don't never really misbehave. But Ziggy, he's into spectacle. Ever since Diamante touched him to marshal over the whole of Meadowlands and gave him that crew of thugs, he's been flashing his badge more than actually getting his job done. Wants to be Diamante's right hand, he does."

"We need to get him out," Clint said. "We bought our giant fair and square, and have a substantial investment in his person."

The man squinted at Clint. "Well now, that's not true, is it? You're not the kind of guy what buys a giant."

Clint forced himself to stay calm, though his heart was beating hard. They'd carefully disguised themselves, but within a minute, a livery stable owner had seen right through him. What had they left hanging in the breeze? And what else might give them away? Did they have any chance at all?

"What do you mean?" said Clint.

"Well, you're a Realm marshal, ain't you?"

"Um…"

"Friend, look at your hands."

Clint looked down. His right hand was open in front of his torso, gesturing as he talked to the frizzy-haired old-timer. His brain had effectively told that hand to be casual, and since it was his dominant hand, it had obeyed. But Clint's non-dominant left hand, idle, had remained on autopilot. Right now, it was poised in a long-fingered claw at his side, his elbow cocked outward, hovering above a pistol that wasn't there.

"My grappy was a Realm marshal," said the stable owner. "He retired with honors after years and years and years of service to the royals and came out here to the Sands to start a simple life, and here he met my grammy and they had appy. Till his dying day, long after he turned in his guns and surrendered his unicorn, grappy held his hand like that, like he was ready to draw. Said it got into his blood. Grammy thought it was funny, tried to break him of it since he always looked like he was waitin' to strike. She'd give him things to hold in that hand, but his draw stance never totally went away."

Clint forced his hand to hang at his side. "I'm just a merchant," he said.

"Hands."

Clint looked down again. This time his right hand was poised. It was the correct hand this time, given that it was where he wore his single pistol, but nobody other than a seasoned gunslinger literally *couldn't* keep his hands from being constantly at the ready.

"Look," said the old-timer. "My name is Percy Noodle, and I'm your friend. I ain't gonna tell nobody about whatever you're doing, since no Realm marshal that weren't renegade would ever pretend to be nothing else. And no Realm marshal who were still with The Realm would be looking to spring that there giant, what folks say was mouthing off about Diamante."

Clint started to object, but Noodle held up a wrinkly old hand and continued.

"It's okay. I been here since before Fat Ziggy, back when this town was wind spit. This city may be in love with the new baron, but that's only because all that matters to them is steam and spark and that fancy black train they think will make 'em rich. But I can see how The Realm grows more visible, and I know from my grappy what that means for the magic — and, hey, what *The Realm* means for the magic true."

"I don't know what you're yapping about," said Clint.

Noodle extended a finger, pointing at Edward. "*You* know, don't you?"

Edward opened his big supposed-to-be-a-horse lips and said, "Yar, I know."

Noodle showed no surprise at the talking gray horse. Instead, he walked over to the side of the barn door, retrieved a bottle of apple brew from a crate filled with ice, and shoved it into Clint's left hand. Then he held Clint's shoulder and pointed down the dirty OldTown central street.

"Your man is in the building with the star out front," he said. "And if you ever need anything, Marshal, you come back here to me. You *and* your unicorn."

"He's not a unicorn," Clint said, grasping at straws.

"Keep that brew in your hand to occupy it and you'll be fine," said Noodle. "And if you'd abide some advice, I'll offer you this: try not to kill them lawmen until they need killing, no matter whose pocket they're in. In Meadowlands, one thing's nar changed: If you start something, you'd best be prepared to finish it."

CHAPTER FOUR: MERCY BARLOWE

They had to buy Pompi to free him from jail.

Clint was counting on the law's corruption in Meadowlands as the key to the giant's emancipation and wasn't disappointed. It didn't matter what Pompi was in jail for, and didn't matter that his contract was with the railroad. It didn't matter that he'd been publicly expressing reservations about the benevolence of the great Diego Diamante and what he was doing with the railroad. Lawless towns were far more honest than places like Meadowlands. True, Meadowlands had law and order, but crooked lawmen never served the greater good. They served the man with the biggest whip or wallet, and on the day Clint stepped inside the station, his wallet still held plenty of Paladin Havarow's gold coins.

The two identical albinos manning the station looked askance at Clint and the apple brew inexplicably clutched in his left hand, but once he pulled out his coins and offered to buy back "his giant," the Teedawge archetypes forgot all about the prisoner's supposed offenses and who he may or may not belong to. The lawmen had bills to pay after all, and should anyone come later to claim the giant, they could always say they'd accidentally killed him during torture. He was only a giant, after all.

Pompi had been beaten beyond beaten. His big eyes were swollen shut and black. His face was a mess of scratches and scuffs. His clothing was torn and bloody, and one arm and one leg seemed either badly sprained or broken. With the help of a giant attendant (one of the two giants who'd beaten him, Clint noticed while gripping his apple brew almost hard enough to shatter the bottle), they were able to get him outside, but once outside and unsupported, Pompi couldn't stand. He was semiconscious and didn't seem sure who Clint and Edward were. He was bleeding from his ears. One of the women who came out to watch the commotion said that between the dizziness and the bleeding ears, it probably meant a concussion — something that was extremely rare for a giant on account of it being so hard to do, and often fatal. The woman suggested they rush Pompi to the town doctor, who lived out on the edge of OldTown in a white ranch house with a picket fence.

Clint looked at Edward, silently asking if there was anything he could do. The gray horse gave a subtle shake of his head. He couldn't heal Pompi in front of so many witnesses, and even without the witnesses he had to remain inert. Using magic inside of Meadowlands would be like ringing a dinner bell for Dharma Kold.

Pompi couldn't walk, and Edward couldn't help to carry him other than as a normal horse. He was strong, but without magic, he wasn't strong enough to drag a giant up a sloping dirt street. But Percy, the livery stable owner, had been watching, and once Pompi fell, Percy ran back to his stable and returned with a team of four horses and an extra saddle girth (especially long and wide, used on his draft horses) and looped it across Pompi's chest and under his armpits. He tied the girth to his team of horses, then used a second girth to pin Pompi's hands to his sides. And in that way, they dragged the giant to see the doctor.

Doctor Mercy Barlowe was a thin man with a short, neatly trimmed beard and squeaky clean spectacles. He saw Noodle, Clint, Edward, the four-horse team, and the ailing giant on their approach and ran outside to greet them, bag in hand. He said he'd never treated a giant, but promised to do his best. And his best, in the end, turned out to be good enough.

A few hours later, Barlowe yanked a blanket over the unconscious giant, who he'd had to leave in the front yard. He promised Clint and Edward that Pompi could stay until he recovered, adding that Diamante wouldn't like it. But the spiteful way he said it made Clint feel as if Diamante's displeasure was reason enough, on its own, for Barlowe's allowance.

Clint reached into his pouch for gold, but Barlowe held up his hand.

"I won't take your money," he said. "But there is one thing I'll accept as payment for this service rendered."

Clint raised his eyebrows. "Name it."

"Your party's company," he said. "I have extra beds. And a stable."

Clint shook his head. "We couldn't impose."

"I insist," said Barlowe. "Besides, you won't be doing yourself any favors by staying in OldTown tonight. No innkeeper will want you. They all know why this giant was in lockup to start with. OldTown is afraid of Diamante."

"And you aren't?"

"I'm the town's only doctor," he said. "All that steam and alloy and spark and growth? They bring their money. They bring their supplies. But they did not bring doctors, and none among them have what they need to learn. They have a few Magic Aid kits, of course, and those ointments will heal cuts and even a broken bone if it's not snapped right in half. But this town teeters on the unsustainable. They don't think of health and medicine in the same way they don't think on other things of good sense. Unless they can open The Realm like Diamante promises or until they can scour the Sands and persuade another trained physician to come here, I'm all that stands between Diamante's men — or any of the people down there — and death by a slow-bleeding gunshot, or a heart issue, or any other among a thousand things."

"I can't believe that," said Clint.

"Believe it." Barlowe pushed the spectacles up high on his nose. "This town is full of magic, but none where it matters. It's like false magic, which can light sparks but cannot heal. The only true white magic in this town is what you brought with you."

Clint looked around, again feeling like he'd been punched in the face. Even with the apple brew clutched in his hand, he'd never felt so transparent.

"Don't worry," said Barlowe, reading the gunslinger's reaction. "Nothing gave you away. Percy Noodle told me, is all."

"Percy told you — !"

"Oh, don't be mad at old Percy. He comes off like a coot, but he's sound of mind. He won't share your secret, and the only reason he told me is because he knows I'd want to help."

Clint sighed, then closed his eyes. Never before had he felt so out of control for so long. Barlowe didn't seem like a threat, but Clint felt as if he and Edward shouldn't have bothered to disguise themselves at all, for all the good it was doing them. They could have ridden in as a two-gun marshal on a white unicorn, magic blasting. Even if Kold came at them, at least Clint wouldn't feel like an impotent actor caught in a bad role.

"Why?" Clint asked. "Why would you want to help us?"

"Marshal," said Barlowe, "I've devoted my life to easing pain and suffering, but now there are men in town who live and breathe it.

They won't hurt me. They need me. So please. Stay. I will tell you what I know, and mayhap in return, you can help me with my mission, as a healer."

"Yar," Clint said, patting his ordinary pistol, "as long as you don't mind that I use different instruments to do my healing."

CHAPTER FIVE: WORLDS WILL END

Clint told Barlowe that their party was incomplete, and that they had to ride out to retrieve another. Barlow said he had plenty of room at his house, and invited the gunslinger to bring back all the subversives he wanted. So Clint mounted his gray horse (a horse which complained endlessly about its tack, saying it itched something fierce) then rode out into the open range to retrieve Mai.

When they found Mai, she was sitting cross-legged in the dirt, her hands on her knees and palms to the sky. Her eyes were closed, and her hands were glowing. In the dark, the glow was bright. Clint was surprised to see she hadn't lit a fire, but when he walked up and touched her, he found her warm. She didn't respond to his touch.

"Mai."

Behind Clint, Edward's horn re-emerged and his coat flushed white, popping into its usual brilliance. A pink bolt of energy shot toward the saddle and reins, which fell to the ground. Edward sighed and heaved with relief.

"Mai," Clint repeated. He tapped her cheek.

Her eyes opened, and she looked surprised.

"What are you doing?"

"Sitting," she said. She looked around, confused. "How long have I been sitting like this? It's dark out!"

"What do you mean?"

She stood, looking briskly at the campsite. "I don't know. I don't remember. I watched you leave. I ate some turkey pie from the pack. I remember preparing to make the fire, but then… then this."

Clint asked a few more questions, but Mai had no idea what she'd been doing, how long she'd been doing it, or what it all meant. Clint, admonishing, told Mai she could have been killt. But when he said it, she locked eyes with him and told him quite sternly that being killt was never a danger true.

Edward had no idea what had happened either, but it was late and they were tired, so they gathered their supplies, obscured the camp, and walked back toward Barlowe's as two humans and a unicorn. When they got close enough, Edward concealed himself again to buffer his magic from Kold and the Triangulum's vision. He refused to wear the saddle, and instead dragged it in the dirt behind him.

A mile or so from Barlowe's, Edward stopped. He turned, looked at Mai, and told her that he could feel her radiance and that her magic was going to give them away. If they got much closer to town, Kold would sense her for sure. So he ran forward alone, leaving Clint and Mai to wait behind in the dark.

A few minutes later, he returned with a vial and gave it to Mai to drink. She asked what it was. Edward said it would suppress her new abilities just as Edward had suppressed his own by hiding his horn. She asked why a country doctor would have an elixir to suppress magic, but Edward simply repeated his order to drink it. She might already be too powerful and too close, and every passing second threatened to expose them. So Mai did as Edward instructed, and almost immediately she told them she felt a chill through her marrow. Edward protruded his horn slightly, seeming to test her, then declared her safe. Inert and more or less powerless, but safe. Then he added that with Clint's sidearms buried back at the old camp and with Mai's magic subdued, the pair would be defenseless if separated from Edward. Clint tried to tell him that he had a sidearm (be it conventional or not) and that he was still plenty deadly. Edward murmured in an unconvinced way and walked on.

They arrived at the doctor's house to find Barlowe waiting at the door. He took Mai's hands in his, then led her to a chair on a patio lit by a conventional lantern. The spark lines, he said, didn't run out this far.

The doctor seemed quite interested in Mai. Clint wondered at this and even felt his own hand twitching near his gun, but the doctor's motives seemed true, and Edward had vouched for him on the trip out to retrieve Mai. Clint had asked Edward how he could vouch for a man he didn't know. Edward gave him a stern look and said that once upon a time, he'd partnered with an ugly man he'd never met before — and that partnership, founded immediately and based solely on a probing of the man's honor — had been bound by magic and had done quite well so far.

"How much did you get?" the doctor asked Mai, sitting with his knees very near hers.

Mai looked confused. "Get?"

"Edward asked for an elixir of repression. I know you have the consumption. It's all right. I have enough elixir to keep it down, and I can make more."

Mai shook her head. "I'm sorry. I don't know what you're talking about."

"Magic consumption," Barlowe said to Mai. Then he turned to the unicorn. "Did she touch a vein?"

"Nar," said Edward.

"Too near a stitcher? Did she catch a spray?" His eyes darkened. "The railroad. You were at Diamante's railroad."

"It's not consumption," Edward said.

Clint looked from the doctor to the unicorn and back. Edward was still disguised as the gray horse. He wouldn't be able to extend his horn until they confronted Kold, and by then it probably wouldn't make a difference. Edward had already warned Clint that if Kold had the Triangulum, which he almost certainly did, they'd be outmatched. Accordingly, Edward claimed to be working on a plan to thwart Kold and Cerberus without facing the dark rider and his unicorn of a different color. Clint kept asking how it was going. Edward kept refusing to answer.

"What is magic consumption?" asked Clint.

The gray horse turned to look at him, sidelong. "You remember outside of Nazareth Shiloh, when I stitched the magic vein?"

"Yar."

"And afterward, do you remember how I lost my memory of who I was and what I could do?"

"Yar," said Clint. Edward had forgotten how to use his magic and had believed himself a horse. Clint refrained from mentioning that right now, Edward *was* a horse. It would only infuriate him.

"That kind of thing comes from an overabundance of magic. I got a kind of feedback when I stitched the vein, but unicorns can withstand such a thing… apparently. But the same amount of magic would have killt you, had it struck you directly."

"It's like cancer," said Barlowe. "You know cancer?"

"Yar."

"It's like that. Magic consumption spreads and suffocates the natural energies of the people it affects. There was once magic everywhere in the sand, but now it's concentrated in veins. The magic veins aren't supposed to be exposed, but when Realm operations open them, they're not just breaking earth. You can't dig to find a magic vein. It takes magic to open them, and magic to stitch them back. So when they're exposed to the world after a fracture — or a willful cutting — they're dangerous. More and more, men are coming to me with exposure. Usually those working on stitching rigs or on top-secret projects that seem somehow related to Diamante's railroad. It's fatal if allowed to spread. Elixirs will keep it at bay, halting its scatter by suppressing the magic from expression. I assumed that was what it was with you." He touched Mai's hand.

"She hasn't been exposed," said Edward in a "and that's all I have to say" tone of voice. Clint noticed the unicorn didn't say that Mai wasn't infected in some way, though, and thought back to the drink she'd taken from the Rio Verde back in Baracho Gulch. Edward had described it like a magic kickstart — a hard reset of her nature. But what *was* Mai's nature?

They sat outside for a long while, until the doctor finally headed for bed. Once gone, Edward nodded to Clint and Mai and led them a short way away from the house. Clint carried a lantern, and they made palaver in the doctor's backyard, well away from the porch. The unicorn's intent was clear. He'd told Clint and Mai how much he believed in the doctor's soul, but added that what he wanted to discuss was too delicate to entrust with anyone beyond the three of them.

"Mai," said the disguised unicorn as they sat around the lantern, wrapped in blankets. "It's time you tell us what happened when you rode with Kold."

She shook her head. "I don't remember. I told you."

"Try."

"I can't."

Edward sighed, then stared at her. "Try harder. I can't use magic and you can't use magic. So be as human as you can be. Look back. After Solace, what do you remember?"

After a moment, she whispered, "Nightmares."

"Tell me."

"It's vague. I remember a house so large that at times, I'd be running down hallways unable to touch the walls. A great space, with a spiral staircase wrapping downward toward forever. Something was behind me. I remember a maze. Or a game. It's… it's vague."

"You're doing fine." The unicorn's nod said to continue.

"You told me that I rode with Kold for years, but to me, it felt like one night. One long dream. You know how time stretches in dreams. One moment I was in Solace, and the next we were in Baracho Gulch. I came back so fast, I might not have believed you about the years you swear passed if I couldn't see it in your face and eyes. You are a different man than you were on the day we nearly hitched. A different man, even, than the hard piece of leather you were when we met. Then, you were battered. Now, it's like something in you has died. Like parts of your soul have been tortured to death."

Something squirmed in Clint's gut, but he pushed it down. It was nar for a man of sand and iron to feel.

"But that's all I have. One dream, one night, barely remembered. Every so often I come across a kind of vague recollection, something new I'd forgotten, but it's like a daze inside a dream. *Beyond* forgotten. Like a memory from another life. I see things that I know I've never witnessed. And I remember Kold as you must have fought him. I remember the dark unicorn as if…"

"Yar?" Clint prompted.

"I don't know. I remember fighting him."

But she'd never fought Cerberus. She'd been magicked onto the dark unicorn's back, where he'd plundered her soul.

"Maybe it's part of the dream, but I remember fighting him. Fighting him like I can fight now. With magic. I seem to remember a battle. Like maybe *he* was the beast stalking my dreams."

"And you won?"

"I don't know."

Clint looked at Edward. In the lamplight, his face looked long and hollowed-out, like the man in the moon.

"What is this, Edward?" he said.

Edward kicked at the dirt around the lantern.

"I've been trying to make sense of what I know to be true and what I suspect," he said. "Kold has the Triangulum; I can feel it. He has the third Orb. So why hasn't he breached the wall?"

"Mayhap he's building an army," said Clint. "The people of this town seem to think he's up to something. We know he's building a railroad. He could be gathering numbers, waiting until he can storm inside in force."

"Mayhap," said Edward. "All I know is that I feel the Darkness more than ever." He turned to Clint. "But do you remember what I said the Darkness wanted?"

"More Darkness," said Clint.

"Right. It wants to release more of the dark Core magic. It wants to upset the balance. We know it's working with Kold. We saw it in Independence Lee's birds and I suspect it was also at work, indirectly, through El Feo and his drones. The Darkness doesn't care about getting into The Realm, but it *does* care about opening cracks. That's most possible at the fractures, and the largest fracture is where The Realm broke away."

"So you're saying…"

"I think that one reason — not the whole reason, but one reason — that Kold hasn't breached the wall yet is because he wants to let his partner have its play. The Triangulum, even at partial power, would work like jamming a pry bar in a crack and splitting it further. Darkness escapes, joins the Darkness that's already here. It powers the city, but while it does, it secretly pries at the cracks, leaking dark magic that goes into birds, bandits, maybe archetypes. Parson Jarmusch clones; I have no idea. But why? And all I can conclude is that if Kold controls the Triangulum and the Darkness is with Kold, the two are working toward something that Kold believes will serve them both. Something that will release Darkness, *and* build soldiers, *and* upset the dark/light balance on this plane, *and* allow Kold to return to The Realm to do whatever it is that he wants to do. Mass the power at the fracture, and only then turn it up and rip down the wall. Darkness storms in. The cracks widen."

"That doesn't sound good."

"I could be wrong," said Edward.

"But you don't think you are."

Edward looked at Clint and Mai across the light of the lantern. "Nar."

"So now what?"

"We have to find him. We have to find the Triangulum. We have to see what he's doing. Until then, it's all just guesswork."

"And then what?"

Edward looked at them for a long time. "I don't expect you to understand this, but magic cannot be created or destroyed. It can only be converted from one form to another, and can really only be moved around. It's like a game of Risk. Each team starts with equal forces, but in this game, none of the armies can be removed from the board. Magic Risk is a game of misdirection and gathering of forces. Incidences of light and dark — an individual unicorn or an individual sand dragon, say — can be destroyed. But the amount of magic itself remains constant. In the end, neither force can win, and neither can lose. But just as a storm gathers when there is too much warmth meeting too much cold, so is there turbulence when magic clumps and congeals."

Clint couldn't follow any of it, and based on what he could see of Mai's face, neither could she.

"Are you saying that Kold is preparing for the apocalypse? Why would he do that?"

"Kold is out for Kold. But he's toying with powers he nar understands. No man can understand it. If he plays his game well, he'll use the Darkness for his own purposes without shearing the world wide open and creating such an imbalance that it will bring about your apocalypse. But I don't think that's likely."

"And then the worlds will end," said Mai.

"Life will end. The societies we've built will end. The beings that represent clumps of dark and light in mortal bodies will end. Everything you know and see and remember and believe and touch and smell and taste. All of *that* — every last bit of it — *that* is what will end. But the worlds? The magic? Nar. Those things will be just fine long after all we've built is dust."

CHAPTER SIX:
ONE COWBOY AND
ONE HORSE

Clint missed Sly Stone.

Stone, with his giant orange hair and twin magic shotguns, would have been upbeat as they left Barlowe's house. He would have narrated tales of chili and times on the trail, making days a few months distant sound like polished memories from his childhood. He would have looked forward to their task, simultaneously seeing it as hopeless and eagerly anticipating a challenge. He would have said things like, "This is where we separate the men from the boys" and "Time to see if you have hair in your pits." Then, because he was Sly, he would have looked at Mai and added a feminine version of both aphorisms, stepping all over his words with two left feet and making himself look foolish.

As they rode into town with their daunting mission, Stone would have been cheery. He would have fingered the grips of his guns and said that it was about time they did something difficult for a change. Even today, if Clint were to say to Stone's ghost, *Do you mean more difficult than the fight in which you were killt?*, Stone would have smiled his wide, pale-skinned smile and said *Yar, harder than that milk run*.

In case there was any doubt, Edward spelled out the situation's reality as they approached Percy's livery:

We can't use magic. If we use any magic, Kold will see us.

Then:

If Kold sees us and comes to us, we will die because he possesses the Triangulum and we do not.

Clint, feeling the single six-shooter on his belt as light and benign as a child's pop gun, nodded. Edward, still disguised as the gray horse, couldn't see him nod, but that was par for the course. It mattered nar to Edward if Clint agreed, so long as he obeyed. Whenever Clint bothered to concur, he did so knowing it was only for himself. And as they rode, Clint found it fitting — if not futile — that after years of trials and terrors, in the end it had come down to one cowboy and one horse against the world.

Edward wouldn't let Mai go with them. She put up a fight, but because she was still suppressed by Barlowe's elixir and wouldn't be able to use her magic anyway for fear of giving them up, her protests were easy to ignore. Edward said that she was too unpredictable. Despite the elixir, she kept falling into trances, and Barlowe had to keep upping her dosage. She couldn't even trust her own abilities. What if she fell into a trance in the middle of a battle? What if she got herself killt — seeing as she'd just be one more unmagical woman, untrained with a gun and with no protection? None of this sat well with Mai. She yelled at Clint as she'd done back in Solace, but it hadn't worked in Solace and it didn't work now. So Mai tried to hurt him. She told him that the last time he'd left her, she'd been carried off. But Clint kept his face straight, walking off before she could turn his mind, pointing out that Kold had discarded her and wouldn't carry her off again. Kold had taken from her what he needed, and she had nothing left that he wanted.

Still, Mai caught up with Clint before he could escape. She grabbed him by both upper arms and shook him, her eyes wet with tears as she told him that she couldn't stand to lose him and that it wasn't fair. She spoke of her dream, about the beast in the dark and massive house. She said that in a new dream, she'd seen the gunslinger die. But Clint couldn't listen. He blocked her out, forcing himself to think about what might lie ahead instead.

They left, leaving Mai as she broke into Barlowe's stock of Fanta and began drinking.

One man, with a single six-shot iron and conventional bullets.

One horse, with hooves and speed as his only weapons.

And to this, Sly Stone would have said, "How can you know your true mettle if you always fight with an advantage?"

Clint and Edward had always had an advantage. Today they would not. Today, in fact, they would have a distinct *dis*advantage. And Clint, who seldom showed emotion, felt his hands beginning to shake. His voice was higher-pitched than normal. He would have to shoot mortal lead. And if he were shot himself, he would have to die.

There would be no magic healing. As long as one of them lived, that survivor would have to continue on in secret. Edward would watch Clint take a bullet in the neck and die in the dust. He'd have to. Worlds were at stake.

They walked to Percy Noodle's barn, summoned the wild-haired old-timer, and asked him if they could stash some guns and supplies. Noodle said yes, of course, and promised to help with his rifle where he could. Clint set Stone's shotguns — now mere lead-shooters — in a corner of the barn with a box of plain old shells and a handful of illegal pistols they'd scavenged from the archetypes back when they'd battled El Feo. Clint wondered if the sinking sensation in his gut was what his foes felt. What was it like to face a man whose bullets never wavered or shanked from their trajectory? What was it like to face a man who, if shot, could never die so long as his equine partner were nearby? What was it like to face a man who could hide behind shields, fold from one place to another, and attack with magic?

Clint looked at the plain lead shells with their copper casings and wondered if wishing he still had that advantage made him a coward.

"You are still fast," said Edward. "And that gun? It was El Feo's. It shoots true. He subdued a village for years with that iron."

"Yar," said Clint, feeling heavy and slow.

"You know," Edward said, "Stone would have loved this."

"I was just thinking that. I wish he were here."

"His guns are," said the unicorn.

It wouldn't mean much to most men, but to a gunslinger, it had tremendous import. A man's guns were like his soul. Clint looked down at Stone's guns. Then he picked them up, still in their long holsters, and decided to strap them to his back instead of leaving them at Noodle's livery. The sawed-off butts protruded above each of his shoulders like an angel's wings.

"It's illegal for a commoner to carry more than one gun," said Edward.

"About as illegal as plotting to kill a land baron," Clint replied, snugging the big holsters tight.

Edward walked outside and stood by a hitching post outside of Fat Ziggy's station. There was little he'd be able to do, owing to his lack of thumbs and trigger fingers, so he offered himself as a lookout. This assuaged Clint's fears not at all. Then Edward walked away from the gunslinger and circled the building, then returned and reported a moment later.

"I looked through the back window. It's just Ziggy in there, plus a pair of matching deputies. Teedawges. I don't see the giants."

"Three shots," said Clint for no reason. He realized he was

whistling in the dark, trying to make himself feel more confident than he was. With his old seven-shooters and the promise of shields and healing, he would have felt perfectly confident even if the Teedawges had numbered to twenty, but now it was as if he were walking on a narrow board between two skyscrapers. Sure, he could walk that board. But the fact that there would be no do-overs in case he fell from it made his mortal heart beat like a war drum.

So Clint crossed the dusty street toward the station, suddenly wishing he'd at least taken some target practice with the rinky-dink six-cylinder gun. He felt woefully underprepared, and as if he were walking to his own execution. But hadn't Stone been a plain old bandit before he'd moved on to magic theft? Of course he had; he'd told Clint and the others his many stories over and over and over again. It was as if Stone had been speaking of old family memories. Good times of mortal peril, firing simple lead without a safety net.

So Clint asked himself: *What would Stone do?*

Instead of stepping into Ziggy's station, Clint knocked on the batwings. Then he swung himself to the side, his back to the wall. He felt himself mentally stepping into Stone's ghost. He was simply here to create a great tale for later storytelling — mayhap when he was eighty years old, spinning yarns from a rocking chair by the fire.

From inside the station, Fat Ziggy said, "What the sands was that?"

Teedawge: "Sounded like a knock."

Ziggy: "A knock? But they're batwings!"

Clint knocked again.

Teedawge (the same one? Clint didn't know): "That's a knock, marshal."

Ziggy, unbelievably, calling out: "Who is it?"

Clint tried to imagine himself with a giant stupid head of orange hair. *What would Stone say?* So he called back, "Bacon delivery!"

Ziggy: "Bacon?"

Footsteps approached the door. An albino face appeared above the batwings. Clint grabbed the head, yanked it down so that it wedged between the batwings, then raised one leg and pushed hard against the doors. The archetype struggled, trapped at the neck. Clint hit him hard over the head with the butt of his gun.

Ziggy, farther back in the station and apparently not within sight of the door: *"Where's that bacon?"*

Clint peeked into the station, saw no one else in the reception area. Nobody had seen him attack the archetype. So he pulled a glass vial from an inner pocket of his vest, used it to wet a rag, and held it over the unconscious Teedawge's face. Barlowe had given him the vial. It was filled with chloroform. Edward had protested, saying that shooting was easier. But Clint had argued, more successfully, for stealth.

He crept into the station's front room, then peered into the back. The other Teedawge and Fat Ziggy sat behind the desk, side by side, cards in their hands. The other Teedawge's cards were face-down on the desk as the others waited for his return.

Clint grabbed the unconscious man under the arms, dragged him into a chair, and propped him up. Then, since it seemed like something Stone would do, he took a woman's hat that was hanging on the wall for some reason and set it on the man's head.

Clint pitched his voice into the other room, trying to approximate a falsetto similar to the Teedawge's voice.

"Hey, you guys want some of this bacon or not?"

Clint ducked into a corner, drew both of Stone's shotguns, and waited. Ziggy barreled into the room much faster than made sense. The Teedawge was behind him, his gun drawn but facing the wrong direction. By the time the two newcomers saw him, Clint had both shotguns pointing at their chests. The Teedawge paused, then slowly lowered his gun to the floor.

"Gentlemen," said Clint, keeping his shotguns centered. "Let's go to jail."

Five minutes later, with Meadowlands' marshal and both Teedawges locked in their own cells (tied, gagged, and dreaming sweet chloroform dreams), Clint stepped out of the station and mounted the nondescript gray horse that anyone, if they'd looked closely enough, would have seen wasn't actually tied to the hitching post. The tall newcomer with the oiled hair and too-clean shirt then rode up the high street as if he hadn't just tied down the town's law with his own two hands.

Diego Diamante — AKA Dharma Kold — lived in a citadel in the mountains north of NewTown. That, Edward said, would be where they'd find the Triangulum. It might be possible to climb up and peek down on the citadel (and maybe even sneak in and locate the Triangulum by homing in on the magic), but they'd have to take out the law's communications first. Kold wasn't stupid. He'd be waiting for Clint, Edward, and Mai, knowing that it was only a matter of time before they caught up to him. Clint and Edward were disguised, but if their cover slipped in any way, the law in town would "ring" (Barlowe's word) to Kold using one of the spark-fueled communication devices they all held. If that happened, Kold would be waiting when they arrived at the citadel, and the game would be over.

Taking out Fat Ziggy and his men in the station at least ensured that their rings wouldn't make it to Kold, but there was another problem. Rings in Meadowlands apparently went through a dispatching center and were broadcast out to the town's other officers. If they didn't handle that wrinkle before heading into the mountains, any discovery would mean that dozens, scores, or hundreds of Teedawges could be summoned to face them.

"The dispatch is beside the saloon," Edward whispered as they walked — slowly, since they wanted to appear as just one man who was not worth noticing.

"Why is everything in these towns beside a saloon?" Clint said, his fear coming out sounding like irritation.

"There are a lot of saloons in old towns," said Edward. "Are you afeared?"

Clint swallowed, then decided it wasn't worth lying. Edward knew him too well.

"Yar."

"Me too. But this is hero stuff."

"We were heroes before this. Back when we were invincible."

"Not really. We didn't have a flaw. Heroes have to have a flaw in order to be heroic, and now we have one: death."

"For me, anyway."

"There are ways that unicorns can die," said Edward, "and one way is if he doesn't use his magic to prevent it. If I'm shot but you aren't — and if there's still a chance you could use stealth to succeed — I wouldn't heal myself so that you could go on."

Clint thought about that, wondering if he could be so noble. He decided he probably couldn't be, so it was good that he had no magic at his disposal. It would mean he'd have no temptation to cheat.

"For a long time, Stone did this all without shields," Clint said. He felt as if Stone were riding beside him, offering guidance. And with that thought, the gunslinger realized with shock just how attached he'd become to the outlaw. For an unknown, unknowable number of years, it had only been Clint and Edward. But over the past months, that twosome had become a threesome, and now Clint felt hobbled, greatly resenting what had once felt like independence. From another human, anyway.

"You're pretending you're him, aren't you?"

"In a way. That way, he'll die if I get shot. Which is okay, since he's already dead. He'd agree with me. I can practically hear it."

Edward snorted. "You sound like the Leisei."

They approached the dispatch office. Clint dismounted, and

Edward circled to the rear. Clint drew both shotguns and peered through the open door. Inside, he saw a handful of men and women working in front of large crystal devices — apparently the communicators that Barlowe had mentioned. All wore implements over their ears and were staring at small screens, jabbing wires into a series of holes. Realm technology, all of it. Clint also counted eleven Teedawges around the room that were either on patrol or acting as guards, but none of them were alert. All had their weapons holstered and their eyes away from the door.

Leading with his shotguns, Clint stepped through the doorway and into the room. No one looked up. He took two more steps, now fully inside, pointing his shotguns around at the room's occupants. Still nobody turned.

"I have come here to kick butt and chew tobaccy," Clint announced, channeling Sly Stone, "and I'm all out of tobaccy."

The Teedawges' heads came up. Their heads were fully raised before vigilance lit their eyes and they realized what they were seeing. Clint locked eyes briefly with each man, mentally daring them to reach for their weapons. If they all drew at once, they'd kill him easily, but of course they *wouldn't* all draw at once, and none of them wanted to be the first man killt.

Clint felt confident of his reflexes and speed, even with the oversized guns. He didn't feel his usual certainty (in fact, his heart was beating so hard that he was sure the room could hear it), but he was cool enough to always keep his weapons trained on the men who moved their hands closest to their holsters. When he did, the men he aimed at would draw their hands back. Then others would inch their hands down and Clint would aim at them instead, repeating the cycle. The room was quiet enough to hear a matchstick drop and skitter on the floor. He wished he could hand out chloroform and instruct each person in the room to whiff from the hanky, but he was out of hands.

There was a clatter at the rear of the room as Edward stuck his head through the back window and said in a loud monotone, "HELLO. I'M MISTER ED."

Several of the Teedawges turned to look. As they did, Clint fired matching shotgun blasts into two of the crystal devices, causing both to explode in a shower of glass. Each made a puff of orange smoke which rose to the ceiling, where it hung like a cloud. Then the Teedawges, their paralysis broken, began to turn toward him and draw. Clint fired and struck two in the chest, driving them hard against the wall. But the Teedawges were machines, not men, and returned to their feet immediately. There was one crystal communicator left. Clint fired at it, saw it explode, then dove back toward the door, pulling himself around the corner. The archetypes didn't immediately follow, likely assuming the gunman was still ready to end the first one who walked out. But once outside, Clint reholstered his two big guns and drew his pistol. Without Sly's magic inside them, Sly's weapons were just oversized scatterguns. While they might work well against men, they were much less useful against the Teedawges. Unless he fired at close range, the gunslinger couldn't reliably hit their thinkboxes using scattershot, and until he could, they'd simply keep coming.

El Feo's six-shooter felt small in his large gunslinger's palm, but it would have to do. He ducked behind a rain barrel, suddenly aware of how hard it was to breathe. His vision wanted to blur but he fought it — along with a kind of red-hot panic that he could sense trying to eclipse his thought. He couldn't let the doubt and fear in. He was still a trained marshal. He had plenty of training and conditioning to keep him cool when under fire without a unicorn, and the fact that it felt so hard now just meant that he'd gotten complacent. He needed to focus, and did. His vision became crisp. His thinking and heart focused. He even seemed to recall some conventional arms training.

He could do this.

Deep breath.

Deep breath.

A Teedawge poked his head out of the dispatch office. Clint fired. Black smoke belched from the thing's head and it fell, this time for good.

Inside, Clint heard commotion as the people who had been manning the crystal devices cried out and shouted, ringing for backup that — if Clint had judged the things' explosions accurately — would neither be able to hear nor respond. Which, of course, had been the point of this little errand.

Four Teedawges streamed through the door. Clint fired and hit one in the leg, but the thing simply stumbled, recovered, then ran on, making for cover behind a stagecoach. Clint tried firing on the others, twice, but only ended one's thinkbox and was forced to scramble back as three more burst outside.

One of the Teedawges stepped into the street, calmy sighted on Clint, and fired. The round struck the rain barrel, punching a hole through the wood and spraying the gunslinger with water.

"You made a mistake deciding to shoot up Meadowlands, my friend!" the Teedawge shouted, the anger in his voice reminding Clint that the things were as much man as they were machine. The archetype fired twice more. One of the shots came too close to Clint's shoulder. The rain barrel was poor cover and the man was shooting right through it.

Clint thought: *This must be what it's like for me to be shooting at anyone, no matter what they're hiding behind.*

Oh, how the marshal missed his guns.

Hiding behind the rain barrel was like hiding behind a sheet, so while he still could, Clint cocked his weapon and leapt out from behind it, sideways, preparing to tuck and roll when he struck the ground and make for a pile of dry goods in front of the general store. While in the air, laid out and weightless, the gunslinger drew a breath and squeezed his trigger. The shot struck the Teedawge between the eyes. There were sparks, then black smoke. One more down.

Clint struck the ground, rolled, came up and fired again. Now he was shooting through a stagecoach, judging his aim based on the legs he saw down by the wheels. But the bullet didn't stay true, and he missed. Legs moved and readjusted. Marshal's bullets would have taken out Clint's target, but the simple lead slug must have veered once inside the coach, or possibly never even gone through it at all.

Clint already felt overwhelmed. How many more archetypes were there? And where was Edward?

Now that there had been gunshots, commotion began to stir all around him. Some of what he heard might be townspeople, or it might be a fresh wave of Teedawges. Or birds carrying bits of the Darkness. Or Independence Lee with his mace, for all Clint knew.

Clint scampered around the dry goods.

A Teedawge followed him behind the pile. Clint ran around, ducking under the boardwalk decking. He crawled on his elbows and belly, keeping his pistol up and clean. When he came up, the Teedawge was still watching the dry goods. He hadn't seen Clint scamper away.

Clint stood behind him, aware that this would have been an excellent time to say something deliriously Stone-like. But he had nothing, so he simply raised his weapon. The Teedawge, his gun still aimed toward the dry goods, looked over with shock. Clint pulled the trigger, then heard a hollow click.

Six shots.

Not seven. *Six.*

He turned to run, but by the time that bit of remedial math passed through his consciousness, Clint had waited a heartbeat too long. The Teedawge raised his gun. Something huge struck the archetype from behind, knocking him flat. A huge gray horse nodded at the man with the empty gun.

Clint ran. Shots chased him. He ducked behind a pile of lumber, his heartbeat raging. His head wanted to spin, but he wouldn't let it.

He was a gunslinger. And no matter the number of rounds in his chamber, *he was a marshal true*.

Deep breath.

Under protection, Clint closed his eyes and drew another inhale. He imagined a target, saw it falling. He opened his eyes and reloaded his weapon, resetting the count he'd learned to keep in his head, mentally reminding himself he had six shots before empty, not seven.

He peeked out. Clint could see them now, growing bolder, barely bothering to hide. He could see their pale and menacing faces. How long before they simply charged at him? They must have realized he didn't have his magic on hand. He'd seen hundreds of these things swarm back in Baracho Gulch. It didn't matter that he'd taken out the communicators; the gunfight itself was making the broadcast.

A bullet careened from nowhere. It struck the lumber, caromed, and crashed into Clint's left side. The gunslinger grimaced, grasping at his ribs. The harder he held the wound, the better it felt, but he needed his hand. He watched, waiting to see who had fired and who would soon fire again.

The ground started to shake. Clint looked up, saw a giant charging toward him. The giant was still far down the street, but he was approaching quickly. It seemed to be one of the two who had taken Pompi back in the glass and alloy alleyways of NewTown.

Clint cocked his newly-reloaded pistol. Looked again, scanning for pale faces. Counted six. Found no others, and noticed how the eyes of the six flicked toward the approaching giant.

The gunslinger stood, held the pistol in front of him, and fired. One of the archetypes belched sparks and smoke. His left hand, undistracted by the pain in his side, fanned the gun's hammer. The remaining shots came off faster than any gunman he'd faced, no matter what kind of iron hung at his side: *twothreefourfivesix,* each beat was counterpointed by a plume of white, ordinary gunsmoke.

Six shots, six men down, but the giant was now very close, still charging. His massive fists obliterated the stack of dry goods Clint had hidden behind a moment ago. Clint ran, but his legs were much shorter than the giant's. He might be able to take it out with a shot to the eye, but he hadn't had time to reload. The gun was still in his hand; the tumbler flung open. As he ran, empty casings spilled to the dirt.

Clint hid behind a stagecoach, but the coach exploded under a massive punch, becoming kindling.

Into a store. The store's facade caving in. A massive hand entering, followed by an even more massive head. The giant couldn't come inside, but now Clint was loading, his back against the wall. His face, back, and chest were all dripping with sweat. His heartbeat pounded in his ears.

Through the shattered doorway, Clint watched as the colossus backed out and unsheathed his giant hammer. He was going to level the store, and send Clint to oblivion in a puff of smoke.

Before the giant could swing, there was the booming of a scattergun and the giant fell. Clint waited to see what would happen next, but then Percy Noodle came through the door with a shotgun clasped in both hands.

"You're carrying shotguns too, you know," he said.

Clint had forgotten. For so long, he'd only had the irons as his side. But Noodle didn't wait for Clint to reply. "Come on!" he yelled, beckoning.

Clint was still smarting from his wound, but the bullet seemed to have gone straight through. He could barely feel it, but he was sure he would feel it plenty once his adrenaline faded.

They ran outside and were greeted by a hail of bullets. Noodle dove, then reported without being asked that he was fine behind a wall of sandbags. Clint found nothing to hide behind, so he darted back inside the mercantile. He noticed the shopkeeper at the back for the first time, cowering with his hands in the air. Then the shop suddenly exploded — another giant had arrived and had swung his hammer as the first intended. Noodle again fired his scattergun and the giant turned. Clint ran and yelled to draw the giant's attention back to him, making for another stagecoach and diving behind it, knowing that a single swing from the hammer would turn it to toothpicks.

Before Clint could make the coach, he tripped and fell. He was finished. He rolled onto his back, waiting for the hammer blow. But then above him, the giant paused with his hammer overhead. Then he lowered the weapon and stowed it. There were Teedawges in the square. Too many to fight, but none took aim or fired. All of them were staring at something behind Clint.

Clint rolled over and looked up.

"Clint?" said the man in black.

The gunslinger couldn't speak.

Inexplicably, Dharma Kold spun, leapt onto a brown horse, and began to gallop away in a cloud of dust, heading up the trail toward the mountains.

CHAPTER SEVEN: PURSUIT

Someone, very loud, screamed, *"GET OUT OF MY WAY!"* preceded by an enormous flash of brilliant white light.

Teedawges flew like leaves in a breeze. Most struck something as they landed, then staggered to their feet, stunned. The giant again raised its hammer, but before it could swing, it was struck by what looked like pink taffy. Then, hopelessly entangled, the enormous thing tripped over itself and fell writhing to the ground.

Edward, now appearing fully himself again, charged past Clint without slowing. The gunslinger felt himself lifted into the air, then flung onto the unicorn's bare back. Edward was in full gallop. Clint was forced to adjust himself on the fly, holding on for dear life.

"I'm hit," he said.

Edward's horn glowed. Clint's side glowed in echo. His skin knitted, and his pain vanished.

"No point in hiding now, I guess," said Edward. "I have a sneaking suspicion that Kold knows we're here."

"My guns," said Clint.

"... are buried outside of town. You'll have to use your charming wit to fight him."

"You didn't go back for them?"

"When was I going to go back? Kold appeared six seconds ago. Don't worry. Your guns won't matter and neither will his, although those things are true for exactly opposite reasons. This should be a fun fight we have coming. I hope you enjoy futility."

"If I had my guns, I'd be able to shoot through shields."

"*Certain kinds* of shields. And when both men fighting have unicorns to heal them, shields are pointless. Try not to be insulted, but this is going to be me versus Cerberus if it's going to be anything. Kold will be there, possibly shooting lightning bolts or something impressive. He shouldn't even need the magic he stole from Cerberus anymore. Not with the Triangulum on his side. They will both be superpowered. You, on the other hand, will be useless."

"You're saying we can't win."

"Exactly."

"So why are we chasing him?" said Clint, aghast.

"Because," said Edward, "my keen powers of observation have shown me that *he* is running from *us*."

Clint tried asking Edward why Kold would be the one running — and, for that matter, why he'd be riding a horse instead of his unicorn partner Cerberus — but between Edward's thundering hooves and the blowing of wind around his head as they ascended the trail behind Kold, it was difficult to speak and took Clint's full concentration to simply hang on. Edward seldom ran, and this was the fastest the gunslinger had ever seen him go. Without the loathed saddle, Clint needed his leg muscles and hands to stay horsed, and it was taking everything he had.

They rounded one bend and then another, always with Kold at the horizon of sight. They were gaining on him. His horse was mortal and tiring, whereas Edward was magic and tireless. The unicorn seemed to sense this and galloped with renewed vigor. They could soon see massive gates — slowly parting — in the path before them. Clint felt as if they were racing time — that maybe Kold needed Cerberus to fight true, or needed the Triangulum close at hand. Mayhap if they overtook him now, they could end him, then take on Cerberus separately. Mayhap the unicorn of a different color, once deprived of his dark rider, would abandon the citadel. Mayhap after his poisoned bond with Kold was severed, Cerberus would slowly regain his natural balance and return to his coat of white. It didn't seem logical that Cerberus would care about taking over The Realm. After all, what interest had Edward ever shown in Clint's human ambitions?

"If we catch him now, will he be easier to defeat?" Clint shouted, leaning low and trying to avoid getting his nose broken by the unicorn's pistoning neck.

"I don't know."

"Does he need to be near the Triangulum to use its power?"

"I don't know."

"Is he drawing power from the Triangulum now? Can you feel it?"

"I don't know."

"Can you sense Cerberus?"

"Nar."

If there was a time limit on their catching Kold, the sands were almost through the glass. Kold leapt from his horse without slowing, landed in a pile, and scrambled toward a massive set of stone doors that seemed to lead into the core of the mountain itself. Clint and Edward pursued, holding their union as rider and mount. The doors were plenty large enough for them both. Edward's horn began to glow. As he watched Kold retreat, Clint — even as a mortal man with mere lead-flingers on his back and hip — felt his confidence growing. Kold was on the run, with clear panic in his every movement. Clint leaped from Edward's back and drew his pistol. Sighted. Fired. Kold ducked behind a pillar in the massive hollowed-out entranceway to his baron's palace, but there was nowhere to go. They walked forward. Clint could see the black sleeve of Kold's shirt billow around the pillar, could see how it heaved as the man fought for breath.

There was a cacophonous crashing from behind them as the massive doors heaved closed.

Clint and Edward spun. The brown horse had wandered into the lobby behind them, and as they watched, its coat darkened to black and a long spiral horn of obsidian emerged from its forehead.

"Thanks for coming," said Cerberus.

CHAPTER EIGHT: THE TRUTH

Kold stepped out from behind the pillar. While Clint Gulliver had aged during his time in the sands, it appeared that Dharma Kold had not. He still had his handsome face, uncharacteristic of his gnarled heart, and kind green eyes that did nothing to bely the evil inside them. His cheeks were smooth, light, and clean-shaven — almost rosy, glowing in the room's flicker. The corners of his mouth twitched with false compassion. He fixed his gaze on Clint, washing the gunslinger with a sudden flash of memory of the day they found themselves together on the wrong side of the wall.

Kold's hair was askew, so he smoothed it. His shirt had come unbuttoned at the top, so he tried to button it, but then realized his button was missing.

"Oh, dagnit," he said. "This shirt was expensive."

Clint couldn't help himself. He already had his gun aimed, so he fired. The shot struck a spot in the air several inches in front of Kold's eyes and exploded into red sparks and twirling streamers.

Kold looked at Clint, wounded. "Oh, come on. That's hardly polite. And look at you. A guest in my house, and you didn't even bring me a sparkling bottle of Fanta. Didn't your mother ever teach you manners? Wait. Don't answer that. Of course she didn't. You were always a jerk."

"Just like your unicorn," said Cerberus behind them.

"I'll let you keep those pop-shooters if you enjoy them," said Kold, gesturing at Clint's pistol and twin shotguns. "But don't fire them again, pleasem and thankoo."

Cerberus circled around so that he stood behind Kold. The man in black and his dark unicorn made for a matching set. Clint had a bizarre thought that he should have coordinated better with Edward, but here he was in denims and a light chambray shirt with fancy scrolling on the breast.

From the side of his mouth, Clint said to Edward beside him, "See if you can get through his shield. I'll fire when I can."

Edward sighed and lowered his head. "There's no point. You'd know it true if you could feel the magic."

"Yar, the *magic*," said Kold, overhearing. "The famous *Triangulum Enchantem*. The instrument that will get me into The Realm."

"So that you can end the worlds."

"So that I can restore balance," Kold corrected. He walked to the side of the chamber, then sat on a ledge carved into the wall, perching as he casually swung his legs.

"So that you can take your revenge," Clint countered.

"Clint… if I may still call you Clint…?" He waited for Clint to give him permission to be familiar, then pushed on when he didn't. "I know your memory is fogged and you won't remember our youthful chats, so let me tell you a story we once passed back and forth in our palaver, back when we dreamt through endless days and nights."

Kold smiled, and Clint felt an odd sense of wonder. Then the man in black continued.

"Once upon a time, there was harmony between good and evil. The two offset each other like cold and hot, up and down, before and after. They offset one another the way —" He gave a nod to Cerberus. "— that unicorns and their riders offset each other. Two halves to a whole, with each lending meaning to the other. Today, we talk about 'dark magic.' But think about it: without 'light magic' to compare it to, 'dark magic' would just be 'magic.' Without dark there is no light, and without light, there is no dark. It takes both, and each is necessary for the other. But one day, in this binary world of co-existing opposites, one side of one particular pair decided that it wasn't happy being a mere half of a whole. This side wanted more for itself. It wanted to be 'the thing' instead of 'the thing that is the opposite of — and defined by — some other thing.'"

"The Darkness, yar," said Clint. "I know."

Beside him, Edward was surprisingly docile. "Nar, you don't," he said.

"The pair I'm talking about isn't light and dark," said Kold. "I'm talking about beings. Specifically, *us*. Humans decided to try and manipulate the magic for their own ends. They gathered it. And that seemed harmless at first, because it was only *gathering*, after all. They created small reservoirs of white magic and learned to manipulate it, to make it do tricks. That meant that somewhere else, there was a bit more dark magic than light, but it mattered nar; it was only the work of a few human hands. Those few learned to summon spells with the magic. They found they could use it to levitate heavy objects and make it do their bidding. They could use it to warm food, to hunt... all sorts of things. Magic was the ultimate tool to give a spartan life more comfort."

Something that might have been sadness crossed Kold's face. Clint could feel Edward's growing discomfort — or was it uncertainty? — beside him.

"But you know how these things go. Centuries passed. Millennia passed. Humans started to cluster. They did so slowly. And as they clustered, they drew their magic-gathering abilities together. They taught each other the tricks they'd learned with the white magic. Soon they learned to harness that magic to power machines. And this was all strange, but it still didn't seem terribly troublesome because there was so much magic in the worlds, and the humans were brushing but a corner of it. So the guardians did nothing, and let the humans be humans. The unicorns moved in to work alongside them, hoping to shepherd their magic-sifting knowledge, to keep it sensible and not let it get out of hand. You see, unicorns themselves are pure white magic, but here's something not many people know true..."

Kold leaned further from his perch, as if conveying a secret.

"Did you know that unicorns can use *both* types of magic? It's true. It took me a long time to understand that, since for a long time Cerberus spoke only in riddles. He withheld information from me, and told me that 'I'd never understand.' " The dark rider laughed. "It was infuriating. But eventually I realized that when he spoke about the same magic being good or bad depending on the user's intent, I started to see that he meant there was really no such thing as black and white — and here, I speak of meaning. Darkness isn't always used for evil, if 'evil' is even a real thing when there's no 'good' to compare it to. Light isn't always good, for the same reason."

Kold leaned back against the wall, making himself comfortable.

"Anyway, the humans, being humans and limited in their human way, could only use the white magic because they were never intended as guardians or users. So the unicorns tried teaching them balance, but the humans liked the new things they'd created with the white magic and knew they ran much better if they didn't 'pollute' them with darkness. And besides, they didn't want *darkness* in their towns and cities."

Clint didn't know what to say. He had to end Kold, but didn't know how, and he couldn't understand why Edward had given up so completely.

"You're talking about The Realm," said Clint.

"The Realm! Yar, the glorious *Realm*. I'm talking about the pinnacle of human progress — a civilization so greedy that it hoarded and hoarded even as storms started brewing. A civilization that created so much polarity in the magic that it managed to fracture the worlds."

Clint shook his head. "Ridiculous."

"Really?" said Kold. "I thought you rode with a savant?"

Clint thought of Sly Stone, and what Edward had told him about Stone's family line holding an archive of knowledge in their genes. That's the word Edward had used: *savant*. He looked at the unicorn, but Edward said nothing.

Kold shifted on his plinth, now leaning forward, opening his body, going for friendly.

"Clint, do you remember the first time we fought?"

Clint tried to recall. He remembered Kold's anger outside The Realm as they'd chased it. He remembered the futility of pursuing a city that was like a mirage, that never came closer no matter how long they marched toward it. He remembered how anger over The Realm had twisted Kold's soul and started to slowly turn Cerberus's color. But he remembered no fights. One night, he and Edward had simply gathered their gear and left. There hadn't been a confrontation until…

"Solace," said Clint.

Kold shook his head sadly. "Nar. But I don't blame you. As magic-addled as the time was, I doubt even Edward remembers. See, that's the advantage of embracing the dark, as Cerberus and I have. Darkness allows you to see the truth even when it's reprehensible. Legitimate solutions to a scenario like 'kill an innocent man for the greater good' are visible inside a shroud, whereas light never allows you to so much as consider them."

Beside Clint, Edward kicked at the stone underfoot. It was as if he'd surrendered.

"The first time we fought," said Kold, "was over Mai."

"In Solace."

"Nar. Years before. Years before you met her, even. You were only aware of her reputation back then. But see, you *knew*, Clint. You *knew* that she was the Orb of Benevolence."

It was a lie. The first time he'd met Mai had been in Solace, when she'd come to town as a traveler. She'd made fun of him within five minutes of meeting him. He'd acted annoyed, but actually he'd been enchanted. That had been the beginning.

Kold's eyebrows were up, waiting. Edward was still looking at the floor.

"It's true," said Kold. "Look inward. You will see."

The air was gone from his lungs. His long fingers found Edward's side, to steady himself.

"Lies," he said.

"Lies? Nar. Truths. We knew who and where she was. We were going to take her, then take the other Orbs. *I* wasn't going to do it, gunslinger. *We* were."

"Lies," Clint repeated, his knees growing weak.

"*Truths*," said Kold more emphatically. "But you were too noble to do it. So as Cerberus and I began to darken enough to see the best solution to the unwinnable scenario, you and Edward departed. But I was right, you see. This was for the greater good. I needed her to complete the Triangulum, and I needed the Triangulum to breach the wall of The Realm."

"So why haven't you gone in?" said Clint. "Couldn't find the third Orb? And now you want our help to find it? Well you can forget..."

"Oh, I have the third Orb," said Kold. "It's below this mountain — deep, deep down under tons of rock. It took the giants weeks to find it, even with Cerberus pointing the way. It's an ancient, ancient machine that fills a room this size. The giants called it a 'generator'; they have legends about the machine under the mountain. A 'generator,' they say, is a machine that begets energy, but first requires power to do so. Like keys. To start the generator, I needed the other Orbs. But something happened. When I fed the generator the Benevolence Orb I'd taken from Mai, it hitched and sputtered. It ran, but just barely. It gave me enough power to run the city and to command the magic Edward is so afraid to face, but I couldn't build the bridge or breach the wall. So I studied until I saw the problem: *benevolence can't be taken*. It must be *given*." Kold laughed. "It's so obvious, right? The concept of benevolence is *all about* giving. Why did I ever think I could *take* it?"

A strange realization was beginning to seep into Clint's mind. He looked over at Edward, and saw the same realization settling into the unicorn's eyes. Edward lifted his head. Mayhap they couldn't defeat Kold and Cerberus. But now, at least, Edward looked like he was willing to try.

"You still need Mai," Clint said, his hand moving subconsciously to his gun.

"Oh, still your gun hand, Marshal," Kold said, waving as he leaned back. "Even if shooting me would make a difference, I'm not going to seize Mai while she's relaxing at Barlowe's house outside of OldTown. It wouldn't work, remember? I can't *take* the Benevolence Orb. She must give it to me."

Clint shook his head.

"I need you to convince her, Clint. I need you to get Mai to give it to me."

"You're insane," Clint growled. "Nothing but evil."

Kold shrugged. "Another half of a polarity. What is 'insane' other than something arbitrary contrasted against something equally arbitrary that people call 'sane'?"

"You dragged her through the desert for years, impaled by Cerberus as if on his horn itself. And now you want my help. *Her* help."

"Hey, it was hard on me, too," the black unicorn interjected. "All that concentration…"

"Clint, you used to believe in this!" Kold said, standing and marching over to Cerberus. "Think! Push past the fog and the blank spots. We plotted together! We only separated because you weren't willing to do what we both felt was necessary to get what we needed from Mai — a girl *you didn't even know* — for the good of all the worlds!"

"Torture that made no difference anyway," Edward said, his eyes fierce as he stared at Cerberus, his voice dripping blood. His lips were pulled back, showing his teeth like a predator. As he watched, Clint found himself remembering how the dark unicorn's perversion had bored into Edward's chest like a spike, and how Edward had been unable to so much as approach the abomination. Cerberus was everything Edward was not, and Edward hated him for it.

"Well, I didn't *know* that I wouldn't be able to take it by force," said Kold, now addressing Edward. "Magic rules are so complicated and ritualistic. But *you* wanted this once upon a time too, Edward the Brave. Don't pretend you didn't, no matter how addled and proud you may have grown since. The four of us had a plan, and together, we could have done it. We could have reunited the Triangulum. We could have opened The Realm!"

"And then done what?" said Clint.

"What we could!" Kold shouted.

"And fracture the worlds in the doing," said Edward.

"And what if it did?" said Kold, his veneer beginning to crumble. "What *if* the worlds had ended? Would that be so bad? It's happening anyway, with us doing nothing and The Realm taking more and more for itself. Would you rather die a slow, certain death or take a risk to save what you can? Maybe if we get past the wall, we can reverse the

damage that's been done. We could open a valve and allow the magic to leak into the Sands, down the vein. Let the worlds start healing themselves. Release the pressure before it builds to an exploding point! You knew this, Clint! Magic has become so pinched off from itself that the Darkness has grown restless. You've seen it! You've faced it! The world *wants* entropy. When there's imbalance, great pressure builds to equalize it. One way or another, that pressure must be released if the imbalance isn't fixed. The event will be catastrophic, and turn the Great Cataclysm into a forgotten hiccup. If we get past the wall, *at least we can help to diffuse the bomb!*"

Something inside Clint ran cold. He'd heard the *so-what* sentiment before. Specifically, he'd heard it from Sly Stone. It even had a certain sense to it. Who would perish if The Realm were catapulted into the abyss? Nobody other than The Realm, and only after digging their own grave.

"You are *evil*," said Clint.

Kold waved a dismissive hand.

"*Perverse*," Edward added. But he wasn't looking at Kold when he said it. The unicorn was staring at his opposite, at the dark steed that had surrendered his power and become like a hole in the world. Something born of light, yet betraying that light with every breath.

"That was always your problem, Edward," said Cerberus. "You were too timid, too unwilling to get your nose dirty."

Kold held up a hand to Cerberus, easing him down. The subservient way Cerberus obeyed the man's gesture and backed off made Edward snort and strike at the ground. Clint knew better than to ask his own partner to stand down. If Edward struck at Cerberus, then so be it.

"Help us," said Kold. "I know she rides with you. I know she's been restored to normal."

"Beyond normal," said Clint.

"We thought that might happen when we left her," said Cerberus, still staring at Edward.

The back of Clint's neck prickled. *They'd left her for them to find.*

Suddenly, Clint understood everything in one gestalt leap. Kold hadn't been able to get what he wanted from Mai. He'd drawn something weak from inside her — an inferior version of the Orb that was just enough to start the machine and power the city, but not enough to assault the Realm wall — and then had left her behind. But Kold hadn't left Mai because he was done with her. He'd left her because he wanted Clint to find her, to nurse her back to health, and to convince her to give up what Kold had been unable to seize by force.

"You needed us," said Clint, quieter than he would have liked.

Kold rolled his eyes, gesturing vaguely with his hand. "Oh, yar, we needed you, you needed us, our unicorns need us, we need them. It's all one big, happy family. I've gotten that over and over from this one, impudent though he may sometimes be." He jerked his thumb at Cerberus.

"All I *need* is Edward's mom," Cerberus said.

Edward took an automatic step forward, but Kold continued.

"Who are you without me, Clint? You're the good guy only because you have a bad guy to chase. But yar, I suppose I needed you. But *she* needed me, too, in order to become what she was supposed to be."

Edward gasped. Finally, the white unicorn had been surprised.

"What did you say?" said Clint.

Edward answered for Kold. "The Orb," he said. "Mai wasn't actually the Orb of Benevolence until…"

"It's all a rich tapestry," Kold said with heavy sarcasm. "*Magic.* Magic and its *rules*. I could make a dozen flowery metaphors: some forest seeds can only crack and germinate once there's been a destructive fire, and so on. Mai wasn't the Orb until we killt her soul, yar, yar, yar. So why did we need her at first, if she wasn't the Orb yet? It'll make your head spin and leave you wondering if you have any free will at all. The irony is that even if she'd wanted to give me what I needed when I'd taken her, she *couldn't* until after we'd left her for you. Can't you see, Clint? This was meant to be. The four of us are a team whether you like it or not. Cerberus and I will do what you and Edward won't, but only *together*, as a foursome, could we reunite the Triangulum. She's become something powerful, but look what it took! Death is part of life, Marshal. The white in Mai couldn't flourish until Cerberus killt all that she was. A phoenix only rises from ashes, and that means that before it can flourish, it has to burn. It makes me feel like we're all just living out a performance. Like this. Watch."

Kold drew his pistol and fired it directly through Clint's heart.

Clint felt everything blacken. His legs collapsed beneath him and he spilled to the floor. His head swam. He forgot where the ceiling was, where the walls were, who was with him. He felt as if he were floating. But then there was a great white something above him, like a beacon, like firelight, and he saw that it was Edward. He looked at his chest and found it whole, his shirt ripped and wet. He touched his skin and his fingers came away red.

"You see?" said Kold as Clint stood. He still held his gun. He gestured around the room with it, looking amused.

"We're going to die," Clint whispered to Edward.

"Nar," Edward replied. "We *can't* die. I finally understand."

"Right through the heart!" said Kold, giddy, looking at Cerberus for approval. "Do you know how hard that is to heal, even with a unicorn standing right beside you? You should be dead already, gunslinger. Beyond saving! But if I *need* you, you might ask, why would I try to *kill* you? And how could I know you wouldn't die? Would you have lived if I hadn't tried to kill you, or died in some other way? Was the shot necessary? It's shown Edward something, I can see. Oh, it's all so *much!* What's necessary and what isn't, who needs who, what's a man's choice and what isn't. Which came first, the turkey or the egg? You think on it too long and your head will hurt something fierce."

Edward's lips a breath from Clint's ear, the unicorn whispered, "We were supposed to end up here."

"So you see, Clint, you can't be bothered by what we did to Mai. We're your other half. You couldn't do it, so we had to. At first, there wasn't an Orb of Benevolence. But now, thanks to all four of us, there is."

Edward whispered, "We are here to play a role, and we must play it."

"For the record," Cerberus said, tossing his black mane and pawing the stone floor with his horn toward Edward, "I look down on your lack of spine just as much as you look down on my lack of mercy."

His equine breath like the fog of fire in Clint's ear, Edward said, "You must do as he says."

That was enough. Clint pushed away from the unicorn, stared at Kold enough to make him stop strutting theatrically, drew his finger like a pistol, and pointed it at all three of the others.

"I can do what I choose," the gunslinger spat.

"In a matter of speaking," said Kold.

"Gunslinger, listen..." Edward began.

"I CAN DO WHAT I CHOOSE!"

Edward stopped. Kold lowered his hand, holstering his gun. Even Cerberus stopped pawing at the stone and waited. Clint was powerless. He had no magic, no decent guns, no ability to heal. But he'd been shot through the heart and was still breathing, and he suddenly he felt as if he held all the dice.

"I'm here for a reason," he said.

Edward nodded slowly.

"And my reason is to defeat you. To take back the Triangulum. To stop what you are doing."

"Predictable," said Cerberus, rolling his eyes.

"I don't know how, but this means that Edward and I *will* defeat you. We will fight you until we can fight no more. Right, Edward?"

Clint looked over at the unicorn. At first the gunslinger thought Edward would contradict him like always — inferior, ignorant human that he was — but instead the unicorn did something that made Clint feel as if Kold had shot him again. Edward extended his right foreleg in front of the other, bowed over it, and said in a sighing voice, "As you wish."

Kold looked at Edward. Clint looked at Kold. Cerberus gaped, insofar as a unicorn could do so. Clint turned from Kold, forgetting that he'd pursued him for five long years and considered him a mortal enemy, and exposed his back to his foe. Edward was still bowing. Clint stood in front of him and shook his head.

"We came here to fight," the gunslinger said, his voice filled with disbelief.

"We did," Edward said, rising back to standing.

"And we will not surrender Mai," he said.

"As you choose," said Edward.

"You did not come to fight," Kold said from behind him.

"You came to surrender," said Cerberus.

"Or to join us," Kold finished.

Clint drew the very small, very light, very insignificant six-shot pistol from his hip and aimed it at Kold's forehead. He'd fired it at Kold earlier and the bullet had simply sparked away, but the gunslinger was suddenly certain that it wouldn't happen that way again.

"This is the wrong choice," said Kold, staring at the barrel. "I don't want to fight you."

"I do," said Clint.

"You can't defeat us," said Kold.

"We will," said Clint.

"With a pistol? With a unicorn who carries a tenth of the magic we carry?"

Clint's long thumb came back and cocked the tiny gun's hammer.

"I will fight with the gun of my enemy," said the gunslinger. "And when it is empty, I will fight with the guns of my friend. And when those are empty, I will fight you with my hands. I have traveled for five years to fight you, Dharma Kold, and when I die, it will be with my fingers around your throat."

"Fine," said Kold, shaking his head. "We will dance."

CHAPTER NINE: THE DANCE

Before Clint could pull the trigger, a great wave of energy struck his body, propelling him sideways. The gunslinger struck a wall and felt his left arm break. His head glanced the rock and concussed, then he fell to the floor as something enormous flew above him — Cerberus, dueling with Edward. Feet stomped by him as if he weren't there or as if he didn't matter, which he didn't. One hoof struck the hand on his broken arm, making it crack. Clint curled up in pain, knowing Edward was too distracted for healing. But after being shot through the heart, what did he have to lose?

He stood and marched toward Kold with his pistol drawn. He fired six rapid shots. Kold no longer had a shield; Cerberus was just as indisposed as Edward. Clint had wanted to shoot Kold between the eyes, but as he fired, the dark rider's pupils rolled up and something — some great force — seemed to shimmer out from him to stop the gunslinger's bullets, one after the other. As the slugs neared Kold, they slowed like they were swimming through syrup. The sixth bullet struck the second and kicked it forward like a billiard ball. The slow bullet tapped Kold on the forehead like a reprimand, and then the shells fell to the floor.

"You can't hurt me, Clint!" Kold bellowed. "Stop fighting!"

Instead of stopping, Clint tossed the spent revolver aside and used his good arm to draw one of Stone's shotguns from behind his back. He started to aim, but a great ball of black and white rolled toward him, knocking him back to the floor. Spells shot from the fighting unicorns, smashing into the hollowed-out cavern walls and sending rubble like rain to the floor. Clint's shotgun was knocked from his grip and skittered across the floor as if gliding on ice. Clint rose to his hand and knees (the other arm hung limp at his side, his pain present but held at bay) and began to chase it, part of his mind yammering at him for his irrationality.

Somewhere deep in his head, Clint heard Edward's voice: *Intention matters to magic.*

Stone's guns were symbolic. His own fighting in spite of literally impossible odds was symbolic. Edward's bow had been symbolic, odd as it was. His determination and spirit were symbolic. And he'd lived after being shot, which Edward seemed to have taken as a sign that he was here for a reason. His reason wasn't yet finished. And with that, he heard Edward in his head again: *We can't die.*

Clint reached the gun, held the slide, racked it by shaking it down hard. A shell clicked into the chamber. Clint leveled the weapon, remembering how effortlessly Stone had fired them one-handed. That was fortunate, since one hand was all Clint had. He was mortal. He was vulnerable. He couldn't be healed, and yet it also seemed that he couldn't die. The gunslinger had nothing to hide, no reason to duck and cover. He held the shotgun before him and fired at Kold when Kold turned to watch the unicorns, which obliterated an entire wall in their tussle.

Man versus man. Unicorn versus unicorn.

The shot tore an enormous hole in Kold's side. Then there was a diffuse orange glow and the dark rider was once again made whole. But Cerberus was across the room, unaware. The magic was coming from Kold himself. And Kold, Clint realized, hadn't so much as drawn his pistol.

"Clint!" he said. "Don't you understand? We left The Realm together! Don't you remember why? Don't you remember how we talked and plotted and planned?"

Clint, striding forward, racked the gun again with his good hand, shaking it hard.

"We're in this together, Clint! As we have been from the start!"

Clint aimed and fired. Kold's head vanished, then came right back. The dark rider didn't so much as stagger.

Against the wall, the unicorns parted. Edward directed a blast at Cerberus, but Cerberus looked almost bored as he parried. The dark unicorn returned fire, still looking bored as Edward was propelled several feet hard into the chamber wall. While encumbered, Cerberus fired again. Multicolored blood soaked the floor.

"I don't want to hurt you," Kold said.

Clint racked the gun. "Hurt me," he growled, and fired again. This time he racked and fired, racked and fired, until the gun was empty.

Kold was almost bare-chested; all Clint could do before Kold healed himself was shred some more of his clothes.

He tossed Stone's gun aside, fished for the other. For his last.

"Why do you keep fighting?" Kold almost screamed.

"Because I choose to."

Clint fired. And fired. And fired. Kold staggered backward — not in fear, but like a man holding back a dog, for the protection of others.

The second gun clicked empty. Clint tossed it aside. The unicorns came forward, but Edward was clearly outmatched. Cerberus had him in some sort of a cloud and was tossing him into walls, faster than Edward could heal. His energy all seemed to be funneled into his survival; he was casting no offensive spells. The dark unicorn cackled and laughed.

"This isn't like our fight in Solace," said Kold.

Clint stepped forward, toward the rider he'd pursued for a long half decade.

"We might have been even then. But now, with the Triangulum…"

Clint's hand formed a claw. He was fifteen feet from Kold. Ten. Seven.

"Don't you understand, Clint? There is only one way!"

Clint's hand closed around Kold's neck. He wasn't impeded; there were no shields as his fingers found flesh, sinew, and muscle. Kold's skin felt like jerky. The gunslinger started to squeeze.

Kold roared, shoving him across the room with unbelievable force. The gunslinger struck the back wall, hearing more bones break. The pain was unbelievable. He felt torment taking over, felt life fleeing his body. Kold was suddenly above him. There was a glow from somewhere and Clint's sharpness returned, key systems knitting enough to keep him alive, albeit barely.

Kold stood above him, his boot on Clint's neck.

"Yield."

Clint's hand formed a new claw. He hooked it to expose his fingernails and began digging into Kold's leg. "Prepare to die," he croaked.

"Yield!"

"It's just a flesh wound," Clint said, his head swimming.

Kold pointed to the unicorns. Edward was once again above the ground, and Cerberus was using his magic to swing the big white unicorn around like a weight at the end of a string. Edward struck the wall, the floor, the ceiling. Cerberus laughed a sadistic equine laugh.

"Yield, and I will stop them," said Kold.

Something inside Clint snapped into surrender as he watched

Edward break and smash and whinny. And, knowing the proud unicorn would never want pity or beg for mercy, Clint gave him both.

"I yield," said Clint.

"Now tell Edward not to fight."

Clint looked at the unicorns as if outside of his skin. When Edward and Cerberus had faced off in Solace, there had been a moment where a spell had reversed Clint's lights and darks and he'd seen the world in negative. When that had happened, he had thought Edward was Cerberus and Cerberus was Edward. Was that happening again? Why should he call off *Edward?*

"Do it!" Kold repeated, pressing harder with his boot.

"Edward, stop fighting," Clint croaked. It was barely audible, but the moment he said it, the tumult at the other end of the room stopped. Kold raised his hand, palm down, and lowered it for Cerberus's eye. The dark unicorn lowered Edward to the floor.

Almost immediately, the white unicorn rocked to his feet, shook, and became as good as new, healed entirely. He walked toward the men. On the way, he gave Cerberus a glance and said, "Buttface."

Above Clint, Kold said, "I can end you at any time. Do you understand?"

Edward stood between Kold and Cerberus. Despite the room's condition and the fact that Clint was still in unbelievable pain, it was hard to imagine they'd just concluded an epic battle. Edward didn't so much as flinch toward Kold or Cerberus, and the dark unicorn didn't so much as cast Edward a glance.

"Yar," said Clint.

"You're a fool, gunslinger," Kold said, removing the boot.

"Yar."

Clint felt his bones and skin begin to knit, then looked up at Edward as his horn stopped glowing, cycling down to pearlescent white. The gunslinger stood and brushed himself clean, now nearly as shirtless as Kold. Any more fighting and they'd both have ended up as naked as the unicorns.

"The worlds will die," said Kold. "The Realm will grow stronger."

"So what." It wasn't a question. It was simply what it was. Clint was beyond tired.

"Talk to Mai. Convince her."

"Nar."

Kold shook his head, heaving a heavy, disbelieving sigh.

"It doesn't make any difference anymore," Edward said, gesturing around the room with his head. "The battle of wills. He's shed blood. The decision is cast."

Clint looked at Edward. The unicorn turned, silent.

"What?" said Clint, finding Edward's eye.

"You made the wrong decision."

"Oh, is that what you think?"

Edward seemed too tired to argue. "Yar. That's what I think."

"I'll think about it," the gunslinger said.

"It's too late."

Edward's manner sparked something inside of Clint. The unicorn seemed defeated, utterly and completely spent, as if the worlds had ended already. Clint had never heard such desperation and resignation from the proud, noble, arrogant creature.

"If you agreed with him, you should have told me," said Clint.

Edward shook his head. "It had to be your choice."

"Then I'll change my mind," said Clint. "I'll talk to her. I'll go to her now, if you think that's best, if you…"

Edward kept shaking his head. "I told you. Intention matters to magic. Things have been set in motion, and you have consecrated your decision with blood."

Cerberus shook his big black head and muttered, "Humans."

Clint turned to Kold. "You should have told her. Not me. *Her.* When you captured her, you should have explained it. Whatever it was that you thought. Whatever Edward is saying. Mai might have seen it as true. She might have understood."

Quietly, sounding not at all like himself, Kold's green eyes looked into Clint's blue ones and said, "What makes you think she didn't know? Did you think she found you in Solace by accident?"

"I…"

"Clint, we separated years before Solace. You didn't want to pursue her. I did. I found her. Years before. *Years.*"

"I…"

"So she ran. She ran, and she hid, and eventually she sought out the one man who she thought might be able to protect her."

Clint felt like all the air had fled from his lungs. He wanted to say more, but couldn't summon the breath. He wanted to fold up and die. It felt like someone had grabbed hold of his entire life and yanked the soul from inside it, leaving his body where it was to carry out its various chemist's reactions as the elements willed, like a machine.

Kold turned to Edward. "Gather the unicorns," he said. "It is time."

Edward nodded his assent. "How many?"

Kold looked around the room, at Cerberus, at Clint, and finally back at Edward.

"All of them," he said.

UNICORN WESTERN 8

CHAPTER ONE:
THE MAN IN THE MIRROR

The man in the shack stared into the mirror above his sink. He'd built the shack with his own two large hands, back when such things had mattered. When he'd finished the house, the man's wife had decorated the place in a way that suited her, and appalled him. The mirror was one such appalling item. It had a heavy wooden frame with ornate, scrolled edges, painted in garish colors ranging from red to blue to orange to yellow. It was an ugly, ugly thing. Mayhap as hideous as the face of the man in the mirror.

The top of the mirror's frame was a blue, darker than midnight and pocked with pinpricks of white that were supposed to be stars. That symbolized eternity. The bottom was green, symbolizing the ground, grass, or world. Mayhap *worlds*. The other colors were somewhere in between. There was something on the mirror that looked like a white horse, though if anyone made that observation, the something would have been deeply offended. Guns were scrawled on the mirror, but their shapes looked clumsy and stupid. The mirror, when taken as a whole, was a child's rendering of the man's life: all rainbows and good times when viewed through one set of eyes, but very little happiness when seen through the eyes of the truth.

The man's face was long and deeply creased — more wrinkled than the man himself remembered. He wore a gray beard, streaked here and there with stubborn strands of brown that refused to surrender to age. The man reached up and ran his hand across the beard, thinking as he did each time he saw it that he should shave. The thing was scraggly, not at all trimmed. His neck was covered in stubble, with nothing beneath but tendons and rough skin like the skin of the turkeys in his pen out back. The face in the mirror was deeply tanned, testimony to a life lived under the unforgiving sun. The man's hair was the only thing that had more or less held firm. It was brown flecked with gray rather than the other way around, as his beard had chosen. The hair looked strange to the man because he almost never saw it. On the rare occasions the man had seen the whole of his head in a mirror, he'd worn a hat — flattened, beaten, and brown — that was almost as much a witness to his life as his own two eyes.

The man leaned forward, peering into the blue eyes that were set deep in the leathery old face. Those hadn't changed, and had remained piercing and cold. As the man watched himself, meeting those eyes, he imagined them as the eyes of an enemy — which, in a way, they were. He tried pretending he was staring down a foe, trying to put himself in the shoes of the many men for whom those same eyes had been the last things they'd ever seen. He tried seeing past the gray beard and wrinkled skin and into the eyes themselves — into the soul of the gunslinger who'd protected The Realm, roamed the Sands, pursued his foe, then spent decades trying to forget it all. Everything was there. Looking close, feeling weightless, the man could see it writ in those blue eyes like words in a long book.

He pulled back, again running a hand through his beard. The beard made him look older than he was, and he was plenty ancient. For the thousandth time, he decided it wasn't worth the effort to fill the sink, wet the blade, or make the lather. He never looked in the mirror anyhow — not when he could avoid it. He hated the mirror almost as much as he hated the face.

The man turned from the mirror, walked back into his small bedroom, and pulled on the same basic outfit he'd worn nearly every day of his life: denims, a long-sleeved shirt (today's was brown), and a vest. He pulled on his boots. He kept his pistols in their holsters, left the holsters on his gunbelt, and left the gunbelt with his hat, slung over a chair. Once, someone had come to the shack to tell him he should turn them in, that he was no longer a marshal and would no longer be able to carry those guns. That stranger had told him that he'd have to trade them both in for a single six-shooter. At that time, the man had still worn the guns on his hips whenever he was awake, so as his visitor had blathered on, he'd rested one hand on his right pistol — not at all agitated but also not at all moved — and had told the small, bald official that one time in the past, he'd used a single six-shooter and what he'd done hadn't made a difference. The twin seven-shooters, he'd continued, always had. Then he'd spread his arms and told the official that regardless, if the ex-marshal would no longer be allowed his guns, then the man should go ahead and take them from him. The man had looked at the man, had looked at the pistols, and then had left without a word or whistle.

The man walked through the shack, his movements barely noticed, going through nothing more than rote habit. He turned on the spark lights and started a timer on the steam cooker. There was a small spark receiver on the counter that would broadcast music if you turned it just right (they'd begun to re-sing Joelsongs in the city, which the man enjoyed, but they had also changed the beats, which he loathed), but he'd never managed to figure out how to work the thing so he barely noticed it. The receiver, like the mirror, had been bought by his wife.

While his cooker heated, the man dropped to the wooden deck inside the shack and started his daily pushups. His joints popped through the first few repetitions, then warmed and went silent as he hit number twenty. Like always, the pushups started with pain, transitioned into a lulling middle, and ended with more pain. The second round of pain was harsher than the first, but that was the part the man most enjoyed. It was rewarding, and it punished him. Both were good.

By the time the former marshal and one-time gunslinger reached eighty repetitions, his arms and chest were burning in earnest. Lately, his back had also started to scream in protest. The man pushed through the pain, feeling it fill him. He relished it. He closed his eyes, refusing to grit his teeth as pain flooded his frame like an acid burn. With every beat of his heart, the pain told him that he was still alive. The man wanted to remember that. There had been many times when he had wanted to die, but it was more painful to keep living, so the man did his pushups to sharpen the invisible blade that felt as if it were permanently stuck in his chest. The pain reminded his body that his tenure in this world had yet to end, and that life was meant to hurt while he continued to live. It was a man's duty to bear the pain and to keep breathing. Beyond that, little else mattered.

Once he finished his pushups (topping out and unable to move after 138 repetitions), the man moved on to situps, wedging his feet under the large steam cooker. A kettle boiled on its top as he moved his torso up and down, running through the same routine — popping joints followed by shock-like discomfort, then a lull in the middle, ending with the growing agony of acid seeping into his exhausted midsection, thighs, and hips. His back screamed through the situps but he pushed on anyway. The kettle atop the cooker wobbled as he worked. One day, the kettle would fall, and the boiling water would scald him. Today was not that day.

Because the man had to think on *something*, he thought every day at this point about what the morning had waiting for him. The answer was the same as every day since he and his partner had retired. The retirement — of both partners in the partnership — had happened quite by default. Neither had planned it. They had simply returned to Meadowlands — the man to his shack and the unicorn to his own abode with his new bride — and then had never gone out riding again. They hadn't exactly decided to stop heading out into the Sands. They had simply done so.

Secretly, Clint suspected that Edward's new mare had something to do with their unspoken retirement, but he never outright accused Edward or the mare (her name was Cameron, though Clint preferred to think of her as Yoko — an ancient term referring to a female Judas) of falling into domesticity and growing soft. For one, unicorns were incapable of growing soft. And for another, Clint suspected that whatever resentment he felt had less to do with his own feelings and more with Edward's bliss. How many years had he ridden with Edward? How long had the two known each other? How much of each other's souls did the other possess, and how much would live within the other until one of them (that would be Clint, of course) died? And through those many long years, how often had Edward expressed joy, or been kind, or shown compassion, or even been reasonable? Clint could count the number of times Edward had given him a kind word on one finger. That single instance of empathy had happened three years after the encounter in Dharma Kold's citadel, around the time Clint first realized he hated his mirror true, even though he could nar bring himself to discard it.

But now Edward was a changed unicorn. These days when Clint saw him (which was rare), he accused Edward of blowing pink bubbles, shooting fairy sparks, and not only bleeding rainbows... but now farting them as well. In the past, that kind of observation would have earned the gunslinger a hoof in the chest. Now it brought a laugh that Clint had never heard during his many years atop the unicorn's back — a laugh that said affectionately that the former marshal had gotten him, and that the marshal spoke true. Edward would nuzzle his Yoko and send bile to rise up Clint's throat. But instead of gagging, Clint would open the straight slit in his face that passed for a human mouth and mutter something about being happy for his former partner. In the past, the unicorn would have laughed at that too, mocking Clint's deadpan sentiment and calling him a curmudgeon. But now he never did. Now Edward simply asked after Clint's turkeys and pumpkins, and inquired about his proficiency at distilling his own brew from the apples that grew from the largest tree in his yard — the tree on Clint's hilltop, once dry and brown but now bearing fat apples as if magically brought back from the dead.

The cooker was still heating, so the gunslinger curled his long, thin fingers around the doorjamb overhead and started his pullups. He wanted triple triples (having gotten 138 pushups and 141 situps), but he'd never managed more than 48 fingertip pullups, then another 34 from the bar before his arms finally quit. Today he managed 49 and 35, but they felt like a lie, since Clint knew the numbers he wanted to achieve and had subtly cheated to make them.

He dropped to the floor and bent forward to stretch, feeling every muscle scream. He was six-foot-three and weighed 145 pounds. It was far too little. He had no fat on him, with nar enough muscle. He barely ate and lived too lean, and his body had been trained not to allow him to gain more tissue than was strictly necessary. His body felt it was inefficient and greedy to carry more than a man needed. To hoard tissue was to do as The Realm did, hoarding magic. But then again, Meadowlands was becoming a lot like The Realm, too.

Edward felt that the comparison was a bit much, and said so on the rare occasions when they palavered like the old days. Clint grumbled that Meadowlands had grown soft, that Kold had turned his playground of a city into a miniature Realm. Edward said that while The Realm pinched magic away from its source (and the Sands, of course) in order to sustain itself, Meadowlands was fueled by the twin (and still warring) factions of steam and spark. Kold had funded both enterprises, just as he'd funded the training of doctors under Mercy Barlowe and just as he'd continued to fund those doctors so that they could provide their services to the people of the city for free.

Kold no longer even used birds or bandits to funnel wealth into the city. That was something Clint pretended he'd persuaded the baron to do, but in truth, the baron had done it on his own after the Darkness, for reasons unknown, had vanished into the desert... or into the Core below it. Ever since Kold had failed to breach the wall and the train project had stalled (because how good was a Sands/Realm train when one couldn't reach The Realm?), Kold had turned the incomplete power of the Triangulum Enchantem toward the city. The Triangulum's magic was at least balanced, Edward said. Clint felt that he was being naive.

Beside the old gunslinger, the steam cooker dinged. Clint pulled his pie from the cooker's compartment, let it cool, then took a slice and poured himself a cup of tea from the kettle. The old Edward would have mocked the tea, but tea had become a part of Clint's ritual. The tea comforted him in ways that he'd never admit to wanting — mayhap *needing*.

He took his mug and went outside, staring out across his vast field of grass, past the pen of squawking turkeys and into Meadowlands. The Realm was always visible now, thanks to the Triangulum's power. But without the full strength of the Orb of Benevolence, The Realm would remain nothing more than a shimmer bewitching the sky. A city no one could reach, unknowingly (or uncaringly) brewing an apocalypse that none on the Sands side of the wall could prevent.

Behind Clint, there was the distinctive clicking of a pistol being cocked.

It was the kid. The kid he'd heard approach. The kid he could smell on the wind. The kid whose presence he could feel in a way he couldn't explain, in the way that he always, nowadays, simply *felt* the presence of people around him.

A voice said, "You don't look like no rootin-tootin', finger-twitchin', cold-blooded killer."

Clint sipped his tea and sat down, looking out over the city, slowly deciding whether to kill the kid or allow him to keep breathing.

CHAPTER TWO:
THE BEGINNING OF THE END

"You're only twenty feet in back of me," Clint told the voice behind him without turning, "but if you pull the trigger in the way you *will* pull it, with an unpracticed dominant hand, you will anticipate the kick and compensate for it without meaning to. You'll miss high and to the right." Still looking out toward Meadowlands and the wavering shimmer of The Realm behind it, Clint raised a long, bony finger and pointed at a lantern hanging from a beam above the porch. "You will hit that lantern. And if you do, I'll have to lay you stone dead, because I love that lantern."

"Are you Clint Gulliver?"

Clint took a bite of the pie sitting beside him on the deck. He chewed slowly, then swallowed. "Yar."

"Like I said, you don't look like no cold-blooded killer."

"Shoot my lantern, and you'll find out whether or not I am."

"What if I hit you, and you're wrong?"

Chew. Swallow.

"Meh."

Clint could make out every noise the kid made while fumbling with the gun. He was an idiot. Clint could hear the quaver in his voice just as he'd heard him drawing his weapon. The kid had almost certainly never pointed a gun at a man. He'd probably shot cans from fenceposts, and he probably thought he could shoot straight. But ending a life was something different, and the kid was nervous enough about it to twitch. He thought he could squeeze the trigger instead of jerking it, but Clint knew he couldn't. He'd jounce and miss.

Clint heard the kid lower the gun's hammer and holster his iron. Then he heard footsteps — not approaching, but going around, down the porch's other steps. While Clint looked out on Meadowlands and chewed his pie, the kid stepped into his peripheral vision. He seemed about seventeen and had the look of someone who couldn't grow facial hair if he tried, yet had tried anyway. He had a scrubby little mustache and cheeks that were smooth and water-fat, as if he'd never seen sand. He seemed fit but untested, shorter than Clint but broader. Clint thought he might be able to out-draw the kid as they stood, even with his own guns still inside the house.

"I didn't mean nothin' by it," said the kid, staring into Clint's steely, appraising gaze. "I just wanted to see if you was who they say you are."

"Who I *once was*, kid," Clint corrected.

"I came about your unicorn. About Edward."

The retired gunslinger swore inside his head. What, was he Edward's social secretary? The unicorn had grown too comfortable for his own good.

"He's not *my* unicorn. If you'd said that to him years ago, he would have run you through with his horn. We were equals, if that."

The kid stared at Clint, waiting for him to continue. Clint didn't. He didn't want the kid here, and wanted to make it obvious. If the kid had business, Clint didn't want to have to ask on it. Nor did he care.

"I'm Billy. Billy Bristow. You fought with my grappy around the time Baron Diamante — I know his real name is Kold — first came to Solace. Grappy lived in Solace all his life and said they still tell legends there about you. Is it true you once took out a team of fifty bandits alone? That your uni… that Edward didn't even help? They say you walked through like a gauntlet, not even bothering to duck or hide since they could only come at you from three directions and you knew you were too fast? That it was like one of those popup shooting galleries where none of the targets shoot back?"

"That was a long time ago, kid. I'm not like that anymore."

"They say your holsters aren't made of leather — that they couldn't be, because your draw is so fast, it'd burn the hide."

"My holsters are leather."

"Can I see them?"

Clint chewed. "What the sands do you want?"

The kid seemed to resettle, too awed for rebuking. "Oh. Well, I live in Meadowlands. Not in the city, you see. Out on a ranch, like you. My grappy taught me to shoot. We don't have spark, just a few steam machines." Clint rolled his eyes up toward the kid, feigning the sort of interest that speaks loudly of indifference. The kid was trying to show him that he wasn't like the others and that he was a hard man. Like the marshal.

"Well like I said, I live in Meadowlands, see, and, well, there are rumors. About the magic. I live on that main road there —" He pointed. "— where the rails were laid. The old rails. By the main road into town, see? And people have been coming into town, by us, lately. They stand out because... well, you know how it's been since the new fractures, even before the big fractures a few years back. Not as many people on the road these days. Realm, Meadowlands, then everything else, like we're reaching for three tiers. I haven't ridden out to see for myself, but people say you can't mostly pass the Rio Verde no more, that soon we'll be as broken off as The Realm. They say that soon we'll need a shimmer to reach Baracho Gulch. It's happening all back through Baracho, San Mateo Flats, Aurora Solstice, um...

"Nazareth Shiloh," said Clint.

"Yar. And beyond. But the travelers, see, there ain't many no more most of the time. But there have been in the past days and weeks, and so my appy, he asked them, and all they'd say is that they felt called. They don't know why they're coming. But Appy, he says he seen The Realm shimmer brighter and brighter, and the rumor is maybe the baron's gonna open the Realm and the railroad."

Clint laughed a dry laugh, still sitting, then looked up at the kid.

"I've been hearing that for a long time, kid. Go home."

"But anyway," said the kid, barging on, "Appy said to go see Mister Edward, since he's the shaman, and so I said that were turkey stupid since the unicorns don't palaver with humans unless *they* call to *us*, and that the last man what went to the unicorns unannounced got himself turned different colors for his trouble, and had to walk around like that forever. But Appy said that Grappy palavered with Edward back in the olden days, and then he said the baron keeps company with *all* of the unicorns. Is that true?"

"That's a rumor, nothing more," said Clint. It *wasn't* a rumor, of course. Kold not only kept company with the unicorns; he'd once plotted alongside them, strategized with them, and asked them to stand ready to help in a conflict that had been brewing — but never boiling over — for decades. Kold had called the unicorns together and then, adding a few forces of his own, referred to the works as The Army of the Triangulum. Clint, however, thought of them as the Army of Frustration. The once-enthusiastic cooperation between Kold and the unicorns had soured when the futility of marching anywhere with the so-called "army" had become painfully obvious. After it became apparent that Kold's supposed "plan B" to breach his way into The Realm was beyond useless, the unicorns had more or less gone back to doing their own thing and Kold had gone back to trying to figure out how to breach the wall. He'd made no progress and practiced mostly politics these days. That's what Clint had heard, anyway, though he didn't care to ask further.

"Anyway, Appy is all superstitious about the fractures like most older folks, saying that it weren't this way when he married Ammy and they had me. So he got all a-jitter enough that I finally said okay, okay, I'd try to gather some answers, but that I couldn't go to the unicorns. And that's when I remembered you and Grappy."

"I don't remember your grappy," said Clint. And at that, the kid started to open his mouth to explain, so Clint barged on. "Nor do I care," he added. "But the magic? Kid, the magic has been getting worse for years. If you feel something out there, it's because it's finally all starting."

"Starting?"

"The end," said Clint. "The beginning of the end. The leaking is getting worse."

"But if it's just that magic from the cracks is coming out, then that's no big..."

"Magic isn't always good, kid. Even white magic."

"I don't understand."

"And I don't want to explain," Clint said, feeling deja vu. He had an odd sense of role-reversal. In the past, it was always Clint who didn't understand and stodgy Edward who didn't want to explain. He knew what the kid felt like, but now he also knew what Edward must have felt like, too: he simply didn't care.

"You've *got* to explain, though, if you know something. The magic..."

"Sands to the magic," said Clint.

"You were once a marshal! Isn't that still in you? Your duty..."

"Sands to *duty!*"

"But the stories about you and Mister Edward — the *legends*, pleasem and thankoo, about all you did after you and the baron became a team again..."

"We did *not* become a team again."

"... all those stories! In the land outside of OldTown, we tell them around the fires! They'll tell your stories for generations — about your quest to save the worlds and heal the fractures, to stop the leaking and open The Realm, how you were bound by duty and honor and..."

Clint jabbed two long fingers at the gray whiskers on his chin.

"Kid, don't you see this beard? This beard says that I'm full of regret and that *I don't care!*"

The kid stopped speaking, his body drooping. "I see. Well, sir, it was nice to meet you, anyhow."

"Thanks for not shooting my lantern. Now go away."

The kid mounted his horse — a pathetic, snaggletoothed thing that looked approximately one billion years old — and plodded down the hill. His body language was so pathetic that Clint and his beard wanted to mock it. He wanted to call after the kid, shouting at him, *Yar, sulk like a baby; now you'd better go off and cry in your apple brew, wah, wah, wah.*

Once his porch and land were deserted, Clint sat for a moment longer, watching The Realm. It had, indeed, seemed brighter and more present of late. The leaking and fractures *were* getting worse, of course. But what was to be done? Nothing. Nothing at all. He looked at The Realm and wondered if, when the bonds finally broke, the moments before the apocalypse would actually bring The Realm closer to Meadowlands, curling the worlds into a tight ball before the entire works dropped into a bottomless abyss.

The magic. He heard it in his mind as if said by a whiny, annoying voice. *Of course* the kid and his family could feel the magic. The all-powerful, all-amazing *magic*. The magic to which all beings must bend, because it was so dagged important. The magic, to which Clint had subjugated his life. For which he'd *thrown away* his life, in fact. And it had all been for nothing. Meadowlands was growing and prospering under a wise and paradoxically benevolent leader while the world continued to end. And as to the other thing the kid had said? Well, it was true. Clint *had* been a cold-blooded killer. But the good guys and bad guys had grown confused over time. He'd served The Realm early in his life and had later killt its officers; he'd freed a terrorist murderer from a Realm knight and had become the terrorist murderer's friend. So really, how was Clint any different from Kold in the end? How exactly was Kold *not* the good guy now, in these strange new days?

Clint hadn't thought about Sly Stone for years.

Or Buckaroo.

Or Pompi Bobo, who at last rumor had returned to Baracho Gulch to marry his love, Paloma, after the railroad project had stalled.

The former marshal looked out across the city with all its alloy and glass, sensing Kold in the mountains beyond, fighting his futile fight and trying to breach the unbreachable wall. The kid had said that there was new magic in the air. And no matter how Clint felt about the kid and his fool errand, things *had* changed lately. He'd been feeling a kind of magic aura all around him for weeks.

Mayhap this *was* the end. Mayhap Kold had found a way to power the machine after all, and this was the beginning.

Clint stood, suddenly feeling every year of his age. He took his plate and teacup inside, set them by the sink, then mounted his brown horse for a ride down into the valley.

CHAPTER THREE: BLOOD AND TEARS

Edward lived in a unicorn house, which was very different from a barn. It was like a human house but much larger, with extra headroom and no low-hanging overhead lights. There were no steam or spark lines coming in, because neither steam nor spark was needed in a house that was rich with magic. There were all sorts of appliances in the kitchen (which had wide counters and floors made of a gritty, friction-rich stone) that simply worked when their owners wanted them to. The lights throughout the building lit as needed, powered by the unicorns themselves.

It had been weeks since Clint had seen his old partner, and when he arrived, he went through the same two-phase experience as always. At first, he sat down with the great white unicorn, felt comfortable, and wondered why they didn't palaver more often. Then Edward's unicorn wife Cameron walked in (they were hard to tell apart, though Edward had a stronger jaw), and Clint remembered the reason.

"You don't like her," Edward said after Cameron left them alone on the wide patio. The house was picturesque and lavish, but that could be said of any unicorn house. Unicorns didn't need to save money in order to buy fancy homes. They could simply magick them up.

"Nar, I don't," said Clint. It was an overly-direct answer, but Clint was old and was therefore allowed to be cranky.

"Why not?"

"Well, just look what she's done to you. What have you become, anyway?"

"Head shaman, like my father before me. Unicorn ambassador to the Army of the Triangulum." He said both with gentle self-effacement, as if he didn't believe in his own titles.

"You forgot 'Jerk'," Clint added.

"I'm less of a jerk now."

"That's the problem," Clint said, sipping his tall glass of Fanta, feeling it sparkle into his head. He loathed Fanta. Once upon a time, he'd liked it, but times changed. Cameron always brought it to him because he was human, and Fanta was the premier, most elegant drink a human could sip. It was an annoying assumption. She would, of course, immediately stop bringing Clint Fanta the minute he asked her to, which was exactly why he didn't ask. It was more satisfying to hate her.

Edward said, "Well, it's easier to be less of a jerk when you're happy."

Clint looked up at the unicorn, then rolled his eyes.

Edward looked exactly the same as he had throughout the entire time Clint had known him. He didn't know how old the unicorn was and had never cared enough to ask, but he knew that unicorns were nearly (if not literally) immortal. Edward, it seemed, would never have to get old and bitter because he'd never have to get old. He'd already done his 'bitter' time with Clint, so now he was going to be happy. It was obnoxious. Clint knew he shouldn't be rude, but he couldn't help himself. He found Cameron annoying. But what was even worse, Edward said that they were thinking of having foals. And so rather than congratulating Edward on his fabulous new life, Clint had made a biting remark about how painful unicorn births must be. Edward, who was farting too many rainbows to notice the gunslinger's apathy, simply replied that unicorns only grew their horns after they were born.

"Mmm," Clint grunted, remembering the day in Solace that he'd worn a strange outfit and had nearly surrendered his pistols, thinking how strange it was to feel happy. He'd worn that happiness like another man's hat. Now Edward was wearing that hat, and it was every bit as strange.

"Try," said Edward. "Try to like her."

"Mmm."

"I liked Mai. The least you could do would be to try and do the same for me." Then the unicorn stopped, seemed flustered, and turned away.

"I'm sorry," he said.

Clint grunted. "Mmm."

"I just meant that..."

"Don't worry about it. It was a long time ago."

"But I know how…"

"I said forget about it." Clint crossed his arms, looking out into the valley. Edward's porch was open and oversaw a small, non-magical river. Clint watched the water. A stick floated down the river, caught on a rock, turned, and continued in the same direction backward.

The unicorn sighed. "You never understood. About any of it."

"I understand fine. She died. I buried her under my tree. I pursued Kold for five years to rescue her, then was hitched to her for three. That seems fair."

"It's not about fair. It's about…"

"Yar, yar. The *magic*. The precious *magic*. Why has everything in my life revolved around magic, Edward the Shaman? Edward the Brave? Edward the Ambassador? Tell me. I never asked for a life of magic, other than riding a unicorn. And yet everything has been about rules and rituals and restrictions and… and *SANDS TO THE STUPID MAGIC!*"

"Your life was enmeshed with magic the minute I chose you. It's true for all marshals. I am the light. You are the dark. Together we are whole, just like the elements of the Triangulum."

"Oh, yar. The Triangulum. Because *that* mattered. Five long years in the sand, chasing something that, once assembled, powered a city and made life better for its citizens. It's too bad we failed to prevent *that*. The Triangulum, for which Mai gave her life. Only that's not true either, is it? She gave her life to become what would power the Triangulum and mayhap seal the breach across the worlds by opening a door in The Realm's wall, but then she never deposited her 'Orb soul' or whatever it was into it. And why, Edward? Because of 'the rules'? Who makes these rules?"

"There are things you don't understand."

Clint stood and slammed his Fanta onto the table. The glass cracked at the base, and the orange liquid seeped onto the tabletop.

"Oh, that's an understatement!" he spat. " 'Things I don't understand.' As if there were only a few! How much truth did you tell me over the years, Edward? Do you remember back in San Mateo, in that barn, with those crows outside waiting to kill us? You told me you knew what was happening, then said you wouldn't explain it to me because I'm a poor dumb mortal. Well, I gave my life to the service of your stupid magic, and I gave it my wife, and I rode with you in ignorance as your lackey because I was just too dumb to understand. Why did you choose me, if I'm so stupid? I'm ugly, I'm dumb, I never understand…"

Edward rose briefly onto his rear legs, flailed with a foreleg, and struck Clint in the chest. The gunslinger stumbled backward, tripping over his feet before smashing through the sliding glass door that opened into Edward's house. Clint felt the glass shards slice his skin as he struck the ground. When he looked up, the unicorn was standing over him. His cheery demeanor had departed, and he was the old Edward again.

"Stop feeling sorry for yourself," he said.

"Edward?" Cameron called from inside the house.

"It's nothing. Stay where you are," Edward yelled. But hoofbeats continued to approach, so he yelled louder. *"I said it's nothing!"*

The hooves slowly retreated. Above Clint, Edward's horn glowed. But Clint didn't want to be healed. He pushed up onto his rear, then climbed to standing. He was bleeding from a dozen places, but waved Edward away.

"Don't heal me."

"You'll bleed to death."

"So I'll bleed."

A glow struck Clint. He looked up at the unicorn, furious.

"You were bleeding on my patio," Edward explained.

"You see?" Clint said. "Magic makes everything pointless. You kick me through a window, then heal me. So why do it? What's the meaning? To make a point? You know what Stone said? He said we had it too easy. 'You and Edward don't know what it's like to ride for real,' he said. 'It doesn't mean anything if you get shot. You can shoot through walls.' And on and on. And he was right. What difference did it all make, in the end?"

"It made a great deal of difference."

"I'm still a grizzled old gunslinger who will die alone. You're still a jerk who will kick me through a window if it suits you. And you still think I won't understand. You still won't tell me everything."

Edward sighed. "Sit down."

Clint, disarmed by the sudden resignation in Edward's voice, sat.

"First of all, I didn't know it all from the start. I learned it along the way, same as you, except that I was usually a few steps ahead. And when, back in San Mateo Flats, I refused to tell you what I'd realized — namely that Kold hadn't gotten the Orb out of Mai, that she would likely recover, and that when she did, she'd finally be the pure Orb that she was supposed to be — I didn't refuse to tell you because I thought you were too dumb. I didn't tell you because in the end, what happened had to be your decision."

"I don't und..."

"Magic has rules. You know that. You also know that it's not inert, and that it responds to the will of the soul who wields it.

Unicorns are the white. There is no conflict inside us. But you? Humans? You are rife with conflict. Unicorn 'free will' means little. But *your* free will means everything. I couldn't pollute your decision in the final reckoning. I had to follow your path, whatever it turned out to be. You sealed our fate when you set me to fight Cerberus. I knew it was wrong, but did it anyway."

"Moronic! You should have told me!"

"In the end, I did."

"But by then, I couldn't change my mind! What sort of idiocy is that?"

"Conviction. Belief. Decision. Intention. All matter. I know it's cruel. But once you chose not to try to persuade Mai, it was all over."

Clint shook his head. "It's not fair."

"Nar. It's not. But what you must understand, Marshal, is that as I've told you over and over and over again, *Mai is in a better place*."

Clint waved a dismissive hand, exhausted by the ancient discussion.

"I'm not talking about superstitions and legends, Clint. I'm not talking about NextWorld. You thought the new magic growing inside Mai consumed her like a cancer, but it's more like she outgrew her body. When I was overpowered by the magic south of Nazareth Shiloh at the open vein, I felt a small portion of the same thing. What you saw was that I forgot myself. But what it felt like to me was that I was in the wrong place. I didn't know where to go. It was as if I was wearing 'Edward the unicorn' like a costume. I didn't know how to wear that body with the magic so intense, and if I could have left my body, I would have. Same for Mai. We saw it from the start. Her abilities. Then her fugues and blackouts. Hours and days gone missing. You knew it when you hitched her. Her condition was very advanced by then, but when she died, she didn't just die. She *evolved*."

"Evolved into a box under my apple tree."

Edward shook his head. "What you buried was just her husk. Like what we found in that lean-to before her purified soul returned."

"And all for nothing."

"She knew it, Clint. You know she did. Kold found her after we split from him, way back at the beginning after we left The Realm. Kold knew, even then, what she was. So she ran. But she didn't run without direction; she ran where her magic told her to go. And when she found you, she held your arm for protection. She fought him for years as we followed — enough fighting to strip the soul from her bones. But in the end, she knew what had to be done. The fight was necessary. She had to die, so that she could be reborn as the pure being she was intended to be."

"And then because of me, she never even fulfilled whatever destiny she was supposed to have."

Edward sighed again. "Mayhap."

Clint felt a drop of blood fall onto his hand. Another landed on his leg. But when he looked down, he realized that it wasn't blood that had fallen. The liquid was clear, like water. It had rolled from the end of his nose. He was surprised, but made no effort to wipe the tears from his eyes.

"I miss her. Even after all these years."

"She's all around you," Edward said.

"Platitudes." Clint shook his head.

"Truth," the unicorn countered.

A long, quiet moment passed between them. Edward hadn't yet fixed the shattered glass door. In the quiet, a gust of wind caused a sliver of glass to teeter from the frame and fall with a clink.

"A kid came to see me. He says the magic is gathering in town."

"Yar. The unicorns know about it."

"And Kold knows?"

"Yar."

"Is this it? Is this how it ends?"

"I don't think so. This is something else. Whiter. More powerful. But most importantly, more *focused*. Things are growing. Literally *growing*. New fields. Crops coming to maturity in days rather than months, and producing huge yields. Different parts of town at different times. At the hospital in OldTown, all of the patients' plants began to bloom long after they'd died and been forgotten. Incurable patients healed. A woman with a broken neck stood and walked out, unharmed, as if cured by a unicorn, back before we got disgusted enough with the human population to cut off most contact. But then whatever it was moved on. The next day, the plants at the hospital again started to falter. The patients who had begun healing reached a plateau. And on that day, a row of azaleas bloomed from a long, hairline crack down the center of Main Street."

"What is it?"

"I don't know."

"*For real* you don't know, or *I'm not going to tell you because you won't understand* I don't know?"

"The former. I've run out of foreknowledge. Your decision was the end of it. This is all new to me."

"But what do you suspect, oh wise and great unicorn?"

Edward tossed his head toward the open end of the patio. "Come on. I'll tell you on the way."

"On the way?"

Edward nodded. "We're going to the river."

CHAPTER FOUR:
DOWN TO THE RIVER

Clint's horse was very excited to go to the river.

"Yippie! Mee-sa wanta walk in the water!" said the horse.

The horse was named Joe. Joe's grappy (who was also named Joe, same as his appy) had followed Clint, Edward, Mai, and Pompi all the way from his herd of slow talking horses who drank from the magic Rio Verde river to Clint and Mai's front door. When Clint tried to shoo him away, Joe (generation 1) had explained his life's purpose versus Edward's life purpose in what had sounded like a sea islands accent, getting most of the facts wrong. He even got Clint's gender wrong while standing directly in front of him. Then Joe had foals with a local horse, and Joe Jr. had foals with another local horse. After the third generation of talking horses with inexplicable accents, Edward had concluded that the genes that dictated stupidity could not be diluted away. Edward was still with Clint at the time, but all three generations of Joes had grown on the unicorn despite their idiocy. They had all come in handy on occasion. Joe Jr. thought he was a stagecoach. Edward tried to explain the difference to him many times, but a man could ride a stagecoach the same as he could ride a horse, so it didn't end up mattering.

Clint asked why they were going to the river. Edward said it was because he stank.

"I have a tub at the house," Clint said.

"Yar, but I fear you've not learned how to use it. Besides, the river is on the way to town, and bathing this way gives me an opportunity to dunk you under water."

"We should go to the Verde," said Clint.

"Mee-sa wanna see the green riva, Meesta Clint!" said Joe.

Edward looked briefly backward, first at Joe and then up onto Joe's back, at Clint.

"I've been to the Verde," said the unicorn. "It's almost impassible. I had to do something like a half-fold to cross what was essentially a half-shimmer — basically a huge fracture back near Baracho. The path we came in on all those years ago is gone. People, elves, giants, and others are managing to cross it on the days when the worlds are close, but I can't imagine how many others simply walk off the end of the road and into the abyss. The fissure is barely visible to the non-magical eye, but it's most certainly there. The crack is especially deep, too. You should feel what's leaking from it."

"I want to drink from it so that I can get magic cancer and die," Clint said.

Joe gave a shrill shriek of alarm.

Edward ignored the horse. "Tell me something. What made you come to talk to me today?"

"The kid. I told you," he said. And Clint *had* told him, in full, on the ride down. He had to keep shouting the story to Edward because Joe wanted to veer off course. Joe's meandering was bad enough that the old gunslinger wished Edward would just hurry up and invite him to ride again. He'd even mentioned it to Edward, and Edward had said that he would, but that they'd lost a bit of bonding that would have to be re-established first. And also, Clint stank.

"You didn't come to talk to me about the kid. You came to talk to me about Mai."

"I came to talk to you about the kid," Clint said. "And the magic he said was brewing."

"Do you even know who that kid was? Billy Bristow?"

"Townie kid. It nar matters."

Edward turned his big white head to look at Clint. "That's Teddy's grandkid. You remember Teddy."

Clint did. Teddy was Solace's town kid all those years ago. The young orphan who'd had that dumb, googly-eyed horse.

"That annoying kid," said Clint. "Yar, I remember him."

"I heard the story from Teddy's appy years ago. Teddy followed us. That's how he ended up in Meadowlands, after it was all over. He followed us all that way, all those years. Sniffed out our trail. Asked folks after us. Tracked us like a hound. He was months behind at best, but he was there. And why not? He didn't have anything else to do. Kid was an orphan."

"Kid was *stupid*," Clint corrected.

"When Hassle Stone came back to Solace — and I'm talking at

the beginning, when it was just Stone and we didn't even know about Kold — we tried to round up a posse. Nobody would stand with us. Do you remember? Nobody but Teddy."

"Kid was stupid, like I said."

"Kid was *noble*," said Edward. "I didn't like him much at the time, but I've had many years to think on it. And I've realized that until we found Sly Stone, Teddy was the closest thing we had to an ally."

"A *stupid* ally."

"A *loyal* ally. Do you remember what you told Teddy the last time we saw him? Do you remember the last command you gave him?"

" 'Go away'?"

"You told him to protect Mai. You said it to get him out of our hair and get him into Solace because we thought we were meeting Stone and Kold outside of town, but he took it seriously. And so when Teddy heard what had happened — apparently Kold bound him with some short-lived magic until he was gone — he went after us. But even more than that, he went after Mai. *Because that's what his marshal had told him to do.*"

Clint looked away. "Meaningless."

But Edward wouldn't drop his gaze. He said, "After all these years, why did you finally choose today to talk to me about Mai?"

Clint grunted.

"I sense an answer in you," said Edward.

"Well, I can sense one in you too," Clint mumbled.

Edward stopped walking, surprised. Joe kept walking, so Clint reined him in.

"What are you talking about?" said Edward.

Clint settled in Joe's saddle. "Over the past few weeks, I've been able to sense things I couldn't before. I could feel the kid's presence on my porch before he showed himself. I could feel his hesitation. I could tell his gun sights were crooked, because I could hear his mind worrying about it as he aimed at my back. I knew he'd never shot a man before and that once, mayhap a year ago, he used paint to scrawl 'Sands to The Realm' on the side of one of their alloy buildings in NewTown, then felt stupid because he realized that the poor man who owned the building was just a citizen, with no strong feelings one way or the other about The Realm… other than anticipation of trade, of course."

"How did you know those things?" said Edward.

"I just did."

"And *today* you wanted to talk about Mai."

"I didn't *want* to," said Clint.

Edward paced around the rider and his horse.

"Do you like it when you 'know' things? Or does the knowledge feel unwelcome, like an intrusion?"

Clint hadn't thought about it. So now, nearing the river, he did. He tried to recall the sensation of sitting on the porch with the kid behind him, reading the kid's every thought, knowing that he would never shoot. Clint had been annoyed, but his annoyance had been at the kid, not at the knowledge itself. The knowledge actually felt good, because it hadn't felt like he'd acquired it himself. The feeling was more like something that had been whispered in his ear by a friend, so they could laugh about it together. He could think of another dozen times he'd felt something similar, and each time, he'd felt not a sense of strangeness, but a sense of intimacy. It felt (and it was hard to admit this, but it was true) as if Mai were standing beside him.

"It felt comfortable," he said.

"Describe it."

Clint did.

"Why didn't you tell me this earlier?"

Clint shrugged. He hadn't told Edward because those odd bits of foreknowledge — as strange as they seemed in retrospect — had felt normal at the time. But regardless of the reason, Clint was enjoying the fact that for once, *Edward* was mad at *him* for withholding information.

But instead of protesting, Edward paced faster, quickening his pace toward town as if goaded. Clint felt an invisible hand pull him from Joe's back and toss him roughly onto Edward's. Edward yelled at the horse to go home. Clint told him that Joe would almost certainly get lost on the way. Edward said that he knew. Joe said that hee-sa a good walker and that Meesta Clint didn't have to worry.

As soon as Clint was on Edward's back, the unicorn began to move even faster. Clint struggled to keep his balance. His muscles were strong and tough, but it had been a long time since he'd had to squeeze with his thighs to stay horsed without a saddle or stirrups. He'd also forgotten the trick of weaving his long fingers through the unicorn's mane. He tried but grabbed too low, and when Edward gathered speed, the slack in his arm couldn't catch him and he rolled sideways. He fell as they were fording the river. Clint suddenly found himself soaked from head to toe.

"Good idea," said Edward. "You stink."

"I didn't fall on purpose, you idiot!" Clint yelled. But since he was down anyway, Edward used his magic to hold him under, and to scrub him with invisible brushes. Then, before the old marshal could object, he used his magic to shave off what Edward called his "depression beard."

By the time they began to approach the OldTown section of Meadowlands, Clint, now clean and smooth-chinned, decided what must be happening. The magic Clint had been feeling must be an extension of what the kid had told him was happening and what Edward had said was going on in the city. The increase in magic meant that something was happening, or was about to happen. *It's Kold*, he thought. It had to be Kold. Kold had found a way to make his Plan B work. He'd found a way to power the generator after all. He'd discovered a way to breach the wall, and the magic suffusing Meadowlands had to mean that Kold was coming down from the mountain to open The Realm.

But as it turned out, that wasn't what Edward thought was happening at all.

"It's Mai," he said. The newly cleaned, still-clumsy gunslinger was atop his back, trying gamely to hold on. He was still strong and lightning fast with his guns, but falling from his mount wouldn't do much to instill fear in any potential foes.

"It's *Mai?*" Clint felt like he'd been punched.

"I've been pondering it for years on and off," said Edward. "Do you remember how I said we couldn't die when we faced off with Kold? That was because you had to make a decision, and you couldn't decide if you were dead. We were like people playing our roles, and all of it was necessary. You, me, Kold, and Cerberus were like four hairs in a braid. Four threads in a tapestry. You know how when you see a stage show, they say that a knife you see toward the beginning means the knife must be used at the end? It was like that. And because of that sense of fate, we could have answered a few questions backward — considering the future to be the *cause* of the past. Why was Mai taken by Kold? Because she would be needed later, as the Orb. Why did you meet Mai? Because you would be the one to make the decision. Predestination is like that. Everything truly does happen for a reason. So when I said we couldn't die, it was because there was a god in the machine of our worlds. We'd lived to that moment because we had a purpose."

"You're not making sense," said Clint.

But Edward sounded excited. He was somewhere between the no-nonsense companion he'd always been and the rainbow-farting goody-goody he'd become in the past decades. How he sounded, as they walked into town, was *giddy*.

"Nar, I finally *am* making sense! You said it earlier, about Mai: 'It was all for nothing.' But don't you see? It *can't* be for nothing! The fact that it seemed to be 'all for nothing' was a clue, and neither of us saw it. Everything happened as it was supposed to. Mai was a mortal with an Orb soul. She was taken by Kold, stripped bare, hollowed out. That had to happen, so that she could become the magic creature she needed to be. So why would we think it would stop there? Everything else happened according to plan, so why would that sense of purpose fail at the finish? The knife was there at the beginning, so it must be used at the end!"

"What the sands are you saying?" Clint said, annoyed. He felt more alive than he had in years now that he was back on the unicorn's back, but it wasn't enough. Edward was being entirely too cheery for him.

"You were *supposed* to deny Kold! She wasn't ready. *She had to die!*"

Clint wanted to strangle Edward for that last sentence, but if he tried, he'd fall. So he gripped the unicorn's mane harder, hoping it hurt.

"You didn't do anything wrong, Clint! You *couldn't* do anything wrong! Her transformation wasn't complete, don't you see? She was too mortal, and she still needed to grow into more. You thought she died in vain, but she didn't! Mai died because it was *meant* to happen, in order to fulfill her purpose. So tell me, Marshal Clint Gulliver: if you could do it all over again, would you still like to change your mind as you've wanted to since that day?"

The town was getting close. In the distance, Clint could see the marshal's station where he'd once chloroformed and locked Fat Ziggy and two Teedawges in their own cells. The station still stood, even after all this time.

"If I could do it all over again, then yar, I'd change my mind," Clint answered.

"You can!" Edward blurted as the town neared. "It wasn't time to open The Realm back then — but it may be now, and it's not too late!"

CHAPTER FIVE: THREE BANDITS

The citadel that housed Dharma Kold's aborted attempts to enter The Realm had become a kind of fortified base and had acquired a reputation in the city as a secretive, reclusive, and maybe even abandoned place. Nobody seemed to go there much anymore, and it was closed only to authorized entrants and intruders wishing for a painful death. Clint, still nowhere near forgiving Kold for what he'd done to Mai and countless others, wanted to storm the place in force. Edward said it was unnecessary, and that he could secure a pass at the marshal's station. Clint scoffed. If he needed further proof of how soft Meadowlands had become, he needed only to look at its bureaucracy and paperwork.

By the time they reached the station, Clint was feeling nearly strong enough to fight. He felt something else, too, but he wasn't sure if it was real or if Edward's exuberance had influenced his mind. Specifically, he felt a warm presence behind him, seeming to press into his back as if riding at his rear. He could smell a fresh, light scent on the air and thought he could feel breath on his neck. He felt comforted as if someone were whispering encouragement into his ear. Once, he even found himself cracking a smile. But the smile was defenseless and visible without his beard, so he stowed it, shoving it down into his boots.

He didn't want to name what he felt because he knew how ridiculous it sounded — but truth be told, it felt as if Mai were riding behind him.

When they arrived in the OldTown section of Meadowlands, the road in front of the marshal's station was blocked by a crowd. Clint hopped down and he and Edward skirted the masses, searching for holes. As he passed, a few people turned around, looked at Clint with a double-take, and whispered to the people beside them. Then, as they moved further around the circle, more and more whispers could be heard. A few men and women and children — *especially* children, toward the back of the crowd and with parents who should be ashamed to have them exposed and in the open — started to point.

The crowd was arranged around the square, clustered in front of the marshal's station and leaving a large open space for four gunmen, who stood in the middle. Clint shook his head. *Idiots.* Any of them could take a stray bullet. But Meadowlands wasn't a town that saw much gunplay anymore, and the people were complacent. They they knew nar of the old ways. People like Clint were relics of a past most had never known.

In the square's center stood three bandits. Across from the bandits stood the town's marshal, who Clint recognized as Little Bill Taylor. Little Bill was fast on the draw and cool with his head. It was even said that amongst the people of Meadowlands that Little Bill had attained almost as much status as the old gunslinger himself.

As Clint stood behind two men with large drooping mustaches, he overheard one say to the other that those men should have known better than to tussle with Little Bill, and that they'd soon find themselves killt. As Clint moved down to stand behind a small man with a bald head and a sprinkle of black moles atop his scalp, this one literally rubbed his hands together and said he'd better get back to his shop and start making coffins because he was about to strike paydirt. A woman to his right chastised the bald man for being morbid, and he said, "Not for Bill, fool woman. For the Troika!"

Clint remembered.

Five or six years back, a bandit named Kid Richard had terrorized OldTown Meadowlands. He'd stayed away from NewTown, which had long ago grown its own police force (staffed by Teedawge archetypes and giants) that only patrolled NewTown, leaving OldTown to fend for itself. Kid Richard's reputation said that he was faster than scattershot. Rumor said that twice, shopkeepers had pulled guns from under their counters and had fired at the kid, but that he'd outrun the lead. It couldn't be true, of course, but the shopkeepers who'd fired the shots didn't argue. After the encounters, both men had been dead by Kid Richard's hand.

Kid Richard was working the west side of OldTown when a brazen older gunslinger (younger than Clint, but still with gray in his beard) nicknamed Doctor Death had come through NewTown as Kid Richard hadn't had the guts to do. The reason the older bandit was named Doctor Death was because he approached crime with a surgeon's precision. He would enter a new area, quietly assassinate the giants, Teedawges, and human lawmen protecting the area, and only then find people to rob after the law was scrambling to regroup. Doctor Death's right-hand was a short man named Cold Hand Charlie. The kid who'd come to Clint's ranch earlier had said that *Clint* was a cold-blooded killer, but Cold Hand Charlie's ruthlessness made Clint look like the tooth fairy. The stories of how Charlie did his work set citizens of Meadowlands to locking their doors and boarding their windows from the inside. During Charlie's time in town, sales of heavy door locks and firearms tripled. Hardware and gun store owners were delighted… until their shops were robbed and their buildings were burnt.

There was a tale told in Meadowlands about the day Kid Richard finally ran into Doctor Death and Cold Hand Charlie. According to folk legend, a black hand had reached out from the fissure between Meadowlands and The Realm and nudged the three gunslingers together — at which point they then shook hands and became the infamous group known as the Troika.

Now, staring at the Troika as they faced off against Little Bill Taylor, Clint could smell weakness on the gunmen. Their hands were poised over their irons (each wore an illegal three), but all of them led slightly with their dominant shoulder so as to present less of their chests and protect their hearts. To Clint, an opponent's cocked posture always meant an opportunity. It told him that the men had something to lose, and that they didn't want to die. A man who had nothing to lose, on the other hand — who stood straight-on, able to draw and aim true from both holsters — was always deadlier. A man who didn't mind dying wouldn't flinch, or double-clutch, or duck, or dive for cover. A man with ice in his blood would stand and fire until his cylinders were empty… and usually because of his steeliness, he'd win.

Little Bill was also standing cocked, but that made sense. Bill wanted to live too (Clint had heard he was building a house), but Bill also had only one iron. He only had to worry about shooting true with one hand instead of both, and he could fan the hammer just fine no matter how he stood.

Clint felt a resentful frown forming on his face as he watched Bill's right hand hover over his single firearm. Each of the Troika wore three guns — their fifty-four bullets to his six — but that was how it was with law. Law said that a lawman had to disarm himself to face criminals who would carry as much iron as they pleased. Law said that a lawman had to lock a criminal up if he could, rather than shooting him dead as the criminal would do to him. In many ways, law was like magic. Magic said you had to follow this or that unfair rule, and that if you didn't do it perfectly… well, then it would kill your wife.

All his life, Clint had been bound by both — by law on one side and magic on the other. His actions had never been his own, which was probably why toward the end of his travels with Edward, Clint had done his best to defy both magic and law.

"Bill's gonna kill 'em," said a townie to Clint's left.

Bill was watching the bandits' shoulders, waiting to see who'd draw first and where their bullets would go. Bill knew what he was doing, and the townie was right — he almost certainly would kill 'em, despite his significant disadvantage.

"Yar," said Clint.

The townie looked at Clint. His brow wrinkled and then, slowly, his mouth opened. But before he could speak, Clint moved on, eager to find a spot where he could see better.

"My arm is getting tired," Little Bill called from the middle of the circle. "Someone draw."

The short, bearded man opposite him spoke next. Both hands were near his holsters, hovering above them like claws.

"*You* draw, Little Bill," he said.

"Or just back off and let us go," said the younger gunslinger standing beside the bearded man.

At this, the first bandit shot the younger man a look. It would have been a perfect time for Little Bill to draw. He could have ended two of them right there for sure — the man who'd given the dirty look and the younger man he'd looked at — and could have dove for cover to face the remaining man one on one. But he didn't draw. Clint rolled his eyes.

Bill said, "I don't want you to go. I want you in shackles."

At this, Clint actually groaned aloud. Several people around him turned to reprimand him for his disrespect, but when they turned, their eyes became fixed and they stared harder. A kid behind Clint tugged on his pants and said, "Are you Marshal Clint?"

"Nar," Clint replied.

The kid's mother pulled the kid back with an apologetic look. "Hush, Bobby," she said. "Marshal Clint would be dead by now."

Now *Clint* was the one giving a glance — this one all the way toward the back of the crowd, to Edward. Edward was using a sharp rock beside the street to clean his hoof, not even watching the standoff. He'd gotten used to Clint commanding him not to interfere in matters of lead, now that he was too good for magic.

"I heard Marshal Clint could fly," Bobby said to someone behind him. "Without his unicorn's help!"

Another child's voice, probably one of Bobby's friends: "His unicorn can fly too!"

At this, a puff of breath billowed from the gunslinger's mouth. It wasn't quite the laugh it wanted to be, but it was enough to make Bill's eyes twitch. An opportunity lost for the Troika. So all four of them were slow to pay attention, then.

"Nuh-uh! Unicorns don't have wings. You're thinking of a Pegasus."

"Pegasuses don't have horns," said the second kid in an I-told-you-so voice.

Their mothers shushed them, reminding them that Pegasi weren't real and telling them that if they couldn't be quiet, she'd take them home and they wouldn't get to see *anyone* killt.

A moment later, Bobby said, "Marshal Clint's guns can fire two bullets at once."

Well, that was true. They could, in fact, fire *six* bullets at once, but only backward... toward the shooter... if the shooter wasn't the guns' owner.

"Stand down, Bill," called Cold Hand Charlie.

"I'll stand down once you're in my cell, Charlie," Little Bill said.

"Or once you're dead," said Doctor Death. Doctor Death, in contrast to his macabre name, had a voice so proper it sounded like he was ordering high tea.

"Just step away, Little Bill," said Kid Richard. "Nobody's going to win here."

"Mayhap," said Little Bill. "But I'm not stepping down."

"Just move your hand away from your iron, Bill. We have nine guns to your one."

"Fired by six slow hands," Bill said.

"Oh, for Providence's sake," Clint blurted, shoving his way through the crowd.

The bandits looked up, but Clint, who did little with his days other than fire shells and practice draws, saw everything happen in slow motion. The small bearded man's hands were closest to his guns, but his body language said he was a lefty and would draw from that side. That man's shoulder dipped, but it was Kid Richard, the youngest among them, who would have his pistol up soonest. The kid had a shorter draw — more from the hip, flipping his iron more from the wrist than the shoulder. So Clint drew, fired, and struck Kid Richard in his draw hand.

The bandit spun and fell to the dirt. He'd bear watching, but Clint could already see his gunbelt turning on his hips as he struck the ground; if he were to draw now, he'd have to fumble with his uninjured, non-dominant hand. If Clint had learned anything about two-gun bandits over the years, it was that the second gun was almost always for show. Few men could fire worth a spit in the wind with their opposite hand.

The other two men now had their hands on their guns, their fingers curling around the wooden grips, their fingers finding their way behind the trigger guards. But the second thing Clint had learned about bandits through the years was that even those who carried double-action pistols were never as fast with their guns uncocked as cocked. The fastest men fanned the hammer before firing, and a man who squeezed the trigger both to cock and fire was always less accurate. Clint's fingers were very long and very strong. He was rare among shooters: a man who was as fast double-action as single.

His guns were both out. So were the guns of Cold Hand Charlie and Doctor Death, but they both had the same long trigger-pull that Clint did. They'd slow down to squeeze their rounds off accurately, but Clint wouldn't.

Clint aimed both guns at once and fired in unison. Pistols spun. Then the old, tall, lean-as-leather marshal walked calmly over and placed his boot on Kid Richard's good hand, crushing it into the dirt. His guns were still out, so he aimed one at each of the other bandits, both of whom were starting to cradle their injured hands rather than reaching for their weapons. And then, for dramatic effect, he reached back with his long thumbs and cocked both pistols.

The bandits' hands reached into the air. Little Bill came up behind him, dragging out shackles.

A moment later, amidst many cries of pain as Bill handled the men's red hands, the Troika was in custody. The crowd cheered as if a sporting event had been won by their favorite team. Amongst them, Clint could hear murmurs about himself, and could already sense the legends about himself growing like a disease.

Little Bill looked back, taking in the marshal from head to toe.

"Marshal Gulliver," he said.

"I thought I trained you better than that," Clint replied.

CHAPTER SIX: A RAINBOW OVER MAIN STREET

Bill shoved the bandits toward the station. Clint followed. Once the men were inside, Edward simply obliterated the station's door so that he could enter as well. Once inside — big white unicorn in a not-terribly big space — he repaired and closed the door behind him.

Little Bill escorted the Troika to the back — to the very cells in which Clint had once locked Fat Ziggy and his men — and returned a moment later to wash his hands in a basin. Finally he sat in a chair behind his desk and smiled.

"The famous Marshal Clint and Sir Edward," said Little Bill. "It *has* been a long time."

"Where is Fat Ziggy?" said Clint. "I thought he'd want to see me."

Bill stared at Clint, then shook his head. "Clint, Ziggy died twenty years ago."

"Was he killt in duty?"

"He died at his house. Of old age."

"Old age? He wasn't that old."

"Clint," said Bill, leaning forward, "he was *eighty-seven*. Have you lost track of days? Or have you discovered the fountain of youth? Because I've got to tell you, you look good for a walking corpse."

"First time anyone has ever said that to him," Edward muttered.

"You must be over ninety yourself."

"One hundred and twelve," said Edward from the floor. "That's why I stopped putting candles on his birthday cake. That, and I don't have thumbs." Then Edward whispered to Bill, his voice taking on some of the recent, new-Edward joviality. *"He doesn't like magic anymore."*

Clint shrugged. Time ceased to matter when you lived alone, seeing no one. Even when he and Edward were traveling, it had seemed like time stood still. Edward never aged, and they never saw the same people twice. He hadn't been into Meadowlands for any meaningful amount of time for nearly thirty years. Those decades of wandering following Mai's death had felt like their five years following Dharma Kold, just dilated and stretched. Sand followed sand. Mesa followed mesa. Bandit followed bandit, and blood followed blood. The changes exposure to the Triangulum had impressed upon his body made it so he aged slowly, but that was small comfort when a man was tired of living.

"Well, regardless of whether you like it or not, magic has been good to *you*. I would have guessed you were sixty-five if I didn't know better. And a strong, lean sixty-five at that."

"Better and faster than certain lawmen," Clint said.

"I didn't want to kill them. You understand that, right? Dead bandits are more trouble than they're worth. Dead bandits become legends. But letting them rot in jail so people can see that their tormentors are mortal? Well sir, that's priceless. This isn't the old Sands anymore, Clint. Your kind is a dying breed, as are folks like the Troika. It changes out in the deeper Sands near the Sprawl and the Edge, of course, but here near Meadowlands, the Whitney Doctrine has made significant improvements in law and order. How often do you hear gunshots up at your place these days?"

Clint thought. It was difficult to notice the absence of a thing, but now that he pondered on it, he realized he *didn't* hear gunshots much anymore, though he'd heard them plenty when he and Mai had first built the place.

"In the old days — and by 'old days,' I mean twenty years ago, being a mere babe of forty-two myself — I would have killt them all. Don't think I didn't see it, Marshal. The way they led with their dominant shoulders, the flicker of distraction when Doc looked over at Kid Richard. But I could never do what you did, disarming them with lead. It was a significantly harder task."

"So if I hadn't come along, what would you have done?"

Bill shrugged.

"They would have killt you if they could, you know," Clint told him.

"Of course."

"But *you* refused to kill *them*."

Bill shrugged again. "Such is law. But it works."

"Soft," said Clint with disgust. "Everyone has gone soft. The leaking and fracture have become critical, and the worlds are about to blow apart right next door, down at the Rio Verde. But the people here, they're concerned with the Whitney Doctrine and making sure their steam and spark service is nar interrupted. What does the apocalypse matter if a man can still get flicker talkies in his home and a roast cooked true in an hour?"

"The apocalypse is abstract, Clint. Comforts are concrete and true. I see what you're saying, but your average Meadowlands citizen can't stop the fractures. So what should he do? Panic? Nar, he watches his flickers and tries to be nice to his neighbor and runs his business with a smile. The law has a responsibility to reflect that reality. Yar, the world may be ending, but at least a lawman can keep life orderly while it does."

"Like making a dying man comfortable while he rots, rather than trying to fight the disease," Clint muttered, shaking his head. He meant it as an absurd insult, but Bill nodded, saying he was precisely right.

"Speaking of orderliness," Edward said, "we need a citadel pass. The living legend here wants to see Diamante."

Little Bill opened a drawer in his desk. "Oh, of course." He withdrew a paper, scrawled on it, signed it with a flourish, stamped it with a seal, then handed it to Clint. Clint looked it over and nodded. More paperwork. More laws. More shuffling of useless documents. Time was, he'd walk to the citadel and demand to be let in. Denial would make his guns start talking.

"Out of curiosity, Edward," said Little Bill, "what are you going to do up there? Nobody really knows what Diamante's up to. We hear rumors, but the place is full of secrets. I wouldn't even bother to give you this pass if Diamante hadn't made a point to tell me that the minute you showed interest, I was to hustle you on up there pronto."

"Save the worlds, mayhap," said Clint. It was meant to be sarcastic, but it fell serious from his lips, and Bill seemed to take it as such.

"Or end them," said Edward.

"For the record, I prefer the former," said Little Bill, leaning back and crossing his hands behind his head.

They left the station. Clint felt his feet sink into something as he stepped into the street and looked down to see that it was grass. He wondered at that, since he hadn't remembered crossing a swath of grass as they'd led the bandits inside, but he stopped wondering once he looked around and saw that the entire area was green. There was grass in the center of the square, where the Troika had faced Little Bill. There was grass in horseshoe courts along a side street. Grass grew in the tops of rain barrels, floating on debris like islands. There was grass on mud walls and suffocating the plants already in streetside planters. All of it was greener than green, as if colored bright by gods.

"What does this mean?" Clint asked the unicorn.

Edward smashed the door again to exit the station, then magicked it whole and walked unheeding through the grass. He stood beside Clint, waiting, and said, "It means we need to keep going."

Clint climbed onto Edward's back, slowly finding the old fit of his bones to Edward's, feeling the unicorn's mane familiar through his fingers. As they marched up the main street and into the winding mountain path toward the citadel, years seemed to slip away. Clint found himself feeling their old time-arrested set point. What Bill had said seemed right: Clint felt like a strong and lean sixty-five, like a warrior's battle-hardened grappy. And owing to constant practice, his hands — his most important part — were even faster than they'd been when he and Edward had stopped riding together. The Triangulum magic in his body had even been particularly kind to his eyes. While his skin had wrinkled, his eyes, like his hands, felt sharper than ever. He could see into a bird's winking eye as it crossed the sky.

"Tell me again about Mai," Edward said as they traversed the winding mountain road.

The unicorn's question seemed random yet clearly wasn't, but Clint was tired of playing the information game with Edward. He was tired of pretending that his heart was stone, and that he didn't care. He was tired of subterfuge and lies. So while he watched the trail ahead, wondering what the citadel would hold and why they were headed there, Clint did something that was rare between them: he answered the question without evasion, without scorn, without resentment, and without rancor.

"She was my wife. She was the Orb."

"I mean, tell me about her *now*."

"Now she is under the tree in my yard."

"That's not what I mean."

"What do you want, Edward? I'm human. Fine. I'm not all grit and stone and alloy. It hurts."

"*Also* not what I mean. You're talking from your head. Think about what you told me earlier. About feeling her near you."

"It's just a feeling. She's gone."

"She's in a better place," said Edward.

"Yar, yar."

"Come on. Clear your head. Just let everything go. And tell me, forgetting ration and logic and the rest — *tell me how you feel her now.*"

Sitting atop the unicorn's back, Clint closed his eyes and tried to do as Edward instructed. It was impossible. Despite what he'd just said, his middle felt like grit and stone and alloy — and for good reason, since he'd built those walls himself. A man's heart had to be hard to do what he did. Gunslingers didn't cotton to whims of emotion or to soft sheets and flowers. They responded to gunsmoke and bullets. To fists and harsh sun and tough jerky.

But little by little, as he kept his eyes closed, as he heard himself saying this was stupid but keeping on anyway, Clint felt a softening. He felt a sense of intuition run through his mind. He felt a presence like a quiet voice inside his brain. He felt his skin crawl and prickle. Something was there… if he'd let himself see it.

"How do you feel her?" said Edward. His voice was low, almost meditative. He was still walking, and the rhythm of the unicorn's steps beneath Clint was like a metronome, soothing him into a trance. "Don't think. Just answer with the first thing you think of."

"Like a rainbow over Main Street," Clint blurted.

Then he heard himself say it, and the absurdity of the sentence snapped him fully awake, fully back to grit, and stone, and alloy. He wanted to take it back, because he didn't like to feel or act ridiculous. He'd ridden with a unicorn whose every magic trick was adorned with fairies and sparkles. He fired pink smoke from his guns, but he'd also laid graves along his path and suffered more pain himself than any of the men laying inside them.

He started to object, to make the silly sentiment go missing, but when his mouth opened, he stopped as he found himself staring into a rainbow. He felt a warm hand on his newly-shorn cheek. Then he saw her face, and her hand, and her body, and she was like a ghost beneath the rainbow and still paradoxically right before him. She whispered his name with affection, and whatever it was — whatever *she* was — leaned in and gave Clint a soft kiss.

She was there. Somehow, Mai was with him as she had been all along. She'd simply gone elsewhere for a while. To a different place. A better place.

"Told you," said Edward.

CHAPTER SEVEN: MACHINES AND CREATURES

In the middle of Main Street leading out of town, with the buildings behind him and the road turning from paved rock to packed stone, Clint felt himself weaken. His fingers fell from Edward's mane. He started to spill from the unicorn and there was nothing to be done, but a hand cushioned him as he came to the ground — Mai's, not Edward's. Clint landed mostly on his knees, some on his hands, and for a moment he couldn't look up because he couldn't take seeing the street empty. But then he did, and she was still there.

"I'm dreaming," he said.

Edward kicked him. "You're not dreaming."

"I'm dreaming, Mai. You're dead. Almost sixty years dead."

Mai's spirit (or whatever it was that Clint saw in front of him) had maintained Mai's biting humor and her ability to mock the gunslinger's stern voice. " 'You're sixty years dead,' " she said, putting a sourpuss expression on her shimmering face. "What a cliche. You've nar changed, Clint Gulliver."

"I missed you."

Her expression softened and her ghostly body knelt before him, taking his large hand in hers. The hand looked transparent, but felt real. He could see his own wrinkled, weathered, ugly hand through hers. "I missed you too," she said. "But I was always here."

"Why didn't you show yourself?"

"But I did," she said. "The days you struggled to face the world, I helped you to rise. The three times you turned your weapon on yourself, I turned it away. The day a bullet pierced your heart because you wouldn't let Edward protect you, I pulled the bullet back so he could heal you — not that you didn't struggle when he tried."

"I would only let him keep me from dying," Clint recalled.

"But not from suffering," Mai agreed. She touched his cheek. "You shouldn't have tried so hard to pay your due. It wasn't *your* due. This all happened for a reason. Same reason you couldn't die by that bullet. You could suffer, if you insisted on it, but you couldn't die. It couldn't be allowed. Because there was work yet to be done."

"I'm tired, Mai. I missed you. I don't want to be here anymore. I don't want any more magic. I want to be with you."

"That's what I'm saying," she said, sounding less tender and more direct, as she'd been in life.

"You need a body," Edward said.

"Yar," she said. "For long enough to do a job."

"But you had a body," Clint said, now looking up at her. "It failed you."

She nodded. "Any body would fail. Like trying to fill a single mug with ten mugs' worth of brew. I can't inhabit a corporeal body for long, and I can't stay like this. So enjoy me while you can, strong marshal, swollen with pride as you are."

Clint felt like subverting his every drop of dignity and pleading. Here she was, real and alive — in a way, anyway — and now she was saying that she couldn't stay. He wanted to get on his knees and turn her words untrue. So why not beg?

"But you just said you needed a body."

Mai smiled. "You'll see."

The rainbow seemed to collapse as if slurped from the sky and into Mai's ghostly body. She became slightly more corporeal, but remained transparent and indistinct. She was, Clint noticed for the first time, wearing the pink hitching dress she'd worn when they'd first tried hitching back in Solace, before Kold had taken her. It was how he thought of her most often. That dress, he realized, bookended the hardest years of his life prior to her death. First, she'd worn it in Solace. The next time he'd seen her over four long years later, she'd still been wearing it — in that shack north of Aurora Solstice, after Kold had drained her. Or killed her soul so that she could rise again, or whatever he'd done.

The hitching dress she'd worn when they'd finally managed to hitch for real had been a powder blue. Nar traditional, but by then Clint had had enough of ritual and rules. He'd seen the scribbles on the wall; after recovering and growing powerful, she'd worn her mortal body like an old shoe dragged through the Sands. Mai had been sick even on the day she'd worn that powder blue dress, and Clint had felt the clock ticking, his own mind as brimming with anger as it was with joy.

Now, as he watched her, she seemed to climb onto Edward's back behind him. He felt her against him for real, the same as he'd felt her presence before. Her ghostly but somehow substantial arms circled his waist. Edward began to move. But where to, Clint couldn't imagine.

"You've been angry," she said, whispering into his ear.

Clint turned, so he could see her face. Somehow, her eyes were as real as they'd ever been.

"I grew a beard."

"You were angry *with me*," she said, as if he hadn't understood.

"I mourned you."

"But you were angry. When you came back from facing Kold that first time, I could see it in your eyes. I was at Doc Barlowe's, in the comfortable chair, sitting and doing nothing because I'd drank Barlowe's elixir and because my power might have alerted Kold to our presence. I was sitting in that chair while you fought for me. The irony is, Kold knew I was there all along. It's why he allowed you to find him. It's why he gave us a trail. He left me in the desert because I wouldn't give him what he needed. *I* wouldn't give it to him. *Me*, not you. Yet *you* had to fight while I rested in that comfortable chair."

"You couldn't have given him the Orb even if you'd wanted to. You had to be scooped out first, and left for us to find."

"But later, at the citadel, I could have. I stayed at Barlowe's. But if I'd gone with you, if I'd spit out my elixir and trailed you, I would have been there. You wouldn't have needed to coerce me to surrender. I'd have simply done it, and you wouldn't have had to decide."

Clint turned to reply, but when he looked at Mai again, a small smile lit the edge of her mouth. He turned forward, seeing motion, and saw Edward give him his equine version of the same smile.

Clint looked back at Mai. "That's *why* you weren't there. Because you would have surrendered yourself, and I wouldn't have had to decide."

Mai raised her eyebrows and said nothing. Edward faced forward. They rode in silence, plodding along as if the world's time was theirs. Which, as far as Clint was concerned, it was. They'd continued up the packed stone road to Kold's citadel, and both Edward and Mai seemed to intend for them to end up there just as he and Edward had originally planned once leaving the station. The faster they went, the sooner they'd reach the gates. The slower they went, the longer he would be allowed to linger in discussion with his long-deceased beloved.

After a few minutes filled with nothing but hoofbeats, Mai said, "You never confronted me."

Clint blinked, again looking back. He'd been woolgathering, enjoying the feeling of her arms around him.

"I never told you that I'd met him before. I knew who you were when I came to Solace, same as everyone else. But I also knew the rest. Things you yourself didn't know. I knew who you'd ridden with. I knew what he wanted. I knew the mission he'd set, and I was afraid. I only knew I had something in me he wanted, and so I ran. But you must understand, gunslinger, I've always loved you, regardless of how it started."

Clint didn't answer. Edward's hooves made dull noises on the dirty stone-packed path. It was something they'd never discussed, but it had been a constant presence between them. He knew she'd sought him for protection from Kold, but never said it true. She always seemed to suspect his knowing, that Kold had told him. But Clint said nothing, shoving his resentment into his boots with the other useless, non-gunslinger emotions. There were three things he knew about Mai, and six months after he'd spoken to Kold, only two of them still mattered: that he continued to love her, and that she was slowly dying.

"I didn't care," he said. After the moments of quiet, his response seemed jarring and out of place. She twitched, and Clint found it comforting to see that even all-knowing spirits could still be surprised. "A marshal doesn't have much use for a past. The past creates attachment. We were what we were. It nar mattered how it started."

"I see," Mai said. "Yet today, you're more attached than ever."

Clint grunted. But true to Mai as she'd always been, she didn't rub it in. Mai had always loved making her points and usually insisted on being right, but she always let things go once her battle was won.

Ten minutes later, they arrived at the citadel's entrance. The place had been heavily, heavily reinforced since Clint had last seen it. The large alloy gates had been replaced by absolutely massive stone ones. At either end of the new stone gates, a tall wall ran down from the side of the raised path and around the mountain's slope. He could see giants patrolling the top of the wall, walking the perimeter while slapping their giant hammers into their massive palms. There were a series of holes in the wall near the top, and from the holes, Clint's sharp eyes could pick out the occasional face. Those would be elves, standing on the wall's top near the giants' feet, completely obscured by a half-wall. They'd be sitting with bows at the ready, likely nocked with their deadly arrows.

In front of them were two guard houses, one on each side of the gates. Each guard house was staffed by two giants. The giants wore armor — something which to Clint seemed patently unnecessary. One giant on each side had his hammer out. The other carried a spear that looked large enough to be most of a tree. One of the spear-bearers also held something that seemed out of place: a board with an alloy clip at the top, with a stack of papers between the clip and the pressboard.

As the unicorn and the two riders approached, the giant with the board held out his palm. It was larger than Edward.

"Halt," he said.

"Surely you recognize me," said Edward.

"Yar, Mister Edward," the giant said. "But Silas knows nar the old man."

"We have a pass for him," said Edward, magicking the paper Little Bill had given him toward the giant. Clint wondered how a slip of paper could possibly prove his permission to enter, but he also didn't understand the new insistence on paper in general. How could the giants be sure that Edward hadn't forged the paper, or that they hadn't coerced Little Bill into giving it to them, or that Little Bill himself wasn't part of a conspiracy true? But then Clint remembered the stamp Little Bill had used to put a mark on the paper and wondered if it was a kind of magic bond. Everything in Meadowlands these days was powered by magic or spark or steam. It was just one of the many reasons the gunslinger stayed away.

Clint watched the giant study the paper, knowing he couldn't possibly be reading it. Many advances had been made over the years, but an increase in giant intelligence wasn't among them. Regardless, the giant must have been satisfied because he clipped the paper to the board and made a large X on it with a sort of glowing stick. So that meant Clint was fine, but he wondered how they'd explain Mai's presence. He also still wasn't sure why they were here. Were they going to help Kold? Or had Edward's years of working with Kold been his way of setting the baron up for a coup?

Clint looked down at Mai's semi-transparent hands, still clasped around his waist. He looked back at her. She smiled with excitement, as if they were headed on a family adventure that promised to be nothing but fun.

"The old man is okay," said the giant. He turned and gestured toward the others, and the giants on both sides of the door pushed their hammers into large indentations in the wall behind them. The enormous stone doors started to open. Clint looked down at the ghostly hands around his waist, then at the swinging doors. Apparently Mai was A-OK.

"They can't see her, can they?" Clint asked Edward.

"In a way," said Edward.

"Why are we here?"

Mai gave him a playful punch to the kidney and answered first. "You always want to ruin the surprise."

The doors weren't moving particularly slowly, but they were so thick that scant light had yet to appear between them. Clint looked up. The air was hazy beyond the patrolling giants' torsos, meaning there was some sort of magical protection above the wall. While Clint watched, the giants moved themselves to a state of heightened alertness and looked down toward the gate. Below them, the elf archers in the windows could be seen pulling back their bows. The place certainly didn't look to be abandoned, as the rumors claimed. What, exactly, had Kold been up to all these years?

"Tell me this, at least," the gunslinger said. "Do I ever get to do *anything* that isn't totally and completely expected by one of you?"

"You constantly surprise me," Edward said. "You know, with your spontaneous hilarity."

Mai whispered in his ear, "If you haven't seen it, it's new to you."

"The more confusing but honest answer," said Edward, "is that your choices matter a great deal, despite the feeling of predestination. Up until now, there were things I knew had to happen — though I seldom knew exactly how or when or where — but there are only two such things left. Then I'm out, and I'll be as clueless as you've been all these years."

"What are those two things?" said Clint.

Mai punched him again in the kidney.

When the doors were open far enough for them to pass, the guards motioned them forward. Clint looked at the doors as he passed. It would take five Edwards end-to-end to span their thickness.

They stepped into a courtyard. The doors started to close behind them. Ahead was a set of large open stone doors that seemed to lead into the center of the mountain itself. After passing through the enormous gates, the stone doors in the mountain looked like toys.

Clint looked around. He'd seen this place before — once at a sprint as they'd chased Dharma Kold and once as he'd plodded out with the weight of many worlds on his shoulders. He thought he'd recognize the room in the mountain if that's where they were going, but he barely remembered the courtyard at all. He didn't recall it wearing a carpet of grass as it did now, for instance, but he'd nar been at his most observant at the time.

Once inside, they seemed to be on their own. Clint was still surprised they weren't being escorted by guards, but nobody seemed to care that they were there once they'd passed the gates.

Edward started to walk.

"We'll go through the mountain here," he said, indicating the doors. "This part will be familiar to you. But what Kold didn't have when last you were here was the tunnel that now leads out of this chamber and into the mountain's cone."

"Cone?"

"It's a dormant volcano, with a crater in the center. You'll see."

They passed through the stone doors and Clint looked around, waiting for it all to seem familiar. It didn't. The chamber had to be the one where he and Edward had battled Kold and Cerberus, but Clint's memory of the place was either entirely gone or the place had totally changed.

The chamber was enormous, with massive white stone pillars scattered across it like men on a Risk board. Their tops were high and buttressed against the ceiling. The walls weren't hewed stone, but flat and painted a bright white like the pillars. Clint watched as the bandit Teedawge walked by in some sort of a blue uniform, then watched a second later as the bandit Teedawge walked by wearing a fancy man's clothing and shoes, like Alan Whitney's fabrics back in San Mateo. Then he saw several Teedawges holding palaver in a corner.

"It's hard for me not to kill these things," Clint said as he watched the identical archetypes, his hands itching for pistols. He held them in hooks above his holsters.

"Yar, but they don't hold grudges and neither should you. We're on the same side now."

It was a strange thing for Edward to say. What "sides" were there? And why would Clint want to be on a side of *any* kind with the man who had stolen and tortured his bride? Clint thought of the Teedawges that had killt Sly Stone. He put his hand on his right pistol.

"Don't," said Edward. "The archetypes we fought in Aurora Solstice and Baracho Gulch have long since expired. These are new. They make them here."

"They *make* them here?"

"It's fascinating," said Edward. "Officially, of course, I loathe it. It's an abomination. But once I get past my supposed loathing, the process is fascinating. They now share collective memory. Dispatch one and the others keep coming, fully aware of what you just did from the viewpoint of the other. Imagine an enemy that can see all sides of you at once."

Clint did. He shivered, despite Mai's sun at his back.

"Why is he making Teedawges?" Clint asked.

But Edward forged on. "You should see what the ropers can do now. They're an elite squad, trained practically from birth. Competition is fierce to get in. There are scimitar squads and gunmen. And men who might be able to outdraw even you." He smirked, a small tweak of the new, chipper Edward sneaking past his serious demeanor of the past few hours. *"Might."*

They passed through the foyer and into a smaller but still-cavernous passageway that was far larger than what seemed warranted. But of course, giants would use this corridor, and unicorns, and Providence knew what else.

After a long walk, they emerged into the open, and Clint's jaw fell open.

They stood at the edge of an enormous crater centered in the mountain, just as Edward had described. The place was so mammoth that Clint could barely see its other side, where the mountain again rose toward the sky. Kold had flattened the floor so it resembled a vast plane of flat stone, stubbled with a knobby surface for traction. It was truly impressive, but the crater itself wasn't what had shocked Clint. What had shocked him were the things that filled it.

The space was packed with all manner of machines and instruments of battle. Clint spotted a regiment's worth of zeppelins far across the field. Rows of battle-adapted thinking machines sparred to one side, their alloy skin a bright pink. A group of unicorns on the other side cast multicolored, sparking spells as foot soldiers (all Teedawges, from what Clint could tell) marched past in formation. Clint heard gunshots and explosions that had to be artillery. He saw two-legged, loud vehicles on fat black wheels that seemed to run on steam. He watched a team of balloons lift off from in front of the zeppelins, and beyond the zeppelins were a team of enormous three-legged machines, jet black, that towered above the other gear on three long, spindly legs. The bodies of the strange things were sleek and swept back, making them look like venomous spiders. One machine turned, and Clint's eye picked out a round spot of white light on its front that seemed to stare at him like an eye. Clint met its gaze and then — surely by coincidence — the thing made a hollow, frightening bellow that turned the eyes of all in the crater. Then the machine turned back and a powerful beam shot from it, annihilating some sort of practice fodder. Clint couldn't see what the machine had obliterated because his line of sight was suddenly blocked by a team of beasts that Clint had never seen, but believed to be a fearsome subterranean species known as morlocks.

Looking into the crater gave Clint a queer melding sensation, as if past and present and fantasy and reality had blended together into one enormous joke. But because the joke's teller didn't know when to stop, he'd beaten the joke like a rented mule, taking it to ridiculous lengths. The combinations facing him were more than absurd. Clint saw unicorns walking by machines that were like huge alloy birds — things that, based on the lights lining their bodies, probably ran on spark. He watched a party of elves (all of them the height of one of Edward's legs, dressed in green, holding bows — and, he knew from experience, notoriously ill-tempered) rush past a darker green device with what had to be an enormous canon at its top. The machine's locomotive parts were long and made of interlocking alloy slats that rolled around a set of smaller wheels. As Clint stared, the thing belched steam from its top.

The gunslinger had lived a perilous, tough, sorrow-filled life that he'd nar wish on anyone, but he'd at least felt like he *fit* when riding the dusty Sands, as a lone gunman atop his mount's back. But here? He was a cowboy thrust into the future, worthless and useless or worse. Older than ancient. In the six decades since Clint had last been at the mountain, the world had rolled frighteningly forward while he'd been out in the Sands or inside his shack, growing whiskers and doing pushups.

"Edward," the gunslinger whispered, "what is all of this for?"

Behind them, a deep, seductive voice said, "War."

CHAPTER EIGHT:
BENEVOLENTS

Clint turned, looking around Mai, and saw Dharma Kold standing behind Edward with Cerberus beneath him.

Kold hadn't changed since Clint had last see him. At all. He looked as if he might have stepped directly out of Clint's memory. He appeared to be in his early forties, and his deceptively kind face had a few small wrinkles at the edges of his mouth. His hair was still a near perfect chestnut — unlike Clint's, which had gone mostly gray. Kold's hands, which were just as large as Clint's, didn't have the prominent veins and loose spots that the gunslinger had started to see on his own. Kold had traded his black trail shirt and denims for a slightly different version of the uniform Clint saw on a few of the Teedawges, but otherwise he was the same man Clint had faced so long ago.

Cerberus also hadn't changed. He was still darker than black, his coat so bleak that he seemed like a hole in the fabric of reality. Clint knew what that blackness meant, and it filled him with chills. Cerberus hadn't used the past sixty years to gain humility, or compassion, or an iota of white magic. His color also meant that his magic was still surrendered to his rider — something that Edward had, once upon a time, found repugnant. It dawned on the gunslinger that Edward had never severed relations with Kold, but had instead been helping him to build his army in secret. That meant that Edward had now been working with Cerberus for longer than he'd fought against him. Clint felt his respect for the white unicorn wanting to ratchet down a notch. Why had Edward dropped his standards? He was once so proud and principled, despite his rankling nature.

"Well," said Kold, eyeing Clint from head to toe, "you look old."

"Well," said Cerberus below him, speaking to Edward, "you look white."

This latter seemed to be an insult for reasons Clint didn't understand (if he had to guess, he'd say Cerberus was calling Edward a weak do-gooder), because Edward took a step forward. Clint hadn't anticipated the movement and rocked backward. Mai's weight wasn't making it easier, but he managed to hang on and stay upright.

Clint looked back at his old foe. "I have nothing witty to say. This is all too much."

Kold shrugged. "You were exposed to the Triangulum and it's slowed your aging, but *I've* been living here with it. Cerberus keeps telling me it can't actually make me grow younger, though, which is a shame."

"Mayhap being a terrible person keeps you from going younger," said Clint.

Kold's eyebrows went up. "Apparently it's *not* too much. Sixty years gone, and still you have your strength and sharp wit. Bravo."

Clint stared. He had nothing to say.

Behind him, Mai stirred, but Kold didn't flick his eyes toward the movement. He'd said nar about the ghostly woman behind him, so the gunslinger figured the dark rider must not be able to see her. Even stranger, Cerberus gave no indication of being able to see or sense her either. Clint assumed he could see Mai because she and he had been close and that Edward could see her because he was a unicorn.

"War," Kold repeated to fill the silence, gesturing toward the machines. "Glorious *war*. You've seen how The Realm shimmers in the sky these days? Most people assume it's because we're powering the city with our 'mysterious magic' and that our power is chipping away at the wall like water plinking onto a stone for millennia. But it doesn't work like that. We aren't building an army to storm the gates. We're building an army to wage war once we get inside."

"But you *can't* get inside," said Clint.

Kold gave him a small smile. "We'll see."

"And what about the train project?"

Kold waved the thought away. "The train doesn't exist and never did. Well, *a* train exists. But not *the* train that everyone expects. The black engine you've seen on the tracks is just that — a black engine. The tracks are just tracks. We had to explain the new magic in the air somehow, especially once The Realm started growing more visible. But that's just the Triangulum at work." He sighed theatrically. "The partial, ineffectual Triangulum."

Kold hopped off of Cerberus and began to pace.

"See, I know it might look like I'm a dog with a bone about this whole 'getting into The Realm' thing, but I just can't give up on my dream… despite my past failures. You've seen how close The Realm is these days. You can almost reach out and touch it! It has presence now, too. Try to walk toward it and you will now get nearer. At some point you'll seem to go under it, and then it will be behind you. Not like the old days, when it was forever in retreat and always leaping off to somewhere else. Not that we can reach it, still, you understand — believe me, my flying machines have tried — but it's… it's so close!"

"It doesn't matter how close it is," said Clint. "Closeness is just an illusion."

"*Exactly*." Kold pointed at Clint like a student who'd just given the perfect answer. "And that's why the main source of my continued faith that one day I will enter is Reason Number Two, given to me by my good friend here." He slapped Cerberus's black neck. "And that's a belief that one day, *you* would bring me what I needed to make it all happen."

"Me?" said Clint.

"*Us*," said Edward.

At this, Cerberus gave a snort of disgust. "I can't take this," he said to Kold. "He smells. Don't tell me you can't smell that." He turned so his profile was facing Clint, and it was as if the big, ominous sphere of the dark unicorn's eye bored into the gunslinger's soul.

"I don't know what you're talking about," said Clint.

"Lollipops and fairies," said Cerberus, indicating Edward. "He positively *reeks* of sparkly goodness."

Clint exhaled. "I meant that I didn't know about the other thing."

"I always wondered why she'd run to you, Clint," said Kold, still pacing. "I was the same as you, you know. We were both men from The Realm, full of pride and adventure and duty. We were both tall…" He rubbed a hand across his smooth chin, then looked meaningfully at Clint. "… and *handsome*. Cerberus was still ashy when we first found her, not yet totally black. But still, despite our innocuousness, she was afraid of us. I didn't even have time to explain everything to her before she fled. It wasn't like I held my hand out to her in a claw and said, 'Give me your soul!' " Kold spoke theatrically, making his voice warble as he laughed. "But she still ran as if she could sense my intention. It was like —" This time, he gave a dramatic gasp, mimicking shock. "— like she was a unicorn!"

"Meaning that she was like Edward," said Cerberus. "But that's not a comment on her magic. It's actually because Edward is so much like a human woman."

Beneath Clint, Edward held his calm, not rising to the dark unicorn's taunt. His quiet was no longer simple silence. It now felt deliberate. If he fought with Cerberus, whatever was about to happen might crumble. Which, Clint thought, might actually be what Cerberus wanted to happen.

"Of course, she *wasn't* a unicorn," said Kold. "I could tell by the lack of a giant horn on her head and her number of legs. But have you heard the Genesis legends? About how there were original lines of seven humans, each cultivated with a purpose in mind for the worlds' requirement later?"

Clint thought of Sly Stone and what Edward had told him about Stone being a savant — a walking, talking human archive of knowledge. That knowledge had been buried in every member of the Stone line since the first.

"Nar," he lied.

"Apparently there was an intuitive line. One that possessed the unicorns' ability to determine worthy souls and pair with them. You've heard that intention matters to magic? Well, they say that the intuitive ones, called Benevolents, were the embodiments of that intention. They carried magic, but they would use their human minds to decide when to allow that magic to blossom — 'when the time was right' is how the texts are written, which makes sense since magic never makes things straightforward."

Clint looked down at Edward, trying to read his response. Finally Edward said to Cerberus, "I'm not sure what's wrong with you to tell him all of that, but I'm sure it's hard to pronounce."

"*I* didn't tell him about Benevolents," Cerberus countered. "He's big on research. He found the texts himself."

Edward's eyes narrowed at the black unicorn. "Lies. It's nar written down."

Cerberus's horn glowed, but instead of glowing pink or red or yellow like Edward's, his magic shimmered with black on black, like smoke from an oil fire.

"There are ways of uncovering information that those of us who aren't burdened by your... *moral qualms*... have access to," said Cerberus. "If you'd loosen up a bit, you wouldn't be so ignorant yourself."

Watching Edward and Cerberus dicker, Kold smirked.

"I've had over sixty years to ponder my failure with you and Mai," he said. "And something deep inside of me said to keep building, to keep preparing to wage war once we got into The Realm — because one day, we *would*. I listened to it like a compulsion. I pondered, I built, and I pondered more. There was much power in the

Triangulum — even as underpowered as it was with only an inkling of Mai's full Orb — and in six decades ruling a city, there's only so much power you can stand to funnel into turning lights on and off, healing people, building infrastructure, and making business boom. The world was ending, Clint, and these people refused to see it. So I pondered, and I weighed my power, and eventually, I used some of that power in ways you wouldn't approve of — upstanding and *righteous* as you are. But it was right of me to do, because my compulsion to build the army you see here grew stronger and stronger as I did it, and then one day, it all came together. I learned of the Benevolents, and then I knew why Mai ran to you. It wasn't just because you were a marshal, and a marshal is bound to 'protect and serve' and to lay killt those who oppose him and those he shepherds. It wasn't because you rode with a unicorn. Nar. It was because *she could sense who you were at your core* in the same way that Edward first sensed it."

Clint leaned forward, keeping an eye on Kold, and whispered to Edward, "What the sands is he talking about?"

"He speaks of the Union."

"Meaning?"

"When we paired, we swapped a bit of each other. It's why pairings between unicorns and gunslingers are permanent. Permanent meaning *permanent*, meaning until one of us is dead — and then, even beyond that in ways you can't yet understand. Forever is forever. You will always carry a part of me in you, and I will always carry a part of you. I read you the rites before you first climbed atop my back. You remember, yar?"

"The memory is gone. Along with the rest."

Mai's hands tightened around Clint's waist. Her voice whispered in his ear, soft, her words carried on warm breath: "My *mother* was the Orb."

Kold said, "The reason I said she was like a unicorn was because she could *sense* me like a unicorn, just as she could *sense* you... as your own unicorn had done."

Behind Clint, Mai whispered, "My *grandmother* was the Orb."

"Mai didn't just *find* you, Clint. She *chose* you."

Still whispering, Mai said, "All the way back to the beginning, *all of the women in my family* were the Orb."

"She *paired* with you, gunslinger."

"But the Orb in me had to flower," Mai whispered, her chin brushing Clint's cheek. "It only reached maturity after I was taken by a man and a unicorn who were dark and evil enough to kill my soul so that it could rise again — finally exposing it, like a seed that requires a great fire in order to crack."

"You *had* to be there for her to find, Clint," Kold said. "For all of this to work, *you had to be there when she ran to find you.*"

"*Forever,*" Mai whispered, touching his chest.

Clint ignored Kold, leaning forward against Mai's embrace. He could feel her fading, becoming less solid. He wanted her to stay, but most of him knew it didn't matter.

"He knows, doesn't he?" Clint asked Edward. "About Mai being here with us."

"He knows," Edward agreed.

"He can see her. Or Cerberus can sense her."

"Close," said Edward. "Except that she's not actually here."

"Or perhaps more accurately," said Kold, "she's *always* been there."

In one massive gestalt leap, everything stitched together in Clint's mind. Everything made sense. Mysteries that had been sprawling since Solace suddenly fit together like pieces of a puzzle. Countless moments of frustration suddenly healed like old wounds and lost their scars. And finally, for the first time, Clint found that he didn't have to tell Edward he didn't understand.

"You and I paired, meaning that you are in me for always," he said, speaking to Edward.

"Yar."

"And *Mai* and I paired, meaning that *Mai* is in me for always."

"Yar."

"So when she died... and then when her magic grew strong enough to flower today... I... I..."

"Correct," said Edward. "*You* are the Orb now."

CHAPTER NINE:
THE ORB OF SYNTHESIS

"You understand," Kold said as they walked into the mountain's beating heart, down a winding stone passage with the unicorns' hooves clicking on the stone underfoot, "that I don't know how this will work. It may open a door up top, allowing the armies to pass into The Realm. It may simply create a new sense of power for us to command later and to open a door at will. Or it mayhap be no door at all, and be more like a bridge. You understand there *is* no wall, exactly, just an obstacle. Something that stops us from going in."

"And *you* understand," Clint answered, "that I hate you true — more than anyone ever."

"Of course," said Kold.

"Then yar, I understand."

The passage wound down further and further. They reached a corner, cut back, and turned to head deeper in the opposite direction. There were no *lights* in the tunnel, but there was *light* in the tunnel. It seemed to breathe from the air itself. Clint could feel it brushing his skin like sunlight. Edward said that what he was seeing and feeling was the Triangulum's magic. He said that they were experiencing but a sliver of its power now, and that it would grow much, much more intense. Clint asked if it was dangerous, recalling the way in which Edward, when exposed to overly intense and pure magic, had lost his identity. Edward's reply to the last question was strange. He didn't answer directly and instead said, "It's waiting for us."

The walls were dark gray and ribbed with sharp, facet-like angles as if sheared from the surrounding stone by a massive chisel. The passage was square, with perfect corners. Clint assumed it was fashioned by giants when Kold first arrived in Meadowlands and took the name of Diego Diamante, the wealthy land baron. He could imagine the giants working tirelessly with their massive, magical hammers, carting stone from the mountain's center to uncover the ancient third Orb.

"Edward hates me too," said Kold. "We've been working together for sixty years, and he hates me every day."

"And I hate Edward," Cerberus added.

"But we continue to work together because as much as Edward hates us, he knows that our teams are two halves of a whole. He knows that none of us can accomplish our mutual goal alone."

To Clint, Edward explained: "You and I aren't vile enough."

"And Dharma and I aren't soft and pathetic enough," Cerberus snarled.

"*Both* qualities are needed," said Kold. He turned his eye from one unicorn to the other in a way that suggested this sort of bickering happened every time the two were in the same place at the same time. "Without you two, we wouldn't have the support of the white magic."

"And without us," said Cerberus, "you'd fight The Realm's death machines with bubbles of glee and party streamers."

Edward snorted, whipping his head toward the black unicorn. Down in the tunnels, Cerberus was like a negative mote of presence. Because light bled from every direction, the unicorns and riders cast no shadows. So as he walked beside Edward, it was as if Cerberus was *Edward's* shadow, his negative true.

"I could make you *scream* with a bubble of glee," said Edward, his horn starting to glow.

Before Cerberus could offer his witty retort, they reached a rusty-looking alloy contraption that reminded Clint of Rank's liftbox out in the desert near the shifting Edge. Cerberus, with Kold on his back, stepped inside. Edward, on the other hand, stopped.

"Step inside, Edward," said Kold, gesturing toward the box. "It's plenty strong."

Edward hesitated. He'd already whispered to Clint that he hadn't seen the Triangulum Enchantem during his time training unicorns for Kold's army despite sixty years' worth of visits to the citadel. For one, Kold didn't permit anyone to see the Triangulum, but a second reason was that Edward seemed to be afraid of the powerful object. He'd told Clint that it could be used for light or dark depending on who commanded it, and to what end. Kold's motives — light or dark? — seemed ambiguous at best. Edward was helping him, but only because they were marching in the same direction... for now. The Triangulum sounded downright terrifying in Kold's hands no matter whose side

Edward and Clint were tentatively on, and Edward seemed to be nothing if not conflicted.

The white unicorn stepped into the box. Alloy clanged underfoot as the lift settled an inch.

"This was used by groups of giants every day during construction of this tunnel," Kold said, pushing a giant red button on the wall. A humming started above them, and Clint looked up to see some sort of a spark engine running above the box's frame, feeding out a sort of thick alloy cable. "It can hold much more weight than two unicorns and two men."

The vibrating, descending box made Clint feel nervous and confined. His hands could still easily reach and fire his guns, but the deeper they went down Kold's rabbit hole of armies and Orbs, the more his guns felt like useless relics. In the Sands, a marshal's guns were an unstoppable force feared by any man who had sense enough to be afraid. Against Kold's army, against Kold, and against Cerberus, however, they seemed ridiculous. Clint felt embarrassed just wearing them, as if he were attempting to project menace that he couldn't come close to delivering.

An impossible time later, the box clanged against another floor of stone. Cerberus and Kold walked out, with Edward and Clint a step behind. It felt beyond strange to be riding a unicorn through mountain tunnels, but he was simply following Kold's lead. The tunnels, having been made by and for giants, were plenty tall enough for clearance.

As they crossed another corridor (this one horizontal), Clint felt his ears pop. The sensation was odd — something he'd never experienced. The air felt like it was trying to squeeze into his head, as if the weight of the mountain was pressing onto him.

"The air is funny," said Clint.

"It's flat-out hilarious," Cerberus countered.

"We've very, very deep," said Kold, turning to Clint. "They really wanted the final Orb to be hard to find. It couldn't be magicked out. Before the giants reached the chamber that's ahead, they couldn't keep their lanterns or spark lights lit and were were forced to work in the dark. Once we found the chamber, though, things started working again, but lanterns weren't necessary once it lit up like this. The air also wouldn't be breathable if the Triangulum weren't making it fit for our lungs. Giants, as it turns out, can hold their breath for hours, so that's how they worked — in the dark and air-deprived, running to the surface every so often to breathe. But the fact that the Orb cleansed the air and the dark once we reached it carries a very important message..."

"We're only here because it's allowing us to be," said Edward.

"Here and alive, anyway," said Kold, nodding.

When they reached the chamber, Clint felt a shiver run up his spine and found himself missing Mai's presence at his back. She'd begun to wisp away with his dawning realization that she'd never actually been there, and had been completely gone by the time they'd left the surface to head toward the Triangulum. Clint decided that if Mai had never actually wrapped her arms around him or physically appeared before him — and if she'd always just been a mental projection of whatever spark of Mai was deep inside him, speaking to her larger energy as it blossomed recently out in the aether — then he might be able to make her reappear. So he told himself: *She's in me. Her spirit was always there. If that magic, lately, could become strong enough to fool me into seeing her, then I can fool myself again.*

Clint closed his eyes and tried to imagine her very real hands at his waist, but nothing happened... except that he did hear a voice deep down in his head, giggling with amusement. He could almost imagine that voice mocking his intense, spiritual concentration.

The Orb of Synergy was a massive machine that filled a hollowed chamber in the mountain's core, easily thirty feet high, thirty feet across, and covered in grease-clotted gears, motors, and chains. As he watched, cogs meshed and ticked forward against each other like clockwork. Chains clattered across toothed wheels, turning unfathomable machinery. Clint hopped down from Edward's back, fascinated, and approached the apparatus, leaning forward to look inside it. The immense machine had no casing; Clint could stare into its middle and see more chains, more wheels, more intermeshed cogs, all of it ticking minutely forward. In its heart was something that looked like a great flywheel, spinning fast enough to create a breeze. On one side were two cams that were wound with chains, rocking in semicircles. Something ascended the machine's side on a pulley, like a counterweight. As Clint looked into the machine, he held a respectful distance and kept both hands behind his back. It looked like the kind of thing that might tear a man's arm from its socket if he got too close.

Kold dismounted and began circling the giant machine. The chamber was large, but the Orb — which had become the Triangulum when Kold had fueled it with the other Orbs, incomplete though Mai's may have been — dominated most of the space. Past it, there were a mere ten feet on all sides. The unicorns stayed near the walls, watching the thing motor and clang.

"It doesn't run on steam or spark or anything else that I can tell," said Kold, his hands also behind his back and his voice elevated to be heard over the machine's ticks and clanks. "We also didn't turn it on.

When they broke through, the air lit and became breathable, but the Orb itself was still. Then I came down and added the other Orbs here —" He pointed to a huge, rusted funnel protruding from one side. "— and over there. Cerberus didn't tell me what to do, if he even knew. It was just obvious. I felt, if anything, *inspired* to do what was required. And when I did, it started up. Everything began to wind up and move. This power you feel thrumming through the rocks behind and beneath you began. And at the same time, up top, throughout the city, old machines started to light up and run. Everything we built after that simply worked how we wanted it to. It was as if we'd been given magic clay. But the Triangulum responded to my will above anyone else's, and it felt like I could talk to it." Kold closed his eyes, inhaled deeply through his nose. "Oh, but I can feel it now! I can hear it, too, inside my head, like a presence."

Clint could feel the power Kold described, and then he realized that he was beginning to hear a second voice inside his head as well — or possibly a third, if he counted his own. The Triangulum gave him no actual words, but he could feel its *sense*. It was as if the Mai inside him was speaking to the Triangulum without the need for words. He simultaneously understood their conversation and didn't understand it at all. He looked at Edward, who was looking at him. No meaning was exchanged in that glance; the great Edward was finally as much at a loss as he was. Mayhap even more.

"I've never felt it," Cerberus said, staring at the ancient, clanking machine.

"You wouldn't." Edward glared at the dark unicorn. "Your magic has been surrendered."

Cerberus turned to Edward, his eyes full of hate. Cerberus's arrogant shell had thus far been imperturbable, but that jibe had gotten to him.

"We could find out if I still have magic enough," said the black unicorn, his horn starting to glow like a black cloud.

Edward shook his head. "Triangulum magic doesn't count."

Cerberus's horn continued to glow, but Edward's interest was already elsewhere. He looked at the great dirty thing as it worked, grease clinging to cogs and dripping into its works. It sped up as the cogs moved faster.

"I don't know exactly how this will work," Kold said again, as he'd told them on their walk down through the tunnels.

But, Clint thought, that didn't matter. Kold and Cerberus didn't need to know. Edward didn't need to know. Even Clint didn't need to know, because…

"Mai knows," he said. And once he said it, he felt the

Triangulum's power begin to reach into his mind, wrapping tendrils of force around and into him, embracing him. The Orb inside of him talked to the Triangulum. The Triangulum talked to the Orb. To Mai.

In front of Clint, inches from his face, the air wavered like heat above a desert mirage. A horizontal sliver of light appeared at his feet and then scrolled upward, like an overhead door opening from the bottom. It was very familiar. Something he'd seen before.

"It's a shimmer," he said.

Kold looked around the room as if searching for something. Clint looked into the bright doorway and realized that just like in Aurora Solstice, he could see what was on its other side as plainly as looking through a window. He saw a street paved with yellow stone leading toward a massive, shining green tower. He saw green, green grass.

Then, spotting Kold from the corner of his eye as he searched the room and scoured every bit of wall and floor, he wanted to laugh. Or more correctly, *Mai* wanted to downright guffaw.

He can't see it, Mai said. *He commands the Triangulum, and yet it won't let him see what it's showing us.*

"Just like how he couldn't see you," said Clint.

Kold peered beneath the machine as if looking for a lost coin, then poked his head up at Clint and said, "What did you say?"

He's not supposed to enter. Not yet.

"Of course not."

Someone else must enter first. Like a sacrifice.

"Like us at the Rio Verde."

Kold marched forward, sounding urgent, almost angry. He stared at Clint, looking through the shimmer, oblivious. He said, "Who are you talking to?"

I knew what I was doing when I found you, Clint. But I always needed you, regardless.

"I know."

In a very, very real way, I was fated to love you. It was meant to happen.

"I know." There was something on his cheek. He resisted the urge to wipe it away.

Kold yelled, "WHAT DO YOU SEE?"

Go inside.

"I don't know what will happen next."

Nobody does. Not even Edward.

"It frightens me."

I'll be with you. And then, just as the gunslinger had felt her physical presence before, a small, soft hand seemed to squeeze his big, weathered one.

"Okay."
Go.
So he did.

CHAPTER TEN: UNFORGIVEN

Clint found himself standing on a road paved in bright yellow stones and surrounded by grass — grass that was deeper-green-than-green, so jade it turned the new life in Meadowlands dead and brown by comparison. The grass seemed to wave in the air as if speaking, whispering to Clint and sending him well-wishes.

The gunslinger turned his head, drawing the reality inside of himself and waiting for memories of The Realm to return. None did. It was as if the place were completely foreign and he'd never seen it before. It was as if he'd never marshaled behind the wall, never ridden a unicorn down Realm avenues, never been on the side of "good" and "right" back when it seemed The Realm had embodied them true.

In front of Clint towered a massive green castle. It wasn't made of stone; its construction seemed to be crystal and it shimmered with an internal, ethereal light. Overhead was the same sun he'd always known, but it seemed closer and somehow warmer. Clint found with surprise that he could look directly at it without fear or damage. His skin prickled with soft fire. He felt like a man returning indoors from the cold, except he'd nar been aware he was cold in the first place. Clint had been out in the cold for so long he'd grown numb — and now, saved, his dying skin was returning to life.

The castle's grounds were carpeted with the magical green-green grass to compliment the castle's sparkling emerald facade, but beyond the grounds, beyond a fence (ornamental, not security; Clint could feel that there would be no need for security here, as the entire place seemed to be draped in peace), he could see a beautiful city of alloy and glass. In that it *was* alloy and glass, it looked much like NewTown in Meadowlands… but this city was different. Whereas Clint had sensed prejudice and ugliness when seeing NewTown through Pompi Bobo's eyes and since, he could tell that this city was friendly, clean, and brimming with welcome. The feeling true was in the sweetly scented air.

Clint had stayed out of Meadowlands (and especially NewTown) as much as possible since Mai had died, but the few times Providence had sent him to visit he'd found that much of the veneer had peeled from the city. It was rich, and had all the luxuries a city-dweller could long for, but the laminate of wealth seemed to be paper-thin. There was crime in the alleyways between the expensive towers. Gangs ruled the underworld. There was garbage in the streets. People in fancy clothes, who seemed like they had it all, were rude and angry. Magic rose to the tops of the tall towers, with those in the highest buildings having the most and not wanting to share. Little sunk to the streets, to the underground train tunnels, which stank with an unceasing reek. But the city in front of him had none of that. Clint's sharp old eyes could see every shining face and rosy complexion, every outfit with nar a tatter in its fabric.

The signs of decay that were prominent in the Sands and even around Meadowlands were entirely absent. The ground felt solid in a way that Sands ground never had. Clint saw no crumbling or destruction. He turned toward the horizon, looking down a long avenue and across a park splitting the glistening city. The gunslinger saw nothing beyond other than more city, rolling hills, and bright, colorful houses. He wanted to walk down the avenues as far as he could, to see where the sidewalk ended. He wanted to peer from The Realm's edge to see if he could spot other worlds below as he'd seen The Realm in the sky for over half of his life. Did this place even know the other worlds were still there? Of course they would; they'd been sending stitching crews to repair veins in the desert. But did they know that at least one of the worlds below them was preparing for war? Was this paradise he found himself in even *capable* of war? He knew they had paladin knights, and he knew they had marshals. He seemed to recall being one, being a man who dealt death. But the thought was far off, drowning in a sea of bliss.

Clint was finally back behind the wall. He couldn't believe it. He'd wanted to return to The Realm for all his life, and now he was finally here. He wanted to lie in the grass and stay forever. He'd kept his promise. He'd brought Mai home.

Mai.

Something cracked in the feeling suffusing him, and it was as if he'd remembered her from another life. But it hadn't been another life. It had been mere minutes earlier. Seconds, mayhap.

Clint turned to look behind him and saw nothing but city and horizon. The doorway he'd come through had disappeared. Mai had said she'd be with him. So was she?

The gunslinger searched his mind, looking to find her. When he did, it was as if she'd been buried under debris. She gave the mental version of gasping for air, then seemed to surface as if she'd lain there forever, long forgotten.

"Mai?"

I'm here.

"We made it. We made it home."

I know. But you must keep moving.

She seemed unappreciative, and Clint felt a frown carving across his face. But as Mai's memory pressed into him, he felt her touching parts of his mind that had been buried for... oh... several seconds at least. It felt strange having those parts return, like feeling a numb limb prickle to life. Harsh and sharp, those parts of him agreed with Mai's seeming lack of appreciation. He felt something slide away from himself, and recalled the time he'd surfaced from Edward's bubble of glee back in the Dinosaur Missouri.

"What is this place?" he said. And of course he knew; it was The Realm, and the castle before him was Castle Spires, where the king and queen lived. But that wasn't truly the question.

You're feeling the magic, Mai said inside of his head. *Don't let it have you. Fight, Marshal. Stay angry and true. Remember the worst of what you've known. The men you've killt. Remember burying my body, planting my headstone. Pursuing Kold. Finding the Leisei, after the dooners had visited them.*

Mai's words, inside Clint's head, were like embers from a fire dropped onto his skin. They sizzled, burning holes in the feel-good magic wanting to bury him. They felt heavy, like weights on his feet or iron on his belt.

He reached down, suddenly frantic. His guns were gone. He looked down and saw that his pants, shirt, and boots were the same, but that he carried no weapons.

You're not a marshal here. Now go. Go to the castle.

As his mind sharpened, Clint began to notice that there was a presence inside his mind. It wasn't himself, and it wasn't Mai. It was, he thought, the Triangulum itself. The Triangulum had known he was coming; it had summoned him; it had expected him just as surely as he expected the sun to rise each morning. The Triangulum had given him the door he'd walked through, which meant that the Triangulum got a share of him… whatever that ended up meaning. Magic had intention and intention mattered to magic. But Kold had said the Triangulum was his — Kold's, not Clint's — just as Cerberus was Kold's. Clint shook his head. It didn't matter. The Triangulum's aim was same as Kold's, just as Mai's aim was the same as Clint's.

Somehow, some way, the gunslinger had to open a door and let the others in.

He walked toward the castle. There were two guards standing out front, both with bright pink hair, dressed in red uniforms and carrying tall staffs that looked like tridents. When he'd first looked toward the castle, the guards had held their tridents in an X across the doorway. But as the dusty, unarmed man approached, they pulled the tridents back, then tipped their heads and smiled.

"Welcome back, Marshal Gulliver," said the one on the left. Clint looked at him in disbelief. If Mai hadn't prodded him to conjure all those unpleasant memories to pop the bubble that the Realm magic had put him in, he imagined this would all seem very sing-song normal and happy. But now it just seemed suspicious.

"Welcome? Really?" he said.

The other guard used his right hand to gesture through the open door, into the castle. "Of course. His and Her Highness are expecting you."

"You knew I was coming? And you *want* me here?'

The first guard smiled an insultingly large grin. His hair was spun sugar pink. It looked artificial, like a candy tuft perched atop his head. "Our most famous hero," he said. "Our prodigal son. Sent into the Sands on a pilgrimage."

"On a journey," said the other guard.

"A journey to determine the extent to which our worlds have been damaged."

"A walkabout."

"A vision quest!"

"And now you've returned. And the king and queen will be so happy to have you back."

"And soon, to have Sir Edward back."

"Edward the Brave!"

Clint stepped forward, eyebrows low, watching the guards. "You know Edward?"

"Of course!"

"And you want him back, too."

"With great expectations!"

The first guard gestured again, now with a pointed finger. "Go forward. You will see them." He winked.

Clint consulted the voices of Mai and the Triangulum, which nudged him forward despite his doubts. He'd been sent here — by Kold and the others, not by the guards or Realm royalty — to warn the king and queen. At first that made no sense when Kold had proposed it, but then he realized that if he warned them, they'd ready their troops. They'd begin sending those troops out. And there, finally, would be the door Clint needed. So he wouldn't tell them about the army. He'd just tell them about Kold. Enough of a threat to warrant heading out to fight, but not so much of a threat that it could be considered a danger to whatever forces this bubblegum kingdom might have at the ready.

He looked at the guards once more, then marched inside.

The castle was more than lavish. The entrance hall was as tall as the Triangulum chamber under the mountain, but was otherwise its opposite. The place he'd come from had been dark, dirty, and secretive. The castle was brighter than bright, its entrance hall pocked with endless skylights from which shafts of gorgeous yellow light shifted and churned with motes of dust. Still, despite the motes in the sunbeams, the hall itself wasn't dusty. It was as if the dust existed only inside of the shafts, as if the light had been captured as decoration, specifically meant to lend the beams substance — open and welcoming, white and clean. The hall itself, from end to end and top to bottom, was fashioned from smooth white marble and bright emerald green. He could see the city through sections of the castle walls, tinged green by the crystal panels. Elegant tapestries plastered a few of the walls. Clint passed a table set with golden flatware and tall, lit candles. His feet whispered on a long, single-piece runner weaved in crimson and gold.

At the end of the chamber stood a man and a woman, both young and beautiful, shoulder to shoulder with their hands clasped in front of their waists. Giant white smiles sat on their faces as they watched him. Each wore green robes trimmed with white fur, speckled with black.

"Marshal," said the king. "It is good to see you home."

"So good," the queen agreed.

Clint listened to the voices in his head, then blurted, "Dharma Kold is preparing for war."

The king laughed. "Marshal Kold can huff and bluff all he wants. He's been doing it since before he left. It's why he was exiled." The king cocked his head, looking almost apologetic. "Of course, you don't remember, do you? He did something to you. He and that unicorn of his."

"There's nothing he can do," said the queen. "We sent him out because he was an insurgent. A malcontent. We sent you after him."

Clint looked over his shoulder, seeing the castle's front door down the long entrance hall. He turned back to the queen. "The guards said I was sent out to assess the fractures."

The king laughed again and waved his hand dramatically. "Oh, they speak in riddles."

"You were sent after Kold," said the queen. "And now you're back. And we are so happy to have you."

"And Edward," said Clint.

"Of course. We will send for him."

"When?"

The king smiled. "Soon enough. But first you must share our feast. As a welcome."

Clint looked back again, seeing the sprawling castle lawn through the front door. The voices were speaking to him, but he couldn't tell what they wanted to say. The Triangulum voice was most insistent. He felt it shape his lips — and so, because it seemed prudent, Clint said what it seemed to want him to say.

"How will you get Edward back here?"

The queen said, "Through a doorway. Like the one you came through."

"You know I came through a shimmer?"

She giggled. "Oh, you sound like the commissioner of a stitching crew!"

"Of course we know," said the king. "And of course we will open one for Edward. But first, we must celebrate." He gestured toward the dining table.

"And you knew I was coming? I mean... that I was coming at all?"

The king nodded. "Of course. We opened your door."

"The Triangulum Enchantem opened the door."

"It may have seemed that way," the queen said. "You control the Triangulum, so you spoke to it and it spoke to us. We heard. We opened the door. It's the only way. Realm doors only open from the inside. You didn't know that?"

"Nar."

The queen giggled at his word, and part of Clint remembered that in The Realm, they didn't use it. The king said, "Of course. It's always been that way. We sent Kold out from the inside. We sent you out from the inside..."

"To assess the fractures," Clint interrupted.

"Yes." This time, Clint was the one who almost laughed at the word.

"I thought I went out after Kold."

"You did."

"It was both," said the queen, now seeming flustered.

"And we opened the door for you from the inside," the king said, continuing as if Clint hadn't interrupted. "So you see, Kold can bluster all he wants. He can build his army as big as he wants. He…"

"You know about the army?"

"Yes, we know it all. But it doesn't matter. Unless a door is opened from here, in The Realm, he can never get inside. The wall isn't an actual wall, and it's entirely impervious."

The king finished speaking, and both he and the queen re-clasped their hands at their belts. The white smiles re-formed, and it was again as if they were statues, left here for Clint to find.

The gunslinger listened for Mai inside his head. He didn't know what should come next. He was flying blind. But she was silent. Clint could only hear the Triangulum. The Triangulum that was, now that he thought about it, growing louder and more insistent. More insistent than even his own voice. The Triangulum, he thought, that the king and queen said Clint had called to, and which had, in turn, called to them, telling them to open the door. The Triangulum, they'd said, that Clint controlled.

But he *didn't* control the Triangulum. Dharma Kold controlled the Triangulum.

Clint felt a strange, incredibly powerful force seize his arm and thrust it upward, palm facing the king and queen. He had no control over it. He could feel the dark force inside him grabbing his muscles and channeling its tremendous power into him, through him like a portal. A web of blue light, like lightning, shot from his hand and struck the king and queen of The Realm, knocking them backward. They fell onto a raised set of steps, their eyes shocked.

Clint opened his mouth, felt a presence fill him like the hand of a puppeteer. And he heard himself say, in the deep voice of Dharma Kold, "You expected me to mass an army in the Sands. But you didn't expect this."

The king's veneer broke. He looked at Clint, bug-eyed. *"Kold?"* he said.

"In the flesh." The power made Clint chuckle. "Well, in *Clint's* flesh."

"This isn't war," the king cried out. "We're unarmed!"

Clint carried a small knife on his belt that the doorman hadn't taken from him. He felt the force control his muscles, opening the knife and tossing it to the king. The king caught it. Clint felt Dharma Kold's sadistic humor crackle through his mind as a ball of lightning made thunder in his open palm.

"Now you're armed."

The gunslinger raised his other hand, and blue lightning again shot toward the monarchs. The king and queen convulsed on the floor, screaming in pain. Clint tried to fight, desperate to lower his hands. But the Triangulum, with Kold behind it, was too strong. Clint couldn't resist or hold his tongue. He couldn't fight the force, or the cruelty, or the lightning. The bolts ended and the lightning retreated, sitting in his palms, making small, concussive booms like thunder.

They watched him with wide eyes, breath bursting from their lungs in harsh gasps. Dharma Kold's force looked down Clint's arms, sighting with them as if holding a rifle. The thunder boomed in his hands. Sunlight outside dimmed as if in response. Clint's consciousness, impotent, sat back, helpless.

The king, seeing what was coming, calmed his breath, swallowed, and looked into Clint's eyes with resolve.

"I'll see you in UnderWorld, Dharma Kold," he said.

The lightning in Clint's palms crackled blue fire. Thunder boomed.

"Yar."

Thunder erupted again as Clint's palms delivered the final blow. The king and queen jerked and spasmed, then writhed and lay still.

Clint felt his palms lower and his face go slack. Kold was gone. The Triangulum was gone. Even Mai's voice — for the moment, at least — was gone. He was himself again.

The guards with the tridents came sprinting down the length of the entrance chamber. They looked at Clint, then at the king and queen's bodies.

Clint didn't resist as they put him in shackles and led him away.

UNICORN WESTERN 9

CHAPTER ONE:
A PLACE FOR CRIMINALS

As Clint sat on an alloy bench clean enough to eat off of, the gunslinger felt stripped of the power he'd felt while he'd watched his hands crackle with spark, as they had when he'd unwittingly assassinated The Realm's monarchs. The lightning in his palms had gone missing when the guards came to claim him.

Not for the first time, a random thought ran through his mind:

(Catherine)

He'd had the thought — strange, disembodied, nonsensical thing that it was — six times in the past fifteen minutes. He was nervous, knowing it was only a matter of time before he'd be killt by Realm authorities. After all, The Realm couldn't give the impression that actions such as those Dharma Kold had so recently perpetrated using Clint's body would be tolerated, but it wasn't his own death that had him nervous. The gunslinger had been prepared to die since the day he'd first belted two seven-shot pistols to his hips, and for the last six decades, he'd actively sought death like dessert after dinner. He was, after all, a man of one hundred and twelve years, and each year he could remember seemed far too long. He didn't feel those years in his body thanks to the Triangulum Enchantem's power (and in fact, he looked half his actual age), but he felt the pile of years in the whispers of his soul's every breath. He was tired of living, tired of dealing death and trying hard not to deal *with* death. Tired of living alone, and seeing hardships in the worlds that his guns couldn't solve. So yar, Clint was ready to leave and take his place wherever he was headed next — in NextWorld or UnderWorld as Providence willed it.

What made the gunslinger nervous, rather, was what would come of the others.

(Catherine)

But *not* Catherine, whoever that was and whatever that stray, random thought bouncing through his mind might mean. Nar, the gunslinger thought of Edward, and of Mai.

But that was absurd. Edward was a unicorn. It didn't matter that his powers were now a mere trifle compared to those of Cerberus, Dharma Kold's unicorn of a different color. He was still a unicorn (some sort of a *special* unicorn, mayhap, given how he seemed to have a secret title he'd never explained in "Edward the Brave") and unicorns were, so far as Clint knew, essentially or entirely immortal. Besides, Edward was quite literally a world away, across the mother of all fractures, back in Meadowlands.

And Mai? There was no sense in worrying about her, either. Mai was no longer corporeal. The gunslinger had buried her beautiful body beneath the apple tree in his yard in the farback of six decades, and now if she was anything, his one time bride was simply a presence inside him, or possibly "out there" in the aether. Clint doubted she'd be harmed — if such a concept had meaning for one such as Mai — if the gunslinger were killt by a Realm executioner.

Still, Clint worried. He fretted the notion that an advanced civilization such as The Realm would have faced many tricky issues that involved magic, and hence would have developed corresponding solutions. Based on what Edward (and even that sand-rattler Kold — oh how Clint wanted anew to kill him) had said over the years, The Realm had prospered only after it had learned how to sequester and use white magic. But nature preferred entropy, so the more The Realm siphoned off white magic, the more dark magic gathered elsewhere. Clint had trifled with the Darkness. He'd lost it over the years since Mai's death, but it had to still be out there, and The Realm must have faced it in the past. It must have developed protections against Darkness. And if The Realm could face Darkness, was it really so unreasonable to imagine that it would have developed ways of dealing with troublesome unicorns, too?

Clint worried because while he'd been in his cell, the lightning had left his palms, the power of the Triangulum (and of Dharma Kold) had left his body, and the voice and presence of Mai had left his mind. He worried because mayhap in The Realm, such things could be defeated. Maybe they could be blocked, traced, or dealt with. And if that was the case, then maybe Mai and Edward were in danger after all.

Or, he thought, mayhap it was something simpler. Mayhap the gunslinger could no longer feel the Triangulum because Dharma Kold was finished with Clint and no longer needed him now that he'd assassinated the royals. And mayhap Clint could no longer hear Mai because as it had left Clint's body, the power of the Triangulum had snuffed her out like a flame.

(The Catherine wheel revolves slowly, rotating on an axle with no wheel on the other end, the works set out from the wall at an angle. The man is bound upon it, arms and legs wrapped back and tied on the wheel's opposite side. A man in a black hood hefts a heavy two-handed hammer, like a sledge. A scream dies in the air as the man's contorted face looks up and begs, "End it; use your guns and end it.")

Clint closed his eyes, shoving the thought from his mind. It was foreign, like the dozens of other alien thoughts that had forced their way inside him since he'd entered The Realm. Mayhap the walls of his cell weren't impregnated with anti-magic protection, but rather false memories as some form of

(Catherine)

torture. Mayhap there was a machine in the next room broadcasting images into his mind that were designed to confuse and unhinge him. The gunslinger actually *hoped* that was true, now that he thought on it. Because if nothing was projecting the strange, disturbing thoughts into his mind (like the image of the dying man lashed to the slowly revolving wheel), then he was losing his sanity. He had no genuine memory of the man, no genuine memory of a Catherine throughout his travels, no genuine memory of a room filled with millions upon millions of books, no genuine memory of an owl wearing a strange bejeweled mask. Yet all of those visions and more filled his mind as he sat and waited to learn what The Realm would do with him.

Were the thoughts projected phantoms? Were they real things happening right now that, possibly thanks to Mai's presence in his blood and the Triangulum's power as he'd unwittingly wielded it, he could sense? In this prison, was there a prisoner, right at this moment, lashed to a wheel and being tortured by a man wearing a black hood? It seemed unlikely. The Realm appeared to be insultingly cordial. When the guards had taken him after Kold had used his body to murder the king and queen, they'd asked if he'd mind coming with them, had warned him to take care with his footing as he'd exited the castle, and then had led him through an office of men wearing the guards' same pink bubblegum hairdos who'd smiled and waved at his passing before placing him in the cell and bringing him a large plate of cookies. On his way through the prison, Clint was sure he could hear jumprope songs chanted in the distance.

Mayhap he was losing his mind after all.

He focused, and inside his head, he said, *Mai?*

But there was no answer. No comforting voice of his beloved, as he'd so recently heard her speaking to him, keeping him company, urging him forward. Clint had learned that thanks to Mai and her presence inside his body, the gunslinger himself had become the Orb of Benevolence — unlikely to Providence as that seemed. But without Mai's presence inside of him, how "benevolent" could the gunslinger actually be? He wanted to protest, to yell at the guards that he shouldn't be here. He'd been allowed inside The Realm because he controlled the Triangulum and because he was the Orb of Benevolence. But without Mai, he was hardly the Orb. And the Triangulum? It was clear he'd nar controlled that at all. From the beginning, Kold had controlled the Triangulum. But of course, *Kold* wasn't the man in the cell. *Clint* was in the cell while Kold was back in Meadowlands, rallying an army that would never be able to cross the void and reach the land they planned to attack.

Nar, Clint alone would pay for the crime his body had committed and Dharma Kold's arrogant revenge. And with that thought, Clint wondered: *Does Kold still need to make war? Or was this spit in The Realm's face enough to satisfy his bloodlust?* Clint could even picture Dharma Kold laughing as the royals died, wringing his hands in victory while he stood across the fissure, safe and sound.

"Mai?" Clint said out loud.

In answer, instead of hearing Mai's voice, Clint saw a sequence of images — another bolus of memories rich with sight and sound and smell and taste. They swallowed him entirely. He clutched his head in his hands, waiting for the false images to end.

A man with perfectly-groomed hair wears a wide, friendly smile and an expensive suit of tailored clothes. He stands before a cheering throng filled with adoration — a throng of people in multicolored shirts, all of them chanting. The chants are innocuous, like slogans, but still raise a feeling of foreboding.

Vendors' stalls line a street fair like that in any Sands town, but with richer wares and dew-covered produce. A hand — mayhap his own — holds a fruit that seems to be called a "papaya." From the right, a woman laughs.

A great room is filled with men with long, white beards staring into what look like gigantic viewers that ripple to the touch, like a Sands water reader dipping his fingers into a rain barrel to read the shifting of the sands.

Clint held his head, watching the images cross his mind. They were all so vivid and real, like things he himself must have seen. But he didn't remember these memories; they felt like someone else's.

He saw a shooting range and watched his own large hand squeezing the trigger of his very own gun. The memory of the range was unfamiliar, but in the memory — if it was indeed one — Clint could feel the weight of the iron in his hand, and knew it to be his own pistol true. He saw a group of women sitting around a horseshoe-shaped table, facing into the middle. Each had what looked like a spark device before them — silver and black, standing tall like a cobra. Some scribbled with their hands, seeming to write. Some looked sad, and some looked vengeful. He saw unicorns. Many, many unicorns. He saw a pool that was black like ink.

Images followed one after the other, all of them new and yet not new at all.

Unicorns. Black pool. Foreboding.

Then it was all gone, and Clint was again just a man in a cell.

As he continued to sit, he slowly came to realize that he wasn't truly alone. He could tell Mai was still there, but she was deep, deep down and not speaking. He didn't know if she could speak. He didn't even know if she was an actual person in her current form or something less literal, like intuition with his bride's voice. Clint shook his head. It had all seemed so clear a moment before.

After enough time passed, the confused gunslinger laid in a cot along the cell's wall and slept.

When he awoke, he felt better. He had no idea how much time had passed, because there was no window or clock within sight, but his body told him that it had been at least an hour or two, maybe more.

He sat up, running his big hands through his hair, trying to assess his state and whereabouts. He remembered being nervous, but didn't seem to be nervous now. He remembered something involving a woman named Catherine (he assumed) but that now seemed unimportant. He'd been nursing a memory of a bothersome dream, but it was over.

He felt nearly fine. A murderer, sure. But more or less okay otherwise.

There was a clanking noise outside his cell, past a solid door framed in a solid wall, and Clint realized that the noise was probably what had woken him. Someone was unlocking a lock, or turning a key, or sliding back a deadbolt, or doing something else that meant he'd soon have company. It had seemed, not long ago, that company would be bad, but now that he'd slept, Clint found himself almost eager for it. It was too quiet here. The gunslinger remembered passing other cells when the guards had brought him in, but all had solid walls and doors and he'd heard noises from nar a one. Either The Realm didn't have many prisoners, or the prisoners they had were all very courteous. That wasn't how it was in Sands prisons, where criminals were rude and riotous, banging against the bars and yelling out crude to all who passed. But things in The Realm weren't like they were in the Sands. Where Clint was could almost be an office. The mattress on the cot was quite comfortable — more comfortable and cleaner, in fact, than any bed Clint had slept in, anywhere, ever, in his memory. The comforter was pure white and seemed to be filled with feathers — but not turkey feathers, he felt sure.

As Clint waited for the cell door to open, he felt The Realm's courtesy and pleasantness suffuse him, and suddenly realized that there was a way out.

He didn't feel the Triangulum's power (which was good, since Kold controlled it) and didn't really feel Mai (which was fine, since he'd learned to live without her for six decades anyway), but even without those ghosts inside of him, he still saw a way out. He would simply explain what had happened. *Dharma Kold* was the one who had killed the king and queen, not Clint. The authorities would believe him. Why wouldn't they? The guards had welcomed Clint into Castle Spires. The king and queen had been delighted to see him return. Clint didn't recall the specifics of his exile (yet), but everyone here seemed to expect his return. They'd actually opened a shimmer across the worlds for him! Surely, they'd be predisposed to believe that something extraordinary and terrible had happened in the castle. They'd believe him when he said it wasn't him who had killed the king and queen, and then everything would be okay.

(Unless they take you to the Catherine wheel.)

As the door continued to clank (mayhap trouble with the lock? Clint for some reason imagined the scene outside as being slapstick and wanted to laugh for a reason he didn't understand), Clint's random thought of the wheel caused a kind of delusion around him to pop. When it did, his formerly rosy thoughts wisped away like smoke. As if he'd come out of a bubble of glee, the situation and the cell's stark reality reasserted themselves with vigor. The mattress was not as pillowy as he'd thought it was a moment earlier. The comforter was not, in fact, pure white. He could have sworn that it was as snowy as Edward, but looking at it now, he saw that it was somewhat gray and plain — like the walls and the floor and everything else. The air, which had smelled beautiful, once again seemed ordinary, or maybe even unpleasant.

And as to his arrest and his crime? Well, clearly there would be no simple explaining. That had been an odd and uncharacteristic flight of fancy for one as hardened as Clint. The people outside would be officers of whatever law was sworn to behind the wall — mayhap even marshals — and those officers would, if they weren't idiots, see the situation as plain and straightforward as it was.

He was going to be killt for regicide. He was going to be put on the wheel, and tortured until he was dead.

Clint looked around the cell, desperate to locate something that might be used as a weapon, but there was nothing. They'd left no belongings on him (he'd been thoroughly searched before being sent — politely and pleasantly — into his cell), and naturally a prison would be criminal-proofed.

The door finally opened. Behind it, Clint saw five guards in paladin uniforms, all but one wearing sleek black helmets with opaque face-shields. The helmetless knight — a tall, broad-shouldered, handsome man with a square jaw and sandy blond hair — hung back, still fiddling with the cell door. It almost looked like he'd gotten his finger stuck in the lock. When he finally came unstuck and turned to join the others, Clint saw that he wasn't holding a key.

Clint, now feeling sharp, wanted to make a dumb-paladin joke about mistaking fingers for keys, but he stopped when a sixth paladin entered.

Instead of a helmet, this one wore a black hood.

CHAPTER TWO:
THE PROPHETIC OWLS

"Get up," said the square-jawed man.

"Nar."

Without hesitation, the paladin smacked Clint hard across the face and the gunslinger's head struck the wall behind him.

"You're probably seeing us as pink fluffy bunnies or friendly pixies right now," said the man, "but you'll do yourself a favor to snap out of it and see us true: six knights who have come to escort you to the Wheel of Fortune."

Clint decided that he wouldn't walk to his own execution as a mopey, subservient lump. He was a marshal, and marshals were better than mere paladins. So Clint looked up at the square-jawed man and said, "Hello, kitty."

The man hit him again.

One of the other knights removed his helmet. This one looked like he'd just woken up. Standing beside the perfect-looking man who'd raised his hand to Clint, the new man was a mess. His hair was askew, his features homely. His voice, when he spoke, sounded as if were made of gravel.

"Do'n h'tm, Morph," he gurgled. "Hesjuss messin' wid you."

"He's not *messing with me*, Brooce. He's bewitched."

"Yar, Morph," agreed Clint. "I'm bewitched. Look out! There's a spider on you!" Clint's old but still lightning-fast fist shot out and punched the square-jawed man in the groin, sending him to his knees.

"Don't worry; I got it," he added.

Two of the other paladins removed their helmets. One was good-looking and held himself as if he knew it. He had broad shoulders and a careless mop of dark hair above mischievous eyes and a confident smile. The other, shockingly, was a thinking machine. It had silver skin instead of Buckaroo's gold, and it looked like a bullet. Clint had never heard of a thinking machine being a paladin.

"Churchill!" snapped the man with the mop of hair. "Hickory dickory dock, put your dagged helmet back on. Anyone sees a machine in that uniform and we'll be hearing a hundred hens howling at a high-noon hee-haw!"

Although the man's words made no sense, the thinking machine complied. Before it did, Clint saw that its every surface was so bright that it looked shiny with oil. The machine also had a fussy little mustache like a circus conductor's.

"He's not bewitched," said the man in the hood. He was taller than the others and was not wearing a paladin uniform. Instead, he wore black pants and a matching leather vest. His arms were exposed from the shoulder, large and bulging with muscle. "Get up, Morph. And you, Marshal, get up too. We're going on a little trip."

"I don't want any fortune. I'm good. You can keep your wheel."

"You can walk with dignity, or we can carry you," the hooded man said. "But you're *going*. There are six of us and one of you, and you're old and unarmed."

Beside the executioner, the paladin who hadn't removed his helmet looked up, then turned his visor toward Clint. His features weren't visible through the face shield's tinted glass, but Clint imagined the eyes behind it assessing him, sizing him up for a fight.

The gunslinger tried to feel the Triangulum's power inside him again. Mayhap he could blast the paladins like Kold had blasted the king and queen. But he felt nothing. Either the Triangulum was no longer flowing through him, or The Realm had somehow blocked its power as he'd feared earlier. Either way, he couldn't fight without a weapon, and the paladins knew enough to keep their hands on their own weapons lest the trained marshal try to grab them.

"Tell me," said Clint as they left the cell with his wrists bound, with three of the party to his front and three behind, "what kind of a paradise executes people on a 'Wheel of Fortune' — without trial and through torture?"

The dark-haired man who seemed to enjoy speaking in nonsense said, "The kind that's a crockpot full of rich and creamy crap."

"You don't know what you've gotten yourself into, Marshal," Morph said. "You might want to keep your mouth shut. You're just one man, and Kold can't send you anything to fight with until we open another door. So just go with the flow, okay? Believe me, we're on your side."

"I see," said Clint, unconvinced.

But despite his jaded exterior, Clint couldn't help but feel that Morph was speaking true. The group knew what had happened in the castle, but it also seemed to know about Dharma Kold and maybe even the Triangulum Enchantem's power being funneled through Clint. Yet nobody had been near enough to see or hear what had transpired in the castle firsthand, and Clint had been too shocked to speak when he'd first been hauled to his cell. These paladins were the first people (and, apparently, one machine) that the gunslinger had seen or spoken to since his arrest. And yet somehow, they knew. They knew it all.

They marched quickly down a long hall lined with small cells until they reached another heavy door. Morph stepped to the head of the group and Clint heard the rattle of a key in a lock. Again it took Morph a surprisingly long time to open the door, but finally it swung wide and then they moved on. The whole time, Morph's hands never approached his belt or pockets.

"What are you, a lock-picker?" said Clint.

"Of a sort. Keep moving."

They crossed an empty space lined with devices that Clint didn't understand or recognize. There were large machines that had screens lit with green lines, pocket-sized devices set on a counter and beeping, and a sort of sparking generator. The area looked like it was partly meant for staging and partly meant for storage. Clint saw stacks of chairs and tables against one wall, the tables halved with their legs collapsed.

The entire route they were taking seemed unofficial and undignified. Clint had killed the king and queen. Surely he'd be punished publicly. Shouldn't he be dragged to his execution in front of jeering crowds so that he could be pelted with rotten food and debris? Or was his logic wrong? Was it better, in a paradise such as The Realm, to do the dirtiest deeds behind closed doors, hidden from the eyes of the populous?

They approached a set of large ash-colored doors that were recessed into a high wall. The hooded paladin pressed a button, which lit with a white light from within. The doors slowly parted. Behind the doors was a tiny room. Morph, the funny talking man, the two masked paladins (were they both thinking machines, or just the one?), and the scraggly-haired one — Brooce — stepped inside, dragging Clint.

"This room looks less comfortable than my cell," said Clint.

The big sleeveless man with the black hood stepped into the box behind the gunslinger, squishing him into the middle of the group. Shockingly, Clint felt the press of the bodies and realized he was smelling lilacs. All six paladins smelled fresh and fantastic.

The doors closed and the box began to inch upward, but nobody in the box was yanking a pulley. It seemed to be a liftbox, powered by spark or magic. Behind Brooce was an orderly row of buttons like the one the hooded man had pressed to open the doors. The one at the bottom had a K on it. The one at the top, which was lit, read *OWLS*.

The man in black reached up and removed his hood, revealing an accountant's face and a shock of bright red hair. His eyebrows were large and fuzzy, like caterpillars. Without the hood, his hair stood in a sloppy mess, wetted with sweat.

"Okay, Churchill," he said. "If we're caught now, it'll hardly matter. Nobody sees the G's without the Senator's permission. So if you wish to take off your helmet, go ahead."

Clint turned, curiosity getting the best of him. Inside the packed liftbox, one of the paladins removed his helmet to reveal the same shiny silver head Clint had seen before — round like the business end of a bullet, slick and too shiny. Clint wanted to touch it, to see if the machine's skin was actually oiled or if it just looked that way. He stared at the fussy pencil-thin mustache. It seemed to be made of real hair. The gunslinger wondered if the makers had pasted it on, or if they'd found a way to cause hair to sprout from the machine's lip.

"Bad enough to have to wear something like this outfit," the silver machine said, glaring at the helmet as if it had insulted him, "but if I'm caught, I'll get deactivated. That's just plain unnecessary. Having to dress like this should be punishment enough."

"Hush little baby," the dark-haired man said, turning to Churchill. "Don't say a word. It took cracker jacks and kung-fu to collect these uniforms for us."

Clint wanted to ask what was happening, but he refrained. Based on the conversations the others were having, he wasn't sure whether he was in custody or not. They had removed his shackles, but the square-jawed man had hit him back in his cell. They were forcing him to go somewhere, but they were concerned about getting caught. Because Clint had precisely zero guidance (from Mai, from Kold, from Edward, from anyone at all) and could do nothing to change his situation, he opted to wait. Things would, hopefully, resolve themselves.

Some time later, the doors parted and Clint found himself shoved into an enormous chamber of stone that looked both timeworn and well-preserved. It had the feel of an ancient, holy place that someone had restored over the years to keep the elements at bay. There were huge windows built into recessed arches, and there seemed to be no glass in the windows. For a moment, Clint considered rushing toward one and leaping out, but moments before doing so, it dawned on him that he was very, very high above the ground. He could make out the tops of the tall buildings of The Realm below. They were practically in the clouds — strange, seeing as the liftbox ride hadn't seemed long enough to raise them so high.

"Don't jump," said Churchill, seeming to read Clint's mind. "If you were on the ground and looked up, you wouldn't see this room because it's not really here, but that don't mean you wouldn't have a long drop ending with a splat if you went out that window. Perception matters with magic."

"Like intention?" Clint could hear Edward in his head, laying the loathed rules like stones on a path. Even after all these years, with the gunslinger so old, the unicorn would mock him until he was salivating for answers.

"Like: whatever you think this room is, it is. But in its natural state — whatever *that* means — the room isn't actually the way that we, as a group, perceive it right now. This time, our collective expectation put it way up in the sky, but I've seen it underground before. Sometimes it's covered in vines; sometimes the floor is dirt or carpet. It all just depends on what it wants to be and what we expect it to be. Like this guy." The thinking machine gestured at Morph. "Wait until you see *his* natural state."

The tall, broad-shouldered paladin with the square chin turned to Churchill. "Stop mouthing off, Churchill. Wait'll we talk to the G's. We don't know that we can trust him yet."

"Jack sprat could eat no fat," said the dark-haired man. "He's seen our faces, so they're a fricassee of familiar, no matter."

"What?" said Clint

The man in black answered. "Boricio is saying that if it turns out you *can't* be trusted, you'll need to be disposed of since you've seen our faces." He turned back to the other, who was apparently named Boricio. "I'll let you handle him if that happens."

"Well, hot cross buns," Boricio said, smiling.

They kept walking. The chamber was very long and very clean and echoed with every step. The party mumbled about the chamber's current size and wondered aloud where "they" were, referring to "the G's" and cursing "the G's" for placing themselves in a room so large when time was short. Boricio declared loudly that they were "a couple of crystal-farting cooked chickens," which was probably supposed to earn a laugh but didn't. He tried again with something about "pat-a-cake" and a "baker's man" to continued silence. It seemed like Boricio probably said things like this often, exhausting the others.

Finally they saw a pair of flat, vertical stones, each nearly the size of a man's chest, mounted atop thin pillars. The group shuffled over, stopped in front of the stones, and waited. There was a sort of squeaking noise and the stone blocks atop the pillars turned slowly around. When they'd fully turned, Clint realized the stones had been the backs of chair-shaped pedestals that had a set of matching owls sitting atop them. Each owl had what looked like feathery horns at the corners of its head, and each had bright yellow eyes that were visible through a bejeweled cat's-eye mask.

"Well, this is nice," said Clint. "Thank you all for bringing me here. I've always wanted to feed fancy birds."

The owl on the left jerked its head forward and bit his finger. "We don't *have* to give you advice, you know," it said. The owl had an impossibly deep, resonant voice. Clint could tell the voice was coming from the bird, but it also filled the room, as if broadcast for drama.

"Yes we do," said the other owl. This one was identical to the first, with the same exact voice.

"We don't have to give *good* advice, then," the first owl said.

The big man in leather cleared his throat. "These are the prophetic owls, Garrett and Gareth," he said, waving a hand at the birds. "But nobody knows which is which."

"I'm Gareth," said the first owl.

"No, I am," argued the second.

"Then I'm Garrett," the first amended.

"Shut up," the second squawked. "Garrett is *my* name."

The first owl looked over, annoyed, and then said, "One of us always lies, the other always tells the truth."

The second owl shook its head. "That's a lie."

"Okay, it's a lie," agreed the first.

"I know what you're thinking," the big man said, talking to Clint and gesturing at the birds, "but this isn't a riddle you're suppose to solve. These owls aren't riddlers. They're idiots."

"No we're not," said the first owl.

"That's a lie," said the second.

The first nodded. "Okay, we are."

"The Ministry consults them on every decision of consequence, so they're both important *and* idiotic," the big man continued. "They arrived at the Ministry one day and announced that one represented dark magic and the other light. For a long time, the Ministry believed them, until they eventually decided that they were just jerky talking owls." He said this last as if jerky talking owls were commonplace. "But our water readers were, after a lot of reading, able to determine that they flew into a fissure as one bird, then flew out like this. Their psyches are split down the middle, but the division that turned one owl into two mimicked perfectly the split in magic that made them this way."

Clint shook his head.

"The upshot is that they tell prophecies," said the big man.

"One of us tells prophecies that always come true," said the first owl, "and the other tells prophecies that never do."

"I'm the true one," announced the second owl.

"No, I am," said the first.

"Technically, their prophecies are *both* always true," the big man interjected, "but because they're essentially two half-birds, each bird only gives *half* of the prophecy. You need both halves to get the full truth. If you only hear what one of the owls has to say, you'll end up with a half truth. Until this was understood, their prophecies were considered highly unreliable. Once a contractor asked them how long a staff needed to be in order to pole for a magic vein. You can do that in The Realm, but you have to nail the vein perfectly the first time. In vein repair work, missing a vein can result in months of lost time. But the contractor who came to the owls didn't know that he had to listen to both owls and so only listened to the first, which told him that his staff needed to be sixty-two inches long. The other owl added that the staff must be six inches shorter than that, but the contractor had already gone, without hearing the rest. He went on to the poling job and missed the vein."

"His staff was too long," said the first owl.

"He was digging in the wrong place!" said the second.

"Anyway," the big man said, waving his hand dismissively, "the contractor was executed."

Churchill rolled his alloy eyes. The thinking machine had an entirely different set of mannerisms than Buckaroo had. Buckaroo never rolled his eyes. He was also servile and would do pretty much whatever any human told him to. Churchill, however, seemed to enjoy condescension.

"So. Garrett. Gareth," said the big man, speaking to the owls and gesturing at Clint. "Who is this?"

"The answer to that question is not a prophecy," said the first owl. (To make things simpler, Clint mentally named him Garrett.)

"It's a prophecy if he remains who he is tomorrow," said the other owl, who Clint mentally named Gareth.

"Well then," said Garrett. "This man is *not* who you think he is."

Boricio reacted immediately, reaching for a knife on his belt.

"... if you think he's the king," Gareth added.

Boricio stayed his hand.

"But if, on the other hand, you think he's Marshal Clint Gulliver, then you're correct," said Garrett.

The other owl started cleaning his feathers. Eventually he looked up and saw the humans watching him, waiting.

"Period," he said.

The party relaxed. Morph turned back to face Clint. The executioner's shoulders fell. Only Boricio looked disappointed as his hand dropped away from his knife.

The big man turned to Clint, still holding the hood in his hand. He touched his own chest, his fingers tented. "I'm Oliver," he said. "I apologize for not explaining things earlier, but it was necessary to take certain precautions while in the Keep and to maintain those precautions until we were certain you were who we believed you to be. There was always the chance that this was a conspiracy, like the conspiracy that covered up the killing of the old Senator. Most people think the old Senator's assassination was straightforward, but I know better. See, there's a flicker talkie that clearly shows a puff of pink smoke coming from behind a grassy knoll..."

"What he's saying," Morph interrupted, "is that there was a chance you were a shape-shifter. We didn't think so, because these two told us you would be returning. But the killing of the king and queen? Well, we didn't see that coming. These two might have known, but they won't volunteer information unless they're asked directly. So we had to bring you here to make sure you were... well... *you*. But now we have official word: You're *not* a shape-shifter."

Morph extended a hand. Clint moved to shake it, but as he did, Morph's hand became a fish. Clint grasped the fish and recoiled. Behind him, Boricio laughed.

"*I* am, though," Morph said.

Oliver gestured around the group. "Anyway. You probably know about us from my great uncle. We represent the Conspiracist Faction."

"Your great uncle?"

"Sly Stone," said Oliver. "We heard from one of our water reader scholars that you rode with him, and that you learned the truth about what he was."

Clint glanced up at Oliver. Now that Clint looked him over anew, he realized that he could see much of Sly in the man, starting with his mop of red hair. Sly's giant head of orange had been so distracting it was hard to look past, but now that Clint thought about it, he could see that Oliver did indeed resemble the man he'd ridden with all those years ago. Oliver had Sly's pale, freckled skin and narrow, upturned nose. He had Sly's lips, which always looked at least mildly amused, or possibly mischievous.

"You're in the Stone family line," said Clint, a realization dawning. "So that means you're a..."

"A savant, yes," said Oliver. "Or 'yar,' if you prefer. The things in my head are... downright scary." He tapped his skull and gave Clint an ominous, knowing look. "Anyway, introductions! Morph you know. This one's Boricio," he said, pointing to the dark-haired man who talked in rhymes. "We're all glad that we're on Boricio's side because he used to be a torturer. Although according to his Realm designation, he was a 'decorator.' Officially, there is nothing as base as a 'torturer' in The Realm."

Next, he set his hand on the shoulder of the scraggly-haired man with the voice full of gravel. "This is Dylan Brooce. Dylan is a scent manufacturer. You can thank him for all those pleasant smells you smelled on the way here."

"I alzozing," said Brooce. Clint interpreted his mumble as "I also sing," but with a voice like he had, Clint couldn't imagine the man carrying a tune for more than a foot.

"That's Churchill," said Oliver, indicating the silver thinking machine. "Machines with enough years of service can be granted sentience in The Realm, and that happened with Churchill. Once he was able to think for himself, he left his position as a butler and met Dylan one day in a cafe. They got to talking, since Dylan's music is deep and Churchill fancies himself a deep-thinker. He's not, though. He's actually a cretin."

"Usually, machines don't reach the necessary level of service and are scrapped before they can choose sentience," Churchill offered. Then he added, "Coincidentally" with a look that swore there was more to the story.

Lastly, Oliver set his hand on the shoulder of the remaining party member — the man who still hadn't spoken or removed his mask. Looking into the black visor on the sleek helmet, Clint felt as if he might be looking at anything, and wondered what kind of eyes were staring back at him.

"This," said Oliver, "is Z. Z is part of the family, but you won't get much conversation from this one. Good with a scimitar, though."

Z nodded politely, then tapped the alloy tube at his waist. All of the paladins carried light swords, but the scimitars were notoriously tricky to wield and were nearly useless in untrained hands.

"The Conspiracists have been fighting to crumble The Realm for centuries…" Oliver began.

"Great job you're doing with that," Clint interrupted, "seeing as you've only had centuries."

"Hey," Morph snapped, "stow your snide remarks. This is a cause that I risk my life for every single day. We took out the head of the Royal Guard over a year ago, and I've been taking his shape and filling his role since then. Nobody's had any reason to come up here and check me against these two," he said, gesturing at Garrett and Gareth, "but if they did, I'd be put on the Wheel of Fortune in a second. How do you think we opened the door for you when we sensed the Orb? And who do you think got you in to see the king and queen?"

Clint blinked. He didn't think that anyone had gotten him in to see the king and queen. He figured he'd simply walked right in.

"Everyone knew you were returning," said the owl on the left — the one Clint had mentally named Garrett. "It's been prophesied forever. And it's also been prophesied that banditos will break the crystal castle into small gems and sell the kingdom off piece by piece."

"That's a lie," said Gareth.

"Okay, it is," said Garrett.

"But the first part was true," said Gareth. "The part about you, Marshal Gulliver. We've been waiting for you for a very long time."

"Well, not just us," said Garrett. "Other prophets, too."

"And also some who weren't prophets, like Dave the Ruiner."

As much as an owl could scowl, Garrett did. He said, "Dave the Ruiner waits for no one. I spoke to the other prophets. They told Dave the prophecies and Dave said, 'Yeah, we're all going to die.' He's an utter ruiner of all prophecies."

" 'We're all going to die' *is* a prophecy," said Gareth.

"True," said Garrett. Whatever had passed for a scowl vanished. Clint got the impression that Garrett hadn't so much forgiven this Ruiner person for his cynicism as forgotten he'd said anything about him in the first place.

"The minute these two owls arrived, they started telling us about an exiled marshal who would return and bring with him the Triangulum's power to seal the breach between worlds," said Morph. "The Realm knows how bad the fracturing has become, and they know that they're making it worse. Most people in the Sands think the leaking started after the Great Cataclysm and that only The Realm has managed to hold onto its magic, but they don't know that The Realm actually *caused* the Cataclysm in the first place. But The Realm's rulers know the truth. Even the citizens of The Realm know the truth, but they have mostly chosen to forget. One day, all of the worlds will sunder, but it doesn't matter to the people here. They've grown too used to their magic."

"Every day," Oliver added, "this kingdom faces a choice. It can keep going as it always has and widen the fissures, or it can surrender its magic vehicles and cookers and age-defying creams and its pleasant potions and stand a chance. The entire Realm has heard the apocalypse prophecy for years, from dozens of oracles. They know the timeframe. They know that if nothing changes, the apocalypse will happen during this generation. But as each new day dawns, they can't bring themselves to put down the magic they've become dependent on and let it return to the source. Every day, they decide that one more day won't make a difference."

"That's senseless," said Clint.

Oliver shrugged. "Most people here live in what is essentially a permanent bubble of glee. They do it to themselves, willfully becoming addicted to a euporite — a scented ointment called PermaBliss that you dab behind your ears like a woman with scent. It's both an amnesiatic and a dillusional. People know they're choosing to forget, but after a while, it ceases to matter to them. They become unable to stare at reality. There are few PermaBliss addicts in the prisons of the Keep, and there are few non-addicts who remain in their old blissful lives. It's not hard to see the terrible truth when the bliss releases you, and because of that, those who remain off PermaBliss usually end up joining us."

"How many of you are there?" Clint asked.

"Not enough. Dave the Ruiner, who the birds mentioned, is our leader. Dave is immune to PermaBliss, and managed to live amongst the populous as a normal citizen for long enough to put down roots. But there is another group of people in The Realm who are clear-headed but who *don't* join us, of course. Those people see things for true but want them to remain as they are. People like the Ministry."

"Barrel of babbling baboons," Boricio said. He'd pulled out his knife and was spinning it in his hands, staring at it as if it were dinner.

"I don't see where I come in," said Clint.

"Oh, that's easy," said Garrett the owl.

"Quite easy," Gareth agreed.

"You see," said Garrett, "You're the Chosen One."

Clint looked at the two owls, shocked. He wasn't a chosen anything. He was a gunslinger. He carried iron. He dealt death. And even then, he'd left his weapons in the Sands, his woman in the ground, and his unicorn partner behind. He stood in front of the owls and the six Conspiricists as an old man who should have died decades earlier, useless.

"It's true," said Gareth.

"But I don't have my guns. The Realm exiled me. I've no way to fight, and no power. What exactly am I supposed to do?"

"You beddastart swimmin', or you're gonna sink lika stone," mumbled Dylan Brooce through a mouthful of gravel.

"Yes," said Garrett. "Do that."

Gareth looked at his partner, then swiveled his head to face forward. "Period," he added.

CHAPTER THREE: MEMORIES AND PERMABLISS

Clint's shoulders were draped in epaulettes with hanging, yellow, yarn-like fringe. His uniform was blue, bedecked with medals that weren't even gold or silver, but pastel — pinks, light oranges, powder blues, and lime greens. One of the medals his uniform had earned, Clint noticed with revulsion, was for "politeness." Another was for "good cheer." A third was for "perfect attendance."

A beard was back on his face, too — this one fake. Oliver explained that The Realm was so completely filled with bliss and white magic that any spell used in an underhanded way (say, to magick up a beard so that Clint could conduct criminal activities) would cling to its user like stink. Everything unpleasant or borderline here, he said, was magnified when magic was involved. A spell used to steal a single dollar would, to the PermaBliss addicts on the street, feel like a massacre.

Five of the paladin Conspiracists were again wearing helmets, including the mysterious and silent Z, who had yet to remove his. Morph was now a different man — shorter, pudgier, and with a complexion that was uncomfortably rosy — and was wearing a uniform identical to Clint's. Both Clint and Morph wore name tags. Morph's said "Captain Wallace" and was bedazzled with fake jewels.

Clint fussed in his uniform, and hadn't stopped complaining.

"It would be logical, in the privacy of the Keep, for five guards in helmets and a torturer to take you from your cell," Oliver explained, "but if we're going out into the streets, seven helmeted guards will look odd if there aren't a least two officers leading them. When guards go out alone, citizens get nervous because they seem like an undirected forceful presence. But if they're with officers, the citizens relax because they figure the guards and officers could be on any number of errands. Like shiny, happy people holding hands."

"So while we're out, try to look delighted," Morph added, practicing a too-wide smile in the mirror's reflection.

"Wallace is the Royal Guard captain that Morph spends most of his time impersonating, so that's who he is now," said Oliver. "Luckily, you look a lot like Wallace's second, John Prince, so that's who you get to be — and fingers crossed that we don't run into the real Prince. The rest of us are too recognizable and look nothing like the other captains, so we're going to be faceless guards, and that'll fit just fine with protocol. And by the way, this will go most smoothly if you can act giddy. Pretend you're surrounded by singing children skipping rope at all times. Or holding kittens."

Clint — who didn't normally like children or kittens and who became sore after smiling — grunted. He stood behind Morph, glaring into the mirror at the ridiculous uniform with its dumb yellow epaulettes. He looked like he was going to do a song and dance. Which, quite horribly, he realized he was indeed about to do.

Before they'd left the chamber in the sky, the owls had told Clint something the Conspiracists already knew — that Clint's arrival was foretold to herald the beginning of the end. The way that end would unfold, however, was open to interpretation. One of the reasons the royals had allowed Clint to enter The Realm was because their interpretation said that Clint would return in order to defeat the Darkness, which constantly threatened The Realm and its abundance of white magic. Clint, who never understood even half of what Edward told him about magic and its rules, found that idea turkey stupid. Was The Realm really so blind as to believe that Darkness could simply be pushed aside so they could keep using magic cookers and magic construction and watching all the flicker talkies they wanted every day? But the answer seemed to be yar — or "yes," in parlance of The Realm. Dylan Brooce said you should never overestimate a person's ability to accept lies that spoke of what he wanted most to believe, then started singing a drawling song that lamented the changes in the world. Clint had to admit that despite his odd voice, Dylan's song was quite good.

The Conspiracists, on the other hand, interpreted "the beginning of the end" to refer to the fall of The Realm and a violent re-equalization of unbalanced magic — a reconciliation with Darkness not as a friend or a foe, but as a necessary equal. They saw a collapse of power structures and the shocking return to reality for millions of blissed-out addicts. They saw harsh lessons in survival for those who'd forgotten how to live without magic. And, of course, they saw the final fracturing of all worlds — and the end of days — if the balance wasn't achieved in time.

The Realm, Oliver had told him, had water readers like those Clint had known out in the Sands, but Realm readings (made on large, sophisticated water pools) were considered so accurate that the scholars who made them were more or less seeing events unfold live. They'd been watching Clint since his exile, but could only see him during periods of low magic interference. Thanks to Edward's and the Triangulum Enchantem's presence, those blind spots were blessedly wide early on, but the scholars knew the basics: where Clint had been, where he'd traveled, many of the enemies he'd fought, and most of the quests he'd undertaken. Especially vivid to the water readers were the last thirty or forty years, since those were the decades in which Clint had mostly eschewed magic. When he and Edward had ridden together in those years (slowly becoming figures of legend in Realm and Sands alike), Clint had allowed Edward to use shields, umbrellas, and healing spells far less often than the unicorn wanted. So Realm readers knew much of those years, after Mai had died and Clint had begun to spend his days trying to join her.

The scholars watched and waited, knowing that Clint would one day return. Morph, who could become whoever he wanted, infiltrated the readers and made friends among the more disenchanted of them, following Clint's legend as it unfolded, watching with eyes of a skeptic. He took his information to Dave the Ruiner, who interpreted what he heard as a cynic true. And so when Clint arrived, the underground was prepared. They'd anticipated The Realm's moves and had decided, in advance, how they would counter them.

As the group rode the liftbox down from the owls' chamber (and then as the Conspiracists dressed Clint in his fussy blue uniform) Clint began to see even more flashes of memory that had been hidden from him. Things he'd forgotten — or been made to forget — all those years ago.

He seemed to remember a marshal partner he'd had while riding behind the wall — a fellow by the name of Bellows. Clint nar remembered his first name, but did remember that Bellows had turned traitor. Clint recalled that part clearly, including the language Clint had used to describe Bellows's traitorous actions. Bellows had been *a traitor* in Clint's mind, not *a member of the underground*. Bellows had said something against The Realm (or possibly *done* something?) and had been caught at it. Clint had been young, newly starred, and brimming with duty and honor. He remembered being aghast at his partner's dissident actions. He remembered turning his back, condemning Bellows along with the rest.

At first, Clint couldn't remember what had happened to Bellows, but then further flashes of memory began to arrive. Bellows had been sent to the Wheel of Fortune. Clint had gone to watch. Given that Bellows was a traitor, his punishment seemed fair and just. Clint had *wanted* to see his partner pay for his crime, which at the time had seemed heinous. Most of the Wheel encounter was still missing from the gunslinger's mind, but Clint remembered Bellows begging, pleading with the gunslinger to end his torture by using his guns. But Clint had been young, and Bellows had been a traitor. So Clint had done his duty, and hence had done nothing.

Then Clint remembered the way in which the shoe had moved to the other foot. He remembered a group, like a jury, judging *him*. He saw the king and queen — and a man who his mind called "Senator" — at the head of the jury as they sent him out in exile. It had been the same king and queen, barely any younger. Did time move more quickly in the Sands? Or did the people here age slowly due to the abundant magic in the air?

As the Conspiracists pasted Clint's fake beard onto his face, the gunslinger's mind continued to send him disjointed images that, as of yet, had no meaning:

A man and a woman, above him, smiling, handing him a set of toy guns. Toy seven-shooters, of course.

Vast playgrounds filled with magic rides, including a sort of trolley that touched the clouds, then plummeted back toward the ground.

Bliss. Endless sprawls of bliss. Too much bliss. And a girl. A woman. Her hair was the sort of blonde that edged on yellow.

A man in uniform, associated in some inexplicable way with marbles.

Clint tried to force the flashes of thought and learn more, but whatever was blocking his memories apparently didn't work that way. He wanted to see Edward. He tried to imagine the unicorn walking on the street's yellow bricks, to see him entering the green crystal foyer of Castle Spires. He would have been permitted inside, right? He was Edward the Brave, wasn't he? Clint tried to see what Edward's title might mean, too, and wished he'd pushed the issue with the unicorn in the near-century he'd had with him. But he had no truly coherent Realm memories of Edward other than a single flickering image that might just be a distorted recollection of his encounter with Kold sixty years earlier: Edward with one leg forward, bowing.

Up in the sky's stone chamber, the six members of the Realm underground had turned to Clint, waiting for direction from their supposed Chosen One. Clint asked what he was supposed to do. Oliver said that they didn't know; *he* was the Chosen One and must be the one to decide. So Clint had said, "I want to find Edward" and Oliver had replied that the water readers — the scholars — might know where he was and maybe even how to contact him. And so Clint had said, "Then we will go to see the scholars" with more certainty than he felt, and the others hadn't questioned him. They had simply led him away, doing their best to follow his arbitrary decree.

So Clint allowed himself to be dressed in the loathed captain's uniform, to have his fake beard applied, and to have his brown hat replaced by a blue cap with a crest on its front. Then, after dressing as two officers and five guards, the group headed out of the hidden room, down another long and apparently underground corridor, and came up through another lift that rose into the middle of an open lawn. He stepped onto the greener-than-green grass and found himself facing a circle of buildings that crawled with ivy. Then he watched as the other six left the liftbox, and as the liftbox descended beneath the grass. Once below ground, the box vanished and grass appeared above its top.

"Harden your heart," said Oliver, speaking through his streamlined helmet. "The edutoriums are less whimsical than the city, but the air is still thick with bliss. Bliss doesn't only come from balms sold in stores. It's actually engineered into the grass. Walk on grass in The Realm for long enough without turning your mind to unpleasant thoughts, and you'll soon find yourself rolling on the ground, dreaming of pirouetting with fairies and pixies."

"Think about leaving people killt," Boricio suggested.

"And that will keep me from succumbing to bliss?" said Clint.

But Boricio wasn't listening. Clint decided it might simply have been one of the man's standard suggestions.

As they crossed the lawn toward one of the ivy-covered buildings, Clint felt the magic begin to work on him. He found himself wanting to be happy. It was as if the strange emotions he'd felt in the farback of Solace's saloon on his botched hitching day were suddenly everywhere, pungent like an overused perfume. They pressed in on him, insistently pleasant and comfortable. So Clint thought of bullets. Of lost friends. Of Mai, and how he hadn't heard her voice inside of him since he'd gone into prison. Had she gone away again, now that her role as Orb was complete? He didn't think so. He thought he could feel her deep inside, but that might just be the bliss talking. He didn't want to hope. Hope would be bad now. So he thought of the worst, about how there was nothing to live for, and when they finally arrived at the ivy-covered building, Clint once again wanted to die. He found the feeling strangely comfortable, like a well-worn shoe.

As they entered the building, a man with a white beard greeted Morph and told the group that he'd seen them coming in his viewer and he knew what they wanted to learn. He told them that he could answer their query, that he knew exactly where Edward the Brave was.

Edward, he said, was being held in the Realm stables. His horn had been sheared from his head.

CHAPTER FOUR:
A NEEDLE THROUGH A
STACK OF CLOTH

They were in a dark room. There was a huge pool of water in front of them, churning slightly in a basin that looked less like a basin and more like the frame of a viewer. The water, Clint decided, was magical. This seemed logical, given that the basin was mounted to a wall and the water wasn't spilling.

"He's in the stables," the scholar repeated. He stared into the water, two fingers in the corner of the pool, submerged to the second knuckle. Clint looked into the water and saw nothing but ripples and swirls.

"There's a pool of black water outside the stables," said the scholar. "I've never seen the pool before; it's new since the last time I've looked on this place. I do not know what the water is, but the unicorns in the stables seem to fear it. All are backed away, toward the rear of the stalls. The stalls are locked and are holding despite the fact that a unicorn can melt a lock into a puddle of alloy. I do not understand the magic I see. The stalls are not all filled, and those that are have unicorns in them that do not belong. This is no longer the marshals' stable. It's a prison. I see Edward the Brave, yes. But I also see Harley the Pure, James the Vengeful, and many others."

The scholar pulled his fingers from the water, then turned to Oliver. "I do not know what it means, but there are many powerful unicorns being held in those stables and they are not trying — or are unable to — escape. This will not help your cause, savant."

"Thank you, Bemis," said Oliver.

"Thank me only by telling nobody that I read for you and your Conspiracists," the scholar replied.

Clint pushed his way forward and spoke at the back of the scholar's head.

"What is the pool of black water you saw?" he said.

The white-bearded scholar turned to Clint. He looked briefly into the gunslinger's blue eyes, then replaced a wire-framed set of spectacles he'd taken off to read the water. "I do not understand the magic," he repeated. "I do not know what the pool is. But it is as I said: the unicorns in the stables have been shorn of their horns, probably so they cannot broadcast a call for help. I do not understand why they cannot regrow their horns, but mayhap it is the same reason they are not trying to escape. It is strange, seeing these unicorns captive. Most of the pure unicorns have left for the Sands by now. Only a few have remained in The Realm as marshals' partners, and those who have stayed are all ashy or gray. The captive unicorns I saw were pure white. This suggests to me that they are probably dissidents who would be — or already are — friends to your cause."

"How did they capture Edward?" Clint asked, thinking of how impossible the notion of "capturing Edward" sounded to him. "Did he come to The Realm after me?"

"No. The door can only be opened from the inside. *They* went to *him*. The move was obvious and predictable. So after I learned of your arrival, Marshal, I started looking for your companion. I could not see him at first."

"I left him with the Triangulum Enchantem."

"Ah. Then there would be far too much interference. So when I couldn't find him, I consulted the forecast tables and my own knowledge of the minds of the Senator and the Ministry and began to search for his mate. I found her at her house and waited, watching. A shimmer opened and paladins entered with several ashy gray unicorns. They took her easily. My reading barely wavered, there was so little magic used. She surrendered because they told her they had Edward, which they did not. I do not know where they took her; mayhap she is in the stables and I did not see her. Then later, when Edward returned to his home, they were waiting for him. They told him the same thing: they had his mate. Sir Edward did not surrender as she had. I do not know how they captured him because there was a fantastic explosion of magic and I lost my view, but somehow they did. My reading of the stables is proof."

Clint looked at the frame filled with water defying gravity on the wall. Colors swirled, showing him the same nonsense patterns he'd seen beyond the fingers of many a Sands reader, including his own kin, Kullem the Brew.

"You are sure of your reading?"

The scholar didn't look insulted, but Clint suspected that it was only because he was too well-bred. "Positive," he said.

There was something else Clint needed to ask, but he was afraid of the answer. He took a deep breath and said, "Why haven't they killed him?"

"You would need to ask the owls," said the scholar. "I traffic in the present. The future is their domain."

"It's not a future question," said Clint.

"Nor do I read minds," the scholar added.

"I can answer your question," said Oliver, stepping forward. "I can't access everything that's in here, in my codex," he said, tapping his head, "but like Sly, I've seen bits and pieces of the information that has been buried in the genetic material of my line. I know which event the prophecy says will herald the start of the apocalypse, and it's the death of Edward the Brave."

Clint squinted, fighting an urge to declare the entire endeavor — prophecies, readers, Chosen Ones, and everything else — ridiculous. "You're saying that by keeping him alive," he said, "they hope prevent the apocalypse? That's turkey stupid."

"I've verified it with the owls," said Oliver, "but…"

"… but if ids meant ta be, ids gonna be," mumbled Dylan Brooce.

"True, but they don't see it as an inevitable thing," said Oliver. "Fate isn't an easy concept to grasp — especially for the people of The Realm, who aren't used to thinking of the future. The Realm deals only in *today*, and thinks only of what will make *today* most pleasant. They think they can fight what's 'meant to be.' So it makes a kind of sense. They might have imprisoned Edward to protect him. 'Put the unicorn in a cell and keep him safe, because as long as no harm comes to him, the worlds will keep ticking.' It's dumb, but it's how they think. The story of The Realm is rich with blind failure to understand the forces that underly The Realm's very existence. It's as if the founders, finding themselves in the dark, discovered a mysterious blob of substance that could light a room for them… and so they used that mysterious glowing blob to light their way, never stopping to think that the power that made it glow might also make it fatal."

"You're saying magic is fatal?" said Clint. But he didn't really need an answer to that one. He'd seen what magic had done to Mai.

"Yes," said Oliver, Brooce, and Morph together. Churchill beeped. Z, still wearing his helmet, nodded.

"Gonna leave us killt like a cockroach kicked to the curb,"

Boricio added.

Then the six Conspiracists looked at Clint, waiting to see what he'd make of everything he'd heard. Waiting for instructions, or maybe for an ill-suited savior.

"We have to go and get Edward," said Clint, breaking the silence.

Oliver shook his head. "We can't. Not if he's at the marshals' stables. We got you out of the Keep because of Morph and his position with the Royal Guard, but we have no insiders with the marshals."

"You have me," said Clint.

Oliver continued to shake his head. "You're a legend, but that's exactly the problem. Everyone knows who you are, and knows that you're no longer one of them. There have been many changes to marshal training since your exile. What you may not realize is that you and Dharma Kold represented catastrophic failures to the system. You can't imagine what a blow your exile was to them. For a system based on honor, loyalty, and an impeccable moral code, having to send their own away — and execute another — was very, very bad. From what we've pieced together from that time, the failure of your training and conditioning undermined the confidence of *all* of the ranks. We're raised here to believe that the people of The Realm are special, and that those in the Sands are lesser beings. They exist to serve us and to send us magic. Everyone — still today, despite mass defections — trusts the purity of white unicorns. And so back then, for one of them to be... well, you know the story."

"I know enough," Clint said, not wanting to head further down a tangent. Some day, when they were out of this, if they survived, Clint promised himself that he'd finally sit with Edward in whatever shards of civilization remained and have a long, tall brew and recount the story from start to finish. But now was not the time.

"Your kind are flat-out brainwashed now," Oliver continued. "Modern marshals are raised from babes under the Ministry's care. Nobody knows that, of course. The public image of the marshal program still makes it appear elite, like something a child might aspire to, and every kid still grows up watching flickers and believing that one day he might become a marshal true. But it's a lie, like almost everything on the flickers, glossy books, and telescreens is a lie."

"Conspir'cies," mumbled Brooce.

"Unpleasant truths," Oliver countered. He turned back to Clint. "Did you know that most of our entertainment is borrowed from cultures in worlds we know nothing about? It's true. The Founders discovered magic and used it without understanding it, so why stop

there? The tunnel system, accessible through portals, pierces an untold number of worlds like a needle through a stack of cloth. Magic opened the tunnels, and Realm pioneers found and heard things in them — thoughts, memories, broadcasts, ideas — that they decided to repurpose and to re-broadcast as flickers. The Smurfs? Seinfeld? Even Risk and Joelsongs? Sands, even the formula for Fanta is from somewhere else. We know not where any of those things are from. What if they're poisons? What if they were sent from other worlds with the purpose of mind control? But that's not how The Realm thinks, and never has."

Boricio shook his head. "History is heaped a haystack higher with chaos than conspiracy, Stone."

Oliver shrugged and tapped his head. "It's not paranoia if everyone really is out to get you." He turned to Clint. "Don't listen to them. I'm right about this. People think the marshals are essentially highly-trained Hill Streets, but they're not. They're closer to drones, and they can't be reasoned with. They *will not* let us pass, and we can't fool or infiltrate them, even with Morph. As long as Edward is in those stables, we cannot get him."

Clint thought of the marshals, imagining them as the unstoppable drones Oliver portrayed them as being. The thought made him recall the Teedawge archetypes. Clint (and Pompi Bobo, and Sly Stone, and Mai, and Rigo Montoya, and Buckaroo) had faced *those* drones in vastly superior numbers and had triumphed. He wondered how the new-and-improved Teedawges would fare against the new-and-improved Realm marshals. The marshals would be better, sure, but how much better could they be? How many Teedawges would it take to simply overwhelm them with superior numbers?

"We need Edward," said Clint. Then, because he had an ace in the hole he'd yet to play, he added, "I *feel*, as your 'Chosen One,' that we need him."

"It's impossible," said Oliver. "We'd need an army to get into the stables."

"Well," said Clint, tapping his chin, "it just so happens I have one."

CHAPTER FIVE:
THE RED ROOM

Clint asked the scholar how people in The Realm — vein-stitching crews, the soldiers who had nabbed Cameron and Edward, even those who'd welcomed Clint himself — opened shimmers into the Sands. The scholar looked at the others in the group and laughed. The others laughed back — all except for Z, who stood motionless with his arms crossed, his blank helmet visor cooly assessing Clint and his intentions.

"It's easy," said the scholar. "You just need to find the Red Room. Once you find the Red Room, you can open any door out of The Realm that you want."

"Okay. Where is the Red Room?"

Everyone laughed again.

"Oldest joke in The Realm," said Oliver, reading Clint's annoyed expression. "You've heard the expression, 'Who is John Galt?'"

"Nar."

"It's okay," Oliver continued. "Nobody knows where that expression came from anyway — probably one more stolen bit from yet another world. It refers to an unanswerable question. Like the Red Room. People talk about 'running to the Red Room and back' when they want to say they went very far away, or on a long errand. People say, 'Consider me in the Red Room' when they want people to leave them alone for a while. Parents tell their kids they'll send them to the Red Room if they misbehave. Once I got lost on the way to a party because the hosts had given me poor directions, and when I yelled at them about it after missing the party, my friends said, 'it was in the Red Room; didn't you look?'"

Clint's blue eyes steeled as he gazed at Oliver and the scholar. "You're joking with me?"

Churchill held up a silver hand. "There is a real Red Room," he said. "People use it as a joke, but it's a real place. But no one knows where it is other than those in the Ministry. The man I used to work for, when I was a serving machine, was in the Ministry. Once I gained my sentience and met Dylan, I searched my employer's files, which is very easy when you're a machine. His files were full of references to the Red Room, but no indication of its whereabouts."

"I've tried to infiltrate the Ministry, but it's as impossible as infiltrating the marshals," said Morph. "The Royal Guard is easy to get into, relatively speaking. The Guard are only soldiers. But I'd never match a marshal's skill, and I'd never be able to bluff my way through the Ministry. It's as Oliver said — the Ministry is seen as a body of angel-like leaders. They're considered benevolent and infallible by all of the Bliss-heads out there. Some even consider the Ministry to be holy, descended from NextWorld to take care of the chosen people. But in reality, they're power-hungry, sadistic, and full of dark ritual. Just ask Churchill what else he found in those files."

The thinking machine nodded its silver, shiny-looking head.

"Our best guess," said Oliver, "is that the location of the Red Room is never written down or recorded in any way. Unless you turn a member of the Ministry, you'll never learn it."

"So follow a member," said Clint.

"You can't. They move through spatial folds, like shimmers."

Clint closed his eyes and shook his head. He'd never felt so completely and totally out of his element. "We can't open a door into the Sands unless we find the Red Room?" he said.

Oliver nodded.

"And there's no way to find the Red Room."

Oliver nodded again.

"My exile," said Clint. "You say it's legend?"

Finally, the stoic figure of Z gave a satisfyingly surprised reaction. He'd been standing in the corner, leaning against the wall with his arms crossed, but when Clint had mentioned his exile, Z had slipped and had to put out a hand to catch himself.

Oliver looked from Z to Clint. "Yes," he said. "But what does your exile matter in terms of finding the Red Room?"

"It matters," said Clint, "because I think I've been there."

CHAPTER SIX:
REALM, OTEL, AND SALAD

They left the ivy-covered building with a thankoo to the scholar (who found "thankoo" to be quaint) and walked out into the warm Realm air. Since his arrival in The Realm, Clint had never been too hot nor too cold. The temperature was always exactly perfect. He looked around at the others and took in their range of clothing, wondering if any of them were too hot or too cold. Somehow, he doubted it. There was magic in the air, and he suspected that if he were to strip naked, he'd still be plenty warm. If someone standing beside him wanted to don furs, that person would find him or herself cool and content.

They wandered off the edutorium grounds, to where the grass underfoot gave way to yellow stone.

The place of learning seemed to be in the city's center — an oasis of green amidst glass, crystal, alloy, and stone. Yet the city didn't have an odor like Meadowlands had. The air was fresh and new. Clint smelled vanilla — his favorite scent — and was suddenly sure the other six in his party were smelling their favorites, different though they may be. Even Churchill, perhaps, was smelling machine oil.

Clint stood where two streets crossed, looked up one and then the other, then marched forward.

He didn't have the slightest idea where he was going. Not even an inkling. Both streets were equal to Clint — the buildings and vehicles shining with the same strange inner glow, and every citizen wearing a wide, pleased smile. Colors on both streets were vibrant. The music Clint seemed to hear — again his favorite: Joelsongs — came from neither street, but instead from every corner of the very air around him. He took in the music as he walked, having no idea where he was going or why. He thought of what Oliver had said about The Realm borrowing from other worlds, and how Joelsongs were among those borrowed items. Where had they come from? Who had first sung them? The gunslinger realized he had no idea. Joelsongs were like the sun and sand to him and everyone he'd ever known. They'd been in the world since always.

Clint led their group straight, right, left, left. They made a near perfect circle, but no one asked why or expressed any doubt. None of the citizens found the procession of helmeted guards and their uniformed escorts in any way odd. They passed several lesser paladins — those Oliver referred to as Hill Streets — and the paladins waved. They even passed one particular paladin thrice and he waved each time, apparently not finding it at all suspicious that the group was walking in circles. On the second and third pass, Clint grew curious about the paladin, and tried to determine what the man was doing with a pad of papers and some sort of pencil or quill. He'd seen lawmen in Meadowlands doing much the same. In Meadowlands, if a man left his stagecoach or motorized vehicle on the street for too long, a lawman would write a fine on a slip of paper and pin it to the vehicle. But the Realm paladin — the Hill Street, out on his rounds — wasn't writing fines on his pad before adhering the notes to vehicles he passed. Instead, he was making small drawings: round smiling faces; flowers; once, a butterfly. Clint dared a greeting, sure even as he did it that it was unwise. The paladin raised his hand again and in reply said, "Beautiful day to you!"

They went up streets, down streets, up and down stairs to elevated walkways. Nobody asked about what he'd said about his exile, the Red Room, or their connection. There was a spell over the group, and the others seemed to think that Clint was homing in on something, or possibly in a trance. But Clint wasn't in a trance. He was walking with faith.

Earlier, he'd had a flash — a tiny, tiny, infinitesimal vision of a room inside his mind. He hadn't seen red walls, but something inside him said that the non-red room was the Red Room anyway. The flash was there and then gone. Clint had the memory hours before, in the tunnels of the Keep, but for some reason, he kept thinking on it: a single frame from a flicker of a thought. A whiff of smoke that went in one ear and out the other.

And then, there was another thought that was particularly sticky: Mai, and a bookseller. Clint had never, as far as he could recall, been to a bookseller with Mai. Solace hadn't had one, and he'd only known her in Solace and Meadowlands and the border towns between, all of the last entirely too poor for a store solely devoted to books. Meadowlands had booksellers of course, but during their time there, Clint didn't think they'd gone to one. By then, Mai was too sick with the magic. Too ready to burst from her body and become whatever it was she'd become.

A room that wasn't obviously red, barely seen.

A false thought, involving he and his dead wife in a bookseller.

Those two things — and those two things alone — led him as he ushered the six Conspiracists through The Realm with nowhere to go.

But that wasn't true, was it? There was a third thought, too... but that one was more of an impression than a thought. It was something he'd taken for granted, because it had become part of him. It was a recurring memory of something Mai had told him, over and over and over again.

She always used to say: "It will all work out."

Telling Clint that it would all work out had just been one of those things she'd done, like how she mocked him when he grew too curmudgeonly. But as the years passed, as his guilt over Mai's death grew worse, Clint found that he could almost hear her in his mind. Over and over, he would think that all hope was lost and that he couldn't survive without her. And when that had happened — and when, three times, he'd turned his guns on himself and feathered the triggers with his big, callused fingers — he'd remembered her saying, "It will all work out." Those memories felt like phantasms at the time, but now he wondered if they might have been more. Maybe she'd never left him at all. Maybe Mai had always been with him through those difficult times.

It will all work out.

Just like Edward telling him, *Things always happen for a reason.*

Coming from Mai, the platitude sounded like naive optimism. Mai could be crushed by a boulder, and in her last moment, she would tell the worlds that it would all work out. Coming from Edward, on the other hand, the idea that things happened for a reason sounded prophetic. Clint would flat-out believe it if Edward said it. Why? Because Edward was in touch with magic true. Yet wasn't the sentiment exactly the same? And wasn't Mai — mayhap even more than Edward — in touch with the magic, especially now? And on the heels of that thought, Clint became suddenly convinced that despite Mai's silence inside him, she was still there. He was sure of it: *She was still there.* She was deep down, seemingly suffocated by white magic of The Realm. But she was *there.*

A room that wasn't obviously red, barely seen.

A false thought, involving he and his dead wife in a bookseller.

And that assurance: *It will all work out.*

Clint walked and waited. Then he waited, and waited some more. Behind him, the wild bunch of conspirators kept pace and trusted their Chosen One. Two owls in a tower had told them that this old, disgraced marshal was special, and they had believed it. Clint couldn't help feeling as if it were all a joke, but because he didn't know what else to do, he kept walking, kept leading them. Was it really any less bizarre to pace in circles and wait for capture than to waste away in a cell? At least they were getting fresh air.

Something grabbed the gunslinger's eye. A purple street sign, which he'd never seen before.

He turned left. Six people turned behind him.

At the end of the street, dead ahead, was a massive glass door on an enormous gleaming building. Like all buildings in The Realm, this one glowed down on him, seeming to wish him well and welcome him inside. They walked closer. And as they did, Clint got the distinct impression that he *knew* this door. He didn't know *how* he knew it, but was certain he did.

The building was some sort of an Otel, but the lower level looked like a glass and alloy saloon and had no beds in it. People watched Clint's group approach, then held the doors and smiled. The people wished them well. Once inside, Clint felt less certain, but he saw a group of citizens to the left and followed them. The hallway narrowed. City people in fancy clothes surrounded them, all wearing sparkling jewels. Clint could sense their bliss hanging in the air like a smell.

To the right, a room with screaming bright red walls.

A woman held guard at the door, blonde hair piled high on her head. She wore a tight black dress and stood in front of a sort of half-desk with papers in a mountain on its top. Her hands were atop the papers, fingers sparkling with diamonds. Clint tried to see past the woman, craning his neck into the crowded room. It didn't seem like the right place, so open and unlike what the scholar had implied of the secretive Red Room, but it had red walls, and Mai — or whatever — had led him here. So he approached, and he cleared his dusty old throat.

"Yes?" said the woman. The gunslinger studied her face, which added a P.S: *What do you want?*

"Is this the Red Room?" said Clint.

The woman turned, looked for a long moment at the bright red walls, and said, "Yes. It is indeed a red room."

Clint turned. Oliver and Morph were already stepping forward, ready to enter. Boricio's eyes were hungry, mayhap starving. But entering the building had been a mistake, and he knew it.

"It's not right," he said.

They left. Clint took a few steps down the street, disappointed. The doors had seemed so familiar. He could almost feel Mai deep inside him, struggling to fight her way to the surface.

This was it. It had to be it, even though it so clearly wasn't.

He was about to walk back into the glass Otel to try anew, but before he could, something else caught his eye. To his right was a small, rusty staircase that seemed entirely out of character for The Realm. It wasn't polished and clean and fresh and new. Instead, it was dirty and old-looking.

Clint walked over to the staircase and looked it over. The stairs went down, below the level of the street. Clint grasped the railing and put his foot on the first step, and was immediately assaulted with very non-Realm sensations. He could feel the grit and rust of the railing under his hand. He could feel the grinding of dirt under his feet. The noises were wrong. The walls around him as he led the group to the basement door were made of old brick, and the sounds of his footfalls bouncing around the space were too muted. Everything up top was crisp and sharp and bright and friendly and new and polished, but the space below the street was none of that.

He opened a squeaky, scratched glass door and entered a small shop at the bottom of the rusty staircase. The others followed.

The small room was filled with shelf after shelf of books. There was a counter at the store's front. Behind it sat an obese old man — too fat for the The Realm's polished glitz — eating a salad.

"I'm Clint Gulliver," said Clint, unsure why he was saying it.

The old man was in mid-chew, his head bent low over his bowl to catch whatever lettuce he didn't manage to shove into his maw. His lips were painted white with creamy dressing. He paused, fork out and face pointed into the bowl, and slowly his eyes rolled up to look at the gunslinger. He looked like he was in a standoff, afraid to move.

"I know," said the man. "I used to work at the Ministry building. I cleaned the halls. On the day of your trial, they were one man short on the jury and pulled me in to sit. My vote would never matter. They were already decided and unanimous against you, but they needed a full jury to make it official." He said it quickly, without stuttering or breaking pace, delivering the words without being asked. He said it as if singing a song he'd sung many times before — as if this were a story he was known for, that people who knew him rolled their eyes at when he lapsed into it like a seizure.

"I remember now," said Clint.

"I was the one vote against your exile."

"I never got your name," said Clint.

"Ron House."

"Ron, I know this will sound ridiculous," the gunslinger said, sighing deeply and feeling stupid, "but we're looking for the Red Room."

Ron House set his fork on the counter. "This isn't it," he said.

Of course it wasn't. The walls of this room, such that they were visible, were yellow and filthy.

"Oh."

"This is the *Reading Room,*" he said, pointing to a sign that displayed the book shop's name.

"Oh," said Clint, feeling more and more like an idiot with each passing second. Was there something else he was supposed to do? He felt that Mai — or, again, whatever — had definitely led him here. The coincidence of finding a man who'd been at his trial seemed too large to ignore. So was there something else he was supposed to get from this man? Clint searched his mind, but found nothing.

Ron House stood and shuffled around the counter, knocking books from shelves as he went.

"The room you want is this way," he said.

CHAPTER SEVEN:
THE ROOM YOU WANT

Churchill wanted to be the first to state the obvious.

"This room isn't red," he said.

Ron House had led them through the back of his small store, through a second room much like the first, then down a very tight-fit spiral staircase Morph had to adjust his body to fit through. Ron didn't bother to close the shop or put a sign on the door. It didn't seem like he got much business anyway. Or any business at all.

At the bottom of the stairs was a large, dingy room under a store that was mostly underground to begin with. If the Reading Room book shop didn't look like it belonged behind the wall, then the basement room looked like it should have been forcibly ejected to its other side. It was filled with cobwebs (there were spiders in The Realm? Somehow that seemed wrong) and the paint on the ceiling was flaking. Every surface was thick with shelves, and every shelf was overcrowded with books that were packed so tightly Clint doubted he could force a single one out. Additional books were piled on top of the stacked volumes, their spines horizontal. Books were on the tops of the shelves and in piles on the floor. The room was large, but still the eight people in it had to watch their feet because there was so little room to stand.

"Not red like the color," said Ron, looking at Churchill. "R-E-A-D. If you *read* a book today, then tomorrow, you can say you've *read* it. There is a 'Red Room' somewhere, I imagine — that one being red like the color — but nobody knows where it is." He laughed. "There's also a Reed Room, filled with reeds, in the Ministry. The people there always confused it with the Read Room —" This time, he pronounced it like *reed*. "— but only because the bathrooms are beside the Read —" (R-E-E-D) "— Room in the Ministry."

"I'm confused," said Boricio.

"Ain' no doubt," said Dylan Brooce.

Churchill was still appraising the room. He'd removed his helmet when, as Ron took them toward the back, the group was blanketed with an instant sense of trust. Ron House seemed to feel bonded to Clint because of his story (a story, Clint suspected, he told often but that nobody believed), so the portly shopkeeper had immediately begun spewing information it seemed unlikely he'd tell anyone other than close friends. Ron's candor turned out to be catching, and the Conspiracists seemed to feel that their secret was safe with Ron.

"This isn't what we meant, though, Mr. House," said Oliver. He turned to Clint. "This isn't the Red Room. Not the one that will help us, anyway."

"Maybe it's not the one everyone speaks of, but this place is just as forgotten, and it does the same," said Ron. "You know why?" He didn't wait for a response. "Well, have you ever seen another used bookseller in The Realm?"

"Of course we have," said Churchill, seemingly annoyed. "There's one on First, and one on Marsten, and one on..."

"Not antique stores," Ron interrupted. "Actual stores that sell books. *Only* books. For *reading,* not displaying on a shelf as decoration."

When Churchill looked confused and nobody answered, Ron turned to Clint.

"People in The Realm don't read. They know how, but they don't," he explained. He shifted, putting one hand on his plump hip and another against a bookcase. "Marshal, the reason I was able to be in your trial was because I cleaned up at the Ministry. They need humans to clean there because they have an enormous magic generator in the building that does something to scramble thinking machines. So how do you get happy, joyous, bliss-filled citizens to scrub toilets in paradise? Answer: you don't get those people to do it at all. Instead, you pick someone like me — someone who wasn't happy to begin with and has become used to it. Someone who's immune to PermaBliss, and to the magic in the grass."

"Like Dave the Ruiner," said Oliver.

"Yes, like him. In fact, people have tried to get me to join the resistance," said Ron, tipping his head toward Oliver, "but I enjoy staying alive despite my station in life, and so I did what the rest of the immunes do: I took jobs that others who are blissed-out and won't face the grit that still exists in the worlds' corners refuse to do. The latest such dirty job is this — keeping an eye on a loose end."

Clint stood in front of Ron House, then looked around the place to see if he'd missed something. "What do you mean by 'loose end'?"

"The Realm is pretty close to perfect on the outside," said Ron. "They're able to fold things around pretty well, using magic like the Ministry and even the readers and scholars possess, keeping the gritty parts out of sight. But below the surface, The Realm is unraveling. If the wall ever fell, you'd see that our paradise is perforated with cracks and holes. They can cover most of it up, but there are still places where the worlds are thin and touching. And oh, I suppose they could find ways to cover those holes too, but then what would happen to the home flickershows? What would happen to the big flickerscreens? Where would we get our products? Most people here wouldn't want to live without their BryCreem and their Revlons. If they closed all the thinning areas, where would they get Seinfeld? What of jingles and music? The people of The Realm would have to make all of those things up themselves, or we'd see some very polite riots. But do you know what, Marshal? I don't think they can. People love Seinfeld, but I don't think they understand it. I have a few immune friends, and there are things we laugh at when we watch that show that I've never seen another Realm citizen laugh at. *Most* things, really. Average Realm folks will laugh when someone wears funny clothes in a flicker, but not when George gets himself into trouble because he's said something that bothers someone else. Why would they? They have no experience with feeling awkward, offended, or embarrassed." He rolled his eyes. "Nobody says anything that bothers anyone else up there."

Clint looked around the room with new eyes. Ron spoke of the majority of The Realm as occurring "up there" as if it were a different world. As they stood in the Read Room, the group was mayhap twenty feet below the street's surface, but what Ron said was true; it was a different place altogether.

"After your trial, they uprooted me from my cleaning job and began to shuffle me around," Ron continued. "I think they regretted having me inside privileged space simply to add another warm body to the jury. So they moved me here, still in the Ministry's employ. The Ministry owns all of the thin places. They're easy to spot. Where the shine fades, that's a thin place. Where you feel grime underfoot or touch something and your fingers come away dirty, that's a thin place."

"And you're here to keep an eye on it?" said Clint.

"Yes, to keep an eye on it — and to gather what comes through. See, there's a crystal recorder in the other room (another thing I suspect nobody understands aside from 'Push this button and the magic does the rest') that draws broadcasts from beneath this place and spools them for later use. But one day, as I sat up top behind what used to be a counter and a large, empty space carved in the rock, I started to notice that there was a draft coming from below. The Realm didn't build this space, you understand. This store was here before the Otel above, before the scent store on the corner, before the fine eatery and the Thuben across from it. They had to build around it. They noticed that this spot was ripe for catching broadcasts, so they placed the recorder and an attendant —" Ron pointed at his chest. "— and then they left it at that. They didn't explore because they're not exploration-minded. They're not curious. And so, they never found this."

Ron reached to his left, gave a nudge to one of the bookcases, and stepped back. The bookcase swung away as if on a hinge, like a door. Oliver, Morph, Churchill, Boricio, Brooce, and even Z, all of whom had seemed to be merely indulging Ron up until this point, suddenly stood straight with interest. Oliver leaned forward, staring into the newly displayed space — a long, dark hallway with a single overhead spark light visible in the distance.

"I was upstairs, felt the draft, then came down here and found the door. It's the source of the thinness, where the broadcasts come from. But unlike so many thin places, broadcasts aren't simply wafting through. The hole here is large enough for passage. I've gone down there a few times, but the tunnel just goes and goes and I get scared. First time I opened it, I found a book just sitting there on the doorstep. The book was called *1984*. After I read it, it felt to me as if someone had walked through this corridor from the other side, from a world very unlike this one, and left that book here for me to find. And so the next time I came down, I got curious and opened the door again, and I found more books — this time further down the passage, against the wall and open, as if they'd blown there on a breeze. I brought them in. I started my bookstore above after I had enough of those alien books, mainly just to kill the time. I wanted to read them all, but they came too fast. So when my shelves upstairs filled, I started putting the books I'd read down here, to keep track of which were which. It didn't matter in terms of the store's inventory. Since this place has been open as a business, I haven't sold a single book. Not one. And like I said, I started here not long after your trial."

"The *Read* Room," said Clint, his head spinning. "And it even has a door."

Ron shrugged. "I didn't even think of the homonym — 'red' and 'read' — when I started this collection. But I swear, things seem to happen for a reason, as if there were a divine hand out there moving pieces on a Risk board. So this became the 'Read Room.' And yes, I'd say that this room will do what you need."

"How do you know what we need?" said Oliver, suspicious.

"Oh," said Ron, smiling broadly, "I've been having the same dream at night for fifty years or more, since back when I was a young man. The dream I've had is of a beautiful woman with long brown hair who comes into my shop and wants to buy that first book — that tattered copy of *1984* with its green cover. In the dream, I tell her it's the kind of book that could send her to the Wheel of Fortune if anyone learns she possesses it. But she doesn't answer. Instead she takes the book, and tells me that the book isn't for her. It's for you — the legendary marshal Clint Gulliver — because he needs to head down the path of AllWorlds. I tell her that she still shouldn't have it, that I shouldn't have it, that you, Marshal, shouldn't have it, and that I'm frightened. But all she says before the dream ends is…"

Clint knew what was coming.

"… that it will all work out," Ron finished.

CHAPTER EIGHT:
RAILS AND DOORWAYS

Oliver looked at Clint, silently asking the gunslinger if they could trust the old, pudgy shop owner. Clint didn't know for sure if they could, but what he said rung true. Besides, Clint had started the day figuring on a trip to the Wheel. The worst that could happen, really, was that he'd end up there after all.

The gunslinger nodded. Oliver nodded back. It was good enough. They'd taken him to see the owls; they'd taken him to see the scholar; they'd followed him aimlessly around The Realm's polished city, moving in circles, for over an hour. Clint was the Chosen One. Oliver and the others had grown up inside The Realm, and even though they'd taught themselves to fight the air's pleasant magic, they were still used to following instructions. The best they could hope for would be to follow the instructions of a better leader. The worst that leader could do would be to fail them, but how was that any different from what Realm leaders had always done?

Clint turned, ready to enter the passage behind the bookcase. But before he stepped into the dark, Ron House stopped him with a hand on his shoulder. The gunslinger was so thoroughly stripped from his element that his hand didn't so much as flinch toward where his gun normally hung. He felt like an old man in a new world — a fast draw in a province ruled by people who commanded weapons beyond his comprehension.

The shopkeeper pushed something into his hand. The gunslinger glanced down to see that it was a small book with a green cover.

"Tell that lady, if you see her, that I did my job," he said.

Clint looked at the book. "Don't you want to keep it?"

Ron gave a small smile. "It was on the shelf down here, so that means I've read it."

"Thankoo," said Clint.

"Go with Providence," Ron answered.

They stepped into the corridor. It was floored in rough stone and sloped slowly downward. Once they reached the overhead spark light they'd seen from the Read Room, the passage widened and they realized they could see a second light in the distance. Clint felt a strange sense of repetition. As they walked steadily lower with their boots clacking on the stone underfoot, the sparse light flickered and bounced off of small square tiles on the walls — much like the tiles in the cathedral under the Rancho Encantato in Precipice. The approach to that cathedral had the same slow, downward slope. The air had the same slightly moist feel. The dark was the same, just like the spark lights and the footing and the tiles.

Further on, they even started to see similar signs lining the walls. One sign showed a green creature thrusting its hand from a box with the word "Gremlins" written beneath it. Another showed a drawing of a happy white dog and seemed to be about something called MetLife. Another, impossible not to like, had a woman in what looked like a hitching dress (except that the dress was white), holding a sword. The words "KILL BILL" were written in blood red across the bottom.

Just as Clint had back in the tunnels under Precipice, they found themselves passing dark side corridors that jutted off of the main path. And also as in Precipice, they could hear a whooshing noise and feel intermittent drafts being forced at them from the side chambers.

Clint stopped, coming to a realization. The others looked at him.

"I don't know where to go," he said.

"We're like a battalion of blind mice after a bucket of brew," said Boricio.

"Just guess," Oliver said, ignoring Boricio. "Or, sorry… use your soul or whatever you've been doing."

But Clint had no idea. The main path seemed to be the obvious choice, but it also didn't seem to be leading them anywhere other than down. So the gunslinger kept walking, and soon he found himself facing a wall covered in small tiles. So it wasn't exactly like in Precipice. In Precipice, the main corridor had opened into an underground cathedral. Here, however, it just ended.

"Again, no idea," said Clint. He turned from the wall and found himself staring into Z's dark helmet visor. The soldier's silent presence almost made the gunslinger jump, so he turned to Churchill.

"Do you have any… calculations… about any of this?"

Churchill looked at Clint with loathing — unmistakable even on his shiny silver features. "Oh, I see. Because I'm a machine, right? So I *must* have calculations. But alas, I don't. So tell me, organic being... do you have any 'stinking orifices' on the matter?"

Morph stepped forward. "I might be able to help. But first, I need to know what we're looking for."

"A way out."

Morph nodded, then transformed into a bat. He flew off, chirping, and returned a moment later. Clint had been spoken to in the past by horses and owls, so it wasn't too large of a shock when the bat said, "There's a passage this way."

Morph, still a bat, turned. Clint and the others followed.

Once off the main path, they found themselves in utter darkness. Churchill had lights built into his eyes, so after a terse warning to Clint not to make snide remarks, he turned them on. The darkness was pierced by two cones of light, but they didn't help much. The chamber walls were painted black, and Churchill's lights weren't particularly powerful. They were enough to see by, though, and so Morph led them to an edge in the rock underfoot, warning them to mind their steps. They found the ledge, then hopped down onto a sort of submerged pathway. Clint felt something underfoot and looked down to see a set of rails like those used by trains.

"We're going to be run over," he said.

The bat flapped near his head. "It opens up further down, and I didn't hear a train."

Clint didn't hear a train either, but Morph probably meant "hear" in the sense of bat vision. So they followed.

They emerged into another chamber like the first, climbed out of the submerged pathway containing the tracks, and walked up a path that looked like the main corridor they'd descended a few minutes earlier. The path ended in front of a beaten-up wooden door made of what appeared to be pine boards. Coming through the door, Clint could feel warm air and smell something like grass.

He opened the door, and gasped.

He was looking at Edward's stall. Edward's *stall*, from Solace, from back when he'd actually lived in one. Edward had called the stall a "house" back then and he'd had the entire barn to himself, but it was, in reality, still just a stall. Clint could see the spot where he himself had carved a mocking face into the wood. A lot had changed in the intervening sixty-five years since he'd last seen this place, but it was the same place true.

Something registered in Clint's mind, causing him to spin back the way he'd come. The group was mostly out of the passage and into the barn, emerging from a small door that Clint was positive had never been there before. The door was at the farback and should have opened to the outside, but behind it was the dark corridor — a perfect physical impossibility.

"Don't close the door!" he yelled, holding out a hand. He was suddenly sure that if the door closed, it would vanish. The king and queen had told him that doors to The Realm could only be opened from the inside. Solace was nowhere near Meadowlands, where Kold's army was waiting. Exiting The Realm for good this far out would be tantamount to starting Clint's sixty-five year journey all over again.

He nudged the group back through the door and closed it, certain that the door on the other side, in Solace, had just ceased to exist.

"This must be how they travel," said Oliver. "The Red Room — the *real* Red Room — must connect to this somehow."

Clint shook his head in the near dark as they hopped back down onto the tracks and retraced their steps. "I don't think so. I've been to a place like this once before. It was built by unicorns. Edward treated it like a holy temple — like a *forgotten* holy temple, more specifically. If we were here with Edward, that door probably would have been wider. Everything responds to us. I've seen Realm shimmers before too, and those look like holes in space, not doors. This feels ancient. I'll bet the real Red Room is all buttons and chrome."

"And that's bad?" said Churchill, his light-cone eyes still forward.

Back inside the main corridor, Morph led them to another chamber with a set of recessed train tracks at its end, just like the first. Not all the chambers went somewhere, and Morph reported each as a dead end, so the group wouldn't waste their time.

The next set of tracks led them to a place Clint had never seen or heard of before. Bright blue clouds puffed in a sky with twice as many suns as there should've been. Too late, it occurred to him that the air might not be breathable, but it was. Either the two-sunned place had air like their world, or the magic was protecting them.

They went back.

The next side corridor forked as Morph led them downward. They tried one side of the fork and found another place Clint didn't recognize (a person's house in the sky like a Meadowlands high-rise, one wall completely covered by books, greeted by a friendly dog wearing a tag that read "Murphy"), then tried the other side and found a second fork.

"We're gunna gid lozt," Dylan Brooce drawled.

At this, Churchill grudgingly admitted to being able to track their route and to keep track of which corridors they'd explored. But by this point, Clint wasn't worried about getting lost. He was more concerned about the sheer number of available tunnels. How many exits could there be? How many worlds did this place pierce?

At the end of one tunnel, they found a bucolic scene with a red barn in the distance. The door — still meant for just one-person — had opened in the trunk a large tree.

At the end of another tunnel, they found a room stacked with strange silver boxes with protruding black handles. A massive rat watched them as they looked around. There was loud music of a type Clint had never heard blaring from above. Someone came down a set of stairs — a kid with his hair tied behind his head. Above, someone else shouted down the stairs, calling to the kid: "Tracy?"

At the end of another chamber, they found the cathedral under the Rancho Encantato where Clint and Edward had squared off against the Darkness when it had taken the form of Parson Jarmusch. He recognized the odd SPICEWORLD sign, now ripped at one corner, and could see the bullet holes in the walls and floor from when he'd fired his slugs at the rats. He had a strange desire to pick at one of the holes until he located one of his sixty-year-old bullets, buried deep inside the wall.

At the end of another chamber, they found nothing at all. The door opened into a great black void, as if the world there had been sheared away. This last chilled Clint's soul, and he yanked the door closed as if the void might strike out at him.

As they walked, they continued to hear whooshing noises and feel the press of air from some of the passages. The gunslinger decided that the noises and air must be from trains, and that some were still running, headed Providence knew where.

Just as Clint was starting to think that the door they needed might not exist, he turned a knob and found himself staring at a great, churning, grease-clotted machine. The engine looked ancient, and was covered in cogs and chains.

"What is this thing?" said Oliver, stepping through the door and gaping up at the enormous machine.

The gunslinger smiled. "It's the Triangulum Enchantem."

CHAPTER NINE: RETURN TO MEADOWLANDS

Clint, Oliver, Morph (back in human form as the square-jawed man), Brooce, Boricio, and Z exited the Triangulum chamber, leaving Churchill behind to hold the door open. They headed to the liftbox, ascended, and began walking up the tunnel that had been carved out of the mountain by giants. Finally, after a long climb, they emerged into the heart of the mountain, into Dharma Kold's citadel.

When Clint had been in the citadel before, nobody had paid him any mind. It might have been because he'd been with Edward (who, as it turned out, had been training unicorns with Kold all along) or it might have been because the milling humans and other beings assumed that someone who'd passed the gate was supposed to be there. But this time, people stared. Clint realized it was probably because of the fussy uniforms he and Oliver were wearing. The guard uniforms worn by the others were generic enough to be overlooked, but Clint and Oliver stuck out like sore thumbs. So they removed their coats and tossed them into a corner, leaving only the stupid pants that were too wide at the bottom to identify them. Clint brushed the wrinkles out of the simple white undershirt he now wore and ripped the fake beard from his face, glad to be rid of it.

They had no problem locating Dharma Kold. He was standing beside his black unicorn Cerberus at the main gate to the dormant volcano's cone, overseeing a marching formation of trolls. Clint walked up behind him, tapped him on the shoulder, and then punched him in the face as hard as he could.

Kold's eyes flashed as he turned, but his angry look only lasted a second. He realized who he was seeing and his eyes went wide. He reached out to embrace Clint like an old friend, but when his arms came up, Clint kneed him in the gut. Kold crumpled to the ground, moaning.

"You got this?" Cerberus asked, unmoved.

"Yar," croaked Kold.

Kold stood slowly to face Clint, with his wild bunch of Conspiracists standing well behind him. The two marshals must have made an interesting pair. Clint knew he must look like Kold's father or possibly even grandfather, but Clint also knew he looked tougher. Clint was in white and blue with his clenched fists and a set jaw. Kold brushed his black shirt free of dust and, once settled, made his posture casual… other than the huge bruise and fresh cut on his cheek.

"You're not happy to see me," said Kold.

"Of course I am," said Clint. "Because now I get to kill you."

Kold was obviously allowing this to happen (with the now fully-powered Triangulum on his side, he didn't even need Cerberus to obliterate Clint with a wink), but Clint still felt his ire rise. Even the fact that Kold was allowing Clint to strike didn't diminish his pleasure. The gunslinger considered doing it again.

Kold's skin glowed yellow. As it did, his bruise and cut vanished. But of course, Cerberus hadn't needed to heal him. The dark rider had done it himself.

"You're angry about me assassinating the monarchs," said Kold.

"Using my body to kill unarmed people and almost getting me tortured and executed? Yar, a little."

Kold shook his head. "You were never willing to do what needed to be done, Clint," he said. "The king and queen were the soul of The Realm. They had to go, to send a message. I thought I'd be able to kill them myself, but I didn't realize it was only going to let you through. So when I saw that the Triangulum could still talk to you once you were behind the wall, I moved to Plan B. If I'd told you, you would have fought it. You never would have gone along with it."

"Of course not!" Clint blurted. "I thought the idea was to stop what The Realm was doing — to use your forces to subdue them like an invading army! Shut down their pinching of magic! Destroy the dams, venting the pressure and letting magic flow down the veins and into the Sands!"

"The fractures are everywhere now, Clint!" Kold retorted, returning Clint's anger. " 'Stop what they're doing'? How will that help? The Realm *is* the plug in the stream. The Realm *is* the pinching off of the magic. It's not enough to stop more damage from being done; *you have to remove the blockage.*"

"No matter who dies," said Clint.

"Where is your anger? Where's your indignation? They threw you out! They doomed you to wander forever as an exile!"

"Revenge nar changes a thing," the gunslinger said.

"That," said Kold, jabbing his finger into Clint's chest, "is where you're wrong. What's going to happen in a world filled with fracture and ruin when the magic starts to return, if it ever does? You think everyone will throw up their hands and sing Joelsongs together, sharing magic's spoils around a crackling fire while gumming their lips with marshmallow? Of course they won't. They'll fight over it. Kill for it. The Sands is a pack of starving dogs, and we're talking about throwing a plate of meat into the center of their pack. You think they'll hold tally and assign each person his due of magic? Of course they won't. They'll pounce, like animals. What we do here must make a statement. It must be a decisive strike of power that will chill the hearts of all who will think to defy us. We must control the magic — and the balance of power — so that we can distribute it proper. Those who would hoard must know that we will come at them. They must watch what we do to The Realm now and know later that if they do the same, they will fall beneath our boot. The first strike *had* to be against the royalty. We had to say, 'This is what happens when you defy us. This is what happens when you take what does not belong to you.' "

But Clint was thinking of the citizens he'd seen in The Realm. The king and queen had just been assassinated, and no one seemed to care… or possibly even know. He thought of the Hill Street he'd seen, drawing smiling faces and sticking them to vehicles. He thought of PermaBliss, and tried to remember if it had existed when he and Kold had ridden white steeds down yellow brick streets.

"You've forced them to come after you with everything they have," said Clint.

Kold spread his arms, gesturing at the army in front of him. "Let them."

"This isn't what I signed on for."

"Sure it is," said Kold, exhaling as if tired of having the same argument over and over. "You are the white. You have your purpose. You brought me the Orb — twice. You got them to open the first door. You were their prodigal son, welcomed into Castle Spires whereas I would have had to storm my way in. You can pretend Cerberus and I aren't what make your 'good actions' meaningful, but deep down you know that without us, you'd just be one more old man with a pair of guns. If we did everything my way, we'd never get in or we'd be thwarted when we did. If we did everything your way, we'd be overrun once we were inside. We are both required. We need each other if either of us are to matter. You are the gentle touch, and I am the hammer of war."

Kold beckoned to a passing unicorn. The unicorn looked over. The dark rider jerked his head and said, "Celeste. Thirty minutes."

Clint expected the unicorn (proud, non-subservient creatures that they were) to tell Kold where he could put those thirty minutes, but instead she trotted off into the open crater of the dormant volcano. Clint heard her yelling. Though the gunslinger couldn't tell what the unicorn was saying, every group she passed began to stir, mobilize, prepare.

"Now," said Kold. "Where is the door?"

Clint feigned ignorance. "What door?"

Kold rolled his eyes. "I don't have time for this."

He held a hand toward Clint's head. Fine tendrils of blue smoke bled from his fingers, moving slowly, like tiny snakes, crawling over the gunslinger's scalp and down under his hair. Clint's skin crawled wherever the things touched, as if they were serpents. Clint tried flinching away, but something was holding him as still as a statue. The gunslinger could only stand helplessly as the blue snakes slithered into his ears, nose, mouth, eyes, and then seemingly into his skull itself. He felt Kold's essence climbing into his soul, as if he were donning Clint like a jacket. But something was already inside Clint, and Kold couldn't displace it in order to settle all the way down. There wasn't enough room.

And then Clint realized: *Mai was still inside him*. She hadn't spoken since those first few words inside The Realm, as Kold searched Clint for what he needed, he saw true that she was still there. She'd said that she couldn't stay long — but she hadn't left yet.

Clint tried to fight the fingers he felt in his brain, but it was like an ant pushing against a boulder. Kold had been powerful before, but now with the Triangulum complete, he was hundreds of times stronger. There was no standing against the Triangulum. There was no *attempting* to stand against it. Clint tried hiding his knowledge about the location of the door, but it was no use. Kold found it instantly.

"Perfect," Kold said as his essence withdrew. "But of course, that placement won't do."

He yanked at the empty air with his hands. As he did, his palms glowed white and a brilliant light filled the chamber. The milling army, now starting to power up their machines, looked over. A moment later, Churchill was standing before them. Behind Churchill was the door that had moments earlier been in the belly of the mountain.

"Churchill, close the door!" Oliver blurted from behind Clint.

But Kold was already there, already reaching an invisible hand out to hold the door open. He gestured with his head for the thinking machine to walk away. With a glance at the others, Churchill did. Then he walked over and stood beside Morph, beside Z, beside the others who'd receded when Clint had punched the man in black.

"I'm on your side," Kold said, looking at Clint with what had to be disappointment.

"Nar, you're not."

"We're a team."

"We are *not* a team."

"But you want to end what The Realm is doing, Clint, and so do I. And Edward? Edward and the unicorns want to end it most of all."

Clint's face fell. In the heat of his fight with Kold, he'd almost forgotten about Edward — about why he'd come back to the Sands in the first place. When he'd come through from the path of AllWorlds, he'd wanted Kold's help. A moment ago, he'd wanted to shut the door and keep Kold's help at bay. Which was the right choice — The Realm or Dharma Kold? Neither option felt any good. Both were tipped with a thousand poisoned spikes.

"I saw what was in your head," said Kold. "Unicorns in captivity. A black pool. You want to rescue them. To rescue Edward. You came here to find me and get my help. And so you see, we *are* a team. It's why you came looking for us."

Clint closed his eyes. Yar, he wanted to rescue Edward. But there was more to it than that. In a way he didn't fully understand, he *needed* to rescue Edward. The gunslinger knew in the way he'd known he could find the Red Room — nar, the *Read* Room — that Edward was important to more than just Clint. The story wasn't close to over.

Kold stood in front of him, eyebrows raised.

He'll go in anyway, Clint thought. *He has an open door. He has the Triangulum. He has an army. Nobody will be able to stand against him. I can't prevent it, even if preventing it were the right choice — which it may not be.*

And with the thought, Clint felt a pang of self-loathing, suddenly sure the Kold had been right all along. Maybe the two marshals did have the same goals. Maybe Clint wasn't willing to get his hands dirty, but was more than happy to let someone else do it.

Reluctantly, Clint nodded.

"See?" said Kold, smiling. *"Teamwork."* He extended a hand. Clint ignored it. He turned, not wanting the wild bunch standing behind him to see his face.

"You will use restraint with your army," he said.

Kold pretended to think, then said, "Nar."

"And we will go for Edward first. For the unicorns. For whatever is holding them."

Kold actually laughed. "Of course," he said. "This all begins and ends with Edward. Did you not know that?"

CHAPTER TEN:
THE WILD BUNCH

Clint didn't bother to ask Kold what he meant about things beginning and ending with Edward. It was probably something stupid involving magic, and Clint was tired of feeling like he was at magic's mercy. All that mattered was that Kold thought Edward was important enough to save first.

Kold shouted a command that ran through the Army of the Triangulum's ranks like wildfire. Unicorns rushed from the crater, away from Clint and the Conspiracists, presumably through a door at its far end. Zeppelins lifted off. Burners were fired and balloons started to rise. The enormous black tripod devices — three zeppelins tall at the legs and one zeppelin wide at the carapace — lumbered off in the same direction as the unicorns, but instead of heading through a door, they climbed the mountain's upper rim. They looked like long-legged spiders as they summited the crater's edge, bellowing their hollow, echoing cries that chilled the gunslinger's blood.

The two-wheeled vehicles (he'd heard them called steamcycles) fired their engines and turned. Wave after wave of Teedawge archetypes, most wearing bi-colored goggles and holding high-pressure steam rifles with magic packs like Sly Stone's, filed by. What Clint had mistaken for giant rocks turned out to be crouching giants who stood and turned, unsheathing their enormous hammers. Behind the giants were green-cloaked elves with bows, all of them appearing especially small by comparison. Flying machines lifted off — some straight up, some speeding down long strips of rock flooring until they found flight. Ordinary human soldiers tested their scimitars. A troupe of counterfeit gunslingers checked their weapons — each with only six shots per pistol. The large green vehicles with treads instead of wheels turned their huge guns and lurched forward, belching steam. Ropers filed in front of morlocks, trolls, and more Teedawges. The air was positively thick with magic. Clint could feel it like sweat on his brow.

At the thought of magic, Clint's gaze turned inward, listening for Mai's voice amidst the chaos. He could almost feel her becoming more present, as if stirred up during Kold's invasion of Clint's mind. He couldn't feel her as he had before, but that probably had to do with the Triangulum. Mai had been born a woman with the seeds of magic inside her, then was struck down so her magic could grow. Finally, through Clint, she'd surrendered that magic to the Triangulum Enchantem. Whatever was left of her was diminished and struggling, but that might be a good thing. She was no longer the Orb of Benevolence. Now, whatever bit of her remained was at least all Mai.

Kold stepped toward the doorway to The Realm and stuck his arm through it. An intense expression of concentration crossed his features, and the door shrunk until it was only a small black circle hovering in space around the dark rider's arm. Then he used his other hand to grab the hole and pull it down over his wrist and to his fingers. The aperture grew smaller, finally circling just his pinky. He wrapped his hand around the hole — which not long ago had been a full-sized door — and squeezed. When he pulled his hand away, the thing had become an opaque black ring that Kold seemed to be wearing like jewelry. The only way to tell it wasn't jewelry was the fact that beyond the ring, Kold had no digit. The rest of his finger, presumably, was sticking out of a similar hole on the other side, into the strange trans-world station that Ron House had called the path of AllWorlds.

"Thank you for opening the door," Kold said, wiggling his ring and missing finger. "And thank you for giving me the Orb that will allow me to hold it open."

"You're going to drive this entire army through that door?" Clint asked. He imagined the tripod machines, tanks, and the rest navigating the tunnels back to the Read Room. Ron House would be quite surprised at what came up from his basement.

"He'll transform it," said Oliver, who Clint had almost forgotten was standing behind him. The gunslinger's eyes took in the rest of his new crew — the broad-shouldered leader, the shape-shifter, the gravel-voiced folk singer, the uptight thinking machine, the man with the knife and wild eyes, and the blank-visored mystery man who was still as mute as when the gunslinger had met him. All of them looked worried and confused, despite their faith in their Chosen One.

Kold pointed at Oliver as if he'd guessed a correct answer and was now owed a prize.

"Listen to that one," Kold said, climbing onto Cerberus's back. "You're about to see a neat trick." He laughed, then reached down to slap Clint affectionately on the shoulder. "Come on, partner. Have you ever wanted to ride a unicorn of a different color? Hop on up."

Clint looked at Cerberus. Cerberus looked at Clint. It was obvious by both of their expressions that the proposition of Clint riding Cerberus behind Kold was appealing to neither of them.

"I think I'll walk."

Kold shrugged. "Suit yourself."

Cerberus bolted forward. His dark shape blurred into a long, winding, serpentine smear of black and vanished through a tunnel in the distant rock wall. A moment later, Clint and his small bunch of renegades stood at the end of the crater more or less alone, watching the last of Kold's army exit and prepare to lay siege.

"I guess we should go," Clint said. He'd never been less certain of anything. He wished Mai's presence inside of him was strong enough to encourage him, but he could still barely sense her.

"Okay," said Oliver, looking even less certain than Clint.

"I guess?" said Morph.

"Hang on," said Churchill. Then, "Okay, I've turned off my sense of fear."

Clint didn't know if the thinking machine was kidding or speaking true. Beside him, Boricio was playing with his knife, eyes full of murder. Beside Boricio was Z, who could have been raring to go or well beyond scared. It was impossible to know.

For the thousandth time, Clint's hands reached for his belt, eager to feel the reassuring weight of iron, but he hadn't been armed since he'd stepped through that first shimmer and found himself on the lawn outside of Castle Spires. He wasn't wearing his garb, or his hat. He didn't have his unicorn partner. He was an old man wearing stupid paladin clown pants. Just one man — tough and battle-hardened though he was — on the eve of the apocalypse.

Edward, he reminded himself. The single word resonated in his mind like an icon, like the one solid thing he could hold onto while the walls fell down around him.

The hope of freeing Edward was all he had left. It was the only thing he might still be able to do. He couldn't heal the worlds. He couldn't stop whatever The Realm was doing. He couldn't keep Kold on the dusty side of the wall, and he couldn't keep Kold from laying waste to all those in the city in the sky. Worse, he didn't know if he wanted to. The gunslinger had flip-flopped scores of times since leaving Solace. He wanted to enter The Realm. He wanted to keep Kold out of The Realm. He needed to stop The Realm. He needed to help The Realm. He needed to escort a prisoner to The Realm. He needed to free the prisoner, then join him on his quest to destroy The Realm. He needed to help Kold bring down the wall. He needed to close the door, to keep Kold from bringing down the wall.

And now, as the six Conspiracists waited for his sage advice, Clint didn't know what to think. He didn't know what to tell them.

"Do you have an army to help us on the other side?" Clint asked Oliver.

"The Realm has an enormous army under the control of the Ministry," said Morph, stepping forward. "But... um... aren't we on the side of *this* army? Wasn't getting reinforcements against the marshals holding your unicorn the reason we came here in the first place?"

Of course. He was on *Kold's* side. He fought *with* his archenemy, not against him. He was on the side of the psychopath who had tortured his bride for over four years and now wanted to destroy the worlds, *not* on the side of the pleasant paradise. That was why he'd shouted to Churchill to close the door — because he was happy that he had his reinforcements, and was on Kold's side.

Flip-flop. Flip-flop. It was exhausting.

Clint sighed, shaking his head. He'd never wished more for Edward's counsel, or Mai's.

"Lesser of two evils, I suppose." Clint turned to Oliver. "I don't reckon there's a word in the prophecies about choosing between two equally bad choices?"

Oliver shook his head.

"Just so you understand, I'm not 'on the side of this army.' Nor am I on The Realm's side. I'm on *my* side. I don't want to help anyone other than *me and Edward*." It was the most selfish thing Clint could have thought, but under the circumstances, it was also the only truth he could muster.

"Well," said Oliver, "that's our side, too."

There was a stack of rifles in a corner. They appeared painfully inadequate given the artillery that had just left the crater and all the artillery Morph implied was waiting to meet it. Still, Clint walked over and hefted one of the guns. It had a glowing recharge pack in the stock, like Sly's scatterguns. He could only carry one because it wasn't sawed off like Sly's, but if he would never have to reload, one would be enough to die fighting with.

Clint tossed a gun from the pile to each of the Conspiracists. They wore scimitars as did all paladins, but the rifles would give them the ability to punch from a distance. Even though it was nothing… well… at least it was *something*.

Clint sighed once more. "Just the seven of us," he said. He remembered his magnificent seven fighters in Baracho Gulch, smiled, and then added, "Again."

"Eight," said a voice from behind.

Clint turned to see an old man floating a foot above the ground, wearing ornate eastern robes and an elaborate goatee the color of fresh snow that was long enough to brush his belt. His hair was equally white, long and pinned up with a stick.

It was Rigoberto Montoya, holding Clint's gunbelt in his hands.

CHAPTER ELEVEN: THE CRUMBLING OF THE WALL

There was no time for a tearful reunion, even if gunslingers were capable of tears. There was no time to ask Rigo how he'd ended up with Clint's guns. There wasn't even time, regretful though it was, to ask Rigo how exactly he was managing to float above the ground. Kold had told his armies to be ready in thirty minutes, and at least ten were already gone. The volcano's crater was massive, and they'd need every remaining minute to reach where the Army of the Triangulum had massed if they wanted to join the party.

So they jogged forward, pacing themselves because they had no idea how far they'd have to run after reaching the tunnel on the mountain's far side. The six Conspiracists carried their rifles two-handed across their chests. Clint kept touching his pistols, reassuring himself that the two seven-shooters were back where they belonged. Rigo carried nothing. He was standing with his arms crossed, gazing straight ahead, flying along at the same pace as the rest of the group. When Clint had last seen Rigo, he'd been thirteen or fourteen years old and had been able to do incredible, almost superhuman feats with his body. Was it really so surprising what sixty additional years of practice had done for him? He was clearly in touch with something that only Edward, if he were here, might be able to understand.

"They were in the magic," said Rigo, floating alongside Clint.

The gunslinger was feeling out of breath, but noticed with satisfaction that he wasn't nearly as out of breath as Morph, Oliver, Borico, and Brooce, all of whom were probably half of Clint's apparent age. Z, as usual, was inscrutable. He could be exhausted or full of vigor. Or, like Churchill, he could be a machine.

"Pardon?" Clint said to Rigo.

Rigo answered without turning his head. "Your guns. I found them in the magic in our fields. I was meditating, and as I strolled in the Garden of Thoughts, I came across them. My spirit animal said you had crossed the magic, and that you were shorn of your stingers on entry, the same as your partner was shorn. My animal gave me the guns and told me to go to you. And so I came."

Between heaving breaths, Clint said, "I've no idea what that means."

Rigo's arms were still crossed on his chest. He held his stare straight ahead as he flew upright beside the gunslinger, his long white goatee and dramatic white eyebrows flapping in the wind of his passage.

"It means you have your guns. And that I am here."

That was as good an answer as any, so Clint asked no further.

The tunnel at the crater's far edge was as large as the one at the entrance, and they approached it with ten or twelve minutes remaining. They could see the vast troops at the end of the passage, standing in formation. When they finally emerged, breathing deeply, they found that behind the mountain was a titanic plain — even larger than the crater. It seemed to be artificial, as if Kold's armies had chipped away a second mountain to create it. Sheer cliffs bordered the space on both sides, with the mountain citadel at their backs. On the open side was a wide path leading gradually upward for mayhap a hundred feet, then ending in what seemed to be a sheer drop-off.

At the end of the path — if the path had continued instead of dropping away, which it didn't — was The Realm. Clint watched it shimmer in the sky, clearer and more present than ever. With the final Orb now added to the Triangulum, the generator was bringing the worlds closer and more into alignment. It almost looked as if a man on a fast horse might be able to run up the path, leap the gulf, and land on The Realm's doorstep.

And all around the city in the sky, Clint could see the dusty brown wall. He watched the projected barrier flicker and shake in the magic, as if nearing the end of its days.

Kold stood at the assembly's head, then climbed onto a plinth. A hush fell over the enormous army, draping every soldier and machine.

"I won't make a speech," Kold called out, his voice seemingly amplified by the magic inside him. "I'm not big on speeches. You all know why we are here. You've trained your whole your lives for this moment — and some of your ammies and appies trained before you, never seeing the day we could finally enter. Today is that day, and now we will do what we must."

He turned, fished the black ring off of his partial finger, and seemed to pull it apart from the middle. The black ring widened into an ever expanding circle, the aperture splitting broad enough to eclipse The Realm's form behind it. Kold gestured, and the black circle started to lighten, growing almost translucent, until they were able to see The Realm again, now through an opaque smear. Then the city actually seemed to come *closer*, as if they were watching The Realm approach like the end of a tunnel seen from the front of a locomotive. The city in the sky sharpened, growing increasingly real. Then, all at once, it was like a bubble popped. The shimmery, indistinct, unreal appearance of the city vanished and the old door, now stretched and distorted into a sort of portal, laid flat, and became like a bridge. The wall began to shake, to blur and distort like a spark-fueled mirage. Then it cracked, fell into rubble, and vanished entirely. When it was gone, The Realm became nothing more than a destination at the end of a black road.

"The wall has been breached!" Kold yelled.

The army began to move, spilling across the bridge like water over a cliff. At the lead were the unicorns. Behind them were the green vehicles, which someone called tanks; behind the tanks were the two-wheeled vehicles; behind them Teedawges; behind the Teedawges ropers and gunslingers; behind them trolls and elves. The black, spiderlike giants trod above them all, stepping deftly into holes in the regiments so as not to crush them. They bellowed their terrible, echoing shrieks. Zeppelins lumbered into the sky; balloons sailed with them. The spark aircrafts zoomed forward and were circling above The Realm in seconds. Line after line after line of fighting forces surged across the bridge and into the city.

Inside of Clint, Mai began to feel more insistent, as if trying to resurface.

Stay with them, she seemed to whisper.

"She's right," Rigo said.

"We're only eight people," Clint said, not bothering to ask Rigo how he seemed to have heard. He was making a mere statement of fact, but he was also voicing his sense of futility. The army's forces were overwhelming. Already they were being elbowed and shoved, having to jockey just to hold their positions against the push of the army. Passing troops brushed against his guns, raising Clint's ire nearly enough to make him want to kill the combatants who were, he supposed, the closest thing he had to "on his side."

"Eight people on a magic carpet," Rigo corrected.

Before Clint could react, a rectangular patch ripped away from the upward-facing road and began to float beneath them. The swatch of dirt was paper-thin but felt bedrock-solid. They all stopped walking and looked around, nervous. Then the eight people on the floating section of dirt and rock began to speed forward as casually as Rigo himself had flown earlier. Rigo's feet were on the ground, his gaze placidly forward, apparently steering the carpet of dirt. Below them, the Army of the Triangulum marched forward, eyes steely and teeth exposed, bloodlust in every motion.

Kold and Cerberus had stopped at a crossroads in the path and were directing troops as they crossed the bridge. At first Clint didn't understand what he was seeing, but as their magic carpet came closer, he realized that the bridge into The Realm was actually a giant and multi-faceted shimmer. There wasn't only one path ahead. There were many paths. The air around them had turned black, and holes into various parts of The Realm pocked the blackness like a forest of screens in a darkened room. Meadowlands, behind them, had shrunk to a scene through a peephole.

Kold was sending troops into various holes, into various sectors of The Realm. Distributing forces. Fortifying. Planning his attack to control key areas.

"It's a game of Risk," said Clint.

Oliver nodded beside him. "The wall has fallen, and now you can see the true nature of what The Realm has hidden even from its own eyes. The worlds have fractured, and yet The Realm has stayed whole. How? And now you see how. They've always stitched what is visible, but doing so is like covering rust with a bonding agent instead of fixing the problem. Beneath the surface, their bedrock is shattered. The wall held it together like a thin skin. But now that it's gone? Well, welcome to paradise."

Clint looked down and found himself almost wanting to cling to the others. The dark they crossed as they flew toward the holes seemed so absolute. Beneath them, there was only blackness. It wasn't the blackness of a hole. It wasn't the blackness of space, where the stars shone. It was the fathomless depths of nothing at all.

"Sands," whispered Morph. "It's all falling to pieces."

Small bridges spun out from the path's fork, where Kold stood and directed the troops to the shimmers. The largest machines had to narrow to a single-file line, the troops in front of and behind them glancing nervously into the void. Looking around, Clint realized that the falling of the wall had laid The Realm bare. All of its places were accessible at once. They could march to Castle Spires. They could march into homes. They could march through the city streets, near the saloon Otel and Ron House's book shop. They could march through the edutorium or fields of magically-growing crops or into the Ministry building, or mayhap even into the so-called "Red Room" itself.

Hurry to the stables, Mai said inside Clint's head.

"We will be there soon," said Rigo.

"You can hear her?"

The others looked at Clint when he said it, but Rigo only shook his head. "I hear the magic."

Rigo seemed to know — or to intuit — the way. Their magic carpet sped by the troops, past the flying zeppelins, approaching one of the flicker screens in the void. But as they drew closer, they saw that the shimmer wasn't so much a hole as it was a *cut*. It looked like they were inside of a canvas bag that someone had already ripped their way out of using a knife.

The gash in the fabric of reality grew larger. Clint could see the gates of a compound in the distance.

They cleared the rip, watching as the world re-formed. The Army of the Triangulum entered beneath them. Archetypes lumbered onto green grass. Unicorns, now at the lead, spread out, taking up their positions.

Realm marshals were waiting to greet them.

CHAPTER TWELVE:
THE GREAT BATTLE

The marshal compound entrance was lined with endless rows of men and women atop unicorns, wearing heavy twin pistols on their hips.

Their faces were impassive despite the army gathering at their doorstep. They were unsmiling, hands resting on their hips. The unicorns beneath them ranged in color from dull alabaster to a grave shade of charcoal, indicating they'd turned away from pure. None were as dark as Cerberus, but none were anywhere near as pristine as Edward. The marshals waited, their eyes assessing the group in front of them. Clint could sense coldness wafting from them in a wave, pressing against the exposed skin at his neck and hands. They all looked young and strong and deadly, all lending warmth to the term "cold-blooded." Clint remembered what Oliver had said earlier about modern gunslingers being trained from birth, raised on violence and retribution. Clint himself had had a family once, even though he could remember nar an eye color nor a smile. These men and women never had. They'd known pain, iron, and nothing more.

As the white unicorns stepped through the crack and spread out like a fan, Clint wondered at the confidence he read in the battalion of gunslingers. There were hundreds of them, yar (he could see more circling the stables' perimeter; they had the place locked up nicely), but there were tens of thousands in the army marching on The Realm along with all manner of machines. Why were the marshals so sure? And was this really all The Realm could muster to stand against the Army of the Triangulum?

Then Clint looked back toward the rip and realized why the

marshals weren't flinching: of those tens of thousands of troops, only a portion had come through with them. The unicorns seemed to have come, along with Kold's version of gunslingers. He could see ropers and Teedawges and a single tank. But the vast legions were nowhere, and Kold had sent none of the largest machines. Where had they all gone?

"The Realm is a big place," said a voice behind him. The voice startled Clint, but it was only Morph.

"He sent troops through too many different holes," said Clint, surveying the standoff with fresh eyes. It would be thousands versus hundreds, but they were facing *marshals*. It wasn't enough.

"Mayhap," said Morph. "But he needs to control a few key areas or he'll be overrun by Realm forces. Probably still will be. But personally, I'd be concerned about the Armory, the Ministry, the Core, and a dozen other places."

"The Core?" The word shocked the gunslinger. It was a word Edward used to describe the center of all worlds, the place from which magic sprung.

"Not *that* Core," said Oliver. "*Our* Core. It's what generates the wall. Another artifact nobody understands. It's at the city's center, and this army will want to make sure they don't raise the wall again." Clint noticed how Oliver said *this army* rather than *our army*.

Clint looked around. They had mayhap fifty white unicorns on their side. Three or four hundred Teedawge archetypes. A regiment of elves. One lone giant. Seemingly all of the gunslingers, numbering about as many as the Teedawges, though they all had ordinary pistols. Mayhap fifty ropers. And the tank.

The Realm marshals sat on their mounts and waited, their hands resting comfortably on their guns. No one was willing to fire the first shot.

Beyond the stone-faced marshals, Clint could see the sprawling stable lands. If not for all of the weapons and troops, the place would have looked downright tranquil. There were rolling acres of green grass, one flowing into the next. The place had to be large; the proud unicorns always insisted on having room to roam. To one side was a long, beautiful white ranch house that, strangely enough, had housed the marshal program even back in Clint's day. The house, he seemed to remember, was larger inside than outside and rich with magic. There was an indoor shooting gallery. There were training facilities for the body. The gunslinger seemed to remember training facilities for the mind, too, but his brain didn't want to think on those, and so he buried the memory.

Beside the white house were the stables — all red wood, accented with white. The sprawling building looked like a barn from the outside, but the stalls, he knew, would be lush and lavish. They would be like Otel rooms, lined with pillows and thick floor coverings. The food in those stalls would not be hay or oats. It would The Realm's finest fare.

Clint could see white heads inside those stalls, visible through the windows. He wondered if Edward was one of the heads he could see. Edward was all that mattered. Nothing else mattered at all. The Realm would collapse if they won, and Kold would kill and burn the city, exacting his revenge. If The Realm won, the wall would rise again and magic would continue leaking, and conditions in the Sands would worsen until faults sheared the world into pieces. The apocalypse was coming regardless of who was victorious.

"There's no way to win," said Clint.

"Sometimes," said Rigo, "it's okay simply not to lose."

In the distance, Clint watched as one of the enormous black machines appeared out of nowhere past the ranch, near the buildings beyond, in the city's center. The thing vented an enormous mechanical bellow and belched fire from its front. Smoke rose where the beam struck. Debris flew into the air. A zeppelin joined the black tripod. Fire bloomed as something exploded. Angry lines of smoke rose beneath the zeppelin.

In front of them, the Realm marshals hadn't so much as moved.

Clint looked at the heads of the white unicorns held captive in the stables. If what the scholar had told them was true, those unicorns would have no horns and wouldn't be able to speak with the white unicorns in the Sands party. They were weak, unable to do much (if any) magic. But why? Why couldn't they heal themselves and fight? But as his eyes watched the unicorns in their cells, he realized there was more to the picture. There was something up near the barn that Clint couldn't quite see, above his line of sight. Something between stables and ranch house. Something that hadn't been there before, that was keeping the unicorns weak and in line.

At the party's head, one of the Teedawges slowly reached for his pistol and drew it, pulling it from his belt as the marshals in front remained stone-faced and cold, assessing. The Teedawge raised his pistol to hip-height, his head even with the marshals, watching. And still the marshals stayed frozen.

Oliver looked at Clint, seeming to probe the old gunslinger's mood. But Clint was neither intrigued nor nervous. He simply wanted to see what would happen, same as the Teedawge.

The archetype held his gun in front of him. The marshals, their eyes mostly on the surrounding white unicorns, didn't flinch.

Then the archetype cocked his pistol. In the same moment, a gun fired. But it wasn't the archetype who had fired. The archetype *couldn't* have fired, because none of the marshals had fallen, and the Teedawge lay killt on the ground. One of the marshals must have shot him, but Clint had no idea which. It had happened too fast.

The Teedawges, Sands gunslingers, and ropers began looking at one another, their eyes full of fear. The Sands army's superior numbers suddenly meant nothing — and the Realm marshals hadn't needed to so much as cock a pistol to make that fact obvious.

In the distance, the city's buildings began to collapse, roaring with orange fire.

"Hickory dickory dock," said Boricio. He reached down, yanked a rock from the rectangle of floating path underfoot, reared back, and launched it into the cluster of marshals. The rock struck one of the marshals, who didn't bother to duck.

All of a sudden, the standoff collapsed.

The Realm marshals drew. A hail of bullets mowed through the archetypes and ropers as if pushing through a crowd. None missed. Around the edges, the white unicorns fired spells at the marshals, but the grays seemed to have networked themselves in some way; they had created a single yellow umbrella that undulated the air around them and bounced the white unicorns' spells away from the marshals like rubber from a road. But the white unicorns were more powerful — a few dozen holding more pure magic than hundreds of their ashier, depleted cousins — and soon the umbrella began to sway and buckle. Clint could see it denting beneath the bombardment like alloy wrapping a sandwich. But it was too little too late; in the meantime the Realm marshals were doing too much damage, turning row upon row of soldiers to bodies. The Sands army began to duck behind obstacles, but as soon as they did, the gray unicorns projected red spots onto the other sides of the obstacles and the Realm Marshals pierced the red spots with their bullets. Teedawges fell. Ropers fell.

The white unicorns advanced on the lead group of marshals, smashing into the umbrella with their far more powerful spells. The umbrella dented inward. The white unicorns' spells began to penetrate it, striking those inside. Many of the marshals dismounted, looking outward, humanity finally starting to enter their eyes. They watched the unicorns, watched the Teedawges. They fired their guns faster than anything Clint had ever seen.

Clint's own guns were out, but he'd yet to fire. His bullet supply was finite, and his shots had to count.

He could pierce the unicorns' shield with his bullets, so he sighted and fired, leaving one marshal killt. The other marshals turned to look at him, their expressions sobering. They didn't look precisely afraid, but Clint could see a marshal's version of trepidation smudging the eyes of a few. The look said that despite their inferior numbers, they hadn't expected any of their own to fall so soon. Guns came up, more than one lip twisting into a snarl. Pistols fired. Clint dove for cover.

The white unicorns charged forward, unafraid. A handful of the marshals beneath the umbrella concentrated their fire on the advancing unicorns. Their bullets did nothing; the unicorns' chests peppered with multicolored blood but they didn't slow. Their eyes — all blue — remained steely and determined.

The power held by the pure white unicorns bested that of the more numerous grays by at least a factor of ten. They bombarded the shield, battering it like a can of beans. Clint fired again and again and again, with both guns, staying low. A marshal looked up, found him, and drew. Clint saw the puff of dull red smoke, anticipated a magic slug of lead to fill his forehead. But instead, the bullet exploded in front of him like a firework.

Clint looked over and saw a large white unicorn. It's horn glowed as it nodded at the gunslinger.

Clint's puzzled eyes asked the unicorn what had happened, because marshal's bullets could normally pierce shields. But the unicorn just gave him an amused look — so like Edward's — that told the gunslinger he knew exactly what Clint was thinking but that he coyly refused to share. Surprisingly, the unicorn's big equine eye seemed to wink.

Rigo said, "Ah... the white magic has learned a few new tricks against the dark!"

Clint, now under the new-and-improved shield, stood tall and marched forward, both guns drawn. White unicorns continued to close on the marshals and their grays from the sides while Clint came at them from the front. The marshals pressed in toward each other, involuntarily shrinking their group. Spells battered the umbrella, making it waver until it threatened collapse. Edward had always said that when a unicorn surrendered some of its power and became less than pure white, it weakened. It was true. The grays and the Realm marshals were learning *how* true.

Marshals fired at Clint. Bullets struck his shield and exploded, plinking off the surface into wisps of pink smoke. As more and more fired, the umbrella weakened and a few slugs eked through, falling to the dirt at the gunslinger's feet. A second white unicorn broke from the group and stood beside Clint, adding a second-layer umbrella to protect him further. A third unicorn joined the first two. Bullets ceased their ingress, each new shot blowing to shards as it struck the reinforced shield. Clint's own bullets, coming from inside the shell, were unimpeded. His bullets sliced through the feeble, failing umbrella cast by the ashen unicorns, dropping marshals and stirring their unicorns into a frenzy.

Clint fired. And fired. And fired. Both guns at once, until empty.

The gunslinger reloaded and fired again.

A dozen marshals fell. Fifteen. Twenty.

The gray unicorns panicked and scattered. The umbrella collapsed. Marshals and unicorns (some still paired, some solo) spread out, each now on his own. Clint continued to fire, tracking those he could and bringing them down.

The chaos in front of the gates cleared a path. The remaining marshals from the flanks pressed in to block it. The marshals, though flustered by Clint and the white unicorns, were still strong; their bullets and their unicorns' spells had knocked out a third of the Sands army. But Clint (and now others) had drawn blood, and it was happening too fast for the gray unicorns to heal all of their fallen riders. The Sands army smelled fear in their opponents. The marshals, they realized, weren't made of stone after all. They were fallible, and they were human.

The Army of the Triangulum mustered their numbers and stormed the gates.

The newly reinforced group of Realm marshals rallied as the Sands army charged. They and their gray unicorns continued to fire, cutting down Teedawges, Sands gunmen, and overconfident elves. Ropers flanked them, rushing to the sides, and managed to catch a few marshals by their necks. The marshals rolled, drew seven-shooters, and knocked the ropers to the dirt. Ropers began doubling up, using three or more of their magic ropes to pin the marshals' arms to their sides, but their victories were short-lived because the gray unicorns easily outmatched the humans, blasting them to dust.

The Sands army, populated by soldiers raised through generations of anticipation, was relentless. Ropers encumbered the gray unicorns' hooves, using blunt force to knock them down. The grays righted themselves and returned fire, obliterating barrels and coaches and other obstacles from their path to find their foes. The tank never had a chance to fire. It was struck by an incidental shot from one of the unicorns attempting to hit a Teedawge, evaporated into white mist, and was rendered an oversized joke.

Clint watched the Teedawges advance, firing their guns until empty and then drawing long, glowing scimitar weapons. A few of the Teedawges' attacks struck down Realm marshals with their sheer brute numbers. The gray unicorns, however, began to team up and quickly regained the advantage. Two would stand together, head-to-tail, and the first would take fire so the second could pause to heal marshals.

An imperative began to ripple through the Army of the Triangulum: *Occupy the gray unicorns. Keep them busy so that they can't heal the others. Then shoot at the marshals near them, several gunners to a target. Aim for the head, for an immediate kill.*

Teedawges, Sands gunmen, ropers, and elves surged. White unicorns began to batter the grays. The gray unicorns staggered back to defend themselves, leaving the marshals exposed. The Realm marshals were much better guns, but there were too many facing them, and The Realm's forces began to thin marshal by marshal.

There was a thundering from behind Clint as the giant charged. The gray unicorns and marshals saw it coming. Spells and bullets rained at the beast's head, but the giant wore a helmet of magic alloy specifically designed to turn him into the perfect instrument for a berserker run. Clint had seen them practice the maneuver — ideal as a way to clear forces, but also acceptable as a suicide mission. Giants trained as berserkers were prepared and willing to die.

The giant unsheathed its massive hammer with its juggernaut hands and swung. The blow was devastating and clearly unanticipated. With the gray unicorns' umbrella gone, the giant's first swing turned six marshals to white smoke. Then the giant turned, spells striking it, weakening its knees to a buckle. Bullets tore into its flesh. But as the giant fell, it managed a final swing and — drawing a gasp from all who saw it — its hammer struck two of the gray unicorns. They poofed into white smoke and were gone.

Clint suppressed his shock. There would be time for assessing later. Stowing both fear and surprise, he ran, ducked, and fired.

The giant was down. Small, green-clad elves were swarming the compound, slipping by marshals and unicorns and running between their legs. The marshals used their guns to knock down the elves like pins in a game of heavyball, but there were too many of them to strike them all. So the gray unicorns cast a wall, holding them back. Once the grays were occupied, Teedawges stormed from behind and started firing at the unicorns, emboldened by the realization that the magical steeds could indeed die (or at least be poofed into smoke) and pumped shell after shell into their bodies.

Clint's small, wild bunch of Conspiracists had scattered from the flying carpet when Clint began firing his seven-chambered guns, but as the Teedawges shot at the unicorns that were casting the wall, Clint saw Oliver working his shotgun's slide, pumping rounds into one of the grays. Churchill was on the other side, but Clint was glad he'd given the sliver bullet of a thinking machine a rifle since his chest didn't have a cannon like Buckaroo's. Buckaroo had been built to work the dangerous Sands, but Churchill was made to serve a wealthy Realm family. He did have a weapon in his chest and was using it in addition to the shotgun, but instead of a cannon, it was a small, delicate, pearl-handled ladies' pistol on an accordion arm.

The only other member of his crew that Clint could see was Rigo. The old, white-haired man hadn't moved. He was still on the magic carpet, which was no longer flying. Battle churned all around him without the old man seeming to notice. He stood perfectly still, his long eastern robes flowing and his arms crossed on his chest, his gaze straight forward.

Clint tried yelling for Rigo to take cover, but as he did, something massive struck him and he looked over to see four gray unicorns — their colors ranging from an off-white to one the dusky color of twilight — beginning to focus their assault on him. Another spell struck his bubble like a rock to the face, making him shudder. His protecting white unicorns hadn't faltered; they had continued to hold the gunslinger in their umbrella as the one man who could shoot true and pierce the gray unicorns' shields. But with four firing spells at him at once, he could still be beaten to death.

Clint fired at the grays, finding his bullets as useless as he'd known they would be. Body shots did nothing. Neither did head shots.

Clint ran. The gray unicorns followed. The whites stayed where they were, still projecting their protection over the gunslinger. But there was no evading the grays. Their spells struck his bubble, knocking him down. They were using the same strategy on him that the others were using on the grays: encumber the gunslinger and keep him off balance. They couldn't kill him — four gray unicorns were still woefully inadequate against three white unicorns — but they could keep him from doing more damage than he already had.

Beyond him, Realm marshals swarmed amongst Teedawges, elves, and trolls. Clint saw Morph; he'd transformed himself into a kind of clockwork jaguar and was striking his enemies at their throats. Ropers surged, yanking whatever the marshals tried hiding behind to pieces. The marshals fought back, driving the Sands army toward the rip they'd come through. The balance of power undulated back and forth like a wave. Clint watched as a roper stole one of the Realm marshals' guns, then cringed as the roper caught it and tried to fire. The marshal's gun folded in half and fired six slugs backward, dropping the roper to the dirt.

The grays continued to batter Clint with spells. The white unicorns protecting the gunslinger couldn't strike at the grays because they were occupied in protecting him, so Clint could only run or take the abuse. Inside the umbrella, he was safe from the spells... but being slugged by magic while inside his shell was like going over a waterfall in a sealed barrel. Everything hurt. His head was battered. His shoulders throbbed from concussive blows.

Clint fell to the dirt. Looked up. A gray unicorn reared above him. He fired at it, knowing it would matter nar. He struck the unicorn in its giant eye, but the gray healed itself instantly, spitting the gunslinger's slug back at him as if fired from a pistol.

A red spot of light appeared at the base of the gray unicorn's horn.

It took Clint a moment to understand what he was seeing because the context was so wrong, but then it dawned on him. Edward had projected similar red dots in battle before, to tell him where to shoot. He looked at the white unicorns that were making his shield, then at the dot of light. He looked back at the unicorns. One of them nodded.

Three more dots appeared at the base of the other unicorns' horns.

He found himself remembering something Edward had said when they were leaving Aurora Solstice, before they'd found Mai but after he'd re-gained his memory and regrown his severed horn: *The only magic a unicorn can perform if its horn is severed is to regrow the horn.*

Clint looked at the other unicorns. *Ready?* his eyes asked.

The white unicorn nodded.

Clint swiveled both of his arms as one, leveled his guns, and fired them in unison, severing two of the gray unicorns' horns. In an instant's flicker he fired both guns again. The four gray unicorns, now looking like four gray horses, panicked. Their heads jerked up, seeming to grasp for their magic like a man who's dropped a coin. But the white unicorns were too fast; they surged forward and, letting Clint's shields fall, turned their own magic on the grays. Three white horns glowed. A jet of green fire shot forward and consumed the grays, which tumbled end over end before falling still forever.

"Don't tell anyone about that little trick," said the white unicorn who'd nodded to Clint.

The gunslinger blinked, then stumbled to his feet without reply. He felt the shields shimmer back into place around him. He marched forward, toward the gate, and found Boricio behind a sheared-off piece of something large and alloy that Clint couldn't identify. He looked down, inviting Boricio to join him. Boricio saw the wavering air around Clint and got to his feet, now inside the shield as well. They stood in a hail of ineffectual bullets, Boricio holding his shotgun with both hands across his hips.

"So unicorns can die," he said.

"Apparently," said Clint.

"Well," Boricio said with a whistle, "hickory dickory dock."

"Have you seen the others?"

"From our side?"

"The others who came with us," said Clint. He wasn't willing to commit to sides, except possibly the side of the white unicorns — who, incidentally, didn't seem to truly be on anyone's side, either.

"Well," said Boricio, "there's Jack-be-Nimble over there." He jerked his thumb over his shoulder. Clint turned to see Rigo, still unmoving, still with no weapon or obvious shield.

"What is he doing?" Clint said.

"I don't know," said Boricio, "but I'm not taking my eye off him. He hasn't done anything yet, and you just know that when he does, it's going to be something really cool."

A pair of Teedawges screamed past, firing guns. Both looked at Clint and Boricio, seeming to wonder why they were frozen in battle. The unicorns projecting the shield waited patiently.

"Dylan Brooce didn't make it," said Boricio.

Clint nodded.

"And Oliver is over there, shooting from behind that grassy knoll."

Clint looked over, saw a muzzle flash. "We should go," he said.

"To Oliver?"

"To Edward." Clint gestured forward, toward the stalls. A way had opened. Marshals were shooting in every direction, gray unicorns were lobbing spells, and white unicorns were obliterating everything in their path. The very air was screaming. There were no machines left; everything was hand to hand, gun to gun. Killt men and elves littered the battlefield. Clint stared at the scatter, thinking he could have ended up killt himself thousands upon thousands of times, but something had always protected him — mayhap magic, or mayhap just Edward. Mayhap luck. Or mayhap Mai.

With the thought, the gunslinger searched for Mai inside himself, suddenly panicked. But then he found her inside, right where he'd left her. She was more present, and he could hear her words. She no longer sounded suffocated — possibly because the Triangulum was no longer right beside her, now a world away.

There was a harsh, high-pitched battle cry that sounded like *Hiiiiii-yah!* from behind them, followed by the sounds of a hammer striking meat in rapid-fire succession. A dozen thumps thundered through the air.

Clint and Boricio spun to see Rigo standing exactly as they'd last seen him, now with twelve marshals dead in a circle around him.

"Oh *maaaan*," Boricio whined.

They passed the gates. Through the first pasture. Over a hill.

When the stables were within Clint and Boricio's sight, The Realm finally sent its reinforcements.

CHAPTER THIRTEEN: REINFORCEMENTS

The world shook with a tremendous explosion. The unicorns' protection over Clint faltered as they turned, surprised, and dropped his shield.

Clint spun to see wave after wave of identical soldiers storming toward him. A perfectly square shimmer had opened to his left a hundred yards distant, and what looked like The Realm's entire army and arsenal poured from inside it. There were vehicles that looked like giant clockwork beetles, captained by men sitting in clear domes at their tops. There were flying alloy things not much larger than two human bodies side-by-side, equipped with huge guns. The Sands army was powered by steam and spark. Clint could feel through Mai's presence in him that The Realm's army, on the other hand, was powered by magic. The battle that was about to ensue would be like a bug under a boot heel.

As the ranks of identical soldiers — much larger and stronger-looking than the Teedawges, and carrying weapons that looked like glowing scatterguns — raced toward them, Boricio dove one way and Clint dove the other. He wouldn't have the unicorns' protection anymore, as they'd broken off to regroup. They hadn't run far, though; they'd circled around and had already started blasting at the soldiers from the sides as if trying to chew their lines in half. But the soldiers had shields, so at first all the unicorns could do was to knock them down. A single, directed blast from a unicorn would lay one dead, but there were simply too many of them for single blasts to make a difference.

The soldier things (which had to be Realm archetypes) moved not toward the remaining Meadowlands forces, but directly toward Clint. The gunslinger felt almost flattered by their assessment of him as a threat, but then realized that the soldiers weren't converging on him; they were headed toward the stables, which were behind him. The realization made him think of something Oliver had said: *Put the unicorn in a cell and protect him, because as long as no harm comes to him, the worlds keep ticking.*

The Realm believed that the unicorn's death — that "the death of Edward the Brave" — would herald the opening chime of the apocalypse.

The prophecy.

As he thought on it, Clint realized: *They're here to protect Edward.* And on the heels of that, he again wondered whose side he should really be on.

Kold's army was annihilating buildings across town; Clint could see the tall alloy and glass structures tumbling under bright beams from the giant black walkers. He could see the blasts of spells as the others in distant unicorn corps fought Realm forces. An enormous explosion pounded the ground, causing everyone at the stables to double-take, and a massive black cloud, like a mushroom, bloomed from the city's center. How much of The Realms' forces did those he was seeing around him represent? Had they sent a small brigade to protect the stables, and left a larger one to fight Kold — to keep him from the other targets Oliver had mentioned in the armory, the Ministry, and the Realm Core? If the Core was the center of The Realm's magic, that's where Kold would be. He'd destroy it, shatter The Realm, crumble the worlds, and bring about the apocalypse true.

Clint leapt aside, skirting the advancing troops and taking cover behind a stock of alloy barrels.

Where *was* the Core? Clint scanned the horizon, looking past the burning city, and saw no clue. He turned back to the battle, seeing shots continue to erupt from the grassy knoll. Clint wondered if, without the white unicorns' protection, he could reach Oliver. Oliver would know at least roughly where the Core was. And, Clint thought, mayhap they should head through a shimmer and find it in order to help protect it as best they could. What could go wrong if they left the stables? The forces they were supposedly fighting against would do their job for them, and keep Edward safe. Might it not make more sense to find Kold?

And... what? Fight against him?

It was the same question, and Clint nar knew the answer. Should he find the dark rider to stop him from destroying the Core, or should he assist him in its annihilation? Should he fight with the Sands forces to take the stables, or with The Realm's forces to protect them?

He stopped, thought, and tried to feel Mai's essence as he sat behind the barrels, temporarily protected. He wanted to ask her if anything he did mattered. *For Kold. Against Kold. Against the Realm, which meant against the forces fighting to protect Edward.* Would it really do any harm to let the unicorns be, to let them remain in captivity?

But Mai was silent, and Clint frowned as he recognized that silence. It wasn't the silence of Mai's absence. It was the same silence Edward had given time and time again — a silence that said, *I could tell you, but I won't.*

Before Clint could make up his mind whether to leave or stay, the decision was yanked from his hands. He heard an enormous bass shriek and looked up to find himself staring into the eye of one of Kold's enormous black tripod devices. Out of instinct, Clint drew his guns, but doing so was idiotic. Not only was the thing ostensibly on his side, but he couldn't possibly harm it if it wasn't. So he holstered his guns, then looked past the walker to see where it had come from and realized that a new tear had ripped the world's fabric behind the stables. And this one, unlike the shimmer the Realm archetypes had come through, was indeed a *tear*. The walkers, flying machines and zeppelins, and thousands of Teedawges were raging through it, closing in on their adversaries.

Clint looked into the huge machine's eye, then back at the surge of forces streaming into the yard around the stables. Did the rip mean Kold had already struck the Core with that last big blast, and the worlds were already starting to fall apart? He looked back to the horizon and saw the city's center in flames, the emerald castle no longer standing. The machines and magic were no longer there. They had come *here*.

Then, as if to prove the point, new rips appeared everywhere around the stables. Clint felt like he was inside a bag being shredded by an angry tiger from the outside. Blackness yawned from a dozen fissures, and forces streamed from all of them. Giants. Archetypes. Unicorns. Elves. Morlocks. More tanks; more airships; more steam-cycles; more faux-gunslingers and ropers. They clashed with Realm reinforcements: marshals, paladins, Royal Guards, something Clint hadn't seen before that was surely a troop of wizards. The sky filled with electricity and smoke and the ozone scent of spark. Steam belched. Artillery and small-arms fire crackled. Bodies and machines fell.

Clint's cover was obliterated by one of the clockwork beetles. Clint looked up, saw the driver, aimed his pistol and fired. His bullet glanced harmlessly off the device's clear canopy. The driver smiled, advanced, and fired at the gunslinger. Clint dove, then crawled for cover. The beetle was struck by a blast from a white unicorn, and then a second beetle struck the unicorn, killing it unceremoniously. Clint turned, finding himself facing a regiment of advancing Realm archetypes. If they were like Teedawges, he'd have to hit their thinkboxes to send them down. But they were shielded, and though the unicorns could penetrate those shields with a direct hit, Clint wasn't sure that his bullets could.

He ran across an opening, found cover, and started to fire. His guns thundered and he exhaled; the archetypes he'd struck had fallen and stayed there. So he fired repeatedly, keeping his cover and moving as needed, counting his shots and timing his reload.

But the gunslinger had no bullets left. He'd run dry as the Sands.

He ran back to the gate, knowing a hit would finish him. But there was nothing else he could do. He didn't know who he was fighting for or why, and one man could nar make a difference, but he had to keep shooting. As forces from both sides converged on the stables and as The Realm tattered around them, he knew his only choices were to fight or surrender. And a gunslinger didn't die with his hands in the air.

He rolled, then grabbed at a gunbelt from a pile of killt marshals. He couldn't fire their guns and wouldn't want to, but he *could* use their bullets. Clint took six reloaders — all he could carry — and filled his chambers with loose shells. He pocketed another two handfuls of shells and stood to face a massive line of advancing Realm archetypes. He was a trifle to them; they were after the rows of fighting machines behind him. Clint fired anyway. The archetypes shot their glowing shotguns, which erupted and made craters in the ground that could only come from magic rounds. Again he dove, this time under bodies and through debris, trying to find his way out. They were close, their boots mere yards away. There was a bellow from above and a great beam of energy shot from one of Kold's walkers and scorched through the line of archetypes from behind, reducing them to piles of ash. Its victory was short-lived; several of the small flying machines that had come through one of the Realm army's shimmers (more were opening all the time, turning the stable grounds into something that resembled a sieve) circled the tripod's legs trailing cables. They pulled the cables tight and the great machine teetered and fell into a converging team of gray unicorns.

Bodies fell from every direction. Artillery fired and exploded. Magic fire burned. Clint saw Oliver struck by an archetype's bullet and fall.

Clint found the battleground's edge, skirted it, then approached the stables, as near as he dared. He found an alcove in the storm, temporarily protected, and looked around. He wasn't the only one who'd found the alcove. A bit further down, in repose as if waiting, was a square-jawed man with a dimple in his chin. Beside him was a helmeted guard.

"Clint," said Morph.

"Oliver and Brooce are gone," said Clint without preamble. The battle had exhausted him, leaving no time for niceties. The truth was at least real and distinct, like the blow of a hammer.

"I know," said Morph.

Beside Morph, Z nodded, the movement of his head small and his expression inscrutable behind his black visor.

The gunslinger said, "We're going to lose."

"Well, that depends," said a fourth voice.

Clint turned and was unsurprised to see Dharma Kold standing behind him. Clint was tired and apathetic. He simply looked at his old friend and enemy, waiting.

"Depends on what?" he said.

"On what you mean by 'lose'."

CHAPTER FOURTEEN: IN EDWARD'S CELL

The world turned hazy gray, but it wasn't just Clint's vision that changed. All of his tactile sensations were alive as well, and all were entirely repulsed. Whatever nothingness he was tumbling through was gray and sticky, like wet spiderwebs or the last bit of an ancient dinner that had been left in the icebox to spoil. He flinched as he swam through the stuff, finding it entering his mouth, nose, and the very pores of his skin. And just when he was near losing his mind with disgust, he found himself landing solidly on hard clay topped with straw. In front of him was something massive and white.

Kold was beside him, looking pleased. His hands glowed a light green, then faded to their normal color. On his other side were the two others — Morph and Z. Morph wore the same look of total disgust Clint imagined on his own face. Z's expression was, of course, unreadable. But his body language seemed equally revolted. Clint wished he were dressed like Z. None of his skin was exposed, so he might not have felt whatever had just happened.

Kold said, "Impressive what a little Triangulum control will do for you these days."

Clint's mind was foggy, still stuck in the disorienting experience of whatever had just happened. For a moment, he could barely remember who the other three were. It took the gunslinger a minute, looking at his hands, to remember he'd grown old. Then his head cleared and he started to recognize the snaps and booming of battle, now sounding muted and further off.

He looked at the white thing on the ground in front of him. It was Edward.

The unicorn was sluggish and unresponsive. Once Clint realized he'd somehow gotten inside Edward's cell (which would make what he'd just experienced Kold's filthy version of a fold), he raced to Edward's side, crouching behind his back and rubbing his still-shiny coat. Edward was a lump of flesh. He was alive, but he was weaker than Clint had ever seen him. The gunslinger's hand moved toward Edward's great white head, feeling his shallow, uneven breathing. He touched the stub of his horn, rough at the top as if cut off with a saw.

"Why didn't you just magick him out?" said Clint.

"Because of that black pool of what looks like oil outside," Kold said. "The Triangulum in me is… well… sort of in league with it. We have an agreement — let's just say it's an 'equally beneficial but tenuous alliance.' "

"The pool," Clint repeated. "The pool is the Darkness."

"Well," said Kold. "*Darkness*, anyway. It was on my tail for the longest time. I believe it was also on yours, or perhaps you were on its. You see, Edward doesn't like The Realm. I hate The Realm. But that thing outside? It's *the antithesis* of The Realm. The Realm hoards white magic, and that upsets the balance and causes an equal amount of black magic to accumulate. Nasty stuff. But you know what they say… the enemy of my enemy is my friend."

Clint thought of the times he'd run up against the Darkness and found himself having doubts about Kold's sentiment. Sometimes, it was possible for a man to have two distinct enemies, equally insipid.

"I can't just magick Edward out of here," said Kold. "We have an agreement, your 'Darkness' and I. We first met when Cerberus… well, when he first let me borrow his magic and became his 'different color,' say. Over the past decades, that… *being*… out there has been helping me open cracks. Turns out it rather enjoys doing it, and as it opens more cracks, it grows. The pool out there — have you seen it up close? It's enormous! — has been growing for sixty years, give or take. And while things were becoming all white-magicky and blossoming in Meadowlands — grass growing everywhere, magic machines running at full steam, sick people being healed, and even old dead wives returning to life — the Darkness just kept on growing, too. We're almost part of each other, it and I. And so while I control the Triangulum, it sort of does too."

Clint stroked the big white unicorn's mane, feeling his rough breath, the slow rise and fall of his body. "And here I thought you were 'part of' me and Edward," he said.

"Oh, but I was! We were in this together — *including* you and Edward."

"But the Darkness…"

"... wants to destroy The Realm, as do we."

"I don't want to destroy The Realm," Clint said. Outside, however, the endless thunder suggested he might be the only one.

"And," Kold continued, ignoring Clint's protest, "it understands the prophecy, and the need to keep the unicorns here, frightened by its growing darkness, which prevents them from regrowing their horns. Just like the men outside."

"So now you're in league with The Realm in keeping him captive? The Realm *and* the Darkness?"

Kold shook his head. "Very little is black and white, even magic. The Realm holds Edward captive while also keeping him safe. We came here to destroy The Realm —" He waved away Clint's protest. "— and to prevent the apocalypse. But the Darkness? It *craves* the apocalypse. We have two choices. We can ally with The Realm against the Darkness and allow The Realm to slowly reap the magic from the world, or we can ally with the Darkness to destroy The Realm and maybe have a chance at the magic's restoration. Do we end things now or end them later? Do we let some suffer or let all suffer? Do I help you, Clint? Do you help me? Or are we enemies true? The same goes for that black pool out there. You battled it as an enemy, but it seeks a restoration of balance, the same as you do."

Clint looked down at Edward. The unicorn seemed moments from death. In the past, that wouldn't have worried him, but the gunslinger had seen gray and white unicorns dying all day.

"I didn't want this," Clint said, stroking Edward behind his ears.

Beside him, Morph shifted positions. Z leaned with his back against the wall. Straw crackled beneath them. The Realm. The dagged *Realm*. Edward was a Chosen One in his own right, and here they'd put this proud, vain creature in a horse stall on *straw*.

"If you didn't want it, you have The *Realm* to blame," said Kold. "I'm a bit your enemy, and that dark pool of oil is a bit too. But The Realm is entirely your enemy."

"Not entirely." He rubbed Edward's side.

"*Entirely,*" said Kold, more forcefully. "You don't even remember your exile, do you?"

"I remember enough."

"*Not* enough," Kold countered. "You don't know that you were exiled because of Edward. Because he chose you."

Clint looked up. He searched Kold's surprisingly compassionate eyes for truth. Mai, still inside him, told Clint that he'd found it.

"You've heard the prophecy," Kold continued. "They've known about Edward for as long as The Realm has existed — possibly for as long as *unicorns* existed. They believe that if he dies, the world will end. Not much to have on your head, eh? And so The Realm protected him and then loved him, but they also feared him. They didn't know how to feel about him, just as you don't know how to feel about me. And eventually, they did what they always do with magical things they don't understand: they ignored the issue. Just as they've done from the start, from when they first began hoarding white magic. The early guardians warned The Realm about imbalance — that separating light and dark too much would violate the natural order of entropy. The guardians told them that braid by braid, they would tie their own noose. But it didn't matter. Roasts had to be cooked and flicker talkies had to be watched. People had to be able to get lost in bliss, no matter the cost. So fractures began, and grew, and then the Great Cataclysm occurred. And *still* they kept on, now separated from the rest of the world, repairing damaged veins, fixing the symptoms of the disease and ignoring the cause. And so it was only natural that when they thought on the problem of the unicorn that might end it all, they finally got tired of thinking on it and cast him out. Him *and* the marshal he'd chosen."

"You're saying…"

"You weren't exiled, Clint. Edward was."

Clint continued to stare into Kold's green eyes. Then he looked back at Edward, stroking his neck in a way the unicorn would loathe if he were well, unsure what to say.

"In a way, I pity you," Kold said. "To be so clouded with emotion. It must be terrible. It's liberating to feel mostly blackness. I understand why Cerberus chose surrender rather than keeping his magic and remaining white. It's unpleasant to feel responsibility as you do. It's hard to not be able to see past emotion, to see what's for the greater good."

"Magick him out of the cell," Clint repeated, looking down at the unicorn.

"I can't," said Kold.

Clint looked up at him. "Please."

Kold shook his head. "It's as you said outside. We can't win. Our army is too small. If we magick Edward out and away and try for retreat, the best that might happen would be that their superior armies and technology and magic will let us flee, and the fractures will continue to widen and spread while they rob us blind. What's far more likely, though, is that they *won't* let us leave. The wall has fallen. They can all cross the bridge to the Sands, just as we can now cross to them. The Realm will eradicate us all, gunslinger. One by one. Every man, woman, and child — until *they* are all that's left. There is only one way to get out. Only one way to escape."

"Please," Clint repeated.
"Only one way," he repeated, then sighed and extended a hand.
Blue light shot from his palm.
And Edward was at peace.

CHAPTER FIFTEEN: THE FAMILY STONE

Kold was gone. Clint sat beside Edward's body, his big, callused hand resting on the unicorn's side. Morph and Z had stayed with him, but neither had spoken. It had only been thirty seconds, but it felt like an eternity. The sounds of battle were still raging outside, and a strangely calculating part of Clint's mind wondered how long it would take for a world to end.

He felt a hand on top of his and looked up, half expecting to see Mai. Instead, he saw Z. The opaque visor faced him, inscrutable as always.

Then a voice came from beneath the helmet, saying, "Sorry."

The word shocked Clint. He'd assumed Z was mute, or possibly mangled beneath the helmet with no ability to speak. Z watched him, letting the word hang in the air, then reached back and pulled the helmet from his head. And instead of a monster, Clint saw a tumbling cascade of long red hair, then the smooth face of a woman with soft features, pale skin, and wide lips.

"I'm Emma," she said.

She looked down, took off her glove, and replaced her hand atop Clint's on Edward's inert form. Her hand was small but tough, like a fighter's. Which, of course, she was.

"I'm sorry too," said the old gunslinger.

"Of all my line, I've accessed the most of what's in me," she said. "The process is complicated, and it's painful to rouse things that were supposed to remain sleeping. But ever since Sly found his secret trove and got his message to Oliver, we began to search for information on how to recover the information locked within us. We've tried all the family we have with some success, but I have uncovered the most."

It took Clint a moment to figure out what she was talking about, but then he remembered Oliver referring to Z as "family."

"You're a Stone," he said.

"Yes. Oliver was my brother."

"I'm sorry about your brother."

She looked down at the white form on the straw. "I'm sorry too."

A moment of silence fluttered between them. Then Emma looked at the gunslinger and said, "A lot of what happened, as far as I understand it, was fated in a way. But most of fate doesn't have to happen, and things can go wrong. The best way to think about prophecies are as things that always work out correctly in the end. But *only* in the end."

Inside his head, Clint heard Mai — not as she was now, but as a memory: *It will all work out.*

"You needed to wind up here, but you didn't need to go through the cities you went through. You could have gone round across the Sands. You could have not faced the enemies you faced. You could have gotten married six times along the way. Your journey could have taken six months or six hundred years, if you lived that long. Magic and prophecy seem to be very adaptable, able to course-correct as events unfold, because at the finish, all that matters is what happens at the end."

Clint looked down at Edward's body. "The end," he said.

"But what I don't understand is a glitch in the scriptures," Emma continued. "The Orb was said to require *evolution*." Clint thought of Mai, the way she'd died, then how she'd come back. "And the word that's used, when talking about the Benevolence Orb, is the verb *yersae*, for 'die' or 'evolve.' There are other places where the word used is *brevae*, for 'die.'"

Clint breathed as he listened, knowing he had nothing left. Nothing to live for. He wasn't interested in The Realm. He wasn't interested in how the war turned out. He wasn't interested in whether Realm troops would walk through the Sands and exterminate anything breathing. He wasn't interested in Kold, or the apocalypse, or prophecies, or magic. He'd had enough magic to last an eternity.

"Why are you telling me this?" he asked.

"Because the verb used for the very end of the prophecy — for the death that heralds the apocalypse and hence the last of all we consider predestined — is the same used for the Benevolence Orb. *Yersae*, not *brevae*."

Clint looked up.

"When the king and queen let you in, did they think you

controlled the Triangulum Enchantem, rather than Kold?"

"Yar. Why?"

"Because you control it in the scriptures, too."

A second hand settled on Clint's shoulder. He turned to see Mai's ghostly form beside him, holding a vial.

CHAPTER SIXTEEN:
THE VIAL

"Mai," he said.

"Yar."

"Are you here this time true?"

She smiled. "I'm always here."

"But I mean, are you *really* here? Actually, physically, here?" He turned to Z, then to Morph. "Do you see her?"

They shook their heads side to side.

"I'm here in every way that matters," Mai said.

"But not to stay?"

She shrugged. "A question for another day."

"Are you holding that vial? For real, are you holding it?"

"In a way. Rigo brought it."

"What is it?"

"It's a scent bottle from my dresser."

Clint looked at the bottle. It was purple, nearly opaque, with a high-end Sands brand name written in white scrawl across its front. He'd seen the bottle and many like it on Mai's old dresser in his shack outside Meadowlands and had thought hundreds of times of throwing them away, same as he'd thought every morning about tossing out his loathed multicolored mirror. But like the mirror, he hadn't been able to throw away the bottles of scent, or Mai's clothing, or her trinkets. It felt like tossing a bit of her soul to the dirt.

"Rigo brought a scent bottle?"

"Yar."

"And how did you get it, if you're not here?"

Mai put her ghostly hands on her ghostly hips and gave him her most common expression — exasperation with the stoic, tough-as-leather man she'd hitched. "All the things you've seen with magic, and the transportation of a bottle from one person to another is what has you perplexed?"

"But why would Rigo bring scent?"

"Because I told him to."

Clint watched her still-exasperated look and thought of Rigo handing him his guns back at the citadel. *They were in the magic,* he'd said. He'd been in the field. A spirit animal told him something. Rigo was a kid when Clint had first met him, and he'd been in touch with something behind the wall. It was how he'd learned to fight like a superhuman, or mayhap a wizard. Edward had once said that Rigo's people were saturated with magic. So something inside the magic had told Rigo about the guns — and apparently the scent — and he'd listened.

"Why scent?" he said, taking the bottle.

"It's not scent."

"What is it?"

"It's something I found in your gear after you returned from meeting Kold that first time, after we settled down in Meadowlands — after it made sense, finally, to unpack your dusty bags. It was in an old waterskin. I was about to pour it out along with an ancient, *ancient* slice of turkey pie that had gone green and fuzzy with mold. But as I stood above the basin with the waterskin in my hands, the magic inside me started to protest. It wasn't bad then, the magic, and I still thought of it as a gift, before it consumed me and outstripped the capacities of Doctor Barlowe's elixirs of suppression. But I knew enough to hear the magic speaking to me, so instead of pouring out the contents of that waterskin, I cleaned a mostly-empty scent bottle and poured the water into it, just in case."

Clint opened the vial and sniffed. She'd either cleaned the bottle faultlessly before filling it or the years had leached the last of the scent, because all the gunslinger could smell was water true.

It had come from his old pack. A waterskin, filled with ancient water.

"This is the Orb of Malevolence," he said.

"Yar. I knew that's what it was after I moved out of my body and could finally see clearly. It's the Orb that counterpoints mine, that represents darkness. But of course, malevolence can also be light... the same as benevolence can be twisted to do the work of the dark."

Clint thought of Mai, left depleted and ruined in the shack. Kold had tried to twist her plenty.

He sniffed the bottle again. It had been over sixty years since he'd first collected the water that was under his nose, but he remembered it as if it were yesterday. He'd been in the underground cathedral in Precipice. He'd filled his waterskin after scooping the Orb water from a spring using the Cup of Ages, as Edward had called it. The unicorn had then told him to smash the cup. Clint had even seen the remnants of that cup earlier in the day, when the tunnels from the Read Room had led him full circle, back to that underground cathedral.

Edward had said, *Intention matters to magic.*

Kold had gotten his Orb of Malevolence from an underground river at the bottom of a copper mine, miles from its source. Clint had gone through the whole song and dance, extricating the cup from a cage with a complicated lock in order to collect his own Orb. He'd done it because, as Edward had said, *intention mattered.*

"Kold cheated," said the gunslinger.

"Yar, he did," said Mai.

"He had enough to power the Triangulum, to breach the wall, and to storm The Realm. He had enough power to grow his army and to assassinate the king and queen, but…"

"… but he didn't have enough to power the Triangulum to its true purpose," Mai completed.

On his other side, Emma nodded. "*You* were supposed to power the Triangulum to its true purpose," she said. "Not Dharma Kold — *you*. The Triangulum belongs to *you*, Marshal Clint Augustus Gulliver, chosen partner of the Chosen One."

"What is the Triangulum's true purpose?" he asked.

Mai touched his shoulder, making him turn back. The same exasperated look was still on her face. "Find out for yourself, you skeptical stick-in-the-mud."

Clint shook his head. "How?"

Mai leaned forward, placing her ghostly lips an inch from his ear.

"Drink it," she said.

CHAPTER SEVENTEEN: THE SOUNDS OF AWESOMENESS

The Orb of Benevolence was in Clint already. He'd had Mai's heart from the beginning.

The Orb of Synthesis had opened a door for him and him alone, and had passed him through it. He'd heard it in his head — felt the Triangulum's power in his nerves and blood. He'd heard it speaking with Kold's voice, but it also spoke with a voice of its own, buried and suppressed.

He touched the pure Orb of Malevolence to his lips, willing the dark magic to obey his intention, to turn malevolence into benevolence and to turn the Triangulum Enchantem white — to wrench it from Kold's grasp.

Clint's eyes lit. Everything was suddenly pure and clean. He heard explosions and artillery outside, but was oblivious to their presence. The guards outside didn't know they were in here, and that the very thing they were protecting was already dead.

Dead, using the verb *yersae*, not *brevae*.

Clint saw the Triangulum's true purpose blossom before him. He didn't know if Emma knew what it was intended to do or if she had simply had faith, but the answer was so obvious to Clint that he didn't have to think twice. The Triangulum was meant to cause the world to *evolve*, not *die*. To cause a *change*, rather than an *end*.

He put his hands on Edward's side.

The unicorn's head jerked up. The stump where his horn had been glowed pink, then reshaped itself and became its familiar long, pearlescent spiral. His blue eyes opened. Then he looked back at Clint and said, "You're even uglier after the sweet sleep of death."

"Get up, you stupid, legendary horse," said Clint.

"The Darkness is outside," said Edward. "It made me weak."

"I know."

"But now, *it* will fear *me*."

Clint chuckled. Laughing was such a foreign motion for his diaphragm after sixty years of sorrow that he felt almost as if he'd fractured a rib for the sake of levity.

"Let it fear your super-powered jerkiness."

Edward tossed his mane. "Get on."

Clint climbed up, then looked at the wall in front of him and remembered that they'd gotten inside by folding, and that there were scores of troops outside. "The place is totally surrounded," he said.

"Not totally."

"You haven't seen it out there. There's all sorts of magic. Unicorns are dying. We can't simply blast our way out."

Edward chuckled. "I have news for you, gunslinger. I've kept one more secret from you. But it's okay. We've kept it from all humans until the time was right to show you true. You've no idea how hard it has been to willfully keep this one in, dying if necessary to keep the secret."

Clint rolled his eyes. "It hardly matters."

"You'll want to hold on. This will require some changes to your riding style."

Clint was about to ask what he meant, but then Edward's sides began to bulge, nudging the gunslinger's legs wide. He moved them back, away from the growing protrusions, finally finding himself flat on Edward's white back, his legs across the unicorn's rump and his face full of mane. The lumps on Edward's sides became massive triangular shapes, emerging flat from his sides.

"What are you doing?" Clint yelled.

Suddenly everything became louder. Explosions racked the stall, making everything shake. Clint heard shouts as the roof rattled on its frame.

"I'M SORRY," Edward said, "I CAN'T HEAR YOU OVER THE SOUNDS OF AWESOMENESS."

The triangles on Edward's sides grew, puffing out as they thickened. Then the shapes tipped out, away from his body at the rear, and unfolded. They spread wide, testing the limits of the already-large stall. In them, Clint saw feathers. *Feathers*.

Still on the ground, Morph and even Emma gaped and gasped in tandem. Apparently there were some things missing from the scriptures after all.

"Oh man," said Edward, wiggling his back. "You have no idea how long I've wanted to stretch those."

"You have *wings?*"

"Yar."

"You're a *pegasus?*"

"Pegusi don't have horns. The word most humans would use is 'alicorn'."

"You're an *alicorn?*"

"Get a hold of yourself, gunslinger," he said, but he was clearly enjoying the effect he was having on Clint. He sounded positively giddy.

"But the battle..."

"I'm not afraid of the battle," said Edward. "I feel as if I've just came back from the dead."

Edward flicked his head, surrounding Morph and Emma in a protective bubble. Then he flicked it again as he beat his wings, and a tremendous burst of energy blew out from his body. All of the walls of the cell — indeed, of the entire *stables* — blew out as if hit by an enormous shockwave. The building was simply obliterated. As Edward flapped and began to climb, Clint struggled to hang on for dear life. He watched as fragments of wood and stone flew across the battlefield. He shoved his legs behind Edward's wings, trying to find his balance.

The sky was filled with white unicorns. All of them had wings. They had burst through the stable roofs ahead of Edward, finding themselves suddenly flooded with new power. The gray unicorns on the ground below looked up but did not unsheath wings of their own. They either couldn't fly or were afraid of Edward's resurrection, of the Triangulum's return to its rightful owner, of whatever it all meant and what it might unleash. They scattered, fleeing the battlefield.

The battling machines turned at the sound of the detonating stables, but Edward considered them all — the machines of both armies — to be mere trifles. They fired beams of light. They fired projectiles. The alicorns blocked their artillery and magic with shields. Edward concentrated. Another shockwave blew out from his body in a burst of green, like the fire from Sly Stone's sawed-off magical shotguns. Flying machines incinerated. Archetypes fell as if shot, and stayed down. Clockwork beetles exploded as the wave touched them. The troops on both sides ran, turning and heading through the nearest tear.

The melee lasted only a moment, because as people, machines, elves, giants, and the rest watched, the cracks and tears and shimmers around the battlefield began to connect, each spreading out to touch the next like spreading fissures on a sheet of calving ice. A black crack shot across the compound's lawn, grass ripping from grass into a zig-zag of nothing. A split crossed the front of the ranch house that had long been home to the marshal program. The beams broke off and shook. The entire side of the house snapped away and fell into the void.

Parties ran screaming. Entire sections of the ground sundered and fell into nothingness. Troops tumbled into the void. Machines that could fly sped away. Kold's giant three-legged walkers, attempting to find footing as the ground split, tipped and fell and were gone. Crack followed crack; tears connected with open shimmers. Entire sections cleaved away as The Realm fell to pieces.

Below Clint and Edward, on one of the few remaining sections of land, was Dharma Kold atop Cerberus's back. The pair charged forward, propelled not by Cerberus's wings (like the grays, he either didn't have wings or couldn't spread them — but by Kold's magic. He still *had* magic — mayhap resident in his cells or in his memory. But Edward parried their charge effortlessly, dodging both the dark unicorn's spells and the bolts of blue lightning that Kold fired from his palms. Even for Clint, atop Edward's back, things moved in slow motion. Kold held out a hand; it glowed blue. Edward broke it off. Cerberus radiated a huge black spell that came at them like a manta, but Edward struck it with a spell of his own, and it became soft yellow and floated away. Kold drew his guns and fired. His shells struck nothing. Instead, they stopped, hovered for a moment, and fell. Kold's face contorted in rage.

"Go!" Edward yelled. "There is nothing more to be done here!"

"How are you doing this?" Kold screamed back, looking down as the island of land he'd been standing on a minute earlier split in two and fell away.

"*You* did this," said Edward. "By killing me."

Kold stopped, his face changing. "The apocalypse," he said.

"Yar. As you wanted."

Kold hovered in front of them, seeming to think. Then he said, "So we both got what we wanted."

"In a way."

"Because we're a team," Kold said. "Two to open the Triangulum, and two to wield it."

"*One* to wield it," said Clint.

"Clearly, you're not seeing how…"

"I won't lay you dead," said Clint, feeling the Triangulum inside him, filling him, bleeding its power away from its old commander.

"Because you're not like us," said Kold, again looking down. To Clint, it looked as if he'd just realized that he was sitting atop a unicorn that couldn't fly, held up by magic he no longer controlled.

"Yar."

"So we'll go our own ways, our work together completed."

"Yar," said Clint. "We will go our own ways. You will go yours. I will go mine. And we will never see each other again. Agreed?"

Kold fought for control as the last of the world fell away, unsteady atop Cerberus's back. Edward flapped and waited. Cerberus simply floated, looking satisfyingly petrified — quite a change from his usual arrogance.

"Fair!" said Kold.

Clint nodded.

"Now what?" said Kold, still hovering. Clint felt strong. He had the Triangulum. He had Mai. He could feel the power in every cell of his body.

"Now you fly off to greener pastures, same as us," said Clint.

"Yar," said Kold. Then: "Wait…!"

Clint pulled the last of the power of the Triangulum away from Kold and into himself.

Dharma Kold and the dark unicorn tumbled down, down, down, into the abyss and into the pages of legend.

CHAPTER EIGHTEEN: THE NEW BEGINNING

Edward and Clint stood on the porch of Clint's shack outside Meadowlands. They gazed into the distance, past the swatch of front lawn, and into nothing. It was as if someone had draped a black curtain across Clint's land, and that they were waiting for the curtain to rise. Below them, Meadowlands had already begun to crumble. Half of the buildings had tumbled into the abyss. The other half seemed on the verge of a massive crinkle — similar to a shimmer, but with a much more rigid edge — that could fold over at any time.

"The other unicorns will come along," said Edward. "The grays. Give them time. They got distracted. It happens to all beings. But they will return to white if they don't tumble down and die. And if they do, then they will fly, and will be as much a part of the new beginning as the rest of us."

"The new beginning?"

"You might call it the end, but that's splitting hairs. The beginning is the end and the end is the beginning. It's merely a matter of change. We always knew it, though we sometimes tried to fight it true. But Kold would have been happy with the way things turned out, were he still alive. The Realm will fall within weeks, and then slowly, the magic will re-stabilize. With time."

"How much time?"

"I don't know — and I say that for true this time. This is all unknown, for all of us. You have a band of people. You have Emma, and Morph, and Boricio… even Churchill. There are others. Plenty of others. Things don't end here. They change."

"What about the Sands?"

"Strangely, I think the Sands will be fine. They'll see fractures, of course, and the shifting will worsen. But the people who learned to live without magic? Yar, they will more or less go on, I think."

"It's strange to hear you say 'I think.'"

"We unicorns aren't used to hedging our bets," said Edward.

"Alicorns," Clint corrected.

"We always had wings, you know. It's a bit like discovering you have a navel and deciding that the new discovery means you must be something else. 'Alicorn' is a human term. To us, unicorns simply have wings, though we've had to keep them hidden."

"Why?"

Edward gave an equine smile. "The world has ended, but that doesn't mean I'll stop infuriating you," he said.

They sat in silence until crackling reached their ears from far off. In Meadowlands — and certainly in The Realm above, now fully open and seeming to hang in the air by many fragmented threads — fires burned.

"Mai?" said Edward.

Clint searched his head. "Gone," he said. But he couldn't help it; he turned his head to look at the apple tree where he'd planted her grave, which was still standing. "Like the Triangulum."

"Oh, nar," said Edward. "The Triangulum isn't gone. It'll always be in you, just as I will. And Mai. If Mai is gone 'like the Triangulum,' then she's not gone at all."

Clint shrugged. It didn't matter.

"What about the Darkness?" Clint asked.

"It fell into the abyss when the stables cracked. I watched it slide down, like a slug."

"Into to the Core?"

"Mayhap," said the unicorn, fluffing his wings. "But mayhap into another world. There could be any number of fissures in the dark below. The Darkness could spill into nothing. It could go to the Core. Or it could go somewhere else. But I do know this: it's not gone. There isn't enough entropy yet for it to be fully re-integrated, which to your mind would be the same as 'gone.' It will take a long time for the magic to totally re-equilibrate, and the Darkness as we saw it enjoyed the power of being collected together in one place — the same as The Realm enjoyed the feeling of possessing so much of the white."

"So the Darkness is the anti-Realm?"

Edward shrugged his wings. "I don't know." Then he paused, thinking. "It's going to be hard for me to get used to saying that."

"You mean: now that you have become the Chosen One and

fulfilled the prophecy."

"Well, me and the one chosen by the Chosen One."

"So what now?" said Clint.

"We wait."

"For what?"

"For the cooker to ding, and tell us our turkey pie is ready."

As if on cue, the cooker dinged inside Clint's shack. Clint's cooker ran on steam, but it was steam that was kindled from a wood fire below. Having lived for so long without central steam, spark, or even magic had its perks. It meant a man could always have his pie.

Clint stood. "And when the pie is cool enough to eat, will you allow me to have any?"

"It would be pretty rude of me not to, seeing as it's your stove," Edward answered.

"When have you ever flinched from being rude?" said Clint. Then the gunslinger walked into his shack, removed the pie from the cooker, set it on the counter to cool, and walked back out onto the porch to watch the world end.

"Can we rebuild?" Clint asked.

Edward turned his big white head to look at him sidelong, meeting the marshal eye to eye.

"If we've filled the world with unicorns that have wings," he said, "I'd say we can do anything we want."

LET THERE BE UNICORNS.

Unicorn Genesis starts in the Farback as Edward's Grappies tell the beginnings of everything: the first unicorns, the time before the Great Flood that tore the worlds apart, before The Realm, before the Sands, and before Marshall Clint Gulliver … a time when unicorns were all there was, and only story and intention shaped the world.

And there will be more.
Unicorn Apocalypse is coming.

Be the first to know by signing up at
JohnnyBTruant.com/join

ENTER THE TRUANTVERSE

When it comes to stories and the worlds they live in,
books are only the beginning.

**Visit JohnnyBTruant.com/join
for exclusive stuff you can't get anywhere else.**

(My list doesn't suck like most author email lists.
Seriously. It has unicorns … and not just Edward.)

ABOUT THE AUTHORS

Johnny B. Truant is the bestselling author of *Fat Vampire*, adapted by the SyFy network as *Reginald the Vampire*. His other books include *Pretty Killer, Pattern Black, Invasion, The Beam, Dead City, Unicorn Western*, and over 100 other titles across many genres.

Originally from Ohio, Johnny and his family now live in Austin, Texas where he's finally surrounded by creative types as weird as he is.

————

Sean Platt is an entrepreneur and founder of Sterling & Stone, where he makes stories with his partners, Johnny B. Truant, and David W. Wright, and a family of storytellers.

Sean is the bestselling author of over 10 million words' worth of books, including the Yesterday's Gone and Invasion series. Sean is also co-author of the indie publishing cornerstone, Write. Publish. Repeat. and co-host of the Story Studio Podcast.

Originally from Long Beach, California, Sean now lives in Austin, Texas with his wife and two children. He has more than his share of nose.

ALSO BY JOHNNY B. TRUANT

Winter Break

Pattern Black

Pretty Killer

Cursed

The Bialy Pimps

Namaste

The Target

La Fleur de Blanc

Axis of Aaron

Devil May Care

Screenplay

The Island

Burnout

Sick and Wired

———

UNICORN WESTERN:

Unicorn Western

The Wanderers

A Fistful of Magic

Shimmer to Yuma

The Man Who Shot Alan Whitney

The Spectacular Seven

Open Meadows

The Unforgotten

The Magic Bunch

Unicorn Genesis

———

FAT VAMPIRE:

Fat Vampire

Fat Vampire 2: Tastes Like Chicken

Fat Vampire 3: All You Can Eat

Fat Vampire 4: Harder Better Fatter Stronger

Fat Vampire 5: Fatpocalypse

Fat Vampire 6: Survival of the Fattest

The Vampire Maurice

Anarchy and Blood

Vampires in the White City

Fangs and Fame

Game of Fangs

———

INVASION:

Invasion

Contact

Colonization

Annihilation

Judgment

Extinction

Resurrection

Save the City

Save the Girl

Save the World

Longshot

———

THE INEVITABLE:

Robot Proletariat

The Infinite Loop

The Hard Reset

Cascade Failure

Reboot

En3my

———

DEAD CITY:
Dead City

Dead Nation

Dead Planet

Dead Zero

Empty Nest

———

THE DREAM ENGINE:
The Dream Engine

The Nightmare Factory

The Ruby Room

The Pandora Core

The Engine Convergence

The Tinkerer's Mainspring

———

GORE POINT:
Gore Point 1

Gore Point 2

Gore Point 3

———

THE BEAM:
The Beam: Season One

The Beam: Season Two

The Beam: Season Three

The Beam Season Four

The Beam Season Five

Future Proof

Plugged

The Future of Sex

————

THE TOMORROW GENE:
The Tomorrow Gene
The Eden Experiment
The Tomorrow Clone
Null Identity

————

COMEDIES:
Everyone Gets Divorced

Greens

Fiends

Decoy Wallet

————

NONFICTION:
The Fiction Formula
Fiction Unboxed
Iterate & Optimize
The Story Solution
Write. Publish. Repeat.
The One With All the Writing Advice